FIRST

FRUIT PRESS

Content Warning: murder, torture, graphic violence, alcohol use, death of a child in memory, brief scene of self-harm on a supernatural healer, memories of past sexual assault, brief suicidal ideations, and brief sexual content.

This story is a work of fantasy, and while historical, artistic liberties have been taken.

Cover by Miblart

Original map design by Ashley Lambright

Secondary city map by whylia.art

 Formatted with Vellum

THE DILEMMAS OF A DEAD MAN'S DAUGHTER

BRITTANY TUCKER

THE DILEMMAS OF A DEAD MAN'S DAUGHTER

BRITTANY TUCKER

For the generational curse breakers.
It ends with us.

Annie's village!
COLD! BRING A
ROUENN
ENOCH
CAMDEN'S
Best Camping
DON'T GO BACK!
ALMOST GOT STABBED
PORT LEBANON
NEW HAVANA
SHAR CRUE
Oops. Blew it up

THE FOUR CORNERS

SLEET FIELD
TRAVELS

TOO MANY TREES
ADAH'S
ARCHIPELAGO
ITCHY BUGS
BRISTOL
WATCH

ABNER
SNAKES. STEP CAREFULLY

Custom's office
The Modiste
General Store
The Green
Enoch

Hunting Lodge
Waverly Hills Hospital
Mr. Baxter's Lab
Callahan estate

THE CITY OF ENOCH

The growing storm splattered raindrops against the fogged windowpanes.

Alexander Callahan traced the droplets' paths down the glass. Erratic. Chaotic. Fragmented. Everything he couldn't be, or else risk toppling the delicately balanced tower he'd built—his *ancestors* had built—into ruin. There's little he wouldn't do to keep his kingdom from crumbling. Only God knew what he'd done already.

Heavy footsteps echoed down the hall outside his study. Alexander smoothed back his shoulder-length hair, adjusted his pristine three-piece suit, then took a seat at his desk.

The footsteps grew closer, more anxious.

He straightened a pen that sat out of line beside his color-coded stack of notebooks before opening his newspaper until it was about a third of the way through. Far enough to make him appear just settled, but not far enough to suggest he'd planned on heading out any time soon.

Alexander scanned over the words printed on the page. There was nothing new—just the same old reports of turmoil in the streets, looting and violence. The footsteps stopped, and there was a knock on the door.

He sighed. *Let's get this over with.* "Come in."

David—one of the staff—peeked his head inside, raindrops staining the shoulders of his black overcoat.

"M-my lord." David had always had a stutter, but he was a loyal boy. Clever. Maya had insisted on his help, and Alexander had grown to tolerate him. "Representatives of The Order are here, sir. I told them you were unavailable, b-but they insisted."

With a slight smile, Alexander set down his newspaper, removing his spectacles and setting them neatly on the edge of his desk. The scar beneath his finger itched. He forced himself not to scratch it as he slid on a pair of leather gloves. "Thank you, David. They may enter."

The boy nodded and ducked back into the hall.

Alexander reopened the newspaper, forgoing the glasses this time. His eyesight had begun to fail of late, but The Order didn't need to know that. The less they knew about anything and everything, the better. He pursed his lips. *They're bloody thorns in my side.*

They'd been getting bolder with him recently—talking back, questioning his decisions—but he'd let it slide for now. Matters were too sensitive to poke the hornet's nest. He'd never been afraid to stir up trouble—he'd never have held the continent this long if he had been—but he was also smart enough to know when to let sleeping dogs lie.

Several sets of footsteps approached now, some wearing boots.

Alexander smirked. *They brought guards.* Good. Fear was good.

David's black-haired head reappeared in the doorway after another soft knock. "Sir, I have The Order with me."

Alexander didn't look up from his paper. "Send them in."

David stepped aside, and six suited men entered his study, all stiff-backed and solemn. The three larger men in the back, he didn't know, but by their look, they were the protection unit. Alexander noted their features in his mental catalog. He never forgot a face.

The three other finely-dressed gentlemen he *did* know—The Order's spokesman and his two assistants, a shorter, balding councilman and a blond Revenant.

The younger, brown-haired man in the front—Henry Bale—grimaced at him, smoothing his satin waistcoat. He supposed it was meant to be a smile. "Governor."

"Bale." Alexander again set down his newspaper, crossing his legs and steepling his fingers. "Nice to see you again." He let his gaze trail slowly over Henry's entourage. After his father, Harrison, passed away just over a year ago—an *unfortunate* heart attack—Henry took over as Enoch's chief of police, alongside his affiliation with The Order.

Alexander had hated Harrison, and he liked Henry even less. "I'm surprised you risked venturing out in this storm with such a large party, and all."

"Well, yes," Henry huffed as he pulled out a folded bit of parchment from his coat. He set the letter on Alexander's desk and pushed it towards him. "Some matters are worth the risk. I assume you've seen this?"

Raising an eyebrow, Alexander took the letter, flipping it open. He didn't need to read a single word, though he made a good show of scanning over the contents. He had seen the original report. He'd read it half a hundred times, several weeks ago. Despite that, a thrill ran through him at seeing it again. He kept his expression deceptively blank as he pushed the letter back to Henry. "I'm aware. What of it?"

Henry glanced between his companions before clearing his

throat. "Your *son's* ship was spotted sailing up the coast. If he stays his course, he'll arrive outside Enoch within the week. You don't think this is cause for concern?"

Alexander leaned back and inhaled. "If I thought it was of concern, wouldn't I have warned you?"

Henry rubbed his narrow chin, exasperated, his usually clean-shaven jaw etched in stubble.

He's stressed. Good. He needed to be reminded of his place. Especially now. Alexander stared Henry down. "Is there anything else?"

"You may remain cavalier." Henry didn't dare break eye contact. "But The Order *does* have concerns. Reports say Camden Callahan is captaining a damned warship."

Alexander couldn't stop the smile spreading across his face. "He is."

Henry looked aghast. "And not only is he a Fire Brand now, but it's said he has two other Revenants on board with him, though their identities are yet to be determined."

"So, I've heard." Alexander didn't let his cold smile falter. However, *his* informants had been able to identify those on board. Camden had acquired quite an interesting mix of talent around him. "It won't be a problem."

"Not a problem?" The Revenant—an Ice Brand—sputtered. "They say he destroyed half of New Havana!"

"It won't be a problem," Alexander repeated, painfully slow. "I'm taking care of it. Now—" He gave Henry another pointed stare. "Is there anything else?"

Henry let out a frustrated exhale, smoothing his waistcoat again. "That will be all."

"Splendid." Alexander returned to his newspaper. "David will see you out."

"Governor?"

He glanced up at Henry, brow raised.

Henry scowled, a bead of sweat making the trek down his temple. "Just remember where your alliances lie."

Alexander's eyes narrowed. "Are you threatening me, Chief Bale?"

"Take it however you like." Henry straightened. Alexander had to admit, at least the kid had a backbone. Henry raised his hand, flashing the phoenix tattoo on the underside of his left ring finger. "But my superiors aren't quick to forgive the debts owed to them. Neither am I."

Alexander ran his tongue along the inside of his teeth. "Get out."

Henry's lips quirked up at the corners as he bowed, turning on his heel to exit the study, his pack of miscreants at his back. David followed them out, shutting the door behind him.

Moments passed, and Alexander's chest rose and fell as his breath quickened, rage leaking into his blood, into his limbs. A roar ripped from his throat as he jolted up and flipped his desk, scattering his pens and notebooks across the study.

Pages of the newspaper gently fluttered to the floor as he rubbed his hands over his face. Black and white photos stared up at him—a city in decay. Blackened with hate and disease. Enoch was falling apart. *He* was falling apart.

Alexander tugged his engraved, golden pocket watch out of his coat—his great-grandfather's watch—and checked the time. Four more months. That's all he had left.

There were still so many loose ends. So many pieces of the puzzle left to fit.

Camden is coming. Alexander slumped to the floor.

He'd always known Camden would come one day. Now, only time would tell if his prodigal son would become his doom or his salvation.

Only time would tell.

And Alexander didn't have much time.

CHAPTER 1
ANNIE

Annie's stomach rolled with *The Elaina*.

She closed her eyes, fighting back the darkness at the edges of her vision as the massive ship swayed. *You're here, not there. There's nothing to fear.* And yet, she was still afraid.

They'd been at sea for weeks. Cam had given her the large captain's quarters above deck, where a brilliant amount of sunlight shone through her rounded windows most days, where the salt breeze cooled her overheated skin when she woke from her nightmares.

Today, the sky was grey and dull. Only the darkening of the clouds showed that evening was approaching.

She'd tried to nap but woke to a cold sweat dampening her brows and sides—more nightmares. She'd told him it was just a bout of seasickness, that she needed time to adjust.

She'd lied—even after they'd promised to be truthful to one another.

Annie didn't want him to know of the faces that haunted

her in the night. That the noise and smells of the ship brought back memories of her years spent on the slave vessels. That sometimes she swore she could *feel* their hands on her again, shoving her face into the blankets, suffocating her.

No, she wouldn't tell him. Not yet. Not when he'd been nothing but kind and caring to her, Jenny, and the refugees they'd saved from New Havana. Cam could be harsh on the crew, but they'd grown to adore him—respect him.

Annie sat on her large, plush bed, arms wrapped around her shins. She fought off another wave of nausea, pressing her forehead against her knees. At least, she really was seasick this time. The farther north-west they sailed, the rougher the waters became. Late summer had given way to autumn, bringing cooler temperatures along with it.

Fine with me. Annie leaned back, resting her head against the wall. *I'm done with the heat.* She was done with the South, too. Done with islands, done with her old life. It was fitting that she'd died before leaving it all behind.

She flexed her hand, the light filtering through the window glittering off the dove-grey brands swirling across her palm and fingers.

Revenant.

She was Revenant now.

Why God had given *her* a second chance, she'd never understand.

After all she'd done . . .

Tip, tip, tap. Annie jumped at the familiar knock on her door—Jenny.

"Annie?" Jenny's fiery curls entered the room before she did, whipped over her shoulder by the screeching winds. She frowned when she noticed Annie curled up on the bed. "Sick again?"

Annie nodded. She didn't bother locking her door. She had

nothing worth stealing, and it wouldn't stop someone who wanted to hurt her, anyway. A lesson she'd learned a long time ago. "I'm fine. Just a bit queasy."

Jenny gave her a sympathetic smile as she sat on the bed. She'd forgone wearing the veil over her face to hide the burns Frank Boyle had given her—her marred cheeks now on full display. The crew wasn't afraid of her scars, so Jenny had decided she wasn't either.

"Do you think you'll be well enough to come onto the deck?" Jenny sucked on her lips. "Cam was looking for you. He said he wanted to show you something."

Camden. Annie's brands pulsed at the sound of his name. Being near him chased the evening horrors away . . . for a time. Whatever power that lived inside her now knew it, too. It craved his heat. She'd told herself that was the reason she always sought him out, why she'd rather stand in the storming rains beside him than be in her cabin alone.

Yet she found herself in here anyway, not wanting to bother anyone while she got herself settled. If, after all this time and pain, being settled was even possible.

"Annie?" Jenny's golden eyes filled with concern. "Are you okay?"

Annie snapped back to attention. "Yes, I'm fine. Give me a moment." She rose and tugged on her heavy coat, thankful they'd found one that fit her, packed in Elias Bennett's things. She'd rarely needed heavy layers on New Havana.

She gave Jenny a forced smile. "Let's go."

Jenny smiled back and took her arm, leading Annie out of her quarters. The wind smacked into her side as she stepped onto the deck, ripping strands of her moon-white hair loose from her braid. She and Jenny braced against each other as they walked.

Even after weeks on board, *The Elaina's* size still amazed

her. Once called *The Armageddon*, black smog billowed from the steamship's two massive smokestacks. Dozens of sailors darted from port to starboard, keeping the ship in line. Some had been part of Elias's crew. They'd been quick to come to Cam's side when he'd given them the option to shift loyalties or die. Others were volunteers from New Havana's harbor, desperate for a free trip off the island.

Men bowed or tipped their hats to them as they passed. Annie offered them small, close-lipped smiles in return. The slaver's crew had acted politely enough during the daylight hours. That hadn't stopped them from becoming monsters as soon as the sun went down.

"Ladies." Twelve-year-old Timothy called to them as he hopped off the mast, stumbling as he hit the deck.

"Timmy." Annie's smile was genuine this time. Timothy had been a powder monkey for the old captain. Now, Cam assigned him to work as Pulley's assistant, a navigator in training.

Timothy fell in step beside them, already as tall as Jenny. He smiled and wiped his runny nose on his sleeve, giving himself a soot mustache. "Heading to see the captain?"

Jenny nodded, grinning as she bundled deeper into her coat. "Yes. Do you know where he went?"

"At the bow." The boy jerked his head toward the front of the ship. "Careful. He's cranky."

Annie huffed a laugh.

His brows rose as if he wasn't sure if she was joking or not. Annie sighed. "I'll talk to him. Thank you."

"Anytime." He nodded. As he turned to leave, Annie caught sight of the dark stain spreading on his sleeve.

She froze and reached for him. *Not again.* "Wait."

He paused, giving her a curious look.

"Your arm." She nodded to the stain. "You're bleeding."

"Oh." Timothy glanced at his sleeve, then shrugged. "I cut myself on the rigging. No big deal."

Annie gestured for his arm. "Let me see it."

"It's fine," he protested, but he rolled up his sleeve all the same, revealing a deep gash on his forearm. "It barely hurts."

"Shush." Annie examined the jagged edges on the wound. It was too deep to heal on its own. It would need stitches.

Unless.

Her stomach clenched, hands buzzing at the thought of using her powers—of what little she had learned she could do with them.

I can't leave him like this. She flashed Timothy a warning look. "Stay still."

He swallowed but nodded, wincing as Annie placed her hand over the wound. A jolt ran through her as energy rolled down her skin, filling her fingers with an icy cold. Her brands shifted from grey to black as a faint glow passed from her to Timothy. She removed her hand, and he let out a small gasp.

The wound knit closed as they watched, sealing into a raised, pale line.

"That's always so . . . strange." Timothy rubbed his fresh skin. "Thanks."

It hadn't been the first time she'd healed him. He was always falling off of something. "It is for me, too," Annie admitted. "Now go change your shirt."

Timothy tipped his cap to them before trotting off.

Jenny tightened her grip on Annie's arm, huddling closer. "The others are watching."

Annie glanced around to find at least ten sailors gawking at them—at her. When they noticed her staring, they dropped their gazes to the floorboards and returned to work.

Annie pursed her lips and tugged Jenny forward. *That's enough making a spectacle of myself today.* "Come on."

It didn't take long for them to reach the bow. Annie's breath hitched when she caught sight of Cam, standing at the edge of the deck, his back to them, the wind dancing through his sandy, blond hair the same way she sometimes imagined her fingers might. The spray of the sea splattered against his knee-length leather coat—another of Elias's things.

Beside him, Nathan was going on about something or another, damp curls clinging to his dark skin. Annie peeked over to find Jenny smiling, her scarred cheeks flushing a pretty pink. Nathan noticed them. A smile curled his lips.

Cam glanced over his shoulder, his jaw set, a fire glowing behind his usually green eyes.

Annie's brows furrowed. *Timothy was right. Something's upset him.*

"Miss Jenny. Miss Annie." Nathan nodded to them, then offered his arm to her sister. "Walk with me? I've got to make the rounds in the brig and could use some proper company."

"Of course," Jenny giggled and took his elbow. She shot Annie a giddy look before falling in stride beside him.

They strolled back across the deck. Jenny nearly floated, laughing at whatever the quartermaster had leaned in and whispered to her.

Annie's brands flared as Cam's warmth rubbed against her like a cat. He stepped beside her and nudged her with his elbow, his voice rough. "Adorable, aren't they? Makes my heart all warm and fuzzy."

Annie blew out a heavy breath. "It just amazes me how she can be so comfortable . . . after all that's happened."

Cam cocked his head, his sunset brands stark against tanned skin. "Good for her. Why let a tool like Frank Boyle be the one to ruin your life?"

"I suppose." Annie glanced up at him, at the fire climbing up the veins in his neck. *He's tense.* "You were looking for me, I hear?"

"I was." Cam backed toward the ship's railing and pointed out across the sea, a crooked grin spreading across his face. "Look."

Annie gazed out over the bay, only to have an electric hum shoot down her spine and into her limbs. Not her powers this time. Just a wave of pure awe.

A sprawling city—larger than she'd ever seen—lingered on the edge of the storm, partially hidden behind the fog. Massive, stone towers rose above the mist, disappearing into the heavy clouds. It dominated the land around it like an infection spreading through flesh. Aggressive. Overwhelming.

She hadn't realized her jaw had gone slack until she'd forced her mouth shut. "Enoch?"

"The one and only," Cam said with more than a bit of disdain. "The crown jewel of the West. Home sweet home."

She couldn't imagine him growing up here. It was so rigid and harsh. No wonder his mother had tried to escape. Instincts had Annie looping her pinkie through his. Cam's eyes flickered to their conjoined fingers.

"You don't like being back, do you?" Annie asked.

He scoffed. "What gave that away?"

She gave him a look.

Cam sighed. "I'd rather sink to the bottom of the ocean than set foot in that city again."

"Then why are we here?" She'd wanted to ask him that several times. He'd promised her citizenship, a place in Western society, but she would have followed him if he'd decided to sail in the opposite direction. He'd called her his friend. Though she was still processing that fact, she was safer with him than anywhere else. "You could turn this ship around right now if you wanted to. Why don't you?"

The breeze snapped his hair across his eyes. "I've thought about it half a hundred times—I won't lie—but I need answers. *You* need answers." He chewed his lip before slipping Elias's ring from his pocket—the emblem engraved with a phoenix. Cam rubbed his thumb over the design. "Even if we turned tail and ran, whoever *these* people are will find us, even if only to get revenge. It's a small world. We can only hide for so long."

He was right. She examined the ring as he fiddled with it. She had a feeling they were only beginning to scratch the surface of whatever Elias Bennett and Charlotte Duskin had gotten themselves into.

Cam lifted their adjoined hands then, scowling at her fingers—at her brands that had darkened to black. "Who did you heal this time?"

"Timmy, of course." She took her hand back, rubbing her fingers. "He cut himself on the rigging again."

Cam shot her a mischievous look.

Her brows furrowed. "What?"

"You know he only does that so you'll patch him up, right?"

Annie crossed her arms. "He does not."

"Please," Cam laughed. "At his age, I would have broken my leg at least six times by now if it meant you would fix it."

She glared. That was just like him. Always teasing and making playful jokes, yet never getting *too* close. Always keeping a safe distance. Never pushing past where he thought she might run.

She wasn't stupid. She knew what he was doing—testing waters that both of them were too afraid to travel.

Sometimes, though, she wished he'd be brave for her.

Cam hesitated, as if he meant to say something else, then a low voice interrupted him.

"There you are." They turned, and Julian Price strode towards them from across the deck, winds whipping at the tails of his cream coat, at his long, black braid. An Air Brand who'd served Lord Duskin alongside her, tearing people's lives apart—until Cam had changed everything.

Mr. Price gestured for them to follow, unfazed by the weather. She wondered if the wind sang to his power. If it called to him like Cam's fire called to hers. "Come on." He called over the storm. "I have something to show you both."

Below deck, Annie's eyes scanned over the crisp document for the tenth time, over the handwriting she knew so well—Lord Richard Duskin's. Nausea threatened to bend her over, and it wasn't from the motion sickness this time. She swallowed, murmuring, "Are you sure?"

"Positive." Mr. Price rubbed at the dark stubble growing on his chin. "He left it to you. All of it."

Mr. Price had led them to his cabin on the third level of *The Elaina*. She'd barely seen him outside of mealtimes the entire week. He'd been consumed with digging through the papers he'd brought with him from New Havana—Lord Duskin's personal files. *Obsessed* was the word that Cam had used.

Mr. Price's room was a mess. Clothes and books were tossed haphazardly across the floor. His bed unmade. Candle wax had dripped and dried on the plush, expensive carpets, not unlike his chambers in the Duskin's manor.

Annie passed the paper to Cam. His eyes widened as he read, some of the color leaching from his golden skin. After a moment, he blew out a sharp breath, gently setting the document down on Mr. Price's cluttered desk. "Did I just read that Richard *bloody* Duskin named Annie the beneficiary to his patent?"

Annie's heart flipped, and she rested her hand over her throat.

Price nodded. "Yes. Which means, Miss Annie here, is now the only person alive legally able to purchase and transport Pearl Dust in the Four Corners."

Father, why? She hated that she sometimes still thought of him as her father. Her actual father was dead. He and her entire family had been murdered by Elias Bennett and his mystery counterpart the day they'd kidnapped her.

Annie winced. *Don't think of that now.* She brought herself back to the present, voicing her thoughts. "But why me? Why not you or Charlotte?"

"Why not you?" He leaned against his desk and crossed his arms. Richard Duskin had been his half-brother. "You were by his side every step of the way. Richard probably hoped you'd continue with his work if something ever happened to him."

"He also painted a *massive* target on her back." Cam gave her an apologetic look. "Half the population will be scrambling to kiss or kill you now, Kitten. Sorry."

"Don't frighten her," Price snapped.

"Would you rather I lie?" Cam shot back. "Coddling won't solve anything."

He opened his mouth to argue, but Annie raised a finger to silence him. "Camden's right, I need to know what I'm up against." She took the document off the desk, folded it neatly, then tucked it into her coat pocket. *And here I thought I was free of the Duskins.* "Who knows about this besides us?"

"If anyone had known, it would have been Charlotte." A hint of sadness flashed across Mr. Price's features. *He misses his sister.* "Besides that, only the patent office would know."

"Good," Cam smiled, but there was a nervousness to it. "We keep this quiet, then. Annie can tell who she wants when she's ready."

Ready for what? How could buying and moving Pearl Dust ever benefit her? She'd hoped she'd never have to deal with the substance again.

Pearl Dust—a powerful narcotic. Capable of soothing horrifying pain in small doses, but when combined with The Rot—the disease still haunting The Four Corners—there was a chance it could predict Revenency. To show what someone might become after they die.

Like it had Frank Boyle.

Like it had she and Cam.

Annie inhaled, tucking loose strands of hair back into her braid. "I need to think about this."

Mr. Price just nodded. "As you wish. We all should be preparing. We'll reach Enoch's harbor by morning." He gave them both a quick smile. "And of course, there's the ceremony to prepare."

Beside her, energy rippled off Cam's body—his brands flaring erratically—but an instant later, he wore his usual, cocky smile.

"That we do." He offered her his elbow. "Shall we be off?"

She took it gladly. He gave Mr. Price a dramatic bow before leading her out of the cabin.

The halls below *The Elaina's* deck were narrow and metal. If it weren't for the gas lamps lining the walls, they'd be walking in total darkness. Annie closed her eyes and breathed. She avoided coming down here. It reminded her too much of the lava tubes beneath New Havana manor.

She'd never be in total darkness, though. Not if Cam was with her. His fiery brands cast a deep orange glow over the metallic walls, basking them in warmth. He squeezed her arm, and she glanced up. His expression was still tense. "Are you hungry?"

That had been his way of asking if she wanted company lately. Annie gave him a close-lipped smile and nodded. She didn't want to be alone with her swirling thoughts. "I am."

Cam's shoulders relaxed. "I'll find something for us, then."

After they reached the wide staircase leading up to the top level, Annie climbed it herself as Cam headed toward the kitchen, hands in his pockets, whistling a bawdy tune she'd heard the crew singing.

The wind howled across the deck, ripping at her hair and coat. Annie's throat tightened. Why did it have to sound like screams? She clutched her chest, forcing her breath to remain steady. *You're safe. You're safe. You're here, not there.*

She could hear them, the sailors still working in the dark. Predators hunting. The lights swaying on the lamp posts illuminated her path in sporadic shifts of dull light and shadow. Her heart pounded so hard it hurt. *You're safe.* It took everything she had not to sprint for the captain's quarters when it came into view.

She couldn't breathe. *There it is. You're safe. You're safe.*

Was she? The sailors were probably waiting to ambush her just as soon as she opened the door. Maybe they were already inside, crouched beside her bed. *Stop it. You're safe.*

She ran the last few steps to the cabin door and slammed it closed behind her, her breath coming in ragged gasps. Her hands shook as she lit her oil lamps, the soft glow revealing that no monsters waited for her in the dark.

No. No, now that she thought about it, monsters didn't frighten her. Humans did.

A firm knock on her door made her jump out of her skin. Annie wiped the sweat dripping down her temple on her sleeve. *It's just Camden. You're safe.* She fixed her expression back into its usual cold mask and only hesitated once before opening the door.

Cam stood outside carrying two covered trays and a large flask beneath his arm. He looked her over quickly, a hint of concern in his eyes. *I must look a mess.* His heat brushed against her arms—a question—and she relaxed.

"Dinner is served." Cam grinned, but it didn't reach his eyes, as he waltzed into her room. Her own brands flared in response, pushing her towards him. He set the trays down on her small dining table and poured each of them a glass of iced tea. She watched him, her pulse finally slowing.

He's here. You're safe.

Cam pulled out her chair. "Annie?"

"Oh." She hadn't realized she'd been staring. "Sorry."

She sat, and Cam tucked her into her seat. She still wasn't used to that. None of this was normal for her.

"So." He sat across from her, resting his ankle on his opposite knee. His full lips curved up mischievously. "How does it feel to be the Queen of the Underworld?"

"I am no such thing." Annie picked at the hem of the table-cloth. "No one needs to know that Richard made me his bene-ficiary."

"I think it could be fun." Cam shrugged and lifted the lids of their trays, revealing healthy portions of roasted chicken and fresh vegetables. At least Elias had kept good food stores on the ship. Cam shoved a forkful of chicken in his mouth and chewed thoughtfully. "I mean, can you imagine the look on men like Elias's face? I'd pay to see that. The world needs more queens."

Annie nibbled on a carrot. She really was hungry. "I'm glad you're so easily entertained."

After some small talk, Cam began to chew on his lip, his knee bouncing as they spoke.

Annie's eyes flickered to his mouth.

Something was bothering him, but she didn't push. She never pushed. Like he never pushed her, and she'd never be able to express how grateful she was for it. *But maybe now you should?*

Turned out she didn't need to. Cam sipped his tea, then sat back. His words came out in a jumbled rush. "A-are you ready for tomorrow?"

"I think so." Annie glanced up from her plate. "I admit, I'm a little nervous about getting to port, but I'm ready to be off this ship."

Cam fidgeted nervously.

Her eyes widened. *Oh. Ohh.* "You're not talking about that, are you?"

Cam picked at the split he'd put in his lip.

Slowly, Annie finished chewing, then wiped her mouth before answering. "Is that what's had you out of sorts today? You think I'm going to get cold feet on our deal?"

Cam's gaze darted around the room before finally settling on his lap. "I wouldn't blame you if you did. Nor would I stop you if you decided to back out. You have lots of options. Especially now."

Especially now with the patent, he means. Annie glanced down at his mother's ring on her wedding finger, the red-orange stone sparkling in the low light. Marrying Cam had been one of the things she'd been looking *forward* to, even if the marriage was only a way of gaining her Western citizenship without any questions.

Every time she looked at him, she reminded herself that she was doing this for a new life. That there was nothing between them but a solid friendship. Every time, it felt like a lie. She didn't know what the truth looked like anymore.

Her cheeks heated as she sipped her tea. "No, I'm ready."

"Really?" His voice cracked with relief, then he cleared his throat. "I mean, as long as you're sure." His irises returned to green again as he changed the subject. "I also wanted to ask your opinion on something else."

Annie cut into her chicken breast, juice spilling over her knife. "Yes?"

"I haven't been able to decide." He rested his chin in his palm and made a face, still flushed. "After we manage our way through customs, should we march straight to my father's door or linger in the city for a few days? Make him sweat?" He popped his lips. "Maybe both of those ideas are stupid, and no matter what, I'll make a fool of myself. Maybe I shouldn't be doing this at all."

Annie set down her silverware and sat up straight. *What would I do if it were the other way around?* If she knew she was about to confront her family's killer, or the slaver who'd tormented her? If she had a chance to fight back against every terror they'd been forced to endure? That *she'd* been forced to endure.

After a moment, she went back to cutting her chicken. "Don't wait."

Cam's face brightened. "No?"

She nodded. "Waiting just gives him more time to plan. Plus, you'll be stressed about it. Why delay the inevitable?"

Cam's smirk widened into a smile. "I'm glad you're with me. Someone has to be the brains of this operation. I'll need you there."

Annie's brows rose. *I'm glad you're with me.* She shook her head. "You want me to come with you? To confront your father?"

Somehow, they'd never discussed that.

"Of course, I do." Cam burst out laughing. Her brands warmed at the sound. "Didn't I mention you're also the brawn?

If things go south, you can turn him into a husk like you did Frankie."

Annie winced. She didn't like remembering the way her powers seemed to have sucked Frank Boyle's *life* away. As much as she'd hated him, knowing she had that power at her disposal unsettled her. *I'm still a monster. Nothing has changed.*

Cam noticed her reaction and picked at his food. "Sorry."

"Don't be," Annie corrected. "It's just . . ." She raised her hand and studied the brands webbed over them. How could she explain it? That it was sometimes hard to believe she was still alive? That sometimes she dreamt of Charlotte stabbing her. That she could still feel the blood filling her lungs and her mind slipping away into the dark.

"I understand." He chewed that same spot on his lip. He was going to leave a scar. "There are times I wonder if this is even real, and that one of these days, I'm going to wake up in hell and this was all a sick joke."

"Stop it." Her breath hitched as she reached across the table to touch his hand. She stopped herself and twirled her glass instead. "You're not going to hell."

"I hope not." He stared at her fingers. "I really hope not."

Annie looked down at her plate so he wouldn't see the tears lining her eyes. She knew that feeling all too well. Somehow, she'd finished her food.

Cam noticed at the same time she did and took their plates. "I guess we should get some sleep, aye?"

Ice dripped through her blood at the thought of sleeping. "I can try."

He stopped short. "You don't sleep?"

I shouldn't have said that. She tried to shrug it off. "I've never slept well."

"Me either." Cam let out a low laugh. "It's hard to sleep when you're always expecting to get murdered—" His eyes widened then shot between her and the cabin door, as if he was seeing straight out to the deck beyond. His shoulders slumped, and he cursed. "*Blazes*."

Annie cringed. "I'm fine."

"I believe you." With a quick grin, Cam gently set the plates back on the table, then walked to the cabin's large closet and started digging.

She rose from her chair, chest heavy. "What are you doing?"

Cam backed out of the closet, arms loaded with fresh blankets. He spread them in front of the door, then dumped a load of pillows on top. He pulled off his coat and tossed it over the back of the chair before flopping down on the makeshift bed.

Annie blinked at him.

"I'll feel *so* much safer with you here." Cam stretched, then laid his arm over his eyes with a feline's laziness. "I don't know why I didn't think of this before. Maybe one of us will finally get some shut-eye."

He's staying in front of my door.

To protect her. So, she wouldn't be alone.

I won't be alone. She *should* tell him to leave, but she wouldn't.

Annie fought against the tightness in her throat. "F-fine. But don't look while I'm changing."

Cam just nodded, arm still covering his eyes, as he fought a smile.

She ducked into her bathing chamber to get ready for bed. When she came out, dressed in her thickest nightgown, he *looked* asleep. His chest rose and fell in rhythmic breaths.

I'm safe. Annie crawled into bed, pulling her covers over her head. *I'm not alone.* A plethora of emotions fought for her attention before she finally smiled into her pillow. "You're a terrible actor."

Cam chuckled. There was a rustle and two thumps as he kicked off his boots and settled into his blankets. He let out a long sigh. "I think I'm an excellent actor."

"You're not." She exhaled. *I'm not alone.* "Goodnight, Camden."

"Goodnight, Kitten."

CAMDEN

It took him hours to fall asleep.

How could he? Annie slept only feet away, burrowed in her blankets like a fawn in a patch of reeds. Cam's breathing only slowed when hers did. When she'd finally relaxed enough to doze off.

I'm such an idiot. He'd known she'd been captive on a slave ship. Though she'd never talked about what happened in any detail, it didn't take much imagination to guess what those pigs had done to her. He'd known and given her an unguarded cabin.

Alone—on a ship full of brash, callous sailors.

He'd thought she'd enjoy the open airiness of the captain's quarters, especially after so many years underground on New Havana. He'd been a fool. Stepping onto this ship probably felt like walking straight back into a nightmare.

Cam rolled onto his side, the hard wooden floor digging into his hip through the thin blankets. Streams of light from the lamps hanging on deck posts leaked through the window over her bed, glimmering across strands of her snow-white hair.

At least she was resting now.

Cam's eyelids grew heavy, his heat coiling up deep into his core, a beast hunkered in its cave. Setting up camp in front of her door was an impulsive move. He'd expected her to kick him out, but she didn't. Instead, she'd watched him with that emotionless mask she always wore. The one he was learning to read.

Annie *wanted* him there.

Even if it was only for protection, he didn't care.

Cam smiled as his eyelids closed. It had been a long day, but Annie was sleeping only a few feet away, and the sounds of her soft breathing were the most beautiful he'd ever heard.

Hours later, a lightning pain sang through the back of Cam's skull, and he jolted upright. "*Blazes.*"

Annie was on her feet in an instant, a dagger in her hand—the damascus one he'd given her. It felt like ages ago.

Jenny stood in the now open doorway, mouth agape as her gaze snapped between him and Annie. She'd opened the door right into his head.

"I-I'm so sorry." Jenny gulped. "Annie, it's time to get up."

Annie sagged back onto the bed, quickly tucking the blade under her pillow.

"You know, a knock would have worked just fine." Cam rubbed his bruised scalp. There was no blood. "I'm going to be feeling that for a week."

He didn't miss the way Jenny's eyes shot over his makeshift

bed. Over his discarded coat and boots. She looked back at Annie, smirking. "Should I bring breakfast for two?"

"Jenny," Annie said flatly, a warning.

Cam yanked on his boots and hopped to his feet. "That won't be necessary." He swung his coat over his shoulder, then checked the clock hanging on the wall. They had one hour until they planned to meet for the ceremony. He turned to Jenny, his voice filled with a deadly calm. "Wait outside?"

She curtsied. "Of course."

After she closed the door, he turned to Annie. Her wide, ice-blue eyes watched him warily. After a brief pause, she whispered, "So, I'll see you soon?"

His brands flickered in response to the relief flooding through him. She still hadn't changed her mind. Not yet. He winked. "I wouldn't miss it."

Cam didn't wait to see how she'd respond before he left the cabin. He wasn't sure he could keep it together if he saw any hesitation there.

Jenny waited for him, leaning against the cabin's central archway. The healed burns marring her skin stretched when she grinned at him.

"Before you make wildly inaccurate accusations," Cam said darkly, "I was having trouble sleeping. I find Miss Annie's presence very calming. That's all."

"Sure." Jenny fell in line beside him, thin hands folded behind her back, as he strode across the deck toward the staircase to the lower levels. "You know," she said, her voice high and sharp. "Nathan taught me how to tell when you're fibbing."

"Is that right?" Cam paused, letting out a breathy laugh. When he turned to face her, Jenny had her arms crossed over her chest. *She's grown bold.* His tone dropped."Nathan is the last person you should take advice from about me."

She backed away a step.

He added, "Do you think Annie would be more comfortable in another cabin?"

Jenny's golden eyes narrowed. "Honestly?"

"Always."

Together, their gazes landed on the city across the bay, and she said, "It won't help. I don't think there's anywhere her demons won't find her."

Cam's face fell.

Without a word, Jenny patted his arm before turning and heading back towards Annie's quarters. He watched her, the heaviness of her words sinking into his gut. *Is there anywhere she'll feel safe?*

If there was somewhere, he'd find it. Even if it were some remote island off the coast of nowhere land, he'd find it. He'd build her a castle taller than Enoch's highest towers. He'd lay each stone himself if he had to.

With low spirits, Cam headed below deck. The metallic boom of the waves crashing against *The Elaina's* metal walls drowned out the shouting of the crewman above.

They were approaching Enoch's harbor. There was no going back. If the next few hours went as planned, he'd be married and through harbor customs.

Cam exhaled as his heart seized in his chest. Even if all his plans for the morning went spectacularly, then what? What happened after that? He led all these people here—led Annie and Julian here—with no real plan or assurance of anything. Blazes, Alexander Callahan may be more inclined to put a bullet between his eyes on sight than to have a conversation.

Cam's fire licked up his neck. *One hour at a time.* He survived New Havana without a plan. Cam just prayed that God would show him as much mercy a second time.

Nearly an hour later, he was dressed in his best three-piece suit—it wasn't much—and stood beside Nathan and Pulley in Julian's quarters. Cam ran a hand through his hair, smoothing back the freshly washed locks. He didn't *need* to make such a fuss. It wasn't an actual ceremony. He and Annie would sign the papers, then it would be done, but he wanted to look his best.

For her.

Maybe a little for him.

Either way, he was terrified. They'd be visiting his father after this, the man who murdered his mother. But at the moment, he was more afraid *she* wouldn't come.

There was a knock on the door. Julian hopped up and opened it, smoothing down his signature cream coat.

Cam forgot how to breathe.

On the other side of the doorway, Annie's steely gaze found him as she fingered the jade fishhook pendant, hanging by a black leather cord, around her neck. The pendant that had once belonged to his captain, Edmund Resh. The top half of her hair was braided and pinned into an exquisite pattern, while the lower half fell loose to her ribs in snowy waves. Where she'd found the ribbed, sky-blue day gown she wore, he had no idea, but he didn't care.

She was stunning.

Beside her, Jenny was equally dolled up and lovely, but he barely noticed her.

He found himself wanting to brush his fingers over the color staining Annie's cheekbones. Instead, he reached for her, and she looped her pinkie through his without hesitation, her expression never changing from that of cool indifference. He saw straight through it. She was as nervous as he was, and he didn't know if that made him feel better or worse.

Nathan moved to stand beside Jenny, his eyes nearly bugging out of his head at the sight of her. They'd have to have a talk with him about that later. Annie would kill Nathan if he made a move on her sister.

"Well." Pulley—good, ole' Pulley—rubbed his shiny, bald head before smoothing down his threadbare waistcoat. "I never thought getting ordained for my cousin's wedding would have come so much in handy."

Cam forced his attention back to his navigator. "Pulley, you're a priceless gem. You've got the form?"

The older man nodded. He took a document out of his coat pocket and unrolled it on Julian's desk. "Right." He cleared his throat. "Who wants to start?"

Cam's fire surged, guttered out, and flared again in the span of a breath. *Don't be a coward. What if she hates you? She's doing this for herself. She won't run. Just sign the blasted paper, Camden.* He wasn't getting enough air. He stepped forward, and Julian held out a pen for him. Cam scanned over the document.

A marriage certificate.

She's not going to run. She's not going to run. Cam signed his name on the dotted line. His fingers trembled as he passed the pen to Annie.

She neatly signed her name next to his. Only the death grip on his finger gave an indication she felt any emotion.

After that, Nathan and Jenny signed as witnesses beside them.

Pulley signed below them.

Just like that, it was done.

They were married—the new Lord and Lady Callahan.

Cam could barely keep himself standing. *Annie's my wife.*

He never thought he'd marry. Not after what he'd seen happen between his father and mother when he was young. *But this is just a deal.* He reminded himself. *Another bargain.* Annie was under no obligation to stay a minute more than she wanted or needed, nor would he try to stop her if she decided to go.

He wouldn't forget that. For her sake, he'd keep whatever this was he felt for her to himself.

"I'll take care of this." Julian folded up the certificate and shoved it into his coat. "Are you two ready?"

Cam blinked at him.

Annie's voice sounded as shaky as he felt. "For what?"

Julian smiled broadly, his silver eyes bright. "Enoch's waiting."

Cam stared up at the massive stone archway leading out of Enoch's harbor. The heaviness of the grey rock matched the anxious weight crushing his chest. "I never thought I'd be here again."

Beside him, Annie followed his gaze. Even a city as sturdy as the Western capital had nothing next to the hardness of her granite stare. She cocked her head, nearly resting it on his shoulder, making his stomach flutter. "Life is ironic that way, isn't it?"

From behind them, Julian muttered, "You have no idea."

The line moved forward, and they shuffled along with it.

Hundreds had departed their foreign vessels and were waiting to be granted entrance into the West, into Enoch. Into the land that was meant to be his. They had to wait their turn like everyone else.

"You think they could liven it up a little?" Nathan stated,

too loudly, standing on Cam's opposite side. "I mean, blazes, would some color kill them? Cam, you never told me your people were such stiff necks."

Cam knew the deepest West Nathan had ever traveled was Port Lebanon, and that sat at the very southern-most tip of the continent. He let out a soft chuckle. "You haven't seen *stiff* yet, mate. Just you wait."

Beside Annie, Jenny giggled, and Annie swatted her elbow.

The line moved, and they managed a few more steps.

A few raindrops had started to fall by the time they reached the front of the line. There was only one group left ahead of them.

Annie tipped her head back, closing her eyes, as droplets landed on her pale lashes. Cam leaned in, whispering as he linked elbows with her. "Enjoying the weather?"

She looked so dainty in the oversized coat she wore over her dress. "I am. It reminds me of home."

Curiosity beat out his nerves. "How old were you when you left the North?"

"Thirteen."

Thirteen. Cam suppressed a shudder. He'd already killed by thirteen. Why did the world have to be so brutal? He kept his voice low. "Where in the North?"

"Rouenn."

"I've been there," Cam replied. He remembered its delicate snow peaks, mirrored by a cold so deep, he thought he'd lose his every extremity to the frost. Annie looked surprised. He continued. "It's beautiful." *And so are you.*

She smiled a little. "Yes, it is."

Loud voices drew Cam's attention back to the customs booth, where the head of the group now argued with the harbor official. *Great. Now they'll be in a terrible mood for us.* He looked back at Annie. "You know, it's not a far sail to Rouenn.

We could visit if you wished." *God, why can't I keep my mouth shut?*

Annie raised a brow. "We? Visit?"

He gave her a sheepish smile. "If you wanted."

"Visit." She seemed to chew on the words. "Yes, we could do that. One day."

If we have a one day, he realized. His future—*their* future—depended on how this visit with his father unraveled.

Somewhere his father won't find him. His mother had died to keep him out of the hands of Alexander Callahan. Now here he was—marching straight to his front door. It felt like betrayal.

Annie nudged his side, and Cam startled. She nodded to his hands. A small ring of flames encircled them, turning the now sprinkling rain to steam. He exhaled, calming the itching fire rolling under his skin. He hadn't realized it had flared so much. The ends of his coat sleeves were singed now. *Lord, help me. This is already going to hell.*

A twitch ran through him as he stuffed his fire down, down, *down.* He didn't know what else to do with it. It fought against his restraints, snapping at him like a wild animal waiting to be whipped. He didn't want to contain it. He wanted to *use* it, but he didn't trust himself not to burn down half the city.

"Next!"

His fire quieted as the official called them up.

Here we go. Cam straightened, slapping on a wide, fake smile. Annie fell in close to his side as they stepped up to the customs booth. The spectacled official inside gave them a nervous once-over as they approached. *Three Revenants. He's probably deciding whether to call the city guard.* The man sniffed. "State your business."

But Cam was ready—at least as ready as he could be. He'd been preparing to play this part. He casually leaned against the booth, gesturing over his shoulder to where *The Elaina* was being anchored along the docks. "Private vessel. I'm requesting entrance for me and my occupants into the city."

The official's thick brows rose, his glasses sliding down his nose as he peered out toward *The Elaina*. "You say *that's* a private vessel?"

Cam shrugged. "You know how it is. Family to impress and all."

"Quite." The official shook his head, licking his thumb to turn to a fresh page in his logbook. "State your names."

Cam's mouth quirked. "Julian Price, Nathan Williams, Jenny Duskin, and my bride—previously Annie Duskin."

The official looked up from where he jotted down their entries. "And you, sir?"

Fire filled Cam's eyes as he grinned. "Camden Callahan."

CHAPTER 3
ANNIE

Bride. He'd called her his *bride*.

Her name was Callahan now.

The official's head jerked up from his logbook, where he took in Cam with wide eyes, mouth agape. Even after all these years, it seemed people still remembered his name.

"C-Camden Callahan." The man repeated as he recorded the name. His gaze finally fell onto her. "And you're Lady Callahan?"

Lady Callahan. A shiver ran through her. *Camden's not the only one with a part to play.* Annie had work to do. She leaned into Cam's side, mimicking his wide, charming smile, and crooned. "Yes, and I'd appreciate it if you'd hurry us through. This rain will ruin my gown."

Cam shot her a delightedly appreciative look.

The official just stared at her, his pen leaking ink on the opened page before him.

Cam cocked his head in that vicious way of his. "My lady just spoke to you."

The poor official leaped from his chair. "Of-of course!" He

fumbled with a ring of keys on his belt before finally unlocking the barred gate separating the harbor from the city entrance. "Please, come inside! Shall I order you a carriage, my lord?"

"Please." Cam kept his arm around Annie's shoulder as they passed through the entry, barely touching her. "And quickly."

"Right away, right away." The official nodded to a younger customs worker to take his place before hurrying to find them transport. The low overhang protected them from the rain as they waited.

Nathan blew out a long breath, then laughed. "Well, that was . . . interesting. I can't believe we got away with it. He didn't even ask to see the ship's papers."

Annie's stomach flipped. She hadn't thought of that. If they had searched the ship, it wouldn't have taken long for them to realize it was stolen.

"I had plans in place if it came to that." Mr. Price leaned against the wall. "They would have found all the captain's documents in proper order."

Nathan shot Mr. Price a suspicious look. After the shock of New Havana wore off, Nathan hadn't been happy about working with the very same Revenant that blew apart his old ship and helped murder his crew. Somehow, Cam had gotten them to work together. He had a way with people.

Annie glanced between Jenny and Nathan. They were dressed more finely than she'd ever seen them—or at least as finely as they could manage with the clothes they found on board *The Elaina*. Nathan's suit was too big—he hadn't recovered the weight he'd lost while imprisoned by Lord Duskin—but Jenny was a good seamstress.

They looked like they belonged alongside a lord's son. *If we play our parts right, we may just pull this off.*

Cam crossed his ankles, a heaviness hovering over him.

"What do you want to bet that oaf already sent a messenger to my father?"

Mr. Price frowned. "I would be disappointed if he didn't. Alexander Callahan hasn't maintained his position this long by remaining uninformed."

"He can't have been in office for *that* long?" Jenny piped in, tucked beneath her parasol. " Callahan can't be fifty yet, can he?"

"Being a governor is like being a walking bullseye. Most don't last more than a few years before they're assassinated," Cam said.

"I'm confused. Is the job elected or an inheritance?" Nathan asked.

"An inheritance," Mr. Price answered. "Unless a governor dies without leaving an heir. Then the council must elect a new man into office, and he will pass the position down to his children."

"That sounds overcomplicated to me," Jenny said. "With so much death, why would someone want the job in the first place?"

An enormous, green-paneled coach, drawn by four black horses, approached, their hooves clacking loudly against the stone street.

Annie watched it solemnly before answering, "Power."

Cam tucked his hands in his pockets as the coach pulled alongside them, letting his expression grow bored. The driver was maybe in his early twenties with a patchy mustache.

He dipped his wide-brimmed hat. "Sorry to keep you waiting, my lord." He stepped down and opened the coach door, sweeping an arm to usher them inside. "Where to?"

Cam tucked a few silver coins into the man's coat pocket. "The Callahan estate."

The driver seemed alarmed, glancing between her, Cam,

and Mr. Price as the other two climbed into the coach. Finally, he tipped his hat, and Cam shot him a half smile before turning to her.

As beautiful as it was, she hated this dress. Its ribbing was too thick and stiff. It was hard to move. She accepted the hand Cam offered, and he helped her up the steps. His eyes were hard despite the fire burning behind them. His fingers brushed against her elbow. "Remind me why we're doing this, please?"

Annie paused on the steps, looking down at him, at the water droplets hissing into mist before ever touching his skin. A strand of his blond hair had fallen over his eye, and it took everything she had not to brush it away.

"You're doing it for *her*," she said softly, not wanting to speak his mother's name where someone might hear. "You're doing it for *us*. For Nathan. For Jenny. So maybe one day we can all live a normal life without someone trying to kill us."

"Today might determine if we ever get to *one day*," Cam said. "In fact, we may not even make it to tomorrow."

She almost reached for that strand of hair but stopped in time, brushing his shoulder instead. She could have sworn he shivered. "Then it's a good thing I'm not afraid to die."

The ride to the estate was uneventful.

Mr. Price insisted on keeping the blinds in the coach drawn, lest they be recognized.

The sharp *pitter-patter* of raindrops hitting the carriage roof made Annie's eyes heavy. *But who would recognize us? Neither* Jenny nor she had ever been West, and Cam said he hadn't set foot in the city since he was nine. Maybe Mr. Price himself had gained a decent amount of notoriety over the years. The only detail she knew of his life before New Havana was that he'd been in the military before his rebirth. After being discharged for being a Revenant, he took up mercenary work. She'd only learned that recently, and he'd never mentioned it again or offered up any more of his history.

Nor did she ask.

She and Cam sat on a bench seat across from the others. Mr. Price stared at the shut blinds, as if he could see through them. Nathan and Jenny talked animatedly to each other about the different kinds of fabric Jenny hoped to collect now that they were on the mainland.

Quilts. Annie's lips quirked. The day Frank Boyle had scarred Jenny's face, she'd said she'd wanted to make and sell quilts if she were free. Even below ground in the bunker, covered in hateful burns, Jenny's wants were so innocent.

Today has to go well. Annie's gaze flickered to the covered window. If it didn't, Jenny would never have her shop. If anyone deserved happiness, it was her.

And what about you? The thought jolted her, and Annie shook it away. She deserved nothing but the grave.

Beside her, Cam's knee bounced incessantly, his chin resting in his palm as whispers of fire crawled up his neck, curling around his ear.

He's a mess. Annie watched him from the corner of her eye. Cam would have to look in the face of his own father and know what he'd done to his mother, what his father had done to *him.*

The bouncing of Cam's knee increased to the point of shaking the bench. Reflexively, she reached out and rested her hand on it.

Cam froze.

Why did I do that? Annie's heart shot into her throat. She shouldn't have touched him. She knew better. *What's wrong with me? I can't keep making mistakes like this.*

Slowly, she tried to move her hand from his leg, but before

she could, Cam rested his over hers, his skin gloriously warm against the damp, bitter cold seeping into the coach.

Mr. Price's silver eyes flickered to them.

Just breathe. Her heart pounded in her ears. *He's not them.*

Cam didn't look at her or even acknowledge where they touched, but his body began to relax. Or at least, his knee stopped bouncing.

Annie counted her breaths. *I won't run. Not from him.* She repeated that over and over as she kept her gaze fixed on the window, focusing on the clack of the horses' hooves on cobblestone. She couldn't tell how much time had passed. Twice, Cam stroked the back of her hand with his thumb. Each time her heart stuttered.

Finally, Mr. Price pulled back the blinds, blanketing them in the dim, grey light of evening. Annie's breath hitched as she leaned forward, at the same time as Nathan and Jenny, to peer out the window, taking in their first view of the Callahan estate. Cam's expression darkened, a scowl forming, as he shifted to the farthest corner of the carriage.

Annie had never seen wealth before Lord Duskin had purchased her from the slavers. She still remembered the first time she saw his manor. The awe, mixed with disgust, she felt at the size of his balconies and lavish courtyards. After years of eating nothing but scraps and sleeping on the damp floor of the slaver's hull, it had seemed so excessive. Indulgent. She'd assumed even royalty didn't live as well as the Duskins.

She'd been wrong.

Lord Duskin had been penniless compared to the Callahans.

A perfectly trimmed hedge, tall enough to block out spying eyes, surrounded endless rolling meadows. Cam's grip on her hand tightened as they approached a wide, double gate. The driver said a few words to the man attending the entrance, and the door opened for them to pass.

The heavy clack of the gate closing behind them made Annie's insides squirm. Fear clawed at her already tight lungs. She was trapped again, in another manor. Another place where they could take everything away from her. She shook her head. *This is here, not there. This is different.*

Annie glanced down at her hand, still wrapped in Cam's. At the inky brands that webbed her skin. At the fiery glow that burned under his. *They can't keep me.* She wasn't helpless anymore. She had Cam. She had Mr. Price. For how long, she didn't know, but for now, they were beside her. *You're safe.*

Cam remained silent as they moved deeper into the estate grounds. The narrow, hedge-lined driveway opened to reveal what she could only describe as the pathway to kings.

Acres of manicured lawn surrounded a six-story manor. Visible to the east and west were elaborate gardens filled with marble fountains. Fruit in more varieties than she'd ever seen grew in rows and rows of trees, ripe for the picking. Beyond the orchards, visible just below the rolling hills, were more manors —smaller, sitting alongside the sea—but just as grand as the estate's impressive centerpiece.

It was stunning. It was grand.

And it was . . . empty.

A frown formed on Annie's lips. *This isn't right.* There wasn't a living soul anywhere in sight. The manor itself rose above them in cold, bitter, grey stone. The massive spire, which seemed to grow off the eastern wing, was stained black with lichen.

The coach brought them to a circular courtyard outside the manor entrance.

Beside her, Cam finally glanced out the window as they rolled to a halt.

"Figures," he said. "Ten years, and my father has let this place go to hell."

"If this is hell," Jenny breathed, staring up at the manor in wonder. "What was it before?"

Annie hated the sorrow that filled Cam's eyes when he said, "Something even worse."

The coach door swung open, and the driver ushered them out with a tip of his hat. Once they exited, Cam stretched as his heat coiled up his neck, and he grinned. "Well, best get this over with, yes?"

Annie followed him as he strode toward the grand entrance, hands in his pockets, all signs of his former anxiousness smothered by the overconfident demeanor he wore like a shield.

Mr. Price moved up beside them, Nathan and Jenny a few paces behind. "Have you thought of what you'll say?" he asked Cam. "No matter how this goes, you'll be accusing the Governor of the West of murder."

Cam just shrugged. "You know me. I make things up as I go."

"Indeed." Mr. Price sighed. "And it's that attitude that got you killed the first time."

Cam shot him a glare. "Why are you even here if you disagree? I didn't force you to board my ship, and I didn't make you come along today."

Cam had a point.

Annie often wondered why Mr. Price didn't go his own way after Lord Duskin was killed. Instead, he clung to Cam. Advised him, guided him. He wanted something, but despite her curiosity, life had taught her enough about the dangers of asking questions.

Mr. Price looked away, lips thinning into a harsh line. "I have my reasons."

"As do I," Cam shot back. "Now, can we agree to mind our own bloody business?"

Annie glanced over her shoulder long enough to notice that Jenny and Nathan watched them nervously. *He needs to stay calm . . . for them.* She reached out to brush Cam's elbow, feeling his warmth even beneath the heavy layers of his leather jacket. "Mr. Price is allowed to ask questions."

Cam raised a brow at her.

Mr. Price nodded smugly. "Thank you, Miss Annie."

"And Camden is also allowed not to answer," she said flatly. "So, can you both agree to each other's privacy and remember the real reason we're here?"

Behind them, Nathan choked on a laugh.

"Touché." Cam gave her a wicked grin as they approached the manor's grand double doors. "By all means, Kitten. The stage is yours if you want it." He ignored the doorbell, instead rapping his knuckles so hard on the polished wooden doors that he chipped the varnish. The sound echoed across the empty courtyards, the silence so complete that the raindrops could be heard falling from the trees' leaves.

From somewhere inside, a loud groan rattled the entry. The doors shook, and the hinges creaked, before opening just a crack. A young, male face with a mop of black hair peeked out, his features twitchy. "State your name and business."

"Now that I'm here, this seems silly to ask." Cam chuckled as he ran a hand through his damp hair. "But is my father at home?"

The boy's quick eyes scanned over Cam's tanned face, then shifted to hers, then to Mr. Price—all the while his skin slowly drained of color. "Please, come inside."

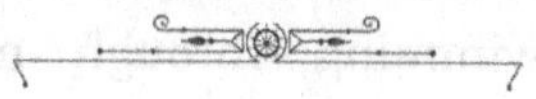

Annie didn't miss the effort it took for Cam to keep his posture loose and relaxed. As the doorkeeper—or whatever he was—led them inside, Cam took in every detail, his jaw clenched tight.

Annie stayed beside him.

There were no words for the interior of the Callahan manor. Castle. Palace. She didn't know what to call it, either. The grey stone entryway continued into the main hallway, but the floors were now stark, white, unblemished marble. Nowhere she looked down the entire trek into the waiting room did she find a streak of grey or black in the stone. She couldn't imagine the cost.

Despite his confident façade, Cam's breaths were too shallow. His fire too close to the surface.

Touch him. Cold energy danced at the tips of her fingers. *Touch. Feel. Take.*

She shook the whispers away, revulsion filling her throat with bile. Since the day she'd been reborn, she'd suspected what this *thing* inside her wanted, what it craved and begged for—power. *For him.*

The man—who'd introduced himself as David—instructed them to wait in a small, cozy sitting area. Annie couldn't stop her eyes from shifting to the fire creeping up the veins in Cam's neck. The energy within her stirred greedily. *Touch. Feel. Take.* Words were exchanged between David and the others, but she couldn't hear them. Not really. Or at least they didn't matter. Not anymore.

"Tea, my lady?"

Annie dragged her stare away from Cam's throat. The movement like swimming through mud. She blinked. "Pardon?"

David blinked back at her. Not judgmental. Just curious. "Would you like tea?"

"Y-yes, please." She placed her hand over her own throat, willing her heart to slow. "That sounds lovely."

David gave her a short bow before exiting, leaving the five of them alone to wait.

Cam let out a low groan before plopping down on a deep blue, cushioned sofa. "And so the games begin."

For the first time since she entered the study, Annie felt awake. She turned, taking it all in. Stacks and stacks of bookshelves lined the walls, filled with worn foreign tomes as well as more modern titles. A long, thin tea table sat before the blue sofa. A second matching loveseat sat on the other side.

"This is . . . pleasant," Jenny whispered, mostly to herself. "Very homey?"

"Claustrophobic is the word you're looking for." Nathan crinkled his nose as he leaned against the nearest bookshelf, arms crossed. "I don't like it."

There were no windows, Annie realized. Just the cheery lights of the pure ivory sconces seated on the walls between every shelf. *It's a room, not a cell. Calm down.*

"It's an intimidation tactic," Mr. Price said and sat on the sofa across from Cam. "The confined space is to make us feel anxious and desperate."

"Well, it's working," Nathan replied. "I'd rather peel my toenails off than spend another moment in here."

Jenny nodded in agreement, picking at the sleeves of her emerald-green gown.

He's not here.

Annie's body locked up. So, so faint. A voice so frail that it barely brushed her ear repeated, *he's not here.* Her power. It was searching for him.

"Alexander Callahan isn't here." The words left Annie's

mouth before she had a chance to think. In her bones, she knew that's what the words meant.

Mr. Price, Nathan, and Jenny stared at her in shock.

Cam just nodded, unfazed. "Figures. He knew we were coming. Waiting is all part of the game."

Annie tried to shake off the tingling sensations running over her skin. *You've seen ghosts. Why should voices frighten you?* It wasn't *really* a voice. Just her power . . . talking to her. *Lord, save me.* She still couldn't get her heart to slow as she said, "But will he show?"

"He'll show." Mr. Price answered, shrugging deeper into his cloak. "He can't risk looking like a coward. He'll show."

Annie's knees trembled as she lowered herself awkwardly onto the sofa beside Cam. Corsets were the bane of her existence. Mr. Price joined the conversation with Nathan and Jenny about a genealogy book they found on one of the shelves.

Annie let out a shaky breath. From the corner of her eye, she caught Cam's gaze trailing over her features. Green-gold eyes filled with concern, Cam faked a smile, his tone low and tight. "You look like you're about to have a meltdown."

She couldn't help the dark laugh that escaped her. Thankfully, the others didn't seem to notice. "So do you."

Cam reclined against the back of the sofa, absently twirling a lock of her hair around his finger. A gentle gesture, but enough to send a chill through her. "Would you laugh at me if I said I feel like I'm going to vomit?"

"No," Annie admitted. "I'd be more concerned if you didn't feel anything at all."

A softness passed over his face just as there was a knock on the door. They both straightened as a petite woman stepped into the waiting room, her expression as tight and rigid as her lean frame.

She was . . . stunning. There was no other way to describe her. The woman's inky-black hair was swept into a sleek, tight bun, accentuating her dark, upturned eyes and creamy-beige skin. The high-necked bodice of her burgundy day gown was buttoned just below her narrow chin, emphasizing her dangling amethyst and gold earrings.

She gave them a tense smile. "Welcome to my home. My name is Maya, the wife of Governor Callahan. My husband is currently out but is expected to return shortly. You are more than welcome to wait and make yourselves comfortable."

A practiced speech. Annie had made similar ones when visitors had come for Lord Duskin.

A thousand emotions passed over Cam's face before it finally landed on maddening rage. "*Your* home?"

A brief flicker of terror flashed through Maya's features as she took in the fire filling his eyes and the brands beneath them. Her mouth parted. "Y-you?"

She'd either heard of him before or knew he was coming.

Cam's smile was deadly, his skin beginning to glow from the heat beneath it. "Me."

No, no, no. Annie reached for him, but it was too late.

The waiting room erupted into a storm of smoke and fire.

CHAPTER 4
ALEXANDER

Alexander grew so tired of the rain.

He leaned his head against the carriage's windowpane, letting the cool glass soothe his pulsing headache. He'd already attended three meetings, and it wasn't yet noon.

With the pro-Revenant group leaders.

With the anti-Revenant group leaders.

With the Enoch police force.

Now all he wanted was to sit in his office with a glass of wine, maybe read a book by the fire, but no. He never got a damn minute to himself. The entire city council was in the carriage following his. He didn't feel like spending a moment more away from home than necessary. He'd told them that if they wanted to meet today, as well, they'd have to make the trek for him. He'd long stopped caring about what they'd make of the inconvenience.

Enoch was the largest city in the West, and the council building was a three-hour carriage ride from his estate. He'd done enough traveling for others over the years. They could cater to him now.

He pinched his eyes shut, praying for the pain to pass. At this point, he'd rather drive an ice pick through his eye than spend the evening with the invalids behind him.

Alexander sighed in relief as his carriage rolled up to the manor entrance. The driver opened the door for him with a deep bow.

David waited for him at the entry doors beneath a black umbrella—fidgeting.

Wonderful. Alexander suppressed a groan. Of course, it would be now, of all times, for something to be wrong. Not much flustered David, and if he was antsy . . .

David shielded Alexander with the umbrella as he stepped out of the carriage, his face pinched with concern.

"Whatever it is," Alexander growled. "Spit it out. I'm not in the mood."

David watched as the council members climbed out of their own carriages and gathered around the entrance. "My lord . . . something's happened."

Alexander rolled his eyes, striding toward the front doors. "I assumed so. Out with it."

David's voice lowered to a whisper. "Y-your son is here."

"Of course, he is." Alexander scoffed. "Kai is a child. Where else would he be?"

Despite just turning eight years old, his second son rarely ventured beyond the folds of his mother's skirts, let alone off the estate. Alexander often pushed Maya to let him take their boy to his meetings in the city, but she always refused. With the unrest, she didn't trust Enoch. He couldn't blame her, but still, Kai needed to learn what it was to be a Callahan.

"No, no." David shook his head. "The other one."

The other one. Alexander clutched his chest. His heart stuttered before starting again. *It's time. I'm not ready.* So much planning. Years of it. Would it be enough?

Alexander grabbed hold of David's collar. "Where is he?"

Truthfully, Alexander hadn't needed to ask.

He'd known precisely where Camden would go.

Cassandra had loved dances and parties when she'd been alive. She'd loved the lights and the decorations, loved to entertain, and was always the center of attention. There was nothing that could compare to one of her balls. The way she could almost make you believe that—just for a moment—time stopped when you entered one of the fantastical worlds she created.

No expense was too high when it came to her guests. She made the most hardened of men smile and laugh.

Cassandra had been a sun. Others followed where she led, revolving around her like planets.

So had he. Once upon a time, she'd been his sole reason to breathe.

Alexander hadn't set foot in the manor's ballroom since the night she'd fled.

The door's handle was hot to the touch, scalding his fingertips. He covered his hand with his sleeve to open it. Warmth leaked through the doorframe, burning away some of the chill clinging to his damp skin.

I forgot to tell the council to wait for me. It wasn't until he stepped foot into the massive, rectangular dance hall that he realized they'd followed, that they were arguing together, alarmed by his unexpected behavior.

Alexander was never unexpected.

Alexander was always everything he was expected to be . . .

and worse. If it hadn't been for that reputation, he'd have been picked off sometime in the last year now that his health was failing.

A twang of regret hit him at the cobwebs fanning loose from the ceiling, at the dusty covers over the furniture. This space had once been so bright, so full of life and beauty and . . .

It didn't matter now. She was dead.

Only the banquet table lay uncovered, long enough to sit one hundred guests comfortably. Now, at its head, a young, handsome Revenant man reclined in the oversized dining chair that had once belonged to Alexander's grandfather—a grand oak piece with red velvet cushions. He'd been a man of fire, too, and Alexander had never been able to live up to him.

With his cheek resting on a closed fist and one ankle propped on the opposite knee, the Revenant's lips curled into an inhuman smile while observing the group of men entering the ballroom.

Cunning. Calculating. Burning sunset brands, like lightning, illuminated the eyes that Alexander knew had once been green, setting them ablaze.

Alexander slid off his heavy overcoat, laying it on the table between them. *The other one.* He kept his voice firm. "Hello, Camden."

The Revenant's grin turned feral. Cruel. "Father."

"What are you doing here, boy?" One of the council members stepped forward, nearly crossing the ballroom doors. He was the same man who had followed Henry Bale into his study days ago. "You're trespassing."

Camden's eyes rose slowly, darkening further.

Fool. Even if he weren't Revenant, only a simpleton would call the creature across from them a *boy.*

The man blathered on. "You are trespassing on the governor's property—"

Camden flicked his wrist, and a wave of blinding heat seared the floor black, dancing around Alexander to slam the doors shut in the council's face. The walls shook. The men cried out in alarm.

They were alone now.

Camden cocked his head, threads of fire bleeding into his veins as he drawled, "I hope you don't mind. There are only so many crusty, old men I can handle in a day. I've already reached my limit."

He's spent much of his time in the South. His slight, rolling accent gave it away. Alexander held back a laugh, his shoulders squared, as he moved down the table. He took the third seat to Camden's left. "Not at all. The feeling is mutual."

He greedily took in every inch of his son, the child he hadn't laid eyes on in a decade. *He looks just like me . . . and his grandfather.* Yes, he had the same sandy hair, the same square jaw. Camden was taller and leaner, built more like his mother, but even a blind man could see what he was—Alexander's heir.

Camden's knee-length leather coat failed to conceal the pearl-finished revolver he wore in a holster on his belt, or the knife sheathed at his shoulder, both well-oiled and polished.

His son studied him as Alexander reclined, taking off his top hat and laying it on the table, before smoothing back his tied-back hair. "You shouldn't have bothered with the weapons. You don't need them, do you?"

"No, I don't." Camden unsheathed his dagger, twirling it between his fingers with a practiced flourish. "But old habits die hard."

"That they do." Alexander licked his dry lips. "Where is my wife?"

"She's with mine. Safe. Well, safe-ish."

It wasn't often Alexander was genuinely surprised. "I didn't know you'd married."

"It was recent."

"Congratulations. I'm sorry to have missed it."

Camden reclined further. "It was a small ceremony. Important people only."

"I see." Alexander copied the movement. "I must admit, I didn't expect you for at least another three days. You must be an excellent waterman." He allowed himself a small smile. Camden mirrored it. *He's learned well.* "And captaining a warship, I hear? Well done."

Camden's smile turned malicious. "Does it make you proud knowing that I've taken nearly as many lives as you?"

Now we're getting to the point. Alexander steepled his fingers. "Immensely so."

Camden picked at the edge of his blade, staining it red, and his eyes sharpened with his tone. "It didn't take you long to replace Mother, I see. Did you even wait until her body was cold?" He ran his tongue along the inside of his teeth. "And don't you dare lie to me. I'll know."

It felt like he'd been stabbed in the gut. Alexander expected this question—these accusations—for years, but it didn't make them sting any less. He kept his expression deceptively blank. "Maya is a wonderful woman. I hope you'll see that."

"I'm sure she is."

"And she's been a wonderful mother to your brother."

As hard as he tried to hide it, Camden's brows rose in shock. "I have a brother? Interesting. Do you beat him, too? Cane or belt?" He let out a manic laugh. "I always preferred the belt. The brown one, in particular."

Alexander inhaled. His finger itched, and he resisted scratching it. *You knew this was coming. Keep it together.* He'd spent his entire life struggling to stay in perfect line. Never once had he strayed from *the plan,* from his purpose. His legacy. He'd done horrific things in the early years in his position to remain in control. He'd never regretted it.

Until now.

Until it had all started falling apart.

Alexander closed his eyes for just a moment. He swore he saw Cassandra staring back at him. His chest shuddered as he reopened them. It was his son watching now, glowing eyes filled with hate.

"I know why you're here, Camden." He sucked in another breath, suppressing a cough. Breathing grew harder every day. "And I know what you've been told, but I never tried to hurt you." His chest seized painfully. "And I didn't kill your mother."

CHAPTER 5
ANNIE

Cam's fire had long burned out, but the waiting room still smelled of it. Of bitter hurt, betrayal, and pain that delved deeper than flesh and bone.

Annie and Maya Callahan sat across from each other, on what remained of the sofas, and waited. Occasionally, Maya brushed a bit of soot off her expensive dress. Annie found herself just watching her. Studying the older woman's casual grace, her ability to keep her features pleasant.

It reminded Annie a little bit of herself.

Cam stormed out in a rage after Maya's introduction, with no explanation of where he was going. Annie meant to follow him, but Mr. Price stopped her with a shake of his head. That had been an hour ago now.

The others kept themselves busy by searching for salvageable books after the inferno. Mainly to avoid the awkwardness between the two Callahan women. Eventually, Maya joined them, filling them in on some interesting tidbits about the authors of the tomes they examined.

Annie's skin buzzed with an electric current. The fabric of

her dress was too rough against her skin. The texture of her mouth felt off. There was a slight ringing in her ears. *My power.* It was searching for him. It wanted him back by her side, where it thought he belonged.

She jumped as Mr. Price sat beside her, far enough away not to touch her, but close enough for her to hear him whisper as he watched Maya with narrowed eyes, "Camden needs to gain control himself . . . and quickly."

He wasn't wrong. Cam's fire had only *grown* since they'd left New Havana. She often wondered how he contained it all, or if sometimes he barely managed to at all, with the way it seemed to boil just below the surface of his skin. It could become a problem.

"Why are you telling me?" Annie chewed her thumbnail. "You talk to him."

Mr. Price folded his hands over his lap. "You're his *wife.*"

"In name only," Annie said sharply. "You know that." *At least, I hope he does.*

Mr. Price gave her a knowing look. "He listens to you. Respects you. I've asked him multiple times to let me teach him how to wield his power, but he refuses. I think Elias soured the idea of a mentor for him."

Annie didn't blame Cam. Letting people in . . . getting too close, it was dangerous. Her brow rose. "And now you want me to convince him?"

"If you can," Mr. Price sighed before his gaze flickered to the ebony-black brands on her hands. "He might be more willing if you two train together."

Now *that* did surprise her. She'd known Mr. Price for as long as she had the Duskins, but they'd never been friendly. He'd mostly ignored her until those last weeks on the island. "I imagine you have much more important things to do than give me lessons. I'm not at risk of burning down a city."

"Maybe not, but I suspect your gifts are no less deadly."

Annie chose not to answer.

"Just ask him." Mr. Price stood as Maya approached. "Please?"

Just as deadly? The image of what she'd done to Frank Boyle flashed through her mind. She gave him a stiff nod, and Mr. Price returned the gesture.

Maya cleared her throat as she sat across from Annie again, crossing her legs. *I wonder if her gown is as itchy as mine.*

"So." Her smile was sweet, practiced . . . artful. "How long have you and Camden known each other, my lady?"

Annie glanced up coldly. Maya's features shifted from anxious expectation to genuine curiosity, then to concern.

A tremor of energy rattled the walls, leaking through the cracks in the door.

Camden. Annie straightened as the wave crashed over her, and she felt it—felt *him*—the disbelief, the sadness, and so, so much hate. The strength soaked into her, her brands flaring in response, absorbing it.

Annie shot Maya—whose face had twisted in fear—an equally practiced smile. "I've known him long enough to know when someone is about to die, *my lady*."

CHAPTER 6
CAMDEN

Liar.

Damned bloody liar.

Cam's bones vibrated as rage coursed through him. He didn't care if Alexander was his father. He'd kill him right then and there. His fire, always waiting at the cusp of his mind, whispered to him. *Release me. Let me char his bones. Let me reduce him to ash.*

Cam shook his head, grinding his teeth. *No. We need answers.* She *needs answers. I—*

"Camden?" His father's voice still sent a shiver of dread through him, just as it had when he was a child. It snapped him back to the present.

He fixed his attention back on Alexander Callahan. On the face that looked so much like his. He hated it.

"You're still lying." Cam let out a harsh laugh as flames burned like acid in his throat. "After all this time, you're *still lying.*"

Alexander cocked his head, looking at him in a way that

would have sent nine-year-old Cam running. "What reason do I have to lie?"

Cam raised one finger. "Because that's what you do. Lie." He raised a second. "Because will your people support a uxoricidal governor? Likely not." A third. "And because that would mean admitting your guilt. We all know you're too much of a narcissistic bastard for that."

"You've learned a lot of fancy words, son."

"I've learned more than that." Cam pulled Elias's letter from the inside of his coat pocket. Addressed by his father to the now dead Revenant. He pushed it across the table. "Explain this."

Alexander unfolded the worn paper, squinting as he scanned over the words. A slow smirk spread over his sallow face.

Cam's brows furrowed. *Has he always looked so gaunt?* In his nightmares, his father had never looked so frail. Maybe he'd remembered wrong.

"What's there to explain?" Alexander laid the letter back on the table. "One year ago, I paid Elias Bennett to bring you home. He failed to do so. It's that simple."

One year? It had only been months since he'd made the deal with Elias that landed him in this mess. *Had he been searching for me for that long?*

Before Cam could respond, a side door in the dance hall swung open. Annie stepped through—her ice-blue gaze instantly latching onto his—followed by Maya Callahan.

Anxiety rippled off Maya as she scanned over Alexander.

Cam scowled. *My new stepmother.* He nearly murdered his father just for that—for replacing his *real* mother like a worn-out sock.

He could also have slaughtered Alexander for the way his eyes lit up at the sight of Annie. At her skin and hair, the color of bleached bone. Her movements, so purposeful and tight, like a viper coiled to strike.

Annie cautiously took the seat beside Cam. "Lady Maya and I grew tired of waiting." She gave Alexander a close-lipped smile. "What have we missed?"

Out of instinct, Cam reached out and looped his pinkie through hers.

Ice . . . that's what it felt like as Annie's power clawed into his veins.

She jumped, but Cam could have groaned in relief as the contact seemed to *leech* the excess energy from him. Beneath the table, she yanked her hand from his, her brands fading from black to dark grey. She stared at her fingers in shock.

God, thank you. Just that slight touch made his head so much clearer. He hadn't realized Julian had joined them until he took the seat to Cam's left, silver eyes never leaving the governor.

Alexander took in every detail of the new Revenants as Maya took her place beside her husband. Cam doubted his father missed the way Annie jolted when they'd touched. He saw everything.

His father gestured to others. "Camden, it seems some introductions are in order before we continue, hmm?"

Cam sucked in a breath, grateful his lungs seemed to be working again. He carefully lifted Annie's hand from her lap again, watching her reaction, making sure his mother's wedding ring—a stunning gold and fire-opal beauty—was on full display.

Annie tensed at his touch, but whatever had happened a moment ago didn't repeat itself. *Too bad.*

She relaxed slightly as he began to speak. "Father, may I introduce you to my wife, Annie Callahan. Previously Annie Duskin." He smiled at her, and to his delight, she smiled back.

A stunning—and very fake—smile, but he would take what he could get.

Alexander's façade finally cracked as he took in the ring on Annie's finger—the ring that once belonged to Cassandra Callahan. His father's steely eyes hardened as they shifted to Cam, filled with rage, but then his features fell back into calm curiosity before he gave Annie a wide, charming smile.

"The honor is mine, my dear." He cocked his head again. "And I must ask, what was your name before Duskin?"

Annie plastered on a convincingly confused look. "What makes you think I'm not a Duskin? Richard was my father."

Alexander tsked. "Don't play the simpleton with me, dear. You're much too clever for that. It was well known that Lord Duskin enjoyed keeping pets. I imagine you were one of them."

Cam tried to hide his surprise. Of course, she had a surname before the Duskins adopted her. *Why had I never thought to ask her that?* Annie hadn't told him much about her life before New Havana, but he should have asked. He'd been more concerned about scaring her off with his questions.

Annie's fake smile fell, instantly replaced with her usual stony mask. Her voice was cold and dull as she said, "I'm grateful we don't have to pretend." She shot Cam a glance. Only he would see the anxiety in it. "My name was Beaumen."

Beaumen. Cam's stomach lurched. *Annie Beaumen.* Who had she been before Elias and his counterpart had slaughtered her entire family and sold her to the slavers? *Do I know her at all?*

"Beaumen." His father repeated, taking her in. "An old name in the North."

"Is it?" Annie's expression remained flat. "I hadn't known."

"Hmm." Alexander's attention turned to Julian. "And you need no introduction, do you, Julian Price? Air Brand. Dishonorably discharged from the Western militia. Mercenary turned infamous killer for hire. I've known many good men who've fallen under your blade. How convenient you found yourself in my son's company. Hoping for a pardon?"

Price is from the West? Cam was an idiot. He'd known Julian to be a mercenary, but an assassin? How little else did he know of the people beside him?

How little do they know of you?

But his father knew. He always knew. And he'd use every ounce of information he had against them.

Julian held Alexander's gaze. "Pardons are for novices. The police know better than to touch me."

"Do they?" Alexander's brow rose. "I have a council judge waiting outside. We could ask him?"

"Enough with the contests," Cam snorted, trying—and failing—to mimic Alexander's calm demeanor. "None of us are saints, and I didn't invite Julian along for his incredible morale-building skills. Now, I'd appreciate it if you'd finish with all the practiced excuses and explain why you hired Elias Bennett."

He could have sworn Annie's lips twitched in amusement.

Alexander's exhale sounded inconvenienced. "I already told you. I paid him to bring you back to Enoch."

Maya sat there wringing her hands, her pale face suggesting she might faint.

"Why?" Cam asked. "Eight times you've tried to kill me, and now you want an elaborate homecoming? What changed?"

"*Again,* I told you, I've never made an attempt on your life."

Cam rubbed his ear. "Sorry, what? I can't hear you over all the bull."

His father's expression twisted in anger, but Maya gently squeezed his hand and gave him an encouraging nod.

Alexander sucked on his teeth before dipping his chin.

"Enoch is . . . in a state of unrest. The pro and anti-Revenant groups are at war with each other, creating friction in the economy and government. To attempt some semblance of peace, I agreed a year ago to meet with both parties and the city council to restructure and cast votes on new Revenant laws." Alexander closed his eyes for a moment. "The meeting is in a few months. Word got out, and now civilians don't know who to side with."

Annie's brows furrowed. "What does that have to do with Camden?"

A thrill ran through him. Cam never got tired of hearing his name on her lips.

"*Camden* is heir to the West." Alexander shot back. "The land, by right, belongs to him, but if the anti-Revenant parties have their way, it could block him from taking his seat at the head of Enoch. But more than that, he's seen the ugly sides of all parties. He's been human and Revenant. He knows wealth and poverty. If anyone can sway the public, it's him."

Son of a gun. Cam let out a dark, rolling laugh. It started deep in his chest before it spread to every corner of the room. *Why am I not surprised?*

Maya winced.

"You *need* me." Cam leaned forward, resting his elbows on the table. "You want to *use* me to clean up the decade's worth of mess you've caused."

"Listen to him," Maya whispered, a plea. "I know of your mother. I also know the complexity of the events that led to her death. Please, before you cast judgments, listen."

"Listen?" Cam's lips pulled back from his teeth. His hands were shaking. "*Obey. Don't question.* I've heard it all before. It doesn't change the fact that I watched my mother bleed out on the docks. That she sold me to pirates to keep me alive and sold herself to worse." He hadn't meant to start shouting. He'd never meant to say those things out loud, at all. *I can still feel her blood on my hands.*

It was Alexander's turn to wince, but he didn't look away. "I didn't kill her, Camden, and if you give me the time, I'll explain everything."

Kill him.

Oh, his fire was so convincing. *It will only take a moment. Only a breath and he'll be gone.* He could relent, just this once, couldn't he? He could succumb to this.

Another frigid jolt ran through him as Annie's hand gripped his, as *all* her fingers entwined with his. The intimacy of it jerked him out of his rage. He couldn't remember the last time someone held his hand. Had anyone ever? More than that, it was *her.*

Her eyes were hard, begging him to see the message behind them as she spoke, "After all this time, I imagine we can wait a little longer." She held his stare, her tone low. "We can *wait.*"

He didn't want to wait. He wanted revenge. He wanted all this hurt to go away.

Instead, Cam smiled at her, mouth dry. He wasn't the only one who needed answers.

He forced his gaze from Annie back to his father. *For her. I can do this for her.* "What are you proposing?"

"The day after tomorrow," Alexander began. Maya released a tense breath. "I'm hosting a ball to showcase the cooperation of the opposing Revenant groups. Attend. Bring your"—He scanned over Annie and Julian— "allies . . . and meet the men and women who are rightfully your subjects. We'll see how they affect your opinions. After you've had a chance to meet them—to hear what's been happening in the city—we'll talk."

"Subjects?" Cam laughed. "You're not a king, Father."

It was Alexander's turn to give a cruel smile. "Aren't I?"

"It's at six. The day after tomorrow." Maya repeated to

Annie, beaming. She probably thought she was the only rational one there. "Formal dress."

Did I just agree to go to a party with my father?

Annie squeezed his hand tighter before letting go. A warning. "We look forward to it." She stood, smoothing her dress, and glanced between Cam and Julian. "Shall we?"

He could barely feel his legs. If it weren't for Annie leading him—arm in arm—he probably wouldn't have made it back to their coach. He sat on the bench inside—smoke curling from his clenched fists—his head between his knees as he just breathed, and breathed, and breathed.

He was a child again. That damned belt cracked across his back, splitting his flesh. After a certain number of lashes, you stopped feeling them. Until the next day. Until your body remembered how it had been betrayed.

I didn't kill your mother. So many lies. He was tired of lies. He didn't want this to continue. This was supposed to be over now.

Nathan and Jenny asked questions. Julian talked *at* him. Cam didn't remember how his tongue worked. Thankfully, Annie answered for him, despite the tension rippling through her own body as she sat beside him.

At some point, he was led to his cabin on *The Elaina.*

His stomach hurt. Did he eat? He couldn't remember. *I'm so tired.* Cam fell into bed, not bothering to undress, and it didn't take long for the weariness to drag him under.

He might have imagined it, but he swore he fell asleep to the feeling of cold fingers combing through his hair. Icy, gentle, hesitant.

He *definitely* imagined it.

Thank God he didn't dream.

CHAPTER 7
ANNIE

Elain watched her, her eyes an endless white void. Annie did her best to ignore her.

The blade of her damascus dagger was sharp enough that Annie couldn't feel the pain as she sliced through the meaty part of her palm. Blood pooled in her cupped hand.

She didn't flinch. She didn't even blink. Her brands glowed as her torn skin began to knit together. Within two steady breaths, the wound was gone.

At this time of the morning, the bow of *The Elaina* was empty. A few gulls chattered in the rigging as sunlight fought to break through the heavy clouds. Waves lapped at the metal hull, far below.

And Elain watched.

She was Annie's adopted sister who'd died on Lord Duskin's table. Ghosts had haunted Annie from the time she'd first come to New Havana, but Elain was different. A friend, almost. Where once the visions of her had been blackened and twisted with death, now she was beautiful. Whole. Just like she'd been while she was alive, except for her pale, empty eyes.

A hint of anger escaped as Annie slid the blade across her palm once more, cutting deeper than she meant to. She only allowed her lip to twitch at the pain before healing herself again.

Annie hadn't seen Elain—or any of the ghosts—since the day she'd died. Since she'd become something *else*. She didn't know why Elain decided to come back now.

Annie continued to ignore her and kept her focus on the energy rolling into her fingers, but her mind wandered back to Cam. Whatever Alexander Callahan had done to him, it still festered far below the surface, consuming him.

She'd been surprised at how much Cam looked like his father—yet at the same time, they were so different. They shared the same coloring, the same cunning eyes. Cam was taller and better built, but Alexander had an air of authority she'd never witnessed in someone—not even Lord Duskin.

Cam had seemed hollow by the time they'd returned to *The Elaina*. She'd followed him to his room—to be a good friend, she told herself—and he'd fallen asleep before she could leave. She kept repeating that it was out of concern that she'd stayed, perched on the edge of his bed. He hadn't woken when her resolve had finally crumbled, and she ran her fingers through his hair.

Annie's stomach clenched. The strands had been so soft—highlighted in gold from the sun—but giving into one temptation only made her want *more*.

She'd wanted to touch his face. To see what his skin felt like. His lips.

Stop it. A wave of nausea rolled through her insides. *I can't be like them.*

The slavers had wanted to touch her, too. It hadn't taken long for those touches to turn into them taking whatever they wanted. The nausea turned to bile in her throat. *I'm not like them. I'm not. Am I?*

She wouldn't be. She refused to be. Her power flickered greedily, and she cringed.

"Miss Annie?"

Annie glanced to her left.

Mr. Price stood a few yards away, tucked in his usual coat. His brow rose as he cleared his throat. "Are you alright?"

She turned back. Elain was gone. Annie nodded and swallowed. "I'm . . . practicing."

"I'm sure there are more efficient ways to practice."

This time, she winced as she nicked herself. The skin was still pink and sensitive. "Do you have any other ideas?"

He sat down beside her with a low groan. He propped his chin in his palm. "How much power do you need to heal a wound that size?"

Annie shrugged, cleaning the bloodied blade off on the corner of her grey, wool day dress. "Not much. I can't even feel the drain . . . if that makes sense."

"It does." He held out his hand, gesturing to the dagger. "May I?"

Reluctantly, Annie passed him the knife.

He examined the dagger. The breeze pulled stands of his jet-black hair from his tight braid. Annie gasped as Julian sank the blade deep into his palm, penetrating the back of his hand. A bright spurt of blood sprayed over his charcoal trousers as he yanked the blade free from his flesh.

"Heal it," Mr. Price demanded, skin turning an awful shade of green. "Now, before I lose more blood."

"How?" Annie grabbed him by the wrist. His blood soaked her sleeve. "Tell me how!"

"Just like you did to yourself," Mr. Price hissed. "Hurry, please."

Shock jolted through her, brands flaring to life, as Annie forced her power to course into Mr. Price's arm. He audibly exhaled as the wound began to seal shut. Annie's breaths were ragged. He gave her an appraising smile as he flexed his newly healed hand, still coated red. "That didn't seem to strain you in the slightest. Interesting."

"What in the blazes was that?"

Annie shifted to see Cam striding toward them, his golden skin pale as he took in the pool of blood that drenched her and Mr. Price's clothes. His hair was disheveled, dark shadows encircling his green-gold eyes, like he'd just woken.

Mr. Price raised his mended hand, admiring the closed wound. "Miss Annie is practicing her gifts. Would you like to join us?"

Cam's eyes flickered to Annie's, his pupils encircled in fire. "Did you willingly stab him? Because if so, I'm jealous."

A thrill ran up Annie's spine. *He's just teasing.* Even so, it didn't stop her cheeks from heating. She licked her lips and shrugged again. "I was already out here practicing. Mr. Price stabbed himself."

Cam let out a sharp laugh, brow arched. "That's . . . odd."

Despite his cheery tone and smile, Annie could see the exhaustion still clinging to him like a flu. In that moment, all she wanted was to take his pain away. To make it better.

Annie lifted the dagger, twirling it between her fingers like she'd seen Cam do half a hundred times, and made sure her smile was genuine. "Would you *like* me to stab you? Stomach or thigh?"

This time, Cam's rumbling laugh was truly wicked. "Don't tempt me."

Mr. Price made an uncomfortable noise, then gestured for Cam to join them. "Healing injuries of this size makes a nearly unnoticeable dent to Miss Annie's energy reserves," Mr. Price said while Cam hopped up on one of the crates beside them, crossing his long legs. "It makes me wonder what she could do on a larger scale."

Cam's lips quirked. "Well, I watched her heal your throat after Frank cut it to the bone, so . . ."

Annie tried to forget when Elias Bennett and Frank Boyle nearly murdered Cam and Mr. Price. She hadn't known that she could heal Mr. Price when she put her hands on him, his body almost drained of life from his open neck, but it had felt *right*. Light had flowed from her body to his, and next she knew, he was whole again.

Alive.

His lips pursed. He didn't seem fond of remembering, either. "What I'm saying is that neither of you are even close to understanding the limits of your power."

Cam rolled his eyes. "Annie, sure, but you act like you've never seen a Fire Brand before. You spent more time with Frank than anyone."

"You're not *just* a Fire Brand," Mr. Price muttered before straightening. "Not that I enjoy inflating your ego, but denying your potential might get us killed. You need to train."

Frank Boyle and Mr. Price had worked together for years. Annie had worked alongside Frank, too. She understood what Mr. Price was hinting at. Cam and Frank *had* been different.

Cam was about to argue, but Annie interrupted. "Mr. Price is right." She stood and smoothed the wrinkles out of her dress. "Your and Mr. Boyle's fire aren't the same."

He inhaled, glancing at her, before locking his warning gaze on the Air Brand. "I already told you—I don't want to spar with you."

Mr. Price's scowl returned, but Annie let her voice rise an octave. "Spar? Like fighting?"

Cam crossed his arms and nodded.

Annie's power perking up beneath her skin. "I think I'd like to see that."

Mr. Price glanced hopefully between them.

Cam gave her a mischievous look as he leaned back onto his elbows. "And what would you get out of watching two knuckleheads beat the snot out of each other, Kitten?"

Despite all her best attempts, Annie smiled broadly. "I guess I'd just like to see how likely we are to survive if things go south."

Cam cursed, then shook his head. "Blazes, I can't say no to that face." He peeled off his coat and waistcoat, tossing them over the crate. He wore a simple gray button-down beneath. Cam's heat flared as he rolled up his sleeves. "I have a feeling one of us is going to regret this, Jules."

Mr. Price's power surge then, not nearly as raw as Cam's, but she could still feel the excitement in it. The Air Brand stood. "Fists or knives?"

Cam snorted. "I thought we were using our powers?"

"We're using both."

"Fine." Cam thought for a moment. His gaze flickered to Annie, to the dagger in her hand. "Knives. There was an unfortunate lack of stabbing on New Havana. I don't want to get rusty."

She tossed the dagger to him, and he caught it by the handle.

Price pulled off his coat, wearing a simple white tunic beneath. Annie wasn't sure she'd ever seen him without it, or some variation of it. He was skinnier than she expected. She stole Cam's spot on the crate, folding her legs beneath herself.

Cam's lips curled into a crooked half smile. "Are you sure you want to see this? Pirates aren't known for playing fair."

She made to reply, but almost faster than she could track, Mr. Price had a knife to Cam's throat. She hadn't seen where he'd pulled it from. He grinned. "Neither do assassins."

Her heart pounded in her ears as Cam bent backward, laughing, as his palms hit the deck and he swung his leg up to strike him in the groin.

Price let out a string of curses but stayed on his feet.

Cam darted back and straightened, cocky as ever. "Thanks. I needed to stretch."

Price raised his blade. "I have no problems maiming you. Keep on guard."

Cam chuckled as he sank into a defensive stance.

Annie had never seen either man fight. They began to circle each other, taunting and jeering. Enjoying it. They held themselves so differently. Mr. Price kept his body straight and casual, like Cam wasn't even a threat. Cam, on the other hand, stayed low—his knees and elbows bent—his form liquid.

A man trained to kill and one who'd learned out of necessity.

This time, it was Cam who took the offensive. He lunged, quick as a cat, and slashed at Mr. Price's thigh. Annie flinched.

Price's leg snapped out of the way—too fast. The strike should have gone straight through his muscle.

He tsked. "Too slow."

"Are you sure?" Cam smiled, but she didn't miss the way his jaw clenched. He swung several more times, but the other man was always just out of his reach. Their dance continued, and sweat made its way down Cam's temple. Price was playing with him. He was better—faster—and Cam knew it.

One moment, Mr. Price was there, then the next, his fist connected with Cam's jaw.

Annie's stomach lurched as Cam staggered.

Breathing heavily, he rested his hands on his knees and spat blood. "Ouch."

Mr. Price sounded bored. "Are you ready to let me teach you?"

Cam flipped him off, and Price laughed. "You're good. I'll admit that. If I were a regular man, you'd have ended me with your first strike."

Cam wiped blood from his lip. "Let me guess. You're not a regular man?"

Price's tone turned serious. "Neither are you, but you still choose to fight like a human."

Human? Annie's eyes narrowed.

"I *am* human," Cam snapped.

"Are you?" Mr. Price surged forward, so fast that he nearly vanished—until his blade was once again at Cam's throat.

This time, Cam flinched, shocked by the movement.

Mr. Price took a step back. "Unless we've been made into something more? A new creation?" This time, his silver eyes flashed to Annie and narrowed. "Our power isn't something that should be called upon only when convenient. It must become *you*. It must flood your muscles, aid your eyes, become your reflexes."

By this time, Cam had straightened—his jaw already beginning to swell—but he was listening. Mr. Price returned to his fighting stance. "Attack again. This time, use your power to *push* your limbs beyond what a mortal is capable of. *Push*."

She and Cam shared a look. She saw the question there—almost as if he was asking permission.

Her chin dipped into a barely noticeable nod. She'd felt the way her power mingled and spread through her body. She'd seen the way Cam's power could scarcely be contained within the shell of his skin. It had to go *somewhere*. Why not use it to their advantage?

Cam turned back to Mr. Price. "Fine." The orange glow of his brands spread into his eyes, setting them on fire. This time, when he moved, the flames snaked up his veins. Despite his newfound speed, Mr. Price easily dodged. He kicked Cam on the side of the knee and sent him sprawling onto the deck.

"*Push*," Mr. Price shouted. "*More*. Use the energy to power your body like fuel."

Annie's mind flashed to the steamship. To the way the sailors shoveled coal into the furnace. She glanced at her hands, studying the dull grey brands covering her fingers. Was the concept the same?

"I don't think you want me to do that," Cam said coldly, clenching his fists. "My fire already wants to kill you most days."

Annie's eyes snapped up to him.

That wasn't the first time she'd heard him speak like that. Like his power had a mind of its own.

Almost like hers.

Mr. Price didn't look concerned enough as he said, "Your power follows your command, not the other way around. Wield it."

Cam let out a sharp breath, hands falling to his sides. "Suit yourself."

This time, when he attacked, Annie couldn't track him. He just disappeared.

She blinked. *He already knows how to use his fire . . . at least this much.* Which meant he'd been choosing not to from the start.

Mr. Price's eyes widened in shock as Cam reappeared in front of him, airborne as he spun and landed a kick straight across Price's temple.

The man's body slammed down onto the deck so hard that

it splintered. He sat up on one elbow, holding his cheek, breath ragged. "Good. Much better."

Cam glared at him before turning his gaze to the ground. The flames crawling up his neck sputtered out. Mr. Price stood and shrugged on his cloak. "We'll meet every morning we're able at this time?"

Cam swallowed and nodded.

Mr. Price stalked off the deck, heading below.

Annie watched Cam's back as his breathing finally slowed —fire receding from his veins— before he turned to her. His eyes were green again . . . and very, very tired. "Did he put you up to this?"

Annie slid off the crate and handed Cam his vest and coat. "Yesterday. He asked if I'd convince you to train with him."

Cam's lips pursed. "Of course, he did."

"I came out here this morning because I assumed he'd follow," Annie smirked. "I was right. I wanted to see what his motives were."

"Clever. And?"

"I think . . ." She was almost afraid to say the words out loud. "I think there's something wrong with us."

Cam let out a long sigh as he reached for her hand. She looped her pinkie through his. He squeezed. "I suspected the same."

Annie squeezed back. His skin was so warm. "Is that why you refused to train with him?"

"Partly," Cam answered. He bit his lip and sighed. "You know him better than I do. Can we trust him?"

We. Annie savored the word. She studied his face. Took in all the fear, tension, and vulnerability she saw there. All of it just for her.

Stop it. She shook her head. Cam watched her curiously.

"I think he needs us." Annie chewed the inside of her

cheek. "Why? I don't know, but if he needs us, he won't betray us. You should train with him."

Cam scanned over her face before nodding. Within a blink, his cocky demeanor returned, and he purred, "I like this side of you, Kitten. So conniving." He held the damascus dagger out to her, hilt first. "I've always had an affinity for dangerous women."

She took it, her stomach doing a little flip, and noted the blood crusted against the pommel. "I learned from the best."

Cam gave her one of his half smiles. "Are you ready?"

Annie's brows furrowed. "For what?"

Cam gestured to his singed suit, then pulled a ridiculously thick cash clip out of his coat pocket. "To go shopping. Dare I step into my father's house tomorrow looking anything less than a governor's son?"

Annie frowned. "What's wrong with what you're wearing now?"

"He'll find something." Cam offered Annie his arm, and she took it. "He and whoever else may be attending. Besides, I'd like to get a fresh look at the city. At worst, it will be fun to go spend some of Elias's money—excuse me—*our* money."

"That does sound fun." Annie walked with him toward the gangplank. *Maybe I shouldn't have wiped the bloody dagger on my skirts.* She paused. "What do you mean by *our* money?"

"What's mine is yours now, remember?" Cam replied, some of that nervousness returning to his features. "Come on, Nathan and Jenny are waiting for us."

Annie felt something tingling in her chest. *Happiness?* "You invited them to go into Enoch with us?"

Cam let out a husky laugh. "Invited? It was Jenny's idea. She woke me up—loudly—and said neither of you had anything proper to wear tomorrow. I gave her a stack of bills to spend as she pleased, but she insisted we come along. I have a feeling she'll be dragging us around past dinnertime."

"That sounds . . . pleasant." Annie smiled. Really smiled.

Jenny was alive.

She was alive.

For now, at least—but for now, she'd be grateful.

Her and Cam's fingers remained entwined until they reached the docks.

CHAPTER 8

CAMDEN

A shiver rolled through Cam's body as he stepped onto the streets of Enoch, the others beside him.

His fire sang at the chance to fight against Julian, flaring to a point he was worried he wouldn't be able to lock it away again. Now it was *hungry*. Clawing at his insides, begging to be freed.

He resisted the urge to scratch at his buzzing skin as their carriage dropped them off at the corner beside a general store —a quaint, squared off building painted a gaudy, matte blue.

As the carriage trotted away, Cam turned to take in his father's city. The city that was Cam's, by right, to inherit. He didn't want it, he never had—but now, seeing it in for the first time in a decade, his bitterness for his title hardened into steel.

At least his father had spoken the truth on one thing— Enoch had gone to hell.

Nathan and Jenny ogled the pedal-powered bicycle on display in the store window as Annie moved closer to his side. "Is this what you expected?"

"Worse." Cam scrunched his nose. "Much worse."

"May I fix this?" She gestured toward his bruised face. It stung.

"Please," he nodded, praying his face didn't turn beet red as she brushed her fingers down his jaw. That icy sensation hummed through him again, but it was gentler this time. Kinder. He rubbed his face when she backed away. The pain was gone. He gave her a grateful smile. "Thank you . . . really."

Her cheeks were red as she turned, cleared her throat, and scanned over the street.

Where the roads had once been pristine and spacious, now carriages dodged potholes at the same time as they dodged each other, trampling garbage deeper into the cobblestone, staining it black.

Unlike the gas lamps that lit the immaculate streets of New Havana, Enoch still used oil lamps. They'd need to be lit in the evening and extinguished in the evening. What an expense to employ so many lamplighters. The money could be used in better places, like cleaning up the filth.

Cam shook his head. *Lord, now I sound like my father.* He didn't want to think about Alexander. He didn't want to think about anything that happened yesterday. Cam shifted, fixing his full attention on Annie. "And what do you think?"

Annie watched with concern as worn-out citizens hurried along the block, ignoring the beggars and newsboys. She noticed the puddles collecting in the cracks of the road, smelling of sewage. Furrowing her pale brows, she murmured, "The city is sick."

"I agree." Cam stretched his arm around her shoulders, but didn't touch her, guiding her toward the store so she wouldn't get trampled by the foot traffic. "Lord Duskin might have been right about that whole sin-causing disease thing."

They followed Nathan and Jenny into the general store, the bell on the door tinkling as they entered.

"There were many things he was right about, but all his wrongs smothered out the right," Annie said.

"True." Cam winced as that bell went off again. His ears were so sensitive with his fire this close to the surface. "He'd have had a field day here. I mean, picture Richard and my father stuck in a room together."

Annie's lips quirked. "Can you imagine the boasting?"

"And the preening." Cam rolled his eyes."What a nightmare." Inside, the scent of tobacco and leather smacked him in the face, seeping out of the slat pine walls. An older, mustached man in a matching, striped shirt and pants stood behind a wooden counter. Behind him, shelves were filled with supplies of all kinds—cigarettes, canned food, tea, coffee, gloves, and candlesticks.

Nathan perused the hunting knives in the glass case as he spoke to the cashier. Jenny's bright red curls were visible over a shelf in the back of the store.

"Annie!" she squealed, "come look at all the candies!"

"Coming," Annie called back. Her expression darkened as she spoke to him. "We weren't allowed candy on the island." The sadness in her eyes nearly took Cam to his knees. "I forget how young she is. How young we *all* are."

"Our childhoods were taken from us a long time ago, weren't they?" Cam mused. Innocence didn't last long in the world they'd grown up in. He touched the deep, orange brands beneath his eyes, zigzagging down his cheeks. "And now we'll be young forever. What a cruel joke."

"*What?*" Annie's ice-blue eyes widened in shock. "What do you mean by that?"

She doesn't know. Cam's heart stopped and started in his chest. Hell, it had been months, and he still hadn't come to terms with the fact that being Revenant meant he was impervious to time—nearly immortal. According to Elias Bennett, they could live centuries.

And they'd never age. Never change—at least on the outside. A fact the government kept hidden from the public to prevent more division.

"Annie?" Jenny's grinning face peered around the back shelves. "Come see!"

Stay calm. Cam leaned in and whispered, "Later. I promise."

Despite her obvious annoyance, Annie took the hint. Folding her hands behind her back, she nodded and strode toward where Jenny waited, her gait silent and graceful, moon-white hair braided down her back.

Cam exhaled as Nathan waved him over to the counter. The cashier's face paled as he approached, taking in Cam's brands, the revolver on his belt. He took a step back.

"Afternoon." Cam smiled at him.

The cashier mumbled something similar before darting into the storage room behind him.

Nathan let out a low laugh. "What an effect you have on people, mate."

"I can't decide if it's a blessing or a curse." Cam knelt to examine the weapon Nathan pointed out to him behind the glass case—a long dagger with a bone hilt, wrapped in a black and red pattern. A similar one sat beside it, the hilt plain leather, but no less lethal.

Lovely. Cam straightened and called over the counter. "How much for the weapons?"

The cashier peeked nervously out of the backroom. "One hundred dollars each, m' lord. Top of the line pieces, those are. A local forge. Handcrafted."

"Lord almighty," Nathan whistled. "Even at Resh's peak, that's more than we made in a year. Too bad."

Not anymore. Cam pulled a crumpled stack of bills out of his pocket and grinned. "I'll take both." He patted his revolver. "Plus, I'll need ammunition. A lot of it."

Nathan straightened. "Both?"

"One for your ugly mug," Cam replied.

Nathan glared. "Says the ugliest bloke I've ever met, but thanks."

The cashier's eyes nearly bugged out of his head. "M'lord?"

Cam slid the cash across the counter. "And may you have them delivered to my lodgings? We have more shopping to do."

"Of course, of course." The cashier swiped the money off the counter before he took the knives from the case. As he began to package them, Jenny skipped over with an armful of candy, Annie a short distance behind her. As Jenny paid for her treats, Annie peered over at the weapons. "Are you sure those are large enough?"

"Never." Cam jotted down the address to where *The Elaina* was docked and left it on the counter. "But they'll do."

"Hmm." Annie *almost* smiled. She glanced over to Jenny. "Where to next?"

"The *modiste!*" Jenny chimed—nearly as loud as that blasted bell—as they exited back onto the street.

"We don't have time to have dresses made." Annie glanced up at the sky. The dull, grey clouds threatened them with rain. "There must be a department store or—"

"No, she's right," Cam said, shoving his hands in his pockets. "Small business owners gossip with customers and each other. We might be able to glean a bit more about the political groups my father spoke of."

Annie nodded, emotionless as ever, and fell in beside him as they continued down the block. People parted for them on the sidewalk—some out of fear, others to gawk—making their trek easier. Annie chewed at her thumbnail, something she did when she was nervous.

She doesn't like being watched. Cam wished there was something he could say to comfort her. That she'd get used to being stared at and feared, but that would be a lie. He hated it. The way onlookers muttered to each other under their breath, some sneering, some with eyes round in awe.

They were Revenants now—spectacles—and the marks on their bodies would never let them hide a blatant, extremely personal fact: they'd died.

Died, and been forced to face life a second time.

He didn't want to be asked how. Was it painful? Where had he gone once everything went dark? Had it been worth it? What was it like having such incredible power now?

The bitterness seeping into Cam's blood set his fire on edge, sending it crawling up his neck. Several pedestrians gasped, and when they met his aggravated stare, their eyes fell to the ground.

Cold fingers brushed his.

When he glanced over, Annie let her hand fall back to her side.

"About that?" Nathan cleared his throat, breaking the tension. "Julian told us what the governor said. That he wasn't the one who tried to kill you or kill your . . ." He let his words trail off. Nathan picked at the hem of his coat. "Do you believe him?"

"No," Cam said flatly.

They all looked at him.

God, he didn't want to talk about this. Cam's lips formed a hard line. "Alexander Callahan is a liar and will say whatever he must to get what he wants. Nothing has changed."

He scanned the rows of shops lining each side of the street until one caught his attention. "Ah." He pointed out a white trimmed shop with a matching lattice archway. "The *modiste.*"

"Oh!" Jenny clapped. "Do you think they have silks? They must!"

"I'm sure they will." Annie took her hand and squeezed. "Hopefully, they have what we need."

Thankfully, there was no bell when they entered the pristine building. A lush showroom greeted them, the hardwood floors covered in thick, petal-pink carpets. Jenny squealed at the endless rolls of fabrics, in all colors and textures, lining the walls. There were so many buttons, pins, and frilly ribbons—nausea rolled through Cam's insides.

"Oh God, this is the worst." Nathan ran a hand through his tight, black ringlets. "Kill me now."

"That can be arranged." A stout, well-dressed woman with shiny, copper locks stepped out from behind the mountain of fabrics. Her dark eyes widened briefly at the sight of Cam and Annie. "I jest, of course. I'm Lydia. How may I assist you?"

"Do you have any gowns ready-made?" Annie's usual low tone became high and sweet. The way she shifted between masks was a wonder. "We just arrived in town and haven't had time to settle. We were invited to dine at the Callahan manor tomorrow. It would be a tragedy for my sister and me to have to wear our sea clothes to such a lavish event."

Cam shot Annie a skeptical look.

Her returning glare said everything: *play the game.*

Lydia clapped her hands over her rouged cheeks. "On my watch? Never! Let me have a look at you all."

Within fifteen minutes, she'd taken their measurements and had darted out of the waiting area. Her voice was faintly muffled as she called from somewhere in the back, "The Callahan manor, you say? What an honor!"

"Sure." Cam barely suppressed a groan as he plopped on the cushioned bench by the window. "If you want to call it that."

Lydia peeked her head out, pin curls swinging. "You don't agree?"

"If only circumstances were merrier," Jenny added, following Annie's lead. "With all the unrest..."

"Terrible, isn't it?" Lydia's voice carried to them. "All the deaths. So unnecessary."

Nathan sat on the narrow armchair beside Cam. "Deaths?"

"You haven't heard?" Lydia returned with several sets of men's clothing over her arm. She shook her head. "Of course, you haven't. Murders, that's what they are. Lots of them. Since the news spread about the new laws being made, it seems like everyone is at each other's throats." She tossed a stack of suits on Cam and Nathan's laps, then pointed to a dressing room to their left. "Go try those on." She gestured to Annie and Jenny. "Come with me."

Fear. That's what Cam felt as he watched Annie disappear out of view.

Nathan must have felt it, too, because he patted Cam's elbow. "They'll be alright. Annie can protect them both."

Yes. He'd seen what Annie had done to Frank Boyle. She wasn't defenseless. She had never been.

Within half an hour, Cam and Nathan found all the clothes they'd ever need. The women still hadn't returned to the showroom. The minutes ticked by, painfully slow. Cam whistled as he sat upside down in his chair, legs stretched out along the wall, ignoring the blood rushing to his head.

Nathan had taken to lying flat out on the plush rug, hands folded behind his head. It had been weeks since they'd sailed away from New Havana, yet the physical toll of months imprisoned beneath the island—and being forced to ingest Pearl Dust—was still plain as day on Nathan's face. Shadows still haunted his eyes, his cheeks gaunt and hollow.

He and Cam had barely spoken about what had happened

on *The Nightlady* or about Resh's death. Or about Cam's death, for that matter, and the suffering Nathan must have endured.

There were times when Cam *wanted* to talk about it, to share the terrors that still plagued him in the night. But maybe it was better this way. To let the past remain the past and just move on.

Cam didn't realize he'd been staring until Nathan shot him a curious look, brows raised, and said, "Something bothering you?"

Damn it. Cam was getting dizzy, but he didn't feel like moving. "Nothing at all."

"You're a liar, too." Nathan snorted and stretched. "I guess we know who you get it from."

He's right. His fire whispered as it clawed for the surface. *You're just like him, and you know it.*

Cam gritted his teeth and looked away.

"Sorry." Nathan sat up, and Cam hated the fear in his eyes. "That was low."

Cam closed his eyes and inhaled, shoving his fire deep, deep down back into its box. "Don't apologize. You're not wrong. I often wonder how many of my hateful traits I've inherited from him."

"You're not hateful."

"Now *you're* lying."

"I'm not." Nathan picked at the pink tuffs on the rug. "Annie likes you. Strange as it is to think, I've known her longer, and she doesn't like anyone." He paused, a flicker of grief passing over him. "Except for Lowana. She liked Lowana."

Does she like me? He hoped so. Cam frowned. "Who is Lowana?"

"Never mind."

"And that's not true." Cam's eyes were getting spotty. He needed to sit up. "Annie loves Jenny."

"It's hard not to love Jenny." A quick smile passed over Nathan's lips. "She's pretty special."

"You like her, don't you?" Cam smiled mischievously. "Actually like her?"

Nathan shot him a bitter glare. "And you like Annie? Even though she murdered Resh?"

Cam's smile disappeared. "Don't you dare blame her. She did what she had to survive."

"That's not an excuse."

"If she hadn't, Jenny would have died a long time ago." Cam snapped back. "Have you thought about that?"

As Nathan opened his mouth to argue, the women stepped out of the back.

Cam fell out of his chair and landed on his head, clacking his teeth together.

Annie was . . . he couldn't breathe.

Her ice-blue eyes flickered with amusement as she watched him fall. Lydia helped her step onto the podium in the center of the room, a massive, full-length mirror set before it.

Lilac. Annie hates lilac. But the color looked sensational on her now. The low-cut bodice, brocade in silver flowers, accentuated her tiny, corseted waist. The skirts were loose and flowing, the sleeves tight and sheer, glittering with tiny jewels.

Nathan's jaw dropped as Jenny stepped onto the podium beside her, dressed in flowing, layered golden silks. "Isn't it extraordinary?" Jenny beamed and twirled. "I mean, God bless, Annie looks like a painting."

That she does. Cam's cheeks burned as Lydia turned toward them, eyes alight. "What do you think, gentlemen? Stunning, are they not?"

"Stunning," Cam repeated. *Get it together.* He shook his head. The heat in his face had nothing to do with his fire. "I don't think Enoch's ready for them."

"My thoughts, exactly." Lydia crooned, laying a dozen more gowns on the counter. "I'll have the clothing delivered straight away, and when Governor Callahan's guests ask who dressed them, you'll send them my way, yes?"

"Of course." Cam paid for their clothes while Annie and Jenny headed back to change. He lowered his voice and slipped her a second stack of bills. "And you'll tell me if these murders have anything to do with an Order?"

Lydia froze, her face paled.

Cam slid the stack closer. "Or am I wrong?"

Lydia seemed to chew on her tongue. "I've heard whispers."

"Only whispers?" Cam pouted.

Nathan moved to watch the door, always in sync.

"Whispers"— Lydia repeated— "are as loud as screams, if you know where to look."

"And where should I look?"

"I think you already know that, Camden Callahan." It took him a moment to register that she knew his name. Her lips twisted into a grin. "Enoch's been waiting for you."

This time, it was Cam's turn to pale.

Annie and Jenny returned as Nathan jotted down their address.

Cam backed away from the counter, fighting against the fire threatening to choke him. "And I assume you'll let me know if you hear any more whispers?"

Annie's gaze glinted from him to Lydia, hard as steel.

"Of course," Lydia bowed. "We are at your service, my lord."

CHAPTER 9

ANNIE

As Cam closed the door behind them, his golden skin drained of color. He flashed her a quick, anxious look before settling back into his usual relaxed demeanor. He ran a hand through his hair before smiling at Jenny. "Where next?"

"Oh!" Jenny beamed. "Can we keep shopping? I've always wanted to—"

Annie wasn't listening. She studied Cam's clouded expression as it fell to the sidewalk.

Something happened. Lydia must have said something.

Nathan and Jenny started down the block again despite the heaviness of the clouds above. Cam followed, still deep in thought.

Annie fell in line beside him, her skirts soaked from dragging over the wet pavement. "What is it?"

"Sorry?" Cam snapped to attention. He blinked at her before regaining his composure. "Ah, it's nothing. Just thinking."

"No." Anger rolled through Annie's insides. *I'm not doing*

this again. She was tired of being a pawn. Always on the outside and only informed when deemed necessary. "Is this how it's going to be? You keep secrets while I struggle to keep up? Because if so, I want nothing to do with it."

"W-what?" He stopped short. "T-that's not it, at all."

Energy rolled through the brands on her arms, down into her fingers. "Then, what is it?"

He exhaled, glancing at Nathan and Jenny ahead of them. "I trust you, it's just . . ." He chewed his lip. "After all those two have been through, I don't want them to worry. They might hear if we talk now."

"I see," Annie said, her stomach sinking. *I shouldn't have snapped at him.* But she needed answers—now. Especially after the bombshell he had dropped in the general store, acting as if it were just a casual comment about the weather. On the ship, there was always someone listening, and she might not get another chance to speak with him alone.

Annie sighed, swiveling toward where Jenny and Nathan had paused to wait for them.

"You two go on by yourselves." She didn't mean for her words to sound so sharp. "We'll catch up with you later."

Jenny pouted.

As expected, Nathan tensed, hesitant. "Cam?"

"What she said." Cam looped his arm through Annie's, making her chest flutter. "I'd like to give the new Lady Callahan a private tour of her city."

Nathan shot her a dark look, then frowned. "If you say so."

"See you tonight," Jenny said.

Before Annie could watch them continue down the street, Cam veered them in the opposite direction, back the way they'd come. When she glanced up at him, he was grinning at her.

Annie frowned. "What?"

"Are you sure *you're* not the lord?" Cam's brow rose. "You could make every man in a room sit like a dog using that tone."

"Don't be ridiculous."

"It wouldn't be the first time I've been called that," he replied. "I'm surprised you'd let Jenny go off alone."

"Nathan won't let anything happen to her." Annie wasn't blind to the way the quartermaster watched her sister, but she didn't mind Nathan as much as he detested *her*. His loyalty to Cam would keep him from trying anything with Jenny.

Cam's shoulders relaxed slightly, letting some of his confident façade slide. Arm in arm, he led her back past the *modiste* and deeper into Enoch. "Can we pretend we're on a pleasant stroll for a while before we talk about serious matters? There's a lot to see."

Annie nodded.

They walked for over an hour. Cam pointed out landmarks and buildings he remembered—places his mother used to take him. A flower shop painted in gold and turquoise, with buckets out front filled with dahlias in every color, along with pink and purple orchids and sunny yellow roses. A bakery tucked into an alley, with more variations of pastries than she could count. No wonder he had such a sweet tooth.

Annie's heart grew heavier as they went inside and he bought some cream-filled danishes, over-tipping the baker by an astronomical amount. She could imagine Cassandra Callahan bringing him here, a mother just trying to escape the stress of home and give her child any happiness she could find. What couldn't be fixed with sugar and flowers?

As much as he tried to hide it, sorrow coated Cam's tongue whenever he mentioned her, no matter how brief.

Annie ate half a danish—stuffed with apricots—and Cam ate the rest as he led her into an alley off the main road. Rats scurried by their feet as they stepped through oily puddles.

Cam seemed to know where he was going, so she didn't question his direction. They emerged onto a side street, the cobblestone cracked and stained with moss. Around them, smaller, abandoned shops were converted into cramped apartments, their doors wide open despite the chill in the breeze.

Cam paused and scanned the street, brows scrunched in confusion. "This is new."

"I imagine a lot has changed." Here—away from the packed main road—Annie's breath came a little easier without so many eyes watching them. "Are you going to tell me what that Lydia woman said?"

"*That Lydia woman?*" Cam laughed. "You truly are vicious, Kitten."

She decided not to argue and glared at him instead.

Cam let out a long sigh and resumed his leisurely strolling. "I tried to bribe her to see if she knew anything about The Order. Or at least if they had anything to do with the murders she mentioned."

Annie followed, heart stammering. "And?"

"Whispers, that's all she said. But . . ." He sucked on his teeth. "She knew my name. She said the city has been waiting for me."

"Hmm." *That could be a problem.* Annie focused on the grime coating her boots as she walked. "I'm not surprised you were recognized after all this time. You and the governor look so similar,"—Cam winced—"but the rest? I haven't a guess."

"Neither do I," he said, "and . . . I don't like that."

The heat of his skin warmed her despite the thickness of his coat. It turned the few drops of rain into steam. It wasn't until she bumped into his side that she realized she'd been edging closer to him, that her power *wanted* to be closer. *Or is it me?* Either way, it had to stop.

Cam gave her a confused look as she jerked to the side, putting a healthy distance between them again.

"And about what you said before?" Annie cleared her throat, stuffing her chilled fingers into her coat pockets. "About being young forever?"

"Ah." A hint of fire lined Cam's green eyes. "That."

The sparse gas lamps did little to ward off the fog hovering over the city like smoke. Cam found a bench and reached out to dry it with his sleeve. He paused, then made a face, before a ripple of heat sucked away the moisture soaking the wood.

He sat and sighed. "I forgot I could do that."

Annie sat beside him, the freshly warmed bench soaking through her clothes. Despite how badly she wanted to push, she waited, watching the death of the raindrops that dared to venture too close to them.

Eventually, Cam rested his elbows on his knees. "We're immortal—kind of."

No. Annie's eyes slammed shut as she fought away a wave of panic. This is *precisely* what she dreaded he'd say. "You must be wrong."

"After I turned, Elias told me Revenants are impervious to time," Cam said. "That we can live centuries without aging. I didn't take it well, either."

Why? They'd already been cursed to live twice, but to live so long? Annie let her eyes flutter open. He watched her anxiously, tearing apart a splinter he'd peeled off the bench.

She did her best to keep her expression bland. "But if that's true, why have I never heard of this?"

Cam shrugged. "Elias said to keep public fear in check."

She chewed her thumbnail. "I'm surprised Mr. Price didn't tell me."

"Maybe he assumed you already knew?"

"Maybe, or perhaps he chose not to." She glanced up. In the

window of the house across from them, an elderly man darted out of view. *Odd.* "I have a feeling there is a lot that he hasn't told us."

"That seems to be the game, doesn't it?" Cam laughed as he shook his head. "It's to keep both of us as much in the dark as possible."

Us. The word still sent her heart racing. She pursed her lips. "I'm sorry for snapping at you."

"When?" He smirked. "I don't remember that."

Before she could reply, a haggard wrinkled face appeared in the window again. This time, he didn't run when Annie met his piercing stare. Instead of being afraid, he looked . . . hopeful? A green, knit cap covered his mat of wiry grey hair and even bushier brows, but it did little to hide his sunken-in cheekbones.

Cam noticed him this time. The elderly man *did* flinch away from his stare. Cam noticed that, too, and plastered on a wide, friendly smile as he patted the bench. "Is this yours, mate? We can leave if you want."

The elderly man moved out of view, only to reappear as he limped through his open doorway. Annie suppressed a gasp at the bloody wrap around his knee. The joint stuck out at an odd angle, the flesh above the bandage—visible through his torn trousers—blackened and weeping.

Despite his condition, the old man smiled back, revealing teeth that were equally rotten. "I don't own nothin' anymore, m'lord. I'm just surprised to see such healthy faces, is all."

A chill ran beneath Annie's skin as her power perked up, woken like a disgruntled cat at the man's words. "Why is that?"

The man peeked up and down the avenue before giving them a confused look. "You know where you're at, lass?"

"Apparently, we don't," Cam replied. Annie didn't miss the

way he angled towards her, shielding. "Would you mind enlightening us?"

"This is The Greens." The man scooted further out of his door, dragging his bad leg behind him. "Get it? Greens? Like pus." He let out a gurgling laugh. "The hospital needed someplace to dump the overflow. You must be new to town to have wandered this far."

Hospital. The word sent a thrill through her. That was part of their original arrangement. That she'd help him against the Duskins in exchange for safe passage for her and Jenny into the West, *and* for a position as a nurse in a local hospital.

It's the only indulgence she'd ever allowed herself. The study of medicine—the complexity of diseases and their cures —had been the only thing to give her any kind of joy during her time on New Havana.

"The hospital's that busy, aye?" Cam replied as his posture changed—becoming looser—a bit of a harbor accent slipping into his speech. He might deny it, but Cam wore as many masks as she did.

"That's what they keep tellin' me." The old man grunted, then patted his wounded leg. "Been tryin' to get this bugger fixed for a year, but they're still full up."

A year. Annie inhaled. The filmly taste of rotting flesh hung in the air. *A year of pain and agony.* It was a miracle he was still alive. Slowly, she stood, removing her hands from her pockets. Energy surged through them, her brands a charcoal grey. "May I have a look?"

Cam glanced at her in surprise.

The man seemed equally as shocked. He patted his leg again. "A look at this mess?"

She nodded. "May I?"

"I mean." The man removed his knit cap and rubbed his

balding scalp. "I suppose it won't hurt nothing, but I don't want you getting this ick all over yeh'."

"Trust me." Annie found herself smiling. "I'm used to it."

Cam followed, wary, but didn't stop her as she approached him. The man leaned against his doorway, grinding his browned teeth as she began to unwrap the bandage. The sickly-sweet stink of pus forced itself up her nose, invading all her senses. He whimpered, pressing his face into the crook of his arm, but didn't budge.

"What's your name?" She asked to distract him. The wrap had grown into his leg, the pus turning pink as it mixed with fresh blood, and she gently tugged the wrap free. Beneath, lay a gaping hole on the side of his knee the size of a grapefruit. Bone was visible beneath the layers of dried fluids and dead skin.

"*Blazes*," Cam murmured behind her.

"Maynard." Pained tears leaked from the man's eyes. "It was a spider bite, is all. A nasty bug, that one. At least I crushed 'em under my boot."

"Mr. Maynard, it is." Annie scrunched her brows. She'd seen these kinds of wounds before. She'd need echinacea, garlic, and honey for the infection—

Power surged into her hands, making them glow. Maynard gasped at the same time she did. *Of course.* Annie rubbed her fingers together. *Why shouldn't I use this?* Maybe *this* is why she'd been brought back. After all the death she'd caused, maybe she was now meant to heal.

Her lips widened into a grin as she retook his knee and released the hold on her power, allowing it to flow freely into his leg. He gasped again as twisting strands of white cut through his ruined veins, burning away the filth, tearing them apart.

She felt it this time—unlike when she practiced on herself

—the pull on her energy as the wound began to knit close. A dull throb spread into her temples, but it was nothing she couldn't handle. Pain was pain.

"Lord above," Cam whispered, his full lips parted in awe, eyes alit with fire—as if his monster enjoyed watching hers at work.

Annie used the hem of her dress to wipe away the last of the blood from Maynard's leg. Beneath the grime, only clean pink skin remained. Closed. Clean.

Maynard let out a sob, shaking as he gripped her shoulder. "W-what did you do?"

"Fixed it, I hope." A wave of dizziness hit her as she stood. "I'd suggest you get some rest."

"Thank you." He dropped to his now healthy knee and kissed her hand. "Thank you, thank you both—" When he looked up, his eyes darted past her, further down the street. A ripple of terror crept over his face before he recoiled back into his house and slammed the door shut.

"The hell was that—" Cam began.

Heavy bootsteps approached.

Annie wheeled around, wiping her bloody hands on the skirts of her dress. Cam had already drawn his revolver.

A few yards away, a different man watched them now—maybe in his mid-twenties, his long, greasy, brown waves tied back with a strand of leather. He wore a stained apron over a brown wool suit, a medical bag in hand. His shocked gaze was fixed on her. "That was . . . extraordinary, my lady." He took a step toward her. "May I—"

Cam cocked back the hammer of his revolver, lips curling into a cruel smile. "You should leave, buddy. Now."

"Forgive me, forgive me." The newcomer dropped his bag before raising his hands. "I'm Van Clarke. I work for Waverly

Hills Hospital, just a stone's throw down the road. Mr. Maynard, there, is one of my patients."

Waverly Hills. As one of the most extensive medical facilities in The Four Corners, she'd heard the name more than once in her life. Even Lord Duskin had respected their work.

"You're a doctor?" Annie blurted.

Dr. Clarke nodded with a smile. "I am."

"Not a very good one," Cam snorted as he lowered his gun. "Poor Mr. Maynard was only a few feet from his deathbed."

Dr. Clarke's face fell. "I do my best. Resources are limited, as is the space needed to treat those in need of our services."

"Out of space? How?" Cam's brows rose. "Waverly takes up three city blocks."

"Alas, our conundrum." Dr. Clarke gave them a quick once-over, taking in Cam's brands and Annie's blood-soaked skirts. "May I ask who you are? I don't often see Revenants, let alone Revenants who wander The Greens."

Annie and Cam exchanged looks, and she mouthed, *"Your call."*

His features settled on defiant confidence. He holstered his revolver, and only she could hear the slight quiver in his voice as he said, "Camden Callahan."

Dr. Clarke blinked once, twice, then beamed. "You don't say? And I thought you looked familiar. I often visit the Callahan estate."

Cam visibly cringed before resting his arm around Annie's shoulders. The warmth of him sent a shiver dancing across her skin. "This is my wife, Annie Callahan."

"A pleasure." Dr. Clarke bowed before taking several steps closer. He wrung his hands, blowing out a sharp breath. "Oh, I hate to sound so deceptive, but I'd stopped at the tailor's to have a seam fixed, and Miss Lydia mentioned I might find you out and about."

Cam glowered, jaw clenched. "Ah. Wonderful."

"Isn't it?" Dr. Clarke beamed. "Please, I'd love to give you a tour of Waverly. As the governor's son, I'm sure you'll have many ideas on how we can recruit more support for the hospital." He extended his hand to Cam for a handshake. "Shake on a yes?"

"We're busy," Cam snapped, ignoring the gesture. "We have an event to attend at my . . . father's."

"Splendid! I've been invited, as well." Dr. Clarke's eyes brightened, letting his hand drop. "Maybe after—"

"How about the following morning?" Annie asked. Beside her, Cam bristled.

"Excellent!" Dr. Clarke clapped. "I look forward to your visit, my lady. I'll see you tomorrow evening?"

"I'm sure you will." Cam flashed a phony smile before steering Annie in the opposite direction, moving as quickly away from Dr. Clarke as they could manage without jogging.

"Cam." Annie tugged on his sleeve. "Slow down, he can't see us anymore."

He didn't seem to hear her as he continued to stalk down the street, his expression twisted in anger.

"*Camden.*" Annie skidded to a stop, slipping on the damp cobblestone. Cam caught her by the elbow before she fell. Her ankle stung, but at least she had his attention. Annie grabbed his hand and squeezed. "Can you please tell me why you just did that?"

"I knew this would happen." He pulled away and ran his hands over his face and through his hair, then began to pace. The now drizzling rain turned into a cloud of steam around him. "That woman already said they—whoever *they* are—have been waiting, and she blabbed to the first person she saw. Hell, they probably are in on it together. They all *want* something. If we go to that hospital, they're going to expect me to fix every-thing, and I can't."

"Who cares what they think or expect?" Annie pulled up the hood of her coat. "If what Lydia said is true, they may have examined those murder victims at Waverly."

Cam paused, studying her over his shoulder. "I hadn't thought of that."

Annie wrapped her arms around herself, a chill creeping over her without him beside her. "You don't have to fix anything."

He inhaled. "And when all those dying men and women expect to be saved? What do we say then? You can't heal them all, Annie. Neither can I."

The images of Lord Duskin's patients flashed through her mind—maddened by my Pearl Dust and ravaged by The Rot, clawing at her from their cells like animals. *I wish I could have saved them.* There was so much she *wished* she could have done. So much she failed to do.

Annie's throat tightened as the pieces clicked into place. *Failure. He's afraid of failing them, failing us.*

Because Cam cared—about her, about Jenny, about Nathan, Julian, and every crewman on *The Elaina*. He saw them as his responsibility, and as much as he'd deny it, he felt the same for Enoch in a strange, twisted way.

Annie held out her pinkie, trying to keep her voice steady. "It's you and me, remember? You don't have to do this alone. We all chose to be here."

His expression softened as he looped his finger through hers. "It's easy to say that when there's still a roof over our heads and food on the table. But when it all goes to hell, what about then?"

Annie burst out laughing. "I've seen and felt hell already, Camden. If no one else, I'll stay beside you." She shouldn't be making so many promises, but the look he gave her took her breath away, so she forced herself to stare at the ground and added, "Besides, you still have a bargain to fulfill. After we're safe, and you get me that nursing job I requested, then we'll see."

Cam huffed and quickly kissed their conjoined fingers, but the fire in his eyes had calmed. "Whatever you want, Kitten. Always."

The touch made her body go hot and cold at the same time.

He let out an irritated groan as he rubbed his face again. "It looks like our schedule is already filling up."

CHAPTER 10
CAMDEN

Time was stupid.

Cam laid flat on the bow of *The Elaina*, watching angry storm clouds pass over the stars in the night sky. It was barely visible through the thick layers of fog blanketing the harbor. The moisture on the deck soaked into the fabric of his new suit, but at the moment, he didn't care. He just wanted to be alone. He just wanted to breathe.

There was so much to do. Soon, he'd be standing in a room full of men and women who cowed to his father. Soon, Cam would be expected to be the man he'd always sworn he'd never become.

Cam inhaled and closed his eyes, attempting to steady the torrential current of power flowing through his blood. When he opened them, he focused on a small space in the air and willed his fire to be there.

It listened for once. A flickering ball of flame formed a foot or two above him, crackling as the energy inside him willed it to grow *larger*. Cam raised his arm and brushed his finger over the fire, feeling its warmth. It danced at his touch.

Elias had been wrong.

After Cam had turned, during those weeks on the island of Shar-Crue, Elias had taught Cam the basics of wielding his fire. How to draw it into existence. How to make pretty lights and fanfairs to impress the noblemen of New Havana.

Elias had pushed Cam to use his hands, to imagine forming the fire into whatever shape he desired.

It wasn't necessary. In fact, it was ridiculous, just like everything else Elias had told him.

Cam focused his gaze higher, further into the sky, behind the clouds. His fire obeyed—rising and growing into its own miniature sun. Cam willed it to move left, and it did. He willed it to rise higher, to disappear out of view. The further it climbed, the muddier Cam's focus grew.

A cloud passed over the fire, staining it in bright oranges and golds. Cam's brows furrowed as he tried to keep the flames alive. Though he couldn't *see* them, he could still *feel* them. The strain of keeping it burning made sweat drip down his temples. He had to try harder. He had to—

"Captain?"

Cam flinched at the sound of Pulley's voice. High above, his fire burst into burning fragments, spreading into the atmosphere. Cam cursed and leaned his head back. Pulley was staring down at him.

"You distracted me." Cam scowled.

"Sorry, Cap." Pulley plopped down beside him, digging into the pocket of the vest he wore over his bare, hairy chest. He pulled out a cigar and held it out to Cam, the spits of moonlight reflecting off his perfectly shaved scalp.

Cam lit the cigar for him, its head burning deep red with ash. After several puffs, Pulley exhaled smoke through his nostrils as he glanced up at the stars. "You're going to run sailors onto the rocks with those lights. Best keep them to yourself."

Cam willed a fresh ball of fire above him and grumbled, "If they're coming anywhere near Enoch, the rocks are a better fate."

"Maybe you're right." Pulley let out a hoarse laugh before glancing off the edge of the ship, into the dim night-lights of the city beyond. "This place has a putrid feel to it. I hope we don't stay long."

Cam wanted to tell him they'd leave soon. That they'd sail away and never set sights on Enoch again, but he couldn't lie to Pulley. Cam fed more into his fire, making it glow brighter. "We'll be here longer than I'd like. Prepare for a long haul."

"As you say." Pulley blew out a smoke ring before glancing down at Cam. "And what about our lady?"

Cam blinked. "What about her?"

"The lady Annie," Pulley clarified. "The sea life hasn't taken well to her, it seems."

Cam glowered at him. "I'd appreciate it if you minded your own." If Pulley had noticed Annie's discomfort on the ship, that meant others in the crew had, as well. "You keep this ship in order. That's what I need from you."

"As you say," Pulley repeated with a nod. He took another drag on his cigar. "And what about you?"

"What about me?"

Pulley smiled a little too broadly. "Who's going to keep you in order, Captain?"

Before Cam could answer, a familiar set of footsteps approached them. Cam reclined his head again to see Julian Price strolling toward them, hands in his coat pockets. With a groan, Pulley climbed to his feet, his backside stained dark from moisture.

"Captain." Pulley nodded to Cam before doing the same to Julian.

Julian nodded back as Pulley left, though his attention quickly fixed on the growing orb of fire in the sky. He squinted, the orb's light casting an orange glow over his sallow skin. "Practicing?"

Cam blinked, and his fire burst into fireworks, raining embers over the deck of *The Elaina*. He scowled as he brushed off a spark before it could burn the sleeve of his new coat. "You could say that."

Julian dodged an ember. "It's good to see you're projecting."

Cam sat up, sitting cross-legged. "I have no idea what that means."

Julian gestured to where the flames had been. "You're maintaining a constant stream of energy, instead of sending it out in quick bursts."

"So?" Cam replied flatly, only because he felt like being an ass.

"So," Julian shot back, unfazed. "That means, before long, you'll be able to manipulate that energy into different forms. Like a weapon, perhaps. Or a barrier."

Cam laughed as he stood. The back of his hair felt damp, and he dried it with a quick brush of his hand. "A fire sword would be a bit old-fashioned, don't you think? Not to mention an eye sore."

"I'm speaking theoretically, of course." Julian cocked his head. "The women are waiting. We should—"

"When were you going to tell me you were an assassin?" Cam interrupted. "Or *are* an assassin, I should say. You happened to leave that detail out."

Julian's expression darkened. He tucked deeper into his coat. "I told you I was a mercenary."

"Those are two very different professions, mate."

"Are they?" Julian asked. "You don't mind me killing to protect a farmer's barn, but killing a specific target for money is out of the question?"

"I don't care who you kill." Cam turned and leveled his gaze on the Air Brand, fighting to keep his temper in check. "What bothers me is that you allowed me to go in front of my father without having all the cards on the table. Bull like that will get us killed."

"And how much have you kept from me?" Julian retorted, a smug smile spreading on his thin face. "How much have you kept from your *wife?*"

Cam couldn't stop the flames that crawled up his neck. "Don't talk about Annie. I haven't kept anything from her."

"Haven't you?" He said as Cam turned and stormed back towards the center of the ship. Julian followed him to the captain's cabin. "You talked to your father. You got an answer. He didn't kill your mother. Your revenge mission is over. How long are you going to string this along to keep her from leaving?"

Cam moved without meaning to, his fire burning through his veins as his fist connected with Julian's jaw. The force of Julian's body hitting the deck split the pine planks in half.

Great. Now I have to fix the ship, too. Cam sucked in several heavy breaths as Julian grinned up at him, his teeth coated red. "Good. That was better."

"Why are you here?" Cam wanted to hurt him, if only to feel something besides fear and forget Julian's question. "What do you want?"

"I need you." Julian wiped the blood from his lip with the back of his hand. "And you need me. You can't navigate your father's empire without me, and you know it."

The beginnings of panic began bubbling in Cam's chest.

Julian was right. As much as he liked to pretend, he knew nothing of politics. Cam sneered, "What use do I have for a washed-up hitman?"

"The same use I have for a governor's discarded son," Julian replied coolly. "Leverage. Let me help you, and when the time comes, promise you'll help me in return."

Promises. Everyone wants something. To rip and tear pieces from him and leave nothing behind to live on. He'd never been anything to anyone but a chess piece to be played with, but still, Cam found himself saying, "Fine." He just wanted this conversation to end.

As Julian climbed to his feet, the door to the captain's quarters swung open, revealing Annie and Jenny standing in the doorway. As Jenny's shocked gaze fell immediately to the splintered deck, Annie's flickered between Julian's split lip and the blood on Cam's knuckles.

She kept her observations to herself. "Are we ready to leave? We're going to be late."

Cam put on the confident smile he was growing to hate. "My father will expect us to be late."

Annie's brow rose. "So, we should do as he expects?"

God, she was beautiful. Cam forgot how to form words. Wearing her new lavender gown, Annie's hair had been swept up off her face in a voluminous updo. A few white tendrils had been left to frame her large, blue eyes, which were now lined in charcoal. The corset she wore beneath her bodice extenuated her petite bustline.

Cam forced his eyes to the ground, face hot. Julian shot him a knowing look and smirked. He wished he could punch him in the teeth.

"For once, Camden's right," the Air Brand said. "Playing into the governor's expectations will create a false sense of security."

"Excellent." Nathan stepped around the corner, coming from below. He looked like a new man in his fitted suit, his dark ringlets freshly washed and set. "I'll take any advantage we can get."

"We're going to do this, then?" Jenny's ruby red locks were twisted into a sleek coil. "We're going to play the ruler of the West?"

"Hang it all." Cam let out an exasperated sigh. "I guess we are."

Their coach dropped them off at the Callahan estate at half past seven. Fashionably late.

Cam sucked in a breath of the cool night air as he stepped out. Even from here, the muffled sounds of conversations and laughter echoed from inside the house and across the courtyard.

That black haired butler—what was his name? David. David stood outside the manor's double doors, as if waiting for them.

Who was Cam kidding? Of course, he was waiting for them. His father had probably ordered the poor man to wait in the cold until they arrived.

As the others climbed out of the coach behind him, Annie stepped up to Cam's side. Her eyes flickered again to his knuckles. She pursed her lips. "What happened?"

Cam flexed his hand. "I punched Julian in the face."

"I can see that. Why?"

She looked so ethereal in the glow of the gaslights surrounding the courtyard. He swallowed. "Because he deserved it."

Annie shook her head, but she did smile a little. "I'm sad I missed it."

Cam offered her his arm and led them up the stairs toward the entry. The others fell in line behind them. He whispered, "Do you also fantasize about turning his nose into meaty pulp?"

Annie let out a sharp laugh, making his stomach flip-flop. "Not exactly, it's just . . ." Her lips twitched. "Never mind."

They reached the top of the stairs before Cam could push the topic further. David bowed as they approached, beads of sweat dripping off his dark brows. "Welcome, my lord. We've been expecting you. The governor waits for you within. Shall I take you to him?"

"I'm sure he is." Cam snorted. David gave him a confused look, and he cleared his throat. "Ah, thank you. I'll find him myself."

"The manor is quite large, my lord," David replied. "You could get lost—"

"I was born here," he snapped. "Open the bloody doors."

David's eyes widened.

He exhaled and forced a smile. "Apologies. It's been a long day. Where is he?"

The man unlocked the manor doors. "In the ballroom. He reopened it just for you."

Annie's arm tightening around his was the only thing that kept Cam grounded. Black spots crept into the edge of his vision, but he focused on her instead, on the lavender scent clinging to her snow-white hair. *He opened it for me.* Because the last time Cam had been to one of his father's parties was the night that he and his mother fled. They'd slept in an alley that night. No blankets. Just shivering as they clung to each other. After a while, when he had pretended to fall asleep, his mother had wept.

A power play. Alexander wanted to make Cam uncomfortable. And it was working.

"David, see our friends in, please." Annie nodded to the others, never releasing her grip on Cam's elbow. "Camden and I will follow in a few moments."

With the doors wide open, gold light spilled out onto the entry. David gave her a quick bow. "My lady." He gestured to the others. "If you'd follow me."

Panic flashed over Jenny's features as David led them toward the ballroom, but Annie gave her a reassuring smile. Neither Julian nor Nathan glanced his way.

Cam's heart lurched and slammed against his ribs as Annie turned to face him, her pale cheeks rouged pink. *She knows you're a coward. She's going to hate you. She's going—*

She hooked her pinkie finger through his, her brands flaring as she ordered, "Breathe."

Cam inhaled, air filling his desperate lungs, chasing away some of the darkness clouding his eyes.

Annie squeezed tighter. "Now again."

He took a second breath, feeling every bit the fool as he must have looked.

Annie lifted his hand, inspecting the bruises forming on his knuckles. Her eyes narrowed in concentration as she brushed her thumb over them. Cam winced as a rush of cold spread through his fingers, and the bruises faded away.

He exhaled, "Thank you."

Annie smiled. She could make him do anything by simply smiling at him. "He's trying to hurt you."

Not a question.

"Yes." He hated the way his voice shook. He hated that the truth spilled out even more. "I don't know if I can do this. If I can spend the entire blasted evening pretending to be who he wants me to be. I—"

"Then, don't." Annie reached out, as if she meant to touch his face, but let her hand fall to her side instead. "Don't pretend."

Cam cringed as more truth escaped. She always made him say more than he wanted to. "If I'm not pretending, then who am I?" *Nothing, that's what. A mistake.*

"You're Camden Callahan," Annie said in that tone of hers. "You're the man who saved dozens from horrible deaths on New Havana."

He met her cold stare. Where some might find her intensity unsettling, he found it calming. An anchor. It had been Annie's idea—her ultimatum—that in exchange for helping him take down Richard Duskin, he'd free the "patients" locked away beneath the island—Lord Duskin's prisoners. Nathan had been one of them.

Cam let out a breathy laugh. "That doesn't count. I didn't do it alone."

"Why would that keep it from counting?" Annie shot back. "I'm sure Alexander Callahan didn't take command of the West alone, either."

"True." Cam's lips quirked, either adrenaline or stupidity making him speak boldly. "If I do it, will you, too?"

Annie frowned. "Do what?"

"Not pretend."

Oh, she tried to hide the flicker of terror that crossed her features, but he'd seen it. They were two sides of the same coin. When had either of them ever been themselves? She was as afraid as he was.

Cam continued, "No acting like the perfect lady. No fake smiles. I'll be me, and you'll be you?"

Annie's frown deepened. "Just for the night?"

He grinned. "If that's what you want."

"Will it help?"

"Will it help me? Absolutely. You know how I hate to suffer alone."

"No pretending, then. For tonight." Annie smoothed her hair, adjusted her dress, then sighed. "Damn it, I didn't prepare for this."

Cam laughed again as he offered her his arm. "That makes two of us."

Annie *almost* grinned back, then bit down on her lower lip. "Let's get this over with."

Just one night. I can do this. If she were with him, he could. Arm in arm, they entered the ballroom.

CHAPTER 11
ANNIE

This was even worse than she thought.

Cam pushed open the heavy oak doors to the ballroom, and Annie squinted as a cacophony of crystalline lights and sounds assaulted them. Beneath her heavy dress, her knees wobbled. Too many colors. Blaring music. Too many smells. Lord above, she even thought she could detect the bottom-feeder stench of crab.

With her arm through his, she felt the shudder that ran through Cam's body. Some of the color had drained out of his tanned skin. His chest rose and fell in rapid breaths. Lined with fire, his eyes frantically scanned over the room, taking in every detail.

Above them, dozens of dancing guests, with strings of tiny, round lights strung between the great, white pillars encircling the room, cast the hall in an eerie, golden glow. Three massive, rectangular tables of appetizers sat on the far left, filled with meats, cheeses, wine—and Lord, she was right—seafood. As her eyes fell to the center of the room, she thought she might vomit.

The dancing had stopped. Even the violinist had slowed his playing.

Everyone was staring at them.

You can't run. You can't run. Annie forced herself to straighten and peer up at Cam again. The anxiety she'd seen from him moments before had disappeared entirely. His expression shifted to his usual overconfidence, touched with an edge of vicious cruelty.

From the dark look in his eyes, she could have fallen for his façade, too, if not for the pounding of his pulse she felt from where they touched.

Cam ignored the stares as he moved toward the dining tables. On instinct, she followed, keeping close, arms still linked. They were halfway across the hall before the music began again in earnest. Cam must have noticed them earlier, because as they reached the tables, she realized that Jenny and Nathan were there, looking queasy as they chatted with a plump woman who was fawning over Jenny's gown.

The woman ran her fingers over the fabric of Jenny's skirts. "You *must* tell me who designed this, I—" She choked when she noticed Cam. Her eyes dropped to the floor before she muttered, "Maybe another time."

Then she was gone. Disappearing back into the crowd that still watched them.

Nathan grabbed a glass of champagne off the table and downed it in one swallow before he said, "You really do have a terrible effect on people, mate."

Some of the tension left Cam as he smiled. "Don't get drunk yet. We've got a lot of night left."

"Where's Mr. Price?" Annie asked.

Jenny shrugged. "Not sure. We lost track of him as soon as we got in here. That woman was the first person to talk to us."

Nathan wiped his mouth. "A chatty wench, she was."

Jenny pinched his arm. "Don't be mean."

Cam wasn't listening. His eyes continued to scour over each and every face in the room. She didn't have to ask to know who he was looking for. She tightened her grip on his arm. His throat bobbed as he finally looked at her, his full lips pursed.

She whispered so only he could hear, "Pretend he's not here."

His brow rose in question.

"He's not here," Annie repeated. "He's just another man in thousands. Nobody of consequence." She used to repeat those exact words to herself back on New Havana. When she'd first arrived on the island, every time Lord Duskin sat at the dinner table with them, she pretended he was someone else. It was the only way she could get through a meal without her mind spiraling back into the horrid memories of what he'd done to her.

Cam's tone lightened. "I thought we *weren't* pretending, Kitten?"

"*We* aren't pretending to be someone else." Annie's lips quirked. "We never agreed upon others."

The tightness in her chest loosened when he smiled at her and replied, "As usual, you're right."

"There you are." A deep, familiar voice called from the center of the ballroom. Alexander Callahan. A slender, brown-haired man walked beside him—the doctor from The Greens, Van Clarke.

Cam's back went rigid as he turned toward his approaching father. As he sneered, his body fell into a practiced, loose posture. "As if you hadn't known the moment we walked in. Don't play stupid, Father, it's not a good look for you."

Dr. Clarke shot Governor Callahan a nervous glance.

The governor sneered back. *He and Cam look so much alike.*

"Forgive me. I'm used to speaking to simpletons." His attention turned to Annie, and he dipped his head. "My lady."

"Governor." She didn't bother to curtsy. She *had* promised not to pretend. "Is Lady Maya here?"

"She wasn't feeling well." The governor answered. He looked to Nathan and Jenny. "Camden, you must introduce me to . . . ?"

"My quartermaster, Nathan Williams," Cam replied, bored. "And my wife's—"

"Sister," Annie interrupted. Jenny blinked at her in surprise. "This is my sister, Jenny Duskin."

The governor's head tilted in the opposite direction. "And here I thought she was your handmaiden."

"Easier through customs this way." Annie held his stare. "You can understand."

Beside her, Cam's heat brushed against her arm in delight. Her own power stirred in response.

"Unfortunately, I do." The governor huffed in amusement. He turned and gestured to Mr. Clarke. "Forgive me, this is Doctor Van Clarke. He's the head surgeon at Waverly Hills Hospital."

"We've met." Cam tsked. "The sick piling up in the streets? I'm disappointed. The slums of Port Lebanon were in better condition."

It was so subtle, only Annie would have noticed the twitch of irritation in the governor's jaw. His eyes narrowed. "The Rot has been hard on us all."

"And has no greater truth been spoken!" Dr. Clarke quipped. "Even I can barely manage to keep the infection from spreading between patients. The hospital beds are full."

"Don't you separate them?" The words left Annie's mouth before she could stop them. Cam's grip on her elbow tightened at the same time the governor and Dr. Clarke gave her strange looks. She swallowed. "The disease spreads by contact. Infected patients must be quarantined."

"My lady has an extensive knowledge of The Rot." Cam tugged her closer, almost protectively. She didn't miss the hint of pride in his voice. "Whatever you may have heard of Richard Duskin, Annie was the driving force behind the . . . success of his work."

"Truly?" Dr. Clarke's brown eyes lit up. "I'd be honored to have you visit Waverly Hills. Even this far across the sea, I've heard of Richard Duskin's research." He frowned and tapped his lip. "Oh, wait, we agreed upon tomorrow already, haven't we? And to think, to have Lord Duskin's daughter at Waverly!"

She and Cam exchanged quick, nervous glances. So did Jenny and Nathan behind them.

Dr. Clarke hadn't forgotten their arrangement to meet. He just wanted to make sure Cam's father knew about it, too.

They can't know about the patent. The last thing they needed was Governor Callahan knowing the results of Lord Duskin's research. How not only the disease—but Revenancy—could be screened by Pearl Dust, and she was now the only citizen legally allowed to own it.

"We're going to . . . mingle." Nathan took Jenny's arm and bowed to Governor Callahan. He patted Cam's shoulder. "We'll catch up with you later."

Annie met Jenny's eye. She knew the plan. They'd prepared earlier this evening that she and Nathan would hover around the party, hoping to overhear any information that might be useful to them.

Before the two men could notice, Annie turned her attention back to Dr. Clarke. "I'm looking forward to seeing the hospital."

"I must introduce you to *my* sister." Dr. Clarke snaked his arm through hers, only hesitating when a lick of fire flared over

Cam's throat. He cleared his throat. "My twin, Violet Clarke. She works as a nurse at the hospital. She's always taken a special interest in The Rot. I'm sure she'd love to speak to you and compare, *ahem,* war stories."

She peered back at Cam. He gave her a look that said, *Your call.* They needed information. They weren't going to get it by standing around.

She turned back to Dr. Clarke. "I'd love to."

"Excellent." Governor Callahan said, "While you two chat, my son and I have some . . . catching up to do." He laid his hand on Cam's shoulder, sending a fresh wave of fire curling around Cam's fists. Honestly, she was impressed he managed to keep from incinerating him.

Dr. Clarke gestured toward the far side of the room. "Shall we?"

Annie let her hand trail down to squeeze Cam's. His skin had become clammy, but he nodded to her as she followed the doctor.

Dr. Clarke continued to talk as he led her across the hall. Annie glanced back to see Cam following his father deeper into the ballroom, a mirage of heat rolling off his body. Nathan and Jenny were dancing together on the ballroom floor, chatting up the couple beside them, Mr. Price nowhere in sight.

Cam will be okay. Annie repeated to herself as she nodded along with Dr. Clarke's chatter. He could take care of himself. In fact, he could burn this entire building to the ground if he wanted to. It was difficult to remember that she was dangerous too, as Mr. Price frequently reminded her.

Dr. Clarke's chatter slowed as they approached a group of five women seated in a circle of green and gold sofas. A heaping platter of pastries and a large, porcelain teapot sat on the low table between them.

One of the women stared up at them, her dark eyes

narrowing. *This must be Violet Clarke.* There was no way she wasn't. She and Dr. Clarke had the same narrow chin and brown curls.

"Brother." The woman—Violet—rose as soon as they were within feet of the sofas. The other women shot Annie suspicious looks. Violet never took her eyes off Annie as they approached. "This is my sister, Violet Clarke. Violet, I have the honor of introducing you to the new Lady, Annie Callahan."

Lady. Annie smirked despite herself. Would that ever stop sounding so absurd?

Violet must have taken her smirking for arrogance because she plastered on the fakest smile Annie had ever seen. Violet's ringlets, pinned into a perfectly relaxed, without-trying updo, fell over the obtrusively full bosom, threatening to spill over the top of her bodice as she curtsied. "I'd heard of your beauty, Lady Callahan, but the reports haven't done you justice."

Reports? Annie ignored the faux compliment. "We've been in port for a day. I doubt you've heard much."

Violet brushed her fingers over her collarbone, her skin like buttercream. "You underestimate my reach, I'm afraid. They're calling you the White Lady in the city, you know."

I promised Cam I wouldn't pretend. Annie kept her expression deceptively blank. "I didn't know, but I imagine the extent of your *reach* doesn't lie far past Enoch's borders, which means not as far as you think. Unless I'm wrong?"

Violet's smile fell as the women behind her exchanged glances.

Dr. Clarke cleared his throat. "As I said before, my sister works as a nurse at Waverly Hills. Violet, did you know that Lady Callahan worked firsthand with Richard Duskin on his research on The Rot?"

"Did you?" Violet replied, her voice high and clipped. She scanned Annie head to toe, rested her hand on her hip, then gestured to the group behind her. "Join us for tea? I'd love to hear what it was like to work with a man of such esteemed . . . character."

I hate this. I hate this already. No wonder Cam had avoided this place at all costs. Annie breathed a sigh out of her nose. "Tea sounds lovely."

Violet dismissed Dr. Clarke with a wave. "Run along, brother. The women are speaking."

Annie froze, shifting to take in Dr. Clarke's expression. Instead of anger, he let out a nervous giggle and rubbed his thin hands together. "Of course, of course. I'll just . . ." Instead of finishing his sentence, he made a quick bow then darted back into the crowd.

Annie stared after him until she heard the stiff shifting of fabric. As she turned, Violet had moved within six inches of her, leaning in. Her gown was a dramatic, fuchsia monstrosity. "Men, am I right?"

Instead of recoiling at the heavy, rose perfume emanating from Violet's skin, Annie held her ground. "I'm not sure what you mean."

Violet scoffed. "You'll know soon enough." She reclaimed her seat at the head of her gaggle of jewelry-leaden geese before patting the seat beside her. "Come. Sit."

Annie did as she was bidden, tucking her own over-priced gown beneath her. The other women stared at her, not bothering to hide their curiosity. They all looked like cheaper versions of Violet. Maybe she chose her friends for that very purpose.

Violet poured Annie a steaming cup of tea and passed it to her. As Annie took it, the rich, flowery aroma clogged her senses, and she fought to keep from sneezing. Out of politeness —Violet wouldn't dare poison her here—she forced herself to take a sip, and it tasted as strong as it smelled.

Pursing her lips, Annie set her cup back in its dish. "Um, thank you."

"Is it true you married the governor's son?" One of the women, a younger, pudgy redhead, asked. "Even though he destroyed New Havana?"

"Of course, she married him, you ninny." Violet did that dismissive wave again. "Why else would she be called *Lady* Callahan?"

The other woman dropped her head.

Violet twisted in her seat, her breasts nearly escaping from her neckline. "My brother tells me you're coming to the hospital tomorrow morning. Will your *husband* be joining you?"

Annie folded her hands over her lap, hiding the rush of energy pulsing through her brands. "Yes, he'll be with me."

"Wonderful." Violet's teeth were too straight, her smile too practiced. "I look forward to meeting him. I've heard he's handsome."

A twist of power moved through Annie's veins, causing her fingers to glow. She tucked them beneath her thighs. "He sure thinks so."

"You've studied The Rot?" Another of the women asked, this one with blonde hair. "That must have been dreadful."

Annie scanned over their expectant faces. *I promised. I promised. I promised.* "It wasn't all bad."

Violet's thick brows pinched together. "A bold statement. How so?"

She picked up her tea again, thankful her fingers were no longer glowing. She blew on the hot liquid before taking a sip. "I enjoyed performing the autopsies."

Again, the women exchanged glances.

Annie continued to sip her tea.

This was going to be a long night.

CHAPTER 12
CAMDEN

Why do I do this to myself?

Not only was he alone at this God-forsaken party, but now he was alone with *him.*

As that sleazy doctor led Annie deeper into the ballroom, Alexander led him up the short flight of stairs to the upper balcony. Guests parted as they passed, some bowing, others trying to start a conversation. Cam gritted his teeth, and he shoved his rage down into the pit of his soul, where he kept his fire. They were here for a reason. The others were playing their part. It was time he played his.

As they walked, Cam skimmed over the room, over the hundred or more stunned faces gawking at him like he was a zoo animal. They indulged in lavish meals, unaware that people like Mr. Maynard lived in nearby hovels, struggling without even the fundamental human right of clean bandages.

Cam blocked them out. Where the hell had Julian gone?

Wait, he can fly. Cam looked up. As sure as the day was long, Julian Price sat on top of the massive, crystal chandelier, surveying the room below.

Air Brands. Cam shook his head in exasperation. Julian noticed Cam's attention and placed a finger over his lips, grinning like an idiot.

He hadn't realized they'd hit the top of the stairs until he felt the weight of his father's gaze land on him. He'd always been able to feel it—like the nauseating crunch of sand in your teeth.

Cam took a note from Annie's book and steeled his expression before facing Alexander. His father leaned against the balcony railing, inspecting Cam as he might a slab of beef. Down below, a roar of raucous laughter echoed through the room—Nathan's laugh. At least he was having fun.

The upper floor was exactly as Cam remembered it as a child. Heavy, crimson drapes were pinned in artful folds between the marble banisters. A small sitting area circled a low-lit hearth—a space where partygoers took breaks from the revelry. Even the bear rug was the same. *I guess Maya isn't much for interior decorating.* His mother changed out the décor every season, along with throwing a ball for every holiday.

Alexander still watched him. With an internal sigh, Cam joined him by the railing. He tapped his fingers on the banister beside them, waiting for some pre-prepared speech.

But instead, his father asked, "Dr. Clarke invited you to Waverly . . . today?"

Cam gave him a slow nod.

"Hmm." Alexander's eyes narrowed before he casually gestured toward the party below. "What do you see?"

Cam hated that his first instinct was to make a cheeky remark. With a sigh, he stared down at the party. Beneath them, couples twirled in and out of each other's arms as they danced. Smiling. Laughing. Men stood along the edges of the room, murmuring to each other as they sipped on booze that probably cost more than they made in an entire year.

But he *felt*, more than he saw, the tension. Revenants—more Revenants than he'd ever seen in one place—separated themselves from the mortals that shot them scathing looks from across the ballroom. They even danced separately. A pang of relief shot through him as he caught a glimpse of Annie's ghostly white hair as she sat with a group of chatting women. She was the only Revenant mingling.

Too tired to argue, Cam rested his elbows on the railing, his brows furrowed. "I see division."

"Good," Alexander smirked a little. "What else?"

Never mind. He wasn't too tired to argue. "I didn't come here for testing," Cam said.

"No, you came here to find your mother's killer," Alexander said.

"I know who killed my mother."

"Do you?" his father shot back, scowling. "So, you know who wielded the blade that took her life?"

Cam fell silent.

"Tell me—what else do you see?" Alexander repeated.

Fire twisted up Cam's throat, making his mouth hot. *Remember, this isn't just about me.* He closed his eyes for a moment before scanning the room again. It looked the same as it had before. *What would he* want *me to see?*

Every few moments, a face or two would glance up at them on the balcony. Some curious, some bitter, some seemed confused. He could almost guess who'd be the next to turn their head.

Cam frowned. "They're watching us."

Alexander nodded darkly. "They are *always* watching us, Camden. They will be watching *you*. You are the heir to the West. If you plan to govern them—"

"I'm not here to clean up your mess," Cam said. "*Your* city falling into pieces isn't *my* problem."

Alexander tilted his head, steel-blue eyes narrowing. "You mentioned eight assassination attempts? How did they try to kill you?"

God, how was he going to make it through the night? Cam clenched his jaw. "Why don't you ask your bookkeepers?"

"Do you really believe that if I wanted you dead, you would still be breathing right now?"

He has a point there. Cam made a show of counting on his fingers. "Let's see—three times were poison. Those were the worst. Twice, I almost had my throat cut in my sleep. Once, when I was a kid, I got shoved in a trunk and thrown into the bay." What was he forgetting? Cam counted again. "And the last two times I got jumped and strangled. Both outside a tavern."

Something like rage flickered over Alexander's features. "Convenient that they wanted your body to be easily moved. A gun would have been easier, but terribly messy."

Cam blinked once, twice.

Alexander smoothed down the front of his three-piece suit. He scratched at his gloved finger. "A few days before you and your mother disappeared, Elias Bennett visited me. He heard what happened when you'd been exposed to Pearl Dust. I imagine you remember that incident? He insisted that I allow you to be studied."

Cam did remember.

At nine years old, he'd snuck into his father's study and gotten into his Pearl Dust stores. He hadn't known what the substance was at the time, only that it was new and interesting and looked so pretty inside the glass vials on his father's desk. All he remembered after he'd smelled the pink powder was the heat that radiated through his body, under his skin. He'd woken days later, covered in burns. Alexander had beaten him for it.

But as Cam recalled the memories, all the pieces began to fall into place. Elias had been obsessed with the prospect of Pearl Dust predicting Revenancy. And if he'd already known Cam had shown symptoms . . .

They'd never planned for Cam to stay dead. Whoever had tried to kill him had known he'd turn. They'd *wanted* him to turn.

Cam gripped the banister until his knuckles turned white, trying to keep from spiraling. *Breathe, breathe, breathe.* "And what did you tell Elias?"

Alexander shifted uncomfortably. "You have to understand, when your grandfather passed and left me Enoch, the city was on the verge of collapse. There were enemies on all sides, and . . ." He blew a long breath out of his nose. "I was in a terrible state of mind. I made bargains with some of the most evil men imaginable to keep this country alive." He sighed. "One of those bargains was you."

Take him somewhere his father won't find him. Those had been his mother's last words, what she'd made Resh promise when he'd taken Cam onto his ship. Alexander Callahan was going to let him become an experiment, and his mother died to keep that from happening.

And they'd followed Cam across the ocean and tried for an entire decade to get what they wanted—for him to die and become something else. They'd succeeded.

Cam's throat burned as his fire curled in his stomach. Absently, he reached into his pocket and pulled out Elias's ring, the phoenix stamped into its silver face gleaming in the lowlight. A phoenix. Rebirth. How very unoriginal.

Alexander reached for the ring.

Cam gave it to him. He really was too tired to argue now. "You sold me to these people, didn't you? Elias called them The Order."

His father rubbed his thumb over the engraving, sorrow dancing in his eyes. "I did. That's a gentle name for them. Now that Revenant laws are again being negotiated, they've begun killing men—good men—on each side of the dispute, manipulating terms into their favor. Of course, the pro and anti-Revenant groups aren't farsighted enough to see it. I guarantee half the people down there are expecting to get stabbed in the back before the night is over."

Cam just wanted to go to bed. "Why?"

"A city in chaos is a city that can be controlled." His father gently set the ring on the edge of the railing between them. "It's the oldest trick in the book. I don't expect you to trust me, Camden, but we want the same thing. Help me stop them."

Help him? Cam let his eyes flutter closed. "You can spin yourself whatever story you want, but Mother still died because of *you*."

"I know."

This Order . . . they were also responsible for the death of Annie's family, for the torment she endured. Cam stepped back, tucking his hands into his pockets. Only for Annie. *Only* for her would he agree to this.

"If I do this, don't forget that I hate you," Cam said. "I'll always hate you. If it weren't for the promises I've made, I'd walk away right now and laugh knowing that vultures are coming for you. Just like you deserve."

Alexander smiled, a genuine smile that crinkled the skin at the corners of his eyes. "Again, I know."

"Governor?"

Cam swiveled as a husky female voice called out to them. A Revenant woman, with russet-brown skin, scaled the staircase, arm-in-arm with Annie. A tall, thin Revenant man trailed behind them. While Annie looked extremely uncomfortable—

the other woman was all smiles and confidence—her poofy, black hair encircling her head like a halo.

As they stepped onto the second floor, Annie moved to Cam's elbow. She shot him a quick, tense look that he mirrored. Turquoise-blue brands tugged from the corners of the Revenant woman's hazel eyes and into her hairline. More rippled from her shoulders down to her toned biceps.

Water Brand. Why, he didn't know, but Cam stepped back until he could feel Annie's arm against his. *She's safe.* Without his permission, his power flared up and reached for her, sending a comforting ripple of warmth down her body. The black brands webbed over Annie's neck pulsed, brushing back against him. He felt the emotion behind the touch—she was intimidated. In no world could he think of a reason she *should* be. Annie had the power to drain the life from them. What was a Water Brand compared to that?

The woman curtsied for Alexander, her lime-green, silk gown clinging to the soft swell of her belly, her accent heavily Eastern. "There you are, Governor. Jude and I wanted to thank you personally for the invitation."

She's pregnant. Cam's eyes shot to the man behind her. He really was a spindly bloke, with a mess of chocolate brown curls and a long nose. His brands were much lighter—a pale, silvery color—and only visible where they swirled just below the length of his sleeve. *Another Air Brand, maybe?* Could Revenants have children? He'd never thought of that. Would the baby be born mortal or with powers? A thought for later.

"Mrs. Hall." His father bowed, brushing a quick kiss to the woman's extended hand, laden with jeweled rings. He shook hands with the Revenant man before gesturing to Cam and Annie. "Son, this is Jude and Reika Hall. They are heavily involved in the argument for extending Revenant rights." He nodded to her rounded stomach. "Congratulations . . . again."

Son. Cam rolled his eyes.

"Thank you. And I would call it a war," Reika said stiffly, her heavy, gold bracelets jingling as she brushed a hand defensively over her abdomen. She gave Cam a devious smile. "I've already had to save Lady Annie from the Clarkes. Seems you already owe me a debt."

Cam snorted out a laugh, reaching back to take Annie's hand. He half expected her to pull away, but she didn't. *Of course, she didn't.* They were both playing parts. Some may be more than others. *Don't think of that.*

He squared his shoulders and outdid the mischief in her smile. "Mrs. Hall, if you think Annie is the one in need of saving, you're even blinder than my father."

Alexander glared at him.

Annie squeezed his fingers gratefully.

Reika laughed, her voice like a bell. "Well said. If you'd commented any less, I'd have deemed you not worthy of her." She gave Annie a quick look before nodding toward the edge of the balcony. "And you can tell your friend there to quit skulking about. If he has questions, he can ask them directly."

Julian. He must have overheard them, because as Cam looked up at the chandelier, gasps had begun to emerge from the crowds below as Julian floated through the air before landing on the balcony. He gave the Halls a quick bow. "Julian Price, at your service."

"Oh!" Jude Hall clapped his thin hands together. "Another wind rider! How have you found the currents of late?"

"Terrible," Julian admitted with a frown. "I've spent most of my time on the ground since leaving the South."

Jude patted Julian's shoulder before steering him toward the hearth. "It really is savage up this way, isn't it? If you don't mind my asking—"

Reika rolled her eyes as her husband wandered away with

one of the deadliest men on the continent. She waved dismis-sively, though her tone was loving. "Jude will talk all night about his preference for air quality from one region to anoth-er." Her cunning gaze gave Cam a once-over. "Camden Calla-han. I'm sure you have many stories to tell."

"More than I'd like," Cam replied. Something in the way Annie gripped his fingers made him pause. He forced a smile for Reika and his father. "If you'll give us a moment."

Annie didn't resist as he guided her to the far stairwell on the opposite side of the balcony. He could feel his father's eyes on his back as he jogged halfway down the stairs, then turned to face her once they were out of earshot. Annie's usually stony expression was twisted with concern.

"What is it?" Cam asked, breathless. More than anyone, he trusted her instincts. They were the only reason she'd survived this long.

Annie didn't look at him immediately. Her stare lingered over the far balcony. "That woman wants something."

Cam relaxed a little. "I assumed as much when I saw your face while you walked up with her—"

Annie waved him off. "No, not her"—She nodded toward the balcony again—"*her*."

Cam looked again and realized Annie hadn't been staring at the balcony, but *above* it. Another woman watched them from the often unused third level. She looked mortal, for as much as he could tell, with brown curls and an absurdly volu-minous gown.

Cam quickly peered back at Annie, brows raised. "Who is *that*?"

Annie let out an angry sigh. It was . . . adorable. "That's Violet Clarke. She works as a nurse at the hospital with her brother."

Cam resisted the temptation to look back at Violet. "And she's bothering you why?"

Annie scratched her neck. "Because she made it *very* clear that she's looking forward to meeting you tomorrow. I don't trust her."

Cam fought, and failed, to hide a smile as he snaked his elbow through Annie's, leading her further down the stairs. "Are you afraid I'll succumb to her—er—womanly charms?"

"*No*," Annie replied, a little too quickly. She glanced back to where Violet had been. She'd moved on. Annie cleared her throat. "It's . . . like I said, she wants something."

Cam tried to ignore all the eyes that followed them as they rejoined the ballroom. "Something we can use to our advantage?"

"I'm not sure," Annie said before her expression saddened. "Sometimes . . . I wish people weren't so terrible."

"You and me both," Cam admitted, surveying the room for Nathan and Jenny. *There they are.* The two sat at a lace-trimmed table together, dining on fried shrimp and scallops as they chatted with another mortal couple.

At his side, Annie watched them, a small smile on her face despite her scrunched nose. "You weren't wrong before. They're handsome together."

Cam rubbed his ear. "Did you just admit that I was right?"

Annie glowered at him from beneath her darkened lashes. "Don't make me say it again." Her expression softened as she observed her adopted sister. "I want Jenny to be happy. I want her to *live*."

"I understand," Cam replied. All he wanted was for Nathan to have a life. For *Annie* to have a life. Alexander's eyes followed them as they reached the dance floor. Reika was gone, presumably to find her husband.

Let him rot. Alexander deserved to sit by himself, miserable. Cam gently tugged Annie towards him, placing her hand on his shoulder as he rested his on her waist. He'd already agreed to help. He wouldn't let his father ruin the rest of his night. "That's why we're doing this, right? So, the ones that we love can live."

Annie slid her opposite hand into his. She shot Nathan and Jenny another longing look. "Yes. I think so."

As the piano played softly in the background, Cam allowed himself to forget about his father and The Order. If he was stuck here for the evening, he intended to make the best of it. He gripped Annie tighter, gliding them into the music. She giggled when he tripped over her foot, making her impossibly lovelier. The mirage of color in the room's décor reflected off her hair, creating shimmering streaks of pink, silver, and gold. Every time her ice-blue eyes flickered to his lips, he convinced himself he'd imagined it.

Tomorrow, they'd be visiting Waverly Hills Hospital.

Cam swallowed. Julian had been right. He *was* afraid of the moment when Annie didn't need him anymore. When their bargain was fulfilled, and she had no reason to stay. She would leave. But not tonight. Tonight, he'd break their promise and pretend that she cared as much as he did, that they weren't the target of a bloodthirsty cult.

Annie held close, molding into him as they danced alongside the rest of the couples in the ballroom. After three or four dances had passed, the guests didn't watch them so closely anymore. In fact, they seemed to ignore them entirely as the night continued. At some point, Nathan and Jenny joined them.

Cam danced with Annie. He danced with Jenny. At one point, he even danced with Nathan, which made the entire room roar with genuine laughter.

All the while, Alexander Callahan eyed them darkly. His body still fixed against the railing of the balcony.

Cam ignored him. He'd lost his crew—the only family he'd ever had. Resh was dead, but for tonight, the people he cared for were with him. He'd enjoy it. He refused to make the same mistakes he'd made in his last life.

And Annie was so . . . breathtaking.

It hurt that she would never think the same of him.

CHAPTER 13
CAMDEN

They danced late into the night. Cam even had . . . fun.

As the dancers wandered off to find cocktails, blurry-eyed and red-faced, even Annie looked content—or at least she wore a slight smile—as she sat on a sofa, nibbling on berry tarts with Jenny.

Nathan was deep in conversation with Jude and Reika Hall. Julian hung in the shadows of a pillar, picking his nails as he listened in on drunken conversations, ever the spy.

And all the while, Alexander Callahan watched Cam from the balcony. He wasn't going to let him leave without having another conversation. There was only so long he could avoid it.

Cam leaned against the wall behind where Annie and Jenny sat, arms crossed. He refused to move. If his father wanted to talk, he could walk his sorry ass down and do it himself.

After a fifteen-minute stare-off, Alexander finally straightened, rolling his shoulders, before taking his time strolling down the staircase. The entire room went silent as the

Governor of the West crossed the ballroom, hands in his pockets.

Cam tried hard and failed to hide the cocky grin spreading on his face. *Checkmate.*

Annie stiffened in her seat—watching from the corner of her eye—as Alexander passed her and Jenny, the latter oblivious to the stand-off.

With a low, tired groan, Alexander leaned beside Cam.

Cam ignored him as he continued to fight a smirk.

His father pursed his lips and sighed. "Don't look so smug. I just don't have all night to play your games."

"Games?" Cam reclined his head back. "Why, I don't know what you mean."

"Right." Alexander exhaled through his nose. "Have you made a decision?"

Annie was doing an incredible job of pretending not to listen, just like she had in the Duskins' manor.

Cam's brow rose innocently. "About what?"

"Are you going to help me hunt down these killers?"

"I already told you I would."

"I prefer yes or no answers."

Cam shot his father a dark glare. "Apologies that I didn't speak clearly enough for you."

Alexander held his glare as he growled, "Yes, or no?"

"Hang it all." Cam pushed off the wall, facing him. "Yes. I will do your job for you in exchange for resources and the promise you'll leave us well alone when this is over. Are you happy now?"

"Very much so." Alexander's shoulders relaxed slightly. "And I agree to those terms. We'll get started in the morning. There's much to discuss."

Cam shoved his hands into his coat pockets. "We're visiting the hospital in the morning."

"Brilliant. We'll meet after, then."

Fire crept up Cam's neck, twisting around his ear. *This would be so much easier if you just killed him.* He shook the words away.

Alexander gave him a curious look.

"Fine," Cam snapped. "After the hospital."

"Where are we going after the hospital?" Annie asked. He hadn't even noticed she'd gotten up. She squeezed Cam's arm and gave Alexander a bored smile. Dare he say she sounded protective? "I assume I'm invited?"

Alexander's lips curled into a wide grin. "Of course, my dear. I would expect nothing less. I'm sure Camden will fill you in on the evening conversations."

Annie scrunched her nose. "He will."

God, these two. He'd never met anyone who could hold his father's gaze the way she did—cold and unflinching. It made his face grow hot.

Guests bid Alexander good night and thanked him for the pleasant evening as they made their way out of the ballroom to the courtyard for their carriages. More than one stumbled on their way out.

"I assume it's time to depart?" Julian Price asked as he strode towards them from across the ballroom, a very bleary-eyed Nathan in tow. Jenny stood as they approached, taking Nathan's arm to steady him. Frankly, they all looked exhausted.

His father gave them a dismissive once-over before turning his attention back to Cam.

"Well, then." Cam gave Alexander a quick bow, grateful for the out. "Until next time—"

"I assume you'll be staying here for the remainder of your time in Enoch?" Alexander interrupted. The question sounded sincere. "The harbor is hours away. It would be much easier for our work and cooperation if you were closer."

As Cam straightened, everyone except Annie looked at him expectantly. It was nearly two in the morning. The sound of a feather bed just down the hall must have sounded heavenly to them.

Cam's eyes seared into his father's. "I'd rather be burned at the stake . . . again."

To his surprise, Alexander flinched. "You wouldn't have to stay inside the main manor. I took the liberty of having one of the villas on the grounds readied for you and your party earlier this evening. Plus, you'll save hours on your trip to Waverly in the morning."

Cam couldn't decide if he was surprised or enraged by the audacity. "You honestly think I'd—" He froze.

The lady Annie. The sea life hasn't taken well to her, it seems.

Annie hated the ship.

He glanced down to where she stood at his side. Annie stared numbly ahead, past them, seeing nothing and everything all at once. He couldn't handle that look. It was the same one she wore so many times on New Havana. She'd worn it the night she'd agreed to help him take down the Duskins, when she'd assumed he'd ask despicable things from her in return for her freedom.

Annie was readying herself for pain—and not all pain was physical. She was expecting him to say no.

Blazes. He couldn't do it. He couldn't make her spend another night where she felt so vulnerable. Even if it meant sleeping within bullet distance of his father.

Cam bit on his lip as he dropped his head, tasting blood. "The villa will be fine."

Annie blinked slowly before she raised her head. Julian

seemed just as suspicious. But Jenny and Nathan sagged with relief.

"Excellent." A flicker of satisfaction flashed across Alexander's face before he smiled. "The estate is well stocked. I'll have your luggage brought over in the morning—"

"Like hell you will." Cam turned to Nathan. "Get our things first thing." He almost pulled away, then paused. "And make sure you bring weapons . . . all of them."

Nathan's smile was droopy from champagne. "Aye, Captain."

Annie remained silent as Alexander instructed his butler, David, to lead them to the estate where they would be staying.

Rain drizzled overhead as Nathan and Jenny dragged behind them on the paved pathways through the grounds. It hadn't occurred to him until now that maybe the reason they were so tired was that they were mortal. None of them had slept much, but Annie and Julian seemed wide awake. He didn't want to think that his death had given him so many physical advantages. It felt like kicking a man while he's down. Not that he was opposed to doing just that.

After a short walk, David held up his lantern, illuminating the villa ahead. "Here we are. You'll find the building clean, stocked, and well-maintained. The master bedroom is located on the top floor, while the rest of the bedrooms are situated below, in the wing opposite the kitchen and dining areas. I will be checking in daily to ensure your needs are met."

Cam still wanted to correct David, to remind him that he'd grown up here, but he kept his mouth shut. Just as he'd expected, the west-side villa looked much the same as it had when he was a child. His father used to house guests here, and that's what he'd become—a guest.

In the glow of the lantern, warm light reflected off the water beading on the ivy climbing up the home's red brick walls, shining off the puddles pooled on the mosaic enclosed patio.

He used to play here with his cousins when the adults kicked them outside. They were always so rambunctious and noisy that his mother called them feral wolf pups.

My cousins. The memory punched Cam in the gut. He'd had cousins. Three of them—his mother's niece and nephews— that used to visit in the summer. Whatever happened to them? Were they still alive? He couldn't even remember their names. *What else have I forgotten?*

He was faintly aware of Annie still watching him as David unlocked the door, letting them into the villa. With a flick of a switch, gas lights rose to life inside the sconces lining the rectangular room, continuing up the red brick staircases to their left and right.

"We've prepared the master bedroom for you and your lady, Lord Callahan," David said, making Nathan snicker. David made a confused face before continuing. "The others will find their lodgings down the main hall."

"Thank you," Cam said without thinking. Of course, they'd put him and Annie in the same room. What reason would they have to suspect that their marriage had been simply part of an arrangement? A deal.

As David turned to leave, locking the door behind him, Nathan stretched and yawned as he wandered toward the main hall. "Goodnight, all, I'm done for today."

"Mr. Price?" Annie's voice shook slightly. "Will you escort Jenny to her room?"

Jenny stilled beside her, strands of her vibrant red curls falling from her tight updo.

Nathan rounded sharply, brows furrowed. "I am perfectly capable of taking her—"

"Of course, Miss Annie." Julian nodded before offering Jenny his arm. "Miss Jenny?"

Jenny shot Annie an irritated glare before she muttered a quick goodnight. As the three disappeared down the hallway, Cam stood alone with Annie in the entry. The others' steps echoed back to them.

"Nathan wouldn't hurt her," he said.

Annie snorted. "Nathan is fine, I suppose. It's Jenny I don't trust."

Cam wasn't sure what to make of that. "You don't have to be her parent."

"I know, it's just . . ." She sighed, the golden glow of the gas lights reflecting in her hair. She chewed on her thumbnail. "I don't think . . . I'm not sure if everything that's happened since we left New Havana has really sunk in for her. All of this is so grand. It's easy to make poor choices when you feel like you're in a dream. I hope that makes sense."

It did. Cam's heart sank. He held out his hand to lead her towards the stairs. "You say that as if you're the voice of experience."

"I've made many horrid decisions, though not *that* one in particular," Annie replied as she slipped her hand through his, following him upward. "But I've seen it happen. Many times. Lord Duskin had many *children* come and go."

God, he wanted to ask. He wanted to know every detail of her life before they'd met, but at the same time, he wasn't sure if he could stomach it without turning the building to cinders.

As they reached the top of the landing, Cam led them down the narrow hallway to their right. Annie didn't argue. He knew this house inside and out. At the end, lay a wide, engraved door carved from red mahogany. He half expected the doorknob to be rusted, but it turned with a well-oiled ease. *What did I expect? Father thinks of everything.*

The room inside was just as immaculate as he remembered. Nothing like the bed chambers in the main manor, but he'd always preferred the hominess of the estate's villas.

The room was decorated in rich shades of gold and brown, with a king-sized, four-poster bed positioned against the far wall, its veils drawn back. A fire burned low in the hearth, keeping the space pleasantly warm. Adjacent to the bed chamber was a fully furnished sitting room, along with a vanity, a bathing area, and an enormous walk-in closet.

Annie scanned the room with a blank expression. "This is . . . quaint."

He knew exactly what she was thinking. There was only one bed. He let out a low laugh. "I'll meet you downstairs at dawn. Better get what little sleep you can."

Annie frowned at him, her lovely, pink lips pursed. "And you'll be?"

"I'll find a room downstairs," Cam answered, too quickly. He took her fingers and pressed a quick kiss to her cool knuckles. "Goodnight, Kitten."

She seemed agitated. "Goodnight, Camden."

With that, he shoved his hands in his pockets and headed back down the stairs. He flicked off the gas lamps in the entry. He'd kill to look at his father's ledgers. With the state of the city, he shouldn't be able to afford such comforts. Cam focused on a space ahead of him and formed a small, round ball of fire —just for a bit of light.

Nathan's snores leaked out beneath his door. Cam kept his footsteps soft as he found an empty room at the end of the hallway. His eyes were burning from exhaustion as he stepped inside the chamber. It looked much the same as the master bedroom, but smaller and less decorated.

There was no fire lit in the hearth, but Cam didn't need it. He was always warm. The only time he remembered the feeling of cold was when Annie's skin brushed against his or when she squeezed his hand. Sometimes—many times—he wondered what it would feel like to have her body pressed against his, with nothing between them. If they'd balance each other, or if one sensation would overpower the other.

Cam shook the thought away as he tugged off his boots. Annie had been through enough. The last thing she needed was someone like him thinking such things.

A weight of sadness crushed Cam's heart as he peeled off his coat, throwing it over the armchair. He couldn't name it, not yet, but a growing sense of dread had been clawing at him since they left New Havana. He thought it had been fear of seeing his father again, but that event had come and gone, and the dread remained. He couldn't shake it.

Cam pulled off his shirt and tossed it on the floor before crawling under the blankets. The mattress was soft—too soft—the quilts smooth against his overheated skin.

I'm such an idiot. Cam rolled on his side and clenched his eyes shut. *Annie is up there all alone. She's alone. And safe. There's nothing to worry about.*

With his biased thoughts aside, they were on the governor's property. The governor ... who wanted them alive for the time being. There was nowhere safer she could be, his logic reminded him, but if that was true, why was every creak of the house settling like an assassin moving down the hall?

The night was so silent, his heartbeat pounded in his ears, radiating into his throat. His chest grew too tight to breathe. Cam rolled onto his back and stared at the vaulted ceiling.

Annie was above him, but she could die without him ever knowing, without him having a chance to stop it. He'd fail her just like he had his mother, just like he had Resh.

Cam shot up with an angry groan. *I could check on her. Just make sure her door is still locked and she's asleep.* No, he couldn't do that. They'd only just gone to bed. She'd think he was insane.

He forced himself to lie back, to close his eyes, to focus on burying the coil of power and fire spiraling beneath his skin, begging to be set free.

An hour passed, maybe two. Once or twice, Cam began to drift off, but woke with a start at the slightest sound—Nathan's snores, the creak of a bed, an early bird outside.

Blazes. He wasn't going to sleep.

Cam rubbed his face and climbed out of bed. After putting his shirt on, he stepped into the hallway. He would check on Annie—just once—then he would sit outside and watch the sky until the sun came up. That's what he used to do on The Nightlady, Resh's ship, when he was young, and the night-mares would come for him.

Although his mind was wide awake, his body was sluggish and reluctant to move. He dragged himself up the stairs as quietly as he could, the glow of his brands illuminating his path.

A jolt of shock coursed through him when he realized there was still a light on in the master bedroom. *She's fine. There's nowhere safer she can be.*

What's wrong with me? Cam pressed his ear to Annie's door. There weren't any sounds of death or violence . . . that was comforting. He took a step back and swallowed. *I can't be doing this. If she knew, she'd hate me.*

His skin itched so badly with the energy burning through it. As he turned to leave, the door to the master bedroom creaked open. Annie stood on the other side, still in her evening gown, her eyes lined with purple shadows as her gaze met his.

Well, now I'm screwed. Cam froze, and his heart vaulted into his throat. "I'm sorry, I—"

Annie's expression softened, and she opened the door wider. "The couch in the living area looks comfortable. I'm sure we can find some blankets."

Cam sucked in a shaky breath.

"I'll feel so much safer with you here," Annie smiled as she repeated the words he'd spoken to her on *The Elaina.* "At least one of us will get some shut-eye."

Cam had never been so close to kissing her. She knew. She *knew.* He managed a smile back, his voice cracking. "We can't let you go without sleep, can we?"

Annie stepped into the giant walk-in closet and returned moments later with a pile of blankets. His hands shook as he took them and headed into the living area without another word. Cam leaned over to pull off his boots again. He'd never put them on.

I'm a mess. Cam curled onto the sofa, covering himself up to the neck in quilts that smelled like mothballs. The couch *was* comfortable.

He listened as she crawled into bed and blew out the candle on her bedside table.

The silence here was . . . good. Cam's eyes had fluttered closed when he heard Annie's soft voice mutter, "Goodnight, Camden."

He'd *never* tire of the sound of her name on his lips. Cam smiled. "Goodnight, Kitten."

CHAPTER 14

ANNIE

hey'll make you love them. They'll destroy you, over and over, to watch you break. Promise me, my little. Don't let them kill your soul."

Annie jerked awake, the fading memory of her nightmare reverberating through her mind.

The fire had gone out. The master bedroom had stayed so warm with Cam in it. Or at least with him in the sitting room.

Annie didn't have to look at the clock on the wall to know the time. She always woke at five o'clock. No matter what time she'd gone to sleep the night before. Her neck ached as she sat up—she wasn't used to such plush pillows. Her heart made a jerky squeeze.

Elain sat at the foot of the bed.

Her sightless white eyes watched her as the gloom leaking in from the window cast her in shadows.

This was the second time Annie had seen her since she left New Havana. Elain's full lips spread into a smile as Annie pulled back the covers and climbed out of bed. The edges of Elain's form murky, not quite solid.

Acutely aware that Cam still slept in the other room, Annie shot Elain a dark look as she sat down at the vanity and whispered, "What do you want?"

Elain's smile widened. As Annie began to finger-comb the tangles out of her hair, her ghostly sister stood and vanished, then reappeared as she perched on the edge of the desk. She reached down and opened one of the vanity's drawers—revealing a hairbrush, a comb, and hairpins lying within. Alexander really had thought of everything.

"Thank you," Annie murmured as she ran the brush through her hair. Elain just watched as Annie braided her locks into a plait that wrapped around her head. She looked over her reflection with a huff. She'd slept in her gown. It was a shame and strange to wear it to the hospital, where it would surely be covered in blood and other such bodily fluids by the end of the day.

Elain made an amused humming sound and pointed to the closet.

Annie made a face. Other than finding some blankets, she hadn't taken the time to look around inside last night. *I'm not in the mood for this.* Annie continued to weave the tail of her braid over her shoulder and whispered, "Why don't you find me something to wear, if you're so clever?"

Elain vanished again, and Annie jumped, nearly falling backward off her seat when, moments later, her sister formed again and dropped a heavy, burgundy day-dress on her lap.

Before she could respond, Elain's white eyes went wide, fear flickering over her features. She dissolved into a cloud of mist.

"What the hell did I just see?"

Lord above. Annie's heart pounded as she swiveled. Cam stood in the doorway of her bedroom, hesitant, his hair a mess and eyes still puffy from sleep. He didn't look frightened, just confused.

Annie's gaze trailed down his golden throat to where his loose undershirt lay only half buttoned, exposing his sculpted chest and the burning brands marking it. Something in her stomach twisted. He looked so *warm*. His skin probably tasted like the sun and a salt breeze—

Stop it. Stop it. Stop it. Annie quickly turned back to the mirror, gripping the edge of the vanity, the tightness in her gut shifting to nausea. *I am no better than they are. I'm still a monster.*

Cam's eyes narrowed. "You alright?"

"I'm fine." *Well, now he thinks I'm crazy for sure. No use hiding it.* Annie kept her expression flat as she tied off the end of her braid. "That was Elain."

Cam's brow rose as he leaned against the doorframe and crossed his arms. "As in your dead sister, Elain?"

Annie nodded. She was just surprised he could see her. "Yes."

"Huh." He cocked his head, peering at the dress on her lap. "Does she do room service? Can you imagine the fortune she could make as a ghost concierge?"

Annie twisted toward him again. "Don't make fun."

"I'm not." Cam sank to the floor and crisscrossed his legs. He rubbed his face and groaned, making her heart do that awful flutter again. "Sorry, I . . . I make jokes when I don't know what else to say."

Annie fought a smile. "Do you think I'm crazy?"

"If you are, then I am, too." His green-gold eyes narrowed. "And I told you before, I like crazy. Does she have anything to do with when you stepped out of that portal? You never explained that to me."

Oh, right. Because she had done that. Twice. On New

Havana, Elain had opened a rip in the world and led Annie through it. Both times, she'd brought Annie to Cam.

Annie rose and folded the burgundy dress over her arm. "What's there to explain? I don't understand it any more than you do."

"Fair enough." Cam stood and walked over to the closet. He peeked inside before letting out an irritated sigh. After disappearing for several minutes, Cam exited in a fresh—but much more casual—grey, three-piece suit and knee-high leather boots. He fidgeted with the deep, blue cravat tied around his neck. "Lord, my father has stuffed enough clothes in here for six people. I have no idea how he guessed our sizes. He has always been such a preener."

"Like you?" Annie replied. *He does look handsome, though.* She wanted to hit herself.

Cam splayed his hand over his chest in feigned offense. "Kitten, that hurts. You know I only preen for you."

Annie turned and walked into the bathroom to hide the pink spreading through her cheeks. "Whatever you say."

Cam let out a husky laugh as she shut the door behind her, only making her angrier.

She hadn't taken the time to look over the bathing room last night, either, but as she expected, it was indulgently over-sized. No one needed a gold-plated, claw-foot tub large enough that she could soak up to her chin. Much like the Duskins, pipes ran down the wall to the tub and sinks, promising hot, running water. There were three sinks. No one needed three sinks. Despite the absurdity, they were pretty—white stone flecked with gold. Whether the gold was real or not, she didn't care to know.

Annie twisted one of the faucet handles, and within moments, warm water filled the basin. With a fluffy towel folded on the counter, she scrubbed her face and neck clean before slipping on her new gown. It fit like a glove. The sleeves buttoned at the wrists, with a high and modest neckline.

That would be Maya's doing, I presume. She'd seen the cleverness in the eyes of the governor's wife. She'd probably sized them all within minutes of their first meeting. It seemed they hadn't needed to buy all those new clothes.

As she left the bathroom, Cam stood by the bedroom door, staring intently at the ground, brows furrowed, as flames danced up his neck and around his ears. On instinct, Annie brushed her power against his, feeling a tinge of sadness coating the heat emanating from him.

At the touch, Cam snapped to attention, his heated gaze scanning her from head to toe before he gave her a wry smile. While she'd been changing, he'd strapped his pearl-finished revolver to his belt. "You look splendid, as always. It's not fair, really."

"Thank you," Annie replied stiffly. She was never sure how to take his compliments or whether she could decide if they were real or just part of his usual banter. She glanced to where she'd laid the damascus dagger on her bedside table. "Do you think I should bring that?"

Cam followed her gaze, lips tugging up at the corners. "Better to be armed than not. Plus, you need to keep up that dangerous image of yours."

"You'll like Violet Clarke if you like dangerous," Annie replied, not able to hide a tinge of bitterness as she slipped the sheathed knife down the front of her bodice. She shrugged on her coat and gloves as Cam opened the door for her. "I imagine she's a man-eater."

"I'm curious to find out why she bothers you so much," Cam said with a sly grin as they stepped out into the hall. "I don't think I've ever seen you so ruffled."

"I'm not *ruffled*," she snapped back under her breath.

"*Ruffled,*" Cam coughed, his brands keeping their path lit as they descended the stairs and into the entry. Her glare only made him smile wider.

Nathan's snores echoed off the brick walls, magnifying the sound. Hopefully, the others were able to sleep through the noise.

Outside, the sky was still dark, but at least the rain had stopped, though the slight breeze brushing against her face and neck was frigid, smelling of imminent snowfall. Annie tucked her chin into her coat, keeping the worst of the chill off her cheeks.

As she did, Cam's eyes snapped to her anxiously. "Do you want my jacket? I don't need it. You look freezing."

"I love the cold," Annie admitted, her breath forming into a cloud of mist. "It reminds me of home."

Cam cocked his head, their pace quick as they followed the paved path back to the courtyard. "You can love it without freezing to death. Let me have your arm, at least?"

With a sigh, Annie looped her elbow through his and nearly moaned at the surge of excellent heat that soaked through the fabric of her sleeves, spreading into her side. With a slight hesitation, Cam slid his hand down and wrapped his fingers around hers, warming her numb fingers.

Just for a moment. Annie let her eyes close. Just for a moment, she'd allow herself to enjoy the feeling of him touching her, as innocent as it was. As the breeze strengthened, she used it as an excuse to tuck in tightly against him. Cam didn't seem to mind. *Just one more moment.*

A breeze, carrying the scent of salt and seaweed, blew in from the coastline, making the trees flutter as their leaves began to change to autumn colors. She could imagine it—the estate colored in oranges and yellows for acres on end. With all the apples, they could make cider and pies. Jenny would be so happy. She'd probably decorate the entire villa in pumpkin-colored quilts. *You have to make this work for her.* Which meant Annie couldn't risk ruining her and Cam's agreement.

The tall gas-lamps illuminated the courtyard as they entered the circle. A horse-drawn coach already awaited them. She almost suggested the governor must have ordered it until she saw the second one behind it.

Cam tensed, gently dropping her hand. A cloaked figure stood beside the horses—Mr. Price.

Cam's lips twisted into a sneer. "You're up early."

"So are you." Mr. Price shot back, a thick scarf bundled around his throat beneath his raised hood. "And here I thought a lordling, like you, wouldn't wake before noon."

Cam frowned.

"We're going to visit Waverly Hospital," Annie said.

"I know." Mr. Price waved toward the second carriage. "I didn't figure you'd want to walk. You're welcome."

"*So* thoughtful," Cam replied. The coach's driver made some annoyed mumbling as Cam stepped forward and adjusted the fit of the nearest horse's bridle. "What would we *ever* do without you, Jules?"

He loves horses. Cam had seemed to be fond of Lord Duskins' sport horses. Annie noted the way Cam smiled at the animal sweetly as he tucked the big, bay thoroughbred's forelock under its browband before giving Mr. Price an accusing look. "And where are you headed off to, might I ask?"

"You're nosy, aren't you?" Mr. Price opened his coach's door. "If you must know, I'm going to see an old friend on the west side of the city."

"You have friends?" Cam gasped.

Mr. Price let out a long breath, then gave Annie a quick bow. "Miss Annie, please try not to let him kill anyone."

Cam scoffed, but Annie found herself smiling. "I'll do my best."

"And here, I thought you were on my side." Cam opened the second coach's door for her. "I'm wounded."

"You'll survive." Annie climbed inside. Mr. Price did the same ahead of them. Cam hopped in behind her, latching the door shut. He slid into the booth across from her and tapped his chin. "What do you think Julian does with friends? Bore them to sleep with ancient war stories?"

"He is an assassin." The coach lurched forward. Annie gripped her seat to keep from falling forward. Cam reached out, as if he meant to catch her. She straightened, brushing off her skirts. "Or *was*. Maybe he has guild members in the city."

"That's possible." Cam reclined, crossing one long leg lazily over the other. He narrowed his eyes at her. "So, this Violet—"

It was Annie's turn to frown. "I *wasn't* ruffled."

Cam grinned at her. "Calm now, I wasn't going to tease you this time. I'm just wondering how she and her twitchy, skunk of a brother took control of Waverly."

He's right, calm down. Annie forced her shoulders to relax, grounding herself in the *clip-clops* of the horses' hooves on the cobblestone street below. "Do you know who owns the hospital?"

Cam shrugged, stretching an arm over the back of the bench seat. "The city, most likely. Which means it's my father's, in all technicalities."

Annie pursed her lips, thinking. "Some distant family tie?"

"Not family." Cam shook his head. "I've never heard of the Clarkes until now."

"Would you have remembered?" Annie replied. "You were only a boy when you were last here."

Cam's smile faltered, almost pained. "Over the years, have you forgotten a face?"

She hadn't. Annie sat back, turning her attention out the window, to the rising sun just beginning to lighten the clouds from black to grey. She knew what he meant. She'd studied and memorized every person who ever walked aboard the slaver's ship. Cam knew who came in and out of that manor, even then. He *would* have remembered the Clarkes.

Minutes passed in silence, dragging on. She wished he'd say something. They had almost an hour to reach the hospital. She liked it when he talked. Why? Why did she like it when he talked?

Because you find his voice so very appealing, that's why. Her power whispered, somewhere deep in her mind, making her shudder.

Annie stilled as Cam's heat brushed against her arm, questioning. When she glanced up, a hint of color had risen on his golden cheekbones, and he chewed his lip. "Can I ask you something?"

She hated that her power was right. His voice calmed her. Annie held his nervous gaze. "I suppose so."

The coach wobbled as they hit a pothole. Cam didn't seem to notice, but what was a carriage ride to the sway of the sea? He leaned forward, resting his elbows on his thighs. "I was hoping you could help me with something. I'm too embarrassed to ask anyone else."

Annie's brows rose. "Even Nathan?"

"Especially, Nathan." Cam stared at the space between them, and an orb made of solid flames formed in the space, casting him in a deep orange glow. He pursed his lips, focused, and the orb shifted into a lily flower, then to a seagull, before turning into a ship on the open ocean.

Without thinking, Annie reached for the fire in awe. It bent around her fingers, her hand, the ship hovering over her skin as it might the waves. Her own brands flared in response, hungry, tugging at the heat as if it might consume it.

Stop it. Annie shook out her glowing fingers and then tucked them beneath her thighs. "What is there to help? You seem to have it handled just fine."

"You'd think so." Cam's expression darkened as he looked away. The shape crumpled. He let a frustrated huff as he turned back, and the flames swirled back into an orb. "I can't hold it in place. Once it's out of sight, I lose control of it."

Annie lifted her hand again, and Cam let the orb settle on her outstretched palm. "How could I help?"

"I don't know." Cam ran a hand through his hair. "Tell me when it starts to go awry so I can try to fix it? Julian did want us to practice, after all."

That he did. Annie sat back, folding her hands over her lap. "Okay, then. Make something."

Cam focused on his fire as it formed into a horse. It snorted, flipping its head. It looked so real, it made Annie smile. She struggled to keep her gaze away from the intensity of Cam's expression as she said, "Now, look away."

Cam did. The fire faltered at the same time as the coach hit another pothole, jostling them.

"How does it look?" he asked.

Annie bit down on her lip to keep from laughing. "It has six legs . . . and I think its ears have melted."

Cam sighed. "Blazes."

"Have you tried imagining it with four again?"

"Yes, but I can't focus that long. Everything distracts me."

"What's distracting you now?"

His eyes flicked to her, then back to the window. "Lots of things."

"Hmm." Annie straightened the horse's flopping ears. The fire molded for her. *Interesting.* "Try."

The rain had begun again, splattering against the window-pane. Cam clenched his eyes shut, breathing deeply, making the fire shift again.

This time, a giggle escaped her. "Well, it only has five legs now."

He groaned, letting his fire dissolve as he stretched out on the bench seat, resting his ankle on his knee. "God, I can blow up an island, but I can't keep a blasted horse in shape."

"May I see it?" Annie said, then clarified. "The fire, I mean?"

Cam gave her a wry smile before closing his eyes and flicking his wrist toward her. The orb reappeared, a contained bundle of destructive energy. Without him watching, Annie touched the fire. Just like before, it didn't burn her. Taking it in her hands, she molded it like she might mold clay until she made a very crude excuse for a donkey. With a satisfied smile, she said, "Look."

Cam cracked his eyes open, only to groan again and throw his elbow over his face. "See, you can do it better than I can."

"But it's yours, though." The donkey started to graze on imaginary grass in her palm. "What did you feel just now?"

"You," Cam said slowly after a pause, his foot bouncing. "I just told it to do what you wanted."

"Stay like that." Annie retook the fire, stretching until it was in the shape of a burning rainbow, her power twirling like dark threads around it. "What about now?"

Cam's lips twitched. "I still just feel you."

She thought back to Cam's snappy attitude toward Mr. Price. Her eyes narrowed. "Imagine Mr. Price. Not any shape, just Mr. Price."

Cam's foot stopped bouncing as his entire body tensed. The fire in her palm twisted into the shape of a coffin with a bouquet of roses laid over the top.

Annie burst out laughing. "That's mean!"

When she looked up, Cam watched her mouth—lips parted—his arm now over his stomach. His gaze rose to hers. "Laugh again."

Annie forced her features back into submission . . . barely. "Make me."

Cam's returning grin was wicked. The fire shifted again, his eyes never leaving hers, as it changed into what looked like a pig with the head of Frank Boyle.

"That's crass." Annie shooed the fire away. "And not funny in the slightest."

"Really?" Cam swung his legs around so he was sitting upright again. "I enjoyed watching you turn him into a dried-out beehive. You're too modest, Kitten."

The coach was slowing. It was raining too hard to see much outside. Annie crossed her arms over her chest. "And you're trying too hard."

Cam mirrored her movements. "How so?"

"As soon as you stopped focusing so much, you were able to control your fire just fine."

"But I was focusing." Cam's eyes dropped to his lap. "I was focusing on you."

Stop it. Don't say that. You're making it worse. Her thoughts were a manic torment she wished would just be still. As the coach came to a rough halt, Annie leaned out to take a better look out the fogged window, and her eyes widened. *Lord Above.* "I think we're here."

CHAPTER 15
ANNIE

Over her three years on New Havana, Lord Duskin frequently spoke of Waverly Hills Hospital. They were the front of scientific discoveries, he'd always said—the forerunners of modern medicine.

Now, as Cam helped her out of their coach and the building was before her, she was sure Lord Duskin had never seen the hospital himself.

This wasn't a place of healing.

It was Death's nest.

She felt it more than saw it—the wails of sorrow and agony seeping through the cracks in the brick. Reaching for her. Pining. It *wanted* her to notice.

As the coach pulled away, the driver promising to return in several hours, Annie backed away from the curb. She craned her head back, fat rain droplets splattering on her face.

Cam hadn't exaggerated. In fact, he'd been depreciating. The hospital took up *more* than three city blocks, curved around a cul-de-sac like a horseshoe. Five stories tall, on a raised foundation of grey-stone blocks, Waverly looked like a honeycomb with thousands of square, white-trimmed windows. A steeple rose over the center of the top floor, brandishing a flag adorned with a leviathan arching over a golden ocean.

Cam must have followed her gaze because he let out a dramatic sigh. "That's my family's crest. Obnoxious, isn't it?"

Annie wiped away the rain beading in her pale eyelashes. "I wouldn't use that word. I think aggressive suits it more."

"You're generous." Cam's eyes widened as he took in her damp face, then looked to the sky. "Hang it all, I'm such an ass. I should have brought you an umbrella."

"I don't mind the rain," Annie said. He offered his arm, looping her elbow through his, again grateful for his heat.

"I know, but I should have thought of it," Cam said as they started down the bare, paved drive toward the hospital's entry. He rubbed his fingers against the insides of her sleeve. "I'm not used to this. Or good at it, for that matter."

Annie stepped through a puddle instead of around it, feeling moisture seep through her wool socks and into the stockings beneath. "Used to what?"

"This"—Cam gestured to her—"being a gentleman. I never thought I'd say it, but I've spent too much time around pirates."

Annie thought for a moment before answering, trying to ignore the oppressive blanket of misery the hospital was trying to lay over her. "I made a deal with a *pirate*. I don't expect you to be something you're not."

Cam's expression softened, though there was still tension behind it. "As much as I appreciate your acceptance, that doesn't negate anything I said. I realize I have a lot of work to do."

What's that supposed to mean? Annie shrugged. "If you say so—"

"Lord and Lady Callahan!"

She looked up to see Dr. Clarke standing in the entry. For as large as the hospital was, the main door was singular and rather plain. He stepped out onto the drive to greet them, wiping his bloodied hands on his soiled apron.

Good thing I didn't wear my new dress. She'd been right about the gore.

"I'm so glad you've made it!" Dr. Clarke reached out to shake Cam's hand, his dark eyes darting between him and Annie. "To think—having you two in my hospital!"

"Er, thank you." Cam didn't accept the handshake. Raising a brow, he nodded toward Dr. Clarke's apron. "Are we murdering people already? I haven't had breakfast yet."

"Pardon?" Dr. Clarke glanced down at himself before bursting into high-pitched laughter. "Ah, forgive the mess! You understand."

Cam made a face. "I don't."

He grunted as Annie elbowed him in the ribs and plastered on a fake smile for Dr. Clarke. *I guess we're back to pretending.* "We're happy to be here." She glared at Cam. "Aren't we?"

"So happy," Cam crooned, rubbing his side. "Overjoyed."

"Splendid!" Dr. Clarke clapped excitedly. "Come, come! Let me give you a tour."

Cam gave Annie a mischievous grin as they followed the doctor into the hospital. He leaned in, and Annie shivered as his lips brushed against her hair. "That hurt."

"Would you behave?" She glared at him again. Cam's smile widened, making her skin grow hot. "We need them to like us."

"I'd almost forgotten." Cam rolled his eyes. The vibrant, deep orange of his brands the only color among the white-washed entry. "Mysteries to solve, and such. I don't think we have to look much further. Van has a mass murderer feel to him, doesn't he?"

Again, Annie shrugged.

The entry opened into a large, stuffy foyer, the air thick and stiff with the scent of vinegar. Besides the glow of the fire burning in the hearth, the only light was the grey gloom seeping in through the high windows. A small sitting area encircled the fire, a kettle waiting on the low table for tea. Hallways led off in every direction, like a star pattern.

A grizzled, older man sat behind a battered desk, overflowing with documents, in the center of the room, the cigar dangling from his mouth, flickering ashes over his paperwork.

"Ludwig, here, is my secretary," Dr. Clarke said, and the man called Ludwig only gave her and Cam a quick, hard look before returning to his work.

"A talker, I see," Cam said.

"Yes, well." Dr. Clarke wiped a small amount of sweat from his brow. "When you have the kind of workload we carry here in Waverly, conversation can become an indulgence we can't afford."

"You must have lots of free time, then." Cam drawled, then hissed as Annie pinched him on the wrist.

"Not at all! We're always busy here at Waverly." Thank goodness Dr. Clarke didn't seem to catch on to the insult. He turned and started down the hall behind Ludwig's desk. "This way, please."

Cam rubbed his wrist then pouted at her, tracing a teardrop down his cheek.

Annie just shook her head as they followed after the doctor.

Dr. Clarke chattered as they walked, telling them bits and pieces of Waverly's history and origins, of important research he'd been a part of. If it weren't for her years spent in the dark in the lava tubes beneath the Duskins' manor, the hospital's narrow, low-ceilinged halls would be claustrophobic.

The bottom floor housed the staff quarters, where most of the nurses rested between shifts, rather than making the long trek home. Dr. Clarke pointed out an operating room, a slim side door which led to the body shoot, and an entire wing dedicated to storing supplies and medicinal ingredients. Before she could ask to see his stores further, the doctor ushered them up a steep flight of steps, with a slippery ramp running alongside it for the gurneys to ascend and descend.

On the second floor, nurses in black uniforms flickered between the dozens of rooms on either side of the hall, the doorways covered with only dark curtains. Low, pained moans followed them, along with several muffled screams that Dr. Clarke seemed not to notice.

Once the vinegar smell began to fade, a stench she knew all too well greeted them—dead bodies.

"How pleasant." Cam's nose crinkled. "What morale your employees must have."

Dr. Clarke beamed at them over his shoulder. "I do try to create a healthy work environment for my staff. I'm so glad you've taken notice, my lord."

Cam's shoulders slumped, and he shot Annie a look that said *this bloke is insane.*

Annie watched the workers. All the nurses were men. Some young. Some older and bearded.

Her brows pinched together. "How many nurses are under your employment?"

"Ah, let me see," Dr. Clarke said without glancing back. "At last count, we had sixty-three?"

"Are any of them women?" Annie asked.

"Ha! Women don't work in the medical field." Dr. Clarke paused as they reached the room at the end of the hall, facing them with a wince. "Apologies, my lady, but you must know that your involvement with the late Lord Duskin wasn't the norm."

What did I expect? That they'd be happy to hire her on the spot? Apparently, not even being the governor's daughter-in-law would grant her that privilege.

"What about your sister?" Cam's voice lowered, gaze hardening. "Isn't she a nurse?"

Dr. Clarke glanced nervously toward the room behind them before muttering, "My sister likes to call herself many things, but that doesn't make them true." He let out that high-pitched laugh again. "But, if the title pleases her, I'm happy to let her pretend."

Bastard. Annie felt a flicker of pity for Violet. No wonder she was so unpleasant.

As he finished his sentence, the door swung open, revealing none other than Violet Clarke. Her brown curls were tied up in a tight bun, blood smeared across her ivory cheekbones, and soaked into the fabric of her simple, black gown, covered with a white apron as stained as her brother's.

"Van, I told you to—" Her irritated gaze snapped from Dr. Clarke to Annie, before finally settling on Cam. Her full-lipped scowl quickly gave way to a charming smile. She yanked off her soiled gloves and extended her hand to him. "Ah, you must be Camden Callahan. We didn't get a chance to meet last night."

Kill her. A ripple of energy made Annie's body tighten.

Her power seethed all the more when Cam kissed Violet's knuckles, as expected of him. "Miss Clarke. A pleasure."

"The pleasure is all mine. You're even more handsome than your wife promised."

"Oh, really?" Cam huffed a laugh.

Maybe I really should kill her.

Violet's eyes fell back to Annie. "Good to see you again, Lady Callahan."

Annie didn't miss the sneer in her words. "Miss Clarke."

Violet gave Cam another hungry look before stepping aside to let them enter. "Come in, we were just about to finish an—"

A solid thud and the squelch of flesh cut her off. Behind her, an *enormous* man—easily seven feet tall and over three hundred pounds—stood over a metal table, a dismembered leg in one hand and a machete in the other. His thick, black brows furrowed at them.

"*Lord above.*" Cam's golden skin paled as he craned his head back. "Where did you find this brute? Fighting for the Philistines?"

Blood poured off the table—spilling from a recently deceased elderly woman—puddled over the man's shoes. His heavy glare never left Cam's as he slammed the cleaver down into the woman's remaining leg, severing it with little more than a quick snap of bone.

"As I was saying." Violet almost looked embarrassed. "We were finishing an amputation. This is my assistant, Robert Lindon."

"Did you have to chop her to bits?" Cam blurted, still staring wide-eyed at Mr. Lindon. "I mean, blazes, what happened to graveyards?"

"Easier to stuff them into the incinerator this way." Mr. Lindon's voice was almost too deep to understand as he casually removed the poor woman's arm, tossing it into the bin beside him. "Graves are messy."

"And overflowing," Dr. Clarke cut in, swallowing. "Though we—with God's mercy—have never returned to pandemic levels, The Rot still haunts Enoch and much of the West. We do the best we can."

"How about we finish this conversation elsewhere?" Violet hooked her arm through Cam's. He gave her a strange look but didn't pull away. *He would offend her if he did.* Annie bristled as

Violet pushed open a curtain to their left and led him into an adjoining room, leaving Annie and Dr. Clarke to follow.

Annie's stomach rolled as they entered a medical ward filled with what could have been one hundred beds, each of them full. Over the sickly-sweet stink of infection, the fumes of feces and ammonia nearly choked her. This was worse than Lord Duskin's cells. Worse than the slave ships. At least there they'd had some form of ventilation. The ward had no windows, only buckets of filthy water and rags between the beds, which sat so close together that the patients could touch each other if they tried. Their coughs were like a wet, phlegm-filled dirge between them.

An angry calm settled over Annie as she wheeled on Dr. Clarke and Violet, the latter standing far too close to Cam. He tore away from Violet, his chest rising and falling rapidly as he took in the state of the patients.

"What is this?" Annie's words came out cold and flat. "These conditions—"

"We're doing the best we can," Dr. Clarke replied. It was the first time she'd seen any sternness from him. "You saw The Greens. Waverly is overflowing with victims of The Rot and other such illnesses. There's only so much we can do. It spreads faster than we can treat it."

I could fix this, or at least, make a difference. With Pearl Dust, she could screen the patients, separate the infected from the clean. *But then you'd have to order it.* She'd have to reveal that she owned the patent. She wasn't sure if she should do that . . . yet. The day was still young.

"You separate them," Annie said through gritted teeth. *And these people are supposed to be the leaders in medicine?* Even Lord Duskin knew to quarantine infected patients. "The Rot spreads by contaminated contact. No wonder you can't keep it under control."

"Don't be ridiculous," Violet scoffed. "Disease doesn't spread by touch."

"Annie's right." Cam stepped to her side, expression dark. "I've seen it, and if either of you had ever spent time in the slums, you'd have seen it, too. Besides that, Annie has spent more time studying and understanding The Rot than either of you could ever hope to comprehend." He rested his elbow on Annie's shoulder, lips spreading into a wicked smile. "I find her mind to be quite impressive. I'd hoped you'd learn from her."

Violet's cheeks reddened, her eyes seething as she gave Annie a curt smile. "Apologies, my lady, I didn't mean to offend."

"I'd have to care for you to offend me." Annie gave Violet a quick one over before turning to her brother. If they weren't going to give her a position, she'd have to carve one out for herself. "Separate them."

Dr. Clarke's eyes shot wide. "There isn't enough space."

"There are five floors," Cam shot back. "How could there not be room?"

"The top three aren't operational," Violet replied slowly, carefully. "There haven't been the funds to repair them."

"Repair them." Cam bowed to them before taking Annie's arm. "Now. I'll have the funds to you by this evening."

"Bless you!" Dr. Clarke grabbed Cam's free hand. "See! What did I tell you, Violet? I knew having Alexander's son here would make a difference."

Cam jerked his hand away before letting out a vicious laugh, his brands flaring as fire crawled up the veins in his neck, as he nodded to Annie. "Thank her. If it were up to me, I'd burn this place to the ground and be done with it."

A bead of sweat dripped down Dr. Clarke's brow as he backed a step. "I see."

The curtain into the ward flew back, nearly pulling it from

its rod. The secretary, Ludwig, barreled into the doctor's back, barely catching himself before hitting the ground. He wheezed, hands on his knees, before holding out a letter toward Cam. "The "—another wheeze—"The governor has called for you. Another killing. Not far from here."

So much for the hospital tour.

CHAPTER 16
CAMDEN

I can't believe I forgot a bloody umbrella. The rain turned into a deluge. The carriage Alexander sent dropped them off outside a multi-family apartment building. A group of uniformed men stood outside, arguing amongst themselves.

As they approached, Cam swallowed down his guilt at the water dripping from the end of Annie's braid, at the dampness of her coat, and her slight shivers beneath.

Later. Later, he'd beat himself up for failing her yet again, but for now, he had to play his part.

His fire crawled beneath his skin, making it itch and twitch, as it begged to break free. He rolled his shoulders, trying to shake away some of the tension, but nothing helped.

Especially not after watching Annie put the Clarkes in their place with an icy cold demeanor that only she could command. Lord, if he'd been on the receiving end of that tone, his resolve to keep a healthy distance may have crumbled right then and there.

Cam smiled widely as the men noticed them, expression stern and more than a tad bit irritated.

"Gentlemen." Cam kept his tone friendly. "I assume the governor has arrived?"

"Upstairs, my lord." The nearest man—a police officer—nodded toward the covered veranda leading into the apartments. "He's waiting for you."

They know me already? Of course, they did. It was hard to remain discreet when you had blasted, glowing brands on your face. That, combined with Annie's unique beauty, he didn't know why he bothered.

Momentarily self-conscious, Cam rubbed the corner of his eye, feeling the warmth of his brands. He frowned and gave the men a curt nod. "Thank you."

A narrow, concrete staircase with iron railings led them to the apartment's second level. Clumps of moss grew at the edge of the steps, the greenery worn in the center where hundreds of steps had trampled it. Cam let out a sigh of relief as they stepped under the cover of the veranda.

"I look terrible." Now that they were out of the rain, Annie undid her braid and shook out her hair, letting it fall in damp waves down to her waist. "Help me, would you?"

Cam gave her a blank look, completely lost in watching the rain droplets trailing down her neck. "With what?"

Her pale brow rose as she stripped off her coat. "Drying off. You're right, I'd rather not freeze to death." A dark laugh escaped her. "Wouldn't that be an anti-climactic way to die again?"

"Oh." *Get it together.* He could feel how distracted his smile must have looked. "I suppose it would."

She handed him the coat, and he ran his hands over it, focusing on burning out the moisture soaked into the woolen fabric. Maybe one day he'd get used to being Revenant. It had been months since he'd died, yet using his fire still wasn't his first instinct.

He passed it back, and Annie tugged on the dry coat and let out a satisfied sigh. "Thank you. Much better."

"You're welcome." Cam chewed his lip. *Don't do it. Don't ask.* Screw it. "What about your hair?"

It was Annie's turn to blink. He considered bolting, but she finally said, "What about it?"

I could still run. Cam swallowed. "Er, just wondering if you'd like that dried, too."

"Oh," Annie replied. They stared at each other awkwardly before she pulled her hair free from beneath her collar and let it fall down her back as she turned. "Go ahead."

Cam had killed hundreds of men in his lifetime—watched even more be torn, or blown, into pieces. He'd been beaten, stabbed, and burnt alive, and none of those events could compare to the terror he felt at touching Annie's snowy locks.

He ran his fingers through it, starting at the scalp and trailing to the ends as he willed the moisture away, combing out the tangles. A shiver ran down her back with each pass. He could have stopped at two, but he'd allowed himself four—just to be safe.

"There." Cam backed away and shoved his hands into his pockets. "All better."

A pink flush colored Annie's cheeks when she faced him. She quickly rebraided her hair over her shoulder as she muttered under her breath, "Thank you . . . again."

Before his nerves could make him vomit, raised voices sounded from down the hall—his father's voice. *Great.* Cam pursed his lips. "We can't avoid him forever, I suppose."

Without waiting, Annie started down the hallway toward the voices. Cam followed. There were three doors on each side, with a second staircase, leading to a third floor at the end.

Intelligible shouting turned into angry curses as the second door to the left swung open. A brown-haired man—

maybe in his thirties—stood on the other side, his eyes widening in surprise at the sight of them. He wore a similar uniform to the men outside, navy blue and well-pressed, but with a row of golden badges sewn over his right breast pocket —someone of authority.

The man stepped back, rubbing a hand over his stubbled jaw, just as Alexander peeked around the doorway. "Ah, Camden, you've finally arrived."

The sound of his father's voice always made Cam's stomach drop, but the feel of Annie's arm against his kept him grounded as he blurted, "Finally? You called for us an hour ago, you impatient bastard."

Annie bit down on her lip.

The brown-haired man snapped around to see his father's reaction, mouth agape.

Alexander just frowned as he sighed, gesturing between Cam and the stranger. "Camden, this is Henry Bale, chief of Enoch's police department. Chief Bale, this is my son, Camden Callahan, and his wife, Miss Annie."

Henry Bale removed his cap and bowed. "My lord, my lady." He straightened, glaring at Alexander as he placed his hat back on his head. "It would have been nice to know you were coming."

Henry wasn't big, maybe only coming to Cam's shoulder, but he had a presence as he stepped aside to let them into the apartment. "I'd also like you to know that the governor is *searching these grounds illegally.*" He shot Alexander another furious look. "My detectives should have first access to every case—"

"Your detectives can wait." Alexander waved flippantly, making Henry's face turn tomato red. "My son and I have work to do."

"Is that what all the arguing was about?" Cam put an arm

out to separate Annie and the police chief as she slipped inside. "Please, we can speak like adults, can't we?"

Henry closed his eyes as he sucked in a deep breath. "I told you—"

"What happened here?"

For as small as Annie's voice was, it silenced them all in unison. She stood in the center of the apartment, studying a sanguine stain soaking into the patterned carpet.

Cam had been so distracted that he hadn't even taken the time to notice the room.

It was nothing short of a nightmare.

The apartment wasn't much larger than *The Elaina's* captain's quarters. Splatters of blood decorated the floral wallpaper and dried over the black, oak furniture. Indigo curtains were drawn back from the windows, the view outside facing southward, letting in the barest trickle of light.

Annie stepped toward the window, glass from a shattered vase crunching beneath her boot heels. She bent over and picked up a white lily lying beside the vase, its satin petals stained with blood. "*When* did this happen?"

Her questions seemed to snap Henry Bale from whatever rage he'd been in. He stepped forward, taking in Annie with a silent awe, as he replied. "The body was found two hours ago." Another glare at Alexander. "The governor *insisted* that he examine the crime scene before my detectives."

His father said something snarky back, but Cam wasn't listening. He moved to where Annie's gaze was fixed on a loveseat beside the window. A lifeless hand hung from the arm of the chair. Cam had seen many corpses, but not many that had the skin peeled off their face.

Terrible way to go. It was impossible to tell how old the victim was in this state, only that someone had wanted him to *hurt.* The male body lay relaxed in the chair, his head reclined, sightless eyes staring out the window as fluid dripped from the flesh still covering his skull.

Cam jumped as Annie brushed past him, her expression fixed in concentration. She leaned in close to the body, unfazed by the stink of death beginning to cloud the air. "Who was he?"

"One of the head members of the anti-Revenant party," Alexander replied as he stepped around beside them, smoothing down the front of his crisp, black suit. "He was also a member of the city council. His name was James Kline."

"James Kline," Annie repeated, almost wistfully, as her gaze fell to where the corpse's left hand lay folded over its lap. The ring finger was missing, cut off at the base.

"He's the sixth victim we've found in such a state in recent months." Henry folded his arms over his chest, stepping to the far side of the loveseat. "Messages are delivered to the barracks, telling us where to find them."

"All pro-Revenant members?" Cam asked, watching as Annie slid on the leather gloves she carried in her coat pocket.

"No." Henry shook his head. "It's been a mix of both parties. The only similarities between the victims are their ties in protesting the upcoming restructuring of Revenant laws."

Odd. Cam snuck a glance over to his father. *What do you want me to see?* Of course, Alexander had already been watching him, an expectant look on his lined face, waiting to see how Cam would react.

"Have you tracked down the messengers?" Cam asked.

"None have been found," Henry replied, frustrated. "Not from any lack of trying on my men's part."

A loud squelching sound brought Cam's attention back to Annie. Completely entranced, she pried her fingers under the flaps of skin still connected by the corpse's ear, studying the severed edges of flesh.

Henry's skin turned an odd shade of green.

"And so, now you see my dilemma," Alexander said, looking as equally fascinated as he was disgusted as he watched Annie's continued examination of the body. "*Someone* is trying to manipulate the results of the voting."

By *someone*, Cam knew he meant The Order that Elias had been a part of. The Order that apparently wanted Cam dead so he would turn, and The Order that had sold Annie into slavery.

Henry bristled, rubbing his weary face again. "If that were true, why kill men from both sides of the debate?"

Cam had spent enough time in the underworld to know the answer to that question. He cocked his head. "Because they don't care about who dies. Whoever's doing this is sending a message." Cam let out a sharp laugh as he turned to the chief. "Someone hates you, Bale. Sorry."

Henry shot him a dark look, then rubbed his chin again. "That's a stretch. We don't even know how this man died—"

"He obviously bled out," Alexander interrupted.

"Or his heart gave out from the pain," Cam said.

"Neither." Annie examined the body's eyes. Her own narrowed intensely. "He suffocated."

They all stood for a moment in silence before Henry burst into laughter. "That's ridiculous."

Annie shifted the body's head to face them, its jaw hanging loose. "Look at the eyes. Petechiae. Swollen eyelids." Her gloved fingers moved down to touch what remained of the body's mouth. "Blue lips. This man was smothered, strangled, or choked."

Henry gagged as she shoved her fingers down the body's throat.

Annie scowled. "There's something in here."

Even Alexander looked a tad peckish. "Should I . . . should I find you some tweezers, or—"

"No, need." Annie pulled the damascus dagger out from the

front of her bodice, unsheathed it, and ran the blade down the front of the body's neck.

As it split open, Henry dry heaved.

Annie prodded around inside the poor bloke's throat, pulling out a severed finger. She grinned, speckles of blood staining her cheeks. "Found it."

"Let me see." Henry rushed forward, sweating, lips pursed into a hard line as she passed it to him. He rolled the finger in between his own, and Cam thought he spotted a flash of a black tattoo on the underside before Henry wrapped the finger in a handkerchief and shoved it in his pocket. Disgusting.

"Good work." He gave Annie's shoulder a gentle squeeze, sending a fresh wave of fire coursing through Cam's veins.

"You can't just take the evidence from the scene," Alexander snarled, stepping around the loveseat so he was standing in front of the chief. "It needs to be sent to the morgue for *public* processing—"

"—I can do what I wish. This is *my* investigation," Henry shot back.

As they flew into another argument, Cam's attention was fixed solely on Annie.

Removing her blood-soaked gloves, she stared across the room toward the long, burnt-out hearth. Her lips moved as if she were repeating something being said to her.

"Annie?" Cam couldn't shake the edge of tension in his voice. "What's wrong?"

She ignored him.

"Annie?" Cam stepped around the other men, trying to reach her, but she moved closer to the hearth, her features fixed in confusion. A thrill of panic ran through him as he reached for her. "Annie?"

Cam halted, sucking in a gasp, as a grey void split the air in front of her like a veil had been torn in half. She didn't pay him the slightest attention as she stepped through it, a ripple of energy swirling around the space she'd been as the void slammed shut behind her.

Breathe. Cam's fire forced his lungs to expand, and he gripped the mantle of the fireplace to keep from falling.

"What the hell?" Henry's voice came out in a squeak.

Cam turned to find his father and the chief staring at him, eyes wide, as if they expected an explanation.

Blazes. Cam let out a nervous laugh, running a trembling hand through his hair. "She, uh . . . she does that sometimes."

CHAPTER 17
ANNIE

Just as Henry took the finger, wrapping it in a handkerchief, Annie felt eyes on her.

She turned her head. A middle-aged man with a missing finger stood beside the fireplace, smiling at her. Blood dripped from his blank, white eyes, streaming down the face Annie knew had been disfigured in life—James Kline. *Ghosts.*

But were they truly ghosts? Beneath New Havana, as Annie's own life had slipped away, Elain had called her, and the image of Edmund Resh, helpers. Whatever they were, she was seeing the image of a man just murdered.

Cam, the governor, and Chief Bale continued to speak together, oblivious to the presence among them.

As she watched, a heavy mist filled the space beside James's ghost. Elain formed a moment later, whispering into James's ear, his empty eyes never leaving hers. She could read Elain's lips. *She sees us.*

"I do see you," Annie whispered back, hoping James would hear her. Since she'd arrived on New Havana at fifteen years old, she'd seen them—the dead. But why was Elain here—*here* —now?

With a hint of a smile, James Kline disappeared, fading away into nothing.

Elain traced a line through the air, opening a glittering tear between this realm and wherever it was the ghosts dwelled. With a mischievous smile, Elain gestured for Annie to follow her through the void.

"Annie, what's wrong?"

Cam's voice sounded so far away.

"Annie?"

She wanted to stop—she wanted him to come with her— but she'd already stepped through the portal. An electric buzz clawed at her skin, a mix of white and grey lights blinding her. Annie squinted as splotches of light clouded her vision. Around her there was . . . nothing. Infinite mists. It felt like she was being squeezed, her lungs unable to expand. *I won't die here.* She'd survived this before. She'd survive it again.

When her eyes regained focus, she wasn't in the apartment anymore. The governor was gone. Chief Bale was gone—

Where's Camden? Annie gripped her chest and moved a step back, a current of energy still coursing through her blood. She knocked into one of the towering bookshelves on either side of her, sending several tomes crashing to the floor. Layers of dust coated the rectangular table in the center of the room, undis- turbed. High, slatted windows along the top of the far wall were the only source of light.

A glimmer of gold caught her eye—Elain's blonde hair. Her sister strode around the table, brushing her fingertips through the dust and rubbing them together like she expected it to leave a residue.

"What do you want?" Annie kept her voice even. "You can't just kidnap me like that."

Elain smiled again, turning until she faced the center of the room. It had been too dark for her to notice before, but now that her eyes had adjusted, the table was stacked with sealed boxes and folders. Newspapers littered the spaces between the stacks, accompanied by the loose papers scattered over the scuffed, hardwood floor.

"Is this what you wanted me to see?" Annie asked, but when she looked up, Elain was gone. She was alone now.

Now what? She wiped her sweaty palms on her skirts before lifting a newspaper off the table. Elain had brought her here for a reason. It seemed her sister had been busy. Annie squinted to make out the writing at the top of the page—*The Enoch Gazette.* It was dated ninety-five years ago. She scanned over the headlines and found what she'd expected—political strife, fear of water contamination, and the first appearances of The Rot.

She picked up another paper, and it said much of the same thing. After sifting through several others, the only new information she gained was that Enoch had a serious sewer problem.

What am I missing? Annie noticed a door on the far side of the room. She could leave at any time.

Or I can stay and figure out what I was supposed to find. As terrible as she felt about leaving Cam alone with his father, he'd tell her to take advantage of the opportunity. With a long sigh, Annie pulled forward one of the table chairs and sat, setting one of the boxes of documents on her lap.

A layer of cobwebs and old ink coated her fingers as she flipped through the papers inside. Receipts for massive amounts of lumber. Obituaries for important community members. Once or twice, she found a recipe for a popular holiday dinner menu—all the documents dating back decades.

Annie set the box on the ground and pulled a second onto

her lap. The flash of a headline made her pause—*Revenant Deaths on the Rise.*

Her brows furrowed. *Revenant deaths?* This paper was dated seventy-six years ago. She shook out the paper and began to read:

—it doesn't seem that the entire community follows the governor's desire to see a union between humans and Revenants. Many share the same concern: allowing beings of such physical advantage to have the same rights as normal citizens sets the building blocks for a tyrannical society. One that promotes men of lesser strength to be bullied into submission by beings that should never have existed at all.

What is the governor's response? He—

Annie skimmed over the rest of the article. The woman she was now, she understood that what she was reading was fear propaganda, but the woman she had been weeks ago? Mortal Annie would have loved to rally against Revenants this way. She didn't blame the citizens of Enoch for being afraid—then or now.

The current governor wasn't old enough to have been in power at the time the paper was written. *I wonder if the governor mentioned was Cam's grandfather.*

Annie tucked the newspaper back into the box when a weathered, folded piece of stationery caught her attention. The outside was stamped with the symbol of a phoenix.

The Order. Annie's fingers shook as she flipped the letter open:

Alexander,

I don't know why you continue to fight me on this—

A faint scuffle outside the door had Annie stuffing the letter down her bodice. *Things haven't changed, have they?* It wasn't long ago she'd been snooping through Mr. Price's things on Cam's directive. She'd be a spy before long.

She stood as the scuffle came again, fainter this time. Setting the box back on the table, she crept toward the door, pressing her ear against it. A female voice echoed beyond it, followed by a smaller, childlike voice.

Annie choked back a shriek, just managing to clap her hand over her mouth, as Elaine reappeared, grinning wildly as she traced her finger over the door.

One moment, Annie was leaning against it. Next, her face slammed into the cold, marble ground.

A shrill scream sounded as she spat blood from her mouth —a lip split. When Annie looked up, Maya Callahan stood over her, hand over her throat, expression as stunned as the little boy beside her.

I'm in the Callahan manor. Annie smiled up at them. She could feel her lip starting to swell. "Hello."

"Hello." Maya wore a patterned robe over a loose, green day dress—casual wear. She hadn't been expecting visitors. She glanced between the closed doorway and Annie. "How . . . where—how did you get here?"

Annie considered lying, but decided against it. She climbed to her feet, dusting off the front of her gown. Quickly, she brushed her lip, healing the wound. "I, um . . . walked through a portal."

"Ah." Maya nodded, her beautiful black hair twisted into a loose knot at the base of her neck. She ran her fingers through the hair of the boy who stood at her hip, hiding behind her skirts. "Well, if that's all," she said.

Annie looked at the boy. He had rich dark-brown hair and steel-gray eyes, his skin the same shade as a buttered pastry. She forced a smile, but it only made the boy retreat even further. "And who's this?"

"This is my son, Kai," Maya replied, stroking his hair again. "Kai Callahan."

Kai. Annie's eyes widened. *Camden's brother.* She inhaled, steadying herself, then offered him her hand. "Hello, Kai."

To her surprise, he stepped forward and took it, kissing her knuckles like a gentleman.

"Nice to meet you, too." He made a face, making his full cheeks dimple. "I, er, don't know what your name is."

"Annie."

"Annie," he copied.

"Miss Annie is family now." Maya pulled him closer, tying her robe closed before she smiled. "Annie, would you like some tea? And maybe a salve for your lip?"

Thank God. Annie's shoulders slumped in relief. "Tea sounds *wonderful.*"

"Excellent." Maya turned and continued down the hall, and Annie followed her. Kai glanced back at her every minute or so, his inquisitive eyes narrowed.

He's staring at my brands. Annie watched Kai. *He reminds me of Cam already.* Though they shared only a few similarities in appearance, they both gave off the same impression that they were thinking more than most men were capable of or bothered to.

Maya led her to a small, homey sitting room at the end of the hall. Wherever Elain had taken her, it must have been close to—or in—the Callahans' private quarters.

The heady scent of chamomile and mint blanketed Annie's senses as they entered. On the low table between the rich, blue sofas, a teapot waited on a solid, silver tray. Three teacups waited atop it.

Maya must have noted Annie's confusion, because her cheeks reddened slightly as she said, "Kai and I have tea at the same time every afternoon. I always keep an extra cup handy, just in case Alexander decides to join us."

"I see." Annie sat on the sofa across from them. Kai snuggled up tight against his mother. "And does the governor join you often?"

"Papa doesn't have time for tea." Kai did a dramatic sniff as he artfully filled their cups from the teapot, careful not to spill a drop. "He says tea is a woman's drink."

"Hush." Maya's embarrassment was evident, but Annie smiled.

"And what do you think?" she asked him. There was something about Maya that made her feel settled, calm. Annie wasn't sure what to make of that yet.

Kai straightened, sipping from his cup, his pinkie extended gracefully. "I think Papa is missing out on good tea."

"He is, isn't he?" Annie lifted her own cup and took a sip. The taste was richer and deeper than any she'd ever tried. Kai couldn't be more than eight. Annie set down her cup before folding her hands over her lap. "If it makes you feel better, your brother loves tea. I've seen him drink it many times."

Maya stiffened.

Kai froze, eyes as round as a plate. "What brother?"

CHAPTER 18

ALEXANDER

The carriage rocked as it flew over the potholes in the street, jostling both Alexander and his son on their way back to the manor.

They'd been alone together for almost an hour, and Camden continued to ignore him as well as he had Henry Bale's persistent questions after Annie had vanished into a cloud of mist. They'd left the rest of the investigation to the detectives, and only at Alexander's insistence did they start the long trek back.

He's a nervous wreck. Oh, a normal man would look at Camden and see only the image of a powerful, high-born turned outlaw. Exactly what Camden wanted them to see.

Alexander wasn't a normal man.

Camden's knee hadn't stopped bouncing since they'd sat down in the carriage. Most would misinterpret the movement for boredom, but that, accompanied by the fact that he would look nowhere except out the window, told Alexander all he needed to know—Camden had no idea where Annie had gone.

The temperature inside the carriage had grown sweltering,

but Alexander resisted wiping the sweat dripping down his temple. He'd learned long ago to never show any discomfort.

Discomfort was weakness. As was fear.

After so much silence, his whispered words sounded deafening. "Camden?"

Camden's eyes flickered to his for only a moment before returning to the window.

Alexander let out a slow breath. "Pretending I don't exist won't solve your problems."

He was glad to see his son's lips finally curl into a bitter smirk.

"You underestimate my ability to commit," Camden replied, his brands flaring. "I could do this all day."

Alexander reclined, folding one leg over the other. "Shall I repeat my previous statement?"

Camden's knee bounced faster, almost in sync with the coach-horses' hooves. "When will we reach the manor?"

"Soon."

"That's not an answer."

Alexander retrieved his golden pocket watch from his coat. "Ten, maybe twelve minutes. Does that appease you?"

"No."

"Annie will be fine. We'll find her."

Alexander finally hit the nerve he'd been looking for.

Fire curled up Camden's throat as his vicious glare snapped to him, his fingers moving instinctively towards the gun on his belt. "Screw off—"

"And if I don't?" Alexander leaned forward, bracing against his knees. "Are you going to shoot me? You need me, and you hate that."

"Need you?" Camden mirrored his movement, the hold he had on his tongue slipping as a harbor accent coated his tone. "This job would be easier *without* you."

"Then why keep me alive?" Alexander returned Camden's cruel smile. "I'm well aware of how easily it would be for you to dispose of me, and yet, you haven't. Won't it hurt your reputation letting your revenge droll on this long?"

Camden sat back, rage flickering over his features.

Got you. "Careful now, son, you might let your cards show."

"Think what you want," Camden replied, "Despite the stain you are on all existence, I don't want Enoch. Killing you now would be stupid."

He was quick, but the momentary hesitation in his response told Alexander everything—his son didn't have a plan. He was acting on impulse, as he always had. Alexander couldn't count the number of times, when his son was young, Camden disobeyed an order as soon as it was given, purely out of obstinacy and a lack of self-control.

And you beat him for it. Bile burned Alexander's throat.

Even as a child, when Camden had wanted something, he'd become driven to the point of obsession to attain it. He only needed to know what his son wanted to control him—and after what he'd watched over the last two days, Alexander didn't need to guess what that was. Just like his own marriage to Maya, he suspected Camden and Annie's marriage had been arranged—a solution to a problem. A neatly fabricated lie, at least for one of them.

His son had a weakness.

"You may come to regret that choice," Alexander said as the carriage passed through the gates into the Callahan estate. "Thrones don't stay empty. When I'm gone, Enoch *will* be taken, ruled by someone else—someone worse—and you'll wish that you'd taken the chance when you had it."

"See, you're lying again." Cam sneered just as they circled to the front of the manor. "There is no one worse than you."

If only you knew.

"Oh, by the way." Camden paused before stepping out of the carriage. "I promised the Clarkes you'd be sending Waverly money for repairs. *A lot* of money."

Alexander slowly frowned.

Cam sneered. "Have fun with that."

His son leapt out with a quick stride and stormed inside the manor before Alexander had even exited the carriage. His chest ached as he hurried after him. When he stepped inside, a wall of heat struck him, forcing the breath from his lungs.

Camden stood just inside the entry, his gaze distant and unfocused, as Alexander watched ripples of energy surge up each staircase, barreling down the hallways toward the west and eastern wings.

As Alexander caught his breath, the skin beneath his wedding finger beginning to itch, Camden's expression softened into one of intense relief as he muttered, "She's upstairs."

He was already sprinting up the staircase, leaving Alexander fighting to stay on his feet.

Alexander followed after him, shoving his gloved hands in his pockets to hide the trembling in his fingers. He and Maya kept their family quarters on the third floor of the eastern wing. His pounding heartbeats slowed to a collected rhythm as he tracked the sound of Camden's rushed steps down the upper hall.

The footsteps stopped before reaching Maya's tearoom, making Alexander smile. As he came around the corner, Camden rubbed his face, then ran his hands through his hair, before he straightened his shoulders, shaking the tension out of his fingers. It was an act. It was all an act.

The same one Alexander played. The same one his father had played before him, and his father before him—one of a man with the weight of the world on his shoulders.

And soon he'd learned if Camden would have the strength

to carry it. All his years of gambles and carefully laid plans depended on it.

Camden opened the door, releasing the calming waft of chamomile into the hall. As Alexander stepped to his side, his two sons locked eyes for the first time.

Alexander let out a relieved sigh. *She's here.* He wasn't sure what he'd have done if the girl hadn't been here. He wasn't ready to face Camden's rage yet.

Annie sat across from Maya, her gaze locked onto Camden as Kai stood from the sofa. His younger son cocked his head as he approached the elder, not a trace of the usual fear or distrust marking his boyish features.

But Maya *was* afraid. Her back was so rigid it looked as if the slightest bend would snap it in half.

Kai craned his neck back, smoothing down his small, tailored suit before looking his brother in the eye, his dark brow rising. "Annie tells me you breathe fire. Is that true?"

To Alexander's surprise—and unexpected delight—Camden smiled so widely and genuinely that it almost made him look as young as he should.

He sat down, cross-legged, bringing himself just below Kai's eye level, as he said, "It's true, but from what I've heard, our father actually likes you, which is even a more impressive accomplishment."

Kai laughed. His gaze nervously flickered to Alexander's before returning to his brother's. He cleared his throat. "I think he likes me sometimes."

Alexander's stomach twisted as if he'd been punched. *I'm so sorry, Cassie.*

"Well—" Camden winked at Annie, whose cheeks turned pink in response, before he tugged on the edge of Kai's sleeve. "—he didn't like me *any* of the time."

Kai's eyes brightened as Alexander's heart continued to crack. "Did he have tea with you?"

"Absolutely not," Camden crooned. "Tea is a—"

"—woman's drink," Kai finished, beaming. "Annie also said you liked tea."

"I do," Cam replied.

"With sugar or honey?"

"Both, if I can get away with it."

Kai laughed again before he reached out and brushed his fingers over Camden's brands. "Do these hurt?"

"No, but neither does this." Cam blew fire onto his palm, using his opposite hand to twist and mold the flames into the shape of a barking dog. The figure crouched, wagging its tail, before darting in a circle around Kai as he laughed and clapped.

Alexander's breath hitched again. Over the years, he'd seen Fire Brands in the hundreds—in the thousands—but this was different. The fire looked *alive.*

He glanced up just long enough to see Annie transfixed, not on the flames, but on his eldest son, her lips parted in awe. *Was I wrong?*

The fire dog settled over Kai's open palm, soundlessly barking, as the boy used the tip of his finger to pat its head. Kai made a face. "I like dogs, but they aren't my favorite."

"No?" Camden replied. "What are?"

Maya watched Kai like a hawk, ready to defend him at a moment's notice. Not that she could.

Kai tapped his fingers on his chin. "Dragons are my favorite. Like in all the stories."

"I've told you," Alexander said out of habit. "Dragons aren't real."

"Of course, they are," Camden snapped, sending him a

deadly glare over his shoulder before turning back to the fire dancing in his brother's hand. "See?"

The fire rose as Camden's gaze lifted. The flames twisted and grew until they formed again into something tangible.

Kai gasped, stepping back, as a brilliant, horned beast stirred by his feet, stretching fiery wings—a dragon, the size of a hound.

Maya and Annie let out a unified gasp.

Its scales were varying shades of reds, oranges, yellows, and golds—its eyes molten as it rose in the air and nudged Kai's cheek with its snout. It looked just like the creature from the stories Cassandra used to read to Camden before bed. He used to beg her to read those damned books over and over again—and she did—no matter how many times Alexander told her not to.

Kai stroked the beast's head, and it twisted and curled around his shoulders, snuggling against his neck.

"It's not burning me," Kai murmured. "It doesn't hurt."

Annie's hand flexed.

Cam's returning smile was tinged with sadness. "Does Father still get angry?"

A small window of silence fell as everyone's gaze fell on Alexander. It nearly broke every careful, defensive wall he'd ever built. He hated himself. Probably more than Cassandra hated him on the night she'd left him.

Kai's voice was barely audible. "Sometimes."

Any light that was left in Camden's eyes flickered out, the fire in both his veins and his dragon's wings burning blindingly bright. He twisted to face Alexander, the threat in his voice tangible. "It won't happen again. Ever."

Alexander gritted his teeth.

"We should be going," Annie said, standing up and effortlessly pulling Camden to his feet as she placed her arm through his. The dragon vanished. Camden's eyes were fixed on the floor, distant, as Annie offered Alexander and Maya a quick, polite curtsy. "Governor . . . my lady."

She smiled at Kai. "My lord."

With that, she turned and strode down the hall, Camden at her side.

Only once they were out of sight did his younger son speak. "Papa, will I see them again?"

"Of course," he replied.

"Are you sure?" Kai asked

"That's what I said, isn't it?"

Kai nodded before heading off toward his bed chamber.

Only once Camden's lingering heat had dissipated did Alexander dare to speak again. "Where did you find her?"

Maya exhaled sharply. "She came out of the storage room. *That* storage room. She stole some papers. I saw them sticking out of her dress."

"Good. Very good," Alexander sighed.

"She also healed herself," his wife whispered.

There is a God. Alexander sometimes doubted. He closed his eyes, trying to hold onto the feelings in his limbs. "Even better."

They may have a chance yet.

CHAPTER 19

ANNIE

She had to get him outside, or there might be nothing left of the manor.

Once they were out of eyeshot, Annie switched from a casual stroll to *dragging* Camden down the staircase. She could feel his heartbeat where their hands were connected, and though he didn't fight her, he didn't come willingly either.

Sweat forming on her brow, Annie studied him over her shoulder. Cam's fire-filled eyes were fixed in the direction of the tea-room. Energy rippled off him, making her ears ring, as the veins beneath his skin turned the color of molten metal. The acrid smell of smoke caught her attention—his coat sleeves were smoldering.

"Camden—" Annie tugged harder, trying to quicken the pace.

He wasn't listening, his gaze still fixed on the third floor.

No, no, no. A flicker of ice spread through Annie's blood, reaching for him. *I shouldn't. I could—*

Where their hands touched, Annie allowed her power to bite down on Cam's—just a little. It wouldn't take much. She only needed to stop him from spiraling. Yet, as the gates between them opened, Annie hissed as a searing pain rushed up her arm, making her now glowing brands *burn*.

More. As they stepped outside, the frigid wind felt excruciating on her overheated skin. *Please, more.* As bad as it hurt, her body drank in his power like it was taking its first breath. She twisted around, their fingers still entwined, but only when Cam let out a low gasp did she pause. A flicker of green had returned to his too-wide eyes, and where their skin touched, it glowed a brilliant white.

"Don't stop—" Cam breathed as she yanked her hand away and shoved him in the chest so hard his back hit the wall. She gripped the front of his shirt, and he grabbed her wrist. He seemed disappointed when no more energy flowed between them.

"Annie." Something like desire flashed across Cam's features as he finally looked at her, and she pushed down the warmth inside her, building in response. Maybe later she'd think about it. Maybe she wouldn't.

"Stop it." Annie's voice sounded empty. His hold on her wrist tightened. "Get it together. You can't help anyone if you lose control every time your father says something you don't like."

Cam's eyes became deadly, the ring of fire around his pupils as vibrant as the sunset brands beneath them. "He's hit him."

Annie blinked. *This isn't just about the governor anymore.* The skin where they touched grew hot again, as if he was pushing energy *into* her.

"He's hit him," Cam repeated, the devastation on his face making her heart ache. "And I *left* him there."

Annie didn't doubt that the governor was inflicting the

same torment on Kai that he had inflicted on Cam. Children were the favorite prey of wicked men.

The courtyard encircling them was empty, silent except for the *pitter-patter* of the evening's first drops of rain. Exhaling a long breath, Annie let her hand fall to her side. It felt so cold without him beneath it. "You can't help Kai. Not yet."

"Why not?" Cam seethed, "If I—"

"There's too much we don't know." Annie shot back, bundling deeper into her coat. "Acting too soon will make things worse—for us and for Kai."

A muscle in Cam's jaw flickered, but at least he wasn't on the edge of hysteria anymore. "What happened? Where did you go?"

Annie glanced around. Just because they were alone didn't mean someone wasn't listening. "Later."

Cam nodded in understanding. He rubbed his tanned face in exhaustion and said, "How did you do it?"

She paused her steps down into the courtyard. "Do what?"

Cam followed as if on instinct, his shoulders shaking. "Look at them every single day after what they did? Richard and the bastards that hurt—" He cut himself off. "Sorry. I shouldn't have asked."

She stared at him for a moment. She'd never talked to Cam about what had been done to her. She supposed she hadn't needed to. It couldn't have been hard to guess, and it was easy to see hurt in someone when you've been hurt yourself. *Maybe you should tell him.*

Annie shook the thought away. No. She didn't want pity.

Instead, she forced a small smile and stepped forward, looping her pinkie through his. "Let's go find the others."

As they headed into the courtyard, Cam's gaze flickered to their conjoined fingers before returning to her face, smiling wryly. He rubbed his chest. "I didn't realize you were so strong, Kitten. Blazes, I think you left a bruise."

Annie suppressed a pang of guilt. "You weren't listening."

Cam chuckled, though it seemed strained. "That's not the first time I've been told that."

They spent the rest of the walk in silence, though with every step, Cam's heat seemed to lessen, as if he was using the time to slowly pack away all the emotions that had flooded to the surface. The sky continued to drizzle, and by the time they returned to the villa, Annie was again uncomfortably damp. Droplets of water dripped off the ivy clinging to the villa's red, brick walls. More fell from the covered gas-lamps, the dim lights making the drops glow gold over the covered patio.

Cam reached to open the front door for her, but before he could, it swung open, revealing Jenny standing on the other side.

"There you are!" Her cheeks were flushed pink, her ruby curls loose over her shoulders. "What took so long? You said you'd only be gone a couple of hours. Dinner is almost ready!"

"It's a little early for dinner," Annie said.

"We were hungry," Jenny answered before ducking back inside.

Through the doorway, Annie could smell potatoes and onions. She hadn't realized how starving she was until the richness of Maya's tea had turned her stomach queasy. She hadn't eaten since yesterday.

Cam's brows furrowed as he slid past her, posture instantly defensive. "Did my father send a cook?"

"Yes," Jenny answered, stepping aside. "And Nathan told him to eat it."

"Jenny!" Annie gaped.

Cam burst out belly laughing. It was good to hear it after

the tension of the afternoon. "You've spent too much time around sailors."

"I'm just repeating what he said." Jenny's cheeks reddened further. "The kitchen was well stocked, though. I'm happy to do the cooking."

Nathan peeked his head around the corner that separated the entry from the dining room. "Finally, you're back. Find anything at the hospital?"

Cam wiped a tear from the corner of his eye as he choked back the last of his laughter. "Let us change into something dry, then Annie can tell you all about how she yanked a finger out of a dead bloke's throat."

Nathan blanched. "Never mind. I don't want to know."

"It wasn't that bad," Annie replied, then paused. *Was it?* Maybe she was just too used to it by now. Before turning toward the stairs, she waved for Jenny. "Help me, would you?"

Jenny's brow rose, but she nodded, holding up her full, flowery skirts so she wouldn't trip as she followed Annie to the second floor.

Cam spoke to Nathan. "Did you bring our things from the ship?"

"Of course," Nathan drawled. "I tossed your luggage in your room, and the big knives and ammunition are in the closet."

"And the tools I asked for?"

"They're in there, too."

What tools? Annie glanced down only long enough to catch a glimpse of Cam watching her, his expression a mix of sadness and longing, before he headed down the hall towards his own room. She swallowed, fighting not to remember the feeling of his power mixing with hers. She could only see the brands on her hands now, but the contact changed from a deep grey to a shimmering, pearly white.

As they crossed over the landing to the second floor, Jenny caught up and squeezed Annie's elbow. "Are you alright?"

"Yes, I'm fine." As they entered her room, she peeled off her sodden coat and tossed it over the chair beside her vanity. "Are you?"

"Me?" Jenny stopped short. "I've been here. Why ask?"

Because you've been here, that's why. Alone. With Nathan.

Annie wanted to trust him. She really did. She'd thought it would be easier after leaving New Havana to know who was safe, but every day that passed without something terrible happening made Annie even more paranoid.

Without Lord Duskin's strict diet hovering over them, Jenny had begun to fill out in the last weeks. Not even the burns Frank Boyle had left on her face could hinder her beauty. In just a simple, floral day dress, she was stunning. It wouldn't be long before she started to look like a woman, and others would notice.

Annie slipped out of her own sodden dress and sat down at her vanity in nothing but her thin shift and corset. She'd shared a room with all her sisters, despite the size of the Duskins' manor. She wasn't worried about decency with Jenny, in dress or conversation.

Annie undid her braid and tugged a hairbrush through her tangled locks. She kept her expression flat despite the snags pulling at her scalp. "I know. That's what worried me."

Jenny scowled, crossing her arms around her budding chest. "Are you insinuating that Nathan touched me?"

Annie avoided looking at her sister's reflection in the vanity mirror as she said, "Did he?"

"Of course not!" Jenny's voice leapt too high. "You always assume the worst. He's my friend—"

"You've only known him for weeks." Annie let a wince slip

as she hit another snag. "You haven't known him long enough for him to be your friend."

"You've known Cam for weeks," Jenny shot back, the furrow between her brows deepening. "Is he your friend?"

With her heart in her throat, Annie set her brush down and twisted to face her. "That's different."

"How?"

"Because we made a deal. It's not the same. We're... business partners."

She was surprised when Jenny sneered. Maybe she *had* been around sailors too long.

"You keep telling yourself that," Jenny said, brushing a strand of red hair off her face. "At least I'm willing not to be miserable."

Annie opened and closed her mouth. Jenny should have just slapped her. It would have hurt less. Before she could respond, her sister had stormed out of the room and slammed the door behind her.

Annie stared at her reflection, watching as a blanket of irritation covered her delicate features. *Am I miserable?* Her father used to say that she'd been born unhappy. That she'd come out of the womb squalling and angry. She used to argue it was because she was always cold and hungry, that it wasn't her fault. Eventually, after years of eating the scraps off of bones, she'd given up hope she'd ever have a full belly. Once she'd been taken away, she'd given up on hope completely. *You always assume the worst.*

Of course, she did. The worst was all there was.

But does it have to be that way?

She didn't know.

J enny had always been a good cook. All on her own, she'd laid out a full meal of ham, mashed potatoes, gravy, and seasoned vegetables.

Annie wanted to tell her that, to apologize, but it was too late now that the four of them sat together at the table. The boys shoveled their food down too fast to leave time for talking.

Later, she'd find a way to tell her that all her questions and accusations were out of fear.

Fear of losing the only family she had left. Even though Jenny wasn't blood, after all they'd been through together, she'd always be Annie's sister, just like Elain had been.

But Elain was a ghost now.

Jenny was still alive. Annie was determined to keep it that way. *Is he your friend?* Cam said he was. Sometimes, she believed it. She wasn't sure how to process what Jenny had suggested, so she decided not to. Even at night, when she tossed and turned, fighting to sleep, only sometimes did she let her mind linger in those places—to remember when she'd been able to lay her head against his chest when he'd carried her out of the bunker. When he'd whispered that they'd be leaving there—dead or alive—together.

She'd been dying then—The Rot destroying her from the inside—and indulging in the feeling of his arms around her hadn't seemed so dangerous.

But then, lying there in the dark, she'd remember how horrid those thoughts made her. In all her years, the only result she'd seen come from wanting another was pain and death. Her mother died in childbirth. Charlotte had hated Lord Duskin.

Annie didn't want to be a monster anymore. She'd been given a second chance, and she wasn't going to ruin it. So, she kept her head down, eating her dinner in silence, only barely listening as Nathan laughed and told his jokes.

They were good jokes, and usually she'd be fighting back laughs of her own, but she wasn't in the mood right now. Not with the way Jenny avoided looking at her.

Cam suddenly sat back in his chair and glanced around the room as he chewed a mouthful of ham. "Hell, I didn't even notice Julian missing. Has he come back yet?"

"Naw." Nathan shook his head before downing half a glass of red wine. "He probably found someone stabbier to spend his time with."

Jenny giggled as she speared a forkful of diced potatoes. "Stabbier?"

Nathan imitated poking a knife through the air. "You know, someone who enjoys death and killing as much as he does."

"So, us?" Cam rested his palm against his cheek before he shot Annie a mischievous look. "Speaking of death, do you want to share your adventures with us, Kitten?"

Nathan made a face. "We're still eating, mate."

Cam popped his lips. "I suppose I should prelude her events by saying Waverly Hills is a nightmare." He gave them a quick rundown of everything they'd seen at the hospital before being called away to the apartment buildings. He told them of Henry Bale and the dead man whose face had been peeled away, which made poor Jenny gag.

Annie set her silverware down, fixing her attention on the lilac, linen tablecloth. She hadn't gone into detail with anyone —even Jenny—about the ghosts she'd seen, or the portals. She still couldn't understand how Cam had been able to see Elain in her room, but not in the apartments. Her only conclusion, so far, is that Elain had *wanted* to be seen, but she couldn't for the life of her imagine why.

The three of them watched her expectantly.

Here goes nothing. Annie sucked in a deep breath, a cold shiver running through her as her brands flared. "After Henry took James Kline's finger, I saw his image standing beside the fireplace, his face still intact, though his eyes were bleeding."

Nathan and Jenny's brows shot high in surprise.

Cam didn't seem fazed in the slightest. His gaze was fixed on her with such an intensity that it made Annie's stomach squirm.

"A . . . second ghost formed beside him," Annie continued, her eyes flashing to Cam. She wasn't ready for Jenny to know about Elain. "It opened the portal and asked me to follow." She told them about the storeroom, the newspapers she had found, and how she had fallen through the doorway to see Maya and Kai.

"I found this. It's from The Order." She slipped out the letter she'd shoved in her bodice along with her dagger, her breastbone sore from where the knife handle had been rubbing against it all day. She set the blade on the table beside her and slid the note across to Cam.

Sandy hair glinting gold in the low light, he unceremoniously flipped it open and began to read out loud:

Alexander,

I don't know why you continue to fight me on this. Your son's reaction to Pearl Dust is the first flicker of hope we've had in decades. We WILL study him. He may be the key we've been looking for.

If this fact, along with the reports we've received from our contacts in the North, isn't enough to convince you to transport him to us, I may have to raise my concerns to my superiors. I will await your

*response before making my decision, but know that if
I do not receive one within the week, I will assume
you've read and ignored my continued requests. You
know how I hate having to force you.
Regards,
Harrison Bale.*

Cam drummed his fingers, letting the letter fall, as he finished reading. "God, I'm tired of these people."

"You're so popular," Nathan laughed. "Who would have thought? They obviously haven't seen how ugly you are."

"Bale?" Jenny pushed her plate away. "Isn't that the name of the police chief you mentioned?"

"Yes," Annie replied. "But it's a common name. We can't assume."

"I say we assume," Nathan said before downing the rest of his wine. "And what about this news from the North?"

"I can't imagine anyone *forcing* my father to do anything." Flames flickered around Cam's wrists as he pushed his chair back from the table. He tucked the letter into his pocket. "I'm going to go think for a minute."

"Good." Nathan shrugged off his own coat. "You're making it too hot in here, and *not* in the good way."

Cam flipped him off, but smiled, before he grabbed his plate and headed out the door leading to the covered veranda.

"Well." Nathan stood, as well. "I'm tired. Goodnight, ladies."

Jenny's brow rose. "It's five o'clock."

"And *that*," Nathan pointed toward the hallway. "Is the comfiest bed I've ever slept on. I'm not going to take it for granted."

They said their goodnights before he headed out into the entry and down the hall toward his rooms.

Leaving Annie and Jenny alone at the table.

Annie chewed the edge of her thumbnail, tasting blood in her mouth, as Jenny poured herself half a glass of wine and downed it in one gulp.

"I've never seen you drink before," was all Annie could think to say.

Jenny stood and smoothed her skirts. "There are a lot of things I haven't done before."

"I wasn't trying to insult you before." Annie winced as she bit too far into the quick of her nail. "I'm just . . . worried, is all."

Jenny's expression softened. "I know, but maybe you should try worrying less and living more."

Oh, Jenny. She was still so young. Annie's body was so tense with anxiety that it felt like it was vibrating. "If only it were that simple."

"I don't see why it can't be." Jenny turned for the entry and called over her shoulder, "I'm going to read the rest of the evening. Goodnight, Annie."

Now Annie was alone.

She glanced at the clock. She wasn't ready to go to her rooms. She didn't want to talk to anyone, but she also didn't want to be alone.

Is that it? The hum of her power asked. She tried to shake the thought away as she stood, absently heading toward the veranda. *Or is it that you don't want to be without him?* The fact that she didn't mind spending so much time around Cam was an issue enough. She didn't need the newfound extra voice in her head, making her doubt herself even further.

Annie stepped outside, grateful as a rush of frigid night air washed over her.

Ivy encircled the pillars supporting the patio's roof, growing over it like an extra layer of protection from the rain.

Cam sat stretched out in a reclining chair near the edge of the veranda, his feet propped up on the railing that separated it from the estate grounds, an empty plate beside him.

Go back inside, Annie. Why couldn't she follow her better judgment anymore?

Cam glanced over his shoulder as she approached and patted the open seat beside him. "Are you here to wallow with me?"

"Maybe," she said on instinct. Despite her screaming sensibilities, she sat beside him and blurted. "Jenny is upset with me."

"Oh?" Cam's brands illuminated the darkness covering the patio. "Why would that be?"

"Because I asked if Nathan had touched her while they'd been alone today."

She thought Cam would be angry at her for suggesting such a thing, but he just gave her a thoughtful look. "And?"

Annie chewed her thumbnail again, ignoring the twinge of pain that shot down to her first knuckle. "She said no, of course."

"I understand why it bothers you." Cam gazed back over the lawn. "I worry about Nathan all the time. I feel—"

"—Responsible for him?" Annie finished.

Cam flashed her a smile. "Something like that."

He knows. Annie's chest loosened enough for her to take a breath, a second one. She even relaxed enough to begin enjoying the sound of the rain pounding against the stone roof.

"Your last name was Beaumen?"

Cam studied her. She'd forgotten she'd told her real father's surname to the governor.

"Yes," she replied.

The ring of fire in Cam's eyes looked so bright against the dark of night. "Tell me about Rouenn."

Usually, she'd hesitate, but his questions didn't feel like prying—just curiosity.

"It's cold," Annie recalled, and the words began to spill out. "We lived in a hut beside the bay. My father was a hunter. Some winters, the snow covered the roof, and all you could see of our home was the little hole in the snow where our door was."

Cam shifted to his side, so he was facing her. "Aye? No wonder you're so strong. Freezing like that would make a warrior out of anyone."

He thinks you're strong. Annie's stomach flipped. "I had two brothers. They and my father hunted most of the day. When they did manage to kill something, I spent most of my time alone, skinning and dressing what they brought back."

It was odd talking about them—her family. Sometimes it felt like they'd never existed at all. That they were just a fever dream she couldn't let go. But now that she was bringing them to life again, she didn't want to stop.

Annie brushed away the tear threatening to fall from her eye before it had a chance to touch her cheek. "I think my father hated me for killing his wife, and my brothers for killing our mother. I think that's why they left me so often."

Cam's heat flared so strongly that it rocked her chair. "And how did you kill your mother?"

Annie tucked her feet beneath her, hoping the movement would hide the tear that *had* escaped. *I'm just overtired.* "By being born. She bled out having me."

"I killed my mother by doing nothing." Cam's teeth gritted so hard she thought they might crack. "In the days after we ran, I remember times when men would give her money and she'd disappear into alleys with them. Only to come back later, covered in bruises, but she'd have food for us." Cam exhaled and sent a wave of power surging across the estate grounds, making the trees shake. "I knew what was happening, but I did nothing, because I was so hungry."

Annie's throat was tight now. "You were a *child*."

"And you were a *baby*," Cam shot back. "Does that fact make you feel any better?"

"No," she said, and was grateful to admit it finally. "It doesn't."

"So, here we are." Cam ran a hand through his hair. She wished she could touch it, too. "Disgraced mother killers, trying to keep the last people we have alive." He sighed. "You'd think it would have sunk in sooner, but it wasn't until we reached Enoch that I realized everyone was truly gone—Resh, the crew, the men I grew up with. All I have left is you, Jenny, and Nathan."

Annie couldn't hide her shock. "Jenny and I?"

Cam scanned over her face, his eyes so bright with fire, and opened his mouth to answer, only to be interrupted by the crunch of grass on the lawn.

They twisted to see Mr. Price approaching, his long black braid dripping over his cream coat. "Oh, good. You two are awake."

CHAPTER 20
CAMDEN

Julian was soaked to the bone as he strode towards them. He ducked under the cover of the veranda, and shook out his clothes, splattering Cam with water.

Cam wiped his face and scowled. *Annie talked to me. Really talked to me.* He could kill Julian for interrupting their conversation. Annie had never spoken of her home before, but of course, the moment would be ruined just as she began to open up.

She curled up on her chair. "Where have you been?"

Julian straightened, spreading his coat out on the railing in front of Cam to dry. "I told you. I was visiting an old friend."

Bloody mooch. Cam kicked Julian's coat off, fighting a smile when the Air Brand glowered. Cam rested his hands behind his head. "And here I am, still surprised you have friends."

"The feeling is mutual." Julian pursed his lips before sitting on the open chair beside Annie. "And now I'm beginning to regret setting a time for you to meet this friend."

Annie perked up. "When?"

Cam's first question would have been *who*, but he kept that to himself as Julian continued.

"It will be easier to show you than explain," Julian replied. "We'll leave tomorrow evening, just before sunset."

"Well," Cam huffed a laugh. "That sounds like a trap, if I ever heard one."

Julian scowled again. "If I wanted you dead, I would have killed you a long time ago."

You already did once. Cam almost shot back, but again, decided to keep his mouth shut. *I can learn.*

It had been Julian, alongside Frank Boyle, who'd burned *The Nightlady,* and Cam along with it. He wasn't sure if he would ever completely forgive Julian for what he'd done, but Cam could shove his bitterness down with the rest of his fire. As much as it pained him to think, he *needed* Julian—needed his influence and expertise.

"I'll be heading to bed, then," Annie said as she stood, smoothing her skirts down before nodding to the two of them. When their eyes met, Cam didn't miss the flicker of frustration he saw there. *She's annoyed over the interruption, too.*

The jump in his heart rate lifted a small weight from Cam's chest, making the fire beneath his skin flicker. Maybe they could continue their conversation upstairs. He didn't care what they talked about as long as he could listen to her.

"Alright," Julian nodded quickly before turning back to Cam. "We need to talk."

Cam blew out a sharp breath. *Figures.*

Annie shot him an apologetic look before heading inside.

Once the door closed behind her, Julian let an amused huff. "I'm sorry, was this a bad time?"

"I hate you," Cam said, only partially joking, and let his eyes fall closed. "What do you want?"

Rain poured down the gutters, making them creak, and

nearly drowning out Julian's voice as he whispered, "I need you to have an open mind tomorrow."

That's not what I expected. Cam opened his eyes, brows raised. "So, it is a trap? Kind of you to give me a heads-up."

"It's not a trap," Julian sighed wearily. "But you're not going to like it."

"Ah." Cam stood, his power making him too restless to sit any longer. "Should I expect torture? Or worse, cucumber sandwiches?"

Julian just shook his head. "Neither. Just . . . try to think before doing anything stupid, please?"

Cam smirked before turning for the door. "Your expectations of me are rather high."

Julian shifted to stretch out on his seat. "Unfortunately, they are."

Ouch. Since he didn't know what to say, Cam went back inside the villa. The halls would be silent if not for Nathan's echoing snores. All he wanted was to talk to Annie again, to learn every tiny detail of her life, and share every detail of his. She was the only one he wanted to talk to anymore.

That thought struck Cam harder than he was expecting, making him hesitate before heading up the staircase. *Why? What changed?* Cam swallowed, trying to fight off the tightness forming in his throat.

He'd changed.

He and Nathan's friendship hadn't been the same since New Havana, not that he expected it would be. Now, even when they laughed together, there was a tension there— Nathan didn't fully trust him anymore. Cam was Revenant now, and it was because of a Revenant that Nathan had rotted for so long in Richard Duskin's prison.

Cam's fire flared so strongly and quickly that it took his breath away. He backed up, struggling to inhale, and continued to back away until he was in the dining room. He didn't stop until he knocked into the table. *I need to get out of here.* He needed to *do* something—anything, before the fire, so desperately trying to break free, drove him to insanity.

Cam swooped into his room, grabbing his new knives and tools before leaving the villa.

He missed the Southern seas—they were so calm, and as light a blue as Annie's eyes.

Cam sat on a pile of driftwood, working on his knife, listening to the waves crashing onto the rocky shore. He'd snatched Annie's dagger off the table. At least the rain had stopped. As grateful as he was that the ocean was walking distance from his father's manor, it wasn't the same.

Here, in the West, the waters were angry and grey—a dark void, promising death to any who was stupid enough to underestimate it. It even smelled different. Dirty. He imagined Enoch's sewers dumped straight into the bay.

Cam laughed as he heated the blade of the new knife until it glowed a golden hue. *The ocean here is as vile as its people.*

"What's so funny?"

"*Blazes.*" Cam nearly leapt out of his skin. Behind him, Annie stood at the edge of the shoreline, half shielded by reeds, her fresh dress soaked to the knee. She must have never gone to bed.

Cam gripped his chest, willing his heart to slow. "Lord above, woman, you're sneaky."

She smiled in a way that made his breath hitch. "Or you're oblivious."

He shrugged. "That's also likely." He narrowed his eyes at

her. "Besides scaring the hell out of me, what brings you out here?"

Annie pointed back toward the estate, to the villa not so far in the distance. "I saw you, out the window, walking toward the ocean with a bunch of knives in your hand. I was a little concerned."

"Oh." Cam raised the knife and winked. "I promise I'm not going to hurt myself. I'm fixing it."

"Is that my dagger?" Annie asked as she picked her way down the beach, trying not to slip on the rocks. She settled beside him, tucking her skirts beneath her, and raised an eyebrow at the damascus blade resting in his lap. "Are you fixing it or destroying it?"

"That's a question of context," Cam replied. He heated her blade again, working the old, bone hilt off the tang. Annie visibly winced at the sound of metal scraping against metal. Cam grinned as it came free. "Most would say I'm destroying it, but I would—" He hammered the new, beautiful red and black patterned hilt onto her dagger—still bone, but a crisp white, instead of yellow—heating the metal to secure it tightly. "—say I'm making it better."

He let out a satisfied chuckle and handed her dagger back to her, now even lovelier than before.

Annie stared at it in shock. "You bought a one-hundred-dollar knife for its hilt?"

"Yes," Cam admitted. "I thought it suited you better."

"An odd compliment." She shook her head before turning her attention toward the ocean, her chest rising as she inhaled the sea air. "At least, I think it was supposed to be one."

"It was," Cam replied, leaning forward to brace his elbows against his bouncing knees. He rubbed his face. God, he just wanted his fire to *stop*. He couldn't think. "I compliment you all the time. You think you'd be used to it by now."

Annie hesitated, and while her expression was flat, a range of emotions passed behind her icy-blue eyes. She turned her dagger over in her hand, inspecting it. "I didn't know you were a blacksmith."

"I'm not," Cam laughed. "Not a good one, anyway. Resh made me learn many things I didn't want to. We'd be at sea for months. If our weapons were damaged, someone had to fix them."

She slid the dagger back into its sheath. "What else did you learn?"

A thrill ran through him. *That's* why she'd come. He hadn't been the only one wanting to finish their earlier conversation. She'd wanted to know about *him*.

"I can sew. The sails were always tearing." Cam was so giddy that he began organizing his tools to keep his hands busy. "I'm a decent carpenter. I'm good at math. I did most of Resh's bookkeeping."

"No wonder he kept you around." Annie gave him a close-lipped smile. Her face fell. "What was Resh like . . . when he was alive?"

Because she'd known him, too. Only briefly, when Richard Duskin had taken him captive.

"He was loud and brash," Cam replied, and his heart sank. "He'd make us train with blades until our fingers bled, and practice our aim until we could shoot the stem off an apple. The crew wanted to kill him most days, but they also loved him."

"That sounds familiar," Annie said.

He looked at her.

Annie's cheeks turned pink. "How did you meet Nathan?"

"Resh adopted him, too." Cam turned back to his tools. "Three years after me. His parents had died, leaving him to care for his sick sister. He sent any money he had back to his hometown to cover her care expenses. He's the only friend I've had."

She paused, stumbling over her words. "Do you consider me your friend, Camden?"

I should have kept my mouth shut. His mind flashed back to the words he'd spoken to her on New Havana. *Friends . . . and whatever else you want. Always.* Cam swallowed. "Of course, I do. I thought we established that fact already."

"Yes . . . I'm sorry." Annie's gaze snapped back to the water, her words coming in a rush again. "Jenny said something to me earlier that . . . I want to trust you."

Cam's heart vaulted into his throat, followed by his stomach. "I want you to trust me, too."

"I don't know how," Annie admitted, but she scooted closer to him. "I've never done this before."

"I haven't either, really." His fire crawled up his neck as he wrapped his pinkie around hers, hoping she understood the meaning beneath his words. Growing up the way he did, he'd been with plenty of women, but had never *cared* for any of them. His crew had never stayed long enough in one place for that to happen, and trust was a dangerous thing. He understood why it frightened her.

He briefly kissed her knuckles. They were so blissfully cold against his lips. "I guess we'll figure it out as we go, aye?"

"Aye," Annie replied, almost teasing. "I think I can live with that."

CHAPTER 21

CAMDEN

"I must admit." Cam cocked his head, shoving his hands in his pockets. "This is not what I expected, yet it makes *so* much sense."

As planned, he and Annie met Julian at sunset the following evening. Their coach dropped them off outside a dilapidated building that may have once been someone's office.

Julian shot him a glare, arms crossed over his chest. The sky was clear tonight, letting the moon reflect eerily on his silver-grey eyes and brands. "What's that supposed to mean?"

Cam gave him a wide smile. "I should have known your friends are vagrants."

Annie scanned over the building with curiosity.

Julian closed his eyes and pinched the bridge of his nose, exhaling a long breath. "Just stay close and remember what I asked you."

Julian headed toward the building, shaking his head. As they followed him, ducking beneath several fractured support beams, Annie murmured, "What did he ask you?"

Cam leaned in. "He asked me to keep an open mind and not be stupid."

Annie's lips curled up at the corners. "That seems a fair request."

Cam faked a gasp. "Again, you wound me."

"Would you two be quiet?" Julian hissed over his shoulder before ducking beneath some more beams. He disappeared into the shadows, and Cam had no choice but to follow him. Though he'd never admit it, he was genuinely curious about this contact, especially with Julian's history.

Cam crouched to fit through some tighter spaces, helping Annie after him. There was a smear of dust over the shoulder of her dark, green dress when she straightened. She brushed off her hands, her gaze rising as a light sprang to life.

Julian stood at the beginning of a narrow, brick tunnel, holding a lantern in one hand as he gestured for them with the other. "Be quick, please."

Cam and Annie exchanged confused glances but continued to follow. The path shifted into a downward stair-case, leading deeper than necessary for a cellar. Cam stepped in front of Annie to brush the cobwebs away, the moisture dripping off the walls bursting into steam as they met his skin.

The path leveled out, and Julian paused. He stepped close enough for the lantern's glow to reveal a heavy iron door with a metal spyhole.

"I knew it," Cam murmured into the dark. "He's going to murder us."

Julian shot him another glare before knocking on the door in a strange pattern.

Annie sidled closer to Cam's side, the death grip she had on his sleeve the only indication of her nerves. Cam was tempted to put his arm around her, but decided against it. He didn't have the excuse of putting on a show for the nobles if she pushed him away.

After a moment, there was a loud screech as the spyhole slid open, revealing a pair of bulging, watery eyes. The voice coming from the other side was high and had an absurdly nasal quality. "Password?"

Julian groaned. "For God's sake, Magnus, I told you we were coming."

"What kind of name is Magnus?" Cam muttered under his breath. Annie bit down on her lips to keep from smiling.

The eyes locked on him before the spyhole slammed shut. After a series of clunks and screeching bolts, the iron door swung open to reveal a squat, balding, middle-aged man in a loose tunic tucked into trousers that came up nearly to his armpits.

He narrowed his eyes at Cam and Annie, shoving his wired glasses up his bulbous nose. "Are these the youths you were talking about?"

"Youths?" Cam let out a dark laugh. "Sir, I don't know what Jules told you, but—"

"Hush, hush." The man called Magnus waved him off before pulling down the front of his tunic. Under his thick chest hair were swirling green brands—Flora Brand. He smiled a thin-lipped smile. "Compared to us, you two are babes."

He ushered the three of them forward. "Come in, come in. I've got tea steeping."

Cam and Annie exchanged looks again, and she shrugged, stepping through the iron door behind Julian. Cam followed, blinking at the sudden brightness flooding the room.

They were in what appeared to be a house—enclosed in solid, metal walls and lined floor to ceiling in draping plants. Lord *above*, there were so many blasted plants. Without any sunlight, Cam imagined they only lived because of the man's

Revenant abilities. What little wall space remaining was covered in knick-knacks—hand-painted models of animals, ceramic mushrooms, and stacks of books organized by color.

Annie's eyes widened as she took it all in. It wasn't often Cam saw her caught off guard.

"Magnus, this is Lord and Lady Callahan." Julian nodded between them and his friend. "Camden, Annie, this is Magnus Baxter. Renowned Revenant researcher."

"World-renowned." Magnus shook his stubby finger at Julian. "Don't embarrass me in front of royalty."

"Magnus Baxter? That's the most made-up name I've ever heard." Cam opened his mouth, closed it, then chose something less cheeky to say, "If you're so well known, why haven't I heard of you, and why do you live in a hole?"

Magnus's bulging eyes sparkled behind his glasses. "There are many different circles, and even more types of fame, wouldn't you agree, Lord Callahan?"

He's got me there. Cam gave him a wry smile.

"Foxglove?" Annie wandered over to a wide pot filled with enormous stalks of pink, purple, and blue flowers. "These are poisonous, are they not?"

"Foxgloves," Magnus repeated. "Fairy thimbles, witches' gloves, dead man's bells—whatever you want to call them. They may be poison, yes, but their uses outweigh their curses."

Annie gently ran her finger on the outside of the nearest petal. "How?"

"They can be used to cure what ails the heart," Magnus said, then gave her a pudgy-cheeked grin. "I'm sure, my dear, you know all about blessings and curses."

Annie's gaze snapped up to his, shifting from wonder to alarm. "Pardon?"

"How about that tea?" Julian ushered his friend towards a tiny seating area. "Then we can talk?"

"Right, right, tea." Magnus shuffled over and lifted a large kettle from the stove. "Make yourselves comfortable."

Julian took the single seat, leaving Cam and Annie to squeeze together on the love seat. Cam tried to ignore the press of Annie's side against his, keeping his gaze locked on Julian. "What in the blazes are we doing here?"

"Patience," Julian whispered back. "Magnus does things on his own time."

"He's Revenant," Annie said, "A Revenant that researches Revenants?"

"And who better to do it?" Magnus set a tray filled with dainty, floral teacups on the table. He tapped his ear. "I also hear well, my dear."

Annie blushed as he sat across from them. Cam fidgeted under the older man's narrowed gaze.

Julian cleared his throat. "Magnus and I came in contact nearly a century ago, after I was stationed in Enoch while serving in the Western military." He swept his long braid over his shoulder and took it upon himself to pour the tea as he continued. "That was before I turned. After my death, I sought him out and we became close associates."

Annie sniffed at her tea before taking a sip.

"Do you like it?" Magnus was near buzzing. "I grew the herbs here myself."

"It's wonderful," Annie smiled sweetly—too sweet. "I've never had better."

Cam sipped his own and almost choked. It tasted like burnt hair. He knew. He'd burned to death.

"You flatter me," Magnus beamed before sitting back and folding his hands over his rounded stomach. As Cam set his tea down, Magnus made a face, his chin tilted. "You both died less than a year ago?"

"Aye," Cam responded reflexively after seeing a flash of anxiety cover Annie's features. "Something like that."

"Hmm." Magnus sniffed, then sipped his tea. "You're right, Mr. Price. They are unusual."

Before either of them could respond, Magnus hopped off his seat and pushed a veil of vines to the side, revealing a door on the other side.

"Come along," was all he said before disappearing through it. Julian gave them an apologetic smile and followed.

Annie set down her cup. "I'm so confused."

"I'm glad it's not just me." Cam offered her his arm. "Shall we?"

"Might as well," Annie said as she looped her elbow through his. "He locked the door behind us."

Ugh. Cam glanced over his shoulder. The door was bolted tight with padlocks. "Hang it all."

Behind the vines—through the doorway—was a second, larger room, also made of metal. Instead of plants and teapots, the shelves were lined with more books, surgical instruments, and one or two taxidermy raccoons.

A desk sat on the far side of the room, covered in box-shaped machines that made an unsettling humming noise, with another room beyond it. In fact, there were dozens of machines Cam had never seen. Some were flashing with green and yellow lights. Some had pendulums that swung back and forth faster than was possible.

Annie wandered toward another desk lined with flasks filled with a strange, purple-black fluid. She bent over, examining it. "What's this?"

"That." Magnus waddled over to her, sighing as he clinked his nail against the glass vial. "Is one of my failures. It's meant to act against The Order's corruption, but I can't get the absorbency right."

Cam blinked in shock. "You know about The Order?"

"Of course, I do." Magnus shot Cam a look that made him feel very, very stupid. "Only fools don't."

"What is their corruption?" Annie lifted the flask, swirling the contents. "And have you tried wood alcohol?"

"Again, of course." Magnus snatched the flask from her, gently setting it back on its tray. "And every affiliate of The Order I've studied holds a certain essence in their blood—we call it corruption."

Julian seemed entirely at ease as he plopped down on the edge of the desk, like he'd done it half a hundred times. Maybe he had.

Cam chewed his lip. "What does the corruption . . . do?"

Magnus's eyes darkened. "I hope you'll never have to know."

"Pearl Dust would work," Annie said, mostly to herself as she continued to study the vials. When she realized they were all staring at her, she blushed again.

"Do you think so?" Magnus perked up, adjusting his glasses. "Pearl Dust is such a volatile substance."

"And it absorbs faster than any I've ever seen," Annie corrected. She hesitated. "I might be able to . . . acquire some for you, if you'd like to try."

Careful, now, Kitten. It seemed her curiosity had gotten the best of her. Cam watched Magnus warily, but the older man just grinned.

"How scandalous," he teased, "But I wouldn't say no. In fact, I'd be most grateful."

Annie nodded, purposely ignoring Julian's pointed stare.

A medical gurney sat in the center of the room, the back propped up, surrounded by more buzzing equipment. Cam considered grabbing Annie and bolting, but then he remembered they were locked in.

"Back to work." Magnus pointed at Cam, then to the gurney. "Have a seat."

Perhaps bolting wasn't impossible, after all. He'd just have to melt the door down.

Cam chewed the inside of his cheek as he asked, "Why?"

Magnus rolled his buggy eyes, as if the answer was obvious. "So, I can start the examination."

"Like *hell* you are." Cam backed a step, reaching for Annie. "You can shove that idea right up your backside."

"Camden," Julian cut in anxiously. "This is what I meant by an open mind. Trust me."

Cam spat. "You just stomped trust into the dirt, mate."

"How can you expect me to help you if I can't examine you?" Magnus tapped his foot before flashing Annie a knowing look. "Maybe the lady would like to go first?"

"Absolutely not," Cam hissed. They obviously weren't getting out of this, and he *was not* letting the old bugger lay a finger on her. With an angry sigh, he sat down, recoiling as Magnus shoved a magnifying glass in his face, examining Cam's eyes.

Annie looked more curious than concerned as she wandered closer, her arms crossed. She scanned over the unique assortment of tools on the table, cataloging.

He snapped back to attention as Magnus began to prod at the brands on his cheeks. Cam gripped the arms of the gurney, cringing as Magnus shoved his head back to examine the flames crawling up the veins in his neck. He yanked up Cam's sleeve, inspecting the rolling heat turning his hands and arms molten.

Magnus made a few grumbling noises before jotting some notes down. All the while, Annie circled them, scowling. Julian didn't seem concerned in the slightest.

Calm down. Cam could feel his revolver rubbing against his hip. He could fight his way out of this if he had to. *He can't hurt us.*

"What are you looking for?" Annie's voice was low and utterly devoid of emotion.

"I'll tell you when I find it." Magnus stepped back and scratched his head. "Tell me, my lord, have you yet reached a stopping point?"

Burn this place down. He can't keep you here, his fire whispered. Cam shook his head, breath coming in too shallow. He wasn't sure how much longer he could keep his fire in check. "I have no idea what that means."

Magnus glanced at Julian, who just gave him an I-told-you-so look.

"At any time," Magnus continued, "have you felt like you were unable to summon your power? Or that you had to rest to regain it?"

Cam's hands shook as he rubbed his face. He had to get out of this blasted chair. "Is that a joke? If so, it's not funny."

Magnus tapped his lips before turning to Julian. "You're correct. He is quite unusual."

Julian began to pace. "Alright, now what do we do about it?"

Cam's head pounded so badly, he thought he might throw up. "If you don't stop speaking in cryptic riddles, I swear I'll burn this place to the ground and laugh while doing it."

To his infinite annoyance, Magnus chuckled and waved Annie forward. "Come."

"Why—" Cam jerked upright, but Annie was already there, standing beside Magnus. He took Annie's hand and placed it over Cam's wrist.

Magnus stepped back. "I assume you know what to do, dear."

Annie's eyes shot wide with shock. "Wh-what—"

"Do it," Magnus grinned, adjusting his glasses. "Or Lord Callahan, here, will be following through with his threats in" —He checked his watch—"around ten minutes, I'd guess."

Cam bristled, "I'd never hurt—"

He didn't get to finish his sentence. Annie grabbed hold, and his eyes rolled back into his head as she opened that space between them—taking, taking, taking—*God,* he just wanted her to keep taking.

Somewhere in space and time, Julian cursed. Magnus was speaking to someone, someone, he didn't care who.

It was just he and Annie. His fire groaned, begging, as her power clawed into his like solid ice, draining it away like infection from a wound. He could die here. He wouldn't mind it at all, actually.

But that space between them was only cracked. He needed her to open it all the way, to take everything he was and twist it into something new—but as he began to push against the gate, suddenly it snapped closed.

Cam jerked forward, breathing heavily as his mind reeled, and barely kept himself from tumbling face-first off the gurney. As his vision came back into focus, Annie stood over him, her entire body shaking, her skin glowing from within.

Magnus shoved her to the side and grabbed Cam's chin, examining his face again before letting it drop and turning to Annie. "Well, I'd say you took the edge off. Once or twice a week with that should keep Lord Callahan away from the deep end for now."

What the hell just happened?

Annie's laugh was slightly manic. "That was just the edge?"

"Just the edge," Magnus nodded, arms folded behind his back. He smiled between the three of them. "Should we have more tea?"

Cam's mind hadn't been this clear in weeks.

After they'd returned to the main room, Magnus sat them down and brought out a fresh pot of tea. Cam drank it gladly this time, barely listening to anything of the man's small talk as he prepared a plate of sugar cookies.

Cam could *breathe*. He wouldn't have cared if Magnus had told him to lie down on a bed of broken glass as long as he could have this slight relief.

Every few minutes, he found his gaze wandering to Annie. She'd been silent, never taking her eyes off Magnus since they'd sat down. Every visible part of her skin *glowed*. It made her all the more stunning, as if the veil had been pulled away, revealing an angel.

Though it still simmered just beneath his skin, his fire seemed content. Resting. It made him sleepy. It was a struggle to stay focused when Magnus set the plate of cookies down between them, taking a seat on his well-used chair near the fire.

Julian sat across from them, nervously picking at the end of his braid.

Magnus folded his hands over his stomach, "Well—"

"Tell me what just happened," Annie snapped, her tone cut to the bone. "I tire of all the games. What am I?" She nodded to Cam. "And what is he?"

God, I love it when she's bossy. Cam shifted awkwardly.

Julian's expression tensed.

Magnus sucked down his entire cup of tea in one swallow before pointing a chubby finger at her. "*You*, dear, are something very old." He shifted his pointing to Cam. "*He* is something very new."

"Care to explain?" Annie's brow arched irritably. "After I . . . died, Elias Bennett called me a Death Brand. That it was only seen from a few families in the North."

"Correct." Magnus shoved his glasses up his nose. "I've been alive over four hundred years, and you are only the sixth Death Brand I've met. Every one of them from the North, and every one female."

Damn, this bloke's old. "Do you know why that is?" Cam found himself more curious about Annie's power than his own.

Magnus yawned. "Why is anything the way it is? I don't have an answer for that. But I've always thought Death Brand to be a lacking term for your abilities. A more accurate description of what you are would be a siphon."

Annie rubbed her glowing fingers, her voice rising in pitch. "What does that mean?"

"You're a conduit," Cam murmured, awed. He knew. He'd *felt* it. "You can take life from one person and give it to another. That's why you can heal."

"In crude terms, yes." Magnus nodded. "In scientific terms, it would be called the transfer of energy."

"But why . . ." Annie sounded alarmed. She shot Julian a nervous look before whispering, "Why do I see the dead?"

Magnus just blinked at her.

Annie's voice lowered further. "Ghosts. I see ghosts."

As the stout man leaned back in his chair, deep in thought, Julian shifted so he was facing her.

"Miss Annie," he began, choosing his words carefully. "You've seen a lot of death. More than a person ever should—"

"If you're insinuating that Annie is imagining things," Cam said, deliberately slow. "I've seen it too. Just one. Annie's sister."

Julian's eyes shot wide. "Who—"

"Elain," Annie's jaw clenched. "She never left."

Julian stared at her for a moment before his gaze shifted to the floor.

He knew her . . . Elain. Sometimes Cam forgot that Julian had known Annie and her adopted sisters for years.

The cat's out of the bag now. Cam rested his arm over the back of the sofa. "Annie likes to teleport, too."

Poor Magnus looked like his head was going to explode. "Oh?"

"Yes." Annie chewed her thumbnail. "Is that bad?"

"Bad?" Magnus leaned forward, shaking his head. "No. Different? Yes. But, dear, I wouldn't be afraid of these abilities. Use them. Explore. There haven't been many, but in my years, I've seen Revenants that have been a tad . . . *more* than their peers." He to Cam. "Which brings me to you."

Cam bit down on his lip. "Uh oh."

Annie shifted just enough to intertwine her pinkie through Cam's. Julian's eyes flickered up, catching the movement.

Magnus hopped to his feet. Even standing, he was still shorter than Cam seated. He hobbled back over to the stove, warming his hands over it. "I haven't met someone quite like you."

Of course. Story of his life.

Annie squeezed his finger tighter.

Magnus pondered a moment longer, the hearth casting a golden glow over his sallow skin. "Fire Brands, Storm Brands, Ice Brands, Air Brands—the more aggressive of elements—tend to land on more aggressive of personalities."

Cam nodded. Elias had told him as much after he'd first turned.

"Lord Callahan," Magnus continued. "I've been studying our kind for centuries. A Revenant's power is limited to what their body can hold—to what their mind can manage."

Cam knew where this was going. "And my fire isn't following normal protocol, is it?"

"No, it's not." Magnus shared a quick look with Julian, who nodded back.

They're in on something together.

"You shouldn't have so . . . much." Magnus took a wilting, yellow flower off his shelf and blew on the petals. They sprang back to life. He set it back in its place. "The amount of energy Lady Callahan absorbed should have killed you, but it barely made a dent in your reserves."

Beside him, Annie stiffened. They both remembered how easily she'd drained the life from Frank Boyle.

"Mr. Price asked me to help find a way to manage your power," Magnus said. "But since I have no answers, I'd ask that you come back after I've had some time to think. Let me run some tests. How about this coming Tuesday?"

Cam's eyes widened. *Manage it?* Why would Julian care what he did with his fire? He'd suggested, more than once, that Cam needed to work on his control, but this was something different. His first instinct was to flat-out refuse, but if there was a way he could live with his fire without feeling like he was going to lose his mind, he was willing to explore it.

The Air Brand still had his grey eyes on the ground.

Cam sucked in a deep breath. "We'll get back to you on a time."

Julian's head snapped up in shock. Even Annie looked surprised.

"Excellent!" Magnus clapped. "Well, if that's it then, I'd like to settle down with something stronger than tea."

"That makes two of us," Julian murmured.

As the three of them turned to leave, Julian raised a hand, swiveling back to Magnus and said, "Did you know the Halls are expecting?"

The Flora Brand's face paled. "No . . . no, I didn't."

Cam's mind flashed back to Reika Hall, to the soft swell of her stomach. "Why the doom-stricken look?"

Julian gave Cam a sympathetic smile. "It's . . . ah . . ."

"Revenant babies die," Magnus said bluntly. "I've known the Halls for many years. This isn't their first pregnancy."

Annie's voice was so soft. "Why would the babies die? It must not be so strange for Revenants to be involved—"

"And all the babies die." Magnus sighed, his attention back on Julian. "Do you know how far along she is?"

"I have no idea," Julian replied. "But she's showing."

"I'll prepare a condolences gift." Magnus unlocked his giant, iron door and swung it open. "Good evening."

Cam's throat tightened. The Halls—

That explained why Reika couldn't keep her hands off her stomach. She was cherishing every moment she had with her child.

The door closed, leaving them in the dark of the tunnel outside. Annie's grip on his hand had become uncomfortably tight. Cam noticed her hand clutched over her chest, a sheen of sweat on her skin as she fought to keep her breathing even.

Julian strode further into the tunnel, ducking beneath the fallen beams.

"Annie?" Cam's stomach twisted, and before he thought to stop himself, he brushed his fingertips over Annie's cheekbone. "Are you alright?"

She jerked away, more out of surprise than fear.

"Oh, yes." She smoothed down her hair. "I was just . . . thinking."

He huffed a laugh. "I think I'm done thinking for this evening."

Annie nodded, smiling faintly. They stepped back out onto

the streets of Enoch. The coach they'd ridden in still waited for them.

Annie didn't speak the entire trip back to the manor.

She didn't speak when Cam led her to her room. The only indication that she was present was when she pointed to the couch in her attached living area, a silent order for Cam to stay.

He obeyed, wishing he could touch her, to pry her mind open, find whatever terrors were hiding there, and suffer them with her.

The couch groaned slightly as Cam curled onto it, burying himself in a pile of blankets. He wasn't cold. He just liked the weight. Even with his mind quiet for the first time in weeks, he couldn't sleep—his heart breaking—as Annie's gentle sobs shifted into the even breathing of slumber.

CHAPTER 22
ANNIE

Let them kill your body. But with a babe, they can kill your soul. They'll make you love them. They'll destroy you, over and over, just to watch you break. Promise me, my little. Don't let them kill your soul.

Annie gasped as she jolted awake, blinking away the memory. She didn't know why hearing of the deaths of Reika's unborn children had smashed through all her defenses, but she'd wept for hours before exhaustion finally dragged her to sleep.

Months ago, the deaths of a few babies would have meant nothing to her. Babies died all the time, but in that moment, she'd seen the hundreds of bodies she'd buried in the tunnels beneath New Havana—seen the white crosses she'd nailed together—and below each lay a lifeless Revenant infant.

The image had stayed with her the entire trek back to the villa, had followed her into her bed.

She'd known Cam had been awake, listening, but she hadn't cared. She just wanted to cry.

When Annie's eyes fluttered open the next morning, swollen from tears, sunlight streamed through the window, leaving panels of gold across the floral wallpaper. She rolled over and looked at the clock.

Eleven? Annie jolted up, her head spinning from moving too quickly. She'd never slept so late in her life. Where were the others? Where was Cam?

She jumped out of bed, still in the day dress she'd worn the night before, and winced at the chill of the hardwood floors against her toes. Halfway to the bedroom door, she froze. Soft breathing came from the other room.

Annie crept with bare feet into the living area.

Cam was still asleep on the couch, his mass of heavy blankets kicked onto the floor, one of his long legs slung over the back as his chest rose and fell in rhythmic movements. Annie found herself grinning. She wanted to push his hair back, to touch his face now that he looked so calm and peaceful.

Stop it. Annie held her stomach as she turned for the door. It ached—actually ached. Scowling, she rubbed her abdomen —the dull ache spreading into her lower back—as she made her way across the hall and down the stairs. Mr. Baxter's horrid tea hadn't agreed with her.

The sounds of clinking dishware came from the dining room. She turned the corner to find Mr. Price alone at the table, a plate of bacon and eggs in front of him. He must have prepared it himself. With all the mystery that surrounded him while she was with the Duskins, it was odd to think of Mr. Price doing something as mundane as cooking. His usual braided hair was loose, falling to his waist in a straight, ebony sheet, his coat folded neatly over the back of his chair. She'd never seen him look so . . . human.

Mr. Price glanced up at her as she entered, a forkful of eggs halfway to his mouth. "Good morning."

"Good morning," she replied, then gestured to the fresh pot of coffee on the table. "May I?"

"Please." Mr. Price grabbed her a clean mug from the tray and filled it for her. "Cream and sugar?"

"No, thank you."

"Black?"

She nodded as she sat across from him.

Mr. Price chuckled as he passed her the steaming mug. "You have a stronger stomach than I do."

It doesn't feel like it. As if on cue, another twinge of pain shot through her abdomen. She took a sip of her drink, letting out a grateful sigh as the bitter roast blanketed her tongue. What a terrible habit Cam had started her on, but she wasn't sure how she'd survived without it before.

Mr. Price returned to his meal. "Are you the only one awake?"

"It seems so." She glanced at the clock again. *I still can't believe I slept so late.* When she looked back, Mr. Price was staring at her brands, still a pearly-white, with narrowed eyes.

"Are you going to tell me the real reason we met Mr. Baxter last night?" she asked, feeling bold. "This can't just be about controlling Camden's fire."

"That was the main motivation," Mr. Price said between bites. "He's a danger to himself and everyone else in his current state."

Annie traced the edge of her mug. "And the secondary motivation?"

Mr. Price sighed. "I wish you two would trust me."

"How can we trust you when you're keeping so many secrets?"

"Now you *sound* like Camden."

"Because he's right." Annie had never argued with him before.

"And you don't have secrets?" He pointed his fork at her. "Do you really plan on supplying Magnus with Pearl Dust, or was that a slip of the tongue?"

Annie winced. She *hadn't* meant to say that out loud yesterday. "If what Mr. Baxter is trying to produce could help us against The Order, I think it's a worthy reason to use the patent."

"And I agree," Mr. Price said, his tone low as if hoping not to wake the others. "Which brings me back to my so-called secondary motivation. We need every advantage possible if we are truly going to stand up against The Order."

It didn't take long for Annie to put the pieces together. "And you wanted confirmation that Camden and I are weapons?"

"I already know you are," Mr. Price corrected calmly. "But owning a weapon doesn't mean you know how to use it. You train. You learn from an expert. We weren't blowing smoke when we said that you are unique." He chewed another bite before continuing. "You want to know my secret? If you can call it that. The Order—this cult—they took my brother from me. They took Charlotte. I will *eradicate* them, if I can."

Revenge, then. "And Camden is your best chance of doing that? That's why you followed him to Enoch."

"That's why I followed him and *you*," he clarified. "Now, will you stop being so suspicious?"

Never. She sat back. "Why haven't you told Camden that? It would have been easier."

"Because if I did, he'd rebel for the spite of it." Mr. Price glowered. "I'm not the only one with secrets."

Annie's brow rose just as a sharp knock rattled the front door.

Mr. Price swiveled in his seat, the silver brands on his arms flaring.

A thrill of fear sprang through her as the knock came again.

Wait. She glanced down at her hands, where her brands were still glowing from the power she'd taken from Cam. She wasn't ready to think about that yet. *I'm not weak anymore.* She could protect herself now.

As the knock came for a third time, Annie stood, smoothing down her bed-rumpled hair as she strode for the door. Mr. Price followed close behind.

He positioned himself against the doorway, hidden from the outside, and placed a finger over his lips as he drew a thin dagger from his belt.

I'm not weak. Annie braced herself, taking a deep breath, then yanked the door open.

She exhaled in relief.

It was only David.

The young, black-haired butler's equally dark eyes flickered to hers before falling to the ground. He held out a folded slip of paper. "For Lord and Lady Callahan."

Oh, right, that's me. Annie forced a smile as she took the note. "Um . . . thank you."

David gave her a quick, twitchy bow before striding toward the manor.

A heavy crash and a loud *"ooph"* on the staircase made them turn.

Cam had nearly fallen onto the landing, barely awake, as he worked on loading his revolver. His hair was sticking up in odd places, his shirt only half tucked, and his voice was thick as he said, "Who was that? I heard knocking."

Annie grinned before she could stop herself. He looked so . . . endearing. *Have I ever called anything endearing before? What's wrong with me?*

"Took you long enough." Mr. Price sheathed his dagger. "Lucky it wasn't a murderer. You'd be dead already."

Cam scowled as he loaded the last bullet into the chamber of his revolver, snapping it shut.

"It was just David." She held the note out as he descended. "A letter for us. I haven't read it yet."

"Oh." Cam rubbed his puffy eyes and yawned as he took the paper from her. He leaned against the doorway. They were only inches apart. Sometimes Annie forgot how tall he was until he was this close—she only came to his collarbone.

He flipped the note open and read over the words. "Blazes."

"Blazes what?" she and Mr. Price said in unison.

"We've been invited to another *tea party*." He passed her back the letter. "This time at the Clarkes. With the pro-Revenant group. I didn't realize the doctor was a sympathizer."

Not there. Not Violet. Annie suppressed a grimace as she read. "Tomorrow at seven." She smiled at Mr. Price. "You're invited, too. So are Nathan and Jenny."

"Splendid." Mr. Price exhaled. "Another waste of my time."

With that, he left for his room.

Cam blinked after him, his lids still heavy with sleep. "Did he just say *splendid*? What a nance."

"Yes." Annie fought back a laugh. "I think he did."

He rubbed his face again, wandering toward the dining room. "I smell food."

She followed him, and as he plopped down at the table, Annie poured him a cup of coffee, stirring in a ridiculous amount of sugar, before pouring another for herself.

Cam tugged Mr. Price's abandoned plate toward him, shoveling cold eggs into his mouth. Annie's brows furrowed as she set his mug in front of him. It was also easy to forget that he'd spent most of his life in poverty. Food was food. You didn't waste it.

Cam let out a low whimper after downing his mug in one

swallow. "God bless you, woman. Not only is it hot, but there's enough sugar in here to kill a horse. You're perfect."

"I pay attention," Annie replied as she sat. *Too much attention.* She'd always watched him, keeping note of his likes and dislikes, of the things that made him smile and laugh.

Cam grinned up at her as he poured another cup. "I'm glad someone is."

"About the Clarkes." Annie leaned back in her chair. "As much as I don't want to, we should go. The sooner we piece these deaths together, the sooner we find The Order."

"You're right, as always." Cam nodded, spooning more bacon onto his plate. "And thank you, by the way."

"For what?"

Cam's eyes flickered to her glowing brands. "For whatever you did at Baxter's. I haven't slept that well in months."

Annie didn't want to think about it. About how *good* it felt to latch on to Cam's power again. Touching him like that, opening that gate . . .

She wouldn't need any convincing to do it again, and that bothered her. The lack of pain in recent weeks was weakening her discipline. She didn't know what else to say, so she just said, "You're welcome."

Instead of pushing the topic further, Cam raised his mug. "Here's to suffering through another blasted party."

Annie clinked her mug against his and sighed. "I hate parties."

nd it wasn't just a casual gathering.

The Clarkes had pulled out all the stops. They lived only a few blocks from the hospital, and while their estate was nowhere *near* the grandeur of even the smallest of the Callahan villas, it still spoke of more wealth than most would ever see in their lifetimes.

Standing outside their crisp, white mansion, all Annie could think of was how much they must spend to keep the exterior walls scrubbed so clean. Endless strands of shimmering, silver garland were wrapped around the outer pillars, creating a festive appeal.

Arm in arm, Annie and Cam entered the Clarke's home—Nathan, Jenny, and Mr. Price beside them. A spindly, thin, elderly man took their coats at the door, ushering them toward the *massive* dining room that was obviously modeled after Callahan's ballroom.

A long oak table ran down the center of the room, where guests sat, eating and drinking. There was a hearth at each side of the rectangular space, surrounded by well-furnished seating areas. The patio doors were propped open, providing access to the covered outdoor verandas.

Despite the size, it felt crowded. There had to be *dozens* of Revenants, their brands in all shapes and colors. She wasn't sure where to look. It didn't take Nathan long to find the appetizers, Jenny hot on his heels. Mr. Price simply disappeared like he always did.

Cam paused in the doorway. Today, he wore a deep navy suit, with a simple black button-down shirt and vest beneath. It looked handsome against his tanned skin. His lips pursed. "God, this is terrible."

"Agreed." Annie pressed tighter against his side. "I changed my mind. Let's leave." She didn't mean it, not when she wore a gown of a matching color, with a wide off-the-shoulder neckline and a beaded black sash around the waist. Jenny had pinned her hair half up, curling the loose tresses into subtle waves. Why waste her sister's efforts? Besides, she felt . . . pretty.

"This was your idea." Cam laughed, "We're going to suffer through it."

"It was not. I just *suggested* we come."

"And I repeat, this was all your idea."

"*Lady Callahan!*" A deep, musical voice called.

They turned to see Reika Hall striding toward them, dressed in a slinky black dress, definitely *not* in fashion, but it accentuated her growing stomach. It made Annie like her all the more.

"Mrs. Hall," Annie greeted as her heart sank. There was a baby in there. A baby that Mr. Price and Mr. Baxter expected to die. She didn't let any of her turmoil show as she continued, "I'm so glad you're here."

And she meant it. She liked Reika, and any company was better than Violet Clarke.

"I wouldn't miss it." Reika pulled Annie in for a hug before raising a brow at Cam. "How dare you bring her late, Lord Callahan. I've had to spend forty-five *entire* minutes alone with these witless ninnies." She nodded toward the group of women in the far corner, surrounding Violet. "A moment longer and my brains would have melted out my ears."

Cam made a face. "But if you take her, who is going to protect me from the ninnies?"

"I don't care." Reika waved flippantly before dragging Annie deeper into the party. "You'll survive."

Cam laughed, raising his hands. "Fine, don't stab me. Just bring her back before bedtime."

Reika blew a kiss over her shoulder at him. "Don't worry, hun, I won't let your sheets get cold."

Lord, help me. Annie's cheeks burned hot at Cam's returning grin. Before she could respond, Reika had her halfway across the room.

"I meant what I said," the woman whispered. She smelled of nutmeg and cloves. "These girls talk of nothing but the difference between metal and whalebone corsets or comparing the size of their men's genitals."

Lord, please, *save me.* Annie pursed her lips. "That's . . . unfortunate."

Reika groaned, rubbing her stomach again. "You have *no* idea how bored I've been."

Annie glanced over at her. Reika's voluminous locks were twisted into an attractive poof on the top of her head, showcasing the starkness of her turquoise brands against her dark skin. She was breathtakingly beautiful.

Annie's eyes trailed lower, over Reika's swollen belly. "How . . . are you well?"

Reika gave her a sharp look, hazel eyes narrowing. "I'm in perfect health. Why do you ask?"

"Just curious," Annie fumbled for a lie, but decided on a half-truth. "But if I'm being honest, I'm terrible at small talk. It was either inquire about your health or the weather, but since it's constantly raining here, that wasn't an option."

Even Reika's laugh was lovely. "You are a treasure, Lady Callahan."

"Just Annie is fine."

Surprise colored Reika's features before her lips twisted into another smile. "Just Annie, then."

As they approached the group of Revenants, Reika leaned in close, her tone pure mischief. "You see that one there?" She nodded to a short, blonde woman with chocolate brown brands. "She's cheating on her husband with a mortal gardener."

"Oh," Annie said.

Reika nodded to the mousy-brown-haired woman next to her, her brands a deeper shade of blue. "That one prefers the company of other women."

Annie's brows furrowed. "Why are you telling me this? That's their business."

She stopped short, turning Annie to face her, expression serious. "Because if you plan to rule, it's your job to know *everyone's* business." She squeezed Annie's shoulders, her tone lowering further. "Your husband has many enemies in Enoch. You'll need to be his eyes and ears."

Annie's breath hitched, the knife in her bodice pressed against her breastbone. "Camden hasn't lived in Enoch since he was a boy."

"The governor has many enemies," Reika said in a way that made Annie feel like she was being scolded. "Which means your Camden has many enemies."

Her eyes rose over Annie's shoulder and darkened. "But I don't have to tell you to be careful who to trust, do I?"

"Lady Callahan, Mrs. Hall!" A high-pitched, slurred voice called for them, too loudly—Violet. Her full hips swayed as she strode towards them, her cheeks patchy and red, a half-empty wine glass in her hand. She gave Annie a crass once-over before shifting her blurry gaze to Reika. "Do you mind if I steal Lady Callahan? There's someone I'd like her to meet."

"Of course not." Reika curtsied before pressing a quick kiss to Annie's cheek, murmuring, "Good luck."

Annie's skin crawled when Violet took her arm, steering her toward the outer patio. The rain poured down on the glass ceiling, the breeze crisp as it snapped her skirts around her knees.

Being several inches taller, Violet had to lean down to whisper in Annie's ear, breath stinking of alcohol. "Enjoying the party?"

Annie wrinkled her nose. "I've been here five minutes."

"Can I get you a drink?" Violet said, almost mockingly. "Wine? Maybe something stronger?"

"No, thank you," Annie replied sharply. Despite stating that she intended an introduction, it took Violet nearly an hour to reach their destination. She stopped to pester every person they passed—Revenant or mortal—forcing Annie to learn dozens of faces and names she'd never remember. Jenny and Nathan continued to mingle, the latter earning a jovial crowd around him with his jokes. Cam was always in her periphery. Right now, it looked like he was playing—and winning—a card game against Jude Hall and two other Revenant she didn't know.

So much power. She could feel it, her own buzzing in anticipation at the collective energy of the men and women surrounding her. Did they know that their freedoms were at risk? How could they not? Mr. Baxter had said that only fools didn't know of The Order. Still, she couldn't understand how so many individuals—with the abilities to manipulate water, wind, and storms—could sit back and allow such evil to take over their country. Either they didn't know, or they didn't care. *But what did you do to stop the Duskins? For years, you committed the same evils.*

She caught Reika's eye from across the room as she sat on the back of the sofa, helping her husband choose his next move. Her thick brows rose knowingly in response. Perhaps she thought the same.

When they *finally* stepped outside, an overpowering amount of cologne assaulted Annie's nose. She turned to see a younger, Revenant man pulling away from the crowd huddled around the refreshment table. Well, young as far as she could tell. He could be hundreds of years old, for as much as she knew.

He grinned at them as he approached, his mouth full of perfect, too-white teeth. Though he was tall, he wasn't quite as tall as Cam, his short, honey-blond hair brushed neatly off his face. His chest was bare beneath his suit coat, revealing a toned chest adorned with icy-blue swirls—a different shade than Reika's.

Violet ran her hand down the man's arm, her smile a little too familiar. "This is Jensen Davis, Mr. Davis, this is—"

"Annie Callahan," he interrupted, taking her hand and kissing her knuckles, his blue-green eyes locked on hers. "I've heard stories of The White Lady all over town. You need no introduction."

"I'd like to know where these stories are coming from." Annie fought a reflexive recoil. *I'm going to need to wash my hands.* "We haven't been in Enoch a week yet."

"Word spreads quickly about women as beautiful as you." Mr. Davis gave her a charming smile. Violet's eyes grew envious as he brushed a strand of Annie's hair off her shoulder. He continued, "And a Death Brand, at that. What a treat."

"Mr. Davis invests a large sum into Waverly every year," Violet said, batting her long lashes at the man. "He was thrilled to hear that you and Lord Callahan pledged to rebuild the hospital."

The way Mr. Davis's lips pursed told Annie everything she needed to know—he gained a lot of influence from his ties to the hospital, and now she and Cam had threatened that.

This cow is trying to set me up. Annie's shoulders stiffened. Fine. If she was going to make more enemies, she'd do it herself. She didn't need Violet's help.

She mimicked Mr. Davis's false charm and crooned, "Violet, by the state of the hospital, you must have squandered Mr. Davis's funds, unless they weren't substantial to begin with." She held his hardening glare. "You should be more careful with your investments."

Mr. Davis cocked his head and tsked. "You have a wicked tongue, don't you, Lady Callahan?"

"What about *my* wife's tongue?" a voice from behind her said.

She felt Cam's heat before his arm slid around her waist. Mr. Davis backed a step as Cam's fire flickered up his neck, sending embers into the night air, his sneer hitting a level of cruelty that other men would never be able to match. "I don't think we've met. You are . . . ?"

"Jensen Davis. I'm applying for the city council." Mr. Davis extended his hand to Cam.

And he ignored it. Instead, his eyes flickered from the top of Mr. Davis's head, down to his shoes, then back up to settle on his brands. "What kind of Revenant are you? Forgive me. I haven't been back from the dead very long."

Mr. Davis suppressed a scowl. A layer of frost coated his fingers, building up until each was adorned with its own personal icicle.

Cam smirked. "Fascinating. I bet you're popular in the summer. Snow cones for everyone."

"I assume you're Camden Callahan?" Mr. Davis said coolly, the frost on his hands spreading up onto his sleeves.

Cam's smirk widened into a half-smile as he guided Annie back toward the dining room. "Who else would I be?"

As they walked away, a wave of bitter cold brushed against Annie's back before Cam's heat slammed down on top of it, crushing it to the ground. Behind them, Mr. Davis let out a low hiss. Though he was smiling, Cam never looked back.

Annie kept her expression flat in case anyone was watching. "As much as I appreciate the rescue, did you have to be so rude?"

"I'm sorry." Cam twirled her around to face him, his gaze turning predatory as it lingered on the patio. "I'm a catty wench when I'm jealous."

"Jealous?" Annie crossed her arms. "Of *him*?"

"He's got nice hair."

"So do you."

Cam ran a hand through his locks. "Did you just compliment me?"

Annie rolled her eyes, shoving him away from her. "You are—"

She froze, her mouth going slack. Across the dining room, Elain sat at the edge of the dining table, her flowing, blonde locks pulled over one shoulder. She crooked her finger at Annie, her empty, white eyes crinkling at the corners as she smiled.

Annie tapped Cam's arm, nodding toward the table. "Do you see that?"

His eyes followed the direction she gestured, narrowing. "I'm assuming by the look on your face, you don't mean more Revenants?"

"Elain," she whispered. His expression shifted from a frown to one of surprise.

"I don't see her," he murmured. "How rude."

Elain stood, gesturing to Annie again, before she disappeared around the corner.

Annie's heart pounded in her ears. "She wants me to follow her."

"Then follow her," Cam replied. "Oddly enough, I trust Elain more than the rest of these sycophants. Go see what she wants. I'll keep these people distracted."

She gave him a grateful nod before stalking after her sister.

The sound of laughter made her peer over her shoulder. Cam sat down amongst another group of partygoers, resting one leg over the other. Whatever he said made them burst out laughing again.

As much as he pretended he wasn't, Cam was good at entertaining. Sometimes, it even seemed like he enjoyed it.

When she rounded the corner, Elain waited at the other end of the hall, leaning against the doorway of a private room. Soft, hushed voices spilled into the space. After all her years in captivity, Annie knew how to keep her feet silent, her breath imperceptible.

Elain shot her a smug look as Annie grew closer, the edges of her form blurred and hazy.

"What do you want?" Annie mouthed.

Elain nodded toward the private room before disappearing.

"You could just tell me," Annie murmured out loud before sidling against the wall just outside the doorway. Now that she listened, she realized the voices belonged to Violet Clarke, and the two other Revenant women Reika warned her about. It sounded like Violet was . . . crying?

Sure enough, there was a sob. "Van doesn't realize how hard this is."

A patting sound. Maybe the other women were comforting her?

Violet's voice grew bitter, obviously drunk. "All of the whispers we've heard have said the same thing—their marriage is a sham. I've even heard she just did it to get citizenship."

Annie's stomach leaped into her throat before slamming back into her gut. *She's talking about us.* But how could she know that? Only their immediate circle knew. Were they being spied on? And if so, by whom? There was no one else in the villa. *Unless a crew member overheard and reported it.* But even that didn't make any sense. There was no reason for it, unless they'd been bribed.

"He'll see that he needs a real woman," one of the others said—the cheater. "You just have to show him. It's not too late for an annulment."

"You're right." Violet blew her nose. "I do have to show him." There was a brief pause, then a sigh, before she continued. "I still have time."

Have time for what? There was the rustling of skirts, then Annie pressed her back against the wall as the three women headed back toward the dining room.

Annie blinked into the darkness, shocked. Is this what Elain wanted her to hear?

Violet is a problem. Annie's power rumbled beneath her skin, purring in her ear. *She wants to steal him from you. Take care of it.*

Annie shook her head. Cam wasn't hers to steal.

Isn't he?

It didn't matter if she had a genuine claim to him or not. Violet was meddling like the witch she was. She needed to learn her place, and that place *wasn't* with Cam.

Anger won out over sense, and Annie prowled after them. When she turned the corner, Violet was settling down next to Cam on the sofa, as if completely oblivious to the other guests already seated beside him.

Cam's eyes grew wide as Violet twisted closer, her heavy breasts in his face. She squeezed his thigh and made some haughty joke that caused the others to laugh.

Annie was going to kill her.

Shadows pooled around her legs as her strides turned stalking, the shadows extending behind her like the glittering train of a gown. Violet's eyes snapped up to her, filling with terror, as Annie stepped behind the sofa.

"Excuse me." She let every ounce of hate she felt spill into her tone. "I need to speak to *my* husband for a moment."

At the sight of her, Cam's expression filled with relief, which only twisted her anger into rage.

"Annie," he said, locking eyes with her. "Would you like to step outside—"

The possessiveness in the way Violet gripped his knee again made Annie snap. She ignored all her pre-rehearsed excuses for why she shouldn't care, as she slid her fingers into the back of Cam's beautiful, soft hair. Nor did she listen to the warning bells screaming in her mind as she crushed her lips against his.

Oh, she'd expected the satisfaction of ruining Violet's petty plans, but what she hadn't expected was the electric current that sparked through every inch of her body at the touch, or the way his lips parted beneath hers as he sucked in a gasp.

What did I do—The thought started to form before he cupped her cheek and pulled her harder against him, making all her worries vanish.

God, his skin was *so* hot. The sensation spread into her limbs, chasing away every night she'd nearly frozen to death in the belly of the slaver's ships. As her own lips parted, smoke filled her mouth—

—Then someone cleared their throat and snapped her back to reality.

Annie jumped back. Everyone stared at them. At her. She exhaled a stream of smoke as if she'd taken a drag on a cigar.

Cam blinked at her—stunned, his fire eating away every ounce of green in his eyes, chest heaving.

Oh no. Only the vile hatred on Violet's face gave Annie the steadiness to let out a low giggle and grab Cam's hand. "Excuse us." She didn't wait before dragging him off toward the patio. He hopped over the back of the sofa to keep up with her.

A series of low laughs followed them, and someone murmured something about *newlyweds.*

Don't think about it. Don't think about it. How could she not when her entire body was still electrified? Once they were outside, Annie quickly shut the double doors behind them.

When she turned, Cam was staring at her, his cheeks redder than she'd ever seen them. His heat was so overwhelming and intoxicating that she could drown in it. His eyes fell to her lips again.

"I apologize for that." Annie moved under the cover of the veranda. "Violet was—"

"Violet who?" Cam let out a nervous laugh, raking a hand through his mussed locks. "Where are we? What day is it? Warn me next time, please, because I almost embarrassed the hell out of myself getting off that couch—"

"She knows, somehow." Annie peered through the window. Violet was still sitting by the fire, pouting. That shouldn't have pleased her so much. "That you married me to get me into the West."

"And what?" Cam's breaths evened out slightly—only slightly. "You decided to teach her a lesson? I knew you were ruffled."

"I am not *ruffled.*" That was a lie. Annie pressed her back against the wall and looked away. "I'm . . . sorry. I shouldn't have done that."

"Yes, you *should* have." Cam stepped closer to her, but not too close. "Blazes, I've been wanting to do that for months."

Annie's heart backflipped. "You don't mean that."

"Tell me you haven't." They were inches apart now, his arm braced over her head. "Tell me you haven't thought about it.

Tell me, and I'll never bring it up again. We can pretend this never happened."

Annie's power reached for his without her permission, mingling with his fire in a way that made the air around them light up with sparks of light and embers.

"I—" Annie couldn't breathe. She didn't want to tell him to go away. She didn't want to tell him he was right. She chewed on her thumbnail. "I don't know how not to—"

Not to be afraid. She was going to say.

But he knew that.

Her pulse spiked again as Cam grabbed the hilt of the dagger peeking out of her bodice and unsheathed it. Before she could panic, he pulled her thumb away from her mouth, shoving the handle of the dagger into her hand instead. He twisted her wrist until the blade was pressed against his throat.

He didn't bother hiding the longing in his eyes. "There. How about now?"

Annie's fingers trembled as she fixated on where the blade met his skin. She brushed it up his throat and rested it against his jaw before she whispered, "I'm not telling you anything."

The fire in Cam's eyes blazed as he leaned over her, close enough that when she slid the blade against his lips, it was the only thing separating them.

The edge of the knife cut into his skin. "Say it. Tell me to forget."

There were people inside who could see them. Hell, there were probably people outside—

But Annie forgot to care. She brushed her thumb over the wound, healing it as she smeared blood across his lips and breathed, "I won't."

Then she moved the dagger away, and Cam's lips were on hers, hot and tasting of copper, making her jaw clench.

Beneath the blood, he tasted like the first rays of the spring sun as it melted away the morning frost. He sighed as he kissed her deeper. She tangled her fingers into his hair as his arm curled around her waist, tugging her body against his.

She could stay here forever. *Here.* Where there were no nightmares, only him.

A loud, piercing crack and wailing echoed through the night. A second crack echoed, causing Cam's body to lurch and stumble backward.

He blinked down—as disoriented as she was—at the blood pouring from a gaping hole in his shoulder.

A gunshot.

CHAPTER 23
CAMDEN

He'd been shot.

Cam stared at the bullet hole in his shoulder, watching the blood spreading over his brand-new coat. Annie's ice-blue eyes widened in shock, her perfect lips flushed. She flinched and turned as a third gunshot sounded, followed by continued screams.

Cam just breathed, and breathed, and breathed.

They'd kissed, and it had taken the breath from him, had smothered out every fear, and blown apart even his greatest fantasies.

She'd kissed him, and some mutton-shunting, ratbag, piece of trash had interrupted them—again.

Worse than that, if the bullet had hit two inches further right, it would have gone straight through Annie's throat.

That bullet hadn't just pierced his flesh—it had destroyed the very last shred of self-control he had left in his damn body.

Cam shoved Annie to the ground as a fourth gunshot tore through the wall, over their heads. She covered her face, but didn't make a sound, as bits of wood and debris rained down on them.

Kill them. His fire rumbled in his chest.

Gladly. "Stay here," Cam growled. He'd shoved an extra pistol in his pocket earlier, just in case, and now he was glad he did. He yanked it out and stuffed it in Annie's hand. "You remember how to use this, right?"

She nodded, taking the firearm. "Yes, but—"

He tried to stand, drawing his revolver, but Annie yanked him down by his sleeve and hissed, "You want me to stay here and do nothing?"

"No." Cam shot back. "Of course, I don't *want* you to, but have you ever been in a gun fight?"

The look she gave him could have curdled milk.

"That's what I thought. Stay. Hide." A fifth shot had Cam climbing to his feet, but she grabbed his arm again.

"Wait." The brands on Annie's fingers began to glow. "Your shoulder."

Oh, right. That. "Don't worry about it." Cam stripped off his coat and shoved his fingers into the hole in his shirt, gritting his teeth as he burned the wound closed. He could feel where the bullet was still lodged in his flesh, but later. He'd worry about that later. "See? All better."

Annie glared but didn't argue. She stared at the pistol, breathing heavily. "Point and shoot?"

"Point and shoot," Cam said as he peered around the door-frame. As the screams continued, water and ice sliced through the air, followed by more gunshots. A table flew past the window—probably Julian's wind.

There are dozens of Revenants inside. Cam listened, counting the voices of those grunting and shrieking. There were at least ten on the opposite side of the wall. *Who would crash a party of immortal magic wielders?*

Idiots, that's who.

Or men who knew how to deal with Revenants, like The Order.

Cam kicked the door open and was immediately hit with the stench of blood and gore. Familiarity slid his instincts into place, bringing him down into a lethal calm.

God, it was like he was on *The Nightlady* again, sacking competing vessels, taking lives at Resh's command. He knew how to kill. He'd done more than he cared to admit.

But now?

Now he was going to slaughter these cult bastards and enjoy every moment of it.

Cam raised his revolver as he swiveled around the doorframe. There were bodies on the ground, male and female, Revenant and mortal, with blood pooling beneath them. Not all of the dead were guests. Several wore black uniforms, their faces covered in dark, eyeless masks. Tables were on their sides, spilling wine and discarded food over the corpses. Most had fled the sitting room. They'd probably run for the courtyard—

Blazes. Why'd he assume that all Revenants knew how to fight? They were civilians, not soldiers. Having powers and learning how to *use* them were two different things. No wonder Julian pestered them so much about training.

A shimmer of ice sparked to his left as Jensen Davis—the arrogant prick—came around the corner, his livid features splattered with blood.

Cam followed his gaze. A masked figure paused as he emerged from the mouth of the dining room, raising his pistol. Jensen began to dodge just as the intruder's finger moved to the trigger—

But Cam had already fired.

The intruder's head popped like a squeezed grape.

"Callahan!" Jensen swiveled, his icy brands flaring as frost coated his fingertips. "There's more—"

Five men poured out of the doorway attached to the dining room that led to the kitchen. All wearing masks, each carrying a defensive shield, gleaming with an oily substance, and automatic handguns.

Like a novice, Jensen raised his own revolver and fired—right into the nearest defensive shield. Instead of penetrating or splintering it, the bullet ricocheted off the metal, sending it careening into the ceiling.

Bullet-proof shields. Hang it all.

Instinctually, Cam reached for his hip—where he usually wore his sword in battle—but no. He wasn't on his ship. He was at a blasted party with an idiot who shot at shields instead of kneecaps. *I can't believe I miss Julian.* He didn't have time to worry about him now, or Nathan, or Jenny, for that matter. The longer these men remained alive, the longer they were in danger.

Five more masked men came in behind them from the main hall. Jensen's eyes widened as they raised their pistols in unison.

Behind the mask, the nearest man's voice was muffled. "Drop your weapons, Stripe."

Stripe. That's what the common folk called Revenants, not noblemen.

"Really?" Cam let out a dark laugh as he waved his revolver in the air. "*This* is what you're worried about right now?"

"*Drop it.*" The intruder growled, stepping closer. "Now."

Jensen slowly lowered his gun to the floor. "Do it, Callahan, before you get us killed. There are too many."

"Fine." Cam tossed his revolver onto the nearby sofa, making the group of men tense. He rolled his wounded shoulder, letting the pain push him even closer to the edge. "To be honest, I didn't want to shoot you anyway. Too quick. If only I had a knife. They are so much more personal."

Wait—

What had Julian said? *That means, before long, you'll be able to manipulate that energy into different forms. Like a weapon, perhaps. Or a barrier.*

God, a fire sword sounded *so* comical, but it also sounded like *so* much fun.

The men pushed in, surrounding them, trying to herd them with their shields as they kicked Jensen's gun out of reach.

Cam refused to budge. Heat radiated through his body as fire curled around his fists, licking up his throat. No one was here to stop him now. If they hadn't wanted him to become a monster, they never should have come so close to hurting Annie.

Cam swung before he felt the fiery blade form in his hand —he knew it would be there. He grinned ear to ear as his new, blazing sword seared through the closest man's neck. The rest of his team froze as their companion's head dropped to the floor.

That moment of hesitation was all the time Cam needed.

A second blade formed in his free hand as he dove, stabbing one man through the gut and slicing through the hamstrings of another. It took that long before they started shouting, readying their pistols, but Cam slammed back against their shields—blinding them—with a wall of fire so hot their shields dripped molten metal onto their arms and wrists.

Shouting turned to screaming.

Cam had two more down before Jensen collected himself, sending a streak of ice to bind the men's feet to the floor. Moments later, they died, too.

"*Camden!*"

Cam wheeled.

Julian Price stood at the top of the landing, leading to the upper floor, his cream cloak splattered in red. Three more masked men tumbled backwards down the stairs. As they hit the base, they scrambled to their feet and bolted for the entry. One of them didn't get up—his neck snapped to the side at an odd angle.

"Blast." Julian flew to the bottom of the stairs and turned. "Don't let them—"

The remaining two made it about five feet down the hall before a deafening crack split the air at Cam's side—another gunshot.

Behind them, Annie staggered—her skin impossibly paler—as the nearest man fell with a fleshy hole in his back.

Blazes. He hadn't even heard her come in. "Annie, hell—"

"Get him!" Julian ordered as he pointed after the remaining survivor. He gestured to Annie and Jensen. "You two, with me. There are survivors in the other room."

Annie backed a step, pistol raised. "But—"

"*They* need you," Julian interrupted, motioning to where pained moaning and weeping echoed out from across the hall. "Camden doesn't. Move."

As much as he wanted Annie beside him, Julian was right. Cam squeezed her elbow. "Go. I won't be long."

Reluctantly, she nodded.

Cam sprinted after the last intruder, leaping over the body blocking his path. The masked man was already halfway across the courtyard by the time Cam caught sight of him.

Cam didn't have his gun. He'd have to run him down.

Revenants are dead. This was a planned attack against the pro-Revenant party. He didn't need to hear one of his father's speeches to know that. Whether he—or Annie—had been the target, it didn't matter. He was going to kill them.

Cam *could* let the man escape, or at least let him believe he did. He could track him back to wherever his cowardly behind was running to, but the fool had made the mistake of threatening his wife.

He wasn't leaving here alive.

Cam's fire spiraled through his limbs, making his hands and fingers glow molten, and he found himself smiling as he relinquished a sliver of control over to the power burning beneath his skin.

A streak of fire ripped through the night sky, punching through the man's gut like a lightning strike. Screaming. The man let out an animalistic sound as he writhed on the cobblestone driveway, gasping for air.

Cam knew his flames would cauterize those wounds nicely. The bloke would have several long, agonizing minutes before he died.

Shoving his hands in his pockets, Cam whistled as he sauntered across the courtyard. He bent over and ripped the mask from the man's face, revealing the blood pouring from the wearer's mouth. He was surprisingly young, not much older than Cam, with a mop of brown hair and a patchy mustache.

Where have I seen him? Cam scanned his memory. It was the carriage driver that the customs official had called for them when they'd first arrived at Enoch.

"I remember you." Cam cocked his head as he knelt. "Does that hurt? I should apologize, but I don't want to."

The man let out a low groan, his eyes beginning to roll back into his head.

Cam slapped him. "Don't die on me now. We have so much to talk about."

As the man's gaze came back into a glassy focus, he smiled, his teeth coated red. "W-w-we've been waiting for you."

The *modiste* owner had said something similar.

"So, I've heard." Cam trailed his finger down the man's throat, blistering the skin until it blackened and oozed, making the attacker sob. "Seeing as your time's running out, I'll get straight to the point. Who is *we?*"

"Blind." The man's voice was a shallow rasp. "You're so blind."

And just like that, he was gone. What little life that had remained in his eyes vanished between heartbeats, leaving Cam alone in the courtyard.

He took one breath, two. There wasn't time to process whatever he'd meant before a blood-curdling shriek echoed across the courtyard, coming from the house.

Julian jogged out of the entry, a limp body in his arms, at the same time as a carriage tore around from the back of the manor. As it pulled to a stop, Van Clarke jumped out of the driver's seat as Violet climbed out of the interior. When Cam caught up, he recognized the man they loaded inside—Jude Hall.

"What happened?" Cam shouldn't have asked. Blood poured from the three bullet wounds on Jude's chest, his already pale skin colorless. "Where's Annie? Reika—"

Reika. If her husband was here, where was she?

As Julian climbed back out of the carriage, Violet applied pressure to Jude's wounds, her teeth bared in exertion.

"They came through the windows." Van climbed back up to take the reins. "It was an ambush—"

"No, really?" Julian shoved him out of the way, his hands slick with dark blood as he pointed at Cam. "Help me."

There was no argument. Together, they jogged into the manor, only to be met again by that horrid screaming. When they came around the corner, Annie had Reika braced against her side, the woman's arm around her shoulder, as they struggled down the stairs.

Reika wobbled, moaning, as she gripped her stomach. "*No—*"

Cam's mind went blank. The baby . . .

"Get her in the carriage," Annie ordered, her voice like steel. "Now."

Within three movements, Julian had Reika in his arms and rushed back outside.

Now that they were alone, Annie's expression faltered, her features filling with terror, as she grabbed onto Cam's elbow. Her brands black as night. "I tried—" She sucked in a shaking gasp. "I wanted to heal him, but he made me heal the others first."

Jude.

"Good," Cam said and led her toward the courtyard. "That's what I would have done."

"I know," Annie murmured. "And that's what scares me."

CHAPTER 24
ANNIE

Jude Hall was dead.

Annie didn't need her powers to know that much. His sightless eyes stared up at her from the carriage floor. She'd wanted to save him—had begged him to let her heal his wounds, but he'd demanded she help the other wounded first. By the time she'd returned to him, it was too late. She couldn't bring the dead back to life.

Annie didn't understand why Violet insisted on holding pressure to his bullet wounds. His heart had long stopped beating. Maybe she was doing it for Reika's sake. If so, she'd misjudged Violet's capacity for kindness.

Mr. Price rode alongside Mr. Clarke in the driver's seat, gun at the ready. Cam hung out the carriage door, waves of fire encircling his body as he guarded against the threat of more attacking cultists.

Annie desperately tried to keep herself present, but the longer Reika wailed—in grief, in agony, in rage—the more her mind pulled away, to the last time she held a pregnant woman's swollen stomach between her hands. As the blood poured from between Reika's thighs, Annie couldn't remember if she was here or there—on the slaver's vessel, years ago.

"Save him," the woman had screamed—a mousy thing, maybe in her twenties—clawing at where her baby protruded from her, feet first. "Save him."

Tawny. She'd served as a scullery maid before her master traded her for a new hunting hound. Tawny had already endured a year and a half aboard the slave ship before Annie had arrived, and this was her second infant, courtesy of the men aboard.

Annie had been thirteen years old.

They were bound to leaking walls in chains, naked, as the ship reeled, tossing them about violently as Tawny screamed.

Annie gripped Tawny's stomach, sobbing, as blood poured from the woman's opening. "What do I do?"

Face steaked with tears and grime, Tawny grabbed Annie's shackled hands, forcing her to take hold of the babe's tiny, tiny ankles.

"When I push, you pull." Tawny cried out as she contracted. "Just do it."

And so Annie did—for what felt like hours.

There were other women down below with them—old women, young women—but none were close enough to help. All they could do was shout advice over each other until Annie broke down under the weight of their overlapping orders, under Tawny's screams of pain.

Annie nearly fainted when the baby finally came free, slick with blood and viscera. Only once she laid the perfect, pink-cheeked baby boy on his mother's sallow chest did Tawny's wailing cease. Her tears shifted from ones of agony to joy as she kissed the baby's slimy head.

It wasn't ten minutes later when the door swung open—

revealing their master on the other side, his head cocked as he smiled from beneath his thick, dark beard.

"Save him!" Reika's shrieks brought Annie back. As she tried to pull away, disoriented, Reika grasped her by the wrists, forcing her hands to remain on her stomach.

Reika let out a shuddering gasp, her hazel eyes harder than granite as she spat. "Save. Him."

Annie blinked. *She's not talking about Jude.* Reika knew her husband was dead. She didn't want to lose her child, too.

"I'll try." Annie matched Reika's granite with steel. *You're here, not there.* She put herself back into the bunker, imagining Reika was just another patient. "You've lost a lot of blood."

"You can't save it," Violet hissed over her shoulder, her arms coated to the elbow in red. "The baby will die no matter what you do. She's Revenant—"

"Shut your whore mouth, Violet," Reika seethed, her grip tightening to the point Annie thought her wrists might crack. She cried out again as her stomach tightened beneath Annie's palms—a contraction. "*Save him.*"

The carriage jostled, sending Violet toppling over Jude's body, but Annie managed to keep steady. She sucked in two steady breaths before letting her eyes flicker to Reika's, and she swallowed. "Stay as still as you can."

Reika nodded, bearing down, as Annie let her eyes fall closed. Her power ripped to the surface, making her fingers glow, as she fought to transfer the power into Reika's body. As it began to flow, Annie could see it.

The darkness behind her lids faded away, replaced with a vision of Reika's womb. It was there, a warm, colorful space inside a void of black. In the center, a tiny form vibrated with the intensity of its pounding heart.

It's still alive. Sweat dripped down Annie's brow. Though

the baby still lived, the walls around it were cracked, leaking fluid just like the walls of the slave ship. It was going to drown.

No. Annie pushed life into the womb, *willed* it. Her power stirred, pouring inside to staunch the cracks, but the leaking continued. Blood broke down the barrier she'd tried to form, continuing to fill the womb with death.

I don't have enough. Annie's head pounded, her own heart fluttering with exertion. There wasn't enough power left. She'd used too much of it healing the others. She pushed *harder*, demanding *more,* until there was nothing left to give. She needed more. Now. She needed more—

More. Annie's eyes snapped open. As she swiveled toward the door, Reika held tight to her wrists. Annie's lungs burned as she cried, *"Camden!"*

Outside, there were gunshots. Why were they still shooting? It didn't matter now. Annie allowed herself to scream, *"Camden!"*

Then he was there, ducking into the carriage beside her. His gun drawn, new blood splattered over his beautiful, tan face. He'd been fighting. More of those men must be attacking. His fire-bright eyes fell to the blood dripping from Reika, his skin paling. "Annie—"

Wrenching one hand free from Reika, she seized Cam's wrist. She didn't have time to explain. Later . . . later, she'd beg his forgiveness. He would forgive her for stealing from him much more easily than Reika if she let her child die. He gaped at her in shock as she murmured, "I'm sorry."

Then she slammed through the gate between them and clawed in deep. Not a crack. It was open wide. Cam's eyes rolled back into his head, his muscles going slack, and he barely managed to catch himself against the coach's bench seat.

God. She'd only allowed herself tastes before—dancing

around the absolute power she knew inhabited his being, but this . . . this was infinite. Like she'd been dumped into the center of an ocean with no beginning and no end.

There was only him, above her, below her, all around her. She felt as his fire's attention fell onto her, more curious than angry. Somehow, she knew this wasn't even the half of it. That if she chose to dive deeper, she may never reach the surface again. She'd be swallowed up by him, consumed.

Save him. Annie didn't give herself time to fear. She grabbed hold of his fire and *pulled.*

The monster inside him laughed, and her entire body *burned* as flames erupted into her veins. It ripped through all her senses, her vision going white. It took every ounce of her will to fight back to the surface, the image of Reika's womb flooding her again.

The baby—its heartbeats so faint as its paradise over-flowed with blood.

Annie exhaled, releasing waves of light careening through the void, breaking apart the darkness, until all that was left was she and the babe. Her light wove around it, through it, shooting up until it sealed shut every crack and tear inside its little world.

A sob escaped her as the baby's heartbeat fluttered back to life. She reeled as something jerked her arm once, twice—then the connection between her and Cam severed, slamming her back into her body.

Annie reeled as her vision came back into focus.

Violet had one hand on Cam's arm, the other on Annie's, her eyes wide with terror.

She pulled us apart. Annie's first instinct was to slap her, but she resisted—Reika.

The Water Brand sucked in heavy gasps, holding her stomach where it still glowed beneath her dress. She exchanged glances with Cam, who looked as stunned as she did, before turning back to Annie, her voice a soft whisper. "Y-you saved him?"

"Yes, I think so." Annie trembled as she reached for Cam. Not to take from him, but to feel him next to her. To remind her she was safe. *Well, as safe as I can be.* "You're right. He's a boy."

And it was. She'd felt it when her power touched him. Reika and Jude were going to have a son.

Reika burst into tears, wrapping her arms tighter around herself. "I knew it."

"How do you know?" Violet grabbed Annie's shoulder and shook. "What did you do?"

"I don't know," Annie said. Tears pricked at her eyes as Cam captured her hand and squeezed it, the surprise on his face shifting to reverence. She swallowed hard and repeated, "I don't know."

CHAPTER 25
ALEXANDER

Alexander ignored the burning in his lungs as he strode across the square lawn toward the Clarkes's home.

At least a dozen police horses were left with an attendant while the officers roped off the dimly lit house—now a crime scene. Twenty or so men and women—all Revenant—sat outside the main entry, monitored by an armed officer. In their evening attire, most wore varying degrees of blood splatter and grime, faces stained with tears or furious expressions as the police questioned them.

An orchestrated attack. Alexander surveyed the grounds, damp with the first drizzles of rain. *Just like the others.* The assaults were growing bolder. Within months, they'd expanded from only singular murders, disguised to look like accidents, to brazen assassinations, and now gunning down an entire party? *They're retaliating against me.*

He'd started this fight. He intended to finish it.

Alexander scowled as he flipped open his pocket watch. *Nine fifty-seven.* Without it, he'd be lost. He couldn't keep track of time anymore.

"Governor?" a voice called across the courtyard.

"Chief." Alexander glanced up to see Henry Bale approaching and shoved his watch back into his coat pocket as he kept pace toward the house. "Care why you've allowed *another* attack to happen in my city?"

"We're doing our best." Henry fell in line beside him. Dark circles plagued the younger man's eyes, his once stubbled beard now shaved into a neat goatee.

Alexander sneered. "I'm sure you have."

"You don't need to be here," Henry shot back, his pointed cap shadowing his face. "We've got it under control—"

"It seems I *must* be here, Chief Bale." Alexander's body tensed at the subtle command, the scar beneath his finger starting to itch. He stopped just outside the main entry, taking in the sitting Revenant, listening in on their conversation, their expressions a mix of awe and fear. He knew each of their faces. Their abilities and the circumstances of how they acquired them. Where they worked—or didn't. Their lineage. Their vices. They weren't responsible for this. He knew it. The Chief knew it.

Where's Camden? Alexander shifted to face Henry. "I don't enjoy making these evening visits, Bale. Not at all. But someone had the gall to make an attempt on my son's life, on *your* watch."

Henry glowered. "There's no evidence to suggest Lord Callahan was the target."

"How about we ask him?" Alexander headed into the manor, instantly hit by the stench of drying blood. "Where is he?"

When Henry didn't respond right away, Alexander swiveled, brow raised. "Where *is* he?"

Henry's mouth opened, then closed. He didn't know.

Alexander pinched the bridge of his nose. "You don't know where he's gone?"

"I—" Henry started, but was interrupted by a rough voice with a heavy Southern accent.

"They went to Waverly."

Seated on the carpeted floor was a dark-skinned boy with black ringlets, handcuffed beside a lovely young lady with vibrant red hair twisted into a tight bun.

The boy jerked his head toward the door. "He, Annie, and Julian left with the Clarkes. Took the Halls to the hospital."

Camden's quartermaster, Nathan Williams, and Jenny Duskin. Alexander had always prided himself on never forgetting a face, yet for a moment, he'd forgotten them. His sickness was getting worse. He glared at Henry. "Why are they being detained?"

"My officers arrested them." Henry's back straightened, his shoulders stiff. "This man fired at my men on approaching the home. The girl is with him."

Jenny squeaked, pushing loose strands of hair out of her face. "We didn't do anything!"

Nathan groaned in annoyance. "I already told you. I thought you were more of those masked bastards."

"Watch your mouth." Henry seethed, drawing his baton. "I'm sick of—"

"Give me the keys to their cuffs," Alexander said flatly and held out his hand. "Then leave us."

Henry blinked in surprise when he realized Alexander was talking to him. "Governor?"

"Now." Alexander let his tone drop. "Or so help me, Bale, I'll gut you where you stand."

A darkness flickered in Henry's eyes as he gave him a quick nod, tossing the keys at his feet. He whispered in Alexander's ear. "*Tick-tock,* old man. Enjoy your authority while it lasts."

With that, he strode out of the house, slamming the front door so hard the walls shook. Several hanging pictures fell, shattering as they hit the ground.

If only I could kill him. With an irritated sigh, Alexander scooped up the keys. He knelt to unlock their chains, but the Nathan boy pulled away.

"Whoa, whoa, whoa," Nathan's eyes narrowed as he positioned himself in front of Jenny. "If this is going to put us on your favor list, I'll find our own way out. I don't wanna owe you anything."

I see why Camden likes him. Alexander chuckled as he unlocked the boy's handcuffs. "Trust me, it's not your favor I'm after."

Nathan snorted, taking the keys from him to undo Jenny's cuffs. "Cam's?"

Alexander ignored his question. "What happened here?"

Nathan rubbed his bruised wrists. "Ask your chief."

"I'm asking you."

"A group of masked men attacked during the party," Jenny said. Nathan glared at her, and she just shrugged before continuing. "They killed a bunch of people before Cam, Julian, and Mr. Davis took them out. Annie healed most of the guests, but the Clarkes insisted they take the Halls to Waverly. Before they left, Mr. Price asked Nathan to keep guard over the rest of the guests. I decided to stay here with him."

Alexander gave himself a few heartbeats to process that information. What bothered him was a name he didn't recognize. "Mr. Davis?"

"Jensen Davis," Nathan replied as he stood and helped Jenny up. "Ice Brand. Kind of a prick, from what I can tell."

"Hmm." Alexander nodded, rubbing his chin. *The Ice Brand.* He'd been with Henry, and Alexander had been too distracted to follow up on his identity. *Mistakes, mistakes, and more mistakes.* He straightened and then turned for the door. "Come along. Both of you."

"Why?" Nathan bristled. "Where are we going?"

"Are all pirates so skeptical?" Alexander allowed himself to laugh, knowing the gesture would put the boy at ease. "You're coming with me to Waverly."

A short time later, Alexander burst into the hospital's back halls, sending several nurses skittering away like pill bugs at the sight of him.

Nathan and Jenny kept close behind. Their eyes were wide as they took in the state of the surgery wing. *It's a disaster.* He should have known better than to entrust so much care to the Clarkes. White paint peeled from the walls. Dark stains marred the hardwood floors. It took a lot to turn Alexander's stomach, but even he recoiled at the stench of death leaking out of the curtained side rooms.

"Clarke?" Alexander didn't hide the fury in his voice as he made his way to the second floor. It was becoming increasingly difficult to contain his anger. "Where the hell are you?"

"Would you stay *quiet*?" A pretty, young woman with brown curls peeked her head out of the door at the end of the hall, scowling—at least until she realized who she was speaking to. Her creamy skin shifted to a shade of green, as if she might faint. "G-governor Callahan?"

Violet Clarke. Alexander pushed past her. *Not the Clarke I'm looking for.*

He didn't miss the seething glare Jenny shot Violet as they passed. *Interesting.*

Inside the first room of the medical ward, the operating tables had been pushed aside to make room for a single bed.

Reika Hall lay upon it, seemingly asleep, covered in multiple thick blankets.

Annie sat on the edge of the bed, a bucket of water at her feet, as she tugged on his son's shoulder with a pair of tweezers, fresh blood spilling over his stained shirt. Camden's eyes were pinched shut, and he breathed through his teeth as he gripped the arms of his chair until his knuckles turned white, his revolver on his lap. Annie let out a relieved sigh as she extracted a bullet from his skin, letting it drop with a loud *tink* into the metal tray beside her.

"There." She wiped her damp forehead on her sleeve, smearing it with red, before laying her palm over the wound. Her hand began to glow, and by the relief on Camden's face, Alexander knew she'd healed whatever lay beneath.

He really did want to kill someone. "You were shot?"

Camden's gaze immediately snapped to his, filled with disdain. "Obviously."

"Governor?" Van Clarke's whiny tone was in Alexander's ear. He must have been right behind the door. As Alexander turned, Clarke bowed, his white apron stained with gore. "What an honor. We didn't expect you."

"A pleasure." Alexander sniffed. Though the space around Reika was clean—probably by Camden and Annie's doing—the state of the rest of the ward was abysmal. Layers of soiled bandages overflowed from a bin by the far door, reeking of pus. He now understood why Camden had so readily pledged funds for repairs. His bitterness over sending David to deliver a check to the hospital this morning faded.

Dull moans echoed from beyond the curtains separating this half of the ward from the other. Nausea made Alexander's throat tighten. The last time he'd spent any significant time here was when they'd found Cassandra's body and brought her back for examination. It had taken him years before he could set foot in Waverly again, and even then, only because there was no other option. Maybe that's why he'd allowed it to fall into such disrepair.

"Quiet," Annie hissed over her shoulder at Van, not even acknowledging Alexander's presence. "You're going to wake her. Again."

Van bit down on his lip, a layer of irritation hidden under his innocent expression. "Apologies, my lady."

Annie's eyes softened, her body visibly relaxing, when she spotted Nathan and her sister.

"Did you come here for a doctor, Pops?" Camden smirked as he ran his fingers down the barrel of his gun. "I've heard city scandals can be very stressful. Bad for your health."

The Clarkes tensed, exchanging glances.

"Not at all. I'm quite well." *He's noticed.* Alexander's eyes narrowed, and he fought against scratching the scar beneath his gloved ring finger. "Anyone whose name isn't Callahan, leave."

"Governor?" Van Clarke questioned.

"Do I need to repeat myself?" Alexander huffed. "Leave."

"Don't feel bad." Nathan patted Van's shoulder as he, too, turned to leave. "He kicked Chief Bale out earlier, too."

Violet dropped her head respectfully before sweeping out of the room, followed by her brother and Jenny Duskin.

Annie flinched, her eyes snapping between Camden and the door, questioning. *Now, why would she doubt her status?* Another interesting tidbit. When Camden didn't budge, she scooted a fraction closer to him, but stayed put.

Camden's grin widened, and he leaned back in his chair, resting his feet atop the mattress. "Nathan, stay."

Nathan paused in the doorway, eyeing Alexander wearily. "Captain?"

A power play. Alexander knew exactly what his son was doing. He'd allow it for now.

Camden stood, setting his gun beside Annie, before crossing the room. He whispered something in Nathan's ear before squeezing his quartermaster's shoulder. The boy glanced between him and Alexander one more time before giving them both a quick bow and exiting.

Alexander nodded toward where Reika slept. "Should we speak somewhere else?"

Annie smoothed her ruined evening dress as she stood, the skirts saturated in blood, and whispered. "She needs to rest. Preferably somewhere that isn't *here.*"

He got the hint. "I'll prepare a room for her at my estate."

She nodded, moving to Camden's side, and the two followed him out of the medical ward and into an adjoining staff lounge. There wasn't much for furniture besides a small, dingy table and four equally ugly chairs, but at least it was private. Alexander slid the curtain closed behind them before taking a seat at the table, crossing an ankle over the opposite knee. It would give off a stronger presence to stand, but his joints ached badly. They always did nowadays.

Steepling his fingers, he held onto his son's haughty gaze. "Are you going to tell me what you said to your quartermaster?"

Camden's brow rose. "Worried I told him a terrible secret about you?"

"I might be," Alexander sneered. "If you *knew* any of my secrets."

Camden rolled his eyes before pulling out a second chair, offering it to Annie. She sat and exhaled, a sorrowful exhaustion clinging to her like a blanket tainted with pox. She began to chew on her thumbnail before she made a face and let her hand fall onto her lap. Her fingers were coated in dried blood.

"If you must know, I told him to wait outside." Camden crossed his arms. "After our discussion here, he will be escorting Annie and Miss Jenny back to my ship."

Annie shot him a quick, nervous look but stayed quiet.

"Hmm." Alexander leaned forward onto his elbows. "And where will you be going?"

"To do your job," Camden sneered. "I don't let those who try to hurt the people I lo—care about to go unpunished. Julian Price is hunting for them now."

"How noble of you." Alexander sneered back before letting his gaze fall onto Annie. "Jude Hall?"

"Dead." She replied without hesitation, her eyes locked onto the far wall, distant. "I couldn't save him."

Sadness flickered over his son's face, not for the Halls, but for his wife.

"Is Mrs. Hall wounded?" Alexander asked.

"She—" Annie shared another quick look with Camden, one that most men would have missed. "Physically, she'll be fine, but grief takes a toll."

Truths and half-truths. Annie had played these games before. They were hiding something.

"Very well," Alexander said and stood. "I won't keep you. She isn't the only one who needs to rest."

Annie stood, as well, and gave him one of her close-lipped smiles. "Thank you, Governor."

"I'm having Chief Bale transfer the attacker's bodies to the morgue." Alexander shifted his attention to Camden. "I plan to look at them before the examiner has a chance to destroy any evidence. Care to join me?"

Camden cocked his head and scoffed. "Don't trust your employees?"

"I don't trust anyone," Alexander replied coldly.

Camden nodded. "Fine, but give us a moment."

Not a question. An order. *Good.* It was about time he started speaking like the heir of the West instead of a simple commoner.

Alexander found himself smiling as he strode out of the lounge. Over his shoulder, he caught a glimpse of Camden kneeling beside Annie. They whispered in a rushed tone, arguing. When she noticed Alexander watching them, she moved in close enough that her cheek brushed against Camden's as they spoke.

Alexander stepped back into the medical ward and tied back his shoulder-length hair. In the bed, Reika had rolled onto her side, tucking one of the pillows against her chest, her vibrant blue brands stark in the dim light.

Jude Hall is dead. He'd liked the Air Brand. He was sorry to hear that the man was gone. He'd prepare a room in the manor for Reika. Maya would be happy to care for her. She often grew lonely with it being only her and Kai at home.

But who is this Jensen Davis? Alexander wasn't willing to admit to Camden that he'd made an error. He should have known every person attending that party. He rubbed his stiff knuckles, the ache spreading through them running deep into his bones. *I've gotten sloppy.*

Not only that, but his thoughts were growing muddier as the months wore on. He was running out of time.

"Governor?"

Alexander twisted to see Violet's face peering through the door. He forced a smile. "Miss Clarke."

"I'm sorry to interrupt." She opened the door wider, tone hushed. "I wanted to catch you before you left."

He slid past her into the hall. The last thing he wanted was to wake Reika. "Speak, then."

"Thank you, Governor." Violet gave a quick curtsy. She was doing an extraordinary job of acting concerned as she said, "I thought you should know—along with the loss of her husband, Mrs. Hall almost lost her child." Violet's eyes flickered up to his from under her thick lashes. "I know Lord and Lady Callahan are too modest to admit to saving her baby's life, but I thought you should know."

So, that's what they're hiding. Alexander wanted to laugh, wanted to scream, wanted to strangle Violet Clarke for being an advantageous witch of a woman that unknowingly confirmed Alexander's every fear and hope since he first saw Camden and Annie together, when he'd noticed the way they'd reacted when their hands had touched when they'd first come to the estate.

"Thank you, Miss Clarke. They are too modest." How Camden knew to keep this from him . . . *either it's a coincidence, or he suspects more than I thought.* Alexander cleared his throat and continued. "Who else knows about this? I shouldn't want to embarrass them with gloating over their heroics."

"Just Van and me." Violet dropped her gaze to the ground. "And Mrs. Hall, of course. Possibly Mr. Price."

Too many. Alexander bowed to her before striding toward the morgue to wait for Camden. *I'm running out of time.*

CHAPTER 26

CAMDEN

The last place in this God-forsaken city Cam wanted to be was in the *morgue* with his father. At least Annie would be safe on *The Elaina* with Nathan. Thirty minutes later, after seeing them off, he'd started his descent into the lower levels of the hospital. The deeper he traveled, the more thick, yet frigid, the air became—clogged with the stink of death and rubbing alcohol.

Annie. His mind was a mess. He didn't want to be here. He wanted to be with *her.* Cam ran a hand through his hair, his finger catching in the dried blood clinging to the strands.

She'd kissed him—hard—twice. Like she'd wanted him, like she'd cared. He was afraid to give himself the hope of that being true, but he couldn't shake the feeling that it hadn't been about teaching Violet a lesson. Annie had been jealous. Just like he'd been envious at the way Jensen Davis's eyes had wandered over her for too long, like she was a prize to be claimed.

She is mine. He can't have her. It's not up to you. Cam shook the thoughts away. His fire had been calm until that encounter.

Now it was writhing beneath his skin, digging at him, begging to be set loose, despite what Annie had taken from him in the carriage.

If you kill him, he can't have her. I can't think like this. Cam shuddered, and the movement made him slip on the damp, concrete steps. He caught himself against the wall, scraping his fingers. Rushed, whispered voices echoed up the staircase—his father and Henry Bale.

Bale. Cam stilled, quieting his breathing. Nathan mentioned that Henry had arrived at the Clarkes's not long after they'd left. Which shouldn't be odd—he *was* the police chief—but he'd been arguing with Cam's father at the previous murder scene as well. Now, here they were. Arguing. Again.

"You knew he'd be there, didn't you?" Henry's tone was low and angry. "*Didn't* you?"

"I wasn't even aware the Clarkes were hosting a gathering." A lie. There was the creak of leather as Alexander clenched his gloved fists. "Isn't that your job?"

"Bull," Henry spat. "The others may trust you, governor, and you may have them convinced that your son's interferences are all part of the plan, but I know better. I'm running out of patience."

Cam's eyes narrowed. Of course, his father had a plan. It shouldn't have surprised him, but he hated not having all the information.

"Your impatience means nothing to me," Alexander said. "Your hands are tied, Henry."

"For now," Bale hissed, and heavy bootsteps thundered toward the staircase.

Blazes. Cam straightened, grabbing the railing, as he jogged down the last few steps. He nearly collided with an enraged Henry Bale. A vein throbbed in the chief's temple, and he shot

Cam a vicious glare before swiveling toward Alexander, slamming his cap back on his head.

"Case in point. I'll be making a report. Good night, Governor." He turned back to Cam and gave a slight bow. "My lord."

Cam watched with a smirk as Henry stormed up the staircase and out of the morgue. Above them, a metal door slammed shut.

Alexander crossed his arms tightly over his chest, brows raised. "How much of that did you hear?"

"As much as you wanted me to, I imagine." Cam shrugged. "I don't think he likes me . . . or you."

Alexander laughed. "That's it? No questions? I'm disappointed."

Oh, I have questions. I'm just not ready to ask them. Cam ignored him for the moment, instead taking in the long, narrow room. A wide, rolling door was propped open, leading into a dark hall on the opposite side—the body shoot. The tunnel likely led to the street outside. The morgue's sheet-metal walls reflected the dim, yellow glow of the gas-lit sconces, which also illuminated the steel operating tables lining the room's length.

Corpses—dozens of them—were laid out over the tables. The masked men, in varying states of mutilation. No Revenants.

Cam tsked. "So, you gave criminals priority seating over your own citizens? And here I thought you couldn't stoop any lower."

"They're dead," Alexander said sharply, frowning. "They don't have an opinion anymore. We'll bring them in later."

"And the Clarkes? I'm sure they'd like their home back."

"They can sleep at the hospital."

Heartless. Cam made a face as he wandered over to the nearest operating table. *Ah.* He let out a short laugh. The man whom he'd blown a hole through. His fire stirred at the memory, flickering at his fingertips, as if asking to do it again. He grabbed the man's chin, tipping his face toward him.

It is the carriage driver. He was sure of it.

Alexander stepped closer, still squeezing his arms over his chest. "You know him?"

"I might." Cam shrugged again. He might have imagined it, but he swore there was a slight rattle in his father's breathing. "Or maybe I don't. Depends on what you were discussing with the chief. You wanted me to overhear you, just like you wanted me to overhear your argument at the apartments."

Alexander smiled. "I'm relieved to hear you've been paying attention."

"Now, here comes the part where I'm supposed to guess what you want." Cam stepped around the table to examine the next body. Without the mask, this man was older than the first, with greying hair and wrinkles around his eyes. Black blood dribbled from the corner of his bruised mouth.

Black blood.

What the hell. Cam's brows furrowed as he leaned closer. Not only was the blood a true, coal black—it *stank*. Like sewage with a hint of boiled cabbage. But he'd seen the men bleed? When he'd stabbed them, shot them. They'd bled red.

Alexander finally dropped his arms before he stepped around to the opposite side of the table.

Cam scanned over the line of corpses—they were all the same. Black blood leaked from their wounds, eyes, mouths, noses, and ears. Even the veins visible beneath their skin had turned black—exactly how Frank Boyle had looked when Annie had absorbed the life from him.

Blazes. Cam's heart sputtered. He grabbed the dead man's left wrist, turning it over. A small, black phoenix was tattooed on the underside of his ring finger, at the base. Just like Elias

Bennett, Frank Boyle, and Charlotte Duskin. Just like the symbol of Elias's ring. He'd suspected The Order was behind the attack, but all of them were members, not just hired thugs.

Cam glanced up at him. "Is this it?"

Alexander cocked his head. "You tell me."

"The Order." Cam straightened slowly, grateful to get his face away from the rotten vegetable stench. "They killed James Kline and were behind tonight's attack. Easy enough." He thought for a moment. "And I imagine the reason Henry hid the finger that Annie pulled from James's throat is the same reason you keep letting me stumble upon your conversations."

Alexander winced as he shoved his hands in his pants pockets. "Now you're catching on."

"Don't trust the chief?"

"As I've said before," Alexander replied. "I don't trust anyone."

"Is he part of The Order?" Cam stepped around to the following table. The third attacker had the same tattoo. "He looks the part with the creepy mustache and all."

"Henry Bale—" Alexander tensed, like he couldn't get the words out, as Cam examined the fourth attacker. He changed the subject. "The Order has infiltrated every organization in Enoch—and most of the known world, for that matter. Everyone knows it, but no one can pinpoint them to a specific location or leader. If they've done that, they have people in the Enoch police department."

This is bigger than I thought. Cam had hoped, coming back to Enoch, he'd be able to avenge his mother, eliminate the threat to him and Annie, then leave. Find somewhere far away to start a new life. But if The Order had people everywhere . . .

There's nowhere we can go that we'll be safe. He could accept a life on the run. Hell, he'd spent his *entire* life two steps away from death, but Annie . . . she deserved better. These men had taken her family away from her, her childhood. *Not to mention her life. And yours.*

Cam swallowed, his jaw clenched, as Alexander began to pace.

"Chief Bale knows I'm withholding information." Alexander shot Cam a look, making sure he was paying attention. "I need you on my side, Camden. I need you watching and observing . . ." He paused, his eyes growing dark. "In case I'm not here anymore before your mother's death is avenged."

"Avenge my mother," Cam stated, the words lighting anger in him like a match. "*You killed her.*"

"*They* killed her." Alexander wheeled, pointing at him, expression seething. "Because I said no. Your mother begged me not to send you away, even after I'd made the deal with Elias. I changed my mind. I told them no, and they killed her."

"And you're *still* lying." Cam's entire body shook, his words barely audible. "You honestly expect me to believe that? God, she *ran* from you! You can delude yourself all you want, but Mother is dead. Because of *you.*"

Alexander's hand went to his chest again, squeezing, as he shook his head. "You don't understand."

"Of course, I don't." Cam turned for the stairway. He had to leave before he did something he'd regret. "And you're just going to drag me along with more cryptic hints and riddles. I don't have time for this. I have a bed calling my name, and my shoulder is as stiff as hell."

"Insolence," Alexander growled.

When Cam wheeled, fire sparked into embers across the floor. His father's aloof mask had vanished.

"It's been a terrible trait you've carried since childhood," Alexander said, deliberately slow. "You've never taken the time to see what's *directly* in front of you."

"Being a murderous back stabber isn't a lovely trait either,

I've heard." *Kill him. Turn him to dust,* his fire purred inside him. Cam inhaled slowly. *I can't kill him yet.* "But you've seemed to master it."

Alexander sighed. "Camden—"

"Father," Cam interrupted.

"For pity's sake." Alexander rubbed his face, the dim light making the strands of grey in his long, sandy hair stand out. "I'm trying to help you."

"Help me?" Rage flared so hot in Cam's chest it nearly choked him. "If I recall, you said the same thing when you were beating me bloody—"

Alexander looked like he might punch him. "We're not talking about that."

"No?" Cam stepped into his father's face, their noses nearly touching. "Do you tell Kai the same thing? How about we talk about that—"

This time, Alexander did punch him—square in the jaw.

Every nerve in Cam's body recoiled, plagued by the endless memories of *pain, pain pain*—but none came.

Alexander hit him, and Cam felt nothing but the edges of his father's knuckles against his skin.

Because he was Revenant now.

And his father was mortal, and sick, and weak, and couldn't hurt him anymore.

They just stared at each other as Alexander's eyes grew wide.

"How embarrassing." Cam pushed his father's hand away. "I'm surprised The Order hasn't done away with you already."

"You need to trust me." Alexander's breaths were ragged. "Listen. If not for yours, or your mother's, for Annie's sake."

"You see, now I need you to listen." Cam's fingers glowed molten, singeing the fabric of Alexander's coat as he plucked a bit of lint from his shoulder. He pressed down hard enough to burn down to the skin, making Alexander jerk in pain. Cam leaned in, smiling as he whispered, "Pretend that you know what's best for my wife again, and I'll burn you alive and toss your ashes into the street for the beggars to trample."

Alexander didn't budge as Cam turned for the stairs. He only glanced back long enough to relish the fear on the governor's face before he left the morgue behind.

CHAPTER 27
ANNIE

*A*nnie sighed in relief as she closed the door to the captain's quarters behind her, the latch falling in place with a satisfying *clink.*

I'm done. She wasn't thrilled about being back on *The Elaina,* but the throbbing ache in her lower back hadn't let up. The events of the night had left her exhausted in a way more than bodily—her soul was ragged.

Jude was dead. Reika would wake up alone, in that reeking room, to find that her entire world had been destroyed.

Not completely. The baby is still alive. Annie glanced down at her hands as she dragged herself deeper into the bedroom. Her brands still shone pearly white, where the essence of Cam's power bled into hers, becoming her own. It would be easy to take the credit, but *they'd* saved that child. She couldn't have done it without him.

Propping herself against the bed, Annie's fingers were clumsy and stiff as she undid the buttons on her ruined gown. Cold, sticky blood—soaked into the fabric—stuck to her skin as she let the gown fall to the floor. It landed with a hard thud. Her boots weren't any easier to remove.

Annie hissed, bent over, as a jolt of pain shot through her stomach. *Lord, what was in Magnus's tea?* Clutching her abdomen, Annie hobbled into the bathroom. Even her feet were swollen and throbbing. A bath—that's what she needed. A hot bath and a long night's sleep.

Camden. Annie's breath hitched as she twisted on the hot water to fill the bathtub. She should *never* have touched him, shouldn't have let him touch *her,* but she couldn't bring herself to regret it.

Many men had kissed her. She'd experienced the hateful, angry force of their lips against hers as they readied to tear her apart—and she'd hated it. Hated it more than the ensuing violations because she couldn't pretend—couldn't picture herself somewhere else—when their tongues were shoved down her throat. But this had been different. When she'd kissed Cam, it was because she'd *wanted* to, and there was nowhere in the entire universe where she'd rather have been than there. Right there. With him.

Stop it. She was so glad that the ship had plumbing. Annie rolled her shoulders, inhaling as swirls of steam curled up from the hot water filling the tub. *You're no better than they are.*

All those men—they'd wanted to be where they were, too. Violating her. Removing, piece by piece, every last shred of dignity she had left in her body. Who were you when you were nothing but an empty shell? No one. That's what they'd made her, and she'd cut her own throat before she did the same to Cam. He was someone—special—and foolish enough to let a rotten creature like her close enough to hurt him.

Annie jolted back to attention as the water rose high enough to brush against her fingertips. She wiped her eyes before stripping off her stockings and undergarments, letting them fall to the tile floor. As she gripped the edge of the tub, about to climb in, another crippling wave of pain made her entire back and stomach clench.

"*Blazes.*" Annie exhaled, trembling. *What's wrong? Did I eat something? Did I—*

A trickle of something hot ran down her inner thigh. She looked down. A trail of red stained her leg—blood.

Why am I bleeding? Annie's fingers shook so badly she barely managed to touch her thigh, reaching between her legs. The blood was coming from *there.* Why? It had been over a year since the last time she'd been hurt. Why—

No. No. No. Annie's eyes widened as she rubbed her fingertips together. The back and stomach pain. The fatigue. *It's my cycle—*

No. No. No. She scrambled to the mirror and wiped the fog away. The horror clawing through snapped fully into place as she scanned over her naked body. Now that she looked—truly looked—her breasts and hips had filled out, not large by any means, but enough that she was beginning to look like the young woman she was. Her cheeks had rounded, no longer pointy and gaunt. God, she'd been too busy noticing how Jenny was maturing to see how much *she'd* changed. She'd forgotten the first rule they'd taught her.

Annie crumpled to the floor, raking her hands through her sticky hair. They'd warned her—a thousand times. Two thousand. They'd warned her, and warned her, and warned her, and she'd forgotten.

The memories came rushing back, smothering her.

The door swung open—revealing their master on the other side, his head cocked as he smiled from beneath his thick, dark beard.

Tawny's eyes grew so round, Annie thought they'd pop out of her head. The master scanned over the two of them, both naked and soaked in blood—Tawny's blood. As he strolled toward them, he tucked his hands behind his back, beginning to laugh. He tutted. "I forgot you were due."

"Get away." Tawny clutched her babe so tightly it was a miracle she didn't suffocate him. "Not this one. GET AWAY."

The master only laughed. "Hand him over. We can't afford another mouth to feed."

"She feeds him!" Annie's voice sounded strangled as she pointed to Tawny's full breasts. "You don't have to pay for anything."

The other women turned away, shoving their faces into the corner, as the master made a face and squinted. "I'll rephrase that. I don't want another mouth to feed."

Tawny wept into her baby's sticky, wispy tufts of hair.

Annie crawled, clinging to the master's boots. "Get rid of me, then. He eats less. Get rid of me and let him live."

At this point, dying would be a welcome reprieve. Annie had wanted to die since her father and brothers had been taken from her, but she'd been too much of a coward to do it herself. She'd gladly, and selfishly, trade herself for the babe.

"Hmm." The master bent over, grabbing her chin.

Tears streamed down Annie's cheeks as he inspected her face. Finally, he smiled, revealing a mouthful of brown, rotten teeth. "No deal."

Tawny's weeping turned to wails. She scratched, clawed, begged, and screamed as the master ripped that boy from her arms. There was no pause or show. The master merely yanked open the rounded port window and tossed the babe outside to the waves.

Annie's entire being narrowed down to that window. Her breath random tugs and pulls of air without rhythm.

The master left. Tawny screamed.

For days and days, she screamed until the fever took her away, too.

She'd forgotten the only rule Tawny had ever given her.

What she'd made Annie promise before she'd taken her last breaths—

"Eat only a quarter of what's given." Tawny's rattle reeked of death. Annie sobbed as the woman brushed her fingers over her matted hair. "Your blood won't come if you have no flesh on your bones." At that, Tawny raised her chin, forcing her to hold her glassy stare. "Let them kill your body. But with a babe, they can kill your soul. They'll make you love them. They'll destroy you, over and over, just to watch you break. Promise me, my little. Don't let them kill your soul."

Jude made Reika love him. He put a baby in her, and now he was gone.

Annie climbed into the bath, the sobs escaping her so strongly that they shook the tub.

She'd forgotten.

Camden had made her forget.

But she'd never forget again.

CHAPTER 28
CAMDEN

The rain poured relentlessly as Cam walked the long distance between Waverly and Enoch's harbor, making him wonder if it had a personal vendetta against him.

Despite being soaked, water sloshing inside his boots, Cam couldn't bring himself to stop one of the passing coaches. Not while his fire continued to cut through his mind like jagged glass, slicing his thoughts into scattered bits of ribbon. He needed to think and have the space to do so without stressing that he'd burn something to the ground.

Only the hazy, orange glow of his brands illuminated the empty, cobbled lane leading to the harbor. The streetlamps had long been extinguished, but he didn't need them. The dark was a comfort, and despite a decade away, he knew every inch of Enoch. Every alley, every hole-in-the-wall pawn shop, drug den, affluent neighborhood, and every tiny, useless detail his father had forced him to memorize about this damn city.

"The West will be yours," Alexander Callahan said as he led Cam, *only eight years old, into his office. He was never allowed in*

there. Cam swallowed, picking at his lip, as Alexander spread a large map over his desk and pinned the corners down with books.

Using a pen, Alexander tapped a random spot on the map, near the northern city gates, leading out toward the pine forests. "Tell me about this location."

Warily, Cam leaned forward to peer at the map, scanning through his memory as if he were reviewing a file folder. "That's where the Bales keep their hunting lodge. Family, friends, and personal invitations only."

"Good." Alexander gave him a rare smile. Lately, all he did was scream at him. His father tapped a second location, further west in the forested regions, about three hundred miles outside Enoch's city limits. "And here?"

Cam blinked at the map, the pen's ink leaking into the parchment. "The . . . Embassy building?"

Alexander frowned. "Why did you hesitate?"

"Because I don't know why you're asking." Cam dared to respond. "We were there last month."

"And you'll be there again. And again. And again." Alexander crouched to eye-level, and Cam flinched, making his father's scowl widen. He straightened Cam's tie. "As governor, your responsibilities will lie far beyond Western shores. Remember that. The entirety of The Four Corners will look to you for strength and guidance."

Cam's heart sank. "What if I don't want to be governor?"

Alexander graced him with another small smile. "In that, my son, you have no choice."

The heavy, kelp-laden scent of seawater snapped Cam back to attention. As he stepped out from a side street, the city peeled back to reveal the open ocean, the pebbled beach just on the other side of a paved courtyard. He was only a mile or two from where *The Elaina* was docked, but he wasn't ready to go back . . . not just yet.

Cam crossed the courtyard and stepped onto the beach, the

rocks beneath his feet slick and speckled white with barnacles. A strong breeze whipped his hair over his face, stinging his eyes. Closing them, he inhaled, letting the sea *fill* him, letting it take him back to a time when all he had to worry over was where his next meal would come from and if he'd be stabbed in the night.

I knew I recognized the name Bale. Cam let his eyes flicker open, listening to the angry waves crash onto the shore. The Bales had been in Enoch when he was a child. Mr. and Mrs. Bale used to come to his mother's parties. Henry had been older and mostly ignored him.

Cam was surprised he'd forgotten them, honestly. He hated to admit it, but he'd clung to his father's every word as a child. Absorbed them. *Worshipped* them. Because . . . because he'd hoped if he'd been able to listen, to never miss a detail, his father would be proud of him—love him—but despite all of Cam's best efforts, they'd always return to the same blasted cycle.

Alexander would expect too much, and when Cam couldn't meet his expectations. He'd rebel instead to spite him, and as badly as it hurt, punishment was better than being ignored.

Cam's entire body began to vibrate as his fire flared up. The raindrops burst into steam before ever touching him. He groaned, scrubbing at his damp face until it felt raw. *I need to use it. I've got to get rid of this. I need—*

Annie. He needed Annie.

Not to drain this power away, but just to talk to her. To hear her low voice and let it tether him back to the earth.

His fire curled around his fists without his consent, the flames spiraling up his arms, over his shoulders, until his entire body was engulfed in it. A high-pitched ringing made the air tremble. Cam could barely breathe over the fire clogging his throat.

The water. Gasping, Cam inched toward the ocean, letting the waves spill over his boots. As he waded deeper, up to his waist, his chest, the ringing turned to screaming as his fire fought against the freezing sea. He sucked in as deep a breath as his lungs could manage, ready to submerge himself. *Better to roast a ton of fish than half the city.*

He closed his eyes and dropped, letting go just as the water was about to cover his head. *Finally.*

An amused voice called over the waves. "I wouldn't do that."

"Blazes." Cam scrambled up at the same time that his fire erupted. A wall of flames, the size of a warship, slammed into the shore, followed by a stream of curses. An unnatural wind crashed into the wall, sending up a storm of smoke and embers, and swung it far enough left that Julian managed to dodge out of its path.

Brick and mortar exploded into the sky as his fire took out a line of abandoned shops along the shoreline.

Cam's breath came in heavy gasps as he waded toward the shore. "What were you thinking?"

Breathing just as heavily, Julian propped himself up, gazing up at the plumes of heavy black smoke spiraling up into the storm clouds. He wiped at the layer of soot coating his face, but only managed to smear it. "The authorities will be on their way to investigate that soon, I imagine."

"We should leave then, aye?" Once on shore, Cam plopped down onto the rocks and pulled off his boots, dumping out the seawater. "And why shouldn't I have done that?"

"Because that's what could happen." Julien let out a rough laugh as he stood, attempting to brush the sand off his trousers. "You still lack control."

"I've been training with you." Cam glared as he laced his

boots back on and slicked wet hair off his face. "I don't know what else you want from me."

"An hour, here and there, in the mornings isn't enough," Julian said, and offered him a hand. Cam took it, and Julian pulled him up.

"We need to see Mr. Baxter again." Julian wrapped himself tighter into his coat, his silver brands stark against the backdrop of the stormy sky. "More time, more dedication—"

"I don't have time for Magnus Baxter," Cam growled as he hopped back onto the street. "Especially now that The Order is killing Revenants in their own homes."

"And when you can't defend yourself—" Julian made sure he caught Cam's eye before continuing—"or Annie, because you can't wield your fire properly? Will you make time on your schedule for training then?"

Cam closed his eyes and resisted the urge to punch the man in the face again. He hated that Julian was right. He opened them again just as he focused his fire into a blade, just as he had at the Clarkes's residence. Julian's eyes widened as Cam twirled his fire dagger between his fingers.

"Is this good enough for you?" Cam never broke stride as he tossed the flaming knife to Julian. The Air Brand jerked out of the way, but the dagger fizzled out before it hit the ground.

Julian stopped and gaped at him. "You can do that, but can't manage to contain a blasted fireball?"

Cam just shrugged and strode further down the street. "I don't feel like arguing, Jules. Can we talk about something else? Did you find the surviving attackers?"

"No," Julian replied, lowering his tone. Despite the late hour, there were more citizens out and about as they grew closer to the center of the harbor. Dock workers most likely. Julian continued, "Despite the sloppiness of their assault tonight, they're organized. They were ready to vanish without a trace. What I don't think they were ready for was us to fight back."

"Why wouldn't they?" Cam thought about that as they wove through the market stalls in the wharf. "And why were you, that Davis plod, and I the only Revenant there that knew how to fight?"

"Truth?" Julian's brow rose as he raised the hood of his coat. "Since the Revenant laws went into place in the West—eighty or so years ago, thanks to my brother—allowing our kind full rights, the Revenants in this corner have grown lazy. There's a reason the West has the highest concentration of Revenant. Power means nothing if you don't know how to wield."

"Way to plug in another reminder." Cam rolled his eyes, but again, Julian was right. He saw it first-hand. All those Revenants . . . Reika, Jude . . . they'd gotten shot down like cattle because they'd become complacent. Comfortable. They'd expected their governor and Enoch's police force to protect them, which was a joke. In his condition, he doubted his father could defend anyone.

That's another matter entirely. Cam chewed his lip as they crossed the gangplank onto *The Elaina.* Several crewmen greeted them, and Cam smiled and nodded in response. Once on the deck, he stopped and faced Julian. "We'll search again tomorrow?"

Julian simply nodded, turning to head for his quarters below. There was more to discuss—the conversation Cam overheard between his father and Henry, the black veins and blood coming from the survivors, but he wanted to talk to Annie first.

As much as Alexander *claimed* to be helping him, and despite all his preaching about wanting revenge for his wife's death, Cam suspected that Alexander was involved with the events happening *now*. He could lie all he wanted about his involvement a decade ago—he was delusional—but there was something deeper happening. He'd admitted that he wished Cam to overhear the arguments, but for whatever stupid reason, he wanted Cam to piece together a puzzle instead of just telling him outright.

And if anyone could see through his father's lies, it was Annie.

Annie had been . . . incredible, saving Reika's child like that. The way she kept a clear head in the midst of chaos. Every day, even when it didn't seem possible, he grew more in awe of her.

God. The simple memory of her siphoning from him made his body tighten in places he wished it wouldn't. In the carriage, in Magnus's lab . . .

The sensation of being weak beneath her beautiful, dainty hands—of releasing his constant struggle to control—was the most exhilarating feeling he'd ever experienced.

And neither time had he wanted her to stop. He'd have given it all to her if she'd only asked.

Candlelight illuminated the windows of the captain's quarters, flickering softly behind the closed curtains.

She's awake. Cam grinned. Annie never fell asleep before smothering her candles. Though he'd hoped she'd be resting, he was secretly grateful she was still up. He wasn't sure if he'd been able to sleep without seeing her and having visual proof she'd made it back to the ship in one piece.

She kissed me. Cam fought away the giddiness filling him as he knocked on her door. He just needed to see her, then he'd go to bed. They could talk tomorrow if she was tired—

The captain's door swung open, and Cam recoiled at the death stare waiting for him on the other side. Annie glared up at him, her eyes swollen and shadowed. Her expression cold, empty, and filled with the same level of hate she'd shown him when they'd first laid eyes on each other on Lord Duskin's porch.

"A-Annie?" Cam backed a step, losing feeling in his limbs. *No, no, no. Something's wrong.*

She continued to stare, emotionless. "Can I help you?"

"What happened?" He scanned her for injuries. She *seemed* fine, physically, but . . . "Are you alright?"

"Nothing happened." Annie closed the door until she was peering through a crack. "Now, do you need something?"

I can't breathe. Something happened. Someone hurt her, or—

Cam's eyes *burned.* "Um . . . can I . . . can I stay—"

"No." She slammed the door before he could finish his sentence.

Annie didn't speak to him the next day.

Or the day after that.

Or the day after that.

He didn't know how to exist anymore.

CHAPTER 29
ANNIE

"This is healing well." Annie gently rubbed a salve over the scabbed wound on Reika's wrist. "A few more weeks and it will be gone completely."

Reika nodded her thanks, inspecting the clean linen. It had been a week since Jude's death, and she already looked gaunt and sickly. As promised, Alexander had provided her with a room in the Callahan Manor. She hadn't wanted to go back to her apartments across the city, not yet. Annie didn't blame her. *Too many memories.*

With Cam and Julian busy searching the city for the men from The Order, Annie had spent the last few days either tending to Reika or to the patients in Waverly. With the repairs to the hospital underway and more rooms becoming available, conditions had already begun to improve. Many of the sick lingering in The Greens had been able to come in for treatment. She'd attended to them herself. Mr. Maynard had visited her twice just to thank her.

With all the busyness, Annie wished more than ever that she had someone to talk to. Cam had tried so many times to speak to her, and every time she'd shut him down. Two days ago, he had begun to avoid her. Nathan wouldn't even look at her. Jenny had confronted her about her change in behavior, but Annie couldn't find the words to make her understand, so now her sister was avoiding her, too.

Annie's eyes burned as she packed her supplies in her kit. She *missed* Cam—missed him to the point that the longing was fighting to override her fear, but it was better this way. Safer. Being alone was easier than feeling.

"You look terrible."

Annie straightened on the edge of the bed, wincing at the dull ache lingering in her lower back. At least her cycle had finally passed. She raised a brow at Reika. "You look worse. Have you been eating?"

Reika snorted, stroking her swollen belly, her turquoise blue brands flaring. "Have you?"

She hadn't.

"Eat." Annie stood abruptly, smoothing her skirts as she grabbed her kit. "The baby can't survive without nutrients. Neither can you."

As she turned to leave, Reika grabbed her hand, gently rubbing her thumb over Annie's knuckles. Despite the sorrow haunting her features, that spark in her hadn't waned. "He's alive because of you. Don't look so glum."

He's alive. Annie glanced at Reika's stomach. Her power reached out, feeling for the life growing inside Reika's womb. He was still there—vibrant, joyful, calm. Yes, *this* babe was still living, but what about Tawny's? He was at the bottom of the sea. She hadn't saved him. She hadn't saved Mr. Hall, either.

She pulled her hand away. It hurt to swallow. "Jude isn't."

"Jude *is*." Reika rubbed her stomach again, her tone low and loving. "He'll wear his father's name well. He's strong. Just like him, and you."

It took everything Annie had not to bolt. "If you say so."

"I'm going home today." Reika fluffed her pillows before settling into a more comfortable position. "I hope you'll still come visit."

"Of course." Annie gave her a brief smile before she strode to the door. As she twisted the doorknob, Reika spoke again. "Annie?"

She turned to find the Water Brand studying her with a stern expression. A thin band of silver lined Reika's eyes. "You are my friend. Don't forget that."

Friend. Annie tried to suck in a breath, but it wouldn't come. So instead, she just nodded and rushed out into the hallway.

Friend. Friend. Friend. The brisk *clip-clack* of Annie's booted heels echoed through the manor's empty halls. *Camden called me his friend, too.* Both of them were fools for choosing to associate with someone as filthy as her. *She* was a fool for thinking she could become anyone else and for allowing herself to grow complacent and begin to hope.

That wasn't true. She hadn't just *begun* to hope. The hope had grown without her consent, its vines and thorns weaving into her spirit. For a moment, she'd allowed herself to believe in the possibility that Cam could be hers. *Hers.*

And that thought alone proved that she didn't deserve him. The master called his slaves *his.* Lord Duskin called her *his.*

Annie choked back tears as she rushed down the staircase toward the main entry. She'd allowed herself to forget that she was as evil as they were—*are.* She didn't know if her master was still alive.

In these weeks, she'd shifted from the prey to predator and was already trying to lay claim to another human being. No, it was better this way. As badly as she wanted him, she'd stay away—for his sake.

"Annie?"

This time, when Annie turned, she found Maya staring at her as she walked toward the main entry. She wore a white and pink floral day dress, a yellow wide-brimmed hat set over her inky-black hair, and a frilled parasol rested over her shoulder.

Her dark eyes scanned over Annie's face before she broke out in a weak smile. "Heading out already? How is Mrs. Hall today?"

"She isn't eating." Annie gave her a quick curtsy, using the time to compose herself. "She needs to eat."

"Grief has a way of stealing our appetites." Maya looped her elbow through Annie's, leading her out toward the courtyard. "She'll come around."

"She doesn't have time for that." Annie squinted as sunlight reflected off the puddles of rainwater pooled between the cobblestones. It was the first truly nice day they'd had since arriving in Enoch. Even the breeze was warm. Across the courtyard, her carriage waited for her, ready to drive her back to *The Elaina*. A weight settled in Annie's gut. She didn't want to go back, but she didn't want to remain here, either. Maybe she'd return to the hospital before—

"Come." With a firm tug, Maya led Annie onto a white-gravel path, heading toward the western wing of the estate grounds. Annie didn't fight. Maya continued to chatter as they walked—about the weather, about the exotic flowers she wished to order, about the stress of the recent attacks. The path continued until they entered a lovely garden, filled with archways woven with the white blooms of autumn clematis. Beds overflowing with giant sunflowers, vivid red mums, and violet salvia enclosed them.

She's lonely, too. Annie peeked at the older woman. She hadn't stopped talking since they'd left the manor. How often did she have company besides her son and David? The governor didn't often seem to be home. He was gone today, though she didn't know where. Maybe he was hunting the killers with Cam and Mr. Price.

Camden. Annie's breath hitched. She didn't want to think about him. She inhaled, interrupting Maya. "Where's Kai?"

"Kai?" Maya paused and blinked before her eyes dropped to the ground. "He's studying with David."

"David's a teacher?" Annie gestured to the chipped, white bench to their right. "I thought he was your butler?"

"David is many things." Maya removed her shawl and laid it over the bench, allowing them to sit without getting wet. "But he plays seven instruments. Kai has grown fond of the piano."

"I can't see Camden playing an instrument," Annie said before she could stop herself, but the hungry way Maya listened made her continue. She sat beside her, clearing her throat. "He can't sit still that long."

Maya tucked her foot beneath her, removing her hat, and reclining her neck to let the sun beat on her face. "Everyone has their strengths and weaknesses."

Annie nodded, folding her hands over her lap. Over the last several days, her brands had darkened to a glittering black. "Some have more weaknesses than strengths."

"I disagree," Maya replied, basking in the sunlight. "I think weaknesses are just easier to linger on."

Annie didn't respond. She kept her gaze fixed on the water dripping off the end of a broad, sunflower leaf. She choked up again as the droplet finally rolled over the edge and splattered on the rocks below.

"You're troubled," Maya said, not a question, eyes still closed. "I know what it's like to be forced into a strange, new country. It's been nearly a decade, and I'm still not sure if I've fully settled into Enoch."

Annie fought back a laugh. "I hated the South. This country is the least of my concerns." A thought struck her then, and she shifted toward Maya. "You are not from the West?"

Maya shielded her eyes and smiled, making the corners of her upturned eyes crinkle. "The North."

"Really? What part?"

"Sleetfield," Maya replied.

"Ah," Annie nodded. She thought she recognized Maya's slight accent. Sleetfield was the capital of the North, and about five hundred miles from Annie's father's hunting cabin. "I am from Rouenn."

"You've come a long way," Maya said. "My brother used to love fishing for cod in the seas around Rouenn."

"Who is your brother?"

Maya's lips pursed. "Someone important. Important enough that he traded me for the governor's favor."

Oh. That explains a lot. Maya's marriage to Alexander Callahan was likely a chess move, not unlike Richard and Charlotte Duskins's. No wonder the governor remarried so quickly. *But Kai?* What would become of the governor's second son now that Cam had returned to Enoch?

That's not my concern. She didn't plan to stick around long enough to know.

"I'm sorry," Annie said, and meant it. "I know what it's like to have your choices taken away from you. At least you have Kai, now."

"Yes," Maya smiled sadly. "I have Kai, and I would do anything for him." She reached out and squeezed Annie's elbow. "I've heard the whispers. Your and Camden's marriage was also arranged?"

This was the last thing she wanted to talk about, but unless she sprinted for her carriage, there was nowhere to go. Annie gritted her teeth. "It wasn't arranged, per se. Camden asked for my help with stopping Richard Duskin. I agreed in exchange for Western citizenship and a place in a local hospital." She didn't know why she was telling Maya any of this, but maybe it was because she was lonely, too. And if anyone, Maya might understand a fragment of how she felt.

What would it have been like to have a mother? To have someone wiser, with more life experience, whom she could turn to for guidance. *But I don't have a mother.* She was dead, and Annie was alone.

"I see." Maya gave her a knowing look. "And he's done that."

"Yes," Annie exhaled, spinning the wedding ring Cam had given her—his mother's ring. "I fulfilled my end of the bargain, and so has he. The deals done."

And it was. Something inside her cracked as the realization struck her. She could continue to work at Waverly. He had no more need of her, or her of him. They'd done their parts.

"He cares for you," Maya said gently. "Very much, I should think."

Annie remained silent. She'd have to find a way to give the ring back. Maybe Maya could give it to him—

"Do you care for him?" Maya asked more persistently.

"I don't see how that is your business." Annie stood abruptly and shook out her skirts. "Apologies, my lady, but I'm tired. I want to leave."

Maya sighed as she stood, as well. "Very well. I'll—"

"Maya?"

They turned in unison to see Governor Callahan rounding the corner into the garden.

His wife smiled.

Annie's heart vaulted into her throat when she realized Cam was right behind him, hands in his pockets and eyes on the ground.

Why is he with Alexander? Annie curtsied to the governor. He leaned in and pressed a quick kiss to his wife's cheek before turning to her. Annie's gaze flickered to Cam. He wouldn't look at her. Dark, purple shadows encircled his fire-filled eyes. He hadn't been sleeping either. His hair was mussed, like he'd been running his hands through it. There was dirt smeared over his cheeks and clothes. Where had they been hunting?

A stab of guilt flooded her. *Remember, it's better this way.*

"I'm glad to see you're still here." Governor Callahan beamed. "I've requested that you and Camden join me for a meeting in the morning. He's agreed to move back to the villa for the evening to save travel time."

Annie's eyes widened. *Maya—*

She'd been stalling. Damn it, she must have known that Alexander meant for them to stay, and Maya had kept her busy until he could return.

"Did he?" Annie shot Maya a glare, but there wasn't even a hint of recognition on the older woman's face. Annie turned back to the governor. "I'd be honored."

"Excellent." Governor Callahan offered his wife his arm. She took it. "I'll expect you both by nine o'clock."

They planned this.

As the rulers of the West strode deeper into the garden, only the slight crunch of Cam's boots in the gravel gave away his discomfort.

Don't look at him, don't look at him. If she did, she'd cry. If she cried, he'd comfort her, and she might not be able to hold her resolve. Annie stared blankly ahead as she shifted past him, toward the courtyard. He followed. Avoiding him or not, it felt important to ask, "You agreed to move us back to the villa?"

"You're talking to me now?" Cam's voice cracked. "What did I do to deserve the honor?"

I earned that. Annie chewed her thumbnail. "Did you find the attackers?"

"No," Cam replied, clipped. "But Father insists we join him in the morning, and I'm tired. Julian's tired. I'd prefer to avoid a four-hour carriage ride so early—" He was rambling, and he knew it. Cam paused before he whispered, "Besides . . . I know you don't like the ship."

Annie inclined her chin enough for it to count as a nod. They'd moved out of the courtyard onto the path toward their villa, Cam a few paces behind. *Our villa.* Annie shook her head. She couldn't think like that. It wasn't *her* anything. Nothing about this city, or anyone in it, belonged to her.

A flicker of heat brushed against her elbow, gentle, questioning. Her brands flared in response, her own power begging to touch him. *God,* she wanted to touch him. He probably didn't even know he was doing it.

Despite this, Annie snapped, "Stop it."

Cam froze as he opened the villa's front door for her. "Stop what? Existing?"

Annie pushed past him into the hallway. "Don't."

"Don't what?" Cam stormed after her. "What did I do?"

She ignored him, the first tears escaping, as she started up the stairs.

"Annie." Cam's heat surrounded her, blocking off her ascent. *"What did I do?"*

"You didn't do anything." Annie gripped her chest. She could run. Lock herself in her room. She could—

"Then why?" His voice was half a sob, nearly bringing her to her knees. "I've replayed it over and over and over. Did something happen on the way back to the ship? Who hurt you? I'll—"

"Stop it." Annie shrieked, lifting her gaze long enough to look him in the eye. She shouldn't have. The absolute despair

on his face made her want to die. *Maybe it would be better if I did.* She forced herself to say the words she'd been preparing for days. "I'm a citizen now. I can work at Waverly. I'll have a room there. Our deal's done."

Cam's fire guttered out completely. His mouth opened, then closed.

"I'll be leaving after our meeting in the morning." She spun away, continuing up the stairs, finally allowing those sparks of hope that remained in her to burn out. She'd leave his ring on the bedstand. "I have no reason to stay here."

"I don't believe you."

She glanced over her shoulder.

Cam's entire body was shaking, his voice colder than her own. "You're lying, but . . ." He sucked in a breath, two. "But I can't decide if it's to yourself or to me."

Annie held his stare, imagining all the ways she could use his knife to pierce her heart. "Maybe it's both."

She watched his heart break.

Cam turned on his heel and strode down the hall, toward his own room, his fire sparking back to life in an angry storm behind him.

CHAPTER 30
CAMDEN

Cam had burned a track into his room's plush carpet from hours of pacing.

She doesn't mean it. She doesn't mean it.

She meant it.

Cam smashed his heel into the face of his antique wardrobe, splintering the wood. He roared and tore the drawers out, his flames setting them ablaze as he flung them against the wall. He stomped the fire out and cursed before it could spread to the curtains. He didn't care how much noise he made. Annie was upstairs, and no one else was in the villa to hear him. If it weren't for her, he'd set this whole blasted estate on fire and laugh at its charred remains.

He'd ruined everything. Whether from getting too close or not protecting her well enough, he didn't know.

But Annie was leaving.

She hates me. Cam sank to the floor and rubbed his face as he leaned back against the bed. Maybe she'd always hated him. Perhaps she'd pretended to care to get what she wanted. He'd always been a pawn, a means to an end—

No. He didn't believe that. Annie *had* cared. Something had changed that. He and Julian had been hunting those masked bastards for days and found nothing. It was an excuse to stay busy, thinking that maybe she just needed some space, but it didn't help.

The only reason he'd agreed when his father had asked him to come back to the villa was because it meant he and Annie might have a minute alone. He'd just wanted to talk, but he'd ruined that, too.

She's leaving.

No. With a growl, Cam got to his feet and resumed his pacing. He'd find a way to convince her to stay, even if it meant begging on his damned knees.

But you promised you'd let her go. He choked back an angry sob. That's what he'd told her. That she could have whatever she wanted, always, and now she wanted nothing to do with him. He had to keep his promise. He cared too much not to.

Every tick of the clock edged him closer to madness. He glared at it as he paced, imagining all the ways he could break it, when a violent surge of power rattled his door. Darkness seeped beneath it. Cam flinched as shadows clawed at his pant leg.

Annie.

"Come."

Cam wheeled, ice prickling up his spine, to find empty, white eyes staring at him. Elain smiled with cracked lips, her spectral form blurring at the edges, as she gestured for him to follow.

He inhaled, but as he opened his mouth to speak, an oily black fluid bubbled up through the floral wallpaper as if it were squeezed from a rag.

What the hell? Cam glanced up at Elain, hoping for answers—just as a nightmarish scream echoed down the hall.

Annie. The shock and terror stole the feeling from Cam's limbs. Only his grip on the bedpost kept him from hitting the ground. A second scream rattled the walls. Cam yanked the door off its hinges and sprinted into the hall. He took the stairs three at a time, a cold sweat breaking out over his skin. Elain never left his side.

Someone's killing her. She's dead. She's dead. Cam kicked in Annie's door without thinking, reaching for his revolver—except he didn't grab it off his bedside table. *Hang it all.* He didn't need it. His fire flared to life, smothering the air out of the room as he stormed inside. Cam's heart dropped into his stomach.

The bedroom was draped in shimmering darkness. Ribbons of viscous black enclosed the space like a spider's web. Inky fluid dripped from the ceiling, burning holes into the hardwood floors.

Annie was in her bed—cocooned in a web—wearing a simple, white nightgown. There were no intruders. No masked men stabbing her to death in the night. It was just Annie. Screaming, and screaming, and screaming, as thundering whorls of blinding light and darkness struck the walls, cracking the stone beneath. The tendrils tore at the floor, leaving deep gouges in the surface. All the while, Annie continued to scream.

"Annie?" Cam croaked, hesitating as he reached over the bed. *What in the blazes do I do?* If he touched her, it would only frighten her more, but Annie's nails were tearing her sheets to shreds. Her back arched off the mattress, her shrieking shifting to guttural sobs. She clawed at her face as if it were the source of all her misery.

"No, stop!" Instinct had Cam pinning her wrists to her sides. She was going to rip her own skin off. "Annie, you're dreaming. *Wake up.*"

Her heel slammed into his stomach. He crumpled on top of her as the air *whooshed* out of his lungs. She kicked a second time, a third, then her hands were around his throat. She threw them off the bed and pinned him to the floor as she straddled him.

Lightning shot through Cam's mind and body as Annie began to *pull,* not with her strength, but with her power. He grabbed her wrists again, trying to break free, but the more places he touched, the more she took. She didn't just open that gate between them—she eviscerated it. Sawed. Cleaved. Destroyed. Just like she would him.

And, *God,* it felt good.

Cam leaned his head back as she squeezed tighter, his lungs shrieking for air. Annie's eyes were clenched shut, her face turned away from him as she sobbed, her moon-white hair brushing over his face.

"Annie—" he managed, but her only response was to squeeze him harder.

She's going to kill me. As he continued to hold her wrists, the veins in his arms began to turn black. She was going to turn him into a husk, just like Frank Boyle, and not because he didn't have enough energy to give, but because his fire wouldn't fight her. Because the only way to stop her was to hurt her, and he'd rather die.

So, die he would—but not until he saw her face again.

"Annie." Cam let his hands drop to the floor. Annie's arms were shaking with exertion, the sweat beading on her brow dropping onto his.

"Annie, look at me." He could barely get the words out. Her muscles were too tired to cut off his airway completely. As the strength in her hands faltered, Cam managed a breath and shouted, *"Look at me."*

And she did.

Everything stopped. The roaring of blood in his head and ears ceased as her grip went slack. Cam arched off the ground as he gasped for air, and Annie's hands settled on his shoulders.

Her eyes and skin were glowing white with the power she'd taken from him. She blinked, her brows furrowing, as she scanned over his face, horror slowly settling onto hers. Annie scrambled backward, away from him, until her back hit the bed. Cam turned onto his side, gasping as his lungs fought to expand.

"No, no, no, no." Annie's words turned into shrieking as she wrapped her arms around herself and crumpled into a ball. *"Nooooooooo."*

"Y-you were dreaming," Cam panted as he managed to get to his knees, inching closer. "It's over—"

"Over?" Annie's hands were on his face then, fingers digging into his cheeks until her nails drew blood, words shifting into frantic wails. "He threw the baby out the window. It *drowned.* He suffocated me. I can feel his hands on my back. He tore me open, over, and over, *and over, and over—"*

Cam's soul *shattered.* He didn't know what else to do but grab her and pull her into his arms. He pressed his face into the curve of her neck, squeezing her so tightly against his chest that as she wept, thrashed, and clawed at his skin, she couldn't budge.

His tears soaked her hair. Blood stained his shirt from the gouges she'd left, but he didn't care. As her weeping began to slow, Cam laid on his side and twisted her until her back was to his chest, his arms locked around her like a vice.

"He threw the baby out the window." Annie's teeth were chattering, her voice like broken glass. "It drowned."

God Almighty. How dare he think he could even *fathom*

what she'd endured? His throat was swollen, and it nearly choked him as he whispered back, "Your baby?"

"My baby?" Annie stiffened, twisting just enough to look him in the face, her own splotchy and red. "No, not mine. Tawny's."

Cam sucked in a relieved breath. "Who is Tawny?"

"A woman on the ship," Annie replied, shifting away again. "She made me promise not to let it happen to me." She subconsciously stroked his arm as her body relaxed, more from exhaustion than anything else. "Starve so I don't bleed. Don't fight. Exist until you die." Hot tears rolled over his arm where she was using it as a pillow. "I forgot, Camden. I forgot."

Forgot? Annie was stunning—no one could question that—but she'd started to look so healthy these last few weeks. Her hair was full and shiny, her curves rounding. It was impossible not to notice. As the pieces started to click into place, Cam didn't know if he should cry or jump off a cliff. "And you think I'm going to hurt you?"

Annie stayed silent far too long before she finally said, "No . . . I don't know. I'm scared that *I'm* going to hurt *you*."

"You can't hurt me."

"I already have." Annie trembled, distant, and squeezed his arms tighter. "I want to be near you all the time. My power searches for you. I'm no better than they are."

She doesn't hate me. She could have pulled a gun on him, and it wouldn't have mattered. She still cared. Cam pressed his lips against her hair as he reached up and pulled a blanket off the bed, laying it over them. "Tell me everything. Please."

And so she did.

Everything.

Of every day on that slave vessel. Of every man aboard it that brutalized her. Of every friend she'd mourned before she'd decided friends weren't worth having. She told him of the hundreds of graves she'd dug beneath New Havana. She remembered each and every patient. Where they came from. Who they'd cried for when Lord Duskin cut them to pieces.

And Cam just listened, face buried in her neck. With every word, his breath grew heavier, rage burrowing itself deeper and deeper into his core.

As Annie's own breathing began to slow, her body warm against his. The hard edge of his voice nearly gave away his anger as he finally asked, "What is his name?"

Annie swallowed, adjusting his arm beneath her, before she sleepily murmured, "Whose?"

"The slave master." Cam tucked the blanket around her to ensure she was well-bundled. "What is his name?"

It took her so long to answer, Cam thought she'd fallen asleep.

"Aman," she whispered, her breath cool against his skin. "Aman Mayer."

Downstairs, the main door to the villa clicked shut. Cam jerked awake. From below, soft footsteps moved down the hall, towards the rooms in the back.

Julian. Cam sagged in relief as he glanced at the clock. Four thirty-seven in the morning. The Air Brand had mentioned that he'd be returning to the villa later. He'd completely forgotten about him.

In their sleep, Annie had shifted to face him. Her lovely face, soft and relaxed, pressed into the hollow of his throat, arms wrapped tightly around his waist.

He'd rather have been shot ten more times than leave her, but slowly—*so* slowly—Cam wiggled out of Annie's grip. He braced himself against the bedframe as he got to his knees. *Blazes*, his head hurt. His throat was burning and raw, his muscles weak and aching, but thankfully, Annie didn't wake as he struggled to lift her back into her bed. Trembling, Cam pressed a quick kiss to her brow before turning for the door—

Oh. He'd kicked down the door. He'd have to fix that tomorrow. Cam climbed over the wooden fragments and stumbled into the hall. Still, Annie didn't wake. Every step down the staircase shot an electric, throbbing pain into his joints, but it didn't matter. Right now, Cam had one purpose— one sole reason for breathing.

He only knocked once before letting himself into Julian's room.

Thankfully, Julian sat at his desk, still dressed in his coat and boots. Though as his silver eyes took in Cam's face, his jaw dropped. "Miss Annie—"

"Is fine now," Cam interrupted, glancing at the dark veins spread across his arms. Julian knew. Only Annie could do that. "She had a nightmare."

"Lord above." Julian slumped in his seat, scanning over Cam's blood-stained shirt. "Are you . . . alright?"

"I will be." Cam smiled wickedly as he snatched a pen and a slip of paper off the desk. He jotted down two words before pushing the note back. "I need you to find someone for me."

Julian's skin sallowed as he took the slip. He read over the words, expression darkening as he peered up at Cam. "Dead or alive?"

Cam exhaled, leaning against the desk for support. "Alive."

CHAPTER 31

ANNIE

Annie's eyes fluttered open, landing immediately on the grandfather clock in the corner. Seven in the morning. She'd slept in. *Again.*

Her body *hurt*—her muscles, her joints, her skin. Even her fingers felt like they were going to fall off her hand. It took several seconds of breathing and *being* before her mind allowed her to revisit the memories of the night. As the layers of fog began to peel away, Annie wanted to crawl into the cracks of the earth and disappear like the worm she was.

Camden. She'd hurt him. Just like she'd always known she would.

He knows. Annie sucked in a rattling breath as she wrapped her blankets tighter over her shoulders. She'd had that same nightmare before. More times than she liked to count, but this time, when she'd woken, her hands had been around Cam's throat. But that—the pain and the phantoms—hadn't been what terrified her.

When she'd realized her body was against his and their

faces mere inches apart, despite what she'd done, there wasn't even a hint of anger or fear in his eyes.

No, in his gaze, she only found an emotion she was too frightened to name, and it sent her into a manic spiral, revealing every secret and defilement she'd ever locked away and promised to never speak of again. Because if he knew, he wouldn't look at her like that anymore. He'd realize she was another man's broken toy and not worth keeping.

But she'd told him everything, and Cam didn't leave. He'd stayed and listened, and listened, and listened, until she didn't remember falling asleep.

He's not here now. Annie winced as she pulled herself back against her pillows. *Just because he stayed then doesn't mean he will now.* Especially after how she'd treated him. Her eyelids were swollen as new tears attempted to form. She would understand if Cam never wanted to speak to her again.

I have to be okay with that. Annie sucked in a loud gasp as the sorrow seeped into her lungs, making them spasm. *I did it to myself.*

A loud *ooph* had her twisting toward the door, just as the black edges of panic began to creep into her vision. *What happened to the door?* It was in pieces. More important than that, Cam had stumbled through the remains, balancing a large, silver tray in each hand.

"Oh, good, you're awake." His full lips broke into a grin. "I would have felt awful if I'd woken you."

Annie almost smiled back until her gaze fell to the thick tendrils of black seeping through the veins on his neck, onto his exposed chest, where his nightshirt lay only half-buttoned. With his sleeves rolled to the elbow, more blackened veins spread down into his wrists and hands. They even plagued his face, darkening the skin beneath his eyes.

His neck—

A deep, purply bruise encircled his throat. Ligature marks. From *her*.

Her brands. She glanced at her glowing fingers. Their brightness a reminder that she'd taken from him—*again*. She hadn't just hurt him. She'd almost killed him.

"Stop it." Cam's smile dropped into a playful scowl as he gently swung onto the end of the bed, setting the trays between them. "I see your cogs turning, but everything is fine. I'm fine."

"Everything is *not* fine." Annie's voice sounded like she'd been scraping her vocal cords with sandpaper. Cam raised a brow. She gripped her throat. "You . . . Frank—"

Because she'd taken everything from Frank Boyle, she'd drained him and had almost done the same to Cam.

"Ugh." Cam rolled his eyes as he took the cover off the first tray. Upon it was a coffee pot, a bowl of sugar, and a carafe of cream. "Please, don't use my and Frankie's name in the same sentence."

"Please stop pretending nothing happened," Annie snapped back. The bruises on his neck were so *deep*. Her power stirred in her fingertips. *I can fix it if he'll let me.* Just like hours before, her words came pouring out. "I don't need your pity, Camden. I don't need your charity. I just need—"

"What do you need, Kitten?" Cam leaned in, eyes darkening as he poured a cup of coffee. "Tell me what you need, and I'll find it. If I can't find it, I'll find someone who can."

What do I need? Annie sank back, watching as he spooned an unnecessary amount of sugar into the steaming liquid, followed by a healthy dose of cream. She didn't know what she needed. She never had. Need was a privilege she'd never allowed herself.

Annie's eyes burned, and beneath the blankets, she curled her knees against her chest. "I need you to be angry at me."

Cam made a face as he removed the lid from the second tray, revealing a *heaping* bowl of porridge, accompanied by dishes of brown sugar, dried cranberries, almonds, and more cream.

His brows pinched together, the skin between them webbed with black. "Go on."

Annie stared as he dumped all the ingredients together and began to mix. It looked disgusting. She swallowed. "You should hate me."

Cam just added more cream and continued to stir. "If you say so."

Tears escaped despite her best efforts, dripping onto her chest. "I could have killed you."

"And?"

"*And?*" Annie wanted to slap him. "Have you looked at yourself?"

"All the time, but not as often as you look at me."

"I asked you to stop pretending."

Cam moved in closer, his lips curling into a cat and canary grin. "When did I give you the impression that I desired saintly behavior from you? I've never expected, or *wanted*, you to be anyone besides the woman I met on Richard Duskin's porch."

Annie blinked at him. She'd told him something similar.

"I made a deal with *that* woman." Cam huffed as he placed the oversweet coffee on the tray beside the porridge. "The one that occasionally scares the hell out of me and makes me want to remember to bring an umbrella. The one that sees things I can't and reminds me to keep my mouth shut. Do you know what I need, Annie? I need you. Not Violet Clarke. Not anyone else."

Annie's lungs stopped working as Cam gently slid the tray across the bed, onto her lap. All that food, just for her.

Oh. A part of Annie's heart cracked—not apart, but back together.

All the excess sugars, creams, and treats . . .

He was asking for trust. For vulnerability. He may not have had a word for what he was asking for—neither did she—but eating as she wished was the level of safety he was offering her. That, at least, she'd never have to be afraid of him.

Annie breathed in deeply before peering up at him. "Let me heal you, and I'll eat."

Cam gave her a crooked half-smile. "Eat and I'll let you heal me."

"Fine." Annie grimaced as she shoveled porridge into her mouth. Surprisingly, it wasn't bad. He watched her longingly as she licked the remnants off the back of the spoon. She offered it to him. "Share with me?"

"Gladly." Cam took a large bite and groaned happily at all the sweets. "I'm starving."

And so, they took turns eating the entire bowl and drained the coffee pot to the dregs.

"No more." Annie's stomach ached as she shoved the trays aside. She'd never eaten so much in her life. She pointed to the settee beside the window that overlooked the sea. The ocean was as dark and grey as the ash in the empty hearth. "Go sit. You made a deal."

"So bossy. I love it." Cam swung off the bed. She winced as his nightshirt slipped to the side, revealing the blackened veins dipping down onto his shoulder. His eyes flickered from her to the dark marks on his arms as he sank onto the settee. "I really am alright. I feel better, actually."

"Better?" Annie fought to keep her breathing even as he leaned his head back against the cushions. Even in the last hour, the bruise had spread further down his throat, tinging his golden skin in deep reds and blues. His voice sounded terrible. She brushed her fingers over his skin and swallowed as the corners of Cam's eyes tightened in pain. *He's such a liar.* But he was lying for her. "Better how?"

"For one, you're touching me," Cam chuckled, the sound raw, as she tipped his chin up to get a better look. When she scowled at him, he sighed and said, "And my fire is quiet. I can breathe again."

"I took too much." The brands on her hands and fingers glowed white as she stroked the bruises on his neck. She could *feel* the damage begin to repair itself at her touch, his flesh ready to answer her call. Annie lingered, transfixed, as she trailed her fingers further up his neck, running them beneath his jaw. *He's so beautiful.* She'd always thought so, since she'd first seen him, no matter how many times she'd tried to deny it.

Annie jumped when Cam's throat bobbed, lifting her gaze to his face. He was watching her, eyes heavy with yearning. Clearing her throat, she grabbed his hand, turning it over to inspect the dark veins in his wrist, and repeated, "I took too much."

"I don't know if you can." Cam's gaze never left her face. "My fire grows as fast as you can absorb it."

"Perhaps. But mistakes cost lives." Annie's brows furrowed as she tried to push her energy into him, to chase away the darkness, but it resisted and pushed back. *What if?* Instead, her grip on his arm tightened, and Annie pulled. Absorbing the darkness back from his body into hers. As it entered her, the darkness was burned away by the brightness of her brands.

Cam flexed his fingers as she stepped back, examining her own.

"That was odd." His expression tightened in thought. "That didn't feel the same."

"No . . . it didn't." Annie sat beside him, still studying her hands. Now that she recalled, it *hadn't* felt the same when she'd killed Frank Boyle as it had when she'd siphoned from Cam. Frank had felt oily, angry. Venomous. Like she'd felt last night when she'd been at the height of her nightmare.

When she'd taken from Cam—in Mr. Baxter's lab, in the carriage—that had felt euphoric. Enthralling.

"Blazes." Cam leapt off the settee.

Annie jumped a mile. "What?"

"I haven't been able to tell you." He ran his hands over his face, through his mussed hair, as he began to pace, sparks flying after him. "I went to Waverly's morgue after you left the hospital the other night."

I haven't been able to tell you. Annie's stomach twisted with guilt. Because she'd been cruel and driven him away. *Never again.* She knew for a certainty that even if she wanted to, she would never be able to stay away from him again. Her defenses had been crushed completely. From now on, unless he told her to leave, she was his.

She folded her hands over her lap. "Tell me."

Cam shot her a quick smile, making her cheeks grow hot. "I overheard my father and Henry Bale arguing."

Annie pursed her lips. "That isn't the first time."

Nodding, Cam continued to pace, his brands burning like a Southern sunset. "Bale thinks my father is withholding information, which proves he isn't stupid."

"I agree with Chief Bale," Annie replied, tone low. "I feel like the governor's been playing a chess game with us since we arrived."

"That's how he works," Cam slowed, chewing his poor lip. "Moves, and counter moves. He *wants* us to know that Bale doesn't trust him. He's waiting for me to ask the right question." He rubbed his wrist, where the darkened veins had vanished. "The attackers at the Clarkes's party were covered in those same marks. They had the same tattoos under their fingers as Elias."

He told her about their connection to The Order, of the foul, black blood that leaked from them, of his father's cryptic warnings. Of his and Mr. Price's unsuccessful hunts through the nights and into the early hours.

Annie listened, absorbing.

All the while—as he spoke and paced—Cam seemed to *decompress*. The intensity of the heat emanating from him slowly lessened. Because he wanted to talk, *needed* to talk— to her.

Do you know what I need, Kitten? I need you. Not Violet Clarke. Not anyone else.

He wanted her.

She didn't know what to do with that fact, but she wouldn't run from it. Not anymore.

Cam finally sat down beside her. There was a smear of blood on his lip from where he'd chewed it. "So, what do you think?"

"I think," Annie exhaled as she reached out and wiped the blood from his mouth, healing it with her touch. "I don't know what to think. If those men's veins were black, like what I did to you and Mr. Boyle, does that mean there's another Death Brand in Enoch? Right now?"

"I don't know." Cam studied her face, his fire smothering out the last of the green in his irises. "That sounds like a question for Magnus Baxter."

She nodded, then let her fingers trail down his cheek. They were covered in scratches. She healed those, too. "I *do* think we need to show your father some trust."

Cam looked bewildered. "What?"

"Think about it," Annie replied. "We came here to get justice for your mother. For us. Correct?"

He scowled. "Justice is a nice word. I was thinking revenge—"

"It's obvious the governor is withholding the information we need," Annie interrupted as she shifted toward him. "Because he wants you dependent on him. Move and counter moves, you said? We can play that game, too. If you open up to him, if we let him believe we're on his side and stop fighting him, we may be able to find The Order before they kill anyone else. More importantly, before they kill us. What we're doing isn't working. Our enemies know how this dance better than we do."

Cam's eyes narrowed, but they never left hers. "You're a devious thing."

"Thank you. I'll take that as a compliment."

Cam peered at the clock, then let out a low curse. "We need to be at that meeting in an hour."

I'd forgotten about that. As Cam made to stand, a thought struck her. She grabbed his arm. "How did you know I was having a nightmare?"

"Oh." This time, Cam made a face as his eyes shot to the destroyed door. "I heard you screaming and . . ." He hesitated. "And Elain showed up."

Elain. Annie's blood went cold. "Elain? She . . . she let you see her again?"

Cam nodded. "She wanted me to help you, I think."

"She trusts you," Annie murmured. Elain. *Elain.* As Annie had died in the lava tunnels, Elain had called herself a helper. In life, Elain would have loved Cam. She was so warm, exuberant, and full of life, not unlike him.

"Do you think . . ." Cam fidgeted. "This may sound insane, but do you think you can *call* her?"

Lord in Heaven. Annie inhaled. "Like summon her?"

"I don't know what to call it." Cam knelt so they were at

eye level. "Annie, you've walked through portals. Spoken to the dead. Why couldn't you?"

"I can try," Annie whispered back. She'd never thought about it. In all these years she'd seen the ghosts, she'd never once tried to call them. And Elain? Would she come?

Not knowing what else to do, Annie closed her eyes. *But how?* She wasn't even sure if they were actually the souls of the living that'd passed or a foreign spirit taking on their likeness.

Cam looped his pinkie through hers and squeezed. Annie exhaled, grounded by the touch. She'd always been able to tell when the dead were near. It was a sense. A heaviness in the air. Annie reached out with her mind, trying to find that heaviness, and asked in her thoughts, *"Elain?"*

"Here." A breathy voice said directly into her ear.

Cam yelped, jumping back, but he didn't release her hand.

Annie's eyes snapped open, only to find Elain's form inches from her face, smiling. Only the solid white, sightless eyes differentiated her ghost from how she'd looked in the living.

Annie stared back and returned the smile. "Can you hear me when I call?"

Elain's grin widened, her head cocking at an unnatural angle. *"Always."*

Cam had paled, his eyes wide but not frightened. They never left Elain.

"Can the others?" Annie asked, remembering all the spirits who had visited her over the years. "Will they come?"

Elain's smile continued to widen into something inhuman. *"Always."*

"The *hell* is that?"

Elain glanced over her shoulder to where Nathan and Jenny stood in the ruined doorway, then she vanished.

All the color left Jenny's ivory skin, her hand jumping between her throat and stomach. "Was that . . . *Elain?"*

"Forget the damned name." Nathan's gaze was fixed on the place the spirit had been. "What the *hell* was that?"

"That was"—Cam scratched his temple and frowned—"my dead sister-in-law."

"God Almighty." Nathan removed his cap, releasing a mass of voluminous ringlets, and placed it over his chest. "Just when I thought this place couldn't get any stranger."

"Annie, how?" Jenny wasn't done. "Why didn't you tell me?"

"I—" Why hadn't she told her? Jenny would have believed her, but after how many adopted siblings they'd lost, she couldn't bear to break Jenny's heart further. Annie held her sister's teary gaze, willing her to understand. "I didn't want to hurt you."

"It's too late for that." Jenny's eyes rose to where Cam and Annie's hands were still intertwined. Her entire *being* brightened. "Are . . . are you two—" She stepped back, a slat of broken wood cracking beneath her booted heel. "What happened?"

"Mommy and Daddy worked it out," Cam smirked before tipping his head back, revealing the slight essence of a bruise that remained on his throat. "Annie may have kicked my ass, though."

Jenny gaped at him.

"Good," Nathan said with a laugh. "You probably deserved it."

Relief colored their every word. They needed them to lead. She and Cam needed to put up a strong front for them.

Nathan shot Jenny a look. "So, I will have a dead sister-in-law?"

Her cheeks turned a brilliant red before falling to the ground.

It took a moment for the statement to register. Annie's head span. "W-what?"

Nathan lifted Jenny's hand. A simple, dainty, emerald ring sat on her wedding finger. "I asked Jenny to marry me. She said yes."

Cam blinked. Once, twice, before throwing his head back in laughter. "You *scoundrel.*"

Annie couldn't breathe. In fact, she might faint.

"Oh, Annie." Jenny hiked up her skirts and hopped over the shattered remains of the bedroom door. She dropped at Annie's side, gripping her hands in hers. "You'll approve, won't you? Nathan loves me."

He loves her. Slowly, so slowly, Annie let her eyes settle on Nathan. His gaze locked on hers as he rang his cap into a knot. He was waiting for *her.* Even after all they'd been through—from being imprisoned in the bunker to now—he wanted, no, *needed* Annie's approval.

Not Cam's, his captain.

Hers.

He loves her. Annie repeated to herself, and she knew it was true. It had been weeks, but Nathan did love Jenny. He always had.

She pulled Jenny into her arms, pressing her face into her little sister's ruby-red curls. "I love you, too. Don't forget."

"I won't," Jenny whispered back.

"Then, you have my blessing." Annie kissed her cheek.

Nathan let out a cheer at the same time as Jenny. Cam clapped his friend on the back before yanking him into a hug, as well.

"We'll talk after our meeting," Cam told them. "You two go to bed, um, separately."

Annie stared at her bedside table as they said their goodnights. Apparently, they'd spent the night hours moving all of their luggage back from *The Elaina* to the villa. They needed to rest.

Cam sank on the edge of the bed after they left and blew out a long breath. "I wasn't expecting that. Not so soon, at least."

Slowly, Annie stood, making her way to the bedside table. "Neither did I."

Cam's brows pinched together in curiosity. "But life is short, isn't it? They should live while they have life to live."

"It's short for some." Annie opened the table drawer and picked up Cam's mother's ring—her ring. She could have sworn Cam stopped breathing as she slid it back on her finger. His brands flared as she sat beside him on the bed, fidgeting with the vibrant fire-opal, wreathed in gold. "I wouldn't have taken it with me . . . if I'd left."

"It's yours to keep." Cam swallowed, taking her hand to more closely inspect the ring. "It was part of the bargain." He traced the jade-fishhook pendant that sat around her throat— his captain Resh's pendant. "A deals a deal."

"Is it—" Now, *he* looked like he might vomit as his eyes briefly flickered to her lips. "Is it because you didn't like it that got you so upset?"

Annie held back a laugh. *He thinks I didn't like kissing him.* She stroked down his jawbone, resting her thumb over his bottom lip like she had her knife only a week ago. Any lingering darkness in his veins was replaced with fire, and every part of him *burned*.

"No, Camden." Annie kissed the side of her thumb, their mouths a mere breath apart. "I did like it. *That's* what upset me."

"And you're going to stay?"

"I'm going to stay."

"Thank God." He grinned. "I don't think I could manage the kids without you."

CHAPTER 32
ALEXANDER

"It's an E. It sounds like *eh*." Maya slammed her pen down on the tea table. She sucked in a deep breath through her nose and released it through her mouth. "You know this, Kai. We've been over it a thousand times."

"I'm *trying*." Kai rubbed his eyes, splattering tears onto his letter sheets. "I just can't remember."

Maya tapped the paper, rattling the tray of teacups resting on the edge of the table. "You can remember, you just . . ."

Alexander watched them over the top of his newspaper. Every few minutes, Kai's eyes flickered to him. Anxious. Overwhelmed. Was that because he was here? He didn't usually join his wife and son for their morning meal in the tearoom, but after the venom of Camden's pointed comments had sunk in, he felt that he should.

Maya wiped a drip of sweat from her temple as she helped Kai correct his spelling, despite his whimpering protests.

Alexander removed his glasses as he rested his newspaper on his lap. "You know you need not go through all this stress. We can hire him a tutor. One besides David."

His wife glared. "I'm fine."

"I never said you weren't."

"He just has trouble remembering his alphabet, that's all." Maya straightened, brushing a strand of black hair off her pointed face. "He's brilliant. He can understand numbers better than most adults."

As they spoke, Kai's round, brown eyes flickered between them nervously.

Alexander studied her for a moment before saying, "You sound like you're defending him."

Maya corrected Kai's *A*. "Do I?"

Alexander considered answering before deciding to return to his paper.

Maya huffed and continued with Kai's schooling.

If I recall, you said the same thing when you were beating me bloody. Alexander visibly winced as Camden's words replayed through his mind. When he glanced up, Kai was watching. He narrowed his eyes at the boy, and Kai swallowed and returned to his sheet.

If only Camden would believe me. Alexander had never laid his hands on Kai. Not once. Every day, he regretted what he'd done to his older son, but repentance didn't change the past.

Flexing his fingers, he remembered the bruises they'd left on Camden's skin . . .

Cassie. He'd give the rest of his remaining days to beg her forgiveness. All those years, he'd justified what he'd done by telling himself it was for their own good. Camden had always been so stubborn—had defied him at every opportunity—and Alexander hadn't been able to handle it.

Now that he was older—and Camden was a grown man— he was beginning to realize why he'd always resented his son so much, even as a child.

Camden was the man Enoch needed . . . not him. Alexander

so desperately wanted to keep the kingdom together, but it wasn't in his power or ability—then or now.

Kai's heightened whimper pulled Alexander back from his thoughts. Maya growled in frustration, raising her hands as if she meant to pull out her hair, but froze when she noticed him watching.

She dropped her hands and cleared her throat before standing. "Come, Kai, let's take a walk in the garden—"

A sharp knock rapped on the door. David. "Sir, a representative of The Order is here."

Maya froze as Alexander glanced up. *Now?* He folded his paper and set it on the arm of his chair. "Thank you, David. Have him wait in the entry."

The door swung open, revealing Henry Bale in the doorway. "There's no need for that." He gave Maya a knowing look. "Lady Callahan. Good to see you again. How's the boy?"

David peeked his head through the door behind Henry and mouthed, *I apologize.*

Kai hid behind Maya's skirts as she plastered on a forced smile, a layer of panic in her voice. "Chief Bale, always nice to see you as well." She ran her fingers through Kai's dark locks. "My son and I were just leaving."

"I won't keep you, then." Henry bowed, then sat down on the sofa, right where they'd been. "The governor and I have much to discuss."

She shot Alexander a nervous look, but he dismissed her with a nod. With pursed lips, she grabbed Kai's hand and dragged him into the hall. David stepped around her, lowering his head. "Is there anything I can get for you and Chief Bale?"

"A fresh pot of tea for the chief, I suppose." Alexander crossed one leg over the other, expression bored. "It seems Henry plans to stay for a time."

"Just a time," Henry replied before shrugging off his coat,

tossing it over the back of the sofa. Alexander frowned as it dribbled raindrops all over his polished floors. "But tea would be nice. I'm on business today, and it's already been a long one."

David ducked out of the room, closing the door behind him, leaving Henry and Alexander alone together in the tearoom. He scanned over the police chief. The arrogant bastard wore a tailored, pin-stripe suit today instead of his usual uniform. On business for The Order, indeed.

"And that business brings you to me? Again." As Alexander picked up his paper, he quickly brushed his glasses out of view. "You've become quite a parasite, Bale."

"Yes, because you seem so taxed for time." Henry surveyed the tearoom. "I apologize for not feeling any regret in interrupting you."

With a low chuckle, Alexander flipped through the newspaper pages. "What do you want?"

"Have we become that informal?" Henry leaned back on the sofa. His usually haphazard, brown locks were neatly gelled back. His goatee was shaved to leave his face clean and smooth. Even his skin seemed fresher, more alive.

"Perhaps we have." Alexander cocked his head. "You seem . . . revived. Did you feed off of *her*?"

"What I have and haven't done are none of your concern." Henry stiffened. "But now that you mention it, you seem quite peckish, my friend. Maybe you should give her a try."

"No, thank you." Alexander fought against the urge to scratch the scar under his left ring finger. "You'll be disappointed to hear that I've never felt better."

Henry sneered. "Of course you do."

After a brief knock, David returned with a fresh tray of tea and cakes. With a bow, he poured Henry a steaming cup and took the old tray away. After he left, Henry lifted the cup to his nose and took a deep inhale.

"Ah, lavender-chamomile." He sipped the hot liquid and sighed before setting it back onto the tray. "Delicious."

"My wife enjoys it." Alexander folded his hands over his lap. "What do you want, Henry?"

"Yes, that." Henry took a bite of cake, chewed, then wiped his mouth on a napkin. "We never finished our conversation the other night."

"Oh yes. How devastating."

"I must confess. You've been a worthy opponent. Having my men murdered one by one, then pushing the blame onto The Order, so your son would start investigating. Dastardly."

If only you knew. Alexander sniffed. "I have done no such thing."

"You're good," Henry admitted. "And since you've left no evidence for me to tie it back to you, my superiors won't permit me to be rid of you. Not yet. Trust me, I tried. They still believe you'll come through on your promise."

Alexander raised a brow. "Chief, did you petition to have me eliminated?"

"No," Henry sneered. "I petitioned to have your innards removed and hung over the city gates, but alas, I was denied. I told you I would be making a report. And since I also can't prove that you're my father's assassin, what you've said before has proved true. My hands are tied."

"Careful now." Alexander threatened. "The West is still mine. Push me and see that I won't have you strangled in your sleep."

"For now. It's yours *for now*." Henry's eyes glinted as he leaned in, his tone low and vicious. "Admit it. Tell me you poisoned him. I know you did."

Resist. Alexander's body went rigid. His blood *boiled* as the command rolled through him, making his scar itch so severely he could have chewed it off. *Resist.*

Henry's grin widened as Alexander's mouth fell open, the confession on the tip of his tongue. *Resist. Do not break.* Sweat poured down his temple. Harrison Bale's control had been absolute. There was no resisting. Harrison commanded, and Alexander obeyed. It had taken him five years to orchestrate his death. He had hoped he'd be free once the wretched man was gone, but no. His authority had passed to his son, but not completely. Alexander still retained some of his autonomy.

It took every ounce of his will and strength, but he snapped his mouth shut.

"Fine." Henry's face twisted in rage. He stood, balling his hands into fists. "Keep your secrets. They don't matter, and they won't stop me."

Alexander collapsed in his chair, panting. He could barely keep his eyes open as he managed, "Camden will. A shame you can't touch him, either."

"About that." Henry spun and knelt beside Alexander's chair. The scoundrel snatched his hand, squeezing so hard that Alexander thought his fingers might break. "Even with all your years scheming, you made a grievous oversight."

Alexander fought to swallow. Even the muscles in his throat were exhausted. "Did I?"

"You shouldn't have killed James Kline." Henry continued to squeeze until Alexander's knuckle popped. "With his death, you left an open council seat. They were quick to give the space to my man, Jensen Davis."

No. He'd forgotten to fill the seat. Alexander let his head fall back, his eyes closing. It didn't matter. He still had time. "That doesn't change anything."

"Doesn't it?" Henry replied. "Mr. Davis can be very convincing. With all of these terrible murders, he was quick to

get the council to agree to reschedule the Embassy meeting to"
—Henry checked his watch for theatrics—"three weeks from now. Which means, soon, our deal will be done."

"No." Alexander jerked up. "I still have three and a half months, you can't touch him—"

"One year," Henry interrupted. "Until the date of the council's assembly. That's what we agreed on." He gave Alexander's hand a loving pat and let go. "You should word your bargains better. Three weeks and then I'm free to deal with you and Camden however I wish."

"No." Alexander croaked. *What have I done?* "But Mr. Davis fought when your men attacked the Clarkes's home?"

"Oh, that?" Henry waved flippantly. "I couldn't allow people to suspect he was affiliated with them, now, could I? Just a bit of dramatics to ward off suspicion. What are the lives of a few low-life recruits to the sanctity of the cause?" Henry stood and straightened his suit. "This is going to be so much fun. Especially now that I've heard the reports of what your son and his wife accomplished with Reika Hall."

"You know nothing about that," Alexander snapped. "Rumors. That's the best you have."

"Rumors or truth, it doesn't matter." Henry's voice was too high. "A Revenant child has reached the second trimester. Longer than any has lived in vitro in the history of their kind. Lord and Lady Callahan are my first glimmer of hope to ascend, and you will not take this chance from me."

The two men stared at each other for almost a full thirty seconds before Alexander finally smiled.

"You're afraid, Henry." Alexander's lungs spasmed as he spoke. "You're afraid because you're not in control. Because Camden is someone you cannot sway with threats and bribes. You're afraid because he is not *me*."

"Afraid?" Henry finished his tea. "I've seen too much to be afraid of a boy and a slave."

"So you say." Alexander pointed out the highlighted article in his paper. *Repairs begin on Waverly Hospital with the efforts of Lord and Lady Callahan. Enoch rejoices.* He couldn't stop his lips from curving up as he said, "You're losing your grasp, Chief. Perhaps it's time you stopped trying to climb so high."

"Says the dead man." Henry turned for the door, then paused, hand still on the doorknob. He glanced back. "I'm surprised you haven't inquired about Mrs. Hall's health."

Alexander's stomach dropped. "Reika Hall went home yesterday in perfect health. I'm sure her servants are taking wonderful care of her."

The ghost of a smile parted Henry's lips. "I'm sure they would if they had the opportunity."

Dear God. "What have you done with her?"

"Lady Hall is safe." Henry slid on his heavy raincoat. "At least until the Head chooses otherwise."

"I don't think I've ever told you this, Bale." Alexander chewed the inside of his cheek. "But I truly hate you."

Henry bowed. "And I consider that to be the highest of compliments. And no more murders. That's an order."

With that, he tugged the door open.

Camden stood on the other side, wreathed in fire, Annie just behind his elbow. His son gave the chief a smug look. "Good morning, Bale."

Just in time.

CHAPTER 33

ANNIE

Annie didn't know why she bothered to be surprised.

Henry Bale stood on the other side of the door, his expression an equal mix of shock and fury. The veins in his neck and temples bulged as he swiveled to glare at Alexander, who sat in one of the tea room's armchairs with a catty grin.

"Chief Bale." *Of course.* Annie plastered on a bland, pretty smile. *More games.* "We didn't expect you so early. Join us for tea?"

Cam sneered as Henry twisted back to face them. "Agreed. What a *coincidence* that we keep meeting like this."

What does he want us to see? Annie raced to study the chief. His glare bore into Cam, and even though his cheeks turned tomato red, his skin looked flushed, like he'd gotten a good night's sleep or just taken a shot of whisky. *What am I missing?*

"Yes, what a coincidence." Chief Bale's tone leaked pure hatred as he pulled his cap out from beneath his elbow and slipped it on. With a stiff bow, he said, "Lord Callahan. My lady."

As he attempted to move past them, Cam caught Chief Bale by the crook of his elbow. The man's entire body went rigid as Cam's burning embers floated into the air around them.

"I realized we've met before." Cam cocked his head, tone deadly. "We were children. Does your family still have that lovely lodge by the northern gate? Hunters, were you not?"

Chief Bale's eyes shot wide as he jerked out of Cam's grip. "The Lodge? It's empty now. I didn't enjoy tromping around the forest the way my father did."

"Hmm." Cam popped his lips before shifting away from him. "What a shame."

With that, Henry shoved past them and stormed down the hall. Cam told Annie about what he'd remembered of the Bales. It wasn't much. They needed more information.

Here goes nothing. She felt silly doing it, but under her breath, she whispered, "*Elain.*"

In an instant, her sister's misty form stepped out of the wall—grinning—gowned in ivory.

"Father," Cam said at the same time as he glanced over his shoulder, his eyes widening as they locked onto her sister.

He can even see her here.

"Camden. Annie," the governor said from inside the tearoom. "Please, come in."

Annie nodded toward where the chief was descending the stairs and mouthed to Elain, "*Follow him.*"

Her sister flashed a wide grin before disappearing from view. Cam squeezed her arm, and they stepped inside together. The flowery scent of lavender and chamomile enveloped her senses, as if attempting to soothe the tension that hung heavily in the room, palpable in her bones.

The governor appeared . . . rattled. Unlike Chief Bale, his skin looked sallow, and the streaks of gray in his long, sandy hair were more pronounced. He gestured toward the empty sofa across from him, its heavy cream fabric printed with dainty, blue birds.

"You both look well." The governor gave her a pointed look. "The villa is still to your liking, I presume?"

She gave him a closed-lipped smile and said, "It is, thank you."

"You look like hell," Cam replied with a cheeky smile, cutting off the small talk. "Spent the night whipping children for fun, I presume?"

Annie admired Alexander's self-control. Instead of snapping back, he said. "Have some tea. It's fresh."

"Thank you," Annie repeated, then glared at Cam as she poured them each a cup. She brushed his arm with her power, hoping he got the hint. *Behave.*

Cam made a face, his heat rubbing against her calf. *Fine, but only for you.*

"I assume you planned that run-in?" Cam scooped three spoonfuls of sugar into his tea. With all the sweets he'd eaten earlier, it was amazing his heart didn't just stop. "Henry looked like he was about to have a stroke."

"I may have." The governor's brows shot toward his hairline as Cam continued to dump more sugar into his cup. "I do enjoy tormenting him every chance I get."

Cam actually smiled. "Finally, something we can agree on."

"Were you raised in a kennel?" The governor took a deep breath through his nose.

"Even worse." Cam licked the loose sugar off the spoon before plopping it back into the tray.. "I was raised here. Thank God the pirates saved me."

"Where is Mr. Price? I requested him to join us, as well."

"He got in late," Cam said. "Even Revenants need to sleep."

The door swung open, and Maya stepped in, wearing a fitted, fuchsia ensemble with puffed sleeves.

"Pardon." She smiled at Annie and Cam before sitting beside Alexander. She brushed back a loose strand of hair and smoothed her skirts. "I thought I'd join you all this morning."

The knot in Annie's chest loosened just a bit. She'd decided she liked Maya. She didn't know why, but she did.

Beside her, Cam's entire body went taut as he set his mug back on the tray. The way his eyes narrowed at Maya was like a fox stalking a rabbit. "Where's my brother?"

No formalities. Just the blunt question. Annie resisted kicking him.

The woman's smile fell. "Downstairs in the parlor. With David."

"Maya schools Kai from home." Alexander placed his gloved hand over his wife's. "David also helps with his studies."

I've never seen him without gloves. Annie thought back to her first meeting with the governor and every time since. He always wore gloves, whether leather, velvet, or satin. His hands were always covered.

"How splendid for David," Cam said with more than an ounce of irritation. "I'd like to see my brother when we're done here." He chewed his lip for a moment, his tone softening as he addressed Maya. "With your permission, of course."

"Certainly," she replied, but her words were edged with nerves. "He's at your disposal."

Cam respectfully lowered his head, enough that his hair fell in his eyes.

Annie sipped her tea, careful not to spill it on her own navy-blue, long-sleeved day gown. "What is this meeting about? I think we're all getting tired of dancing around the point."

The governor's polite expression dropped, revealing a level of exhaustion Annie had never seen from him. "If dropped pretenses are what you prefer, I'm going to be blunt. Did you save Mrs. Hall's child?"

Cam stayed quiet, though his brands flared, filling the space with a suffocating heat.

They'd planned for this. They'd discussed. They were as ready as they could be.

Annie took a breath, grateful for the comfort of Cam's warmth beside her. "We did."

Maya placed her fingers over her mouth, her chest rising and falling in rapid succession. Where she seemed terrified, Alexander closed his eyes, deflating, as he asked, "You can siphon?"

"I can." Annie kept her expression flat. *Stay calm. He can't hurt you.* Cam would never let him.

"It's said that not all Death Brands can." Alexander's eyes opened, and his waning lips cracked into a sad smile. "Yes, all Death Brands can drain, but not in a way that replenishes them. Their power has to return naturally, a process that takes time. Not all can heal, or move life from one person to another. It's not as simple as it sounds. Violet Clarke told me a wild story of how you siphoned power from Camden to heal the babe."

Cam groaned irritably at the sound of Violet's name.

Not all Death Brands can siphon. She'd have to ask Mr. Baxter about that. Annie held Alexander's eye, unblinking. "I did. *We* did."

Maya squeezed her husband's hand, and there was a slight quiver in her voice. "I think honesty would be best now, don't you agree?"

"Honesty." Alexander huffed with a slight shake of his head. "A forgotten virtue." He blinked up at Cam, a slight haze in his eyes. "When was the last time you believed a word spoken to you, son? Believed it without question or hesitation?"

The room was silent except for the chirp of cardinals outside the fogged window.

"Never." Cam's voice caught. "Not until . . ." His eyes flickered to Annie as he pressed his full lips into a line. "Not until Annie agreed to help me take down the Duskins. She wanted to keep her sister alive. I trusted her to keep to that."

Her breath hitched as she held his gaze. They'd planned ahead of time, as they'd walked to the manor, that they'd show vulnerability today. That they'd play into the snares the governor would certainly set for them. Because they couldn't track down The Order without him. Despite this, she hadn't been ready for Cam's first truth to be about *her*.

"Good." Somehow, the weight hanging over the governor grew heavier, darker. "I ask that you believe what I'm about to tell you with that same firmness. I hope you'll believe it because I love Enoch. I love my country."

Cam's tone dropped low enough that Annie knew it wouldn't take much to push him over the edge. "If only you'd loved the people you were supposed to as much as you loved your country."

The governor visibly winced. His weary, worn gaze fell to the ring on Annie's finger as he began to tug off his glove.

"I loved your mother." The governor rolled the glove over his wrist. "I loved her to the point I killed her."

Annie grabbed Cam's wrist as a high-pitched *hum* filled the air—his fire. *Calm.* She let her own power sink into his and *held.* She didn't take. Not yet.

Cam exhaled and flexed his fingers, but didn't respond despite the death in his burning eyes.

The governor noticed, he always noticed, but he continued as he finally tugged off his glove, revealing nothing but an ordinary hand. Thin, maybe—paler than the rest of his body—but nothing strange.

Grief twisted his features. "Camden, do you remember when she'd insist on taking you to the weekend markets?"

"Of course, I do. You always told her no." Cam inhaled at the same time his voice cracked. "She just wanted to see the flowers."

"Yes, she did," The governor replied. Maya squeezed his arm, her gaze on the floor. "And she never realized that there were legions of men who wanted her dead because they hated me. Because they hated your grandfather, and his father before him."

"Why?" Annie's words tumbled out of her. "Why did they hate you?"

The governor's steely eyes softened. "For the same reason every legacy is hated. Because we are what they can never be. Powerful. Not because we earned it, but because that's who we are—absolute authority."

Alexander rubbed his bare fingers, thoughtful. "But that's not why Cassie loved me. She said I reminded her of a thunderstorm."

Only by sheer will and the grasp Annie had on his fire did Cam remain silent. His attention was locked on his father, though, and she knew he was hanging on the governor's every word.

Maya. Annie felt for her. To be the wife of one of the most powerful men on earth, and to listen to him talk about the woman he'd *truly* loved. She deserved better.

"So, I made deals to keep her safe," The governor exhaled, his brows furrowed. "Deals I can never take back."

"We talked about this," Cam whispered. "You said you traded me to stay in control."

"I did." Alexander Callahan flipped his hand over, palm up.

The stench of decay overpowered the flowery scent of the tea. Annie's heart forgot to beat, then tripled its pace, when she caught sight of his ring finger. The outline of a mark was imprinted into his skin—a phoenix. A rot had spread through the governor's finger, where it looked like he'd tried to carve his flesh away. The blackened flesh had spread over his palm, creeping toward his wrist. *The Order.* Alexander Callahan was a member of The Order.

In one fluid movement, Cam was on his feet, and the governor let out a sharp gasp as Cam's knee sank into his stomach. He pressed the mouth of his revolver against his father's forehead. Maya shrieked and stumbled back out of her chair, hands over her mouth as tears streamed down her cheeks.

"I knew it," Cam hissed, leaning in until he and the governor's noses were only inches apart. "I bloody knew it, you sick bastard. You are going to deserve *everything* I do to you."

"Camden," Annie whispered in warning. "Not yet. Wait."

There was no humanity left in Cam's eyes when they flickered back to her, only fire.

The pause gave the governor enough time to catch his breath.

"I do." Alexander pressed his face harder against the gun. "But today is not the day for it." He was eerily calm as he raised his hand, exposing his rotting flesh. "Once you take the mark, they own you. I didn't have a choice anymore."

Cam cocked back the hammer of his revolver and grinned. "Bull. Try again."

Maya sobbed by the door.

Alexander never dropped Cam's gaze. "After the accident with the Pearl Dust, they wanted you for what you would become. I told them no, but Cassie knew I couldn't resist them for long. I wasn't safe anymore." His voice faltered. "I hadn't been for a long time."

Cam tilted his head and brushed his finger against the trigger. "This—all of this—is your fault."

Alexander swallowed. "It is."

Cam's grip tightened. "You have three seconds to convince me not to kill you."

"It doesn't matter if you do," Alexander shot back. "Because I'm dying already."

The heaviness on Annie's chest loosened only when Cam paused, expression twisted in confusion. "W-why are you dying?"

The governor raised his hand again, showing the festering wound where The Order's mark had been, where he'd tried to cut it out.

He smiled weakly. "Because I said no . . . again."

Cam leaned back, breathing heavily. "I don't—"

"I thought if I . . . removed my influence, I would be free of this." Alexander's words were *so* tired. Tight, like he wanted to say more but couldn't. "But I was wrong. It can't be removed. The agreement is a blood contract to the depths of which I didn't understand. I've kept my attempt at defecting a secret from everyone except—"

"Henry Bale." Cam sat back until he was seated on the tea table. His revolver was still pointed at the governor's head. "He knows."

"Yes." Alexander gave Maya a soft smile as she returned to his side. "He does, and he loves to remind me how little time I have left."

"But how?" Annie stood and stepped closer, brushing Cam's shoulder as she leaned in to examine the governor's finger. "Have you tried to treat the wound? Surely, there's a cure—"

Alexander threw his head back and laughed. "I told you. It's a contract, binding me to their will. It's not something that can be remedied."

Cam stared blankly at his father's hand. Only the way his brands flared and guttered gave away the torrent of emotions terrorizing him.

Blood contracts. Incurable wounds. It reeked of black magic, like in children's tales. Her father used to tell her of men who'd sell their souls to devils for gain. Beings of otherworldly abilities. Those devils, it turned out, were Revenants. People like her. Like Cam. Like Mr. Price.

"That's why you want us to stop them," Cam muttered and shook his head. "To save your life."

"No." Alexander slid on his glove. "I'm going to die. It can't be stopped. Enoch will pass to you whether you want it or not. I want you to stop them because they want *you*." His eyes flickered to Annie. "How do you think they create these blood contracts? They siphon, moving life and death between individuals until their life force is no longer owned by its source, but by its manipulator. But it takes energy, an *enormous* amount of energy, to take control of a single person's mind. Imagine if The Order had a way to speed that process? How many others could they control?

"*I've been alive over four hundred years,*" Magnus Baxter had said. "*And you are only the sixth Death Brand I've met. Every one of them from the North, and every one female.*"

Not all Death Brands can siphon. Annie backed up until she felt the edge of the sofa against her knees. *If our transfer of energy creates these contracts . . .*

And if another owned that power . . .

Annie knew what it was to be owned. Whoever controlled the siphon would control the rest. If it was out of willingness or fear, it didn't matter.

Her gaze shifted to Cam. His eyes were fixed on her.

If his power was as limitless as it seemed, and she could harness it and use it as she willed—as they had with Reika Hall—then that made them more than a weapon.

"We're a battery," Annie said out loud.

Cam's eyes fluttered as he sucked in a breath.

"The Order has known what you are for years," the governor said. "They've been hunting for Death Brands, particularly those able to siphon, since Revenants came to be, and when they discovered what Cam had the potential of becoming . . ." He smiled at them sadly. "You two were doomed to find each other, one way or another."

CHAPTER 34
ELAIN

Elain faded between the here and there, caught in the realms of Earth and the Grey as she followed the suited man down the staircase. He reeked of death, and his footsteps left oily, black stains on the marbled floors that only she could see.

My lady. Elain glanced back just as The Healer, Annie, stepped into the tearoom. The fiery boy, who yearned for her, stood beside her. He would protect her. She could trust him to keep The Healer safe.

The suited man grumbled to himself as he strode out the main doors and into the courtyard. Elain kept close behind, her dainty bare feet never touching the ground. The man approached the carriage waiting for him, snapped at the driver, and muttered something about a lodge before climbing inside.

The space where her heart had once been ached. She couldn't leave.

I have to. The Healer commanded that she follow, so follow she would. She glanced back at the manor, vowing that she would return soon. She wouldn't let her lady down.

The carriage circled the courtyard, heading for the city. Elain climbed aboard, invisible to those inside.

CHAPTER 35
CAMDEN

The Order can burn. They will *burn.* Cam would willingly give his soul to the deepest levels of hell before he's let another man lay a finger on Annie.

And his mother.

His mother.

"Take him somewhere his father won't find him." She'd begged Resh. Because if what his father said was true, Alexander Callahan would have sold Cam to The Order whether he'd wanted to or not.

The Order murdered Annie's family, had stolen her in the night, had savaged her, because they'd known what she'd become. Just like they'd known what Cam would become.

Elias Bennett.

Richard Duskin.

They'd been pawns. Tools. Just like him.

Richard Duskin's research on Pearl Dust had been meant to speed the process, and it had worked. Pearl Dust *could* predict Revenancy, and if Elias hadn't died when he did, the rest of The Order would know it now, too.

And Annie owns Lord Duskin's patent. If The Order took Annie, not only would they be able to use her as a siphon, but as a way to obtain all the Pearl Dust they'd ever need.

If it weren't for the fact that he was about to vomit, Cam would have already killed his father, even if only because he'd known and done *nothing.*

You can do it, you know? His fire whispered so sweetly. *It wouldn't take much. He's dying anyway. Then this will all be over.*

No. Cam shook his head, his skin crawling, and he pressed his palms over his eyes. *It won't be over.*

The Order wouldn't stop coming for them if Alexander Callahan died. In fact, his father was likely the only reason they hadn't taken a more aggressive approach.

I need him. Cam exhaled, releasing a wave of energy that made their teacups crack, spilling hot liquid over the remaining pastries on the tray. *I need my father alive, at least until we stop them.*

"Camden," Alexander began. He looked like a corpse. "We need to start planning. Now. While we still have the advantage. The council has rescheduled the Revenant rights meeting for three weeks. We must prepare you to take command of the West—"

"*Shut up.*" Cam squeezed his eyes shut as his fire squirmed just below the surface, fighting to break free. "For once in your damn life, be quiet."

Alexander stopped talking.

"Camden." Annie's voice was low, emotionless, but her grip on his elbow was deathly tight. "Should we—"

I have to leave. Cam stood abruptly, knocking into the tea table. He needed fresh air. He needed space to breathe before his fire decided to lash out on its own. Thankfully, no one tried to stop him as he strode out of the room, trailed by swirling flames.

They did this to us. He took the stairs three at a time, fighting to get air in his lungs. Panic threatened to strangle him. The Order took everything from them. How was he supposed to beat a centuries-old organization that had stomped his father into the dirt?

His father, the one who'd plagued Cam's nightmares since he was a child. The man who'd beaten him. The man who'd controlled the West with an iron fist for decades. Now he was dying. Cam hadn't even gotten to do it himself. The Order had taken that from him, too.

I can't do it. Cam slipped as his boots hit damp grass. He strode towards the garden, looking for somewhere—anywhere—he could be alone. *I can't stop them. I can't save us. I can't protect her.*

Annie.

Cam rubbed the still-aching spot on his shoulder where he'd been shot. How could he keep her safe when he couldn't even protect himself?

Burn it down. Cam cried out as his fire ripped through his veins, filling his mouth with smoke. *We will burn it all down.* He grabbed hold of the closest thing to him—a fence post, maybe—and braced as an explosion of heat and rage and terror tore out of his body.

In that moment, the fear stopped. He wasn't Camden Callahan anymore. No, in that moment, he was simply *fire* —and he would burn it all down.

And he would have if a small, angry voice hadn't cut through his inferno. "You've burnt my strawberries, you brute!"

Just like that, his fire guttered out.

Cam's breath came in heavy gasps, smoke billowing from his nose and mouth, as he swiveled. A few yards away, at the edge of the lawn, his brother stood with his arms crossed, his expression twisted in frustration.

Between inhales, Cam managed a rough laugh. "What did you say?"

"My *strawberries.*" Kai gestured to the gardens, grass clippings stuck to his white stockings. "Look what you've done to it."

Cam turned back and winced. *Incinerated* would be a good word to describe what he'd done to his father's—pardon, *Kai's*—gardens. Nothing remained of the once manicured labyrinth but smoke and super-heated ash.

"Apologies." Cam released the fence, but it crumbled into coals, staining his palms black. "I was arguing with . . . myself."

Kai's dark brow rose. "Who won?"

Cam waved toward the destruction. "Not me, obviously."

Kai smiled. He looked a little like Father, and a lot like Maya.

From the front entry, Annie, Alexander, and Maya watched them. Cam shot Annie a quick look, reaching across the courtyard with his heat to brush her arm. *I'm sorry.*

Even from here, he could see her small, returning smile. He still couldn't believe she was here, talking to him, smiling at him. He worried that if he let his gaze linger too long, she might disappear. That she'd return to hating him. That her promise to stay was just wishful dreaming.

She's staying. You'll be okay as long as she's here. Even using that little of his fire had allowed his mind to clear.

"So." With a deep sigh, Cam plopped down on the grass, not caring if he ruined his fresh suit. "How do I make it up to you?"

Hesitantly, Kai crossed the ashy lawn and sat beside him. He glanced up at Cam, lips pursed, a nervous twinge in his tone. "Do you do much gardening?"

God, I destroyed all his hard work. Cam grimaced again. "I don't, I'm afraid."

Kai pouted. "Oh. Drat."

"I could try, though." Cam quickly added.

"Would you?" Kai's eyes twinkled, then the light vanished when he glanced back to where their father stood. "Father says lords shouldn't spend their time in the dirt."

Cam reclined onto his elbows, crossing his feet at the ankles. "Our father's full of bull."

Kai's mouth made a perfect, shocked O. "We also shouldn't—"

"Use foul language?" Cam's grin widened. "It's a good thing I'm not a lord, then."

"Yes, you are." Kai shot back. "You're my brother. That makes you a lord."

"If being your brother is the qualifying factor for lordship, then I'm less resistant to joining the club."

"Are you really a pirate?" Kai changed the subject, that sparkle returning to his gaze.

"Am. Was. I'm not sure anymore." Cam shrugged, then gave his brother an appraising look. "Would you like to see my ship?"

"Would I!" Kai nearly shrieked, then covered his mouth before whispering. "But Mother and Father would never let me."

"Nonsense." Cam glared over his shoulder. Alexander was gone, but Maya continued to watch them like a hawk. "I'm a pirate, remember? They can't stop us."

"Truly?" Kai asked, amazed. "Do you have cannons?"

"I have one hundred and twenty-four cannons," Cam winked. "Across three levels."

"You're teasing me!"

"I never would."

"Wow." Kai stared wistfully across the estate grounds, towards the sea. "I wonder what would happen if you fired them all at once."

Cam burst out laughing. "You'd explode your eardrums, that's what would happen."

Annie held up the hems of her skirts as she crossed the lawn. Once she was within a few yards of them, she gazed out over the ruined gardens and wrinkled her nose. "I don't think David is going to be happy with you."

"He'll understand." Kai tried to brush the grey stains off his stockings. "I'll make sure he does."

"That's kind of you." Annie sat down on Cam's opposite side, curling her legs beneath her. "We'll pay for the damages, of course."

Cam *wanted* to argue that Alexander could pay for his own damn gardens, but he was too transfixed by how the recently emerged sunlight reflected off Annie's white hair and skin, making them glimmer like snow.

Kai perked up. "Camden said he is going to take me to see your ship."

"Did he?" Annie smirked.

The boy nodded in excitement. "Do pirates really have gold teeth and hooks for hands?"

Cam forced his eyes off Annie long enough to come back to the present. "How do you feel about rotten teeth and missing arms?"

"That sounds . . . not nearly as thrilling." Kai frowned.

"But Camden has something better to show you." Annie gave the boy one of her close-lipped smiles. "Don't you?"

Cam made a face and mouthed, *"I do?"*

She scowled at him.

"Oh, right." Cam groaned as he got back into a sitting position—Kai's dragon.

Since that evening in the carriage—and after Magnus's suggestions— after he and Julian's morning training, Cam and Annie had been practicing controlling his fire. At least they had been until she'd stopped speaking to him. He could hold a shape now without it in his eyesight, but after his last visit with Kai, he'd wanted to give him a gift. Something special no one else could give him.

Even with the small outburst that took out the gardens, his fire felt calmer as he willed the shapes he saw in his mind into existence.

Just beyond Kai's laced shoes, the same dragon formed out of fire, colored in golds, oranges, and reds. It cocked its horned head at Kai and spread its broad, fiery wings.

Without hesitation, Kai leaned forward to stroke the imagined creature's chin. The dragon nipped at his fingers playfully, making Kai squeal in delight. He'd kept the size to that of a large dog. Perfect for keeping inside the manor.

Cam didn't hold back his smile. When he'd crafted the dragon from his fire the first time, it had been on impulse. He hadn't even been sure how he'd done it.

But he'd practiced—a lot. It had been the only thing to keep him from losing his bloody mind this last week.

"He's yours," Cam said, and for once in his life, he felt proud. "He'll stay with you, protect you, even when I'm not here."

"How?" Kai breathed as he examined the spikes lining the dragon's spine. "I've never heard of a Revenant doing this."

"I don't know." Cam shrugged. "I just did. Because I wanted to."

"Your brother is different. Special." Annie ran her fingers along the creature's side. It didn't burn her. It didn't burn Kai. "What are you going to name it?"

Kai paused and blinked. "I'm not sure. I've never had a pet."

"Neither have I," Annie replied, dropping her hands to her lap. "Even when I was young."

"Me either. It would have gotten eaten aboard a ship." Cam shot Annie a wry look. "We should get a cat."

She smiled slightly but didn't reply.

God, he loved it when she smiled.

"I'm going to name him Brantley." Kai beamed and nodded towards the gardens. "It means *burnt meadow*. Are you sure Father won't make me get rid of him?"

"He can't." Cam picked at the grass until there was a small pile beside him. "He'd have to get rid of me to get rid of Brantley."

Kai didn't look reassured.

Cam pointed out some scraps of uncharred wood in the garden. "See those? You and your new pal should go burn them up. Father would want you to make sure the job is done well, aye?"

With a laugh, Kai scrambled to his feet and bolted into the remains of the gardens, the little dragon flying not far behind.

Cam felt a slight tug against his fire as they left. Not in a way that drained him, but more of an irritation. Like an itch he had to learn to ignore. He kept his attention fixed on Annie— who still watched Kai—listening until his brother's running footsteps had faded.

Cam made a face. "Is our friend, Brantley, still intact?"

Annie's gaze flickered to his before returning to the gardens. "Yes."

"Thank God." Cam flopped back into the grass. Heavy, lumpy clouds clogged up the sky above, interrupted by small slivers of blue. There—he'd forgotten about The Order for a full fifteen minutes.

Annie scooted closer until her side touched his. "Are you alright?"

"No." Cam's eyelids fluttered closed. "You?"

"I've been better," she whispered back. "Do you believe him? What he said about the mark and The Order wanting to use us?"

"How can I not? His finger is rotting off."

"There are only three weeks now until all the parties meet." Annie brushed a strand of her hair off her face. "I expect The Order will retaliate. I wouldn't be surprised if there's another murder."

"As long as it isn't us," Cam sighed.

"Camden." Annie's pinkie looped through his. "I think we should go see Mr. Baxter again."

Cam shifted so he could look at their entwined fingers. "Why?"

"You know why." Annie returned to watching Kai and Brantley in the distance, the dragon breathing fire on everything and anything his brother commanded. "I saw it, Camden. You took out an entire acre with a breath. If you don't get this—"

"You think I'll hurt someone," Cam said coldly, daring to brush his free fingers over the back of her hand.

"That's not what I said," she replied. "I was about to say, you're going to hurt *yourself*. Your fire is going to tear you apart unless we can figure out how to keep it contained."

"I like *we*." Cam slowly wove the rest of his fingers through hers. She didn't pull away. "I know, and you're right, even though you sound like Julian."

"Thank you." Annie's own brands flared, a striking pearly-white, as she gently closed her hand around his. "I'll ask Jenny to send him a letter."

They stayed like that for several minutes, hands locked

together. Cam's heart pounded so hard he worried she might hear it.

Finally, Annie sighed, her voice barely a whisper. "What are we going to do?"

He knew what she meant. He let out a long, exaggerated sigh as he stroked the back of her hand with his thumb. "Cry?"

"Crying seems rational," she said, flat. "But not productive."

"They want to use us to power their mind-control scheme," Cam said. "They're using blood magic to kill my father, which I didn't even know was possible, and I have a feeling they're blocking him from telling us what we need to know. They have the entire city divided and at each other's throats—" Cam groaned. "I think we're out of our league."

"And we're going to keep fighting," Annie responded, not a question. "For us."

"Yes." Cam let his eyes fall closed again, enjoying the feeling of her icy skin and the sun on his face. "We will keep fighting . . . for us."

CHAPTER 36

CAMDEN

Three days later, their carriage pulled to a stop alongside the road in one of Enoch's less savory neighborhoods.

"You sure you don't want me to do it?" Cam asked. He'd offered six times already.

Annie sat beside him, Julian across from them. She stared out the window toward the street corner, sweat beading on her brow. She looked like she was about to hyperventilate.

"No." Annie sucked in three deep breaths, then smoothed her already pristine waves. "I can do this. I *have* to do this. You can't."

"Have it your way." Cam opened the door for her and stepped out. "I'll be right here." Close enough that he could protect her, but far enough away to give her the space she wanted.

Annie nodded nervously as she climbed down beside him. Her back was as straight as a board as she waited to cross the cobbled street. After several horse-drawn buggies passed, she hurried across. An elderly man waited on the other side, dressed in a rain hat and a heavy coat. Annie passed him a thick cash clip, and he handed her a small package.

Just like that, it was done.

She looked sick as she rushed back to the carriage and dove inside. Cam followed and shut the door behind them.

"Check it before we leave," Julian ordered.

Annie's fingers shook as she undid the strings holding the crinkly, brown paper in place. Inside were three one-inch-long corked bottles, filled to the brim with a petal pink powder—Pearl Dust.

"Ha," Cam snorted. "You're a drug dealer now."

"I am *not*." Annie shoved the bottles into her coat pocket. "I-it's for a good cause."

The man on the corner had already disappeared into the crowd. Julian reached out and knocked on the top of the carriage, and the driver set them back in motion.

"Why three vials?" Julian asked, completely unfazed. "Surely, Magnus doesn't need that much."

"It's for the hospital." Annie wiped her sweaty face on her wool sleeve. "There are so many patients. They're all infecting each other, and well—" They went over a bump, making the bottles in her pocket clack together. She winced. "—I need a faster way to screen them."

Cam feigned a gasp. "Are you telling us you're planning to illegally drug your patients?"

"No!" Annie's eyes widened. "Kind of. Don't make me hit you."

"You can't," Cam grinned. "You know I'd like it."

She blushed.

Julian cleared his throat. "Do you plan on sharing this information with the Clarkes?"

"I haven't decided," Annie sighed. "To some degree, I have

to. They'll need to know the treatment plans, but I . . . I haven't gotten that far yet."

"One day at a time." Julian gave her a kind smile. "That's all we can do, isn't it?"

Cam and Annie nodded in unison.

An hour later, they rolled to a stop in front of Magnus's dilapidated building.

"I've changed my mind," Cam said as they waited in the tunnel for him to open the heavy, iron door to his prison— pardon—lab. "This is a terrible idea. Let's call the carriage back."

Annie rolled her eyes at him. "It's too late now."

"Miss Annie's right." Julian pursed his lips, tucking deeper into his cream coat as he folded his arms over his chest. "You dragged me out here. I'm not letting you leave."

"Try stopping me." Cam waved a cobweb out of his face. Now that he thought about it, he wasn't sure who'd win in a proper fight between him and Julian. Their first fight, back on *The Nightlady*, didn't count. Cam was still human then. All their time training together proved what a capable fighter Julian was.

Now, if Annie and Julian ever went toe to toe, he'd definitely put his money on—

The rusted metal hinges let out an awful groan as the door swung open, revealing Magnus in all his stunted, spectacled glory.

Wearing those same silly trousers up to his armpits, Magnus scanned them over and grinned. "Ah, Lord and Lady Callahan, I was so happy to receive your maid's letter."

"Sister," Annie corrected. "She's my sister, not my maid."

"As you say." Magnus bowed, ushering them inside. "Still, I have been looking forward to your return since you left. I've been poring over books and records and think I may have found information that could be of use."

The humidity bogged down Cam's lungs as he and Annie sat down on the love seat, Julian on the chair beside them. Lord, somehow there were *more* plants than last time. They were hanging from pots on the ceiling now. Great bushy things full of ferns and dangling moss.

"We're grateful for all your help." Annie fought back a grimace as he poured her a cup of tea. "We need it."

Boxes upon boxes of papers had been shoved into the corners, making the space claustrophobic. A desk had also been added. Atop it sat the vials of that purply-black fluid he'd been working on, each labeled and dated.

Annie seemed to notice at the same time he did. She carefully took one of the Pearl Dust bottles out of her pocket and held it out for Magnus. "Here, for you."

"Thank you, thank you, my dear." Magnus swiped it out of her hand and shoved it in a random drawer before taking the seat across from them and tossing a thick blanket over his short legs.

He continued as if nothing had happened. "After our last conversation, I decided to see if I could track down the last Death Brand I'd met, Clarisse. Of course, that was about two hundred and fifty years ago, but I figured what was the harm?"

Cam ignored his tea. "Did you find her?"

"Of course not." Magnus snorted into his cup. "But what I *didn't* find was more interesting to me than what I *did*. No documents. No letters. No paper trails to prove that Clarisse had ever been anything but a figment of my imagination."

Julian sank back into his chair, solemn. "Sounds like a cover-up."

"Indeed." Magnus refilled his tea, seeming to be blissfully unaware that no one else was drinking theirs. "After that, I started digging into Clarisse's mother—also a Death Brand—but she'd vanished, as well. Clarisse had children, but only sons. As I continued in my newfound obsession, I did my best to find the other remaining Death Brands I knew of—not counting you, my lady—and take a guess what I found?"

"Nothing." Annie swallowed, shifting uncomfortably.

"Nothing," Magnus confirmed. He set down his cup and tossed aside his blanket. He rose, moving to adjust one of the ceramic mushrooms decorating his mantle, his expression contemplative. "Nothing but dust, cobwebs, and forgotten lives."

"Well, I'll take an easy guess of who made them disappear." Cam hesitated. Trusting wasn't natural for him, but Julian had known Magnus for decades. He couldn't see the old Revenant betraying him. "The Order wants Annie and me. My father suspects they want to use our combined powers to expedite whatever world domination plot they're involved in."

Seconds passed, and only the sound of bubbles rolling in the kettle over the fire broke the silence. Moisture dappled Magnus's brow. He turned back to his ceramics and sucked in a heavy breath. "That's . . . concerning."

Cam's heart dropped into his stomach. "That bad?"

Magnus let out an exasperated chuckle. "You can say that."

"You read my letter." Annie cut in, hiding her nerves behind a glacial stare. "We want your help with Cam's fire. Is there anything you can do?"

"Yes, apologies." Magnus shoved his glasses up his bulbous nose before waddling toward the door he kept hidden behind a curtain of vines. "This way, please."

They exchanged nervous looks before following him and Julian into the back room. Just like last time, the plants were replaced with an area of surgical equipment, blinking, humming machines, and steel walls.

Cam tried, and failed, to keep his pulse even as Magnus moved past the tables and gurneys. He kicked back a rug, revealing a small hatch in the floor. With a grunt, he tugged open the hatch and motioned toward a newly unveiled downward staircase. "After you."

Julian descended the steps without hesitation, followed by Magnus.

"If I die," Cam whispered in Annie's ear. "Avenge me."

"No deal." Annie turned her head, accidentally brushing her nose against his cheek. "If you die, we all hang."

Cam managed a smile before offering his hand. She took it, and they followed the others. The tightness of the hall had them walking single file. At the bottom, the stairs led into another square, metal room, this one even smaller than the last. Where the first was clogged with greenery, and the second machines, this one was filled from top to bottom with used notebooks. Some of the stacks were taller than Cam, leaning precariously in one direction or another.

And the room was split in two. The half they stood in—filled with what he assumed was Magnus's research—was separated by a dividing wall, not unlike a zoo enclosure. The bottom of the wall was metal, lined with more whirring machines, covered in twisting dials and knobs. The top half was a glass panel for observation.

Magnus dug through notebooks and journals as Julian found himself a place to sit on top of one of the stacks.

Annie wrung her hands, eyes darting in every direction. "What is this place?"

"My testing chamber," Magnus said casually as he flipped through the pages of a worn, leather binder. "I invite many Revenants here to test their abilities. We will be testing Camden's today."

"How?"

Magnus ignored her, continuing to flip through pages until he paused, eyes brightening. "Ah, here we are."

Notes in hand, he began adjusting various dials, causing the lights on the walls to shift from green to yellow. Next, he opened a drawer on a nearby cabinet and removed a tangled pile of straps and wires.

"We"—Magnus cursed as he struggled to untangle a cord—"are going to test you with these."

Cam popped his lips. "I'm not going to lie, you lost me at the testing chamber."

Julian chuckled from atop his paper pile.

"Revenant bodies," Magnus began, along with more curses over the tangles. "Produce a monumental amount of energy. It manifests in the manipulation and creation of elements: water, storms, plant life, and fire. Aha!"

Magnus held out the wired contraption to Cam.

He sighed before taking it.

"In all of my studies." Magnus returned to his knobs and dials. "I've found that vibrations power Revenant energy—the oscillating motion of an object—and their strength is determined by frequency—the rate at which motion repeats."

"I've read about frequency, back on New Havana." Annie scanned over the machines in fascination. "Lord Duskin was enthralled when scientists discovered the concept. He read all the reports and made me read them, as well."

"Dear," Magnus straightened and smiled. "I *am* the scientist who discovered them—at least in Revenant."

"How could you possibly track frequency?" she asked.

"With those." Magnus motioned for Cam to shake out the straps. The straps themselves were made of leather, the outside of which was adorned with round steel studs spaced every three inches. The insides were lined with short, thin needles.

Cam's heart vaulted into his throat. "I don't like this."

"It won't hurt." Magnus waved flippantly. "Much. You'll wear the harness over your torso, where the needles will be inserted into the skin to record frequency levels."

"I'm done." Cam held out the harness like it might bite him. "I quit. I didn't sign up for being punctured by hundreds of needles."

Magnus snatched it back. "If I don't know the extent of your power, Lord Callahan, I can't help you. That's like asking me to shoot pigeons in the dark."

"Pigeons don't come out in the dark," Cam muttered.

Magnus scowled.

"Excuse us a moment." Annie gave the Flora Brand a grim smile before tugging Cam aside by the elbow. Even just that simple touch set his heart and fire ablaze, his brands bright in the dim light.

"What if this helps?" Annie held his gaze. "We have to try."

"Again, I like the *'we'*." Cam let out a frustrated huff. "But what if I blow this building apart, and stabbing me was a waste of time?"

Her lips curved into an amused, wicked smile. "Is stabbing ever a waste of time?"

"You've got me there," Cam grinned back. "I just . . ."

"Lord Callahan." Magnus turned more dials. "*You* are wasting time."

He'd forgotten about Magnus's excellent hearing.

I don't trust myself is what Cam wanted to say. He didn't trust his fire, or the way it whispered to him, but he'd have to disappoint Annie to get out of this, and he wasn't prepared to do that anytime soon.

"Fine." Cam brushed his fingers over Annie's arm before turning back to Magnus. "What do I need to do?"

"Strip off your coat and shirt." Magnus didn't even

look at him, still transfixed with machine adjustments. "The needles must be inserted through several layers of skin."

Blazes. Annie's cheeks were as red as Cam's as he slipped off his coat and tossed it into the corner. The flush crept down both their necks as he pulled off his undershirt. It wasn't like Annie hadn't seen him half-naked before, but things were different. Before, her eyes didn't scan hungrily over his body the way they did now. Or if they had, she'd done a damn good job of hiding it.

Cam slid the harness over his shoulders, careful not to let the needles pierce him. Another set of straps came around his waist, and the four bands buckled over the center of his chest. His fire writhed beneath his skin, trying to escape. Even it knew this was a bad idea.

"Right." Magnus rubbed his hands together and grabbed the straps on Cam's shoulders. "Now we just press these down one at a time—"

"I'll do it." Annie stared Magnus down—which wasn't hard, she was taller than he was—until he moved aside.

"Thank you," Cam muttered under his breath as the Flora Brand turned to separate wires. With gentle hands, Annie re-tightened the straps. "I think he might be enjoying this a little too much."

"He's a scientist." She huffed. "Of course, he is. Take a deep breath—"

Before Cam could form a response, Annie quickly, but firmly, ran her hands over the straps, shoving all the needles in at once. It wasn't the pain Cam noticed but her arms around him, and her chest pressed against his.

"*Hang it all.*" Cam's sides spasmed and his skin *burned*, but at least she'd gotten it done all at once. He let out a rushed breath. "Ouch."

Julian looked green. He guessed he wasn't the only one who didn't like needles.

"Well done." Magnus came between them and started tying wires to the studs along the outsides, where they then connected the machines. "Once inside the chamber. I'm going to direct you to use your power. When the machine records a reading, I will signal you to release more and more energy until you feel like you've reached your limit. Understand?"

Cam nodded. "Unfortunately."

Thank *God* he'd worn the fireproof clothing Elias had given him in expectation of something like this happening. He controlled his fire well enough that he rarely burnt his clothing anymore, but this was bound to be a disaster.

"Excellent." Magnus patted his elbow. "Head inside then."

I shouldn't be doing this. I shouldn't be doing this. Every warning bell he possessed screamed at him to *flee*, especially as he stepped inside the chamber, and the door behind him began to close. It was like his fire knew its time had finally come. It filled him to the point of suffocation, crouching in wait.

From the other side of the glass, Annie chewed the edge of her thumbnail bloody. Julian didn't look any more confident.

Magnus slid open a glass panel at the bottom of the window. "You may begin."

Let me go. His fire whispered as Cam exhaled, letting a small amount of flames rip free from his body, licking up his limbs. *Just let me go.*

No. Cam stared at the metallic floor, the orangey glow of his fire warbling in the reflection. *I don't trust you.*

A tap on the glass had Cam raising his head. Magnus gave him a thumbs-up, signaling for more.

Cam let his head hang again, his chest rising and falling as more fire poured out from him. The needles beneath his skin *itched,* and it took a tremendous amount of concentration to keep them from melting. Flames erupted higher, spiraling around him like a tornado. He could handle this. Here, he was dangerous, but still safe.

I am you. His fire whispered. *You don't trust yourself.*

That's not true. Cam shook away the thought as the tap on the glass came again. Without looking up, he allowed a bit more fire free. He wanted to avoid the anxiety on Annie's face, the calculation on Julian's, or the expectation that Magnus wore. He just allowed a bit more fire free.

The fire released wasn't even a fraction of what had escaped him this morning. Maybe he'd get lucky and burn out. Maybe the extent of his power was merely hype and assumptions. He would be like every other Fire Brand that had been reborn. That's all he'd ever wanted—to be normal. A nobody. Someone who could live and die without consequence.

Another tap on the glass. Cam bit down on his lip as he let more flames free.

If it's not true, let me go. His fire challenged, whispering temptations in his ear. *Let me go.*

I can't do this. Cam's lungs were too full of sulfur and ash to breathe. He clenched his fists so hard that his nails bruised his palms. *I can't.* As his mind spiraled, he was bogged with visions of his mother's face, of *The Nightlady* on fire, of his own body burning alive, of the hatred in Annie's stare only days before. *I can't—*

Another tap on the glass. More fire.

More. More. More. Everyone wanted more. His father. Julian. His crew. Magnus.

He tried to think of something—anything—else to distract him, but now, all he could hear was that damned rapping on the glass and his fire demanding, *Let me go.*

Let me go.

Let me go.

Let me go.

I can't do this anymore.

So, let me go.

Cam leaned his head back and closed his eyes. The heat was suffocating, even to him. Then the gate holding his fire back cracked open, just enough that it consumed the chamber in a vortex of flame. Perhaps Magnus would be happy with that and let it be.

But no, they'd never be happy. *He* would never make anyone happy.

The pounding on the glass grew louder. Someone was screaming.

But it didn't matter.

Because Cam let out a relieved sigh and finally let go.

CHAPTER 37

ANNIE

Only Annie noticed Cam's quick descent into whatever hell his fire dragged him. As soon as he'd stepped inside the chamber, she regretted ever asking him to go there.

As Magnus continued to push him, Cam's eyes never left the floor. His entire body shook with the restraint, until something like peace washed over his face, and his eyes closed.

She banged on the glass, begging him to stop—

Then she crumpled at the explosion that peeled the roof off Magnus's lab—three floors deep. It tore open in layers, Cam's fire slicing through solid steel like sheet paper until only stars and black sky shone above them.

Annie's ears popped, making her jaw clench, as she forced herself to her knees. The glass panel between them had melted, along with all of Magnus's equipment, as a gale storm of fire spiraled into the night.

Scorched ground encircled her, leaving the space she lay untouched, as a second explosion slammed Mr. Price and Mr.

Baxter into the back wall, denting it with the force of their impact.

Gripping her chest, Annie scrambled to her feet. The metal support beams groaned as they gave way, leaving the remaining ceiling to crumble. *Camden.*

A gap in the flames reflected Cam's silhouette. His back was to her, his entire body glowing like molten ore, the veins showing beneath his skin white hot. As he stared up at the stars, he seemed calm. Peaceful. Free of the rage she expected.

Annie choked on smoke. "C-Camden?"

If he heard her, he didn't respond. Instead, he reached above his head and swiped his hand to the side, as if chasing away an insect. The back wall of the chamber *melted,* instantly turning to liquid. As Cam stepped forward, the liquid metal formed into stairs, one at a time, leading up into the night.

He's leaving. Annie's heart nearly stopped. *No, he's leaving.*

There was no more door to the chamber. It was gone. Mr. Price was fighting to get on all fours. Mr. Baxter had yet to rise at all.

They couldn't stop her.

"*Cam!*" Annie bolted after him, the soles of her heeled boots sticking to the charred ground. "Come back!"

This time, he heard her.

Cam paused, twisting, peering down at her from his molded stairway. There was nothing left of his eyes but flames. No white. No irises. Just endless pools of torrential fire.

Annie stopped short, fighting to breathe through the smoke, and whispered, "Don't go."

Where his posture had once been calm, Cam's shoulders stiffened, his features contorting in anger. When he spoke, his voice was raspy, shredded. "And where would I go, Annie?"

She didn't know how to answer that. In fact, where could *either* of them go?

"I don't know," she replied honestly. When she tried to take another step closer, her boot was fully cemented to the floor. "And I don't care, as long as you take me with you."

One moment, Cam was there, the next he was standing over her, leaning so their faces were inches apart. Lord above, she could feel her skin burning where his breath touched it.

He wasn't himself. She'd met this monster before. On New Havana, when he'd turned Lord Duskin's manor to rubble. She'd caught a glimpse of it again when she'd clawed into his power as they'd saved Reika's child. But she wasn't afraid of him. He wouldn't hurt her.

"Come with me?" Cam snapped, his flames spiraling around them. "You tried to *leave* me once already."

"Don't you dare," Annie straightened, not hiding an ounce of the pain in her voice. "Don't you dare hold that over me. I was scared, just like you are now."

His expression darkened, but a glimpse of *him* appeared beneath the fire.

"Miss Annie." Mr. Price's voice cut through the smog. "You need to get back—"

As he spoke, Cam's attention lifted to him, filled with hatred. Annie only felt a shift in the air as Cam vanished, to reappear with his hand around Mr. Price's throat as he slammed him against the wall.

"You." Cam's smile twisted, and smoke poured from his mouth as he spoke. "You watched me die."

"I did," Julian choked out, his fingers blistering as he clawed at Cam's wrist. "I can't change what's been done, can I?"

Mr. Baxter was on his knees, watching with wide eyes as Cam tossed Mr. Price aside like a rag doll. A blade made of fire formed in his hand. Cam was going to cut Mr. Price into pieces.

"*No!*" Annie scrambled and put herself between them just

as Cam drew the blade back. Instead of stopping, Cam pressed his forehead against hers and pushed until *her* back was to the wall.

Eye-to-eye, she held his furious stare. "I said no."

Cam's grin turned feral, his fire smoldering the hem of her dress. "Say that again."

"No," Annie repeated, unblinking. "You're not killing anyone today."

"*No*," Cam said, mocking. "Is that what you tell yourself when you look at me?"

Annie's entire body went rigid. Cam grabbed her hand and placed it around *his* throat.

"I feel your power begging for mine. I wish you'd just *take* it." He breathed, his nose brushing against hers. He took her opposite wrist, placing her palm onto his bare chest, over his heart. "Take it, Annie. *Please.* Don't make me beg. I don't want to be like this anymore."

"I will." *You've always wanted this.* For so long, she'd wanted *him.* His power mixed with hers. She'd dreamt of it, craved it. Annie squeezed Cam's throat tighter. He grinned and choked out a rough laugh.

Then she threw the gates open, and his fire slammed into her, drowning her, until there was nothing left but him and her and whatever cords on heaven and earth that had forced them together.

Cam sank to his knees, reclining his head to give her better access. Annie's vision went white—but she wouldn't break away. No, she'd take whatever he gave her until there was no space left inside her to fill because he needed her. Because he couldn't be sane without her.

There was a jolt, then they were both on their knees— ragged, gasping. Mr. Price stood over them, his face ghostly white, holding Annie's arm off at an odd angle.

He pulled us apart. Why do people keep doing that? Her entire body trembled, skin glowing like a newborn star. "W-why?"

"Because I told him to." Mr. Baxter wasn't far behind. "Because you'd kill each other if he didn't."

"*Never.*" Cam rasped. The vortex of fire around them had ceased, and a semblance of humanity returned to his eyes. "We can't. We've tried."

Then he collapsed.

CHAPTER 38

ANNIE

It hurt to breathe—not just from the sweltering heat and ash tainting the air—but because as Cam hit the ground, all the fire shining through his body vanished. Snuffed out. Around him, little scraps of paper gently floated to the ground like charred snowflakes.

He's dead. Annie's head spun and drew her down, down, as she struggled to stay conscious. *He's dead. He's gone. You killed him. You made him do it.*

No, no, no, no. Tears poured over Annie's face as she crawled to him, shaking his shoulder, but Cam remained lifeless. Mr. Price and Baxter watched as she rolled Cam onto his back. His usually tanned skin was sickly pale. Even his brands had gone dark. Only training and instincts had Annie checking for a pulse. As she pressed her fingers against his jugular, a wave of relieved sobs escaped her as the faintest of heartbeats met her touch.

Annie wiped her eyes, smearing black soot over her cheeks. "H-he's alive."

"Get him upstairs." Mr. Baxter wobbled as he stood, his

voice taking on a level of authority it hadn't carried before. "We need to get him by the fire."

Mr. Price blinked at him, barely able to answer past his blistered throat. "Are you insane? He *is* fire, you loon."

"Not right now, he isn't." Magnus pointed to Mr. Price, then to Cam. "Upstairs now."

Annie barely reacted when Mr. Price shoved her aside and scooped Cam into his arms, tossing him effortlessly over his shoulder.

Not right now, he isn't. Annie watched as Mr. Price navigated up what remained of the staircase. *No.* She'd seen into the depths of Cam's power, stood at the edge of it. She didn't believe for one moment he'd burnt out.

"He's in shock," Annie said out loud, but they'd already left. She tried to stand, but her remaining boot had melted to the floor. Cursing, she ripped her foot out of it and darted after them in just her stockings.

Praise the Lord, most of Magnus's main dwelling was intact. She'd have never forgiven herself if they'd destroyed all his precious herbs and flowers. Mr. Baxter dragged the love seat in front of the fire. "Put him down here."

"He's in shock," Annie repeated as Mr. Price lowered Cam onto the sofa.

"He's at his limit," Magnus corrected, shoving his glasses up his nose. "You took too much from him—"

"Get out of the way." Annie shook her head and pushed past him. *I have to know.* She grabbed Cam's wrist and opened that gate between them. The flames in the hearth and candles guttered as Cam's fire roared back to the surface. Mr. Baxter yelped and stumbled backward.

Where are you? Annie closed her eyes, keeping hold of Cam's fire, as she wandered deeper inside him. She reached out with her power, searching for places she could heal, where he was hurting, when a rush of heat and darkness slammed down and pushed her out.

Annie gasped as she crashed back into reality. She tumbled over the corner of the rug, but Mr. Price caught her before she fell.

"Tell us what to do." His silver eyes flashed from her to Cam. "How do we help?"

He didn't want me there. Cam blocked her from seeing any deeper. *He doesn't want my help—*

Later. Annie let her old mask fall into place, the one she had worn when tending to Lord Duskin's patients. Gently, she brushed Cam's hair out of his face, his skin sticky with sweat, and ran her fingers along the line of his clenched jaw. Even the corners of his closed eyes were tense. With the back of her hand, she touched his neck, his chest—his skin was ice cold.

Annie nodded toward Mr. Baxter's chair. "Give me that blanket."

Mr. Price tossed it to her. After covering Cam, she twisted to face Mr. Baxter. "Get more."

"Incredible." The Flora Brand didn't seem to hear her, eyes fixed on Cam, mouth slack with awe. "He should have burned out, he—"

"*He* needs medical attention," Annie shouted. *You can care later.* "Get me the damned blankets."

Mr. Baxter almost looked offended as he hobbled toward a small closet in the back, muttering to himself.

Kneeling beside the sofa, Annie rested her hand over Cam's chest. *His breathing is too rapid.* Even through the blanket, his heartbeat—once slow—now felt like a hummingbird.

Mr. Price leaned against the hearth, arms crossed, expression creased in concern.

"Is this what you wanted?" Annie glared up at him, unable

to hide the venom in her tone. "You knew this would happen, didn't you?"

"Not exactly." Mr. Price cocked his head, the fire casting a golden glow over his sallow skin. "But I needed to know. I think we all did. Especially Camden."

Somewhere in the back, Mr. Baxter was still digging.

"What happened?" Annie glided her fingertips over Cam's eyelids, remembering how they'd been consumed by fire. "What was he? Why did he attack you?"

Mr. Price studied her for a moment. "Did he ever tell you how he died?"

"I know the general events, but not the details." Her mind snagged on Cam's comment. *Dear God.* "He said you *watched* him die."

The man swallowed, wrapping his coat tighter around himself. "At that time, I was working against both Elias Bennett and Richard Duskin. Camden's ship was one of the ones we burned. I let Frank Boyle tie him and his crew, who were too injured, to the mast before he set it on fire. Frank had a sick mind, and I let him get away with more than I should have to keep him compliant. I don't think Camden has ever forgiven me for it."

Nausea nearly bent her over. Mr. Price could push the blame onto Mr. Boyle all he wanted, but he was equally responsible for Cam's death. What would it be like if she had to work every day beside Charlotte Duskin? To never be able to repress the memories of the broken bottle that pierced her chest because its wielder was dining with them every night?

And Cam was just expected to live with it. To put it behind him. She knew much of pain. It didn't disappear after the physical scars had faded away. Releasing those bent-up flames had freed other things. Cam was hurting, and she'd spent too much time fighting her own demons to stop and ask about his.

You tried to leave me once already.

"Camden is repressing his fire instead of using it," Mr. Price said, bluntly. "He has since the start."

"But you've been training with him." Annie ran her fingers through his hair, an excuse to touch him again. "He *has* been using it."

"A fraction of it, yes," Mr. Price continued. "And he thinks he's fooling us all with his shows and displays. He's been hiding something since New Havana, and I don't like it. He could have incinerated every man who attacked the Clarkes's home with barely a thought, but he didn't. He used his damn gun."

"Why?" Annie let out a heavy sigh. Mr. Price's words had a level of truth to them. *Maybe that's why he shut me out.* She'd come too close to whatever part of Cam he didn't want her to see.

Mr. Price pursed his lips. "You tell me."

"Here." Mr. Baxter returned with three heavy, woolen blankets. "These should do the trick."

Annie didn't bother thanking him as she took them. Later . . . later she'd apologize for her rudeness. But right now, there was a patient who needed her. She tucked the blankets over Cam's body, making sure his limbs were covered, before tossing another log in the fire.

"Oh, I already have so many ideas." The legs of Mr. Baxter's chair screeched as he twisted it toward the fire and sat. "I could expand upon Elias Bennett's fireproof material design. Create a suit that not only is flame resistant, but that can *absorb* heat, allowing Lord Callahan to continually emit enough energy to keep his power from boiling over—excuse the pun."

Annie was grateful that Mr. Price let their conversation drop, his attention snapping to the Flora Brand. "Could such a thing be made?"

"Of course." Magnus adjusted his glasses. "It will just take research and materials."

"I wonder if Elias left anything behind that could be of use."

"Now there's a grand idea!"

The corner of Cam's mouth twitched, his brow furrowing, and his breathing began to quicken again.

Annie tugged the blankets more tightly around him. "Can you two discuss this somewhere else?"

Mr. Baxter gave her an incredulous look. "This is my living room."

"And you can chat elsewhere." Her glare hardened before she directed her gaze to Mr. Price. "Can't you?"

"Sure." The Air Brand's lips curled into a smile. He stood and patted Mr. Baxter on the shoulder. "Come along, my friend. You can tell me all your ideas as we see what we can salvage of your notes."

"My notes, yes!" Mr. Baxter hopped off his chair. "I forgot them. Blast it all, I had centuries of information down there . . ."

His words faded out as Mr. Price guided him back into the laboratory. Only once they were out of earshot did Annie finally relax.

"There, you can rest now." She slid to the floor and watched him. Right now, it just looked like he was sleeping. *I did this.* Annie lay her head against Cam's side, blinking back the moisture building in her eyes.

"I'm sorry I asked that of you," she said aloud, wishing he could hear her and simultaneously hoping he couldn't. "I just wanted to help, to make things better." A tear rolled down her cheek, and she quickly wiped it away. "The last thing I want is to hurt you, and it feels like that's all I ever do."

Cam just continued to breathe and breathe and breathe.

Mr. Price and Baxter's voices floated upstairs from below.

"What are you afraid of?" Annie whispered to Cam, pressing her face into the blankets. They smelled like rosemary. "I wish you would tell me."

A strong jerk under her cheeks made her jump up. Cam's body was seizing. His expression shifted into pure agony, the rhythms in his chest deep and heavy, as he convulsed. Before she could react, his eyes shot open, his back arching off the sofa, as he sucked in a gasping breath. His brands flared back to life, and surges of fire poured into his veins.

"*Cam*—" She reached for him, but he was already on his feet, the fire in his body flaring in and out like the lights on Mr. Baxter's machines. Cam wobbled. He was going to fall. He needed to lie down. He needed to—

Not knowing what else to do, Annie wrapped her arms around his waist and *pulled*.

Cam glanced at her—his eyes wild and filled with fire—and stumbled. Annie suppressed a shriek as they fell backward. With one hand, Cam caught himself against the edge of the sofa, trying to prevent himself from crushing her under his weight, but it took only a moment for his strength to give out.

He slumped to the floor, landing between her legs, his back against her chest.

Shaking, Annie kept her arms tight around his torso. "Don't move."

Resting his head against her shoulder, his words slurred as he muttered, "I'm sorry, I'm sorry, I'm sorry—"

Annie pressed her cheek against his shoulder as she tried to catch her breath. "You need to stay still."

"I-I can't." His teeth were chattering. He flexed his fingers as his limbs continued to convulse. "I'm twitching."

"Here." Annie reached over her head and tugged the stack of blankets over them both. She squeezed her grip on him tighter. *Pressure. He needs pressure to ground him.* "You're alright. You're in shock, but you're alright."

"Is that why I'm so cold?" He placed his hand over where hers lay on his bare stomach. "*Blazes,* I'm cold. I forgot cold. You're cold." He pressed his head back harder against her shoulder as his back spasmed. If she turned her head, her lips would be against his cheekbones. "I like your cold. I don't think I like this cold."

"Stop talking." Annie wanted to laugh—because he was awake, he was alive—but she forced her tone to stay low. "Just breathe for a minute."

Cam nodded and did just that. He inhaled and exhaled at her count, his tremors finally slowing when they reached fifty. His skin warmed, making her sweat as he lay against her. His voice was thick and muddled when he asked, "What did I do?"

That laugh escaped her. "You destroyed Magnus's lab . . . and most of the building."

"Damn it all." Cam blew out a hard breath. "I thought so."

He squeezed her hand, making Annie's heart flutter. "I'm sorry."

"Don't apologize." Annie nestled her cheek against his, and he sighed, melting deeper against her. "It was my fault."

"No, it was . . . not." His words grew more garbled as he began to fall back to sleep. "I-it's . . . I'm hungry."

"I imagine so." Annie stroked her fingers through his hair, making him melt all the more. *Touch him. Take it.* Her power came alive, reaching for him. She shoved it down and did her best to ignore it. Instead, she made a mental list of all the supplies they had in the villa. Anything to distract her. "We'll go home. What do you want to eat? I'll make it for you."

Cam let out a breathy laugh. "You c-can't . . cook."

Annie frowned. "You don't know that. I've never cooked for you."

"S-silly Kitten," Cam sighed, twisting until his head rested against the crook of her neck. "I'm a-already home."

Annie's brow rose. "We are at Mr. Baxter's."

Cam let his eyes fall closed and smiled. "Sure."

They both startled as a metal door slammed open, allowing Mr. Price and Mr. Baxter's voices to flood in from the other chamber.

Annie slipped out from beneath Cam at the same time he rolled forward, ready to defend her, ready to kill.

"It's fine." Annie squeezed his arm as the two Revenants stepped inside the living area.

"Lord Callahan!" Mr. Baxter's voice was far too loud and cheerful for the given moment. "I think I may have found a solution to your problem."

"Problem." The tension in Cam's shoulders visibly sagged as he rubbed his eyes. He sounded drunk. "S-sorry I broke your house."

Magnus waved dismissively. "Think nothing of it. You've inspired me again! There's so much to learn—"

Cam blinked at him. "Why do I feel like hell?"

Mr. Baxter burst out laughing. "Because you broke my house." He grabbed Cam by the chin and studied his face, scanning over the fire in his eyes and veins. Cam didn't fight him this time.

"To think." Mr. Baxter stepped back. "Lady Callahan is right. That isn't your limit. Your body was just unprepared to use so much power at once. Like a muscle that hasn't been stretched—"

As Mr. Baxter continued to chatter, Cam's face fell. A wave of despair passed over his features as he wrapped the blanket tighter around him.

This is what he was afraid of. Annie watched him, the threads of understanding starting to pull closed. *This is only the begin-*

ning. As Cam continued to get stronger, he would only become more dangerous, not only to his enemies, but to himself.

So will you. Annie shivered, her stark white brands flaring, as her own power stirred. *We are different. And The Order knows it. They've been expecting it. This is what they wanted.*

"Can it be controlled?" she asked.

"In time, I think so." Mr. Baxter said, tapping his chin. "But not without practice. Consistent practice at *that* level, or else Lord Callahan will continue to have repeats of today. As I've said before, the mind can only contain so much energy before it starts to be consumed by it."

"I'm ready to go." Cam lifted himself off the floor, managing to sit on the love seat. "Now."

Mr. Baxter's face fell. "But . . . my solutions—"

"I'll return in a few days." Mr. Price nudged his friend's elbow. "Then we'll hear all about your solutions, yes?"

"Yes, yes, I suppose." Mr. Baxter still pouted. "I expected you'd want to depart, though I'd hoped you'd stay. I had my personal carriage brought around." The Flora Brand held up a scrap of fabric. "There was nothing left of your clothing, I'm afraid. And since you won't fit in mine, you can take a blanket, Lord Callahan."

"That's very thoughtful." Annie looped her arms under Cam's and helped him to his feet. He wobbled for a moment, the blood draining from his face, but he managed to stay upright. Annie curtsied, noticing her dress's singed hems. "Goodnight, Mr. Baxter."

Cam's skin went pale as they walked to the main door, his gait unsteady.

Mr. Price offered him an arm. "Camden—"

"I'm f-fine." Cam shrugged him off and they headed back into the tunnel, leading toward the street. Though he managed his way through the fallen beams just fine, Annie kept close to him. Watching. Shock didn't dissipate that quickly. It could take hours—days—before he felt like himself again.

Rain had begun to fall, drizzling through the heavy clouds of smoke lingering over Mr. Baxter's ruined lab. She let out a sigh of relief to see Mr. Baxter's unfamiliar carriage waiting for them.

"The police will be here soon," Mr. Price muttered with an anxious glance to the sky as they climbed inside. "And Bale, too, most likely. We need to be far from here by then."

"The ugly twat." Cam let out a rumbling laugh as he sat down on the carriage's bench seat. "H-have you seen his mustache?" Cam sighed and curled up onto his side, blanket still snug around him. "I-I wish I could grow a mustache."

Once they had settled, Mr. Price shut the door and made a sharp knock on it. Cam was fast asleep before the driver urged the horses into a quick pace down the dark street, their shod hooves loud against the brick road.

And Annie continued to watch. Watching his sides rise and fall. Watching every shift in his sleeping features. Watching that he didn't break . . .

"He's going to be fine," Mr. Price said, as he undid his damp braid, shaking it out before replaiting it. "You both are."

"Easy to say when you're not the one being hunted." Annie glared at him. "We're walking targets."

"You forget Elias was high ranking in The Order." Mr. Price tied off his hair and then tucked his hands into his pocket. "And he wanted me dead. My own brother, yet here I am."

"And why is that?" Annie whispered back. "If they are so lethal and fearsome, why are you still alive? Why aren't Camden and I in chains? Why are they murdering members of their own Order?"

"Now," Mr. Price smiled at her. "Those are the questions

you should be asking, Miss Annie. Ones that I've been trying to find the answers to for decades."

Her mind reeled as the carriage jerked and bounced over potholes. She'd spent enough time around evil men not to be surprised when they murdered their own. More than once, she witnessed the slavers doing just that, but it was always in fits of anger, greed, or jealousy. The Order was calculated and strategic. They weren't just another criminal organization—they were a cult.

Annie tilted her head, gaze fixed on Cam as she said, "I disagree, Mr. Price. I think those still aren't the right questions."

"And what should I be asking?" he shot back.

"I don't know." Her lips pulled down at the corners. "But we're running out of time."

The carriage driver was kind enough to pull up to the villa's front entry. Mr. Price opened the door and held it for her while she shook Cam's shoulder.

"We're here," Annie whispered, and he jerked awake at her touch.

Cam didn't fight her. He sluggishly nodded and followed her out of the carriage, squinting at the lit gas-lamps hanging from the archway over the door. Mr. Price lit another lamp, illuminating the empty entry.

"Mr. Williams and Miss Jenny must be sleeping," he said.

"Well, it is after midnight." Annie followed after Cam, who was already making his way upstairs . . . towards her room.

Below, Mr. Price smirked. "Do you need help?"

"I've got him." Annie gave Mr. Price a quick curtsy to say her goodnights, then jogged up the stairs after Cam. Mr. Price let out a low laugh before heading down the hallway toward his bedchambers.

Once Annie had reached the top landing, she found Cam standing in the middle of the upper hall, a frustrated look on his face.

Quietly, she stepped up beside him and brushed his arm. "What is it?"

Slowly, he glanced down, tired eyes scanning her face. "I forgot I broke your door."

"Oh." She'd forgotten, too. He'd practically ripped it in half when he'd come for her during her nightmare.

Cam's voice caught, a weariness settling over him. "I ruin everything, don't I?"

Oh, Cam. "It's not ruined." Annie forced a smile as she climbed over the jagged, wooden remains of her bedroom door. "See? It works just fine."

Cam's expression didn't lighten. He just stared at her, jaw clenched, still gripping that blanket like it was the only thing keeping him alive.

Annie stretched her hand out for him. "Come on."

Relief flickered in his eyes, but it was quickly chased away by exhaustion as she helped him over the destroyed door.

Now, on the other side, Cam slid down the wall until he was seated on the floor. He closed his eyes, resting his head against the doorframe. "Goodnight, Kitten."

"You're not sleeping there." Annie wiped a bead of sweat off her forehead. The air was *boiling* as his brands flared and dimmed. "The bed is right there."

"That's y-y-your bed." His words started to slur again. "I'll stay here."

"Don't be ridiculous." Annie grabbed his arm and pulled, but he didn't budge. "Cam, get up. Go to bed."

"You called me Cam again." He burst out in giggles, barely managing to keep upright. "You never call me that."

It wasn't his fire that made Annie's cheeks grow warm. She knelt beside him. "If I call you that again, will you go to bed?"

His eyes flickered open as he gave her a sleepy grin. "I might."

"Cam." Lord, she was *burning* now. He still had that awful harness on him. Exhaling, she didn't give him a chance to react as she began to undo the buckles on the straps. "Cam, I'm going to need you to hold your breath."

"W-why?" He tried to sit up, but she shoved him back down at the same time as she ripped off the harness straps, one by one. He bit down onto his lip until it bled, then let out a string of colorful curses she'd never heard from him.

"I'm so sorry." Annie ran her fingers over Cam's skin, touching every place the needles had punctured, sending a stream of white energy over the wounds, and they quickly sealed shut. "It would have been worse if I'd gone slowly."

"Mmm hmm," Cam mumbled as she gently pushed his shoulder until he leaned back against the wall again. She ran her thumb over his mouth, healing his split lip. His eyes flickered open again, fixing onto hers, and Annie did her best not to look at him. Instead, she noticed his boots. They were coated in an inch of mud from Enoch's streets.

"These have to go." Annie began to untie his boots. "You'll ruin my sheets with these."

As she tugged them off, Cam burst into another fit of giggles. "Are y-you trying to take my clothes off? All you had to do was ask."

Annie jerked back. "What? I wasn't—"

"I'm a mess." His eyelids started to droop again. "Please forget this ever happened."

"Stop that." Annie yanked off his boot, then the other. "Get up. You're going to bed."

With a few stumbling tries, Cam finally managed to fall into bed. He immediately curled onto his side, pulling the blankets over his shoulders.

"Goodnight." Annie hesitated once before running her fingers through his hair, brushing it off his face. Before she could stand, his fingers snagged hers. When she glanced over, he was watching her again, his eyes hazy and sad.

"You're exquisite." Cam sighed, losing his battle with consciousness as the flickering candles cast shadows over his cheekbones. "I wish I could tell you that."

Annie couldn't breathe. "Why can't you?"

Cam's words were barely audible. "Because you wouldn't believe me."

He was fast asleep after that.

And Annie stared at the candle flames until they went out.

CHAPTER 39
ELAIN

The suited man—Henry Bale was his name—stared down at the hot coals still glowing in the remains of the scientist's private laboratory.

Elain watched from the shadows, not that they would see her, but Henry seemed to *sense* when she got too close. The hairs on the back of his neatly trimmed neck would stand up. He'd glance over his shoulder, scanning the corners and dark places. The guards he always kept with him were oblivious. She could pass straight through them, and they'd be none the wiser to her existence.

So, she kept her distance. Listening, waiting, her spectral form always fading between the here and *there*.

Two of his guards were dressed as policemen—even though she knew now that they were *not*—dragged a short, round man out of a tunnel in the rubble. The scientist. A Revenant. One that had seen much and told little.

He struggled, grunting and sweating, as the guards dumped him on the ground at Henry's feet.

"Mr. Baxter." Henry inhaled, slicking back his dull brown

locks before replacing his tall cap. "I would ask what happened to your residence, but I assume you'd lie to me."

"Chief Bale." Mr. Baxter stood and dusted off his knees. "I must say I can't take responsibility if you cannot discern the truth from a lie."

"Well said," Henry smirked, that same oily blackness hovering around the edges of his frame. He peered down at the coals again, kicking some around with the tip of his shined boot. "But since my discernment is well intact, I suppose I will ask. Why is your home in cinders?"

"Oh, that?" Mr. Baxter winced as a blackened beam crumpled, crashing down into the remains of the wreckage. "Just a failed experiment. Nothing of consequence."

"Hmm." Henry shoved his hands in his pockets as he circled the scientist, his guards falling in line beside him like clockwork. "I hope the substance is still intact. I will be very upset if it isn't."

"I-it's safe," Mr. Baxter stammered. "Better than ever, actually. I believe Pearl Dust is the key."

"I won't ask where you acquired it." Henry gestured to the rubble. "Citizens have already inquired about the smoke, but I told them to pay no mind."

"How very kind of you," Mr. Baxter replied, shoving his round glasses up the bridge of his nose. "I'm glad to hear you respect my privacy."

"That's the thing." The guards grinned as Henry knelt, hiking up his pant legs, revealing a knife hilt poking over the top of his boot. "I don't. I've been waiting for you to make the right choice and tell me that you've been in contact with Camden Callahan after I strictly prohibited such an interaction." Henry tilted his head menacingly. "Unless you've forgotten?"

"No." Mr. Baxter paled, his lips wobbling. "I have not."

"See, that's the truth." Henry tapped his temple. "Didn't I say my discernment was intact?"

"You did." Mr. Baxter wiped away the sweat snaking down his cheek. "As for Lord Callahan—"

"And Lady Callahan?" Henry shook his head and sighed. "Or, as I *should* say, the trollop of New Havana. To think, a Death Brand had been on that God-forsaken island for years, and by a misstep of one of our own, at that." After a moment of thought, he nodded to his men, then to the ruined building. "But don't worry, you'll have plenty of time to tell me about Lord Callahan this evening."

"Bale—" Mr. Baxter squeaked as the guards swept him up and stuffed him inside their carriage.

To the remaining guards, Henry Bale said, "Bring the substance with us—carefully. After that, start rebuilding the lab. We're going to need it."

Elain watched as the men did just that, taking in the black tattoos on the insides of their fingers, before fading back into The Grey.

CHAPTER 40

CAMDEN

Kitten, I've tried to write this a thousand times and I still can't get it right—

Cam paused, chewing the end of his pen. *Stupid.* With an angry huff, he crumpled the letter, rolling it between his palms. Despite the chill in the air—fogging the windows—he didn't light a fire. He was broiling hot now that his fire had come back with vengeance.

Bloody hell. Cam dropped the squished paper onto the table and rubbed his face. It was seven in the morning. He'd woken an hour ago in Annie's bed, with the worst headache he'd ever had in his life, and his fire was all over the place. His body *ached.* He was cranky as hell and felt like he could sleep for twelve more hours. It was like when he'd first turned and woken with Elias in his face.

My fire. Cam let a few sparks escape from the tips of his fingers, where they shifted into little sparrows and dragonflies. He glowered at them. "Playing nice now, are you?"

Flames rolled inside him, its version of a response.

His damned fire could have gotten them all killed last night—could have killed Annie . . .

No. He shook his head. Despite everything, he *did* trust his power enough not to touch her. Everyone else?

Cam let his head hit the table and groaned. When Mr. Baxter suggested the test chamber, as reluctant as he was, he'd wanted *so* badly to hit a limit—*any* limit—something to prove that the rest of his bloody life wasn't going to be spent keeping this creature inside him from turning half the planet to ash.

But no—instead, he woke with a new chamber drilled into his reservoir. A deeper level. He could feel it, hovering in the recesses of his mind, waiting to see if he'd dare to touch it.

Hang it all. Cam wiped away the nervous sweat beading on his brow onto his sleeve and grabbed a fresh piece of paper.

Kitten,

I—

"Oh, good, you're awake."

He cursed as Annie peeked through the broken door slats, her brow furrowed. "What are you doing?"

"Nothing." Cam's heart nearly broke free from his ribcage as he snatched up all the failed letters on the table. "Scribbling."

Annie gave him one of those close-lipped smiles that let him know she saw right through his bull. She took the seat across from him. "I've heard journaling can be therapeutic."

"Yeah? Well, whoever said that probably sold ink." Cam forced a smile and set the crumpled papers on fire.

"Hmm." Annie's eyes narrowed at the remnants of paper floating into the air in bits of embers. Her ice-blue gaze returned to him and softened. "How do you feel?"

"Fine," Cam lied. Annie's brow rose, and he slumped, letting out a long sigh and running a hand through his hair. It felt gritty from ash. "I feel terrible. Happy?"

"Yes, actually." His tone didn't faze Annie in the slightest. "I'd be worried if you said you felt like sunshine and rainbows."

Cam pursed his lips. "Dragonflies."

"What?"

"Never mind." He brushed the bits of charred paper that remained in his palm and dumped them into the fireplace—just standing made his legs ache. He couldn't bring himself to look at her, so instead of returning to the table, he sat on the floor, resting his back against the edge of the bed.

"I'm . . . I'm sorry, Annie." Cam reached down to pick at the hem of his shirt. *Blazes.* He hadn't put a shirt on. He picked at the carpet instead. "I'm sorry. I didn't mean what I said."

"Yes, you did." She rose and tucked her singed skirts beneath her as she joined him on the floor. She hadn't changed either. She folded her hands in her lap. "And I deserved it. I haven't been a very good friend lately."

Friend. Cam winced. The word stung way worse than it should. "Even if that were true, I shouldn't have said it. Or tried to kill Jules."

He wasn't sure if she did it consciously, but Annie scooted closer. Their shoulders nearly touched, though her gaze was fixed on the floor. "Mr. Price told me what he and Frank Boyle did to you on your previous ship."

Cam tensed. "Oh."

"Did I ever tell you how Charlotte murdered me?" Her words were thick, as if fighting off tears.

Cam resisted the urge to take her hand in his. "You never did."

Annie smiled wide enough to show teeth. "She plunged a broken bottle into my chest."

"God—" Cam caught the carpet on fire. As he smothered it out, Annie continued.

"She did it at the same time that I shoved the knife you

gave me through her throat." Annie rubbed her chest where he imagined the glass had pierced her. "She died in seconds. It almost wasn't fair. Elain and Resh stayed with me as I bled out."

Cam sucked in a shuddering breath. "Resh was with you?"

Annie smiled again, then nodded. "He was."

Hell with it. Slowly, Cam took her hand from her lap and twisted his fingers through hers. Annie didn't pull away. In fact, her entire body seemed to relax.

Cam still couldn't look her in the eye. "Are you angry with me?"

Annie shifted closer. "Are you angry with me?"

"Of course not," he swallowed.

"Then neither am I." She rubbed her thumb over the back of his hand. She'd never done that before. There was a quiet pause before she said, "I think we've been responding to The Order all wrong."

Cam tried not to feel disappointed at the change in topic. He refused to let go of her hand. "Responded? We've done nothing but react to their psychotic antics since we've arrived in Enoch."

"Exactly." Annie's voice jumped an octave. "Your father has been treating the murders and the attack on the Clarkes's home like a criminal investigation. This is something different."

"It's a message," Cam replied. "I suspected as much, especially after the mess they made at the Clarkes. Then to disappear entirely? It was planned that way. They allowed us to kill their men. What I haven't figured out is why?"

"At the moment, I don't think the *why* matters." Annie chewed her free thumbnail. "It's more than a message. They're testing you, Cam. It's like they want to see what they can get away with. What matters now is that we send our own message."

"Cam. We." He repeated before kissing her knuckles. "You're still spoiling me, Kitten."

For once, as Annie scanned his face, she didn't look afraid. Nervous, maybe. Uncertain, yes, but no fear. She shook her head. The air around her seemed to vibrate. *Frequency.* "That's what you got from that?"

"Forgive me, I was a bit distracted." A moment of boldness had him flipping her hand over so he could kiss the inside of her wrist. Teasing her had always been easier. It felt like when they'd first met, and he never expected to see her truly smile, never expected that smile to make him rethink his entire existence.

Annie's mouth turned downward into an irritated frown.

Cam froze. "Sorry, again—"

"No." Annie grabbed his forearm to keep him from pulling away. "It's just . . . *blazes.*"

Cam burst laughing. "I've never heard you say that."

"It's just . . ." Annie sat on her hands as her scowl deepened. "It's . . . silly."

"Tell me." Between laughs, Cam's lips curved up into a mischievous smile. "Or I'll go insane wondering what it is that you don't want to tell me."

Annie stared at him with her glacier-hard expression for a full ten seconds. Cam never broke her gaze.

Then she was straddling him.

Cam gasped as he was hit with an electric jolt—her power. His fire bent around it, welcoming it in. He couldn't remember how to think, how to breathe, only that she held his face between her hands as her frigid, sweet breath cooled his overheated skin.

She leaned in, close enough that her nose brushed against his, and whispered, "Don't move."

Cam's fire crashed to the surface as he nodded. He was smoking again. Despite his restraint, his hands locked down onto her hips—*God,* he was touching her—and kept her in place as she ran her fingers into his hair. With half a sigh, half a moan, she gripped the strands on the back of his head and held tight.

A hunger replaced her mask. She tugged until his neck was exposed and her mouth was against his throat. "You have no idea how long I've wanted to do this."

Cam swallowed, her lips icy against his skin. "W-why have you waited so long?"

He could die like this. To hell with Enoch. To hell with revenge.

She released her grip, letting her lips trail along his neck until they were eye to eye. And just like that, the fear was back. A wave of it passed across her features. She was going to run. To shrink into her shell and never let him in again.

No. He wouldn't lose her like that. He'd rather go down in a wave of gunfire.

Before she could pull away, he wove his hand around the nape of her neck and crashed his lips to hers. It wasn't graceful, but she didn't seem to care. Annie sighed, her fingers twisting into his hair again as she tasted his mouth.

His free hand wrapped around her waist and drew her more tightly against him. *Here.* Never mind, he would die right *here.*

A sharp knock and the clearing of his throat announced Nathan's presence. "Bloody hell, and you get on *my* case."

Annie leapt back so fast that she smacked her head on the edge of the table.

When Cam spun, Nathan threw his hands up. "Relax, I was just seeing if you two were coming for breakfast!"

Breathing heavily, Cam pointed at him. "If I had a gun."

Nathan rolled his eyes. "Yeah, yeah. Come and eat before the food gets cold."

He disappeared down the hall. When Cam turned back, Annie was staring at him—obviously embarrassed—but not afraid.

Cam could live with that. He smiled, adjusted his pants, then stood, offering her a hand. "Should we go plan how we're going to leave a message?"

To his surprise, Annie beamed at him—her cheeks and lips flushed. She was more beautiful than the Southern seas. "I think that's a good idea."

He helped her up before shoving his hands in his pockets. "I'll . . . I'll meet you downstairs. I need to find a shirt."

She just smiled before ducking through the broken door and heading down the hall.

All he needed was her smile, and he'd live the rest of his life a happy man.

By the time Cam dug out something clean to wear and found the others in the dining room, Annie had changed, as well, into a deep, violet day gown. It was too long. She must have grabbed it from Jenny's room.

Her cheeks reddened when she glanced up at him from her plate, but she said nothing.

Nathan smirked at him as Cam sat across from her and poured himself a cup of coffee. Jenny bit down on her lip as she filled her plate with eggs and toast. She offered some to Annie, who declined, opting instead to sip her steaming tea.

"So," Nathan said. "What's the plan for the day, Captain? Price already left this morning. Didn't say where to."

"Did he?" Cam chewed the eggs he'd just shoveled into his mouth. "Julian can handle himself. I need you to check up on Pulley and *The Elaina*. Annie and I are heading to the *modiste*."

Annie frowned over her cup. "We are?"

"We are," Cam replied. "I want to have another chat with the owner."

"Fair enough," Nathan nodded. "But if you wanted to go shopping, you could just say it. I won't tell anyone what a preener you've become."

Cam pointed his fork at him. "Don't mock my frilly coats."

"I'm not, I'm mocking you."

"Don't mock me either. I'll gut you."

"Try it."

"I'd like to go with you to the *modiste*," Jenny said calmly over a bite of buttery toast. "I decided I finally want to start quilting, but I need some fabric."

With the reverent way Nathan looked at her, you'd think she just said she planned to end world hunger. "If that's what you want. Would you like me to accompany you? I can see to the ship after."

"That's alright," Jenny squeezed his hand, her emerald engagement ring sparkling in the low light. "It will be nice to spend time with Annie."

They're engaged. It didn't settle in until now. Nathan—*his* Nathan—was going to marry Jenny Duskin. Nathan, who joined Resh's crew at the age of ten. Cam had been twelve. Nathan, who'd been Cam's only friend ever since. The only friend he'd ever had, really. Who had played cards with him until the wee hours of the morning. Who'd remained by his side through hurricanes and the ferocity of Resh's temper.

It's not like that anymore. Cam's gaze dropped to his plate.

They'd become different people since *The Nightlady* burned, but he missed his friend. *I'm not sure if I can fix it. It's my fault he ended up in Richard Duskin's bunker.*

Nathan nodded again at Jenny's words, with a hint of disappointment, then went back to his breakfast.

"It's settled, then." Cam downed the rest of his food and then stood. "We'd better get going before the streets fill up."

"I'll call you a coach." Nathan helped Jenny slide into her coat, which hung on the back of her chair.

"I'll go with you." Jenny looped her arm through his as they headed toward the entry at the back of the villa.

After finishing her tea, Cam and Annie stepped out on the patio. She wrapped a thick wool shawl around her shoulders and slipped on a pair of gloves. "What do you hope to find at the *modiste?*"

I guess we're not talking about that. "I'm not sure we'll *find* anything." Cam wrapped his fingers through hers, letting his heat flare to warm her. "The owner—"

"Lydia," Annie corrected.

"Lydia," Cam smirked and squeezed her hand. "She said Enoch had been waiting for us. The Cultist at the Clarkes said the same. At first, I assumed she was a pro-Revenant sympathizer . . ."

"But she could be affiliated with The Order." Annie nodded in understanding. "And just told you what she thought you wanted to hear?"

"Something like that." Cam tucked his free hand in his coat pocket as the *clip-clop* of horse hooves sounded the arrival of their carriage. "You'll help me?"

"Always." Annie's expression softened as the carriage halted in front of them. She studied his face. "How are you feeling?"

Like a wreck, "I feel fine," Cam lied again.

Jenny swung open the carriage door, her round, scarred cheeks pink with the cold. "Hop in!"

Two hours later, they were outside the *modiste*.

Their ride had been easy, filled with Jenny chattering about her plans to open her quilt shop in town and to donate half the profits to nearby orphanages. A level of peacefulness hung over Annie as she listened to her sister, only interjecting two or three times to encourage her.

It was easy to see why Annie had grown to love her over all her adopted siblings. Why Nathan loved Jenny. She was like a breath of spring air, bringing everything around her back to life.

And you're responsible for her. For all of them. Cam's stomach rolled as he helped the women out of the carriage. Jenny would never have her quilt shop if he didn't stop The Order. It wasn't just his and Annie's lives at stake if he screwed this up—it was Jenny's, Nathan's . . . hell, even Julian would be a target. At least more of a target than he already was.

Despite the chill and the growing wind, the door to the *modiste* was cracked open. The rumble of male laughter spilled onto the street—several men. Cam and Annie exchanged hesitant glances before they stepped inside, making the bell on the door chime. He was struck again by the boldness of the shop's pink carpet, of the hundreds of bolts of cloth hanging from an equal number of ceiling-high racks.

Two well-dressed men turned in unison to stare at them as they entered. The owner—Lydia—stood behind the counter, her face flushed from laughing with them.

Cam tensed when he recognized the man closest to her—Jensen Davis.

Father doesn't know him. Nathan had mentioned the uncertainty and frustration in Alexander's eyes when he'd heard Davis's name. If his father wasn't familiar with the Ice Brand, that meant Jensen hadn't been in Enoch long, or he was *trying* to stay out of the governor's notice.

"Lord and Lady Callahan." Lydia bowed, her full bosom on display. "Miss Duskin. What an honor to see you again."

"Lord Callahan." Jensen bowed stiffly, then smiled a little too widely at Annie before gesturing to the pudgy, balding man beside him. "My Lord and Lady, may I introduce you to an honorary member of Enoch's city council, Francis Leigh."

I'll never remember all these names. Cam gave them a brief nod as the man bowed. *Nor will I ever get used to that.*

Jenny sidled behind him and Annie. Cam gave Jensen a cavalier smile. "I didn't see you stick around to help clean up the mess at the Clarkes."

Francis Leigh straightened and paled, glancing at his companion. *I remember him.* Cam had slammed the ballroom door in his face at the manor when they'd first arrived.

Jensen forced a strained smile back, brushing back a strand of his smooth, honey-blond hair. The ice-blue brands peeking over the top of his collar flared. "I trusted Enoch's police force to handle the investigation."

"Hmm." Cam clicked his tongue, wrapping his arm around Annie's waist. "Did you?"

Jensen's smile fell.

"How may I help you, my lord?" Lydia cleared her throat nervously. "I hope the clothing I provided has served you well."

"It has," Cam replied, never taking his eyes off Jensen. "My lady's sister requires your expertise."

Jenny blinked up at him. "I do?"

Annie nudged her elbow.

"Oh," Jenny chimed. "I do." She and Lydia delved into an extensive conversation about various types of fabric. Cam didn't need Lydia now. Not when he had everything he wanted right in front of him.

Annie must have been thinking the same thing, because she turned to Francis and asked, "You're a councilman? I assume you'll be attending the Embassy meeting still now that the date has been moved?"

Francis's wet lips opened and closed. "I am a councilman, my lady, but how did *you* hear of the schedule change?"

"I am the governor's daughter-in-law." Annie let out a girlish chuckle. "I hear *everything*."

The man's face turned a brilliant shade of red.

Cam could have kissed her right then and there.

"Mr. Leigh will be attending. So will I," Jensen replied, more than a bit irritated. "You see, I'm also a member of the council now."

"Since when?" Cam snorted.

Jensen pursed his lips. "Since last week, if you must know. The position opened after James Kline's tragic passing. The council was kind enough to offer it to me after seeing the work I've done with Waverly Hospital."

The murdered man in the apartment.

Annie shot Cam a look. He squeezed her side in response.

James Kline, Order member or not, was in the way of Jensen getting a council seat.

But did Davis kill him? Cam's eyes dropped to Jensen's hands. He couldn't see a tattoo under his finger, but that didn't mean it wasn't there.

He sneered at the Ice Brand. "I assume your *work* on the hospital included The Greens? Annie met a man whose leg was rotting off and saved his life. Have you ever smelled infected flesh, Mr. Davis? It isn't pleasant."

"The Greens were on my list, but it seems your lady had gotten to them before me." Jensen's brands flared again. "And I have no doubts you've smelled plenty of rotting corpses in your previous profession, Lord Callahan. Pirate, was it?"

Francis mumbled something about *unsavory* under his breath.

Cam gave Jensen a once-over and smirked. "*Aye*, and good thing, too, or else I might have become weak-spirited enough to leave justice to a corrupted police force."

Jensen scowled.

"Do you believe yourself above the law, Lord Callahan?" Francis cut in, trying and failing to button his waistcoat over his round belly. "Nonsense like what you're spouting is exactly why we've had to create laws to keep Revenants in check. Enoch's police is above reproach."

Cam laughed, barely acknowledging Francis as he kept an eye on Jenny and Lydia in the back of the shop. "Of course, I'm above the law, Mr. Leigh. I'm a Callahan."

Francis looked as if he was about to have a coronary.

Annie's power brushed down his back and pinched him. *Behave.* Another thing he didn't know she could do.

"I assume you support anti-Revenant law?" she asked him. "If so, it's nice to see you and Mr. Davis on such friendly terms."

"Don't be mistaken." Jensen leaned against the counter. "Revenant, I may be, but believe me when I say I do not support the laws currently in place, allowing our kind to do whatever they like." His eyes flashed to Cam. "Especially when we so *often* believe ourselves above authority."

That made Cam pause. Not that it should have. Jensen had brown-noser written all over him. Men like him would do and say whatever they must to gain a semblance of power.

"Hmm, interesting," Cam repeated, taking Annie's arm. "Enjoy your day, gentlemen."

With that, he turned and led Annie into the side room, where Jenny and Lydia were fawning over a glittering, indigo fabric. He could feel the men's eyes boring into his back.

"What are you doing?" Annie whispered, inclining her head towards him. "We need more information."

"And they'll give it to us." Cam tucked a loose strand of her hair neatly back into her updo. She shivered at the touch. He flexed his fingers and shoved his hand back into his pocket. "If there's one thing influential men hate, it's being ignored."

Annie nodded, gave his arm a squeeze, then broke away to join her sister. As she walked, her fingers brushed along her neck as if chasing the shiver away. That movement alone set Cam's fire boiling.

He inhaled, swallowing down the rolling in his chest, and leaned against the doorframe. Once Annie was in arm's reach, Jenny pulled her closer, gesturing for her to feel the new fabric they were admiring—a deep red silk.

"Why did you come to Enoch?"

Cam glanced over his shoulder. Jensen Davis stood behind him, scowling, arms crossed over his chest as frost crawled up his sleeves. Further back, Francis Leigh rifled through a newspaper at the counter, obviously listening.

Cam shifted his gaze back to the women. "I don't see how that's your business."

"You're the governor's heir." Jensen moved to stand beside him, his navy three-piece suit spotless. "It *is* the city's business."

Cam huffed a laugh. "Then the *city* needs to mind its own damn business."

"It's no secret your father's health is failing." Jensen's words were as icy as his brands. "Have you come to replace him?"

Your father's health is failing. Cam stiffened and shot Jensen a glare despite his best efforts to remain aloof. *My father is dying, and Enoch will pass to me.* Another dire issue he'd been trying to avoid thinking about. When Alexander showed them what the mark had done to him, Cam *should* have been happy —but he wasn't.

He felt . . . wrong. Off. Unsettled. It wasn't supposed to be this way. All these years, he'd fantasized about how he'd want to kill Alexander Callahan. Skin him. Fill him full of bullet holes. Cut him until he bled out slowly, chained to the cold floor.

He wasn't supposed to die by someone else's hands, looking like a sick, old man.

"Lord Callahan?" Jensen's voice cut through Cam's swirling thoughts. "Have you come to replace the governor?"

He startled back to attention to find the Ice Brand staring at him, brows furrowed.

Cam clenched his jaw. "I'm here for my own reasons. None that have anything to do with ruling Enoch."

"That's good to hear," Jensen sneered, his eyes flickering to Annie long enough that Cam clenched his fists. The man continued, "There are those in Enoch who fear that having a Revenant—a Fire Brand, above all—ruling The West will pull the country into a state of tyranny. Others believe Revenant power is exactly what the land needs to return to order."

"That sounds like politics." Cam crossed one ankle over the other. Jenny had already chosen at least eight bolts of fabric. "I'm not a politician. I'm a pirate, remember?"

"Which is exactly why you should have never come here." Francis cut in, stepping toward him. "A world ruled by Revenants is a world where mortals bleed."

Cam's brow rose. "I don't think I asked for your opinion."

"Well, you have it." Francis puffed out his chest at the same time as he slammed his fist down on the counter and shouted, "Enoch should be ruled by its people—not Revenants, and *especially* not by a disgraced son and that fiend, Lord Duskin's, Northern whore."

The room went still.

Lydia's mouth fell open, while Jenny covered hers. Annie's already granite stare went cold. Even Jensen backed a step, eyes widening as they shot between Cam and his companion.

Cam's fire paused, the entire force of it narrowing onto the councilman as he grinned. "Say that again."

Francis blinked twice and stammered, "I apologize—"

"Call her that again." Cam couldn't breathe as fire crawled up his throat. Wreaths of flame swirled around him. "Call my wife a whore again, Leigh."

Francis stumbled back, shaking his head as sweat poured down his brow.

Not even Jensen tried to stop Cam as he moved forward, leaning in until they were face to face. Francis whimpered as his back hit the counter. He tried to jerk away, but Cam seized his chin and held firm.

"Say it again." Cam breathed hot enough to scald the man's skin. "Say it, and I might let you leave here alive."

"A whore." Francis let out a wet sob. "I called her Lord Duskin's whore."

"Yes, you did." Cam patted his cheek, blistering it, as he stepped back and tossed some cash onto the counter before turning to Lydia. "Is that enough to cover the fabric?"

Lydia nodded, still too stunned to speak.

"Good." Cam grinned again and motioned for Annie and Jenny to meet him by the entry. Lydia quickly packed their purchases into a bag and handed it to them. Annie was at his side in an instant, her eyes hiding a level of fury and hurt only he would see.

The bell jingled as Cam opened the door for them, but it wasn't quite loud enough to hide Francis muttering *whore* under his breath as he rubbed his scorched cheek.

Cam froze in the doorway, taking two long breaths before he rounded on the filthy bastard.

Francis's eyes bulged at the same time as he choked, clawing at his fat throat.

"Mr. Leigh," Jensen gripped his friend's shoulder, but leapt back and cursed, his own hand burnt raw. Francis began to scream and scream and scream—until Lydia covered her ears and sobbed. The councilman screamed until his face grew blood red and split open, spewing bubbling liquid down his front. The screaming stopped, turning to gurgles, as Francis's torn face continued to peel back until it crumpled into greasy, grey lumps of ash. Until there was nothing left of him but charred bones.

Annie held Cam's elbow, her eyes alight with something he couldn't name as the councilman's ruined body slumped to the floor.

Jensen stared at what remained of his friend before finally gaping at Cam. He hadn't even tried to save him.

Cam's returning smile was nothing but pure hatred. "I'll see you in a couple of weeks, Davis." Then he slammed the door shut behind them.

CHAPTER 41
CAMDEN

"You killed him," Jenny murmured from the bench across from him, hand still partially covering her scarred mouth. "You killed him."

Cam stared out the carriage window, embers sparking from his clenched fists, jostling as the horses hit a pothole. He didn't want to answer her. Especially not with the way Annie was watching him from the corner of her eye. Yes, he'd murdered a man, and he'd done it for *her*.

"Will you be arrested?" Jenny's eyes were lined with silver now as she gripped the enormous bag of fabrics in her lap.

Is that what she's worried about? Cam forced himself to straighten. And here he'd assumed she'd hate him for it.

"No," he muttered, watching as the citizens on the street gawked at their silver-encrusted wagon. In truth, he didn't have the faintest idea what Enoch's police would do, but he didn't care—and he didn't need her more upset than she already was.

Jenny nodded, turning her attention to her bolt of silk.

Annie remained silent, continuing her observation of him when she thought he wouldn't notice.

By the time they returned to the Callahan estate, the rain had grown into a deluge. Howling winds ripped at the women's skirts and hair as they exited the carriage and strolled into the courtyard.

Then David was there—his father's butler, or whatever the hell he was—with an umbrella. He held it over Annie and Jenny, unfazed as rain soaked his inky-black locks and dripped down his sallow face. "Your father is waiting for you."

Of course, he is. The downpour stung Cam's eyes as he glanced up. Alexander stood beneath the covered main entry, his arms crossed over his chest. The angry crook of his brow sent a thrill of instinctual fear coursing through him.

He can't hurt you. Cam sucked in a breath as he took the umbrella from David, shielding the women as they headed toward the manor. If it weren't for them—and the slight shivers raking Jenny's body—he'd have bolted for the villa.

"Where have you been?" Alexander said as a way of greeting as they stepped out of the rain.

"This whole town is full of busy bodies." Irritation helped smother out the fear. Cam shook out the umbrella before snapping it shut, making sure to scatter a wave of frigid water over his father's pressed suit. "Worry about yourself, old man."

"If only I could." Alexander's lips pressed into a hard line as he flicked droplets off his elbow. "You'll find that's an indulgence not allowed to men in our position."

Our position. Despite Cam's repeated statements that he didn't want Enoch, it seemed that either his father wasn't listening or had twisted his words until they matched what he wanted to hear.

"If you two are going to argue, do it outside." Annie

unstuck the sodden hair clinging to her cheeks. "I'm cold. I'm wet. I don't want to listen to your insufferable bickering."

Cam let out a short laugh, and this time, when his father's brow rose, it was in surprise.

"There's a fire going in the sitting room." Alexander nodded to David. "I'll have tea brought up for you."

David bowed quickly before ushering them into the manor. "Come with me."

Another jolt of fear rattled Cam's bones as Annie turned to follow. She must have felt it because she glanced over her shoulder, giving him the smallest of smiles as her power brushed against his arm. *We'll be fine.*

I know. Cam willed the thought back to her.

She made a pointed glance at Alexander, her power making his skin tingle. *Play nice. Remember the plan.*

Cam just nodded. They disappeared as David led them through the foyer and into the main house. *She'll be alright.* If he had to remind himself a thousand times, he would. He knew first-hand what Annie was capable of. David wasn't a threat.

Cam felt eyes boring into him and shifted to find his father's stare, his expression twisted in confusion.

"What?" Cam growled.

Alexander studied him a moment longer before asking, "Did you two just speak to each other? Without words?"

Cam's mouth snapped shut. Could they? He hadn't given it much thought. It was just their way. With a nervous laugh, Cam pushed his hair out of his eyes. "Delusional, are you? You're closer to death than I thought."

"Hmm." Only the slight tension in his jaw gave way to how badly the comment stung. "Are you going to answer my question?"

"No." Cam spun on his heel, striding into the foyer. "You're not privileged to know all the details of my life."

The grey light, seeping through the foyer's skylights, accentuated the silver threaded through Alexander's sandy ponytail. "I am when your actions affect the fate of Enoch and of our family line."

"To hell with the family line." Cam stopped short, then forced himself to take a breath. *Play nice.* He had a purpose. He had to stay focused. He faced Alexander, fire filling his eyes despite the rein he fought to keep on his temper. "You have Kai. Why not leave the West to him?"

Alexander rested a hand against a pillar to steady himself. "You'd leave an entire continent to an eight-year-old?"

"You spent my entire childhood shoveling my *greater purpose* down my throat. I assume you've done the same to him."

"It can't be Kai. Maybe if he had another decade, but . . ." With a sigh, Alexander pulled his ornate, solid gold pocket watch from his coat pocket. He stared down at it, rubbing the face with his thumb. "As I'm sure it delights you to hear, I don't have much time left. Once I'm gone, and if you don't take Enoch, the West will go to whoever The Order appoints."

Cam didn't respond. Kai wouldn't be able to stop The Order from taking over. With the extent of their corruption in the council, Enoch would be sacked in hours.

He exhaled. "Jensen Davis has been given James Kline's council seat."

Alexander rubbed his stubbled jaw. "So, I've heard. There's a man, Francis Leigh, who was a known—or known to me—Order affiliate. He must have bypassed the voting system for them to get Mr. Davis inside."

Blazes. At least he'd been right about Francis.

"Well," Cam grimaced. "You don't need to worry about him anymore."

Alexander glanced at him. "Who?"

"Mr. Leigh."

"Why?"

"I may have . . . killed . . . him."

Alexander's jaw dropped. "You *what?*"

Cam shrugged as he picked at his nails. "He deserved it."

"I don't doubt that, but . . ." Alexander shook his head and let out a frustrated sigh. "This will complicate things. The Order will see it as an attack against them."

Good. "Is Davis an Order member?"

"He—" His father's words seemed to catch in his throat. "I've sent spies to collect information about him. So far, all they've retrieved is his customs paperwork. He booked passage from Bristolwatch to Enoch around eight weeks ago."

Bristolwatch. The capital of the East. Cam had been there once with Resh and the crew. In those days, Resh had been bold. They'd sacked half the capital's fishing villages before the city guard had caught wind of them. It had been years, but he had a familiar face. He doubted he'd be welcome in Bristolwatch again until everyone left to remember him were long dead.

"Davis made it very clear that he doesn't support Revenant rights," Cam said.

"Again, I'm aware."

"And you didn't think to tell me this?" Cam leaned against the foyer wall and crossed his arms. "It would have been nice to know who to avoid."

A flicker of rage passed over Alexander's features. "And when, my dear son, have you given me a chance to inform you? If you'd just dropped the pretenses of pride, I could have listed every single man and woman in Enoch for you. Their names. Their occupations. Their weaknesses. But no, instead you've been gallivanting across the city like you own it, while doing nothing to take responsibility for it."

Play nice. Remember the plan. Cam repeated Annie's words in his mind, but *God,* he wanted to punch Alexander in the face and keep punching until he was no longer breathing.

Cam grit his teeth. "And when, my darling father, have you given me a reason to trust you? Why would I share anything when, for all I know, you're reporting straight to The Order?"

Alexander looked away, rubbing his gloved fingers. "I don't expect to gain your trust, Camden, but if we aren't aligned, I suspect neither of us will be walking away from the Embassy meeting."

Cam remained silent as Alexander wandered back toward the entry, watching the rain as he continued. "I've been stalling the pro and anti-Revenant parties from coming together for well over a year. The Order knows it. Now that they have Mr. Davis on the council—and with what you've done to Francis Leigh—they'll be ready. They'll convince the others to vote how they wish and prevent you from becoming governor."

"So, that's what this is about?" Cam replied as he stepped to his father's side. Raindrops that strayed too close to him turned to steam with a loud *hiss.* "You've been waiting—you hired Elias Bennett to find me—just so you can bring me back at the same time as the people voted in favor of Revenants, and when that didn't happen, you stalled. You needed their fervor fresh enough that they wouldn't realize they were voting in a nearly immortal leader."

"One powerful enough to force them—and the world— into line, if need be." Alexander shot him a quick smile. "I'm glad to see you've been paying attention."

Bastard. Cam backed a step. "I won't be your weapon."

"You've *always* been a weapon, Camden." Alexander's eyes drifted to the storm. "Whether mine, or The Order's—your mother knew it. *That's* why she ran. Because she wanted you to have an ordinary life." His tone turned wistful, almost dreamy. "But that could never be. I tried to tell her, over and over, but she didn't listen. Just like you're refusing to listen now."

An ordinary life. Cam shuddered, fighting against the fire whispering in his ear. "I hate you."

He wasn't sure who he'd said it to.

"I know." Alexander nodded. "I know."

CHAPTER 42

ANNIE

David had them settled in the sitting room, a tray of boiling tea in front of them, before Annie was able to shrug out of her sticky, damp coat.

"Thank you," she muttered as she began to unpin her hair. It was a mess, and the way her now lopsided updo tugged on the soft hairs at the nape of her neck was making her near homicidal. "You can go."

David didn't react to her rudeness. He merely bowed. "Just ring the bell if you need anything else. I'll be downstairs."

"And how will you hear it?" Jenny asked, mostly to herself. She lifted the dainty, silver bell off the side table. It was the size of a thimble.

David smiled at her. It was the first time Annie had seen him do so. "I'll hear it. Don't you worry, Miss Duskin." His dark eyes flashed down to the emerald on her wedding finger. "Pardon. Soon to be Mrs. . . . ?"

"Williams," Jenny blushed. "I'll be Mrs. Williams."

David gave her a curt nod, then closed the door behind him as he left.

"Careful what you say." Annie let out a frustrated huff as she finger-combed through her tangled waves. "I don't like him."

Jenny snorted as she poured each of them a cup of tea. "You don't like anyone."

"For good reason." Annie stirred a splash of cream into hers. Cam's sweet tooth was passing to her. She paused. "And that's not completely true. I love you. You know that."

Her sister shrugged before glancing around the room. It was decorated much the same as Maya's tearoom, but instead of pale blues and white, the walls were painted a soft lavender, the sofas, ottomans, and chaise lounges a baby pink. The dishware, the rounded mirror, and the desk were all gold-plated metal.

It was hideous.

"It's pretty in here," Jenny said sweetly.

Annie rolled her eyes.

Jenny then gestured toward a bouquet of dried, pink hydrangeas. "It reminds me of Elain."

Elain. That stopped Annie short. She hadn't seen Elain since she'd sent her to follow Chief Bale. *Hopefully she's alright.* Could a ghost not be okay? Annie tugged her white tresses over her shoulder and began to braid. "It reminds me of Rose, too."

Jenny's face fell. "I hate that she died the way she did."

Rose. Charlotte Duskin had killed her. She'd killed their brother—also named Nathan—too. She'd cut his throat to the bone.

Annie tried to shake away the thoughts of his brutalized body as she tied off the end of her hair. "People die all the time."

"They shouldn't have to." Jenny sipped her tea, making a face when she burned the tip of her tongue. "Maybe one day we'll live in a different world."

"Maybe," Annie said before picking up her teacup. The warmth of the cup spread into his stiff fingers, and she held it between her palms. "I'm glad you're so optimistic."

Jenny nibbled on the edge of a biscuit, watching Annie from beneath her lashes. Something was bothering her. She could feel it. Jenny had never been good at keeping her feelings to herself.

After several minutes of silence, Annie slammed her cup down—too hard. She didn't mean to crack it, letting tea leak from the side. She swallowed, using her napkin to mop up the mess. "Whatever it is you wish to say, Jenny, say it."

"I'm not sure why you're so irritable," she scowled. "You seemed fine earlier."

"I'm tired." Annie took in a long breath. "I'm soaking wet. We're stuck in the room waiting with no idea what's going on. I want to go ho—"

Home. That's what she'd been about to say. Annie's stomach rolled. Where was home? Had she ever truly had one? Her father's cabin had been close, but even there, living with him and her brothers, she'd been an outsider, an inconvenience. The slave ships had been hell, and New Havana not much better. The villa was merely a comfort. It didn't belong to them—

Them. *Us.*

She wanted Cam.

She hated being in here when he was out there. Alone. With Alexander Callahan. She was upset at herself for getting carried away this morning, and now she was in here, anger bubbling over all the emotions she had yet to process.

Jenny poured herself more tea. "You know he killed Mr. Leigh for you, right?"

Annie paused, tossing the tea-soaked napkins on the tray. "Don't start."

She didn't want to hear it because she *did* know. Cam had killed a man without hesitation for insulting her, and worst of all, she'd *liked* it.

She'd spent most of her life being insulted and had long since grown numb to it. But Mr. Leigh's words, calling her Lord Duskin's whore, they'd stung. They'd stung when they shouldn't have, and watching Cam burn him alive gave her more satisfaction than she could ever admit out loud.

He had done it for her. *Her*. Despite being Lord Duskin's whore, because that's *exactly* who she was. She'd been the slaver's whore, too. Cam knew that, and he'd killed for her anyway.

And she wasn't sure if she'd ever be able to tell him how much that meant to her.

"Why shouldn't I start?" Jenny bristled. "I don't know why you can't just accept the fact that he lov—"

"Stop." Annie jolted to her feet, knocking her cup to the ground and shattering it. "I can't."

"Why?" The fact that Jenny's voice grew softer, like she was coddling her, made it so much worse. "Why not?"

"What about you?" Annie bent to pick the shards of glass out of the carpet. "How can you marry Nathan after what Frank Boyle did to you?"

Jenny looked genuinely confused. "What does that have to do with Nathan?"

Hot tears leaked from the corners of Annie's eyes, and she tried desperately to wipe them away on her shoulder. "Because . . . because what if wanting Nathan makes you just like Frank?"

Jenny's eyes widened.

And there it was—all Annie's fears laid bare, the first time she'd said the words out loud.

She didn't realize how badly she was shaking until Jenny

bent down and wrapped her arms around hers. Annie hated herself for crying as Jenny brushed a stray hair off her face and smiled, the motion stretching the scars Frank had given her. She used to never cry.

"Those feelings . . ." Jenny wiped Annie's cheek. "One has nothing to do with the other."

"How can you know?" Annie held tightly to her sister's wrist.

Jenny pressed her lips together before saying, "Because it's not wrong if both of you want the same thing, I think."

Annie blinked at her, thinking, before dropping her hands to her side. "I don't want to be here anymore."

"Then let's leave." Jenny looped her arm through Annie's. "Because we can. Because no one can stop us."

They can't stop us. They couldn't stop her. She was here, not there. She was *free.*

Together, they left the sitting room and made their way through the hall, down the stairs. As they approached the main entry, the governor and Cam were still there—and so was Mr. Price.

Cam's eyes were on the ground as the other men argued. Eventually, the governor wheeled, storming down the hall, pausing only long enough to give them a curt nod as they passed.

Annie barely acknowledged him—she only noticed the slip of paper Mr. Price handed to Cam.

Cam curled his fist around the note, the fire in his eyes burning so bright it lit the foyer, before he shoved it in his pocket.

"Miss Annie." Mr. Price bowed at them as they approached. "Miss Jenny. The rain has stopped. Shall we head to the villa?"

Jenny nodded and took Mr. Price's arm as he led her out

into the courtyard. Annie paused beside Cam, where he still stared at the ground.

"What was that?" She nodded to his pocket. "What Mr. Price just gave you."

His eyes met hers, and there was no green left. "It's nothing. Just a location."

"Where?" Hesitantly, she reached out and looped her pinkie through his.

Instead of squeezing back, he wove the rest of his fingers with hers, brushing his thumb over the back of her hand. There was a heaviness hanging over him, a sadness, when he asked, "Do you trust me, Annie?"

She thought long and hard before she answered, "Against my better judgment, I do."

He smiled at her, the curve of his lips taking her breath away. "Good."

CHAPTER 43
ANNIE

The following two weeks passed in a blur, and each day that drifted away led to more tension. There was no sign of The Order, no matter how hard Cam and Mr. Price searched. No more attacks. In her heart, she knew they were waiting, biding their time. The Embassy meeting was only a day away, and she dreaded it. It ate away at her insides, always lingering at the edge of her mind.

Cam was often gone. He said he was working on something special. She kept her curiosity to herself, spending her hours at Waverly, tending to the patients. The Pearl Dust had worked wonders, though the Clarkes didn't seem happy with her decision.

She hadn't heard from Reika Hall, either. She'd even tried twice to visit, but the knocks on her apartment door went unanswered.

So much for being friends.

Neither had she kissed Cam again. Not because she didn't want to, but because she'd needed a chance to process their new normal. They were closer now, no longer hiding whatever was budding between them, but she hadn't been ready to push it further, nor could she stop thinking about what Jenny had said. *It's not wrong if both of you want the same thing, I think.*

Did they want the same thing?

She didn't know, and she was afraid to ask.

She wasn't sure what she'd do if the answer were no.

CHAPTER 44
CAMDEN

Cam woke Annie in the dark by shaking her shoulder. Before she could scream, he pressed a warm finger over her lips, the brightness of his brands making her squint.

"Get dressed, Kitten. I brought these for you." Cam's voice was a low, rumbling whisper as he tossed a stack of clothes on the end of her bed. "They're not fancy, but we're not being fancy today."

As he backed away, her eyes darted to the clock. Three in the morning. She sat up, her voice thick as she held up the loose button-down shirt and grey pair of trousers. "Pants? Where did you get these?"

"They're Timmy's. I had Nathan grab them for me." Cam grinned at her. "Trust me, he was as confused as you are. Bring your dagger. Meet me downstairs."

Annie just glowered at him, her hair a mused, glorious tangle as she kicked off her covers, wearing nothing but a slip of a nightgown. "Where are we going?"

"I can't tell you . . . yet." Cam averted his eyes to the floor. "Remember that trust we talked about?"

"Unfortunately." Annie rubbed her eyes, then huffed. She glanced at the clock once more before shooing him off with a dismissive wave. "Go. Away, please."

Cam chuckled as he left and headed down the hall. He leaned against the doorway, illuminated only by his eyes and brands. Ten minutes later, as Annie descended, he scanned over her before he cocked his head and tsked, "You still look far too lovely."

And it was the truth, even in a boy's clothes, she was breathtaking. Despite being loose, the trousers did a fantastic job of showcasing her newly developed curves.

"I would be more inclined to take your compliment if it weren't still dark out." She made another face at him as she tucked the ends of her braid into the cap he'd left her. She seemed to notice then that he wore an outfit similar to hers, except that his was adorned with a shoulder holster strapped across his chest and a gun belt at his waist. Additionally, he wore a brown leather coat with the hood pulled up and a dark scarf covering the lower half of his face.

Annie gestured to his attire, keeping her voice low. "Is there a reason we're dressed like criminals?"

"Stop trying to spoil the surprise." Cam offered her the peacoat—also Timmy's—he had over his arm, and she slipped it on. "You're just going to have to wait and see."

Annie made an irritated noise before following him out of the villa. An immediate shiver passed down her body once they stepped into the bitter chill of the night. The stars were out, no clouds. No wonder it was so cold. He couldn't feel it anymore. Only the frost blanketing the lawn gave it away. There would be sun today if this continued.

Annie had to jog to keep up with his long strides as he

made his way around to the backside of the villa, to the stables. Two horses were tacked and ready for them. Before she could question it, Cam pulled a heavy, gold-plated candlestick out of the bag at his side and handed it to the stableboy. The boy nodded his thanks, clutching the treasure to his chest like his life depended on it, as he passed the reins to Cam.

Her brows rose as the boy scurried away. "Where did you get that?"

Cam shrugged as he checked the horses's girths. "My father won't miss it."

Annie let out a low laugh and accepted his offer to help her in the saddle. Cam's hands lingered at her waist, his eyes burning above the scarf. "Last chance to change your mind. I'll take you back inside and go myself, if you'd like."

Annie gathered the reins, pulling her coat tighter around her. "How can I make a choice when I still don't know where we're going?"

Cam turned and climbed onto his own horse, a tall, slender pinto. "Stay here or come with me, Kitten?"

With a smirk, Annie nudged her horse forward, calling over her shoulder, "Let's go."

It felt so good to ride again. It had been too long. Even better was to ride beside her, even if it were in the earliest hours of the morning. Annie looked beautiful on a horse. He'd always thought so. Her body moved in rhythm with the animal's gait, flowing, natural, happy, even. Her mount—a dappled grey gelding—didn't seem to mind the chill. He plodded along, keeping a steady pace until they reached the more heavily trafficked streets.

Despite the hour, the city was teeming with people. Cam

kept to the outskirts of the markets, instead of cutting through the center, his gaze constantly scanning over the morning crowds, searching for threats.

"They look terrible." Despite whispering, Annie's words rang too loudly across the alley. She received more than a few glares, causing her cheeks to turn bright red.

"They do." Cam glared back at the onlookers, who returned to their business.

Enoch's people were *dirty*, clinging to sacks full of rotten vegetables, watching with wide, fear-filled eyes as they passed. Packs of children roamed without mothers and fathers to guide them. Scantily clad women lingered on street corners, working to catch the eyes of potential customers. It was nothing new to him, but he didn't remember it being this bad when he was young. Maybe he'd just been too innocent then to realize the extent of the city's desperation.

"How long until we get to the surprise?" Annie asked in her monotone way.

"About twenty minutes." Cam patted his mare's neck. "Getting bored with me already? I don't blame you. You could be doing much more exciting things. Like sleeping—"

"That's not what I said," Annie shot back, watching as town goers prepped their shops for morning business. "I just . . ." She made to chew her thumbnail, forgetting she wore gloves. She pursed her lips before taking her reins in both hands again. "I-I don't know. I thought we could talk. You've been gone a lot, and I . . ."

I miss you. That's what she'd been about to say. Cam's heart vaulted into his throat.

"Talk?" Cam's brow shot skyward, making her face redden all the more. "I talk all the time. I'm not sure what you mean."

"Never mind." She scowled. "Forget I said it."

"No." Cam reached across the space between their horses and brushed her cool thigh. "I was just joking. Obviously not well—"

"Because you make stupid jokes when you're nervous," Annie replied, recalling his previous admission. She gave him a weak smile. "Why are you nervous?"

"You always make me nervous," Cam blurted, adjusting the scarf over his face. God knew he'd do foolish, foolish things if it kept her smiling. Eyes followed them down the street, putting him on edge.

She opened her mouth, but before she could ask the question he'd been avoiding, he interrupted. "What did you want to talk about?"

As she thought, chewing on her words, he lost himself in the petite curve of her nose, of her neck, in the way her ice-blue eyes looked so stark against her white lashes and brows.

Annie cocked her head as she swayed along with her horse, the dove-grey, swirling brands on her throat visible with her hair tucked into the cap. "Um, when is your birthday? I've never asked."

"My birthday?"

"Your birthday."

"Let's see." It took Cam a moment to remember. It had been a *long* time since birthdays felt important. "It was two days ago, actually. October the sixteenth. But I suppose it doesn't matter. If we're truly going to live for centuries, at some point I imagine I'll forget how old I am."

"Of course it matters. We should have had a party. Or a cake, at least." Annie thought for a moment. "How old *are* you?"

"Twenty," Cam replied, tugging his hood lower over his eyes. "When is yours?"

"In the spring. April the third, to be exact. I'll be nineteen."

"Spring." Cam smiled to himself. "That's strangely fitting. Hopefully, we live long enough to celebrate it."

"I've been thinking about something you've said," she said. "You mentioned you and your mother hid in the city for weeks before trying to leave. Why didn't she try to board a ship right away? The harbor is always full."

Cam stared at her in shock. He'd never thought about it, but as she said it, little bits of memories came back to him. "She used to say we were waiting for the *right* one."

Every day, his mother would drag him to the dock's schedule, scanning over the ships coming and going for the day. Every day, she'd leave disappointed. Until one day, she didn't. The day she'd died.

Somewhere his father won't find him.

"Strange." Annie's brows furrowed. "Do you remember where you were headed?"

"East," Cam answered. He recalled that much. "She wanted to go East, but she didn't say where."

Annie nodded, lost in thought.

Several minutes passed, the silence broken by the low hum of distant chatter, the nagging cries of seagulls, and the barking of dogs. Finally, Annie shot him a quick, anxious look before asking, "Camden?"

"Yes, Kitten?"

"Do you think we'll survive this?"

Cam glanced up at the sky as another gull flew over. *Almost there.* He urged his horse forward and replied, "What do you want me to tell you?"

Annie frowned and nudged her mount into a trot to keep up. "The truth."

"The truth? I don't know," Cam said as they came around the corner, the street opening into the harbor. His throat tightened at the sight of grey sails whipping atop the masts of docked cargo ships. Fish merchants called to passing sailors, offering fresh, fried snapper.

Take him somewhere his father won't find him. Cam closed his eyes, breathing past the tears that threatened to fall. The last time he'd been here, in this part of the harbor . . .

"I changed my mind," Cam exhaled before reaching across the space between them and taking Annie's hand in his. She held tight. He gave her a wide, weary smile. "We *will* survive. I promise you that. I'm tired of merely staying alive. I want to *live.*"

With her—though, he was still too afraid to tell her that. Even if she never cared for him more than just as a friend, he would live and spend every day trying to make her happy.

Annie's returning smile was equally as tired. "You shouldn't make promises you can't keep."

"We'll see about that," he said before a flurry of motion caught his attention. A few docks down, a graying man in worn, sailor's slops shouted at the crewmen working to unload the crates from a tied frigate's hull.

Cam zeroed in on the heavy chains dangling from the man's belt. *Right where Julian said he'd be.*

"Follow me." He squeezed Annie's fingers before dropping them, gathering up his reins. He kept himself between her and the ship, blocking it from her view, as they trotted to the small harbor stable. As they dismounted, he tossed a few bills to the stable hand before retaking her hand, leading her back out into the sea air.

She glanced down at their entangled fingers, brows pinched together, as the breeze yanked strands of moon-white hair from beneath her cap. "Is this the part where you tell me the surprise?"

"Yes." His heart pounded as he led her around the side of

the stable. She didn't argue as he prompted her to follow him up the small ladder, leading into the hayloft. Nor did any of the staring passersbys question them. This wasn't unusual behavior for Enoch.

Annie let out a low laugh as Cam jerked open the windows at the front of the loft, looking out over the harbor.

"This . . . wasn't exactly what I expected." She kicked a loose pile of straw. "But if dust and horse shite are what gets you excited, I won't judge."

Cam swiveled and tugged down his scarf to grin at her before splaying a hand over his chest. "Did you say a naughty word *and* make a joke in the same sentence? I'm so proud."

She rolled her eyes, but he didn't miss the color rising in her cheeks.

"Come here." Cam waved her towards the window. "I promise I'm not trying to woo you in a barn."

"That's a relief." Annie stepped to his side, swallowing as she peeked over the edge, down to the streets below. She looked like she was about to be sick. "Why are we here, then?"

Cam chewed on the edge of his lip, struggling to find the words. He inhaled and took her hand again, running his thumb over his mother's ring beneath her glove. Another breath. "It occurred to me that I never got you a wedding gift."

Her pale eyes shot wide, but she didn't let go. "A wedding gift—"

"So, here's your surprise." Cam's heart beat so fast, he thought he might faint, as he pointed across the harbor to the docked frigate. *God, please don't let her hate me for this.* "It needed weeks of planning. Tracking schedules and shipments. I'm sorry it took so long. There—the third ship to the left."

"We don't need another ship, Camden." Annie shook her head as she scanned over the vessels. "*The Elaina* is too large as it is—"

Annie's entire body went inhumanely still as she locked onto the frigate and the crude, black, and maroon-striped sail flying on its mast.

Her pupils dilated, her gaze unblinking, as the greying sailor stepped back onto the gangway, cursing as he shouted orders at his crew. He spat into the sea before disappearing below deck.

Annie wobbled, her knees buckling. "The note Mr. Price gave you—"

"Julian is good at his job, after all." Cam took the opportunity to twist her to face him. "And it just so happens, after a little work, that the underground was happy to give up the location of an infamous slave trader, scheduled to make port in Enoch today, on the search for more cargo."

"He's taking more slaves." Annie gripped her throat so tightly that he thought she might bruise it. "He can't—"

Cam sank onto one knee—like he should have a *long* time ago—and slid the damascus dagger from its sheath on her belt. He removed her glove, revealing her glowing brands, and gently kissed each of her fingertips before curling them around the dagger's hilt. She stared down at him, expression empty, her chest rising and falling faster than the waves.

"Let me do this for you." Cam's lips spread into a cruel smile. "Let me be your monster. Let me show you what ten years of piracy have taught me. He will *never* hurt you again, Annie. Please, let me end your nightmares."

Annie wobbled again, but she caught herself against his shoulder. Slowly, she knelt until they were eye to eye. She slid her hands up his cheeks and locked her fingers in his hair. She rested her nose against his, their heavy breaths mingling as she whispered, "He's mine to take apart, piece by piece."

"Piece by piece," Cam promised, brushing his lips over

hers, reveling in the coolness of her skin. "Anything you want. Always."

She pulled back enough to hold his gaze, her own descending to a deeper level of cold than he'd ever seen them. "Take me to him."

CHAPTER 45
ANNIE

It felt like the winds and the stirring rains paused to watch them cross the harbor. A group of sailors huddled around a fire lit inside a metal drum. As they passed, the sailors twisted away, muttering something about *Stripes*. Cam shot them a glare, catching one's eye, and the man's face drained of color.

"Superstitious lout," Cam smirked, his brands glowing beneath the scarf over his face. Annie's skin buzzed as Cam's fire brushed against it, the touch protective but gentle. Her power purred in response, flaring to the surface. They twined together, filling her with a security that calmed her storming heart.

He's here. Her master. She'd only allowed herself to say his name that one time. Dark sails whipped above them, creating a cracking sound akin to thunder. Beneath her gloves, her palms were coated with sweat. He was here—somewhere inside that ship—and she'd have to look at him again. Breathe the same air. Smell the tobacco on his breath.

Her entire body shuddered, and she would have stumbled

had Cam not rested a steadying hand on her lower back. A younger man with a thick beard stood guard at the gangplank leading up to the vessel.

Cam leaned in, tugging her closer. "Now, I know we agreed that the big guy is all yours, but may I have the honor of picking off the little ones?"

"*Oi.*" The man perked up as they drew closer, scowling as he instinctively reached for his gun belt. "You don't need to be here. Shove off."

I don't know him. Annie didn't understand why she'd expected the crew to remain the same. It had been years.

Cam let out an excited groan as the man drew a revolver. "Pretty please? Do you want me to beg?"

"He's all yours," Annie said. *I'm ready.* "But if I see one that I want, hold him for me."

"Deal," Cam rumbled as the man aimed at them.

"I said shove off," he cried, backing a step when he realized they were Revenants. "Don't make me say it again—"

Cam waved his hand, and a wall of heat slammed into the man's side, flinging him off the gangplank with a guttural shriek before he splashed into the bay.

"Ah," Cam let out a low laugh. "You know, I understand now why Julian does all those stupid hand movements."

"Pardon?" Annie asked as four more men peered over the edge of the ship, their expressions shifting from shock to rage.

"It's *so* satisfying. Watch." Cam cackled as he yanked down his scarf, blowing across his palm as he might dust from a book. He sent an explosion of embers directly into the men's eyes. They screamed, gripping their ruined faces as they ducked out of sight.

"See?" Cam offered her a hand and led her up the gangplank. "Satisfying."

An alarm bell rang, the chime so loud it made her ears ring.

Annie sighed, gripping the patterned bone hilt of her dagger. "Well, they know we're here now."

Cam's grin turned feral. "Good."

As soon as they stepped onto the deck, six more crewmen were upon them. Each wore variations of the same uniform: brown trousers, grey button-down shirts, and heavy wool coats. Exactly like she'd remembered. The master bought their clothes in bulk. They didn't get to pick.

"The hell do you want?" The nearest one sneered and drew his sword, pressing the tip to Cam's chest.

Cam didn't even flinch.

"I should run you through now, but it's your lucky day. I'm curious why two Stripes are so desperate to get aboard." The sailor's sneer grew wider, revealing a missing canine. "And one's a lady. Captain will be happy about that."

Cam's brands flickered and pulsed as he studied the men. He inclined his chin to her. "Anyone you know, Kitten?"

Annie took in each of their faces before shaking her head. "None of them."

His gaze flickered back to the crewmen. "Do you want them dead?"

She hesitated before answering, "No."

"Hmm, too bad." Cam shrugged before gripping the end of the sword. The metal instantly turned molten as he twisted the tip back towards its owner. The man yelped, jumping back as he dropped his ruined weapon, but Cam was faster. He clamped down on the man's wrist, smoke curling up from where he burnt through his coat sleeve. "Is your captain below?"

The five others just watched, wide-eyed, as their companion nodded *yes* and moaned in pain.

Cam kicked the man's feet out from under him, laying him on his back before leaning in and smiling. "As much as I'd like to eviscerate you, my lady said no. I suppose it's *your* lucky day. You all can leave, or you can follow us below and die. I don't care either way."

They were scrambling away before he'd finished speaking, dropping their swords before barreling down the gangplank and disappearing into the harbor crowds.

Flames sparked around Cam's fingers as he let out a long sigh. "Are you sure you want them alive?"

"If we killed every evil man, the world would be empty." Annie's heart thudded so hard it made her chest ache. Across the deck, the hatch leading below hung open. *This ship had looked so large before.* Everything had seemed enormous after she was taken from her father's hut. The woods, the snow, the hunting village . . . they'd been the expanse of her world. She'd never known anything else.

But now that she was here again? Her past seemed so small. Insignificant.

"Why do you always have to be right?" Cam pouted, then froze as Annie closed her eyes and sucked in a deep breath. The bells continued to toll, but no one came for them. *Why haven't the police arrived?* The master—*her* master—waited for them below.

Softly, so softly, Cam brushed away the tear spilling down her cheek. "He can't hurt you anymore. Let's make him pay."

He can't hurt me. Not only because Cam was with her, but because she wasn't a child anymore. No, she was a Callahan now, and she wore death on her fingertips. He'd never hurt her again.

Annie looped her pinkie through Cam's and smiled up at him. "I'm ready."

He kissed her knuckles and nodded. It was only a short flight of stairs down into the hell that haunted her nightmares, but he was with her. Fear couldn't hold her anymore.

The smell hit her first, bringing the memories back to life. She took Cam's hand entirely, squeezing hard enough to break it if he were a normal man. It wasn't the scent of feces or unwashed bodies that nauseated her. It was the *cleaner*—a mixture of white vinegar, seawater, and cheap liquor. From dawn until dusk, she scrubbed the floorboards. Scrubbed it free of piss, vomit, and blood. She could still feel it, burning the sores on her hands and knees.

Annie willed her heart to slow. The sconces were unlit. They were always lit—

Cam drew her back, placing a finger over his lips to silence her. He signaled for her to stay behind him as he took a deliberate step forward, causing the pine boards to creak beneath his weight. Suddenly, a flash of metal descended, stabbing into the floor right where Cam had been standing—just inches from where she would have been if he hadn't stopped her.

Another crewman emerged from the darkness, bursting through a doorway while screaming and swinging his sword. Cam sidestepped and slammed his heel into the side of the man's knee. His joint snapped at an odd angle with a loud crack, and he let out a grunt as he fell to the ground, his sword clattering beside him. Without a word or a moment's hesitation, Cam picked up the blade from the floor and drove it through the back of the man's head, pinning him to the floor.

Before she had time to think, Cam strode into the open room, a supply closet. The wreath of fire he summoned around them chased the shadows away. Three more men waited with their swords at the ready, crouched in the corners, squinting against the sudden light blinding them.

Cam's brands flared as he smiled, and they screamed as their weapons melted in their hands, searing their flesh. They didn't fight—in fact, they pissed themselves—as Cam yanked them one by one by their hair so she could see their faces. "Anyone look familiar?"

"Him." Annie's focus narrowed down to the sailor in the middle, to the scars that crisscrossed his cheeks. She used to stare at them when he'd pin her to the floor, imagining all the ways she could give him new ones. She never knew his name. "He's mine."

Fire filled Cam's eyes, and he grinned at the others, nodding to the door. "I'd suggest you leave while you still can. Good luck finding a doctor who can fix your hands."

They abandoned their companion without a second's thought. Outside, the bell still chimed, a looming threat on the horizon. *The Enoch police will show up soon.*

"We're running out of time," she said, more to herself than him.

"*You* have all the time in the world, Kitten." The remaining man groaned in pain as Cam forced him to his knees. "I've taken care of it."

"How—" Annie paused, then smiled a little. "Mr. Price?"

"Remember, he's good at his job." Cam nodded for her to proceed, near shivering with anticipation. He wanted this as much as she did, possibly more.

As she drew her dagger, the man finally seemed to notice her. His thick brows knit in confusion before recognition passed over his features. "You—"

"Me." Annie knelt, scanning over his scars. He recoiled and cried out as she sliced them open again. He jerked, but Cam held him still as she slid the blade further down his cheeks, mixing the new wounds with the old. He opened his mouth— likely to curse her—but she sank the blade through the open space, plunging it through the back of his throat and hitting bone, before twisting and yanking it out to the side, nearly decapitating him.

There was no screaming. Just a soft gurgle as his yellowed eyes rolled back into his head. Annie stared at his face, waiting to feel something—satisfaction, relief, joy, maybe—but she only felt a strange hollowness. Not numb, but empty.

"Damn." Cam let the body drop to the floor. He gave her an odd look as he wiped some of the blood spray off his face. "I probably should be concerned about how attractive that was."

Annie wiped the blade off on the man's trousers to hide her shaking. "Come on. We're not done here."

Cam bowed, gesturing for her to take the lead.

They'd only taken two steps into the hall before a dozen men poured in through every open space, howling like banshees and armed to the teeth.

This time, she was ready. When Cam moved, his features shifting into a lethal calm, she moved alongside him. She'd never properly learned to fight, but she could wield a knife, and she had her power now.

Cam had already cut three men in half before she'd closed in on her first, an ugly, short lump of a man she didn't know. He swung at her head with a chipped axe. Instead of dodging, she ducked in close to him and grabbed his throat. Her brands flared to life as she began to *pull*, brightening from grey to white as she stole his life from him. It only took seconds for the man to wither, dropping in her grip like a burlap sack.

A second sailor—that was already lunging for her—skidded to a stop as the other fell. It was too late. He was close enough that Annie stabbed the damascus dagger through his eye.

A scalding rush of heat made her turn, and she yanked the blade free from the man's skull.

In the center of the hall, every visible part of Cam's skin glowed like a walking sun. His eyes flickered to hers, a hint of the creature he'd been in Mr. Baxter's lab shining through. The rest of the sailors were dead at his feet. Some in pieces. Others charred lumps of flesh.

Ten. He'd killed ten men in the time she'd taken two.

Touch him. Her power whispered. *Take it.* Annie's throat tightened until she could barely breathe as she fought the urge to crush her lips against his. Instead, slowly, carefully, she reached and brushed his jaw, murmuring. "Are you alright?"

"Never better." Cam sucked in a breath as he rolled his shoulders, some of the fire beneath his skin fading. Blood dripped from the ends of his hair, painting his cheekbones red. "Where to next?"

His skin was uncomfortably hot as he squeezed her hand. She squeezed back, refusing to pull away as she led him deeper into the bowels of the vessel. No one else tried to stop them.

I never thought I would be back here again. The hall narrowed until the walls pressed against Cam's shoulders. While she had a bit more space, it felt like she could have been underwater, struggling for air. The fiery glow of Cam's brands illuminated the tar-stained walls, the light swaying with each step he took. An angry whistle echoed through the corridors, a reminder of the approaching windstorm.

Her feet fell in sync with the worn floor, her muscles remembering every crack or knot that could trip her. There—a slim, iron-framed door began to reflect the gleam of Cam's fire.

No, no, no, no. As Annie's heart stopped and started beneath her ribs, her head grew too heavy to carry. She reached behind her and grabbed hold of Cam's thigh to steady herself. He was the only reason she didn't faint.

"Annie." He wrapped an arm around her waist, holding her back against his torso. He leaned down and pressed his cheek to hers, his voice a low rasp as he whispered, "You're going to walk out of here. He's not."

"He's not." She whispered back, eyes closed, as she continued her fight to breathe. "I will."

"You will." Cam squeezed her tighter, his heat spreading into her muscles, her bones. "And you will set the rest that are in chains free. They'll live because of *you*."

They'll live. The words repeated over and over in her mind. They'll live just like she did. She couldn't let them suffer any longer.

A low, eerie creak made Annie's eyes shoot open. Cam's body went taut.

The door opened enough for a familiar, bearded face to peer through. It was like she never left. He looked the same now as he had the day Lord Duskin purchased her. The same as he did in her nightmares.

Cam's hate was a visceral, physical thing. His chest heaved as his grip tightened on her shoulders, the energy swirling off of him enough to make the extinguished sconces rattle.

Her master didn't seem to notice him. His gaze remained solely on her as he said, "I knew I'd see you again. I don't know how, but I knew." He opened the door wider, revealing himself to be dressed in simple, sailor's slops and no visible weapons.

She'd always thought it would have been easier if he'd been ugly or foul, but he still looked like a regular man. Tired, maybe, and sea-weathered, but perfectly ordinary. If she hadn't known better, she could have passed him in the street and never thought twice about him.

He turned and stepped into the room, leaving the door ajar as he called, "Come in."

Annie's body obeyed without her permission, not hesitating to follow. Cam was behind her, holding the hem of her shirt as if he thought she could disappear. Once inside, her master took a pack of matches out of his pocket, struck one to life, and lit a candle sitting on a nearby desk.

Not that he needed it.

Cam's fire alone was enough to reveal the line of terrified, grimy faces chained to the wall in heavy, iron shackles. Naked. Women. Children. Men.

Slaves.

Cam's expression remained frighteningly blank as her master sat on the three-legged stool in the center of the chamber, facing them. He lit a cigarette, snuffing the match on his boot, before jerking a thumb at the shivering people behind him. "I like to watch them, you see. Get a sense of who each of them is, so I know who best to sell them to." His cold eyes latched onto Annie again. "You'll remember, I expect?"

"I do," Annie managed past the lump in her throat.

He'd watched her for days before he'd first decided to drag her by the hair into his bed chamber.

Crackling, violent flames snaked across the floor and onto the walls, hissing as they sucked up the moisture, warping the wood. The slaves recoiled, their chains rattling, as they edged away from the fire. She'd never known Cam to be so silent.

Her master seemed to notice him, then, giving him an inquisitive look as he folded his arms over his chest.

He smiled at her, "I see you found yourself a dragon." He glanced over the exposed brands on her hands and neck. "If I'd known you'd be a Stripe, I'd have sold you for quadruple the price or kept you for myself as a prize. I miss you. Never had better."

A darkness hunkered at the edge of Annie's mind. The same one that would find her whenever she wanted to stop feeling. The one that would take her continents away, back home to her hut at the edge of the forest.

If it weren't for Cam beside her, she might have let it take her, but not today.

Today, she wanted to feel.

She barely registered drawing her dagger, but she *did* notice the way Cam began to circle her master like a wild cat, his lovely lips curling into a grin.

Her master *hmphed* as he crossed one leg over the other. "That's what I assumed you came for. Get on with it, then."

He wasn't even going to fight her. No, he wouldn't after what they'd done to his crew. What could he do? Where could he go?

His eyes brightened as he puffed on his cigarette. "Do you remember our first time together?"

Annie crept closer, clenching the dagger's handle. "Yes."

"You'll always remember me, I suppose." Sweat poured down his face as Cam continued to circle. "That's my only solace in this. That I'll live on in you." He glanced back at the slaves against the walls. "In them, too."

"Annie." Cam slid a short, slender knife out of his boot. "Tell me how you want him to hurt. Tell me what you want. Let me help you."

That was the first time she saw a hint of fear on her master's face.

Fear—because he was only a man. And now that she looked at him, feigning control as he sat on that ridiculous stool, waiting to die, she realized that's all he ever was.

A man. One whose control over her was only fed by fear.

Cam's blade hovered over her master's throat, ready to cut to the bone at her word.

Annie rubbed her aching chest as she scanned over the faces of the slaves. She may be free in body, but in her soul, she was still one of them. She was still chained to that damned wall, kicking and screaming as they made to drag her into the shadows. Eventually, she'd stopped fighting. She'd given up. She'd also been waiting to die.

But now she was alive.

And he meant nothing.

"You can't hurt me anymore," Annie murmured, testing the edge of her blade against her thumb. "Nor will you hurt them."

Her master swallowed as her eyes snapped to Cam's. "Take his eyes."

Within a breath, Cam carved out her master's eye sockets, leaving only fleshy, empty holes behind. Her master wailed and screamed, curling into himself as he tumbled to the ground, splattering fresh blood over the stained wood.

Cam was grinning ear to ear as she nodded to the slaves and said, "Free them."

They shrank away, but didn't try to run, as Cam heated and ripped off their shackles. There were eight, now that she counted, each with a different level of bewilderment on their gaunt faces.

"You're going to come with me," Annie said to them. "I'm going to get you well. Then we'll worry about what comes next."

They nodded in unison. As the master continued to scream, one of the children—a girl about the same age as she was when she was taken—spit on him and said, "Take his tongue."

Cam gave her a curt nod before doing just that. The master's tongue came free in a wet snap. He tossed it to the ground and stomped on it.

"Tie a millstone around his neck," the older woman said darkly. "Send him to the bottom of the sea."

Cam glanced at Annie for approval.

"Yes," She found herself smiling. She stepped over the master, cocking her head as he writhed at her feet. "Let him sink into the depths, not knowing which way is up. Just like I did."

"Ooh." Cam broke out into a laugh. "I'm always up for a bit of theatrics."

It seemed so effortless as he turned, the slaves scrambling out of the way, and blew out the back of the ship in an explosion of fire and shrapnel. Seawater poured over their feet, filling the hull.

Cam took what remained of the shackles and melted them around the slaver's neck, making a thick, heavy collar. Her master fought and clawed at Cam's limbs as he was dragged to the opening in the hull, the ocean an empty void beneath him.

The older woman and the young girl held hands as Annie lifted her master by the neck. He struggled, letting out an agonized groan as she whispered into his ear, "I will never think of you again."

Then she shoved him over the edge, giving him to the waves.

They brought the slaves ashore, and Cam set the ship ablaze.

She'd never think of it again.

CHAPTER 46
ALEXANDER

A gust of wind whipped through Alexander's shoulder-length hair as he stepped out of his private coach. He didn't bother putting on his top hat. He tucked it under his arm instead. The heavy, dark clouds swelling in the skyline behind Waverly Hospital accentuated the already ominous aura of the curved building.

Lights flickered in every window of the hospital—a recent development—thanks to Camden's outrageously large donation out of the Callahan funds. *For his wife*. Alexander smirked as he made his way up the steps to the entry. He had a feeling that if that girl asked his son to give her the world, Camden would do it. As he should—Annie was special. Special in the way Cassandra was special.

Alexander recoiled at her name running through his mind, his lungs already burning from the incline. Not now. He couldn't linger on her memory. Those times were reserved for late at night, when he could finally have a moment to himself and simply breathe . . . though, even that was getting more difficult.

A flurry of activity met him at the door. Nurses zipped by frantically, carrying alternating loads of clean and bloody linens. The elderly desk manager furiously filled out paperwork as sweat dripped off his balding scalp. Usually, he'd have given the governor a forced, but courteous greeting, but not today. Something, or *someone*, had the hospital in a tizzy.

Raised, angry voices came from the hallway leading into the medical wing, echoing into the foyer. Alexander recognized the voices immediately. *Camden and Van Clarke.* His smirk spread into an amused smile. Trouble followed his son like a dog to its master. He hoped that his son hadn't killed anyone important this time, but it would be better not to get his hopes up.

No one stopped him or even glanced his way as he strode down the hall. The closest he came to any acknowledgement from the staff was the irritated expressions they wore as they had to squeeze past him in the narrow corridor. Dark curtains blocked his view of the adjoining rooms. Even since his last visit, Waverly's cleanliness had improved considerably.

I should have kept up on it. He didn't use to slip on things like Enoch's upkeep, but in recent years, the city had deteriorated as quickly as his body. *But Camden is here, now.* And as much as his son could go on fighting it, Enoch would crumble without him. It was only a matter of time.

"You can't just waltz in here and do whatever you like. There's a *system!*" Van Clarke hollered from further down the hall. Alexander turned around a corner to find Van nose to nose with Camden, who smiled back in just the right way to infuriate the doctor.

Alexander paused, not wanting to interrupt the show.

In response to Van's statement, Cam leaned in even closer, making Van back up.

"See, that's where you're wrong. I *can* do whatever I want.

And if you continue to annoy me, I'm going to take this hospital and give it to my wife. Who, I might add, has done more for Enoch in the weeks she's been here than you have in your entire, flea-ridden life."

"Flea-ridden?" Van backed another step, hand splayed over his chest. "How dare you. I have served this hospital and your family faithfully."

"Then *serve*. Stop nagging me." Camden's eyes darkened. "And you can do that by getting the hell out of my way."

Van bristled, slicking back his greasy, dark hair. "Your wife can't just take over my entire staff to treat a crowd of slaves. If she's trying to make amends for the atrocities she assuredly committed for Lord Duskin—"

"*Ah, ah.*" Cam's smile widened into a careless grin. "Now you've lost it. Waverly belongs to Annie *Callahan* now. So, if you're not going to help treat *her* patients, you can leave."

He's been trained in intimidation. As much as he despised the thought of his son being raised with pirates and brigands, at least they'd taught him how to hold himself. How to manipulate a situation to his advantage. Van Clarke cherished his image above all else and yearned for nothing more than to be praised for his charitable endeavors. Alexander, himself, would have taken the same approach.

Van gaped, sweat beading on his heavy brow. "Y-you can't do that."

"I just did." Cam winked as he turned to leave. "Too bad."

"I will pull my support," Van blurted with more than a hint of desperation.

Camden froze then swiveled, brow raised. "Excuse me?"

Alexander crossed his arms and leaned against the wall as Van stepped around in front of Camden, his back to Alexander now.

"I'll pull my support," Van repeated, a quiver in his voice.

"Don't think I don't know what your father is doing. He needs the pro-Revenant party's support—my support—to make sure you're allowed to take control of Enoch when the time is right. I'll vote against you."

"Oh no, *whatever* will I do?" Camden let out a low, bitter laugh before putting himself back in the doctor's space. When he spoke again, it was almost too quiet for Alexander to hear.

"Vote against me, then. If I want Enoch, I will take it. Just like I'm taking this hospital, and your staff, and your job, and giving it to my lady. Because I can, and it makes me happy to do so." Fire encircled Camden's fists, the only tell of the anger lying beneath this surface. "Now, step aside before I enjoy turning you into a pot roast."

Alexander cleared his throat, stepping into view.

Camden's gaze shot up and locked onto him without a hint of surprise. He'd known Alexander was there.

Van wheeled, his narrow face reddening. "G-governor? You can't let him do this. It's absurd!"

Camden stepped to the side, his entire body tensing.

"It sounds like he already has." Alexander scanned over the doctor. "Are you going to threaten to pull support for me, as well?"

His son smirked a little.

Van's face shifted from red to bloodless in an instant. "I-I—"

"Go." Alexander waved dismissively. "Before I take this a step further and pull your council position."

Without a word, Van dropped his head and rushed back down the hall, disappearing into one of the curtained rooms.

Alexander chuckled, but when he looked back, Camden was studying him, guarded.

Despite the burning ache in his chest, Alexander managed a smile. He couldn't remember the last time he'd smiled so much. *When Cassie had been alive.* He shook his head, making Camden's brow arch.

"What?" Alexander pushed off the wall, stepping closer. "Did you expect me to scold you?"

"Something like that." Camden's tension didn't lessen. "What are you doing here?"

"I saw smoke on the horizon and called my driver." Alexander moved to let a nurse pass. "I assumed it was you and decided to check here first. I'm glad I was right."

"Ah," Camden crooned mockingly. "I'm touched by your caring."

With that, he turned on his heel and headed to the upper floor. Alexander followed, reaching his side just as Camden made to open the door into the medical ward.

He grabbed his son's elbow, bracing to be burned. "Stop for a moment."

To his surprise, Camden did, but he jerked his arm out of Alexander's grip as soon as they came to a halt.

"Is Annie alright?" Alexander asked, slightly out of breath.

"What did I tell you about using her name?" Cam bristled but stayed put. "She's fine. Fantastic, even. You can leave."

It wasn't until Alexander noted the stickiness on his hands that he realized that his son was soaked in blood. It was clotted in his hair, smeared across his tan face, and stained his knuckles.

It's not his. Alexander eyed him curiously. "Who did you kill this time?"

"They deserved it." Camden shrugged.

"*They?*" Alexander exhaled a long breath. "Is this in relation to the slaves Dr. Clarke mentioned?"

"Yes." Camden's fingers hovered over the doorknob. "Annie and I freed them and brought them here for treatment. Van didn't appreciate the extra workload. Annie told him to eat it."

"I knew I liked her." Alexander snorted, then nodded to the door. "Shall we?"

Camden groaned but obliged.

The medical ward was packed, not just with staff, but with patients. Nurses darted in and out—Violet Clarke among them—checking on a group of emaciated men, women, and children. Some were being scrubbed clean, while others nibbled on crackers and sipped at light, flowery tea.

Annie stood in the center of the chaos, grinding something sweet-smelling in a mortar at the same time as she gave two young male nurses orders.

Camden's entire demeanor softened at the sight of her.

A lovely smile began to spread on her face when she spotted him, but it fell when she realized who walked beside him.

"Governor." She set the mortar down and made to curtsy, stopping when she seemed to remember she wore pants. She cleared her throat. "If you need healing"—she gave him a knowing look— "you'll have to get in line. It seems Dr. Clarke has forbidden me from using the newly furnished rooms upstairs."

On the other side of the ward, Violet shot Annie a glare.

"Actually, I've taken care of that," Camden said with more than a hint of smugness. "The hospital is yours, Kitten. Use whatever floor you want."

The entire room went still.

Annie blinked at him in shock. "W-what?"

"It's yours." Camden shot Alexander a glare, as if daring him to say otherwise. "I promised you a nursing position, didn't I?"

"Yes, but . . ." Annie brought her words down to a nervous hiss. "You promised me a job, not an entire damn hospital."

Camden shrugged again. "Tomato, tomahto."

"Congratulations on your new position." Alexander gave her a curt bow. "You'll honor it well, I'm sure."

Camden seemed to relax at that, even if only slightly, but before he could respond, a loud bang came from the corner of the room. A young girl—maybe ten—threw her cup at one of the nurses, shrieking something about *perverts*.

"Hey!" Camden strode towards her, his tone playful. "We've talked about this, Mary. The poor bloke's just trying to treat your foot—"

As Camden knelt beside the girl's bed, she let out a strangled stream of words, her face plastered in tears. He took the linens from the nurse before shooing him off. The girl relaxed as Cam wrapped her badly deformed ankle, chatting happily as he did so.

He's so much like you, Cassie. Alexander's throat grew tight. *You'd be proud of him.*

Annie must have read his expression, because she whispered, "He's good with people. As much as he doesn't think so."

Alexander swallowed, pressing his lips into a thin line. "He'll rule well. As will you."

A hint of concern showed through her granite features. "And if he doesn't? If we don't? What happens to Enoch? To these people?"

"Depending on who takes the city after me," Alexander replied, hunting for her fears. "They'll either perish or find themselves back in the same situation you've just liberated them from. It can't be helped."

Her chest rose and fell, her pale brows furrowing as she watched Camden finish wrapping the girl's leg.

"The slaver." Alexander shot her a sideways glance. "Was he the same one from whom Lord Duskin purchased you?"

Annie met his gaze, her ice-blue eyes filled with genuine shock.

"Come now," Alexander tutted. "Did you really think I wouldn't have inquired about your history before you ever set foot on my soil?"

With a quick huff, she arranged her mask back into place. "Yes, he was the same one."

Alexander nodded. "Is he dead?"

"Yes."

"I'm glad to hear it." He squeezed her shoulder gently and nodded to Mary as he turned to leave. "I do hope you'll try to convince my son to take up his seat. It would be a shame to see that girl in the hands of another."

With that, he turned and strode out of the hospital.

The council meeting was tomorrow, and with Henry's tie on his tongue, he'd done all he could. Now the cards would fall where they may.

Bale. Alexander let out a slow, wheezing breath as he climbed back into his carriage. Once the meeting was over, their deal would be done. He'd failed the terms of their agreement, just like he'd always planned to.

It was Camden's turn now.

Alexander only hoped he lived long enough to watch his son turn Henry to dust.

CHAPTER 47

CAMDEN

The sun had long fallen by the time they left the hospital, exhausted and crusted in dried blood. Every time their carriage hit a bump, Cam jolted awake, not realizing he'd nodded off.

Annie was wide awake, though. She stared intently out the window, brows pinched, her pale skin reflecting golden light every time they passed a streetlamp. The brands visible on her hands and neck still glowed a charcoal grey.

Cam drank in the lovely planes of her face, the curve of her rose-petal lips. Seeing her treat the slaves had been . . . extraordinary.

He'd seen her heal on *The Elaina,* seen her heal Julian, and even Reika Hall, but watching her in the hospital had been something different. Where everyone had panicked when they'd wheeled in over half a dozen badly wounded patients, she'd been completely calm. Focused. A leader. Like she'd been born for it.

Annie's eyes flickered up to him and narrowed, breaking him from his thoughts.

"Why are you staring?" she whispered.

"I was just wondering." Cam straightened and cleared his throat. "Why didn't you use your power to heal them?"

Because she hadn't. Not once. All of their care, she'd done with the tools and medicines she'd had available. That had amazed him, too. He hadn't known half of what the herbs or tonics she'd used were called or did.

Annie rubbed her fingers, gaze returning to the window. "I didn't want to frighten them."

"Oh?" Cam grinned. "Would it have been more frightening than watching me dismember their master?"

She flinched at the mention of him. "It's not that, it's—"

The carriage lurched violently, and she let out a low shriek, bracing against her seat. Cam had already drawn his revolver when the door jerked open, revealing Julian Price. He glanced over their haggard appearances and raised a dark brow. "Successful mission, I take it?"

"Hang it all, man." Cam slid his gun back into its holster. "Damned Air Brands. Don't do that."

Annie's cheeks were bright pink from her scream.

"My apologies." Julian chuckled as he ducked inside and shut the door, taking the nearest, open seat beside Cam. He glanced between them expectantly. "Well? Is it done?"

Hand over her throat, Annie nodded solemnly.

Julian nodded back. "I'm glad."

After an awkward silence, Cam popped his lips, crossing one leg over the other. "So, Jules. Where have you been?"

"Terrorizing Enoch's police," Julian scowled. "Like you asked."

"We sank the ship seven hours ago," Cam replied dryly.

Julian adjusted his cream coat. "Do you have any idea how difficult it is to create six separate false catastrophes in a city this size without getting caught?" He shook his head. "Of course, you don't. I doubt you've ever been discreet in your life."

"You're just jealous because I can get away with it," Cam said. As he watched, Annie scooted deeper into the corner, eyes still fixed out of the window. His heart sank. Something was bothering her.

"Please," he asked Julian, keeping his attention on him and away from her. "Inform me on your heroic acts of subtlety."

Just as he hoped, Julian droned on and on about his favorite stealth tactics. It took little prompting to keep him talking, and the longer he did so, the more Annie seemed to relax. She may have even nodded off once or twice.

When they arrived at the villa, she went straight inside, wrapping her arms tightly around herself, leaving Cam alone with Julian's rambling while tending to the horses, much to the stableboy's dismay. He just wanted Annie to have a moment to herself, a chance to decompress if that's what she needed.

It was an hour later when he followed her inside. Julian was smiling when he said his goodnights. Cam paused in the entry, watching him go. God, sometimes having Julian around felt like Resh had come back from the dead. Resh used to love to shove facts down the throats of anyone who would listen. It drove Cam crazy.

Is that the real reason you keep him close? Because he reminds you of Resh?

Or because having him around felt like having a father? Or as close to one as he could get without acknowledging the father he still had alive. Cam groaned and rubbed his face. He was too tired for this.

Give her some more time. As much as he wanted to check on Annie, Cam dragged himself down the hall to his room. Inside, his dresser still lay smashed to bits where he'd piled its remains against the wall. The bed was unmade from the last time he'd used it. He ran his fingers over the mahogany desk before stepping into the bathing chamber, a layer of fine dust clinging to his skin. The only nights he had actually slept in here were during the hell week Annie hadn't spoken to him.

It won't be like that again. Cam's chest tightened as he brushed the dust onto his filthy trousers. He couldn't assume that every time she was distant, it was because she was upset with him. Even in the past, when she'd pushed him away, he hadn't been the cause. Still, fear wasn't rational. He needed to talk to her—to hear from her mouth that she still wanted him around.

It took another thirty minutes to scrub all the blood off his body and out of his hair, turning the water in the tub a murky red.

You shouldn't be bothering her. Cam dressed in a simple black sweater and lounge pants before heading upstairs. *You should turn around, go downstairs, and go to bed. Leave her alone.*

But he couldn't. No matter how hard he tried, all he wanted was to be near her, to share her air.

Go to bed. He swallowed, tracing the knob of the repaired door as his chest rose and fell. Maybe she'd let him sleep on the couch again. At least he'd be close. Maybe—

"Come in, Cam." Annie's voice called softly from within the bedroom. "I can hear you thinking from here."

Thank God.

"Really?" Cam responded as he opened the door, choking back a sigh of relief. "Because sometimes I wonder if you actually . . . can."

He forgot how to form words. He forgot how to think.

Annie sat at her vanity in nothing but a violet silk robe, yanking through her damp hair with a wide-tooth comb. She let out an irritated huff and twisted, holding out the comb to him. "Would you help me with these tangles before I cut them out?"

Cam blinked at her. His mind was a mud puddle.

The corners of Annie's mouth quirked. "Cam?"

Hearing his name on her lips snapped him back into focus.

"Um, sure." He took the comb, and she shifted back toward the mirror. His attention snagged on the bead of water slowly trailing down her ivory throat, over her collarbone, and disappearing below the neckline of her robe, where his eyes couldn't follow.

Keep it together. Cam sucked in a steadying breath before lifting several locks of her hair. The lavender scent of her soap nearly destroyed him. Her hair really was tangled. He managed a nervous smile, letting his fingers catch on the knots. "Lord, woman, were you fighting with a wild animal?"

"It looks like it, doesn't it?" Annie took a second comb out of the vanity before starting on a separate section, her brows knit together in frustration. "I'd be here all night without you."

"It's my pleasure," Cam replied, and he meant it.

After several minutes of working in silence, Cam rested a freshly brushed section over her shoulder, then picked up a new one. Finally, he asked. "Are you . . . are you alright?"

Annie's ice-blue eyes snapped up to his reflection in the mirror, making his face grow hot.

"Of course," she replied, too calmly, as she resumed her combing. "Why wouldn't I be?"

"Well, I don't know." He let out a dark laugh. "We did just murder half a crew. Some might say that can cause one to become out of sorts."

Annie's mouth quirked up again. That was twice in the same conversation. "It was your idea."

"I'm aware." Cam scowled, laying the following tangle-free strands with the rest. He lifted another lock of her hair and twirled it around his finger before he continued. "I . . . I should have asked before ordering Julian to hunt down—"

"I don't want to talk about him again." Annie peered up at his reflection again. "Ever."

He held her stare, and from where he stood behind her, he could see her ears turn pink.

Kiss her neck. The thought slipped into his mind before he could stop it. Cam ignored his thumping heart by reorganizing his attack on the last of her tangles. "Is that why you seemed upset after leaving the hospital? Because Julian mentioned him—"

"No, that's not why. I'm fine, I promise." Annie replied, but this time she turned fully on her stool to face him. "And, please, don't talk about him. He's dead. He doesn't matter anymore."

"That doesn't seem rational." He smirked, and her blush deepened as he leaned over and laid the comb on the vanity. "Or healthy."

"Says you, the model of healthy coping mechanisms." She smiled wryly, an expression he rarely saw on her face. "And besides, you told me before that I could have whatever I wanted. Always."

God, save me. "I did. And I meant it."

"I know. And I believe you." Annie's features turned serious. She rubbed her arm, revealing the brands trailing up to her elbows. "Thank you. For . . . caring."

"Mmmhmm." He swallowed, fighting to keep his gaze from where the fabric of her robe puckered at her bustline. They stared at each other another moment, her cheeks turning as red as his felt.

Cam huffed, then made a spiraling motion with his finger. "Turn around."

Annie's eyes shot wide, filled with enough surprise that it made him laugh.

He gave her a mischievous grin. "I just want to dry your hair."

"Oh," she said, then cursed under her breath. She spun away to face the mirror again. "Go ahead."

Just as before, he trailed his fingers from root to end, letting his heat suck the moisture away. Annie's eyes closed, and with every tug, she let out a soft humming sound, almost like a purr. *I can't keep doing this.* His fire burned so hot, he had to jerk his hands away, letting her moon-white strands fall in a silky, smooth sheet.

When she opened her eyes again at the sudden motion, they were hazy. Hungry.

They stared at each other's reflections again, at least until his clenched fists started smoking.

"Well." He blew out a long breath, then turned for the living area, where the safety of his couch waited. "Goodnight, Annie."

"Cam." She stood and laid a hand over his elbow. He couldn't bring himself to look at her. He'd break if he did. Her voice was strained as she murmured, "Don't go."

"I have to." He gently—oh so gently—removed his arm from her grip. An electric jolt startled him as their skin touched. Despite, he repeated. "Goodnight, Annie."

"Why are you walking away?"

The question made him turn.

Annie was picking at a strip of bloody skin beside her thumbnail. "And be honest. I don't know if I could take it if you lied."

"Why am I—" He was too shocked to be embarrassed. The words tumbled out of his mouth. "Why am I walking away?

Hell, because I'll lose my damned mind if I don't. Why do you think I'm walking away?"

Annie's chin tilted, spilling her white hair over her shoulder, but she didn't look up from where she was mutilating her thumb. "Tell me you want me."

Cam could count the times on one hand where he'd been speechless. This was one of them.

When Annie's eyes lifted to his, the intensity of them could have brought him to his knees. "Tell me. I know you do."

Cam held her burning stare, his voice thick as he asked, "If I do, will you think less of me?" He could barely get the words out. "W-will you think I'm like *them?*"

She knew who he meant. The slavers, Richard Duskin, the Revenant man who'd killed her family. They'd wanted her, too, and she'd suffered because of it.

Instead of answering, Annie demanded, "Tell me."

Screw it. "I want you," Cam replied flatly.

"For how long?" She stepped closer, pausing just before she touched his face.

"Since the beginning," Cam admitted as his breath escaped him in a rush. Before she could pull away, he grabbed her hand and pressed her palm to his cheek. Another thrill of cold energy lurched into him at her touch. "Since I first saw you on Duskin's porch, and you looked like you wanted to kill me. Since then, and every day after. Hate me for it, but you asked for the truth."

Annie's bloodied thumb brushed over his lip, her eyes far away. "I'm tired of being afraid."

Cam stayed silent as her fingers trailed down his chin, over his throat, stopping where his heartbeat slammed beneath her fingertips. Her brows furrowed again. "But I don't know how to be anything else."

"What do you want?" Cam asked slowly, afraid to move, lest he frighten her away.

"I . . ." She paused, thinking, her hand dropping to her side. "I want you to be brave for me when I say yes and stop when I say no. I don't want to pretend. I don't want someone to take you away from me. I want you to wait with me until I'm ready. All of that is selfish to ask, but it's what I want."

Cam's fire flared and guttered so quickly that the carpet began to smolder. He kicked it out before he grabbed her hand again, weaving his fingers through hers. He leaned down to press his forehead against hers, their breath mingling. "Ask me to kiss you, Kitten."

A shiver ran down her body, and she inhaled. "Kiss me, Camden."

Annie didn't fight when he lifted her, but wrapped her legs around his waist as he crushed his lips against hers. His fire went wild as she let out a happy sigh—happy—and tangled her fingers into his hair. He leaned her against the vanity, her back to the mirror.

God, her lips were everything—the ice to smother the flames that would consume him if she didn't touch him just a little bit more.

Gently, her fingers trailed down his face, his neck, down his chest. Annie broke away, her brands bright silver, as she tugged on his sweater. "I want this off. I want to see you."

Cam obeyed and tossed his sweater into the corner.

"Don't move." Annie's touch was hesitant as she brushed over his collarbone, his chest. Cam braced against the vanity, his hands on either side of her, as he watched her lovely, lovely features slowly shift from fear to fascination. Lord, she was beautiful. Not in the way that all women were beautiful, but like how a mountain blanketed in snow, peaking over the clouds, was beautiful. She was a painting born from the deepest, anguished depths of the soul. One that only God could craft.

Cam closed his eyes, taking steady breaths, as Annie's fingers danced over the planes of his stomach, moving closer to his sides. He braced as she brushed his ribs, but he couldn't help it—

He flinched.

Annie blinked at him, shocked, and Cam could have died from the shame of it.

"Did I—" Her cold mask threatened to return as she scooted back. "Did that hurt? What did I do?"

Cam let out an anxious laugh. "You didn't do anything. It's just—"

Understanding made Annie break out in laughter. A real, genuine, belly laugh that made him long for her more than any stroke of her hand ever could.

"You're ticklish!" She tried to touch his side again, but he ducked away, wrapping his arms around himself like a shield.

"I'm neither confirming nor denying." He dodged as she hopped off the vanity and tried to grab him. Annie beamed as he grinned and continued to back away.

"But if it *were* true," he said. Another dodge. "It would be a carefully guarded secret, and I hope you'd have mercy on such a cursed affliction."

Annie laughed so hard she had tears streaming down her cheeks. Good tears. Not bad ones. He forgot all about his wretched sides as he kissed her again. Softly this time. Her lips parted for him, but before he could taste further, she smiled against him.

"This is what I want," she whispered.

"What?" he began to ask, but she ran her fingertips up his ribs and he broke out in shivers. After another quick laugh, she kissed his throat, his chest, making his fire flare to the surface.

"I want to know all the things you've never told anyone." Another kiss, but this time, she wrapped her arms around him. "I want your secrets to be my secrets."

Cam rested his head on top of hers, holding her tighter. "Well, for my first secret, I think the last person that hugged me was Nathan, not long before I died."

Annie leaned back to look him in the face, squinting in concentration. "I can't remember the last time I was hugged. Or at least, the last time I *wanted* to be hugged."

Cam scooped her up into his arms, carrying her to the couch. Not to the bed—there were too many temptations there. He laid on his back so he could stretch out, lying her on top of him. Her head was against his collarbone as he wrapped his arms around her tightly and buried his face in her hair. Something that was half a laugh, half a sob escaped her as she squeezed back.

It feels exactly like I hoped it would. Even with the thin fabric of her robe between them, the iciness of her skin soaked into the heat of his, making them both break out in goosebumps. It was perfect, she was perfect. She always had been. There was nothing to buffer the feel of her body. Every curve, every move-ment. Despite all his efforts to keep his fire in check, their power seemed to have a mind of its own. It swirled and twisted together until black and white embers sparked in the air like glittering fireflies.

They just lay there, talking until the sun had started to share its first rays over the horizon.

He didn't realize he'd stroked down the curve of her back until Annie stilled against him.

Go to sleep, Camden. Don't ruin this. Go to sleep.

He really should start listening to himself. Instead, a thrill ran through him as he brushed his lips against her ear and whispered, "Have you ever felt good before, Kitten?"

Annie quickly shook her head against his chest, letting out a thick, "*No.*"

When he stroked down her spine this time, he let his touch trail lower. "May I try?"

After a short pause, she murmured, "Yes."

Gently, Cam twisted until she was below him. Annie watched him with a stern intensity as he slowly pushed open her robe. She took his breath away.

Her brands flowed over the length of her, swirling down her stomach, her thighs, encircling her breasts. Again, she was a painting. Flawless. One he shouldn't be touching, yet he found himself tracing her brands anyway. They shimmered and flared beneath his touch. Her power reached for him greedily, and his fire was quick to respond. Annie let out small gasps as his lips replaced his fingertips, starting at her collarbone, moving lower and lower, slowly, taking his time, until when he'd next asked her permission, the answer was an immediate yes.

The morning had fully come before they'd finally fallen asleep.

CHAPTER 48
ANNIE

Annie stared at Cam as the late-afternoon sun filtered through the drapes, illuminating the deep orange color of his brands.

They'd fallen asleep on the sofa, curled up, with their chests pressed together and their limbs tangled until there was no space left between them because that's what she'd wanted. Not to have his body in that way—not yet, at least—but to feel his skin against hers. To be able to absorb his warmth and scent, and to just *be*. To be touched without being hurt.

He had done that. She had never felt more alive than when he'd explored every part of her without demanding anything in return.

Annie brushed her fingers through his mussed locks, smoothing them, as his chest rose and fell against hers. She didn't want to wake him. She wanted to enjoy this moment of peace where he was simply hers. Not Enoch's. Not a target. Hers.

She peered over at the grandfather clock—three in the afternoon. In one hour, Cam would be traveling with the governor for the meeting with the council and the Revenant groups.

She didn't want him to wake yet. Because when he did, he'd have to leave.

I do hope you'll try to convince my son to take up his seat. Alexander's words haunted her. A rush of panic had her tucking even closer against him, making Cam stir slightly. *It would be a shame to see that girl in the hands of another.*

Mary. Stolen at nine years old from some remote town in the South. She'd spent the last year as a slave. Tortured. Used.

Just like she'd been.

You promised you'd never think of him again. Annie shuddered. She had never allowed herself to imagine how many Tawnys and Marys there were in the world or how many *new* Marys there would be, but the governor was right.

When he died—and that time was coming near—The Order would take control of Enoch if Cam didn't. They'd rebuild it into whatever kind of empire they wanted, leaving hundreds of thousands at their mercy.

Annie and Cam had come to Enoch to get revenge for his mother. To destroy the people hunting them so they'd have a chance at a normal life.

Then, she'd imagined a free life would just be her and Jenny—she working as a nurse, while Jenny worked on her quilts—but now she wanted that life to be at Cam's side. She wanted Nathan and Mr. Price in it. She wanted to wake in the morning and not fear what the day would bring.

Cam thought he could destroy The Order, but he couldn't, at least not by clearing them out of one city. As much as he promised to give her whatever she wanted, that would never be possible.

What she truly wanted was to have him all to herself, unburdened by a life of governance. But having what they wanted wouldn't make them safe. The Order wanted them. No, the only chance they had for peace was for Cam to rule the West, and yet, she could never ask that of him.

"I can hear you thinking from here."

Cam's eyes were still closed, but he was smiling.

"Don't use my own words against me," she replied, attempting a light tone, but her words were tinged with sadness. "That's not fair."

"If you say so." He shifted until she was using his bicep as a pillow. He grinned at her as he brushed away the hair that had fallen in her eyes. "But I swore I could see smoke pouring out of your ears. Care to share your thoughts?"

I can't lie to him. She brushed her fingertips down his jaw, down his muscled arm. He sighed, melting into her touch. No, she couldn't lie to him, but she wasn't ready to discuss what his father had asked of her, either.

"I'm nervous about your meeting," she admitted. "With so many known Order members present, they could have set a trap for you."

"Oh, I'm sure they have." Cam sat up, pulling her onto his lap. He smiled sheepishly in response to how wide her eyes had grown, and he kissed her shoulder. "Don't stress about it, Kitten. I'm as prepared as I can be, and my father will have his guard with him, as useless as they are. Plus, I won't be the only Revenant there. I have Jensen Davis's splendid presence to look forward to."

"Telling me not to stress doesn't stop me from stressing." She scowled and lifted his chin. His eyes lit with flames at her touch. "You'll be careful?"

"Of course." His brands flared as his gaze fell to her lips. "Anything for you."

She tried to ignore the way the look made her stomach

clench. "And you'll use your fire, if needed? The full extent of it?"

His eyes darted back to hers, his brows knitting together in confusion. "I—"

"I know you've purposefully been holding back," Annie said, recalling her previous conversation with Mr. Price. "Promise me, if it comes to it, you will spare no one. That you'll do whatever terrible thing you're afraid of doing, because I'd rather you be a monster and alive, than die feeling good about yourself."

Cam just stared at her, a swath of emotions passing over his features, before he finally nodded and said, "Yes, ma'am." His attention shifted to the clock, the corners of his lips curving upward. "We still have forty-five minutes."

Annie's stomach did that odd flip again, her skin growing hot. "You should get ready, then."

"I should," he drawled, a hint of his harbor accent escaping as he traced a heart over her breast. "But I don't want to, and you don't want me to, either."

Annie pursed her lips together, glancing at the clock once more. She *really* didn't want him to leave. Cam grinned again as she opened and closed her mouth, struggling to get the words out.

"Could you do . . . *that* . . . again?" She finally blurted.

She could have died from embarrassment, but Cam let out a low, rumbling laugh as he tugged her closer by the waist, kissing her before his lips moved to her throat, then lower, as he murmured against her skin, "I thought you'd never ask."

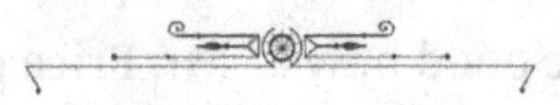

Exactly forty-*three* minutes later, they met the others outside of the villa, ready to head to the manor.

Nathan gave them a curious once-over, making a face. "You two look equal parts elated and depressed, and I don't know how to feel about it."

"Mind your own business," Cam growled. If he was trying to come off serious, the ornery smile he cracked ruined it.

Annie must have looked guilty because Jenny shot her a mischievous grin. They started down the paved driveway. Cam's elbow linked with hers. His other hand casually tucked into the pocket of his crisp jacket.

Today, he really did look like the governor's heir. After scrubbing away all the blood and ash, the fall sunset high-lighted the gold in his skin and hair. His simple, three-piece charcoal-grey suit was perfectly tailored to his tall frame, concealing the pearl-finished revolver on his belt. He didn't need flashy fabrics or jeweled cuffs. His nobility was evident in his confident strides and his relaxed yet alert demeanor. He looked like he could rule a city. She just hoped the council believed it, too.

"Guard *The Elaina*," Cam said to Nathan as they walked, repeating the plan they'd gone over a dozen times. "Watch the ports."

"So, they don't close in from behind and block us in, I know." Nathan nodded. "I've had the crew mixing with the crowds in the harbor for over a week, listening for any hints of an attack coming. There hasn't been a peep."

"Which could be good news." Mr. Price gave Nathan a side-long glance. "Or The Order is better at keeping their informa-tion private than your men are at retrieving it."

Nathan bristled, ready to argue, but Jenny rested her hand

on his arm. "Everyone is doing their best. Picking at each other isn't going to help."

Mr. Price shrugged. The closest he'd come to openly agreeing with her.

Annie bit back a smile. Jenny had always been the diplomat between all of the Duskin's adopted daughters. Rose had been the one to start the fights, where Elain would usually cry in the corner because her feelings had been hurt in some way or another.

Elain. The thought made her jolt, causing Cam to shoot her a questioning look. Annie glanced over her shoulder to where the villa grew smaller behind them. She hadn't seen Elain in weeks. She'd forgotten about her—again.

Where is she? Annie turned her attention back to the road in front of her, the others' voices fading into a low hum. Maybe once everyone had gone, and she had a moment to herself, she'd try to call for her. Last time, she'd come. There was no reason to think she wouldn't do it again.

"I still don't see why you can't just leave in the morning." Nathan stretched, resting his arm around Jenny's shoulder, making her sister smile all the more. "I mean, who holds a meeting in the middle of the night?"

"Half of the men attending have targets on their backs," Mr. Price said. "And the other half are the marksmen. Traveling is dangerous no matter the hour, but at least you're less likely to be shot in the dark."

"Is that your trained assessment?" Cam laughed bitterly. "I've shot plenty of men in the dark."

They stepped into the manor courtyard.

Alexander stood in the covered entry, glaring at them. A line of six coaches waited, his guard already seated inside.

The others waited in the courtyard as Cam and Annie met with the governor. Alexander fiddled with an antique, golden pocket watch as they approached, opening and closing the face with the edge of his thumb.

"You're late," he snapped.

"I am not," Cam shot back. "You're senile."

The governor shook his head in exasperation. He unclipped the watch's chain from his belt and tossed it to Cam.

Cam caught it with ease, raising a brow as he examined the relic. "What's this?"

"A watch." The governor retorted.

Cam's death glare could have withered flowers, making the governor chuckle.

"It was your great-grandfather's," Governor Callahan said. "Don't lose it. Maybe next time, you'll be on time."

"Or maybe I'll melt it," Cam mumbled, but despite this, he carefully tucked the watch into his inner coat pocket. "Let's get this over with."

In response, the governor took Annie's hand and pressed a quick kiss to her knuckles, sending a flicker of rage across Cam's features.

"Take care, dear." The governor strode toward the carriages, only slowing long enough to give Mr. Price a respectful nod.

Once he was out of earshot, Cam let out a long sigh, turning to face her with a sad smile. "If all goes well, I'll be back tomorrow evening."

"If all goes well," Annie repeated dryly. "And what are the odds of that?"

"Julian is staying to protect you," he said instead of answering. "Not that I doubt your ability to defend yourself, but it makes me feel better knowing you'll have someone watching your back."

Annie nodded, frozen, throat tight from struggling to find the words she wished she could. *Stay with me. Don't leave.*

You're safer here. Stay with me. With me. Always with me. Instead of speaking, she stared at the ground, studying the mud staining the edge of her hem, trying to ignore the sound of her racing heart.

"Annie—" Cam took a breath, making her look up. "I—" He rubbed his face and let out a short, frustrated groan before reaching into the opposite coat pocket. He pulled out a folded square of paper and handed it to her. It was torn at the corners like he'd crumpled it up before deciding to keep it.

"Read that when you have time," he said, and before she could answer, he kissed her. Not gently, but like it may be the last time he'd get to do so. He let her go before he wheeled and headed for the carriages, leaving her alone holding a wrinkled note.

As soon as Cam climbed in beside his father, the drivers urged the horses forward, leading the line off the estate.

Jenny stared up at her from below. She'd seen the entire exchange. If the others had, they didn't let it show. They were talking together in low voices. Annie took a steadying breath and tucked the note into her bodice.

It wasn't until later that evening, when she was alone in her bedroom, seated at her vanity, that she gathered enough courage to open it.

> *Annie,*
>   *I've tried to write this a thousand times, and I still can't get it right. As I'm sure you're aware, I'm a damned coward.*
>   *And I love you.*
>   *Telling you this way is despicable, but I don't think I would recover if you didn't say it back, or even worse,*

if you did it only because you felt obligated to maintain our current situation. That would be so much worse.

So, here I am, choosing the easy way out and justifying it by telling myself that at least now you have time to think before answering. If you love me, too, perhaps you can be brave enough to say so. If not, you can say nothing and pretend you never read this. I will respect that.

Below that, another paragraph was hastily scratched at an angle below the others, the fresher ink suggesting the words were recently added:

(I realize last night changes things, but my original thought still stands. I don't want you to have to make a rushed decision. Or maybe I just look like a bigger asshole, now. You can make that decision, too, I guess.)

Whatever you want, Annie. Always.

Cam

Annie's blood went cold as she stared at the letter, reading it over and over until she'd memorized it. She stood, tucking it back into her bodice, before leaving her bedroom. Her power left trails of darkness in her wake as she descended the staircase. The black tendrils spread onto the walls, seeping into the cracks.

She knocked on the door to Mr. Price's chambers. As she was about to knock again, more firmly this time, the door swung open, revealing Mr. Price already in his bedclothes, his braid undone, leaving his long locks loose and flowing to his waist.

"Miss Annie—" he began, but he froze, wide-eyed when he noticed the darkness surrounding her.

"Take me to Waverly," she said coldly.

He tore his gaze away from the darkness long enough to give her a curious look. "Now?"

"Now." Annie spun on her heel, calling over her shoulder as she thundered down the hall. "I need to work."

CHAPTER 49
ALEXANDER

One hour and forty-eight minutes cramped in with his son, even in a spacious carriage, was too much. Camden fidgeted every two and a half seconds. Fiddling with his pearl-handled revolver, which he'd insisted on bringing. Twisting his coat buttons. Picking at a loose thread on the carriage's *expensively* upholstered seats until he'd torn up the corner completely.

Alexander just watched him, taking it in. Beneath the brands and invisible scars, this Revenant was still the child he'd lost a decade ago. Not much had changed.

Camden glanced up when he noticed Alexander staring. He slumped back against his seat with a loud huff. "Are we there yet?"

"Don't start that again." Alexander pinched the bridge of his nose. "It's only been—"

"Are we there yet?" Camden's lips curved into an amused smile. "I'm bored."

Alexander pursed his lips. "Then read a book."

"I don't have a book."

"There are books in the drawer beneath your seat."

"If they're your books, I'm sure they're terrible."

"Or maybe you'll learn something." Alexander sat back as well, resisting the urge to scratch where the corruption had spread onto his hand. "You never were much of a student."

Camden quit picking at the upholstery and shifted his destruction to the brocade paneling. "It's not my fault that the tutors you hired were reprobates. If you'd let Mother teach me, it would have been different."

Outside the fogged windowpanes, the sun hung low on the horizon, coloring the sky with deep oranges and pinks. A clear day. Hopefully, it was a good omen. There were so many things that Alexander wanted to say, but instead, he sighed, "Well, you don't have to wait much longer. We'll reach the Lodge in another ten minutes or so."

"The Lodge?" Camden's brow shot up, his expression calculating. "You mean the Bales's hunting lodge?"

"Correct," Alexander replied. "We'll be meeting Dr. Clarke and several other council members there, then starting our journey to the Embassy building."

"The Embassy building is a week away. I thought we were meeting in the city." Camden's brands flared, filling his eyes with as much fire as there was rage. "You told me we'd return by tomorrow afternoon. I told Annie—"

"I lied." Alexander kept his features expressionless as Camden's twisted in hate. "And I did so with good reason. There are dozens of crucial politicians making this journey, and we don't need our enemies overhearing our comings and goings. Don't fret. You weren't the only one I left in the dark. I've instructed David to inform your companies of the schedule change."

He raised a finger as Camden's hand twitched toward his revolver, and Alexander finally allowed himself a smile. "Also, it won't take a week. I've been busy over the last few years. The train station I've commissioned outside the Northern gate is now fully operational. Days of travel can now be made in hours."

Camden's brows pinched together. "What the hell is a train?"

"You'll see," Alexander replied smugly. "You'll see."

As infuriated as he was, Camden didn't budge the rest of the carriage ride.

The Bale's Hunting Lodge was an impressive sight, even to Alexander. It had been in the Bale family for four generations, as long as the West had belonged to the Callahans.

The brick-and-mortar establishment faced the northern gate, making it the first impression travelers had of Enoch upon their arrival if coming from the forested regions. Although it was only two stories, it carried a presence. Enormous antlers, trophied from some long-gone beast of old, were mounted above the entrance. The colossal stone slabs, carved to encircle the doorway, were etched with intricate designs reminiscent of ancient ruins. The Bales had never shared with him what they said.

Henry Bale stood outside the Lodge, his expression sour, waiting for them and the other councilmen to exit their carriages. Dr. Clarke stood beside him, wringing his thin hands.

As expected, the men in their party gawked at Camden's presence, whispering to each other, some angrily and some with a familiar high note of hope.

The prodigal son had returned home.

As the others bustled with their preparations—checking their luggage, their pockets, their wallets—Camden stared at the northern gate, flames dancing up his throat, curling around his ears, as if he expected to see through to the locomotive beyond. The men jumped in unison—all but Camden—as the train's horn blared, echoing over Enoch's walls.

"Governor." Henry Bale cleared his throat as he stepped to Alexander's side. Dr. Clarke kept behind, just out of earshot. Henry's words were pure venom. "I hope you've thought this through."

"Chief," Alexander answered, keeping his tone cheerful. "I assure you, I know exactly what I'm doing."

"I'm glad to hear it." Henry peered at him from the corner of his eye, his jaw tight. "I'd hate for you to say something you shouldn't. I've heard tempers can be quite tested at meetings like this."

Arrogant bastard. As much as Alexander would like to reply with a scathing remark, the pain in his scar flared, the darkness swimming in his veins burning up his arm until his entire body tightened in response to the silent command.

No. Henry Bale would never have complete control, but he had enough to make Alexander's life extraordinarily difficult.

He shot the chief a glare. "Trust me, *boy*. I'm well-adjusted to the subtleties of politics."

Henry returned the glare. "Again, I'm glad to hear it."

"Bale," Camden called as he strode towards them casually, making it very apparent he'd been listening. Henry's face flushed red as Camden gave him a judgmental once-over.

"You look terrible." Camden's lips quirked up in the corners. "And they call me the scoundrel. Have you been playing in your father's ashes?"

The veins were bulging in Henry's neck now.

Alexander followed Camden's gaze to Henry's knee-high

boots, which were stained with ash up to the ankles. Additionally, the knuckles on Henry's right hand were yellowed from a recent bruise.

I'm a fool. Alexander swallowed. He hadn't noticed. Even a year ago, such obvious details would never have slipped past his attention.

"I've been working," Henry replied shortly.

"In a chimney?" Camden snorted.

Henry scratched his chin, exhaled, then smiled politely. "You really are unpleasant, Lord Callahan."

Camden chuckled, ignoring the comment, his tone mocking as he said, "Will we be having the pleasure of your company?"

"No." Henry folded his hands behind his back, his thin lips pursed. "No. I am only here to remind the governor of all he has to lose, excuse me, all *Enoch* has to lose if this gathering goes sour."

"Ah." Camden's eyes narrowed, just a fraction. "Well, God forbid anything happen to him—pardon—Enoch."

"We best be going." Alexander patted Henry's shoulder, resisting the urge to strangle him. Not that he could. His fingers were too weak for that anymore. The chief gave them both a pointed nod before turning on his heel and heading back into the Lodge.

As he left, Camden let out a low whistle. "Back on the ships, we'd have called him a flapdoodle."

Despite Henry's threat still clawing into his muscles, Alexander cracked a smile. "And what does that mean?"

Cam shook his head. "You don't want to know."

Still wringing his hands, Dr. Clarke followed as they turned for the city gate.

Just outside, black smoke billowed from the train's smokestack, filling the air with the oily stink of coal. Camden's eyes grew round as he took in the enormous machine, its sleek black metal frame, the lines of steel tracks leading out of the station and into the heart of the West. Beyond, the height of the Western forests blocked out the last of the sun, casting the land beyond the station in darkness.

Alexander watched as, one by one, the councilmen boarded the locomotive. Dr. Clarke hesitated as he entered, looking as if he meant to say something, but instead, he closed his mouth and climbed aboard.

Camden watched as well, his arms folded over his chest, an anxiousness slipping through his façade as he chewed at his lower lip. He did the same as a child, often making it bleed. Every time Cassie caught him doing so, she'd take his hand and kiss it. Cradling him in her arms, she'd tell him. *"Never fear, sweet boy. Nothing can ever hurt you as long as I am near."*

The memory made Alexander's breath hitch, and he gripped his chest as pain made his lungs spasm.

Camden's eyes immediately locked onto him. "Are you dying already? I can't believe I'm saying this, but I'd prefer it if you lived a few more days. I don't want to deal with these toadies alone."

"I-I'll do my best." Alexander managed past the tightness in his throat, tasting blood. He made to check the time, only to remember he no longer carried his family's heirloom . . . or its legacy. Alexander sucked in the deepest breath his body would allow. "It's time to go."

Camden simply nodded and stepped onto the train.

CHAPTER 50
CAMDEN

He was a mess.

A ridiculous, bloody mess who couldn't get his act together.

Cam found an empty bench seat near the back of the train, alone, and stared blankly out the window. The trees appeared as smears of various shades of brown and green as the coal-powered machine surged down the metal tracks. He should be impressed by the behemoth. He should be studying the councilmen that swarmed around his father at the front of the train, but no.

No, he was teetering on the edge of insanity because he'd given Annie that damned letter.

Cam exhaled, fidgeting as his heart missed two beats at the thought, followed by a fresh surge of adrenaline as memories of the last twelve hours replayed in his mind for the five thousandth time. If he allowed his mind to drift enough, he could still taste her, could still feel her velvet-soft skin beneath his fingertips. So, he tried to think of something else. Anything else, but it wasn't working.

Annie cared for him—wanted him even—but now she knew that what he felt for her, what he'd been trying to hide since New Havana, she might change her mind and never look at him the same again. After all she'd been through...

The last thing she could want was someone like him. Every day that passed proved that to be true. She'd never be safe near him. She couldn't have the peaceful life she hoped for her and Jenny if she stayed with him. He was a walking bullseye. Death followed him like a shadow and didn't seem keen to leave him any time soon.

The only thing that could save this mess was if she'd chosen not to read it.

Maybe she'd burned it. Threw it in the street. Lost it. He could only hope. Then maybe they could go on as they were. He'd rather stay her friend and plaything than not have her at all.

Cam squeezed his eyes shut as he tried to focus on the babbling of the gathering men stuck inside this screeching hunk of metal.

Watch them. Do something. Cam forced his eyes open. Near the front of the train car, his father smiled pleasantly as a short, round-faced councilman in a top hat told a joke. Hell, he couldn't even muster up the energy to hate his father right now. Not when he looked so . . . ill.

Despite the squared shoulders and clean, pinstripe suit, an air of frailness hovered over Alexander Callahan now, and Cam wasn't sure what to think. He could still picture him as he was —tanned and muscular, his eyes sharper than the edge of any blade. Now he was pale. Shrunken. And growing more so with every passing day.

If the other men seemed to notice, they did well not to let it show. They all continued to laugh, growing more red-faced as the hour passed and they'd taken their second or third refill from the waiters that passed through, carrying trays loaded with whisky, wine, and an array of fruits and cheeses. At least he'd noticed that much. How could he not? Only his father would go through the trouble of having private catering on a train.

The sound of a throat clearing came from behind him.

Beside Cam, Van Clarke loitered at the end of his booth, a crease between his worried brows.

Blazes. Cam scowled. He should have known where Van had sat. More proof of what a disaster he was.

Van must have thought the scowl was for him because he flinched and stepped back. After a pause, he pointed to the open booth across from Cam. "May I sit?"

Before Cam could answer, he did just that, still wringing his hands. It was a miracle he hadn't rubbed his skin off.

"Look, Doctor." Cam crossed his legs and sighed. "I'm really not in the mood to—"

"Please." Van didn't meet his eyes. His greasy dark hair brushed into a neat tail. "I need to apologize for my atrocious behavior yesterday. I was under a lot of stress, and it was undeserving."

It took every ounce of Cam's self-control not to roll his eyes. "I don't care, Van. I have more important things to worry about than your temper tantrums."

A flash of irritation passed over the Doctor's thin face, but he pursed his lips to hide it. "You're right, of course. I'm sure preparing to become the new governor can be quite taxing."

Cam froze, his fire flaring to the surface. "I never said—"

"For years, Alexander Callahan has used intimidation to keep Enoch in line," Van said, some of his usual good spirits returning. "There are many, and I mean *many,* that would risk it all to see the city fall under new leadership. Better leadership. Someone like you."

Cam just stared at him for a moment before raising a brow. "I literally threatened to burn you alive yesterday. I'm still considering it."

Van let out a sharp, high-pitched laugh. "You're honest about it, at least." He leaned forward, resting his elbows on his knees. "Your father tells his council little, and his closest associates less than that. Is that your intention? Do you mean to take control of the West?"

Why do people keep asking me that? Saying *no* was Cam's first reaction, but he held his tongue. Why *would* he ask when, less than a day ago, he was threatening to pull his support for Revenant rights?

As much as he hated to pull the daddy card, Cam said, "If my father can't trust you, why should I?"

"Because I would stand at your side," Van replied, his expression turning serious. "As would all of Waverly Hospital. As would most of Enoch's lower class. The funds you donated have done wonders to clean up The Greens. Most of the council would follow you, as well. They're sick of the tyranny."

Cam didn't know what to say.

Van continued, leaning in closer as his voice fell to a rushed whisper. He held out his hand as if he meant Cam to shake it. "Say that you'll stand for Enoch. For the West. Say yes."

They can't possibly think I'd be a good leader. He'd gotten the entire crew of *The Nightlady* killed. Even now, he had no idea how to stop The Order. Cam blinked at Van's open palm, bewildered. Thankfully, before he could form a response, his father appeared at his side, placing a hand on his shoulder. Normally, Cam would have recoiled, but this time, he was relieved.

Alexander smiled blandly, holding two glasses of whisky in one hand. "Do you mind if I have a moment with my son?"

Van was up in an instant, bowing curtly as he backed away. "Of course, of course. Enjoy your evening."

And evening it was. The moon had long overtaken the sun as the dominant sphere in the sky. Van gave Cam a quick, pointed nod before skittering off toward the front of the car.

Alexander took his seat, offering Cam a whisky glass.

Never mind. Get me out of here. Cam shook his head, letting his gaze return to the window.

Alexander's eyes narrowed. "I thought you were being dramatic before when you said you didn't drink. You're serious?"

Cam scoffed but didn't look at him as he said, "Have you ever been poisoned?"

"No," Alexander answered before setting the two glasses on the ground beside them. "I know better than to accept drinks from strangers . . . or friends."

There were so many ugly, useless retorts Cam could say, but he was too tired. He never let his view stray from the window.

Alexander leaned back, folding his gloved hands over his lap. "What did Dr. Clarke want from you?"

Cam shrugged. "Just the usual wanton betrayal."

"Hmm." Alexander sighed, not elaborating further. He must have sensed that Cam was telling the truth. After a minute of silence, his father cocked his head, giving Cam one of his detached, studying looks. "You're worried about Annie."

Not a question.

Cam shoved his clenched fists into his coat pockets to hide the flames forming around his knuckles.

Alexander took one of the whisky glasses off the ground and drained it in one swallow. He let out a pained moan, gripping his chest, as he straightened. When he spoke, he sounded strained. "I loved your mother."

The hell with this. Cam tried to stand, but Alexander raised a hand to stop him. The strange expression on his face was the only reason Cam remained. His father looked wistful, and that unnerved him more than the rage ever could.

"You keep saying that, but I don't believe it." Cam pressed against the back of his seat, facing toward the window as Alexander continued.

"Even if it didn't seem like it, I loved her." Alexander drained the second glass. The redness in his cheeks said that he'd had too much already. "Believe it all you want, I never hit her. Or Maya. Or Kai."

"You hit me." Cam didn't mean to say it. It just slipped out.

"I did." Alexander just nodded. It was the first time he'd admitted to it. "And I regret it. I've regretted it every day since I lost you."

Cam closed his eyes again, pushing away as far as the space would let him. *He can't hurt you anymore.* Their fight in the morgue proved it. He was stronger than Alexander now. He could kill him in less than a heartbeat, but if that were true, then why did he still feel like a bloody child?

"Listen to me." Alexander pointed at him, unsteady, but he managed not to drop the glass. "I know you love that girl, like I loved Cassie, but if you're thinking about her in the morning, you'll kill her."

Cam glared at him. "That doesn't make any sense—"

"It does." Alexander snapped, a little too loudly, earning them a few curious looks. "Because if you are, you'll make mistakes. You'll make mistakes like I made mistakes. You can't do that." His tone lowered into something lethal, his grey-blue eyes like a storm on the open sea as he hissed, "Camden, these men—despite all their flowery compliments and gifts—they want us dead. They hate us. You cannot be distracted. You cannot let them win."

This didn't feel like it was just about the council meeting.

"Tell me how that happened." Cam nodded toward his father's gloved hand, where he knew that rotting tattoo of The Order lay beneath. "Why did you take that mark? This would all be so much easier if you were just straight with me."

Alexander locked up, the stiffness in his body starting in his limbs and then spreading throughout his body. He closed his eyes, swaying his head back and forth as if to music. He was obviously drunk, but there was more to it than that. It was as if a stream of memories was carrying him away.

"Trust no one, Camden." Alexander finally breathed and clutched his head. "Trust no one but Annie and me."

"I did trust you once," Cam whispered. "I wanted to *be* you, and now becoming you is the thing I fear the most."

And there it was. He should have kept those secrets to himself, but his father was dying. He might not ever get a chance to say it to him again.

That was what he hid from Annie and Julian.

His fire made him everything he was afraid of—an unbalanced scale. He could burn Enoch to dust. More than once, the thought had crossed his mind. He could be a tyrant if he wanted, and that terrified him.

"Good." That was all Alexander said. "You should hate me. Maybe you'll do better." He reached into his coat pocket, meaning to check the time. He blinked in confusion when he found it empty. He'd given his watch away. Instead, he leaned to the side, squinting, as he tried to focus on the clock at the far side of the train cabin. His eyes were lined with silver. "I can't see it—"

Cam slid the gold pocket watch from his coat. He knew enough of precious metals to tell that this trinket was priceless. His family's heirloom. He flipped open the face, adorned with a leviathan, and scanned over the hands. "It's eleven-forty-seven."

Alexander sucked in a breath, not bothering to wipe away the tear threatening to escape down his cheek. "Eleven-forty-seven. Good." He stood, tugging down the front of his suit coat. "We'll be at the Embassy building in a few hours. You should try to sleep."

For the first time, when Cam responded, he didn't feel angry. Just sad. "I'm used to living without sleep. You go get some rest."

"Alright," Alexander replied, bleary-eyed. "I'll find the bed car."

"You do that," Cam murmured.

The councilmen watched as Alexander Callahan stumbled off into the next car. Cam shot them a glare that could peel the flesh off their bones, and they turned back to their drinks.

Van's words echoed in his mind. These men were waiting to eat his father alive, and Cam might be the only one who could stop them.

Cam swayed with the train's movement as it lurched and shuddered, its braking system engaged. The rest of the council tumbled into their seats, holding their hats in place on their heads.

It was near dawn, and pink wisps were slowly invading the night sky. The train rolled into a small station. A tall, slim conductor, wearing yellow and burgundy stripes, opened the double doors and bowed as they exited. Cam hid his smirk as the other men stumbled when they hit steady ground. Land-lubbers.

The air is different here. It was lighter. Thinner. Cam

couldn't remember the last time he'd been so deep into the West. Gone were the sounds of gulls or the scent of the sea. Beyond the now bustling station was nothing but an endless canopy of evergreens. He rubbed his fingers together, remembering how the pitch dripping from their limbs would stick to his skin for days.

Alexander stepped up to his elbow as the other councilmen clamored their way into the waiting carriages. His father's eyes were bloodshot to hell.

Cam allowed himself a mocking smile. "You shouldn't drink so much. Dulls your senses, you know."

Alexander grunted, rubbing at the rotting finger that lay beneath his glove. "You try meeting with these buffoons, day in and day out, for twenty-five years and then you can preach to me about the merits of sobriety."

Cam actually laughed.

Alexander nodded to Cam's suit. "Is that fireproof? I've seen the material before."

"Elias Bennett had it made for me," Cam replied as he watched the coaches fill up, one by one. "I figured today would be the day for it."

"Pray that you won't need it." Alexander's lips twitched. "I've said it already, but I'll say it again. I need you to follow my lead. Speak only when spoken to and keep your snide comments to yourself."

Cam tsked, "You don't know me well at all, do you?"

His father scowled deep enough that his brows nearly touched. "As fatuous as they may seem, make no mistake, these men know how to play the game. They've been playing it for longer than you've been alive. As clever as you *think* you are, you won't beat them. You are a pirate, not a politician."

"There you go using big words again." Cam inhaled the scent of pine on the breeze. The sea was so far away now, and so much had changed. He touched the pearl-finished revolver on his belt. "I'm not sure if I count as a pirate anymore."

"Keep that close." Alexander nodded to the gun. "And covered. The others won't appreciate you flourishing weapons around."

"My lords?" The train conductor called to them before gesturing to the final carriage. It was empty. "Are you ready?"

Alexander let out a long sigh. "Let's get this over with."

Cam couldn't agree more.

CHAPTER 51

CAMDEN

The Embassy building looked just as Cam remembered it—stone, square, and covered in moss. Three stories tall, it seemed to hover over them as no less than ninety men unloaded from the carriages. It had only taken them an hour to arrive from the station. They'd met another line of coaches on the road—also from Enoch, his father explained. He'd had them take an alternative route to prevent the whole of the council from traveling together.

Cam had to admit, as he scanned through the crowd, that Alexander had caution mastered in an art form. Giant, brutish men—one of them being the Clarkes's beastly assistant—patted each of the guests down for weapons before allowing them inside. Cam followed his father's lead and strode straight past them, earning more than a few complaints from the others.

The interior of the Embassy was as ghastly as the exterior. Past the main entry, it opened into a massive ballroom-shaped space with polished, granite floors. The halls of the second and third floors were visible from the first, with only a waist-high railing separating guests from an open-air fall. In fact, onlookers already watched them from above. Groups of men and women—dressed in shades of greys and blacks—whispered amongst each other as, slowly, the rest of the councilmen made their way inside.

They must work here. Cam had never thought of the Embassy having employees. As a child, it had always seemed so empty.

"This way." Alexander nudged his elbow, nodding toward the center of the room. The largest table Cam had ever seen awaited them, big enough to accommodate everyone with space to spare. Dishware had been set out, and as the men began to take their seats, waiters emerged from nearby rooms, ready to serve.

The air vibrated with the sound of so many voices, like a swarm of bees, as the noise reverberated off the stone walls. As he followed, Cam continued to study the faces around him. Across the hall, Jensen Davis's smug features came into view, his honey-blond hair combed back neatly as one of the bodyguards forced the Revenant to turn out his pockets. Blazes, he could even smell his god-awful cologne from here.

Cam leaned in close enough to Alexander to whisper, "I thought we agreed he's working for the Order, and you let him in?"

"All the more reason to allow it," Alexander replied. "Keep an eye on him." As he settled down at the head of the table, he gestured for Cam to sit in the chair to his right.

As Cam took the spot, Alexander smiled. "Did you know I hand-arranged the seating for today? I put Mr. Davis beside you to make your job of watching him all that much easier."

Cam leaned back in his seat, returning his bland smile. "Did I mention I hate you?"

His father chuckled.

"Governor."

Cam suppressed a groan as Jensen shouldered through the crowd. He leaned against the back of the chair to Cam's right and nodded. "Lord Callahan. What an honor to be invited to the front of the table." His blue-green eyes locked onto Cam, tone on the verge of condescending, as he said, "I didn't realize you held me in such high regard."

Alexander shot Cam a look.

Cam forced a wide smile. "Neither did I."

As Jensen's features began to twist irritably, Dr. Clarke appeared and took the seat to Alexander's left.

Cam could have cried.

"Morning, gentlemen." Dr. Clarke was back to his usual chipper self. "Can you feel the excitement? Today will mark a turning point in the West's history."

"I'm sure it will," Alexander replied, but his gaze was locked onto Cam, giving him a second look that said *watch them both.*

Cam gave a subtle nod back. Jensen and Dr. Clarke chatted amicably as the rest of the council found their seats. Cam took the pocket watch from his coat, stroking his thumb over the leviathan before he flipped open the face. Ten till six. Annie would be awake by now.

His fire flared and guttered, twisting up his neck. Only yesterday, it had been *her* beneath his fingertips, his lips—her skin as cold and smooth as a glacial stream. He snapped the watch shut and shoved it back into his pocket, shaking. *I can't think of her now. She might not have read it. Don't think about it. Don't—*

But hell, his skin *crawled.* His fire. Cam slammed his eyes closed, the shiver rolling down his spine making his limbs twitch. He'd done so well controlling it, suppressing it, but now—

The room was so loud. His breaths were too shallow. He wasn't getting enough air. The men carried on, oblivious to how close he was to falling apart.

But his father noticed. He saw everything.

Alexander Callahan stood, and the entirety of the Embassy went silent. He scanned over the length of the table. He knew every man there. Their private addresses. Their vices. Their finances. He held himself straight, shoulders squared, and for that moment, Cam saw the man he knew, the man he'd feared for so long—the Governor of the West.

For nearly an hour, the men chatted about trivial matters. The price of bread. Worsening street conditions. Increased crime rates.

With an air of indifference, Alexander let out a deliberately brief sigh before he began to speak. Cam didn't know why he let them go on for so long. "We are here to address Revenant rights. Not to squabble about Enoch's current state of affairs. If any of you choose to derail the purpose of today's agenda, I will have you forcibly removed. Is that clear?"

A nauseating echo of slapping jowls echoed up the table as the councilmen nodded in unison.

"Good." He sat, steepling his fingers as he leaned onto his elbows. "Because I've been listening to your complaining for nigh on a year, and I am sick of it. This matter will be settled. Now. Today."

Get it together. He had to stay alert. He had to remain calm for Annie.

For Annie.

As if in agreement, his fire crawled back into his core, allowing him to put on a mask he'd grown used to wearing— that of Lord Callahan. *Pretend you're back on New Havana.*

He was good at pretending.

Cam melted back into a lazy sprawl, resting an ankle over

the opposite knee. If they expected a criminal, that's what he'd be. Cam slowly removed his revolver from his belt, twirling it around his fingers as he let his brands flare. "Father forgot to mention that I'd be the one removing you. The thick blokes by the door are just for show."

Eyes widened.

His father huffed.

A man midway down cleared his throat. Cam recognized him as one of the guests who had survived the party at the Clarkes.

Alexander raised a brow. "Did you have something to add?"

The man shook his head, eyes locked onto his lap.

"Very well," Alexander drawled. "If there will be no more interruptions."

"If I may, Governor." Jensen leaned forward and nodded toward the man who'd made the sound. "I think what Mr. Willows *intended* to say is what is on all our minds. You've been stalling this meeting. Not us. The council has been pushing relentlessly for the reevaluation of Revenant rights, and our pleas have been continuously ignored. Correct me if I'm wrong."

Alexander gave Jensen one of his dangerous smiles. "Remind me again where you're from, Mr. Davis?"

Jensen didn't break eye contact. "The East, my lord. Bristolwatch."

"I see." Alexander looked him up and down, then proceeded to ignore him. "It's been eighty years since the laws in the West were passed, allowing Revenants the same rights as mortals—"

"Ordered in place by Elias Bennett, who's since been murdered by *your* son." A balding, heavy-browed man down the table interrupted. Every set of eyes in the room fell onto Cam. "How can we argue rights when there is no justice for murderers? These *laws* have done nothing to protect humans from Stripes."

Stripes.

Alexander opened his mouth to reply, but Cam spoke first.

"You're from Port Lebanon?" Cam asked.

The man blinked in surprise. "Yes, but how—"

"I recognize your accent," Cam said, letting his own natural drawl come through. "Was your family hurt by the lockdown?"

The man nodded, swallowing.

Cam often tried to forget the months he and his crew had spent trapped in Port Lebanon's harbor, the fear of The Rot preventing any ships from coming in and out of the city.

"I was there." Cam's eyes darkened. "I lived in it. Starved in it. Do you know why I killed Elias Bennett? Because he offered me a deal. One I accepted because I was desperate, and he betrayed me. Beyond that, his actions caused an unimaginable amount of suffering to the woman who is now my wife. I killed him because he was a traitorous pile. Simple as that."

Silence returned to the room. So silent that the crinkle of the man's coat could be heard as he nodded.

"Being a *pile*, as you put it, is not an excuse for wanton violence," Jensen interjected, smoothing back his already pristine locks. His eyes rose to Alexander as he continued, "Nor should being a Callahan put you above justice."

"Is he straying off topic?" Cam grinned as he reached for his gun. "I think he's straying off topic. Should I remove him?"

Jensen's eyes grew as round as tea saucers.

Alexander rolled his eyes. "My son is prone to drama." Again, he ignored Jensen. "But a few select Revenants pushing the boundaries of law does not equate to the change of an entire infrastructure. Enoch had lived, and lived well, with Revenants living alongside mortals. As equals."

Jensen's gaze leveled on Cam as he said, lips curled into a

sneer, "But we will never be equals, will we? Can men like us truly resist the temptations of our power? We could be gods. Who will stop us if we are not given restraints?"

Bastard. The others watched as Cam took his time to answer. "It seems you don't trust yourself, Mr. Davis."

"As little as I do anyone," Jensen answered, his icy-blue brands pulsing. "I'm sure you understand the feeling."

Cam held his stare—and he made his decision. *I don't trust myself.* This was his last hail mary to deny Enoch. "I do, which is why I agree with Mr. Davis. Revenants should not have the same rights as mortals within city limits. Similar, maybe, but not the same. And we should not be able to hold positions of power."

Half the table jumped to their feet in an uproar.

He'd never seen two men look as shocked as Jensen and his father did in that moment.

Plates shattered as men hammered their fists against the table, sending food flying.

"Nonsense!" Dr. Clarke finally spoke, his voice rising above the others, and they lowered theirs to listen.

"I repeat, that statement is nonsense." Dr. Clarke wheeled to face Cam, something like terror hiding behind his features. "You are being defamatory against yourself, Lord Callahan. In a matter of weeks, you've done more for Enoch than its current leadership has in years." He flashed a look at Alexander. "Your humility proves your worth. Enoch is the jewel of the West, a symbol of power, and it's dying. You and your lady are the first spark of hope to grace our coast in a generation."

"Be quiet, Van," Cam snapped. "You're embarrassing yourself."

"Maybe," Dr. Clarke continued. Alexander didn't stop him, despite the suspicion filling his eyes. "But your great-grandfather—the city's founder—himself was Revenant. Perhaps Enoch wasn't meant to be ruled by a mortal."

Cam stopped breathing for a moment, remembering to do so only when his ears began to ring.

What little color Alexander had left drained from his face.

The rest of the council, even Jensen, held onto Dr. Clarke's every word as he feigned surprise.

"You didn't know?" He twisted toward the men at the table, holding out his arms. He turned back to Alexander, a wicked curve tilting his thin lips. "It's a well-guarded Callahan secret. One that you didn't share with your own heir?"

"Van." Alexander rose, ever so slowly, to his feet, his expression lethal. "Don't."

"Why?" Dr. Clarke lost all pretense of meekness, his voice growing louder. "Because you want to continue to hold onto something that wasn't meant for you. The West was never yours."

No. Cam fought to keep air in his lungs. He wasn't sure which one of them was lying, but it didn't matter. If his great-grandfather had been Revenant, he'd still be alive. He'd have ruled for centuries, unchanging. Un-aging. He would have still been young in a Revenant's span of life.

Unless—

Cam wasn't sure who his question was for when he asked, "Who killed him?"

"Camden, don't—" Alexander's mouth was moving, as if he meant to form words, but no sounds left his lips. His entire body stiffened, and he forcibly pushed himself back into his chair as his chest began to spasm.

"More proof of his impotence," Jensen chimed in, gaining a few grunts of agreement from the others.

Alexander's mouth continued to move as Van Clarke leaned across the table, his voice just above a whisper. Despite,

Cam was sure every soul in the room heard as Van breathed, "Enoch—the West—belongs to you, Camden Callahan. It always has. Why do you think your father tried so hard to make sure you'd never have it?"

"Don't." Alexander's back was glued to his chair. "Don't."

No. Cam counted each of his chaotic breaths. His father had been trying to force governance on him since he arrived. No matter what had happened before, it didn't explain the last few weeks. Of all they'd worked toward to stop The Order.

Cam's whirling thoughts must have been plain on his face, because Dr. Clarke leaned in closer, his words low enough that only the men at the front of the table—he, Jensen, and his father—could hear.

"He's dying, Camden." Van's voice had a soothing edge to it. "He's dying and better his kingdom go to his son, to keep it in his bloodline, than for it to be taken from him by force."

The realization struck Cam harder than any blade ever could.

He'd begun to trust his father. After all he'd done to him, Cam had still fallen into seeking his approval. He'd been played—*again*—just like the governor had played everyone else.

Dr. Clarke held out his hand like he had on the train. "Rule Enoch. Take it. These Revenant rights, this arguing, it's all his distraction to keep the people from seeing who the real enemy is—him. Take the city, Camden. Let us help you."

Take the city. Cam's mouth was dry as a bone. He glanced down the table and was met with mostly hopeful eyes. Some were filled with terror and confusion, just as he had imagined he must look.

Alexander struggled against whatever invisible binds held him, mouthing words Cam couldn't understand.

Take the city. God, what a way to spit in his face. A vision of his mother flashed in his mind—bright and smiling—only to be replaced by the emptiness of how he last saw her, as Resh dragged him away.

He'd spent nearly every night of the last ten years dreaming of revenge, and what a delicious way to take it.

Alexander Callahan fallen—betrayed by a people he'd lorded over. Just like he'd betrayed him.

If I took Enoch, I could make it safe. Annie might stay with me. The only thing he hated more than who he was supposed to be was the thought of losing her.

Dr. Clarke extended his hand further, near buzzing with anticipation. He smiled so wide that faint, blackish streaks were visible on his gumline. "Shake on it, Camden. Take it. Say yes."

Tears lined Alexander's eyes as he slumped in his chair.

These men know how to play the game.

And that's what this was . . . a game.

Cam slowly lowered his gaze to Van's open, left hand, then back to his expectant face.

The *left*.

Say that you'll stand for Enoch. For the West. Say yes.

Alexander let out a low moan as Cam reached forward, smiling, as if to take Van's hand—but instead of shaking it, he bent back Van's left ring finger until the knuckle snapped. Van shrieked and tried to pull away, but not before Cam saw the phoenix tattoo inked into the flesh near the base, partially concealed by a wide banded ring.

Cam bent the finger back further until he felt the satisfying snap of torn tendons. "No."

Van stumbled back, gripping his ruined hand, as pained tears streamed down his hate-filled face. Whatever hold there seemed to be on Alexander, it fell. He nearly hit the table, gasping for breath.

"I didn't want it to end like this." Van's features twisted into extreme focus, his eyes distant, and a ripple of energy rushed over the room, ascending over the halls above them. All the men and women Cam had seen earlier—dressed in greys and blacks—reappeared at the railings, their veins inky black, hands laden with heavy rifles and shotguns.

Cam drew his revolver, but it wouldn't be enough.

Jensen Davis backed toward the doors, grinning.

"Camden—" Alexander croaked.

"Shut up." Cam craned his head back. There must be one hundred of them, at least. *Not good odds.*

But he'd dealt with worse. He refused to die today.

"It may have been blanketed by jealousy and ambition," Van said, rubbing his ruined finger. "But for what it's worth, I really did like you, Camden."

A symphony of sharp *clicks* echoed through the room as Van's soldiers chambered their guns. From above, they rested the barrels of their weapons on the railings, ready to aim at anyone with the audacity to move.

Cam kept still, breathing slowly, revolver trained between Van's eyes as the doctor took several steps back, a twisted grin still on his face.

"This doesn't have to end in death, you know," Van said smugly. "Put your gun down. My superiors have been anxious to meet you."

Cam just smiled.

This. He could do this. Politics be damned, but he'd been in more shootouts in his life than he cared to remember. On instinct, he scanned the soldiers. Counting them. Searching for additional weapons, just as Resh taught him.

Use me, his fire whispered to him, hungry. It coiled in his stomach, his brands flaring, as it poised to strike.

I can't. If he used his fire, he'd likely kill everyone in the building. He didn't need that. Not yet, anyway.

"Camden," Alexander murmured, his skin sickly pale, as he rose from his chair. "Put your gun away. We can't fight them like this."

"Listen to your papa." Van laughed. He pointed to the group of pathetic, terrified councilmen huddled by the exit. "Put the gun down. If I must ask again, one of them dies."

Jensen was gone, but by the several muffled screams, loud thumps, and the frost creeping beneath the locked main doors, he must have taken out the bodyguards.

"You think I care about them?" Cam let his finger hover over the trigger. "Do it, but I'll hit you first. I can promise you that."

"Camden," Alexander repeated, lower this time. He gripped his chest as he slid around to the other side of the table. "The Order—"

Cam's eyes flickered to the second floor as one of the soldiers shifted their gun.

Alexander froze, noticing at the same time he did. They were surrounded.

"Come with me, both of you." Van held out his stupid hand again. "If you come peacefully, they can go. We're not here for them." He slid off his ring and raised his hand, revealing the phoenix tattoo beneath his finger. "Have you seen the matching mark your father wears? He knew this was going to happen. He knew, and he allowed it."

"Lies," Alexander began, but Cam shushed him.

"I know," Cam shot back, raising a brow. He'd gone into this expecting a trap. Whether his father was part of it or not, it didn't matter. He was tired of running.

Van seemed surprised at that. "You knew?" His gaze shot to Alexander. "Your commands—"

"Never strictly forbade me from sharing my *affiliations* with him." Alexander sneered, edging closer to the councilmen. Above, the soldier's gun followed his every move. "It seems *our* superiors made an error in verbiage."

Alexander sent Cam a pointed look, inclining his chin ever so slightly toward the main door. It was frosted shut.

Ah. Cam nodded just enough for his father to see, a plan locking into place. *I guess I'll be using you, after all.* His fire flared to life before he'd finished the thought.

Cam pulled the trigger.

The gunshot split the tension in the air as he focused all his thoughts on the entry, unleashing his power. A fireball exploded the door off its hinges, just missing the councilmen's shrieking heads.

Darkness spread through veins in Van's face and neck, a blackness pooling around him as he managed to duck out of the bullet's path.

The soldiers cried out, taking fire, but Cam had already put a wall of flame between them and the other men. As they reloaded, a voice shouted from the other side of the firewall —Alexander.

"Leave them, Camden!" The inferno nearly drowned out his voice. Cam thinned the wall enough to see his father's panic-stricken face. "We need to go. If you go with him, they get what they want. Kill them all, and they'll use it as ammo to keep you from taking the governance. Come with me."

"Yes, go with him, Camden." Van straightened his suit coat as the soldiers aimed. "Then what? Your carriages are gone. Shall you run with them like rabbits across the fields?"

Despite everything, Cam burst out into a sharp laugh and shrugged at Alexander. "He has a point."

Before his father could respond, he sealed the wall shut.

When Cam turned back, Van was watching him, the soldiers above waiting for his orders.

"Your father may be a lot of things," he began, brushing back a strand of dark hair. "But he isn't stupid. If you refuse to come, I will force you. If you kill me, The Order will force you *and* punish you."

Cam cocked back the hammer on his revolver. "Oh, *no*. I'm so scared."

"And Annie?" Van grinned when Cam stiffened. "Do you care about her? Let me make this simpler for you. Refuse, and she dies. Today."

Promise me, if it comes to it, you will spare no one. That you'll do whatever terrible thing you're afraid of doing, because I'd rather you be a monster and live than die feeling good about yourself.

All the control, all the fighting Cam had done to keep his power in check, shattered as her words invaded his mind.

A monster.

That's what he was afraid of—becoming one. *Being* one. Just like his father.

To hell with it. Let him be a monster. If he couldn't play the game, he'd break it. He'd always been a sore loser.

His fire ruptured, pouring from his body like tidal waves. The flames crashed over the railings, climbing to the second and third floors, leaving only brief, tormented screams in the wake of blackened corpses, as not a soul was left alive.

Except for Van.

Cam watched the doctor as his fire raged. Watched as he crumpled into a childish ball, wailing, like the coward he truly was.

It didn't take long to char the Embassy black.

Cam inhaled, fists clenched, as he reined in his power.

As the last of the flames guttered out, Van raised his head.

A bare patch of untouched granite encircled him. A reminder of how close he'd come to death.

Cam could still feel the fire in his eyes, taste it on his tongue, as he breathed, "Crawl to me, Van. I want you to burn."

Van let out a sob, but he obeyed, letting out pained moans as his exposed skin split, immediately blistered by the heat of the stone.

It wasn't until Van reached Cam's feet that he noticed his were bare, his boots having turned to dust. He slammed his heel into Van's spine, forcing him to the ground. He grabbed him by the hair and shoved his cheek against the superheated stone. Van shrieked, flailing, but he held him still.

He rolled Van's face until his nose crunched against the floor. "I'm so tired of men like you making Annie's life a living hell."

Despite the agony and the blood pouring from his nostrils, threatening to drown him, Van let out a dark laugh. "It won't be a man ruining her this time."

"Who—" Cam blinked before the pieces clicked into place. *Blazes.* "Violet."

"Back away, Camden."

He glanced up to find Alexander standing there, aiming his own revolver at him. He hadn't realized he'd dropped it. At least his fire had known better than to melt it.

"Are you going to shoot me, Daddy?" Cam cackled as he released Van's hair. "Try it. I dare you."

Alexander nodded to the doctor. "If you kill him, The Order will know. They'll give the command to take her. Back away. We'll bring him back with us. Question him."

A frustrated growl escaped Cam's lips. Alexander was afraid of him. Instead of the satisfaction he should have felt, it only made him angrier.

"Oh, Violet is a jealous thing." Van cut in and rolled onto his back, half his face melted away. "I'd bet on what little life I have left that your pretty, little wife is dead already."

CHAPTER 52

ANNIE

The wound *stank* as Annie peeled back the saturated bandage. A pungent, sweet smell she knew to be infection. The girl from the slave ship, Mary, watched as Annie worked on her ankle, ruined by so long in chains. Several of the nurses peered over her shoulder, equally observant.

They covered their mouths, gagging, as the smell wafted to them. Annie lip's pursed as she prodded at Mary's wound with gloved fingers. The girl winced but didn't move.

She narrowed her eyes at Mary. "Have they changed these since yesterday?"

"Of course, we did." One of the nurses chimed in. "We—"

Annie raised her finger. "I wasn't talking to you."

Mary smirked, tendrils of her stringy dark hair falling in her eyes. A clever, little thing. "No. They haven't. I would have done it myself, but I couldn't walk to get the supplies."

Of course not. Annie glared over her shoulder at the nurses. "Change the bandages twice daily. If I hear that you've failed to do so, you'll be finding work elsewhere."

The nurses glanced at each other, a look of shock crossing their faces.

"Now," Annie exhaled, laying a clean cloth over her lap. "Bring me a mortar, pestle, beeswax, garlic, and oregano."

"My lady, whatever for?" Another nurse answered, dropping her gaze when Annie's brow rose. "S-shouldn't we just bleed her?"

"No, you will not *bleed* her." *Archaic lunatics.* "Bleeding is an outdated practice and will not be used again in Waverly. Now bring me the supplies I requested." She sighed. "Please."

They nodded and ducked away. Leaving her alone with Mary. Well, not actually alone. The rest of the rescued slaves were still in their beds, but most were dozing. Mr. Price lay stretched out on one of the empty beds, arms crossed over his chest, fast asleep.

He's gotten as little sleep as the rest of us. Yet she'd woken him anyway to bring her to the hospital. He'd nodded off not long after they'd arrived. Hours ago. The sun was beginning to rise. One by one, she'd sat down with each patient. Evaluating them and treating them. Now, Mary was the last. She wanted to feel guilty for dragging him here, but she couldn't. Not when Cam's letter, neatly tucked into her pocket, felt like it was eating her alive.

I wished I'd started with Mary. Annie tried to force Cam out of her mind as a nurse returned with the supplies she requested. She pulled her rolling side table beside her and tossed the ingredients into the mortar to begin mixing. All the while, Mary watched her. Silent.

I'm a damned coward.

And I love you.

Annie winced as she ground the culmination of herbs, the heady scent of the oregano clogging her nose. She'd read the letter so many times, she could recite it. She'd read it and wanted to tear it to shreds. To throw it in the fire. To do what he'd suggested and pretend she'd never read it at all.

Because she was angry.

Not because he loved her, but because she loved him.

She'd broken every rule she'd ever made. Every promise Tawny forced her to make. And now it was too late. She couldn't go back to before—when it had been so easy to hate. Cam was a part of her now. She needed him to breathe, and he wasn't here. And for that, she was angry, also. Because he didn't give her a chance to say it back.

Annie swallowed, fighting against the tightness in her throat. After all she put him through, he didn't trust her to love him. Now, if something happened . . . and he didn't return, she'd never have the chance to tell him.

So, she sat there. Grinding herbs until her fingers ached and the mortar's stone began to crack.

"Maybe you should put that down. I think it's done." Mary murmured.

With a huff, Annie set the bowl down on her side table. She soaked a clean rag in fresh, warm water and wrung out the excess moisture before she began to clean the infected skin. Mary let out a pained yelp.

"I'm sorry." Annie glanced over to make sure Mr. Price hadn't woken. He hadn't. "I didn't mean to press so hard. I'm just—"

"Exhausted?" Mary smirked again. She reminded her a little of Cam, which made things all the worse. "You should take a hint from your friend and find a bed to sleep in. You look terrible."

"At least you're honest." She placed the towel back in the bucket before scooping some of the fresh salve on her fingers. Gently, she applied some to Mary's wound. "But I'm fine. I appreciate your concern."

Mary gritted her teeth as Annie continued to clean and apply the medicine. "Maybe if you let the nurses help, you wouldn't have to work so hard."

"I wouldn't have to work so hard if they were competent," Annie replied. "I don't understand why they didn't clean this."

"One or two of them tried," Mary hissed through deep breaths. "But that heinous woman with the brown hair kept chasing them off. Said if you wanted us treated, you could do it yourself."

Annie paused, her brands flaring so quickly and so bright, Mary jumped.

"I'm sorry," Annie repeated, then scooped out some more salve.

Violet Clarke. She knew she shouldn't have allowed her to stay after Cam had given her Waverly, but she didn't have the heart to make her leave. She, above anyone, knew how difficult it was for a woman to gain any respect in this field. Violet was a sow, but she was a skilled physician. Thankfully, Violet wasn't here now. The last thing she needed was to get in a fight.

"Where's the tall, fire Stripe that was with you?" Mary asked innocently, but Annie caught the implication. "You know, the funny one?"

"He's away." Annie kept her features blank as she wiped off the excess salve on her towel. *Stop talking about him.* "He'll be back soon."

That's what she'd kept telling herself. He would be back. He had to come back.

"He follows you around like a swooning maid," Mary giggled. "It's hilarious."

"He'll be back," Annie said, more harshly than she meant.

Mary raised a brow. "When—"

With a loud, metallic screech, Annie pushed her chair back and stood up. She waved her hand over Mary's leg, and the wound instantly closed. "Get some sleep. I'll check on you in a few hours."

Mary blinked at her leg before turning her stunned gaze to Annie. "You've been able to do that the whole time, and you've been squishing *poultices?*"

Annie bit down on her lip. She didn't know how to respond, but thankfully, she didn't have to.

The door to the medical ward swung open with a loud *thud,* startling Mr. Price awake. He nearly fell off the bed.

"There you two are!" Nathan waltzed in, Jenny at his side. She carried a heavy, wicker basket. Mr. Price blinked the sleep out of his eyes as Nathan grinned, his black curls falling over his forehead.

"You should be on *The Elaina,*" The Air Brand grumbled.

"I already was. Pulley has things covered." Nathan plopped down on the bed beside him, making it shake. "We checked the villa for you first, and since you weren't there, this was the obvious second choice."

Mr. Price jumped up and straightened his cream coat, then smoothed his long braid over his shoulder. "Any sign of discord on the docks?"

"None that I noticed." Nathan wrinkled his nose. "But The Order wouldn't be a good opponent if we could pick them out of a crowd that easily."

"This isn't a laughing matter," Mr. Price scowled, going off into one of his lectures. Nathan argued back, mostly to annoy him, she suspected.

"Have you eaten?" Jenny sidled to Annie's side, voice low, and held up the basket. "I brought breakfast."

Annie's stomach growled as if on cue. "Thank you, but I should get back to work."

"You're always working." As if that was an answer. Jenny grabbed her by the hand and led her toward the sward's private quarters. She was too exhausted to resist. Behind the heavy curtain, the air in the enclosed space was dense and stagnant, but at least it lacked the smell of decay.

Jenny dusted off the table with the sleeve of her coat. She emptied the basket, then arranged an assortment of dried fruits, hard cheeses, brown bread, and a tiny jar of honey. She even brought glasses that she filled with a strong, room-temperature tea she poured from a canteen.

She smiled sweetly. "There. Breakfast."

"You didn't have to," Annie grumbled, but went straight for the tea, draining it in one swallow. She *was* starving and had already bitten off a chunk of fruit and cheese together when her sister sat down across from her.

Jenny watched her eat for a moment, a strange look on her face. "You need to take better care of yourself."

"I'm fine." Annie swallowed and poured herself another cup of tea. "Besides, it's my job to take care of you, not the other way around."

"It's okay to let others care, you know?" Jenny sliced off a piece of brown bread and slathered some honey on it. She set it on Annie's plate. "Especially now. I know you must be worried about—"

"Jenny," Annie said flatly. *Please, stop.* Her mouth felt too dry to swallow. "Can we talk about something else?"

"Alright." Jenny twisted the emerald ring on her finger. Her engagement ring. "I miss you. We've barely spent time together in weeks. There's so much I want to talk about, but you're always . . . working."

Shame ate away at Annie's guard. She set her bread down and wiped the crumbs off her lips with her thumb. She couldn't argue with that. *I wish I could make everyone happy. I wish I were enough.* "I don't know what you want me to say."

Tears lined Jenny's eyes as she sipped her tea. "You haven't even asked how Nathan proposed."

"I'm sorry," Annie whispered. How many times would she have to apologize tonight?

"Maya says that you're adjusting." Jenny sniffed. "That it will get better after you've had a chance to get used to Enoch."

Anger burned away some of Annie's guilt. "You talk to *Maya* about me?"

"Sometimes." Jenny straightened, defensive. "When the rest of you are gone, I need someone to talk to. You may forget, but the West is as strange to me as it is to you."

Annie picked her food apart. "I know. I haven't forgotten."

Jenny's expression slowly softened. "Maya told me something. Would you like to hear it?"

She nodded. She knew better than to say no.

"She told me healing was kind of like sitting on your foot," Jenny said matter-of-factly. "That while the pressure is there, you can't feel it, but when the pressure is taken away, and all the blood starts rushing back. That's when it hurts."

Annie froze, staring at her.

"It hurts because you're healing," Jenny continued. "*We're* healing, Annie. We're going to get better."

"We're going to get better," Annie repeated, and she wanted to believe it. *You're healing.* She nibbled thoughtfully on a bite of cheese. "So . . . how did Nathan propose?"

Jenny's entire face brightened.

Out in the ward, the door squeaked as it opened, and a familiar voice scoffed.

"What are you doing here?" Violet Clarke. No doubt toward Nathan and Mr. Price.

"Whatever we want," Nathan shot back. "What are *you* doing here?"

"None of your concern." Her heeled footsteps thundered

toward the private quarters, and the curtain swung back. Violet scanned over Annie and Jenny, her brunette ringlets in a tight bun.

The frustration on her face instantly melted into an amused smile. "Slacking off, I see. I heard you showed up in the middle of the night. Uninvited."

"Good thing I don't need an invitation." Annie nodded to Jenny, but let her tone come out sharp. "Sister, may I have a moment alone with Miss Clarke?"

"O-of course," Jenny stood and swept for the exit, shooting Annie a quick warning look. Violet sneered at her as she passed, letting the curtain drop once Jenny was clear.

"What do you want?" Annie sipped her tea. "You wouldn't be storming in here, all in a huff, if you didn't want something."

"There are so many things I want." Violet took Jenny's seat, swiping a dried apple off her plate and taking a bite. She chewed for a moment, resting her cheek in her palm. "Like you. I want to be you."

Annie sighed and set down her cup. "You don't want to be me. Nor do I want to sit here and listen to all your reasons for why you think you do."

"If I were you, I'd be rich." Violet proceeded, blatantly ignoring her. "If I were you, I'd have a handsome, powerful husband and live in a palace by the sea." Her eyes darkened. "If I were you, Waverly would be mine. Not Van's. *Mine*. I could do and be whoever I wanted, and no one could stop me."

She reminds me so much of Charlotte. Annie counted her breaths, making sure she didn't respond too soon or too late. She'd dealt with mad women before.

Despite her caution, Annie couldn't stop the slight smirk on her face as she said, "Sounds like a pretty dream."

"It is." Violet smiled in response. "One I can still have."

A small *boom* followed by short screams sounded from several floors below. A sound like thunder grew louder with every passing heartbeat.

Out in the medical wing, there was a sharp click as Nathan drew his revolver. "What the hell—"

Another boom. This time it was closer. Close enough that the vibrations could be felt through the floor. Beyond the curtain, Jenny let out a yelp. Mr. Price cursed as a gust of wind rushed through the room as he called on his power.

We're being attacked. Annie stood, reaching instinctively for the damascus blade she kept sheathed in her bodice. *The Order is attacking.* Ice leaked into her blood. *And if they're here...*

As Annie stepped toward the curtain, Violet moved around the table until she stood behind her and grabbed her elbow.

"No, no," she said, brushing a loose, brown curl out of her face. "Best you stay here. With me. You don't want to see this."

Annie froze, heart pounding. The sounds were closer now, and it wasn't thunder. It was the echo of sprinting footsteps. Cultists.

"They're coming up the stairs," Mr. Price shouted to Nathan from the other room. "I'm going to push them back. Don't let them get inside."

"Hide in here. Stay with Annie." The curtain tore back. Nathan dragged Jenny into the private quarters, her pale skin bloodless. Gun in hand, his dark eyes scanned over Violet and Annie, growing wide with horror as he looked *past* them.

"Everything you have will be mine."

Annie turned as Violet removed the large ring from her left ring finger. Beneath the band, a phoenix tattoo was inked into her skin.

But it wasn't Violet's wicked grin that made Annie's limbs turn leaden. It was the six nurses standing behind her. The same nurses whom she'd sent away earlier. Now, their eyes were fixed on her, the whites of them threaded with black. Darkness pulsed in the exposed veins in their necks, spreading into their faces, just like the men who'd attacked the Clarkes's estate.

Annie's own power responded, recoiling.

"I tried to do this privately." Violet's smile grew wider as she slipped a thin blade from her sleeve.

Jenny screamed. Nathan cried out, raising his gun.

Violet was faster, though, and plunged the dagger into Annie's stomach.

A gunshot went off, whizzing by Annie's ear, and hit one of the nurses. They slumped to the ground with a screech, black blood staining the floor.

Violet was too close to her for Nathan to take the shot, even as she twisted the knife deeper.

Not again. That was the first thing Annie thought. What she kept thinking as Jenny screamed again, yanking her back by the shoulder. A blinding, white pain ravaged her insides as they fell and landed on their backs beneath the table.

Not again, not again, not again. She couldn't breathe. Charlotte had stabbed her, too. She'd died once to a blade. *Not again.*

The cultists, clad in nursing uniforms, unsheathed swords from beneath their coats. In a whirlwind of movement, they charged at Nathan, forcing him to scramble out of the private quarters as he fought to draw his own weapon with his free hand. He fired again, and another cultist fell.

Jenny whimpered, tears pouring down her face, as she tried to staunch the blood seeping from Annie's gut. The dagger was stuck inside her.

Annie bit back a hiss of agony as she rose onto her elbow. She had to pack the wound. She had to—

Oh.

Her power hummed through her body, sending vibrations through the wound. A tightness in her abdomen threatened to overwhelm the pain of the blade. In fact, it seemed fixed *on* the blade. Squeezing it, pushing it.

Of course. Jenny shrieked as Annie yanked the dagger free. The steel had barely left her skin before it knit closed. Only a thin red line remained on the bare flesh that showed through the hole in her dress.

I can heal myself. Annie let out a low laugh. Stupid. Of course, she could. And if it hadn't occurred to her, it must not have occurred to Violet, either.

Fingers stained red, Jenny trembled as Annie rose to a crouch. "Are you a-alright?"

"I'm fine." Annie shoved the dagger into Jenny's hand. "Keep this. We need to—"

She lurched backward, landing on her back again, as she was dragged from beneath the table by her ankle.

Violet straddled her, reaching for her throat, but Annie caught her by the wrists before she could.

Annie burst out laughing again, adrenaline chasing away the sleep deprivation and fear. "You've seemed to have forgotten something."

Violet grimaced as she fought to break free of her grip. She was strong, but Annie was stronger now.

"Have I told you how much I hate you?" Violet seethed.

"Not often enough." Annie flipped her onto her back and pinned her wrists to the ground. As Violet struggled, she leaned in. "You also forgot this."

As much as it repulsed her, Annie let her power free. It latched onto the other woman, attempting to drain the life from her. Violet let out an enraged cry as her skin began to crack and wither.

"How dare"—Violet lurched forward, slamming her forehead into Annie's nose—"you."

Stars exploded into Annie's vision, darkness clouding the edges, as hot blood spurted from her nose. She gripped her face, reeling, and Violet shoved her and scrambled off the floor.

As Annie's eyes began to clear, Violet stared down at her sunken skin in horror. "Look what you've done!" She backed away, a welt already forming on her forehead.

Jenny watched, wide-eyed, still hiding beneath the table.

Get up. Annie tried to stand, but staggered, falling back to the floor. *Get up, get up, get up.* She should have trained with Cam and Julian when they offered. She should have done more. She *refused* to let Violet be the one to kill her again.

"N-no matter." Violet sniffed and brushed a curl off her bruised face. She drew a small pistol from her skirt pocket. "I don't need to touch you to kill you."

"*Stop!*" Jenny screamed, but she didn't move.

Get up, get up. Annie managed to get to her knees, but Violet kicked her down again. She shoved her heeled boot down onto her chest, making her sternum crack, and pressed the barrel of her gun between Annie's eyes.

Violet started to smile, but everything happened too quickly. Before either of them could move or speak, a gunshot rang out—outside the private wing, in the medical ward.

Nathan.

The body of another cultist flew through the curtains, slamming full force into Violet's side. Her own gun went off, the bullet hitting the ground inches from Annie's cheek.

Then everything went quiet, the silence replaced by a piercing shriek in her ear. Annie rolled, her head spinning. Violet was still on the ground, struggling to free herself from beneath the corpse.

My ear. Annie scrambled to her feet, fighting to breathe, as that ringing kept growing louder. *I can't hear out of my left ear.* There wasn't time to heal it. She reached under the table and grabbed Jenny's arm. Her sister hesitated, but she dragged her out of the private quarters.

In the medical ward, the patients were wailing. She hadn't noticed before, the sound muffled due to the damage in her ear. Three more cultist bodies lay dead in puddles of black blood. Where was Nathan? She pulled Jenny behind her, heading toward the back beds.

Annie tore back the blankets from one of the empty bunks. "Hide under here."

Jenny did as she was bidden, and let out a soft sob as Annie dropped the blankets back into place. Now that she really looked, half the patients were missing—they'd likely made a run for it. The rest were huddled in their sheets, staring at her in terror. More than one had soiled themselves.

"Let me help."

Annie spun. She hadn't realized she was beside Mary's bed.

The girl's features were set in a hard line. "Let me help. I can distract her."

In the other room, Violet let out another frustrated cry, her heeled boots clacking on the floor as she stormed into the medical ward. On the far side of the room, the back of her head was visible.

Annie ducked lower behind the bed. "You can't help, Mary. You need to stay down until I can get rid of her." Because she *could.* She knew she could. She just didn't know *how.*

"Of course, I can help." Mary hissed. "If I get hurt, you can just heal me again."

"I can't raise you from the dead." Annie ducked lower when Violet swiveled. She looked dazed. "She has a gun."

"All the more reason for me to distract her." Mary leaned

forward carefully. "I've been through enough. I'm not afraid to die."

Annie knew that feeling all too well. She squeezed Mary's hand, then ducked again when Violet took a staggering step toward the back side of the room.

"Does it bother you that he's going to be mine?" Violet giggled, wobbling as she moved right. Her forehead had swelled to double its normal size, already turning shades of purple. "Your husband will be mine. So will your house. So will this hospital."

She has a concussion. Possibly a minor brain bleed. Annie's skull was tougher than hers, apparently. She could use this to her advantage, but she'd need Mary, after all.

Annie held her blade tightly to her chest, turning to the girl. "Wait for my signal."

Mary nodded. Annie moved from one bedframe to another. "You're madder than I thought if you think Camden would be with you," she called. As Violet wheeled, Annie was already crawling under the bed, shimmying her way to the next row forward. She needed to get closer.

Violet wobbled again, her ankle rolling, as she cautiously inched forward, gun at the ready. "He won't have a choice, you imbecile. Once Van gets him to take the mark, Camden will do as he's told."

Annie froze, her chest smashed against the cold floor. *The mark. Their tattoos.* Like Alexander's. Could The Order use it to control him? She sucked in a breath. "I was told you had to take the mark willingly,"—she scrambled beneath the next bed— "He won't."

Violet tried to track her movements but couldn't. She squinted at the faces of the patients, as if one of them might be Annie. They tucked deeper into their blankets, quivering.

"It only takes one yes." She wiped at the blood dripping

into her eyes. "He doesn't even have to know what he's agreeing to as long as he says yes."

No. Annie forgot how to breathe. *That* was the point of the meeting. It had to be. They'd try to trap him with his words and with Cam's mouth and temper . . .

Lord above. She had to find some way to warn him—*now* —but first, she had to deal with Violet.

From across the room, Jenny's bright gold eyes were visible beneath the bed. She watched as Annie slid to her next hiding space, only a few spaces away from Violet. Angry shouts and banging came from the hall. Mr. Price. A wave of relief rushed through her. Help was coming. She just needed to avoid getting shot a little longer.

"I'm going to kill you, Annie. I don't care what The Order wants," Violet muttered, almost to herself. "I'm going to kill you, then be you. Van can't stop me. Camden can't. You can't."

We'll see about that. Annie shifted far enough now that she could give Mary a nod.

The girl broke out into a wide grin. "You're trash, you know that, right?"

Violet turned slowly, her expression equally stunned and enraged, finger inching toward the trigger. "Excuse me?"

"You heard me." Mary leaned back onto her pillows, resting her hands behind her head. "Trash. Like what's thrown into the street. That's why nobody likes you."

Oh no. Slowly, Annie scooted out from her hiding place. If Mary kept this up, she wasn't going to have time to get into position.

Violet reached out and steadied herself against a footboard, a small amount of clarity returning to her hateful gaze. She checked how many bullets she had in the chambers of her gun.

"And you." She aimed it at Mary's head, expression twisted

in rage. "Are dead. You'll be a *corpse* in the street. How about that?"

Mary shrugged. "Whatever."

I won't make it in time. She was still fifteen feet away. With her blade in hand, she considered throwing it, but couldn't guarantee she wouldn't hit Mary. Her power flared, humming to the surface, causing her brands to pulse a charcoal color.

Violet's finger moved. She was going to kill Mary, and there was nothing she could do. If she could touch her, she could stop her. If only—

Annie's power *pulled* again, but this time, instead of at her wounds, it was pulling toward Violet. Violent. Hungry.

In that moment, she could feel the space between them connect. It was hers for the taking. *I can do this.*

As Violet's grip grew tighter, Annie didn't give herself time to think. She opened the gate—letting her power tear across the room and claw into the woman like talons. This time, when she touched the essence of Violet's life, she didn't hesitate. She wasn't gentle. No, she just took, and kept on taking, until Violet crumpled to the floor.

Mary scrambled backwards, mouth agape in shock.

Breathing heavily, Annie closed the distance between them. Violet was still alive, gaping up at the ceiling. Her once plump, ivory face drained into something like the dried apple she'd stolen.

"You can't stop them," Violet choked. "They'll take him from you."

"They won't." Annie brushed her fingers down Violet's leathery cheekbones. "Because Camden is *mine.*"

Then she plunged her damascus blade into Violet's heart.

A soft gasp, a rasping breath, then another, and Violet was gone. Blood spilled over her lips, staining Annie's dress red— red, not black.

"Blazing hell." Mary burst out laughing.

A sharp inhale had her twisting toward the door to the medical ward. Nathan and Mr. Price stood within the frame, soaked in gore.

Nathan took one look at her, crouched over Violet's body, and cursed. "Damn, Annie. No wonder Cam's obsessed with you. Have you ever heard of overkill?"

"She saved us." Jenny slid out from under the bed, still ghost white and shaking. "All of us. Where were you? Nathan, why did you leave?"

"I was dealing with two dozen other cultists." Nathan gestured to Mr. Price. "And saving his ass."

"You did not," Mr. Price spat. "I had already taken out half before you arrived."

"Admit it, old man. I'm the better shot."

"I'm done speaking to insolent children."

"We don't have time for this." *Elain.* Annie jumped to her feet, a wave of dizziness hitting her as her damaged ear began to ring. "I need to get to Cam. Now."

Elain, Elain, Elain, where are you? The others were talking to her, asking questions, but she ignored them. Where was Elain? She needed the rip in the void. To step through that gleaming gap and find Cam before it was too late.

"Elain." She cried out, fear boring a hole into her already sore stomach. "Elain, I need you!"

No response.

Jenny gripped her elbow. "Annie, Elain is dead. What are you doing?"

"You don't understand." Annie pulled away. She sucked in several steadying breaths. "She has to open the—"

No. This power was hers. *Hers.* If she wanted to step through the void, she'd do it. She didn't need Elain.

Just like she'd seen her sister do before, Annie dragged her finger down in the open air in front of her. She didn't know what she was doing, only that she wanted to be where Cam was, and it wasn't here.

A series of gasps echoed throughout the room as the air parted for her, revealing a shimmering rip that led into a grey nothingness beyond.

Later. Later, she'd think about what she'd done and how she did it. But for now, she let her heart lead her into the void.

CHAPTER 53
ALEXANDER

He was so *tired*.

Down into the marrow of his bones, he was tired.

Alexander sat alone in his private booth, his head lolling with every bump and rattle as the train flew down the tracks. If it weren't for all the jostling, he would have fallen asleep. The train was moving too fast, *far* too fast, to be safe. Each time the machine screeched and rumbled, he expected it to break apart, killing them in a fiery explosion.

Not all had survived Van's attack. Seven had died in the hands of the cultists he'd learned the doctor had stationed outside the Embassy building. Jensen Davis was nowhere to be found.

Alexander shifted to look outside the sealed, glass doors of his booth. The remaining councilmen were huddled in the sections opposite, anxious sweat dripping down their faces, eyes darting around wildly, as if they were waiting for the train to come apart, as well.

Camden needs to slow down.

As a child, his son had always been prone to fits of anger. Only Cassie had ever been able to calm him. But when he'd stepped back into the Embassy—after Camden had shut them out—his son had become *wrath*. Had transformed into a different creature entirely. Even after he'd thrown the lot of them back onto the train, terrifying the engineers into pushing the machine to its limits, fire still cracked and webbed across his skin, the green of his eyes completely lost to flame.

Alexander groaned as he forced himself to stand, his joints so stiff he thought they might break. He fought to stay upright as the train rocked and swayed beneath him.

He nodded as he passed some of the physically stronger councilmen he'd stationed to guard Van, locked inside one of the other private booths. Not that the doctor could go far on his own. Camden had burned most of his body and left half his face a melted slab.

Van Clarke. Alexander shook his head, the movement sending a fresh wave of exhaustion through him. He'd never cared for the Clarkes. Van had always been a lickspittle, and his sister a trollop. He'd even suspected that they'd been recruited by The Order—especially after he'd grown close to Henry Bale—but he'd never suspected Van to have the audacity to make a move at the Embassy. Not without Bale at his side. Which meant Bale put him up to it.

But Camden didn't take the deal.

Alexander smiled to himself. Good. If his son resisted them once, he could do it again. There may be some hope after all.

He still had until the end of the day. Then their bargain was up, and he wouldn't be able to protect Camden anymore. *But our meeting wasn't concluded.* That could be a loophole, a way for him to delay Henry just a little longer.

When Alexander finally reached the engineer's cab at the

back of the train. Heat radiated off the door handle, warping the air around it.

Too hot to touch. Alexander let his hand hover over it before sighing and shoving it into his coat pocket. "Camden, open the door."

No response. Only the scraping of the wheelsets against the tracks, making the metal walls vibrate.

"Camden."

A moment later, the door swung open. A wave of heat crashed over him, so intense he choked as it sucked all the moisture from his mouth and nose. Alexander covered the lower half of his face with his lapel and pushed inside, his eyes too dry to blink properly.

Camden never looked at him. He just turned back to his vigil, fire-filled eyes fixated on the grate by the boiler. The flames inside surged, escaping their containment, licking up the top of the boiler and onto the ceiling. Camden remained unfazed, arms crossed over his chest. His brands flared as the fire burned hotter.

Alexander held on as the train surged again, barreling even faster down the tracks. The cab was small, with only enough room for three people, and stained with years' worth of charcoal. The dials and levers were pushed to maximum capacity.

Alexander leaned against the back wall, near the doorway. "Where are the engineers?"

Camden gritted his teeth, gaze still fanning the flames higher. "I told them to leave."

Alexander exhaled. He hadn't seen them inside. "Why would you do that?"

"Because they told me to stop." Camden's brands flared again. "And that wasn't an option."

"You need to slow down," Alexander said flatly. "You won't

return to her any faster if you turn this train into a hunk of iron slag."

Cam's jaw clenched, his eyes growing darker, but he didn't respond.

He's terrified. It was Van's words that now pushed Camden to the point of madness. If Annie was gone . . . if Violet had managed to hurt her . . .

He wouldn't let himself think about it. Not yet. Alexander wrapped his coat tightly around himself, protection from the scalding heat pouring from his son's body, let alone the coal grate. "You didn't listen to any of my directions before the meeting. In fact, you blatantly disobeyed them."

Camden shifted in irritation. "You seem surprised."

"I'm not," Alexander smirked. "But I am proud of you."

That caught Camden off guard. He glanced over his shoulder, giving him a confused look.

"You didn't take the deal," Alexander clarified. "Van tried to play you, but you saw through it."

A flurry of emotions passed through Camden's eyes before he turned back to his fire, pushing the train harder.

They stood in silence for several minutes before Alexander built the courage to ask the question weighing on his heart. "Why didn't you?"

Cam cocked his head, still focused on the fire. "Why didn't I what?"

"Take the deal." Alexander had seen the temptation on his son's face when Van had offered him Enoch. "It would have been an easy way to get rid of me."

Cam huffed a dark laugh. "I may hate you, but if it makes you feel better, I've grown to hate them even more."

It did, actually. Not that Alexander would admit it out loud. He turned for the door. He needed a bed. Maybe he could get a few hours of sleep before either they reached the station or

Camden blew them into oblivion. He may as well try to relax in the short time he had left.

The handle had cooled enough for him to twist it.

Camden's rough voice interrupted him. "Was my great-grandfather really a Revenant?"

Alexander felt the familiar way his body began to lock up, but he managed to fight it long enough to say, "Yes."

Camden twisted toward him. Only his suit coat and trousers had survived his inferno, his chest and feet bare. "Why didn't you tell me? I know you're a liar, but why hide that? It doesn't make sense."

Alexander's tongue began to twist, attempting to silence him. Bale's hold was weaker on him now. He could argue it was distance, but he knew the truth. As his body withered away, so did the constraints.

"Because I couldn't." Alexander's words were thick, strained. "There's a lot I cannot tell you."

"Why can't you?" Camden asked.

Alexander swallowed. "I think you know."

"Bale?"

"Bale."

Because everything was tied to the Bales, and he couldn't even tell him that. He was as useless now as he was then.

Camden nodded in understanding.

"I don't have much time left," Alexander blurted. And it was the truth. The decay in his finger had spread up to his forearm. His body was falling apart. The deal was done.

"I know," was all Camden said. His eyes remained on the coal grate, pushing his fire hotter, pushing the train faster. So, he could get back to Annie. To his life, to everything The Order had been taking and taking from him since he was born.

Alexander left the engineer's cab, ready to sleep until someone woke him or the darkness took him.

Either way, this would all be over soon.

CHAPTER 54
CAMDEN

She's alive.

She's alive.

She's alive.

She's dead.

And it was his fault. He left her behind.

Cam stared into the burning coals. Willing them hotter, pushing the blasted train faster. His fire echoed all his fears, threatening to consume him.

Maybe he would let it. Maybe he would go out like a dying star. Take everyone with him and leave nothing left of this world but ash. He didn't care.

Maybe he wouldn't be so dramatic. Perhaps simple and quiet would be best.

Cam exhaled, allowing the train to slow as the first flickering lights of Enoch's station lit up the horizon. His fire curled with the terror swirling in his stomach.

He checked his new pocket watch. It was just after one o'clock.

He only had to wait a little longer.
Then he would decide.

CHAPTER 55
ANNIE

Time worked differently in the void. Annie didn't know how she knew, but she did. She could have spent a thousand years—wasting the endless days she had to live—inside this empty plain of dark, swirling mist.

But where do I go? Anxiety clawed at her insides. No matter where she looked, there was nothing but the mist. When she'd done this before, Elain had always been with her. Guiding her. Now she was alone.

Listen for him. In her previous trips through the void, she'd been able to hear Cam's voice. Distant. Echoing. They'd been able to follow it straight to him. *Listen.*

So, she did. And there was nothing but silence. A stillness so complete she could hear her blood as her heart pumped into her veins, could hear her lungs filling and emptying, the creaking of her joints when she moved.

And Cam wasn't here.

Annie fought back the first waves of panic, a cold sweat coating her skin. *Focus. Listen.* The longer she stood, the less she heard, but she swore she could *feel* him. Her heart beat even harder.

That's him. It has to be. Strumming beats of his power resonated from deeper in the gloom, brushing over her, his fire coated with a mix of sorrow and grief so heavy it threatened to drown her.

Please. Wait for me. What if she were too late? If he'd somehow said yes, and The Order had taken control of him, she had no idea how she'd free him, but she'd fight to the end of her days trying.

"Take me to him," she spoke into the void, her voice echoing through the abyss. The mist swirled and twisted, as if noticing her for the first time and appreciating its strange new visitor.

"Take me to him," Annie repeated, louder this time.

The mist widened, forming a tunnel with a small flicker of light at the end.

There. Annie sprinted down the path. Her limbs weightless. The light grew closer. Its shape never growing more defined. When she stepped through, gravity crashed down on her once again.

Then she was out.

Annie staggered back as the world reappeared in a flurry of motion, color, and frantic shouting. No one looked at her, despite being soaked in blood, her gown torn. There were so many people. Dozens of men in black or navy suits—

Councilmen. Annie clutched her chest as she tried to catch her breath. Acrid smoke billowed into the midday sky, staining it sooty black. A massive, black machine bellowed over the voices, a piercing sound that shot another wave of pain through her ear.

A train. She paused, staring at the wheels locked down

onto a metal track. Lord Duskin had told her about them. He'd taught her more than she cared to admit.

The sun was high overhead. How? It had been morning when she'd left the hospital.

The men were scrambling through the city gates, only to stop—faces white with shock—when no carriages were waiting for them. They must be ahead of schedule . . . or behind.

But where's Cam? At his height, she should be able to see him above the others. She shoved her way through the crowd, closer to the train, earning angry grunts and curses. The shouting grew louder as she drew closer to the locomotive.

"Move," Annie growled, squeezing herself between two men gawking at whatever was happening in the open space outside the train car. She froze as she broke through the throng.

Three councilmen—younger than the others—dragged Dr. Clarke off the train and tossed him to the pavement. He let out an agonized moan, rolling to his side. His clothes were blackened and burned, blistered welts showing through where his skin was exposed. His face—

Lord above, his face.

The left side was *melted.* Dried clumps of fat clung to what remained of his cheek and jaw.

Bile rose in Annie's throat, a wave of nausea hitting her like a thrown brick. His *face.* She scanned the other councilmen around her. They were scraped up, their clothes charred or stained with flecks of blood, but none of them were burned.

Those three councilmen bound Dr. Clarke's wrists with thick rope, turning him onto his back. She didn't know why they bothered. He wouldn't be running any time soon. They winced at his burns, averting their eyes as their faces turned green.

Camden did this. Annie blinked slowly. Cam had mutilated him, and she felt . . . satisfied. Van and Violet had worked this plan out together—there was no doubt about that—but what kind of person did that make her?

You killed her.

She couldn't think of that now. Not when Cam was still missing—

Alexander Callahan stepped off the train. He looked . . . depleted. She didn't miss the way he swayed as he stepped into the circle, staring darkly at Dr. Clarke, who writhed on the ground beneath him. Ash stained large portions of Alexander's suit. It was smeared across his face and coated his dark blond hair, dulling it.

He pointed at the doctor, addressing the men binding him. "Take him to my estate and lock him up."

Where's Cam? Her lungs weren't working anymore. They'd been attacked, too, and Cam wasn't here. She scanned the crowd again. Nowhere. She couldn't see him anywhere. Pins and needles covered her entire body.

"*Where is he?*" She didn't realize she'd screamed it until everyone turned to stare at her. At that point, she didn't care. She was already halfway across the circle then, striding towards the governor. "*Where is he?*"

Alexander looked up at her, eyes growing wide, before filling with relief.

"Annie—" He reached out for her. Maybe he meant to take her into his arms. Hug her. Herd her off somewhere more private. She'd never find out.

Annie had already punched him. She expected it to hurt, for her knuckles to shatter with the how hard she'd hit him, but she felt nothing.

Alexander hit the ground, though. *Hard.* His jaw instantly turned purple as the blood pooled beneath his skin.

A unified gasp erupted from the crowd. None of the councilmen tried to stop her as she pulled their governor up again by the front of his jacket, her power pouring out of her in sticky, dark shadows that gathered around her feet.

"Where is he?" She seethed, the brands on her hands flaring as her power begged to take hold of him. She shook it off. "Where's Camden, Alexander? Why isn't he here?"

The governor smiled up at her, blood leaking from his lips, and he dared to tuck a loose strand of her hair behind her ear. "He's fine. At least he will be once he sees you."

He's fine. She wanted to fold. To curl up on the ground and cry. *He's fine.*

Annie released her grip on him and staggered back, trying to breathe. "Where—"

She felt him, then. Just before he screamed her name over the crowd. The voice wasn't entirely human. No, it was wild, amplified, like when he'd torn Mr. Baxter's lab apart.

A wave of heat, visible in the mirage, split the crowd down the middle and forcibly parted them. Men cried out in anger, but fell silent when Cam rounded the corner.

She'd been right. He wasn't in control.

His eyes were lost to fire, and flames burned beneath his skin, making it glow.

Instead of pushing, this time, his heat wrapped around her and *pulled.* Dragging her to him, but he need not bother. She was already sprinting across the gap. Cam opened his arms, and she dove into them, wrapping her legs around his waist as her arms wound around his neck.

"Alive," he murmured over and over into her neck.

"Yes," she whispered back, and his whole body began to tremble as he held her. "*We're* alive."

She glanced around. People were staring at them. Alexander was still smiling, despite his swollen jaw.

"We need to leave." Annie squirmed out of Cam's grip, grabbing his hand as her feet hit the ground. "We need to talk."

Cam's eyes were wet, but he set his jaw and nodded.

I did it once. Annie inhaled, exhaling slowly as she carved her finger through the air. *I can do it again.*

Just like before, a glittering, grey opening before them, revealing the void beyond.

"Annie—" Cam's tan skin paled.

People started screaming.

"Trust me." Annie squeezed Cam's hand as hard as she could before she dragged him into the void with her. She'd still been mortal the first time Elain had taken her through. There was no reason to think she couldn't bring another.

Cam's death grip made her fingers go numb. *Where should we go?* She hadn't thought of that. Only that she'd wanted to leave. Before, she hadn't known exactly where she'd *needed* to go. Only that she'd wanted *him.*

"Take us somewhere safe," Annie called out into the mist. "Somewhere we'll be left alone."

Again, the mist twisted, *seeing* her. Another path formed. A new opening—with a dim light at the end—waited for them.

"What is this?" Cam whispered, barely a breath.

She didn't know how to answer. "Come with me."

Cam didn't fight her as she tugged him down the path. He hesitated before stepping through the opening, holding onto her for dear life.

Then reality abruptly slammed back into place, sending a twinge of pain through her ankles.

"How the hell—" Cam gasped.

My room.

Annie's shoulders sagged. They were back in her bedroom at the villa. It was strange to think she'd been here just the night before. For some reason, she didn't expect her belongings to be as she left them. After the events of the previous hours, it seemed as if every aspect of her privacy would be stripped away. Yet, her hairbrush still lay on her vanity. Yesterday's clothes were still thrown on the floor by the bed.

Take us somewhere safe. Over her months in Enoch, this space had become like home to her—with her in here, and Cam just in the other room.

The sound of Cam dry heaving snapped her back from her thoughts. He sank to the floor, bracing his head between his knees.

"Oh, no." Annie scrambled around looking for a waste basket. "Are you going to be sick?"

"I'm f-fine," Cam mumbled without looking up. "Just—" He gagged. "That was . . . something."

"It is, isn't it?" She sat down beside him, their shoulders touching. She brushed her fingers through his hair. She couldn't help it. *He's alive.* "I didn't want to be there anymore."

"I didn't, either." A shiver ran down his back. "Thank you, I —" As he looked up at her, scanning over her face, the blood drained out of his own, and he looked like he'd be sick again.

"Your *ear.*" Cam pulled her up and sat her at the vanity. Now that she had a chance to look, dried blood ran down her cheek and neck, sticking in her hair, staining it red.

He wiped at it with his sleeve. "What happened? Did Violet—"

"She's dead," Annie blurted, surprised at the shame in her words. "I killed her."

Surprise, then something like pride passed over Cam's features. "How?"

She swallowed, leaning back, and showing him the hole in her dress, at the faded pink line on the exposed skin of her stomach. "She stabbed me. I drained her."

"Annie," Cam breathed her name. Exhaustion settled over

him, and he hesitated before running his fingertips over the fading scar, giving her goosebumps. "This is my fault."

"You can't make everything your fault," Annie replied softly.

"I can, and I will." He dropped to his knees, laying his head in her lap. "I should never have left."

She thought for a moment as she ran her fingers through his hair again. Blood and ash clung to his sandy-gold strands. "No, you shouldn't have, but Violet wasn't your fault."

Cam's body went rigid—as if remembering something—and he scrambled back, getting to his feet. His face had gone white again, his hands trembling. "You didn't . . . did you . . ."

His shirt and vest had burned away, leaving his muscled torso bare. The brands on his chest and face pulsed manically, mirroring the thoughts he was so terrible at hiding.

His letter. After everything that had happened, *that's* what he was worried about? Another wave of anger flared up—at him and herself—as she slipped the note from her pocket. His eyes locked onto it, filling with terror, as he took in the creases in the paper. Proof that she'd read it. More than once. Dozens of times.

They just stared at each other.

Cam backed up until he was leaning against the footboard of her bed. He swallowed.

Annie set the letter on her vanity. "Are you going to say anything?"

Cam gripped the bedpost. "What do you want me to say?"

"I . . ." Annie closed her eyes for a moment. *What do I want him to say?* There was no going back after this. She couldn't keep her promises. *To hell with them.*

She picked at the corner of her vanity stool. "I want you to do what I asked. I want you to be brave for me. I want you to say what I've been too afraid to."

Another pause.

"And what if I'm afraid, too?" he admitted.

"Say it, anyway."

His eyes fluttered as he sucked in a heavy breath. "I love you."

Reading it had torn her heart to pieces. *Hearing* it shattered her completely.

Annie glared at him. "Say it again."

Cam fell to his knees. He slid forward, taking her hand and pressing her palm to his cheek. "I love you, Annie. If we weren't already, I'd be begging you to marry me." He kissed her wrist. "Forgive me. Have mercy on me. Just don't tell me to go."

She wouldn't. She never could.

Annie lifted his chin, brushing her thumb over his full lips. They parted for her, desire rivaling the fire in his eyes.

She leaned down, letting her mouth hover over his, sharing his breath. "I love you, Camden. Forgive *me* for being the real coward, and if I hadn't married you already, I would say yes."

"You mean it?" he asked.

"I do."

Cam dragged her onto his lap, sighing as she kissed him, tracing her fingers down his jaw, his throat, his chest, then she pulled off his coat and tossed it beside the bed. He kissed her deeper, pulling her closer.

Annie reached for the buttons of her dress, but Cam let out a deep, rumbling laugh and stopped her.

"Not here." He peppered her neck with soft kisses. "I've ruined enough, I'm not ruining this."

Annie scowled at him, but he swept her into his arms anyway, taking her into the bathroom. He turned on the faucets, letting water pour into the enormous, claw-foot tub. He raised a brow at her, his skin as flushed as she felt, when he set her back onto her feet.

Gently, he took her hand, covering hers with his, as he laid it over her ear. "Can you heal it?"

"Yes." Annie nodded, a thrill jolting through her as he reached around with his free hand and began undoing her buttons.

"Good." Cam cocked his head and let her gown drop to the floor. His brands flared as he sent a rush of his power into hers, their entwined fingers glowing bright, as energy flowed through them. She exhaled as her ear hummed, the ringing slipping away as her hearing returned.

Cam stood back as she shrugged out of her undergarments, and he lifted her again, kissing her as he brushed his fingers through the water, making it steam. She let out a small yelp as he lowered her into it.

"Sorry," he chuckled and drew some of the heat away. He grabbed a basin and a stool and sat behind the tub. He poured water over her hair, squeezing the excess into the basin. "You're a mess."

"So are you," she smirked.

"Yeah, yeah." He dumped her favorite lavender soap from roots to tip and began to scrub. "But my hair isn't white."

God, his fingers felt heavenly on her scalp.

He had to wash it a second time to rinse out all the matted blood and grime. Pushing the full basin away, he spoke again, voice thick. "I thought she killed you."

Annie shifted to face him. His eyes were wet again, and she cupped his cheek. "She tried."

"I had . . ." He chewed his lip, and she followed his gaze to where his gun belt lay beside his coat. "I had plans if I'd come back, and you were gone."

It felt like he'd slapped her in the face.

"Don't ever say that again." She grabbed his chin, and a

tear spilled down his cheek. "Ever. Don't ever think it. Never again."

He sucked in a shaky breath. "I don't want to do this without you."

"And you'll never have to." She kissed him gently. "It's you and me, remember?"

His throat bobbed as he nodded.

"Come in." She patted the edge of the tub. "Please?"

He kissed her again before stripping off the rest of his clothes. She watched, taking in every inch of him. Camden was beautiful, otherworldly—a creature of fire and death, and he was *hers*.

Forever. Because that's what she wanted. It had always been her choice.

He climbed in behind her, and Annie leaned back against his chest as he ran a soapy towel down her arms, her hands, cleaning the blood from beneath her nails.

"I'm sorry you had to kill Violet," Cam murmured into her hair. "I'm sorry for all of it. The slavers. The Order. The Duskins. I wish I could fix it. Undo it all."

I'm not in pain now. It was just a quick thought—one she would usually have let go—but it made her pause. She wasn't in pain. She was . . . happy. Here. With him. Even if The Order took everything, they couldn't take this.

Camden loved her. *Her.* And not even *she* could ruin that.

"I'm not." She twisted and took the towel from him, washing the soot from his face and hair. "Because the Annie I was before I met you is dead. She died below New Havana and never came out of those caverns."

His eyes filled with awe, as if something inside him had clicked into place. "They're gone . . . the people we were before. They're dead."

"They are." Annie straddled him, locking her hands around his neck.

His fingertips danced up and down her sides, over her hips. "And we don't have to be them anymore."

"We don't. Now *we* will live. You and me. And no one can take this from us."

She kissed him, savoring the taste of him, his every touch, the feel of him beneath her. Because she wasn't powerless anymore. Because no pain could ever compare to the joy he gave her.

Her power clawed into him, and his fire was waiting for her. This time, when she opened the gate, there were no secrets. She could dive straight into the depths of his soul, and he would let her. Their skin began to glow, and for that moment, as their power entwined, they were one being—a monster of their own making.

"You and me." Cam let out a soft gasp as their bodies slid together. "Until the stars fall or time takes us away. Even then."

"Even then," she breathed, unraveling, as the chamber erupted in black flames, radiant light, and lovely, waltzing shadows. "Always."

CHAPTER 56
CAMDEN

Cam was afraid to move—to brush away the strand of moon-white hair off of Annie's sleeping face, or else he might wake her. Curled against him, head cradled against his chest, she was more beautiful than all the celestial bodies above, and she loved him.

Him.

They'd spent the rest of the day sleeping and exploring each other. They'd even slept peacefully through the night. Together. In her bed. Not on the couch, which felt like a victory. He'd told her everything that had happened at the Embassy, and she shared the events at Waverly. Now the sun was rising, and Annie hadn't woken once. Not one nightmare.

No, if he moved, and she woke, they'd have to return to normal life again. The Order would still be after them. There would still be more lies to untangle than he could count. So instead, he imagined all the places he wished he could take her. All the places they could see together when they were free.

We may never be free. He refused to think of that. Not now. Instead, Cam daydreamed until he'd dozed off again. This time, it was Annie's rustling that roused him. When he cracked his eyes open, she was perched up on her elbow, grinning.

Cam arched a brow. "You look like the cat that caught a canary."

"I kind of did." She lay back down, curling her hands under her head. "You call me Kitten, after all."

He huffed a laugh.

"What were you dreaming of?" she asked. "You were smiling in your sleep."

"I was thinking about those cinnamon buns we had on New Havana."

"We?" Her grin widened. "You devoured those, not me."

"I offered." He took her hand out from under her, brushing his thumb over his mother's ring on her finger. "Also, I was thinking maybe you'd want a proper wedding when all of this is over."

"Absolutely not." Annie pressed a kiss to his brow before sitting up, her hair frizzing around her like a snowy halo. "The first time was terrifying enough. I don't want to do it again."

Cam rolled onto his back and closed his eyes. "As you wish. You'd look lovely in white, though."

"You could wear it, if you like," Annie replied, then hesitated. "Do you want one? Another wedding?"

Cam peeked at her. "I just want you to be happy."

"I *am* happy." She shot back in her usual flat tone. Her smile returned as he held back a giggle. "I think you just like every chance you can to show off."

"Preposterous." He snorted. "I couldn't outshine you if I wanted to."

"We do have another wedding to plan for," she said. "Jenny will spare no expense. Nor will she have any qualms about spending your money."

"*Our* money," he corrected. "And I have no doubts. A trait she and Nathan share. He'll be drunk for a week."

Annie rolled her eyes before they found the clock. Seven in the morning. She frowned. "I slept in."

"Thank God," Cam groaned, tucking the blanket under his chin. "No one in their right mind gets up at five."

Annie swatted him, but he didn't miss the heaviness falling over her features. She knew as well as he did that they couldn't stay here forever. She scooted closer and tucked herself beside him again, using his arm as a pillow.

"We don't have to leave yet." He kissed her forehead. "I can bar the door. We can go back to bed . . . or do other things, but no one can *make* us leave."

Even as he said it, he knew it wasn't true. People would soon come looking for them. Especially after their dramatic exit at the train station.

"I thought The Order had stolen you from me yesterday," Annie murmured.

Cam made a face. "Stole me? I'm too old to be lured away with candy. Well, it depends on the kind, but you know what I mean."

"It was something Violet said." Annie ignored his comment. "That once Dr. Clarke got you to take the mark, you'd do as you were told. That it only took one yes. That you didn't have to know what you were agreeing to as long as you said it."

Say that you'll stand for Enoch. For the West. Say yes. Van had tried to shake his hand on the train and again at the meeting. *Shake on a yes?* Damn it, he'd even tried it when they'd first met.

Could he have really forced him under The Order's control like that? Hell, his father had tried to warn him, but hadn't been able to say the words out loud.

"That bastard." Cam shot out of bed and tugged on some clean clothes. Van had set a trap for him, and he'd been *this* close to falling for it because he hadn't known.

He hadn't, and he *should* have.

He needed answers—*real* ones—and there was only one place he was going to get them now.

Annie slipped on her robe, and as if she could read his mind, she said, "I overheard the governor order Dr. Clarke to be locked up in the estate house."

"I need to question him *without* my father present." Cam yanked on his boots before strapping on his gun belt. "He's implied more than once that there are things he can't tell me, and since I don't know how much influence Van has, I want him alone."

Annie nodded. "If the governor is there, you'll need someone to distract him and Maya. I'll come with you."

Cam sucked in a breath. "I hate to bring you with me, back into the hornet's nest, but leaving you here is just as dangerous."

"You told me before that this was my choice." Annie glared at him as she finished dressing. She crossed the room and grabbed his collar to bring his face down to hers. "*You* are my choice. Whether that means we leave, or you take Enoch, I don't care. Our enemies don't matter. I'd rather be fighting alongside you than spend the rest of my life drinking tea on a floral couch, understand?"

You are my choice. Cam pressed his forehead to hers. "I don't want the West. I never have."

"You might not get to decide." Her ice-blue eyes filled with sadness. "But know that if it comes to that, I will be with you."

Cam kissed her gently . . . at first. Annie sighed into his touch.

You are my choice. If ruling the West was the only option to keep her safe, then he would do it. With her, he would survive. He could be better.

He lifted her into his arms, pressing her back against the door. She pulled him tighter against her, fingers sliding beneath his shirt.

They didn't have to leave *just* yet.

Van could rot a bit longer.

As they approached the manor, Nathan sat on the steps outside the main entry. Dark circles shadowed his dark eyes.

"Nathan?" Cam slowed as his friend stood, a pang of guilt running through him. "What's wrong?"

"Nothing," Nathan replied too quickly. He ran a hand through his black curls. "Well, nothing at the moment. Jenny is exhausted, and I couldn't sleep. I figured you'd be coming this way. Thought I'd wait for you."

"Jenny and I would have died if it weren't for you." Annie surprised them both by giving the man a quick hug. "Thank you." She glanced at Cam. "I'll get started."

He squeezed her hand before she left, striding into the manor. A wave of terror seized him once she was out of sight. He wanted to grab her and run. Get on their ship and sail to the farthest corner of the ocean where no one would ever find them.

But that's what his mother had tried to do, and they killed her anyway.

A moment of silence passed before Cam finally exhaled. "Thank you."

"Thank you?" Nathan looked genuinely confused.

"You were there, and I wasn't." Cam inclined his chin

toward the entry, and Nathan followed him up the steps. "Also, I'm sorry."

"Where did that come from? Near-death experiences didn't used to make you sappy," Nathan laughed. He slowed, his smile fading. "But you did die, I suppose, and things are different now."

"I did. And they are." Cam turned to face him just outside the doorway. He struggled to get the words out. "I'm sorry I haven't been a better friend to you these last couple of months. It won't happen again."

Nathan's eyes darkened. "You're my captain—"

"And your friend," Cam interrupted. "You're also my quartermaster. I should have kept you better informed. I should have come to you for ideas."

"What is it that Resh used to say? Don't worry about the should-a-would-a-could-a's," Nathan said. "Do you want my advice now?"

Cam fingered the handle of his revolver. "Yes."

"Are you going to find Dr. Clarke?"

"I am."

Nathan's lips curled up at the corners. "Jenny could have died in there, too. Make him pay."

Cam's fire flared to the surface. "You love Jenny?"

"I do," Nathan replied without hesitation. "And you love Annie?"

"I do." Cam gestured to the doorway. "Help me, then. Let's do this together, like old times."

"No . . . like, er, *new* times." Nathan rubbed his hands together.

Cam groaned. "That's the stupidest thing I've ever heard you say."

His friend flipped him off. "While I waited, I overheard

some of the staff talking about bringing food downstairs to their *guest.*"

"What are we waiting for, then?" Together, they headed into the manor. Cam knew precisely where Van would be. The main hall of the manor didn't have a downward staircase. At least not one visible to guests.

"Have you seen Julian?" Cam asked as they passed through the foyer.

"No." Nathan shook his head. "He tore out of the hospital, like a bat out of hell, after Annie vanished into her silver-sky thing. He didn't come back last night."

"Hmm." *I don't like that.* Cam swallowed down his nerves. Julian was known for keeping his own hours, but right after an attack?

The hall was empty as Cam led them through a side door into an adjacent room, filled with dusty, covered furniture and paintings. As a child, he would play here when his father wanted him out of the way. Of course, then, his mother had decorated the room in all his favorite colors and filled it with every kind of toy imaginable. They were gone now. Likely tossed or burned after they'd disappeared.

It also led to a private stairwell attached to the manor's lower level, which consisted of a small infirmary and some extra bedrooms for the family or staff to stay if they fell ill. His father was also often known to use the space as his makeshift dungeon.

"What about the governor?" Nathan asked as they descended the staircase.

"Annie will keep him busy," Cam said. As they entered the bottom floor, lights came from the hallway across from them, where the spare bedrooms were located. "You haven't asked why we're going alone."

"I don't care to know," Nathan replied. "As long as I get to take a swing at Van."

"Deal." Cam kept his voice low, his steps light. His father would have stationed guards outside Van's door. He hadn't thought about how he was going to get around them.

Wait. What am I doing? Cam straightened, dusting off the sleeves of his coat. He was a Callahan. It was time he started acting like it. He patted Nathan's elbow. "Just stay behind me and play along."

Nathan fell in line as they entered the hallway. Just as he expected, two thickly muscled blokes in heavy trench coats stood outside one of the bedroom doors.

They turned instinctively, bristling, but their eyes widened when they realized who was approaching. "My lord—"

"Leave. Now." Cam's fire coiled around him, filling his eyes. "And if either of you says a word, I'll burn your tongues out. Then maybe your eyes. *Then* I'll kill you."

The guards dropped their heads and scurried out of the hall without a fight.

After their footsteps had long faded away, Nathan let out a low whistle. "That was handy."

"If maybe a tad dramatic," Cam chuckled. He turned the door handle. It wasn't locked. *Odd.* Nathan stiffened, reaching for his gun, as he let the door swing open.

Inside, the room looked exactly as it had when he was young. A single bed sat against the right wall, covered in gaudy, magenta bedding. There were no windows. The only light came from a lit candle on the narrow bedside table. A matching rug was tossed over the oak floor.

Van Clarke sat at the four-person table in the center, staring at them, a spoonful of watery porridge halfway to his mouth. As he realized who'd entered, horror twisted the visible half of his face. The other side was wrapped in stained bandages, fluids already leaking through the linen. His left arm was wrapped and in a sling.

Van awkwardly set his spoon down as they entered.

"I didn't realize my father treated his prisoners so well." Cam closed the door behind him, the glow of his brands illuminating the space. "I'd say it's too good for you, Van."

Nathan smirked as he casually leaned against the closed doorway, folding his arms over his chest.

Van watched, wide-eyed, as Cam sat across from him, propping his feet up on the table.

The doctor pushed his bowl away before trying to take a sip from the mug beside it, the contents spilling down his chin. Cam nudged a napkin toward him.

Van wiped his mouth, clearing his throat. "M-my sister?"

"What do you think?" Cam's expression turned serious. "You were right. Violet tried to kill Annie. It didn't turn out well for her."

"I see." Van folded the napkin, laying it over his lap. "I'm sure you were overjoyed to hear it."

"Not really." Cam's jaw clenched. "As hateful as your sister was, she was still a lady. I didn't want her harmed. She's dead because of *you*. Because whatever plan you made failed."

"I'm aware," Van snapped, and spittle flew from his mouth. "Just as I am aware of why you're here."

Cam rose a brow. "Enlighten me."

"I know your type." Van straightened, his voice edged in fear. "You want information, but not until you beat it out of me like a common brute. I will have you know that I have no stomach for violence, despite my profession. I will not stand up well under torture and would prefer to avoid it."

"Close your mouth, Van, your breath stinks of hypocrisy," Cam replied. "You attacked the entire council."

"That was a different situation." Van took another sip,

managing not to spill it this time. He slapped his good hand on the table, sloshing his porridge. "Well, get on with it. How shall you brutalize me first?"

"You just said I didn't have to. I won't beat you." Cam glanced over his shoulder at Nathan. "I *did* promise my friend here that he could take a shot at you, though. See, Violet almost killed his lady, too."

Van went pale as Nathan cracked his knuckles, grinning wildly. Van shoved his chair back, as if to make a run for it, but Nathan was faster. He slammed his fist into Van's cheekbone, making a satisfying crunching sound. The doctor let out a short scream, which turned bloodcurdling as he fell backward and hit the ground, landing on his blistered arm.

"Put a cork in it." Nathan jerked him upright, setting him back in his chair. Van's breaths were ragged as Nathan took his position back by the door.

"There." Cam clapped, making Van jump. "That wasn't so bad, was it? Now you can tell me everything I wish to know. No more bruises."

Van composed himself, rubbing at his swelling cheek. "I have a condition."

"Of course, you do." Cam dropped his feet to the floor. "There's always a condition."

"Protect me," Van stated with a nervous swallow. "I will be torn apart when Henry Bale learns I talked. Take me under your protection, and I promise to hide nothing from you. I've never liked him, anyway."

This feels like another trap. He looked to Nathan again, who shrugged. Cam turned back. "I'll consider it."

"But—"

"Don't push me." He drew his revolver, twirling it around his fingers. "I'm tempted just to be rid of you. Prove to me why you should live."

"Alright, alright." Van glanced around like the walls were listening. "Just don't shoot me."

He's actually going to talk. Cam shifted in his seat. Van's willingness made him uneasy, but they were running out of time. Beggars couldn't be choosers. But where to start?

Cam studied him. "What would have happened if I'd said yes?"

"Are you reconsidering?" Van looked hopeful. Cam cocked back the hammer on his revolver, causing the doctor to lean back in his chair.

"Take it easy." He wiped at the sweat beading on his brow, then hesitated. He raised his left hand, showing the phoenix tattoo under his broken ring finger. "These marks are blood oaths. *Dark magic,* if you will. Your willing 'yes' and the contact with my mark would have branded you. Giving The Order—more specifically, a certain individual *in* The Order—control of you. Temporarily. Until more permanent oaths could be made."

Cam's brows furrowed. "So, *you* would have owned me?"

"Not me, no." Van shook his head. "I'm just a conduit. Control would have been given to the one *I* am bound to."

Blazes. Cam scowled. "Bale."

"Henry Bale," Van said nervously. "Enoch was put under his charge after his father's passing."

Cam had many memories of the Bales's lodge. His father spent a considerable amount of time with them. *Maybe that's who my father was bound to.* He'd mentioned that Henry's father had died . . . one year ago.

At the same time that he'd hired Elias to find him.

"How does it work?" Nathan stepped closer to the table, making Van flinch. "How can ink in the skin manipulate someone like that?"

"It isn't ink, boy." Van showed his hand again. "There are

men—high masters, and later their children—who've had their life forces siphoned. Corrupted. Then when they are mere breaths from death, their life is returned. Returned, but changed. This corruption not only grants special abilities but also the power to corrupt others. To control them." He gave Cam a dark look. "You've seen it before."

"The soldiers at the Embassy," Cam replied. "And the ones who attacked your home."

"Yeah, why attack your own house?" Nathan chimed in, scratching his chin. "That doesn't make any sense."

"I wasn't *attacking* my house." Van nodded to Cam. "I was under orders to capture him and his wife, and to eliminate as many Revenants as possible in the process."

"Why?" Cam asked.

"Because Revenants are dangerous to us," Van explained, cradling his wounded arm. "It takes considerably more power to corrupt them. I wasn't even sure if I could take control of you, but Henry insisted I try." Van let out a laugh. "Did you know that Revenants only began to appear after The Order was created? Like a cosmic balance. Why do you think Elias Bennett was obsessed with the idea of predicting Revenancy?"

Cam must have looked surprised because Van laughed again.

"I know all about Elias's work with Richard Duskin," Van continued. "He thought he could create a Revenant army, loyal to The Order. It could have worked. It did with Frank Boyle. He petitioned Henry for help in corrupting them, but Henry's resources were too slim to share."

The Order has known what you are for years. Cam recalled his father's words to Annie. *They've been hunting for Death Brands since Revenants came to be, and when they discovered what Cam could be . . . you two were doomed to find each other, one way or another.*

He thought he knew what—or *who*—these resources were. Death Brands.

"That's why they're so desperate for Annie," Cam said, mostly to himself. "Because without her, they can't continue the corruption."

"And spreading corruption takes a lot of *power*," Van added. "Which is why they need you. And you're the heir to the West? It couldn't be a more perfect combination."

"But that Davis fellow didn't want Cam to be governor," Nathan said. "He's working with you, isn't he? Why would half of you try to force Enoch on him, while the other tries to rip it away?"

"Henry had his reason. One he didn't share with me." Van gave Cam a once-over. "And where is your Annie now? At this very moment?"

Cam exchanged a glance with Nathan—who looked as unnerved as he felt—before answering. "With Maya."

Van didn't need to know that she was with his father, too.

"Maya," Van tsked. "Did you ever bother to ask why the governor remarried? No? Of course not. You're too arrogant for that."

Cam struggled to keep still as Van leaned forward, bracing against the table with his good elbow.

"Maya Callahan used to be Maya Lee," Van continued. "Sister to the Governor of the North, who, I may add, has long been under The Order's control. Henry's own personal spy, sleeping in your father's bed, bearing his son. How do you think Henry always knows where you're going and when? I've heard she's a good listener. So is the butler she insisted on bringing with her from her homeland."

David. Cam's blood went cold. David checked in on them every damn day. He could have gone through their things when they were out. Overheard their conversations.

"Bale could have taken us captive at any time." Cam pressed the barrel of his revolver under Van's chin. "Why let all this go on for so long? Why send you to do his dirty work when he knew you'd fail?"

"Because he and the governor had an arrangement." Van grinned at the way Cam's hands shook. "Isn't it odd that your father seemed so willing to hand over the West to you after everything he's gone through to keep it? After the governor attempted to defect, Bale offered him a bargain: One year to serve you and the city on a platter in exchange for his life. Elias slowed that down, though, didn't he?"

I'm running out of time. His father had told him that half a hundred times. The corruption killing him wasn't from defecting. It was because he hadn't fulfilled his bargain. That's why he'd hired Elias to find him. Had he been searching for him for that long before Port Lebanon?

"I'm going to tell you another secret." Van leaned in closer. "Yesterday was the last day to fulfill his promise, but now, time's up." He tapped his chin, his hideous bandages creasing as he smiled. "In fact, Henry's probably already waiting at the door to claim his prizes."

Lord above. Cam forgot how to breathe.

"And you're down here." Van scooted back. "And your dearest Annie is up there. With Maya. She's likely already wrapped her in a sweet bow for Henry to—"

Cam pulled the trigger.

Van's head exploded into a cloud of blood and bone.

Cam was out the door before his corpse hit the floor.

CHAPTER 57
ANNIE

Annie clenched her fists, her power *humming* as she strode into the Callahan manor. Her brands were stark white against her already pale skin. Last night, his fire had filled her, consumed her, pushed her to the edge of sanity, and she couldn't get enough. Even now, she wanted more. Because she could *feel* it—she could feel him—and that was the very reason he'd cracked her defenses from the start.

After years and years of nothingness, he made her feel again.

Cam's warmth reached for her as she moved into the entry, silently begging her not to go.

He was as afraid of being separated again as she was. *They won't take him from me.* Annie exhaled, head high. *I won't let them.*

She'd make sure no one interrupted Cam's interrogation.

Annie smoothed back her hair, making sure no flyaways had escaped her neat bun. Her heart was beating too hard. Inside, the foyer was empty. Voices carried from further down the main floor, likely the maids had started their daily clean-

564

ing. Her power stretched out without her permission, blanketing the hall, searching. She couldn't feel Alexander.

But she *could* feel someone watching her.

Annie glanced up the staircase just as a voice called, "Welcome, Lady Callahan."

David.

"I'm glad to see you well this morning." The dark-haired butler gave her a curt bow. "How may I be of service?"

"I need to see the governor," Annie replied, keeping her tone low and emotionless.

"He's not in." David straightened. "Council business. But the other Lady Callahan and the young lord are upstairs taking their morning tea. Would you like to join them?"

"I would." Annie forced a weak smile. David gestured for her to follow. She started up the staircase after him. *Council business already?* After yesterday's chaos, she supposed there would be many ruffled feathers. When she'd seen the governor, stepping off the train, he'd looked fractured and sickly. He should be resting, not bustling across the city.

I haven't seen Kai in days. Despite the villa's proximity to the manor, Kai rarely left the house, nor was he allowed to visit unless Maya was present. *She keeps him close.* But could she blame her? With cultists running rampant, Enoch wasn't safe for any eight-year-old, let alone the governor's youngest son. *Cam's brother.*

Which made Kai her brother-in-law. She hadn't had a real family—besides Jenny—since her own was killed. But she supposed she did now. A family. All her own.

And The Order wants to take it from you. Annie held the thought, fuming over it, before she set it free. Yes, she could understand Maya's paranoia.

She even pitied her.

At the end of the second-floor hallway, David opened the

door to Maya's tearoom and waited for her to step inside. Sitting on the floral sofa was Maya, sipping from a steaming, gold-rimmed cup. Kai was curled up beside her, a book opened on his lap, brown hair askew, as he nibbled on a biscuit. The fire dragon—Brantley—lounged on the back of the sofa, appearing to be napping, as its spiked tail twitched.

It's still here. Annie had forgotten about the dragon. Even after everything that happened, Cam still kept it formed, alive.

Maya's surprised gaze shot up to her, dark circles shadowing her upturned eyes. She smiled and nudged Kai to straighten before gesturing to the chair across from them.

"Annie, please, sit!" She gave her butler a pointed look. "David, may you bring us a fresh pot of tea?"

"And more cookies!" Kai chimed in. The dragon startled awake, blinking at Annie.

"You've had enough sugar," Maya scowled. "Just tea."

"Of course, my lady." David gave another quick bow, then left, closing the door gently behind him.

"Please," Maya repeated, once again gesturing to the chair. Tired eyes aside, Maya was immaculate, even at the early hour. She wore a flattering, rose-gold day gown with a large bow cinched around her waist. Dangling, gold earrings brushed against her neck, her black hair twisted into a tight knot. Even her cheeks were painted pink, a matching hue staining her lips. Perfect. She was always perfect. It wasn't natural.

Annie tucked her skirts beneath her as she sat. Kai watched her curiously, fiddling with the pages of his book. Maya poured and offered Annie a cup of dark tea, the scent full of spices.

"It's not hot," she said as Annie took the cup. "But it's good."

It smelled nice. "Thank you."

After fifteen minutes of pleasantries, Maya smirked a little. "Marriage suiting you well? You're positively glowing."

"Erm, yes." Annie's cheeks grew hot. She finally took a sip. It *was* good, even cold. "Just the two of you this morning?"

"Father left before the sun was up." Kai's steel-grey eyes narrowed. "Where's Camden? He still hasn't taken me to see your ship."

"We will," Annie replied. *Maybe one day, when we leave this place, we'll take you with us.* "When things settle down, we will."

"Pinkie promise?" Kai held out his little finger. "Swear it."

Maya scowled. "Kai—"

How can two people who've hardly met be so similar? Annie looped her pinkie through his and shook. "Pinkie promise."

Kai beamed, sitting back and scratching the dragon's chin. "Camden said that Brantley will protect me. We don't have to worry about bad men as long as he's around."

"Go find David, won't you?" Maya patted her son's elbow. "See if he needs help."

"If I must." Kai nodded, then hopped off the sofa. He gave Annie a curt bow before heading out of the room, the fire dragon at his heels.

Maya let out a long sigh, rubbing her temple. "That creature will be the death of me."

"Kai?" Annie smiled. "Or the dragon?"

"It's *Brantley this* or *Brantley that.*" Maya shook her head. "He plays with it all day. It guards the end of his bed at night. Sometimes I feel like it's watching me."

"It sounds like Kai was lonely. It's good for him to have a companion." Annie took another sip of tea, as sudden tears burned the corners of her eyes. *Just like Cam was lonely. He gave his brother the friend he never had.* Was that piece of his fire sentient from him now, or had he maintained the focus this entire time, keeping it burning, just for Kai?

"So, I've been told," Maya sniffed, a hint of bitterness in her tone. She took another quick breath, her mood returning pleasant. "Tell me, Annie, do you have siblings?"

"I had two brothers." Annie's stomach twisted uncomfortably. "They're dead."

"Your mother?" Maya asked.

"Died giving birth to me."

"No sisters?"

"No." Annie's brow rose. "Why ask?"

"Just curious." Maya refilled Annie's cup and handed it back to her. "I know so little about you."

"I'm sure you know plenty about me." Annie sipped more tea, mostly to appease Maya's persistent stare. She didn't know how long Cam needed to make Van talk, but the staff wouldn't intervene unless Maya told them to. *I need to keep her talking.* "What happened in the city that the governor needed to address it himself? Couldn't he have sent someone?"

"You know how these Callahan men are." Maya shrugged, glancing at the clock. "They're not the most trusting."

"True." Annie's stomach ached. She should have eaten something. "But that still doesn't answer my question."

Maya's dark brows knit together. "I didn't know I was required to answer it."

"My apologies," Annie said, the pain in her stomach shifting to her sides. "I didn't mean to offend you."

"You didn't." Maya glanced at the clock again. "I-I'm sorry. It's not you. I shouldn't have been so cross. It's been a tough several days."

"Did something happen?" Annie asked. "To you, I mean? Here?"

"Plenty has happened here." Maya turned back to her. "Don't fret over it. Finish your drink."

Something is wrong. The pain snuck up into Annie's chest now, making it hard to breathe. She stared down into her cup.

Maya also drank the tea. She watched her. It couldn't be poisoned—

Then Elain was there, solid white eyes wild as she pointed at the door, mouthing words Annie couldn't understand.

Annie shrieked, spilling the cold liquid down the front of her dress.

Maya was on her feet, panicking. "What is it?"

"Where have you *been?*" Annie hissed at Elain through the pain. She didn't care if Maya was listening. "It's been *weeks*. Where did you go?"

Elain's speaking turned to screaming. She grabbed Annie's arms, trying to shake her, but her ghostly fingers passed through her skin.

She understood two words, though. *He's here.*

"*Whose* here?" Annie asked.

Maya paled.

A suffocating heat filled the tearoom, setting the door aflame. Maya screamed, leaping up, as it flew off its hinges, crashing into the sofa inches from where she sat.

Cam—

Annie doubled over and retched. Stars flickered across her vision at the same time as he grabbed her elbow.

"*Sit down,*" Cam growled. The hatred in his voice made her look up. His revolver was trained on Maya's head as he hauled Annie up and against his chest. Blood. She could smell it. It was splattered over his jacket.

"Don't." Maya burst into tears, slumping into the smoldering couch. "I didn't—"

"What did you do to her?" Cam was screaming now, pulling Annie tighter. It felt like she didn't have any bones in her legs. "*What did you do?*"

"He would have killed him," Maya wailed, inching toward the edge of the sofa. "I didn't have a choice."

Kai. She means Kai. Annie's body was leaden.

"We need to leave." With her back to his chest, Cam dragged her toward the doorway, his aim never leaving Maya. "*Now.*"

"Nathan?" Annie managed through numb lips.

"He went to get Jenny." Cam couldn't hide the terror in his voice. He scooped her into his arms. "Bale—"

As he turned toward the hall, Henry Bale stood behind them, grinning as he sank a syringe into Cam's neck.

Cam went rigid, a violent shudder rolling down his body as Henry pulled the syringe free.

Annie cried out as Cam's arms went limp. His eyes rolled back into his head as he dropped to the floor, taking her with him. Annie's back hit the polished marble, knocking the air out of her lungs. Darkness clouded her eyes as she desperately tried to inhale, rolling onto her side.

Cam lay beside her, eyes closed, their limbs tangled together. His brands went dark.

"*No.*" Annie couldn't get the words out. She tried to crawl to him, but her arms gave out.

"Hello, love." Henry crouched down beside her, tilting his head to look at her face. "Time's up, I'm afraid."

"*Cam—*" She managed. *Don't touch him. I can't breathe. You have to get up.*

"Will live as long as you co-operate." Henry rolled Cam onto his back. He pulled a thin knife from his boot, pressing it hard enough against his throat that bright red blood leaked down his tanned skin. Henry glanced up and winked at Maya. "Isn't that right?"

Maya wept, burying her face into the sofa's charred pillows.

I can't stop him. Her body was turning to stone. She tried to drag her power to the surface. It squirmed, muted.

"Do you like that?" Henry held up the syringe. A small amount of a violet-black substance swirled inside it.

No.

The fluid from Mr. Baxter's lab.

"It's a neurological toxin made from the essence of our corruption. Crafted precisely for neutralizing Revenant power." He flexed his fingers, showing the darkness spreading through his veins. With a cruel laugh, he lifted Cam's hand and then let it drop. "You can thank yourself for this. Without the Pearl Dust, Magnus would never have gotten it to work. He's a loyal little man. I may have given our friend here too much, but I'm sure he'll be fine."

Henry tapped her on the nose. This was the most lively she'd ever seen him. "I only tell you because I know you're as fascinated by the medicinal arts as I am. It works when ingested, too, as we've just discovered. Thank you for being my test subject."

"But Maya—" *I saw her drink it.*

"—isn't Revenant." He tapped her nose again.

She'd kill him if she could move. Several sets of heavy footsteps moved up the hall, towards them. She tried to blink, but her eyelids wouldn't open again.

As the last of her consciousness slipped away—slowed by the sensation of someone lifting her—Henry whispered in her ear. "Remember, sweetheart, his life's in your hands."

CHAPTER 58

ALEXANDER

Alexander's driver dropped him off in the courtyard, waiting until he was striding for the manor before pulling the carriage away towards the stable.

Five hours of smoothing over angry councilmen, giving condolences and restitution for lost loved ones, and being the pin cushion for mountains of complaints—now he just wanted to go to bed. Alone. For the rest of the day. Van Clarke would have to wait, though he was sure he'd hear more complaints about that, too, coming from his son.

There was only so long he could push. He couldn't make it any further this afternoon. He just needed a breather.

He hadn't died yet, which meant he still had time.

Henry hadn't come for them last night. He couldn't possibly know the exact hour their bargain would come due. He must have made a miscalculation.

The sky opened up as Alexander dragged his aching body under the cover of the main entry, stopping short when he found Kai sitting on the ledge of its wide, double doors. That dreadful, red dragon splayed out on his lap.

"Kai?" He questioned as he drew closer, gaining his youngest's attention. "What are you doing out here?"

"Mother is beside herself right now." Kai's posture shrank, as if expecting to be punished. "She didn't want me to see her crying. Also, I think Brantley is sick." A tear fell as he stroked the dragon's head, its once blazing gold and red scales now barely glowed. "Everything's wrong. I don't know how to fix it."

No. Alexander's heart stopped and started, making him wobble. He gripped his chest, trembling, as he knelt and touched the dragon's side. It was cold.

"When?" Alexander couldn't look at Kai. Not when he'd failed him, *both* of them. Again.

"Men came," Kai whispered. "Not long ago. Camden's gone."

No, not yet. Alexander tore frantically through his coat pockets, searching for his pocket watch. *I must have hours yet. I was so sure. The deal—*

But the watch was with Camden.

He couldn't think. All he wanted was a damn moment where his skin wasn't *itching.*

I don't know how to fix this, either. Alexander stood and pulled up his sleeve. The corruption had taken over his arm, turning it black. When he inhaled, his lungs rattled.

Alexander had lost track of time. He'd never been good at keeping it.

"Stay here," Alexander said as he knelt and kissed his son's head. Kai blinked at him in shock. "Protect your mother. I'll make Brantley better. I'll bring your brother back. I promise."

Kai grinned and wiped his runny nose on his sleeve. "You will?"

Tugging the boy into a tight hug, he could feel Kai hesitate before hugging him back.

My God, I've never hugged him before. "I will," he reassured the child. "Don't be afraid."

With that, Alexander headed back into the rain, making his way towards the stables.

Whatever time he had left—whether minutes or hours—he'd give it to his sons.

He would make this right.

He refused to die just yet.

CHAPTER 59

CAMDEN

Muffled voices surrounded him, fading in and out. He couldn't decide if they were real, even as he was being poked and prodded. He wasn't sure if *that* was real, either. Occasionally, there was pain. Mostly, there was nothing.

I've forgotten something. Cam knew it in his bones, but no matter how hard he thought, struggling through the thick muck of his mind, he couldn't place it. He curled his stiff fingers. *What did I forget?*

A voice—loud and clearer than the rest—pierced through the fog. "He shouldn't be awake yet."

Annie. Cam's fire exploded, only to hit a wall inside him. He slammed against it, over and over, but it wouldn't budge. His fire crept back, enraged, like an animal in a cage. When he tried to open his eyes, they felt heavier than steel slabs. He winced at the blinding light shining right over his face. His tongue like chewing on a dry sponge. *"An-nie."*

She'd been poisoned.

Maya had done it.

They had to leave.

"Should I inject him again?" The voice was unmistakable this time. Magnus Baxter.

What the hell? Where was he? Cam tried to turn his head, but something kept him from moving. As he blinked through the murky shroud on his senses, another voice answered.

"No, let him be." *Bale.*

They'd been at the manor. Van. He'd found Annie upstairs and she was . . .

"W-here is s-she?" Cam managed as he tried to sit up. He couldn't move. With a groan, he heaved against whatever bound him, and raw pain seared into his wrists and ankles. *Chains.*

"You two are like parrots. Constantly squawking." Henry Bale's voice was flat, bored. When Cam reached for his fire again, trying to melt his binds, Bale laughed.

He rattled the metal links. "That's not going to work, I'm afraid. I made them just for you. Well, our mutual friend, here, did. I shouldn't take the credit."

Now that his eyes had cleared, Cam shifted enough to see Magnus standing in the corner, wringing his knobby hands. Soot stained the Flora Brand's trousers, still hiked nearly to his armpits. Behind his glasses, his eyes were filled with endless regret.

When he noticed him watching, Magnus rushed to the edge of the table—a table, he was chained to a table. He tried to jerk away, but his binds held him.

"Please forgive me, my lord, this was not my intention." Magnus's words were frazzled, panicked. "I beg you and your lady's pardon. You *can* get free, you can. I know you will—" He let out a low, pained squeak when Bale struck him on the spine with the handle of his pistol.

"Get out," Bale growled. "Before you annoy me more than your skills are worth. Leave."

Magnus struggled to his feet, pleading for more forgiveness before he left the chamber.

I recognize this place. He was in Magnus's blasted lab. The ceiling was still split in half, the walls charred black from his last visit. The viewing glass had been repaired. Now it was tinted—separating the testing chamber from the room beyond. He wanted to be angry at Magnus, but it was pretty damn obvious the man hadn't had a choice.

But why bring me all the way here?

And where was Annie?

"Don't listen to that algae-stained fool." Bale leaned against the table, giving the chains another firm tug. "Baxter knows too much, but he doesn't know everything. If it weren't for my superiors, I would have taken care of him a long time ago." He took a syringe out of his pocket, turning it over in his palm, swirling the black-violet contents. "No, you're not going anywhere. He was as wrong about that as he was wrong about this poison. The essence of corruption."

His mouth slowly fell into a scowl. "Baxter promised me it would keep you incapacitated for twelve hours. You started waking after thirty minutes. I've had to inject you six times. *Six.* Such a waste. You have no idea how expensive this was to create."

I've been out for three hours? Cam tried to swallow, but it felt like he was choking on sand. "Where is she?"

"More squawking," Bale sneered, his upper lip hidden beneath his mustache. "Lady Callahan will be fine. For now. How long she stays that way depends on you."

"Of course." Cam let out a raspy laugh. "Is this where you start your villain monologue? You're not even original."

"No." The chief leaned over him, breath giving off a rotten

odor. "I don't have time for all that. This is where I start torturing you. And I will continue to do so until there's nothing left of you but the pieces I wish to keep."

Great. He couldn't do anything with that poison in his system. He could feel his fire trying to crawl back by the second. If he could keep Bale busy, busy enough not to notice when his power returned, he could get out of here. He would find her.

"If that's the case, I'll tell you a secret." Cam spat in Bale's face, who recoiled. "Start with my sides. A feather will do. I'm terribly ticklish."

As Bale glared at him, wiping the spit off his cheek, the vein in his temple bulged. This time, darkness showed through his skin, more of it webbing the corners of his eyes.

"Sir?" A heavily muscled guard peered through the door, the bright overhead lights reflecting off his bald head. "We found Callahan skulking about outside. He's demanding to see you."

"Hell below," the chief cursed. After a moment, his cracked lips curled into a smile. "Bring him in."

Several minutes later, Cam bit back an audible gasp when his father stepped into the testing chamber. Alexander had aged twenty years overnight. His hair had gone completely grey. The lines around his eyes were a crevasse. He wobbled, bracing against the doorframe, tired eyes widening when he took in Cam strapped to the table.

Alexander sucked in a breath as he moved a few steps closer. "Henry."

"Chief Bale." Bale corrected. "I'm about to start carving your son into bite-sized pieces. Have you come to help or beg some more?"

Anger burned through Cam's blood, and the memory of Van's words came rushing back. *He traded me for his own life.*

More betrayal. What bothered him most was that somewhere, in the hidden places of his soul, he'd started to believe his father cared, just like he'd started to trust him. That, perhaps, he'd been a victim of The Order—but that was a lie, too—a trick to get his guard down.

"Let me speak to Camden. Alone." Alexander struggled to breathe. "Give me another chance."

"The answer is no." Bale gritted his teeth. "You've had a year's worth of chances. I've wasted enough time on you."

"Damn it, Henry," Alexander yelled. "I've known you since you were born. Give me ten more minutes. Please."

Bale's hand twitched toward his pistol, face turning beet red. Finally, he sighed. "*Two* minutes. My last gift to a dying man. You're welcome. But remember, I will be watching."

Henry pushed Alexander aside as he stalked out of the chamber. His father broke out into a coughing fit, red spittle dotting his pale lips.

Kill him. Cam's fire surged, clawing for the surface, and he couldn't agree more. If it weren't for the chains, he would have already ended the precious life he'd traded for him.

Alexander took another step toward the table. "Camden—"

"Burn in hell." He refused to look at him.

"You need to listen to me." Alexander was at his side now. "There isn't much time."

"There is no more time." Cam struggled against his chains. "Now get closer so I can spit on you, too—"

Alexander punched him in the stomach. Cam gasped as his breath left him in an audible *whoosh*. The pain made his vision flicker.

How? Before, in the morgue, when his father had struck him, he'd felt nothing. It had been less than a fly bite.

The corruption. The substance didn't just blanket his power, it smothered out pieces of his Revenancy completely.

As long as he was drugged, he would endure Bale's torture like a mortal. *I'm so damn screwed.*

"*Listen to me.*" Alexander grabbed Cam's chin while he still fought for air. "Henry needs to think I'm trying to convince you to bow to him. Play along. Annie is being held at the Lodge. Do you understand me?"

Bastard. Cam managed to nod between ragged inhales.

"Below ground, the Order keeps a sanctum there," his father continued. "I think I can get her out, but I need more time. Bale will come for her, but only once you've taken the mark."

"I won't—"

Alexander punched him again, this time in the jaw.

Cam blacked out for a moment, only to wake to Alexander's furious whispering.

"He will torment you, Camden." God, his father smelled like putrid flesh. "Not just your body, but your mind. He will make you see things that are worse than death, but you *must not take it.* No matter what he shows you, what you hear. He won't *kill* Annie, but he will turn her into something worse than the Duskins ever could. He'll tell you submission is the only way to keep her safe. Alexander made Cam look at him. "*Do not take it.* Do not do what I did."

Cam tried to blink away the dark spots in his vision. "Annie …"

"Endure," Alexander answered. His entire body was trembling. "Do not break. Do *not* break. Keep that ridiculous dragon you made for Kai alive. I will send a signal, then you will blow them to hell. Get to the Lodge. Do you understand?"

Do not break. Cam dipped his chin only enough for him and his father to see.

A wave of relief washed over Alexander's features. "Good."

He shouldn't have said it, but the words rushed out before he could stop them. "How could you bargain me away . . . *again?*"

Alexander's face crumpled. Whatever hold Bale had on his tongue seemed to be slipping. "I made that bargain to keep you free for a little while longer. I wanted you to have a chance."

"You wanted to keep yourself alive."

"I did," he admitted. "I needed time to fix this. I needed you to learn who not to trust—"

The door opened before he'd finished speaking. The bald guard stormed in and roughly grabbed his shoulder.

Bale swept in behind him. "You had your two minutes. Now it's my turn." He waved the guard away. "Toss the governor outside. Let him die with the rats."

Before he was dragged away, Alexander shot Cam a last desperate look and mouthed, *"Do not break."*

He wouldn't. He refused to.

Once they were gone, Bale leaned over him again, smiling. "Has anyone ever told you what you are, Camden Callahan?"

"I'm sure you're going to tell me," Cam drawled.

"You are but another in generations and generations of puppets." Blackness crept up the veins in Bale's neck, onto his jaw, spreading across his face. "I will own you, like my father owned your father, and my grandfather owned yours, on and on and on. You were always meant for me. Like a pet." A viscous black mist spread across his open palm, his eyes alight with madness. "You will rule the West at my command. All while fueling Annie's power, allowing my Order to spread further than it's ever had the strength to reach."

"That's all very interesting, but I don't understand your lot." *God help me.* Cam swallowed, staring at the darkness whirling in Bale's hand. "Why use me when you could rule Enoch yourself? What's stopping you from taking it?"

"What is it that you called me before? A villain?" Bale laughed. "Most don't like bowing to villains. No, it's much more fun to pull the people's strings from the shadows." He rolled back his sleeves, revealing blackened veins up to his elbows. "I've been waiting for this for a long time. Let's have some fun."

Cam thrashed as Bale placed his palm over his face. The darkness latched onto him, drilling a hole of gnawing agony through his temples until it had burrowed so deep into his mind that there was nothing left but him and Bale and whatever hell that was threatening to drown him.

He gasped, panting, as his eyes shot open. The pain had faded, but he was no longer in Magnus's lab. He was in a chair. The dark-paneled walls creaked against a howling wind, allowing rain to seep through the cracks in the window glass and rot the floorboards beneath.

This is a warehouse. He'd been in enough of them to recognize the lingering stink of booze and gunpowder. When he tried to move, his muscles were locked in place.

This can't be real. Yet, he wasn't sure if visions could mimic the salt spray of the sea and his thundering heart. He gritted his teeth, straining against his invisible binds, but no amount of force made any difference. He was trapped.

"Don't hurt yourself."

Cam froze. Behind him, Bale squeezed his shoulders.

"Struggling won't work," he murmured in his ear. "Trust me."

If he wasn't panicking before, he was panicking now. He couldn't even move his head enough to look at him. "W-what the hell is this?"

"My playground." Bale stepped in front of him, grinning. "What I say here goes. Do you like it?"

"You're a sick freak, you know that?" Cam didn't sound nearly as confident as he wanted.

Bale shrugged. "I've heard it takes one to know one. I think we'll get on wonderfully."

Cam shuddered when the man stepped behind him again.

"There are some things I wanted to show you." Bale pointed over his shoulder. "I thought they might help change your mind."

As Cam watched, the center of the warehouse blurred, as if it were losing its shape. The space remained empty . . . until he blinked.

Then a woman was there, sitting on the damp ground, wearing a grey cloak.

His mother.

His *mother*.

Cam's vision began to fade until Bale gave him a firm shake.

She looked . . . perfect. Not like she had in the days before she'd died, but when they'd been happy. When she'd dance with him, read to him, and remind him again and again that she loved him more than eternity itself.

Her cheeks even dimpled when she smiled at him, her thick, dark curls spilling over her shoulder. "Hello, Camden."

He'd forgotten her voice.

She smelled like rose petals. He'd forgotten that, too.

"This isn't real." He choked out.

"No." Henry squeezed him tighter. "But it feels real, doesn't it?"

A solid weight dropped on Cam's lap. He managed to glance down. A butcher knife lay over his thighs.

"*No.*" He slammed his eyes shut. "*Don't.*"

"Don't be like that." Henry tugged at his eyelids, pulling them apart in time to see his mother's gaze fall onto the blade. Her face went pale. Henry chuckled. "I thought you'd be happy to see her again."

"Stop." Cam's body moved without his permission, grabbing the hilt of the knife. Then he stood. *"Stop."*

"So soon?" Henry's laughter grew louder. "You know exactly what you need to say for this to stop."

"Camden?" His mother's words were a plea. Begging. "Please."

Do not break. No matter how hard he tried, he couldn't close his eyes again as he stepped across the warehouse. His body wasn't his anymore. And he knew this was what his life would be if he failed.

Bale hovered at his elbow as he stood over his mother, shaking, the knife clenched in his fist.

It seemed she couldn't move either. She just stared up at him, her voice the melody that used to sing him to sleep. "Goodbye, Camden. Remember, I love you."

"I know," he whispered, strangled by the tightness in his throat.

When he blinked again, fighting back tears, Annie appeared beside her, features cold and unyielding, dressed in layers of pure white—a wedding gown.

Endure. His mind cracked. "Please. Don't."

"You can make this end at any time." Bale pulled up the chair and sat, crossing one leg over the other, before he clapped. "Now begin."

It wasn't long before Cam started screaming.

CHAPTER 60
ANNIE

Annie snapped awake with a jolt.

She sucked in a ragged breath, attempting to stand, but her limbs weren't working right. Her wrists were bound behind her back, chaffing at her skin. Reflexively, she reached for her power, but it was still muted. Awake, but weak.

"Evening, Princess."

You've got to be kidding me. When she looked, Jensen Davis sat in the booth across from her. She was in a dim carriage, its windows locked tight.

"Before you ask," he said, swaying with the jostling gait of the horses pulling them. "Henry Bale has him. Don't worry, I'm sure your Camden will be fine. As long as he cooperates."

Cam. Annie swallowed back the terror crawling up her throat. Cooperating would mean taking the mark. *He never will.* She knew him better than that. The only way she could help him now was to get free. She had to stay focused.

"Where are we going?" Her lips were numb from the lingering poison in her blood.

"To your new home," Jensen replied. "I'm sure you'll love it."

"What does it hurt to tell me, then?"

Jensen rolled his eyes. "We're going to The Lodge. There, are you happy?"

The Bales's hunting lodge? Cam had mentioned it. Annie quickly scanned the interior of the carriage. There were no weapons she could see. Jensen was dressed in a casual jacket and trousers—no gun belt or knives holstered. *He doesn't expect me to be much of a threat.*

And at the moment, she wasn't one. Not with her power smothered and her limbs so stiff she could barely move. She glanced over her own clothes. Nothing looked out of place, and besides the ache where she'd landed on her back, her body felt fine. They hadn't hurt her. *Yet.*

She flexed her fingers, her brands now a dull black. *The substance drained all of my reserves.* "How long?"

"Until what?" Jensen's brow rose.

"Until we arrive, you idiot."

"That wasn't very ladylike." Jensen rested his elbows on his knees. "You should stop hanging out with pirates. They're a bad influence on you."

"How long?" Annie kept her expression blank.

Jensen sat back and huffed. "Fifteen minutes, at most."

Annie nodded. She tried to call her power again. Just a whisper of it answered back.

A short time later, the carriage lurched to a stop. The driver pulled the door open and bowed to him, the wind ripping through his curls. "My lord. My lady."

Jensen said nothing to him. He stepped out, reaching back inside to lift her into his arms.

"*Don't touch me.*" Annie scrambled away. "I can walk."

"Can you?" Jensen sneered at her as she stumbled out of the carriage. "You can barely stand."

Rain mixed with the wind, sticking her hair to her face. With her hands tied, she couldn't push it away. "I will walk."

"Suit yourself." Jensen shrugged. "You'll just wear yourself out."

Or move the substance through my body faster. Jensen grabbed her elbow, shoving her forward. On New Havana, Lord Duskin used to tell her and her adopted siblings that if a venomous snake ever bit them, they should stay calm, not run or panic. That would only make the venom work faster. This could work similarly. Maybe she could burn it off. It was worth a shot.

The Lodge looked just as Cam described it. *Massive* antlers were mounted above an arch of white stone, covered in runes. The pain in her joints made her move slowly, but she used the time to examine the carvings as they passed. *These are Northern.* There were marks like this on the well in her old village. She couldn't read them. Her father—her *real* father—could.

"*It's the history of our people,*" he used to say, pointing to a more recent carving in the rock. "*Every life. Every death. One day, a rune will be carved for you.*"

But a rune would never be carved for her. No one would even remember her. Was this the Bales's history? *Or The Orders?* She gave the stone one last, long look before Jensen dragged her inside.

She was overwhelmed by the scent of tobacco as they stepped into the main entry. It emanated from the pine slat walls. A brown bear-skin rug was tossed over the equally unfinished floors, its mouth agape, revealing teeth as long as her little finger. Jensen nudged her in the back, and she winced as her muscles spasmed.

I need to bide my time. Then she'd drain the life from him, down to the last drop.

He guided her around the corner, toward the west wing. Two men carrying rifles stood outside a door, pistols and swords on their hips. They nodded as they approached and opened it for them. As they stepped aside, Jensen gave them a curt nod.

She squinted as rows of gaslights sprang to life, illuminating a downward staircase. As the door closed, Jensen whispered, "I'm going to carry you now. I don't have time to watch you hobble down these like an old woman."

"Fine." She glared at him, but allowed him to lift her, only because she wasn't sure she'd make it on her own. He held her against his chest as he descended, and she recoiled at the unnatural cold spreading into her skin wherever he touched.

He chuckled at the movement. "Not what you're used to, I imagine?"

"No." Her teeth began to chatter. *Just a little longer.* "C-can we get this over with?"

"Quit wiggling, and I will." Jensen gripped her tighter. It was six flights down before they came to the bottom. He didn't waste time dropping her like a sack of flour. Annie barely managed to stay on her feet.

"Come on." Jensen grabbed her upper arm this time, dragging her further down the hall.

Annie's power stirred at the contact, hungry, but not quite strong enough to take hold. Already, she was walking faster.

Down here, so far beneath Enoch, only the gas lamps illuminated their path. Variations in the shadows indicated that adjacent hallways were splitting off from the main one. Every ten feet or so, they passed ornate numbered doors on either side. Her skin felt sticky with humidity, and the deeper they traveled, the more pungent the stink of chemicals grew.

Annie counted each step, imprinting it in her memory. She

glanced up when she felt eyes on her. Jensen was staring, his blond brows knit together in frustration.

"Why is this place so empty?" she asked.

"It's not empty." Jensen looked away, lips pinched together. "There are others. They don't want to be anywhere near you."

Interesting. Her wrists burned from the ropes, her shoulders aching. "Why?"

"Because of what you are," he answered.

"If I'm so dangerous, why did Bale leave you to transport me alone?" Her curiosity got the better of her. "Why not bring me himself?"

"To answer your first question, because he trusts me," Jensen replied smugly. "To the second, Bale's business with your prick husband is personal. Don't worry. He'll come for you when he's done with him."

Jensen stopped at the third-to-last door to the right, framed in red. He waved his hand over the heavy brass knob and winced when a cloud of darkness latched onto the phoenix tattoo beneath his finger. He hissed in pain as it released him. The door swung open, and he quickly undid the binds on her wrists before he shoved her inside.

She turned, only catching a glimpse of his face—which had gone bone white—before he slammed it shut again. He hadn't been looking at her this time, but *past* her.

"And who are you?" The voice was female, equally youthful and ancient, tinted with fatigue.

Annie stiffened and slowly twisted to face the center of the room. Though small, this one was well-lit. The walls were painted a deep burgundy, matching the upholstery on the sofa and pillows. Another bear rug lay on the floor—a black one, this time—and a four-poster bed sat against the center of the far wall, covered in thick fur blankets.

They were wrapped around the shoulders of a thin, white-haired woman, her locks tied in a haphazard knot on the top of her head.

She sat up straighter as Annie blinked at her.

"Who are you?" The woman repeated. She slid out of the bed, wearing nothing but an oversized nightgown. Swirling, black brands covered her exposed calves and arms, just like hers. From a distance, she could have been young, but as she drew closer, her age became apparent in the wrinkles around her eyes and mouth, the sagging in her jowls. Her glacier blue eyes scanned Annie.

"You're a little dove." Her shoulders drooped in relief. "I see they've finally found my replacement. Praise God."

"Your replacement?" Annie followed the woman as she wandered toward the sofa. She plopped down with a tired sigh and poured two glasses of clear liquid from the decanter on the table. She offered one to Annie, smiling when she noticed her hesitation.

"It's just water." She took a long drink of her own, smacking her lips. "Nothing nefarious here."

Slowly, Annie took the glass and took a sniff. It smelled fine. Her mouth and throat were painfully dry. She sat down on the rug before taking a careful sip. It tasted fine, too. The woman watched as she chugged down the rest of the glass.

"You still haven't answered my question," the woman said, offering to refill the glass.

Annie let her. "You haven't answered mine."

"I asked first."

She looks like me. Or at least, what she could look like if she had the chance to grow older. "My name is Annie Dus—Annie Callahan."

The woman cocked her head. "What name were you born with?"

"Beauman," Annie replied. "That was my father's name."

"Ah." The woman's eyes brightened. "By your look, I thought you might be mine. My sons only had sons. And those sons had more sons. Glad to see one of them finally had a daughter."

After our last conversation, Mr. Baxter had said, *I decided to see if I could track down the previous Death Brand I'd met, Clarisse. Of course, that was about two hundred and fifty years ago.*

Dear Lord. Annie's eyes shot wide. "Are you Clarisse?"

The woman threw back her head and laughed. "The only person outside of these walls who would remember that name is that old codger, Magnus Baxter. He used to grow me the loveliest pink roses. Small ones. They fit perfectly in a pot on my windowsill. Tell me, is he still alive?"

"He is." *And he betrayed us.* Wetness built up at the corners of Annie's eyes. If she was telling the truth, then Clarisse was her grandmother, generations back, and the only blood relative she had left.

"Did you know that he came all the way North to visit me?" Clarisse beamed. "I'd never left the country before they took me away." She gave her an inquisitive look. "Another man used to visit me. Here. His name was Elias. He said that they'd found a girl from my line, but his partner got greedy and sold her before they could bring her back to Enoch. He said he would find her, but that was years ago. I assumed she'd died, but that was you, wasn't it?"

"It was." *Elias Bennett.* Rage curled in her gut, and her brands flared. "It was Elias and his partner who killed our family. He's dead, too, now."

Clarisse scowled. "I'm sad to hear that. All of it."

Wait. Annie stared down at her glowing hands. *My power!* She could feel it, humming inside her, making her blood sing.

She leaped to her feet, her muscles still shaky, but strong. *There has to be a way out.*

Clarisse watched, brow raised, as she rushed to the door. She tried everything, even pouring her own darkness over the knob, but it didn't budge.

As she started working at the hinges, Clarisse asked. "What are you doing?"

"Leaving." Annie cursed and backed a step. The door was solid. "And you've yet to answer my question, though I know the answer. I refuse to be your *replacement.*"

"Sit down." Clarisse waved at her. "If there were a way out, don't you think I would have found it?"

That made Annie pause. *Of course, that was about two hundred and fifty years ago.* She ran her hands over the walls, searching for a weakness. "Have you really been here for over two centuries? In this room?"

"Not entirely in this room." Clarisse shook her head. "The Order has moved me several times, but now I'm getting old. I was old when they were formed. I was old when Revenants started being born by the thousands."

Annie grunted as she shoved the bed aside—nothing under there. "And you've been using your power to corrupt people's minds, steal their free will, and enslave them? Forgive me if I have little sympathy."

All the kindness drained from Clarisse's face. "You think I had a choice?"

"There's always a choice." Annie sat down on the rug again, folding her arms over her chest. "And I'll be damned if they're going to take mine."

She wouldn't tell the woman all the evil *she'd* done on New Havana to keep herself alive. Right now, she just needed a solution. One she wasn't getting.

Clarisse's expression softened. "You're a fiery thing, aren't you?"

"No." Annie's heart twisted, her throat growing tight. She glanced back at the door. "But my husband is."

"He can't save you, little dove. Not here."

"He will." Annie shot back, and she knew it was true. "We will get out of here, and he will come for us. He will."

"I wish I could believe that," Clarisse muttered.

She didn't have the energy to try to open a portal yet. Annie closed her eyes. When Bale came for her, she would be ready.

She'd never be a slave again.

CHAPTER 61
ALEXANDER

Henry had done exactly what he'd promised—he'd thrown Alexander into the street like trash.

His carriage was gone. They must have chased away his driver. Venomous pain lanced through his every muscle as he did the only thing he could do.

He walked.

For hours.

And though every step felt like his last, he didn't stop. Nor did he have to ask where Annie would be. He knew. He was well acquainted with the underground sanctums that The Order had carved out beneath his streets. He'd even met the Death Brand they kept below, the day he'd lost his freedom to Harrison Bale.

It had been six hours now since he found Kai sitting on the doorstep, and every minute that passed, his body grew weaker. He tasted the blood in his mouth with each breath, the constant racing of his heart, on the edge of failing.

His time was up. He wouldn't last the night.

He nearly collapsed in relief when The Lodge came into view.

I made it. Cassie, I made it. Frigid water pooled on the steps as he made his way toward the foyer, soaking into his boots. Alexander gripped his chest, willing his lungs to function. As focused as he was, he didn't notice the man lingering in the shadows by the door until he'd grabbed him, forcing his back against the wall, a dagger to his throat.

"Governor." Julian Price nicked the blade into his skin. "Fancy meeting you here."

"Price." Alexander held up his hands, showing that he was unarmed. "I hope we're here for the same reasons."

"I should bleed you like a pig." Julian squeezed the knife tighter, making Alexander wince. "You betrayed them—"

"I'm trying to save them, damn it," he growled. "And it would prove much easier if you'd get that blasted thing out of my face."

Julian cocked his head and smirked before taking a step back, pressing the tip of the dagger against Alexander's chest. "Better?"

"Don't be haughty," Alexander snapped. "You sound like Camden."

"Where is he?" Rain dripped down Julian's braid, soaking into his cloak. "I thought they'd transport them together, but from the chatter I've overheard, Miss Annie is the only one here."

And where were you? Alexander wanted to ask. *Why didn't you protect my son?*

The question escaped him. "Why weren't you there?"

"Why wasn't I—" Rage coated Julian's features. "I was trying to catch Bale, but he got away from me."

The creak of footsteps inside made them both freeze.

Alexander pulled Julian further away from the foyer and under the archway.

"I've spoken to Camden," he whispered as he listened for any more movement. "Henry has him. We have a plan. I'll send him a signal as soon as Annie is free from the building. He'll find us."

"Why wait until she's out? He'd have an easier time breaking in than we will. You've seen his destruction. He's like a toddler with building blocks."

"The Order designed the lower levels of the Lodge to collapse in the case of a Revenant breach," Alexander replied. "Annie would be crushed before we could get her out."

Julian cursed, sheathing his blade. "And how did you plan to rescue her? The entries look empty, but the interior of the building is crawling with guards. I'd rather not get in a gun fight."

Despite the pain radiating through him, Alexander smiled. "You forget that I'm still the Governor of the West, and a member of The Order. They can't stop me."

"And if they've been ordered to arrest you on sight?"

"Then, I guess, that's what you're here for."

"Fair enough. Lead the way, then." Julian bowed. "It's time for you to make amends."

Yes. Alexander headed for the main door. *I don't have much time left, but I can still do that.*

Julian fell in line beside him, his chin low, adopting the stance of a bodyguard. Alexander held his head high, maintaining a straight posture, as he shoved his hands into his pockets. As they entered, two armed guards stepped out of a side room, their faces drawn, veins threaded with corruption.

One of them hesitated as they recognized him.

The other didn't seem fazed by his status in the slightest. "The Lodge is closed today. Screw off."

"It's open for me." Alexander removed his glove, flashing the tattoo beneath his finger. Despite his rotting flesh, the outline was still visible, an ever-present reminder of his cowardice. "Step aside."

The guard flashed Julian a look. "No Stripes allowed."

"He's with me." Alexander brushed past them. He'd played this game long enough. He wasn't about to be slowed by a couple of hired thugs. "If your master has a problem with it, he'll know where to find me."

Julian's expression never changed as they continued down the hall.

From the corner of his eye, Alexander watched the two men exchange glances and a shrug. They turned and re-entered the room from which they came. *Henry should have hired better security.*

"That was too easy," Julian murmured, reflecting his thoughts. "I don't like it."

"Neither do I," Alexander admitted. "Stay alert. There will be more."

Just as he suspected, another set of guards—dressed in heavy suits—stood outside the door to the lower levels. They stiffened when they approached, reaching for their holstered pistols.

"Let me pass." Alexander flashed his tattoo. "I'm on Bale's orders."

One of them grinned, drawing his gun. "The chief mentioned you might show, Callahan. *Our* orders were to take you into custody if you caused trouble."

Well, damn. Price was right.

"I don't have the patience for this," Julian growled and flicked his wrist. The two men's eyes bulged, faces turning red. They clawed at their throats, desperately trying to inhale.

Julian's brands flared, the silver in his eyes brightening, as the men fell to the ground, their lips blue. Lifeless.

Alexander paused. "Did you just steal the air from their lungs?"

"I did." Julian wrenched the door open. "I prefer not to do that. Lead on."

Six flights of stairs waited for them, and every ten feet, Alexander had to stop for a breath, clutching his spasming chest. It took much longer than he'd like for them to finally hit the bottom. Gas lamps sprang to life, illuminating a lonely, dark hall lined with numbered doors.

Keep going. Alexander forced himself to keep moving. Every step felt like a small victory, his last rebellion.

Julian's silver eyes glowed in the low light. He did a third glance over his shoulder, voice low. "What is this place?"

"Hell," Alexander whispered back. "This is just one of many levels of The Order's sanctuary. They have locations like this all over The Four Corners."

Julian's expression grew more uneasy. "Then why is it so empty?"

"Because Bale knew I would come." Alexander noted the lights shining from beneath the doorframes. It felt good to admit the truth out loud. "As soon as we try to escape, he'll send his armies down on us."

"And you're still going through with it?" Julian tensed, though he never broke his stride. "Why?"

"Because there is no other way." Alexander slowed, turning to face him. "You still have time to change your mind. Leave. I wouldn't blame you." He cracked a crooked smile. "Camden might, but he's not here to see you go."

"Eat shite, old man." Julian spat. "We're doing this. You said that you were sending a signal. How?"

"Oh, yes." Alexander held open his coat. A quick snort, followed by a cloud of smoke and embers, revealed Kai's fire dragon tucked neatly inside his inner pocket. It peeked its horned head out, blinking up at them innocently. It didn't look well, but it was alive.

Which meant Camden was still alive, holding on.

Julian's eyes filled with disbelief. "How, in all that is good, did you get that blasted thing in your pocket?"

"On a whim, I asked if it could shrink itself." Alexander closed his coat. "It listened— better than both of my damn sons. I'll send it to him once we're clear of the building."

"Clever," Julian replied.

A murmuring voice carried down the hall, coming from one of the rooms.

"It's not far." Alexander kept a rhythm of steady breaths to distract him from the pain coursing through his insides. It was only another four doors down until he found the one he was looking for.

The Death Brand's room. What was her name? *Clarisse.*

Bale, despite his intelligence, was predictable. He'd want to show Annie a taste of what she was to become, to heighten her fear, before he proceeded to tear her apart.

He wouldn't let that happen.

They stood outside a beautifully carved, red door. Its brass knob polished and shining.

Julian's brow rose. "This is it?"

"Yes." *Let me pass.* Alexander closed his eyes, focusing on his hate, his rage, of all that had been taken from him—all the parts of him The Order had exploited and twisted. He passed his hand over the knob. Darkness latched onto him, eating at him. He grimaced, gritting his teeth hard enough to crack. *You will open for me.*

Alexander sagged when the door clicked open. It may have drained the little strength that he had left, but he'd have to make it. He would endure for just a while longer. Then he could die.

Julian drew his dagger as Alexander cracked the door open. Then the sirens began to sound.

CHAPTER 62

ANNIE

Sweat dripped over Annie's temples, down her sides, as she concentrated all of her energy into creating a path to the void. A silver line shimmered in the air, taunting —but every time—before she could open it, the portal collapsed.

Just like it did again.

The opening fizzled out with a loud crack, sending an electric shock up to her elbows. Annie tumbled back onto the carpet, panting. *I don't know how long I can keep doing this.*

"How many times have I told you?" Clarisse still sat on the sofa, thumbing through a novel. "At least eight, I believe. It's not going to work, little dove."

"It has to," Annie hissed and got to her feet, shaking the tension out of her arms. "I've done it before, I can do it again."

"And it *won't* work here." Her grandmother snapped the book shut. She stood, stepping to Annie's side, strands of her bone-white hair falling loose from her bun. She raised a finger, tracing a seam. The air crackled, light and darkness twisting together, in response to her silent command. A mere beat of hope filled Annie's heart as the void began to open—only to snap shut a breath later.

"The Order has sealed this space with whatever power they have access to." Clarisse turned and flopped back onto the sofa, crossing one slender leg over the other. "It won't work."

Elain watched them from the corner, her empty white eyes narrowed, mouth twisted downward.

Some help you are. Annie shot the ghost a glare before taking a seat beside Clarisse. Elain had reappeared hours ago, saying nothing, and *doing* nothing, but watching them.

Her sister gave her a grim smile, then vanished.

Annie swallowed her frustration, rubbing her eyes. She'd barely slept, only drifting off on the couch for an hour at a time. She wasn't sure how long she'd been here. Every time she closed her eyes, when she'd begin to fade and her guard would fall, she'd be consumed with terror at the thought of Cam in Bale's hands.

She swore she could hear him screaming, could *feel* his pain.

Don't think about it now. Annie's heart sprinted in her chest, making it ache. *You can't help him if you fall apart.*

"Tell me how the corruption works again." Annie ran a hand down her face and stared up at the ceiling. "Distract me."

Clarisse arched a pale brow at her. How could a person look so old, yet so infinitely young?

She gave her grandmother a small smile. "Please?"

"You know how it works," Clarisse sighed.

"Tell me again."

"They'll use you to drain a person's very essence," Clarisse began, reopening her novel and finding her page. "You'll transfer it to one of the elders. They'll poison it. Destroy it. Leave that person's soul in fragments, then force you to transfer what remains back into the individual. The elder will own the person, body and soul. That person can then corrupt others, but only if they're continually replenished by the life that The Order will have you take from others. From useless civilians, in their eyes."

Useless civilians. Why did power so often cost empathy?

Annie exhaled through her nose. "Is Bale an elder?"

"Yes." Clarisse turned the page. "But he's not satisfied with that. You have to control a city to become an elder. Once Bale takes your husband, he'll control a nation. Then he'll ascend, like his father, into a master. Likely, he'll make you do the life transfer on your husband, just for the enjoyment of it."

"The agreement has to be made willingly."

"On your husband's part. Not yours."

"Camden will never agree." Annie sat up. "He won't . . . he can't."

"I hope that's true." The older woman patted her arm. "I really hope so."

The doorknob jiggled.

Annie's blood went cold.

Slowly, she looked to Clarisse. Her grandmother's eyes were equally wide. The door clicked this time. She wasn't imagining it. Someone was coming in.

Clarisse touched Annie's thigh, mouthing, *"Bale."*

No. If Bale was here, then Camden . . .

Don't think of that now. She let rage replace the fear. It didn't matter if he'd taken the mark. She'd kill Henry. She'd get Cam back.

"Stay here," she whispered to Clarisse, who nodded. Her power roared to the surface, setting her brands aglow, as she crept across the room, silent as a phantom. Her blood pounded in her ears as she leaned against the edge of the doorframe.

You can do this. And she would. She'd do whatever it took.

The knob twisted, and the door gently swung open.

She braced herself, darkness pooling around her.

Then sirens blared—from somewhere above—followed by a string of low curses.

She didn't wait. Annie wheeled, and as she reached through the doorway, her hand connected with a man's chest. Her power latched on to him, and he cried out as she burrowed deeper, aiming for the heart.

"Annie, stop—" A second man clamped down on her wrist and pulled. "It's us! For the love of God, let go!"

Blazes. Annie bit back a sob. If it weren't for the hand holding her, she would have fallen to her knees. The sirens continued to scream, piercing her ears, as Mr. Price came into view, horror coating his sallow features.

"Let go," he repeated, prying her fingers off whoever's chest she still held onto. She sucked in a heavy breath and let her power fall. The second man doubled over, gasping, as color returned to his skin—the life she'd tried to take from him. Alexander.

"Governor." Annie's voice shook, barely audible over the sirens. "I would say I'm sorry, but I'm not."

"Of course, you're not." He shook his head, limbs quivering as he straightened. "This is what I get for trying to save your bloody lives. We need to go. *Now.*"

Annie couldn't believe she was looking at the same man. Alexander's hair had turned silver. The corruption had spread to his neck and jaw, his grey-blue eyes bloodshot.

"Right now." Julian yanked her through the doorway. "We don't have long."

"Wait—" She jerked free and spun. *Clarisse.*

Her grandmother was on her feet, hand outstretched like she'd meant to help. She looked ready to faint when Annie ran forward, grabbing her shoulders.

"Come with us," Annie begged. "Don't die here. Come with me."

Clarisse's gaze rose, locking onto Mr. Price and Alexander. She pointed at the governor. "I know you."

"And I you," he shot back. "Let's not make this our last meeting. Follow us, or serve The Order for the rest of eternity. Your choice."

Your choice. Camden had said those exact words to her once, back on New Havana. They had been her salvation, the reason everything changed.

Annie gripped Clarisse tighter. "You *have* a choice. Come with me. *Please.*"

Footsteps thundered on the floors above, making the ceiling shake.

Still in her nightgown, Clarisse nodded. "I will follow you, little dove, and only you. Lead on."

She took the woman's hand and dragged her through the door. Julian took a cautious step back, watching Clarisse warily. All the legends he'd probably heard of her . . . it must be like seeing a myth come to life.

The ceiling rumbled again, showering them with dust.

She stopped short. "What was that?"

Alexander sighed. "The foundation is crumbling."

"It's—*what?*"

"Let's go." He started down the hall towards the exit. "Bale's soldiers will come, but if we can funnel them in the stairwell, we might have a chance." He glanced back at them, his eyes wilder than she'd ever seen them. "What's one hundred men against three Revenants?"

"Nothing." Mr. Price pushed past him. "But it will be more than that if we don't hurry up."

Clarisse's eyes shot in every direction as they moved, taking in every crack and shadow. When was the last time she'd left her prison? Halfway down, she froze, bringing Annie to a halt.

She touched her ear, pressing her finger to her lips. "Do you hear that?"

Price paused, listening. "All I hear are those bloody sirens."

"No." Clarisse cocked her head. "*That.*"

Annie closed her eyes, focusing. *There.* Another voice, screaming. Fists banging on wood. She knew the voice, the lilting accent . . .

"It's Reika Hall!" She wheeled. There were so many rooms. "We can't leave her!"

"Yes, we can." Alexander scowled. "Annie, we need to go—"

I'm not leaving her here. Reika had been through enough. She turned to Mr. Price. "Can you open these doors?"

He blinked at her. "All of them?"

"Unless you plan on doing it one by one, yes, all of them!"

"You're going to get us killed." He shook his head as his brands flared. He inhaled as wind balled in his fists, swirling, growing, ripping at their clothing, before he finally exhaled. A torrent of air exploded outward, blowing the doors off their hinges. There were more screams as wooden shrapnel lodged into the walls. Four doors down, a woman stumbled out of her room, holding her swollen belly—Reika.

She's still pregnant. Her baby was still alive. Her stomach had grown so much larger in the weeks since she'd last seen her. *There's no way she'd be able to keep up in her state.*

Mr. Price must have thought the same, because he rushed forward, scooping Reika into his arms as if she were nothing more than a child.

"Miss Hall." He dipped his chin to her before turning to Alexander. "How does four Revenants improve your odds?"

Alexander frowned, making a *hurmp* sound before continuing. Another tremor caused more dust to fall.

"I can still fight." Reika grinned wearily, her vibrant blue brands pulsing. "Don't count me out, yet."

"Never." Annie squeezed her hand. She was surprised at how genuinely happy she was to see her. "What happened? How did you get here?"

"*Ha*," Reika laughed. "I was dragged out of my damned apartment by a bunch of goons in suits. Babe or no, I'd taken half of them before that blasted chief showed up."

"We can catch up later," Julian said as they reached the stairwell. "We've got company."

A dozen men swung their rifles over the stair railing, aimed at their heads. She hadn't even heard them with the sirens. The veins on their hands and faces were black. Cultists.

Alexander skidded to a halt just as one of the cultists fired, missing his foot by inches.

"Let me." A wicked smile curled Reika's lips. She stretched out her hand, fingers spread. A tidal wave erupted out of her palm, washing *up* the stairwell. The men screamed as they were swept away. Reika clenched her fist, and the water wrapped around them, pinning their flailing bodies to the ground.

She drowned them, leaving their corpses strewn over the stairs.

"That was . . ." A mix of emotions passed over Price's face. "Impressive."

"Thank you," Reika said sweetly in that accent of hers. "I impress myself."

They smiled at each other.

"That won't be the last of them." Alexander was already up the first flight of stairs, clutching his heart. "Hurry."

Annie kept hold of Clarisse's hand as they climbed upward.

They were nearly to the top, the sirens deafening, when the door to the upper floor kicked open. Another twenty cultists aimed.

Darkness curled over Annie's shoulder, chilling her to the core.

Clarisse's face twisted in concentration as the darkness passed over them, swallowing them, followed by muffled shrieks. When it passed, there was nothing left of the men but bones.

Reika pouted. "Show off."

Could I do that? Annie felt sick. What Clarisse had done . . . they were both Death Brands. Could she harness her power like that?

"Come to me in another five hundred years, girl," Clarisse said to Reika as she stepped over the cultists's remains. "Then we'll see how you compare."

"Wait until you meet Camden." Annie squeezed her grandmother's hand, allowing the flicker of hope. "You'll love him. There's so much you can teach us."

Clarisse's returning smile wasn't nearly as hopeful, but she squeezed back anyway.

They were nearly to the exit. Alexander opened his coat, revealing Brantley snoozing in his pocket. Annie gaped in shock as he shook the dragon awake—Cam's dragon—and whispered, "It's time."

Just like that, the dragon vanished, leaving a small ring of soot on Alexander's palm.

"Where do you think you're going?"

Jensen. Annie turned just as the Ice Brand came into view, countless more cultists at his back, rifles raised.

If we move, we're dead. Annie kept still as Jensen stepped forward, his smile widening into something cruel.

"You weren't planning on leaving, were you?" His eyes

danced over them before settling on Alexander. "Bale was right. You did come. I didn't think you had the balls."

"Stand down, Davis." Alexander never lost his composure, despite struggling to breathe. "You're making a fool of yourself."

"Says the King of Fools," Jensen laughed, spreading his arms wide. "I don't have to riddle you full of holes. Submit, and I'll let you each return to a cell. You can even pick which one you like best."

"Insolent child." The darkness swelled around Clarisse. No—she *was* darkness. "How dare you."

Fear flashed in Jensen's eyes as the darkness blanketed the hall, stretching toward his army. It surged, lunging for them. Jensen cried out as a gunshot went off—

—and a bullet tore through Annie's knee, shattering it.

"*Oh.*" That was all she managed to say as agony burned through her senses. She didn't realize she'd hit the ground until someone grabbed her face, shrieking at her. She couldn't see them.

I'm alive. She blinked, her eyes coming into focus. Alexander tugged her upright. Blood gushed from the hole in her leg, soaking through her dress. Hurricane-force winds blew over her, ripping her hair free. Mr. Price. Dizziness threatening to put her down again.

Reika was on her feet, fighting alongside him.

Shards of ice tore through a sea of darkness, crashing into the Air Brand's windstorm. Jensen stepped out of the blackened fog, his face sunken from Clarisse's drain, only to be driven back by Reika's waves.

Annie jolted. Alexander was pulling at her again. She couldn't stand.

Then her grandmother was beside her.

"Little dove." Clarisse's voice broke through the shock, straight to Annie's heart. "Look at me."

Annie obeyed. She wished she hadn't.

Cracks weathered Clarisse's face, splitting down her cheeks. She was withering away before her eyes, crumbling into powder. The older woman looked down at herself and let out a soft laugh.

"I told you I was old." She lifted Annie's chin. "There's a reason they wanted my replacement. I didn't have much life left, I'm afraid."

"No, no, no." Annie reached for Clarisse, but she swatted her away.

"Stay still." She clamped her hands over Annie's ruined knee, blood gushing between her fingers. Light poured into Annie's skin, into her marrow, sewing all the fractured bone back together. Alexander watched in awe as her flesh sealed shut.

The aching pain was still there, the bruising, but she would be able to move again.

Strands of Clarisse's white hair broke off in clumps. "You made me proud, little dove. Meeting you was worth all of my years in chains."

"*No.*" Annie grabbed hold of her. She could heal her, she could.

The ground shook, followed by a wave of heat so intense the edges of Clarisse's nightgown began to smolder.

The fighting stopped. When Annie looked back, the three Revenants—and the remaining cultists—stared off toward the heart of the city, faces twisted in horror.

The shockwave first pushed her to the ground. Alexander tried to shield her as the skyline erupted in flames. A deafening explosion, then in an instant, half of Enoch was gone— consumed by a fire so intense, the stone melted beneath it.

Tears fell from Clarisse's eyes. "Is that—"

"My husband." Annie grinned and took the woman's hand. "You should meet him."

"Maybe in another life." She kissed Annie's knuckles. "But not this one. Go. Your friends will keep The Order busy." Clarisse spoke to Alexander. "Keep her alive."

"I will." Alexander hauled Annie to her feet. "You have my word."

"Keep it, son of the West." Clarisse waved them off. "Make it count."

Annie's knee buckled, barely holding her weight. She hissed through the pain, and as they hobbled deeper into the city, she glanced back one last time.

There was nothing left of Clarisse but dust, ripped away in Mr. Price's wind.

CHAPTER 63
CAMDEN

Do not break.

Cam stared at Annie's broken body slumped against the dock. Slaughtered. Blood saturated her hair, spilling into the sea. Her empty eyes watched him. Beyond, *The Nightlady* floated in the harbor, aflame. Aboard, the crew screamed for him, begging him not to burn them alive.

Again.

And again, and *again.*

He glanced down at the bloody knife in one hand, his fire in the other. *What have I done?*

"You did this." Shadows swirled around him as Bale's fingers curled over his shoulder. "You destroy everything you touch."

Cam let the knife clatter to the boardwalk. "I do."

"It doesn't have to be that way," Bale murmured so sweetly. "I can fix you. I can make you *so* much better."

Endure.

When he didn't answer, Bale dug his claws deeper. "I can make it stop."

Cam sucked in a shuddering breath, nauseated as the darkness enveloped him once more.

Then the world went still, leaving him stranded on that cold table again.

He blinked up at the light hanging just above his head. He didn't care if it blinded him. If it did, maybe he wouldn't have to see those things anymore. Hot liquid pooled around his wrists from where he bled, thrashing against his chains. He couldn't feel the pain anymore, either.

He didn't feel much at all.

Cam squinted as Bale yanked the light away and stood over him, mouth twisted in frustration. "We don't have to keep doing this, you know?"

Do not break. How long could he continue to bend without snapping in half? Cam closed his eyes and swallowed, ashamed at the tear that escaped.

"Oh, Camden, was that too much?" Bale laughed and wiped away the tear. Blackness oozed from his fingertips. "I know, why don't we return to the slave ships? You seemed to like those better."

"Eat it." Cam braced as Bale struck him across the face. He'd expected it. He could handle *that*.

His fire roared just beneath the surface, pleading to be set free. Cam shoved it down, down, down. If Bale noticed, if he realized his power had woken, he'd drug him again. He'd lost count of how many times he had.

Endure. He wasn't sure how much longer he could.

Over and over, Bale scourged his mind. There was no will but his, and every passing moment proved that the visions would become his reality if he caved.

Bale would own him. He would take orders. He would obey. He would kill. A puppet, just like he'd said.

Just a little longer. God, he was so tired. He just wanted five minutes of peace. Just five, damn minutes. Bale would wear him down.

The chief picked at his nails. "I never told you who killed your mother."

Cam managed a glance. The movement made his back throb.

"Besides you, of course. We can't forget *that*." Bale chuckled before hopping up to sit on the edge of the table. "I looked into it. My father ordered the hit—a little warning to get the governor back in line." He tapped Cam's nose. He wished he could rip that bloody finger off. "Her killer was a thug. A lowlife, scourge of the earth, nobody. Just like you."

Just like me.

It wasn't long ago that he wished he were no one. Now he wished he were enough.

"Disappointing, isn't it?" Bale brushed away some of the blood leaking from Cam's split lip. "All your anger, and scheming, and lust for revenge, it was all for not. How does that make you feel?"

He didn't answer.

Bale sighed, then leaned down until their faces were inches apart. "I'm bored with your moping. How about this? I'll make you a deal. If you say yes, I'll let you keep her."

Do not break. He wanted to. Cam's voice cracked. "W-what?"

"Does that make you happy?" Bale sat back and grinned. "I've been hard on you, and you've held out longer than I expected. Much longer than your father. He crumbled in minutes, I've heard. As a reward, if you say yes now, I'll let you keep Annie. You can live together. I'll even allow you to have a little family, if that's what you want."

He raised his hand, more blackness curling out of the tattoo beneath his finger. "Say yes to me, and she's yours."

He won't kill Annie, but he'll turn her into something worse than the Duskins ever could. He'll tell you submission is the only way to keep her safe.

But it would be so easy to say yes. He could do that.

Then she'll be safe. Safe from him. Safe from me. Henry would never let me hurt her. Because he didn't know anymore, and Bale was right—he destroyed everything he touched.

Maybe it was better this way.

"You promise?" Cam's mouth tasted of blood, his throat raw from screaming. "Swear it."

"I swear it," Bale crooned. "Annie will be yours. She will serve when she's needed, but you'll remain together. Forever."

Do not break.

Forever.

Cam stared up at the ceiling. He hated Bale, but he hated himself so much more. At what point did enduring hurt her more?

Forever.

He wanted forever with her. That's all he wanted.

And he'd do whatever it took to keep it.

Cam swallowed, ready to say the words he thought he never would. *Do not break.* He choked back a sob and snapped his mouth shut. He wouldn't break. Not yet. He'd endure just a while longer.

Do not do what I did.

His father's words were all he had left. The only thing that kept his broken pieces together.

"Terrible decision." Bale placed his palm over Cam's forehead. "To the slave ships, then."

Cam inhaled.

A flicker of light formed beside the table. Not just light, but *fire*. His fire.

Kai's dragon, now the size of a grapefruit, fluttered by his face. Then it was gone. He would have thought he had imagined it if Bale hadn't jumped back in surprise.

"What the hell was that?" He wheeled, enraged, and pointed at him. "What was *that?*"

I will send a signal, then you will blow them to hell.

Cam began to laugh, deep at first, until it turned manic.

Bale backed a step, reaching into his pocket for another syringe. He thought he was going to drug him again. "What was that—"

Finally.

"Your death sentence." Cam let the madness take him as he ripped one arm free, his fire burning straight through the metal.

Bale ran for the door as Cam wrenched his body from the table.

Let me destroy him. His fire purred. *Let me destroy them all. Let me ruin them like they ruined you.*

Blood rushed to Cam's head, making it spin, but it didn't matter. Seeing Bale cower in the doorway was enough to get him to his feet. He gasped, trying to get oxygen into his lungs.

Bale shrieked as the door handle melted to his skin. He glanced back, eyes filled with terror. He didn't look so dangerous now as he said, "You can't kill me, Camden."

Cam grinned. "I can try."

Let me go. His fire was a vortex, consuming the chamber.

Let me go.

And he would. Because he was just like his father and didn't care who died.

But he knew the truth now. His father had wantonly killed

because he had to. He *tried* to save him and his mother. He'd done terrible things to try to keep them alive, but The Order had beaten him. They'd won.

They wouldn't win today.

Maybe being the son of Alexander Callahan wasn't the worst thing he could be, after all.

As Cam let go, his fire tore out of him, forcing him to the ground. The flames howled as they annihilated what remained of the ceiling, burning it away. It would rip him apart. Destroy him, just like he'd destroyed everything else.

Promise me, if it comes to it, you will spare no one. That you'll do whatever terrible thing you're afraid of doing, because I'd rather you be a monster and alive, than die feeling good about yourself.

He would be her monster.

Whatever Bale had broken, she would fix.

Cam cried out as he took hold of his fire, letting it fill him, consume him—not to ruin him, but to *become* him. He refused to be owned.

He pushed the flames outward until the chamber shook, raining rubble over them. It couldn't touch him. It burned away, melting into slag. When he looked up, there was nothing but open sky around him, filled with dark clouds.

Bale was gone. He either escaped or was buried beneath half a ton of melted stone.

It didn't matter now. *She* was all that mattered.

Step by step, Cam clamored out of the chamber, out into the streets of Enoch.

Somewhere far away, a siren echoed across the city. *The Lodge is over an hour away.* And that was in a carriage. On foot?

I'm so tired. Smoke billowed around him. People were screaming, scattering out of the way like roaches. Enoch's sprawling buildings and towers blocked out his view of the horizon. He'd have to guess his way there. He'd—

"Freeze."

Armed cultists poured out of the surrounding structures. They circled him, guns raised, shouting orders for him to stand down.

Of course, Bale had backup. Cam looked out over their faces. Frightened, but not nearly enough. Each of them had chosen to serve The Order. Whether it was willingly or under duress, the kindest thing he could do was remove them from the face of the earth.

You never trusted me. His fire crooned. *Because you never trusted yourself. I am you.*

Yes. He didn't wield fire—he *was* fire, in the flesh—and he wanted his damn wife back.

Cam exhaled, and flames surged through his veins, infusing into his soul. There would be no separation between them anymore. No more shoving it down and locking it away. No longer could he pretend that he didn't have the power to burn cities to the ground.

He became the creature he was when he was pushed too far, because that's who he'd always been. A calamity. He couldn't hide it anymore.

The cultists continued to shout at him as Cam's gaze met the skyline. There was too much in the way. He wouldn't get to her fast enough. Unless . . .

It took only a breath to shake Enoch's foundations. An inferno crashed over its tallest towers, bringing them low. The men's screams changed from rage to terror, then to silence as the fire swept away their charred remains.

And Cam felt nothing. Their lives were only a blip in his existence.

Because he was endless, a devourer of worlds.

His skin glowed molten, webbed, and coursing like lava flow.

A wasteland—that's all that stood between him and the Lodge. He would make it. He would find her.

Endure. Despite the exhaustion eating him alive, Cam started across Enoch's scalded ruins. *Do not break.*

More men came, demanding that he surrender.

He'd leave none of them alive.

CHAPTER 64

ANNIE

The ground quaked as buildings continued to fall.

Enormous crowds emerged from great clouds of black smoke. Screaming.

Everyone was screaming.

Annie pulled Alexander into an alley as another roof collapsed, blanketing the street in ash.

"He's lost his mind." The governor braced against the brick wall, his limbs shaking as he struggled to breathe. "We've got to stop him."

He's alive. Annie peered up at the flames overwhelming the city's western districts. *He's alive, and if he loses control, there won't be anything left of Enoch.*

Even now, thousands upon thousands would be without homes.

But Cam wouldn't take their lives, not the innocent ones, at least. She knew him better than that.

Even now, people sprinted through the fire as they scrambled to avoid the soldiers streaming into the ruins. In their panic, they didn't even seem to realize that they were unharmed by the flames.

Gunshots sounded in the distance, echoing down the avenue.

No, Cam wasn't on a random killing spree. He was hunting cultists.

And me. Annie turned, her knee nearly giving out with the movement. Clarisse had done her best, but it hadn't been enough to heal her completely. She could try to finish the job with what energy she had left, but Alexander wouldn't make it, and she refused to leave him behind.

"Give me your hand." As she reached for him, the governor jerked away, sweat dripping off his face as he shook his head.

"No," he grunted. "I'll be fine."

"Be quiet and give me your hand."

"Annie—"

"I won't make it without you," she snapped. "Will you please just give me your hand?"

He stared at her for a moment before relenting with an irritated grunt.

There's so much corruption. She took hold, and light soaked into his skin, into his veins, but it did little against the darkness that inhabited him. Despite his protest, Alexander took a long breath, an easy one, and closed his eyes. Whatever she'd done must have given him a slight bit of relief.

"Thank you." He steadied himself and wiped his forehead with his sleeve, smudging it with soot. "Enoch's police are under Bale's control. They'll be in full force by now."

"We don't have to stop them. We just need to get to Cam." That's all she wanted. To see him, to touch him, to have proof that he was sound. "We'll figure it out from there."

Annie checked around the corner. "The crowds have cleared. Let's go."

"Follow me." Alexander pushed his now silver hair out of his face. "This way is faster. The gunshots are coming from the market."

Gunshots. They took off onto a side street, avoiding the main road. *Men are shooting at him, and I don't know how to stop them.*

Frightened faces watched them as they passed, huddling inside their houses. There wasn't time to warn them, not with cultists behind them as well as ahead. The ground trembled again, sending shingles flying from the roofs and shattering at their feet.

Alexander navigated the backways with expert precision. He knew every inch of this city, every twist and curve. An elderly man with a beard, dressed in rags, barreled past them and knocked Alexander against the wall, not even realizing it was his own governor. Alexander grimaced, holding his bruised shoulder, but continued.

Smoke mixed with the clouds, turning the sky as dark as night. The end of the alley opened into a small square, usually filled with market stalls, but not today. Today, it was blanketed in dust, stone, and splintered lumber. Beyond, toppled buildings had become an enormous wall, blocking the square from the city beyond.

"Wait—" Annie swung her arm out and Alexander crashed into her, making her knee pop. Voices were coming from outside the alley—several of them, and too calm to be friendly.

Alexander nodded. He heard them, too. With a finger over his lips, he crept to the end of the alley and peered around the edge. She followed, murky puddles soaking into her blood-stained skirts.

Four cultists were crouched about fifty feet away, reloading their rifles. The red haze of the remaining sunlight reflected off their blood-splattered uniforms, their faces stained grey.

"Baxter's place is gone," one of them said as he rammed a bullet into the chamber of his gun and snapped the bolt shut. "Nothing but a pile of rocks now."

The second one straightened, taking a sip from his canteen. "Is the shite dead? Baxter, I mean."

"Naw," said the first. "We already searched the rubble for bodies. He wasn't in there. Neither was the chief."

Oh no. Annie shot Alexander a look, who pursed his lips in response. Henry Bale was still alive. *But how?* Flames still crested over Enoch's towers. How could he have escaped a blast like that?

"Where is the chief now?" said another.

"A long way from here, we can hope," the first replied and stood. "Doesn't matter, anyway. We have our orders. We're taking the Fire Brand down and not leaving here until we do."

Like hell you are. Annie swiveled to face the governor. "I can drain them."

"Absolutely not." He frowned. "You'd have to touch them. I'm not going to sit here and let you get shot."

"I don't have to touch them," she said. With Violet, she'd been able to strike from half a room away. If she'd done it once, she could do it again. She rubbed her knee. It was swollen to twice its normal size. "I can do it from a distance. I don't have enough energy left to repair my leg . . . but I could use theirs."

"*Or* we could avoid them. Go around. That would be wiser."

"And leave us with four more cultists to kill later."

"Which wouldn't be an issue if Camden were with us."

"We won't *make it* to Camden if I can't walk."

Alexander glared at her before he cursed. "Fine." He drew a revolver from his inner pocket. It was Cam's. "But you're not doing it without my help."

She blinked at it, stunned. "Where did you—"

"Bale had it tossed aside." Alexander managed a grin and pulled out a golden pocket watch from his opposite pocket. "Along with this. I'm not losing a family heirloom so easily."

"Thank you." It was all she could think to say. She turned back toward the square, sinking lower. *How am I going to do this?* They'd shoot her if she stepped out of the alley. Could she wield her power that far?

An electric current coursed through her blood. Her power wanted to *take*. To feed. *If Clarisse destroyed all of Jensen's men, I could take four.* It had to work. There wasn't another option. *What would Cam do right now?*

He'd get them shot at. The thought made her smile.

Annie blew out a hard breath and focused. *I can do this.* She would not be afraid. Alexander reached for her arm as she slid out of the alley, but she was faster.

The cultists spotted her immediately, their gazes snagging on her hair before moving to the shadows swelling around her. Maybe they mistook her for her grandmother. Either way, they raised their rifles.

"Halt!" The first commanded as his finger slid over the trigger. "Get on the ground—"

I will not die today. Darkness surged out of her, ripping across the square in a silent torrent. Three of the cultists dropped as her power took hold, leeching their life away.

Three.

She missed the fourth. She pulled, and as his companions withered away. The fourth made to fire—

A gunshot rang out.

Blood gushed from a hole in his head with a sickening *pop*.

Alexander stood beside her, trembling, as smoke poured from the barrel of Cam's revolver. "Well, I know why he likes this thing now." He let out a shaky laugh. "It's got some kick to it."

Something's wrong. A wave of nausea threatened to overwhelm her as their life flowed back into her. Instead of growing brighter, her brands darkened, webbing. *No, no, no.* There was no life left inside them, only poisoned death. It ravaged through her bones, her teeth, making them ache.

Her heart pulsed in her throat—too hard—and she began to wobble.

"Annie?" Alexander caught her under the elbow before she fell. "What's happening? What's wrong?"

"You were right." God, even her lungs hurt. "That was a bad idea."

"Hell." He sighed, scanning over the corpses. He passed her Cam's revolver, then took one of the rifles for himself, slinging the strap over his shoulder. "Can you keep going?"

"Yes." She brushed her thumb over the revolver's pearl handle. *I'll get this back to you. I promise.* They had to keep going. "I'll manage."

"Good." Alexander nodded. "I—"

The world exploded in fire. Raging over them, around them, bringing the remaining buildings to the ground. The streets fractured as they shook, creating deep holes down to the sewers below. Brackish water sprayed out of damaged pipes, soaking them. Another barrage of gunfire sounded from just outside the market—right on the other side of the crumbled towers.

"Cam!" Annie cried out, dragging her ruined leg behind her as she raced for the towers. She'd dig through them if she had to.

Her fingernails cracked against the rough stone as she began to climb. Every movement had her eyes watering in pain. Beyond the throbbing, her knee started to *burn*—internal bleeding. *It doesn't matter.* Annie continued to climb. She was used to pain. She could survive a little longer.

She was gasping for air by the time she reached the top, Alexander close behind her. Blood dripped from his lips. He spat, staining the broken bits of stone red. The corruption was killing him from the inside out.

The destruction had turned the city below into a valley of ash. From their distance, the cultists looked like fluttering moths, drawn to the flames. Cam was at the center of them, their beacon, his fire a massive cyclone around him.

They fired their rifles, but the bullets couldn't touch him.

He was . . . magnificent.

Fissures formed in the earth beneath his footsteps, the valley a mirage from the suffocating heat radiating off his body.

Annie laughed through a sob. He was alive. Alive, alive, alive and fighting. Even from here, she could feel his rage. His eyes were lost to the fire, his body molten and glowing. He'd transformed flames into blades, cleaving cultists in two with a single swing. He ducked between them, teeth bared, soaked in black blood, as he cut them down in droves.

"My God." Alexander gaped in awe. "I wish Cassie were here to see this."

She didn't. No one should have to see their son kill this way.

Terror coated the cultists's faces. They were losing and they knew it, and yet still more came. Because they had to, their orders were that Cam had to die, and they would continue to fight until they'd accomplished their mission.

Annie couldn't sit here and do nothing.

Alexander let out another stream of curses as she began to climb down the other side of the tower. *Slid* would be more accurate. Her dress tore, the stone tearing into her skin as she continued to fall.

The remaining cultists moved in from the east side—at Cam's back.

A cry bubbled in her throat, but Cam spun, his eyes ablaze. He threw out his arms, and the valley was again bathed in fire. It ate up the ground, moving over her, around her.

Even now, it would never hurt her.

Then the cultists were gone—dissolved into smoking remnants.

Cam's chest heaved as his arms dropped to his sides.

"Cam!" Annie scrambled to her feet when she hit the bottom, sprinting for him, every step undoing the work done on her knee. *"Cam!"*

Alexander wasn't far behind.

Cam noticed them, and his rage disappeared as quickly as the vortex around him. His smile was like the first rays of dawn. "A-Annie—"

Time slowed as another wave of dark figures crested the hill to their left, followed by the echo of more gunfire.

The light in Cam's eyes vanished as he collapsed with five bullet holes in his chest.

CHAPTER 65

ALEXANDER

Annie's scream could have cleaved the world in two. For a breath, the sky tore, leaving glittering ribbons of silver in the air, paths to nothingness.

And Camden fell, his fire winking out like a snuffed candle.

Dozens more soldiers poured into the valley, but they didn't have a chance.

She was the apocalypse.

Darkness—an infinite, breathtaking force—crashed over the land like a tidal wave, submerging the remaining cultists beneath its fury. Those that survived were swallowed by the rippling currents that followed, over and over, until only they remained.

Then she was sprinting across a bloodied battleground, screaming his name.

Camden didn't stir.

Not like this. Alexander couldn't breathe past the fluid filling his lungs, but he ran anyway. His bones splintered with every stride, the shards embedding into his tendons and muscles. But he would make it. He had to.

Annie dropped to her knees beside his son, listening for a heartbeat as she attempted to staunch his wounds. There were too many for her dainty hands. Blood pumped over her fingers, pouring onto her lap.

Alexander's mouth tasted of iron when he crouched beside her. *Please no.* He held pressure on the bullet holes she couldn't reach, but it was too late.

Camden's eyes were glazed over and lifeless. Open. Staring at nothing. Gone.

Alexander's throat bobbed as he stared at his face. After all these years, he'd finally gotten him back, and now his son was gone.

I'm so sorry, Cassie. I failed you.

He'd failed them all.

He gripped Annie's shoulder. "Annie—"

"Don't you dare." Her brands flared white then sputtered out, turning dark again. "He's *alive.* I can feel a pulse." Light danced around her fingertips for a moment, then vanished. She broke down into sobs. "But I don't have anything left. I can't fix him. *I can't fix him.*"

She can't heal him. Because she needed life to heal. Life the cultists didn't have. Life that he *did.*

They deserved to have a millennium together, to grow old in the strange way Revenants did. They deserved everything he and Cassandra never got to have.

He would not let his son die.

He took Annie's hand in his and squeezed. "Take it."

"Take it?" Annie blinked at him, dazed, the ends of her moon-white hair stained crimson. The realization slowly sank in. She pulled away. "Governor—"

"Alex," he corrected and smiled. "That's what Cassie called me. Let me do this. For them both."

"I could kill you." Her eyes turned back to Camden. "And your corruption . . . I don't even know if I could."

Alexander squeezed tighter. "I haven't lost all of my humanity. Not yet. Do it."

Annie hesitated only once. Her brands flared, her features fixed in concentration. Alexander grimaced, scrunching his eyes shut, as invisible talons violently clawed at what little remained of his soul.

He remembered this feeling—when the other Death Brand woman dragged him to the edge of the abyss and gave his life to Harrison Bale.

This time, though, there would be no getting it back. Nor did he want it.

Take it. His body began to wither. It felt like that moment just before sleep, that last consciousness before emptiness takes you. The talons started to lift. He tried to push more, but then they were gone.

Alexander sighed, and when his eyes opened, he had collapsed.

The pain is gone. In fact, he felt nothing. He could barely move, but managed just enough to watch Annie glow as she lay her hands over Camden's chest, kissing the corner of his mouth while whispering words meant only for them.

The bleeding slowed to a stop, but his skin was still too pale.

Please, be enough. He was so, so tired, but he refused to slip away. *It has to be enough.*

Annie cradled Camden's head, rocking, weeping, as the last of the light in her brands faded to black.

Nearly a minute passed before his finger twitched, then his back arced off the ground as he gasped for air.

Annie continued to weep as his brands flared back to life.

She tried to steady him, but he pulled her down to kiss him, wrapping his arms around her waist.

As she broke away, Camden let out a raspy, nervous laugh. "I think those bastards shot me."

"They did." Annie's voice quivered as she held him. "But they're gone now, and we're still here."

"We're still here," he repeated as he held her. "We're alive."

He noticed Alexander, then. Camden's green eyes widened. The same color as Cassie's. It was good to see them again. He let out a pained groan as Annie helped him sit up. He dragged himself closer, panting, a layer of thick dust covering his skin and hair.

"W-what did you do?" Camden grabbed the front of Alexander's jacket. "You can't—"

Annie covered her face, choking back another sob. She looked like a little girl. It was so easy to forget how young she was. How young they *both* were. *Time has not been kind.*

Alexander gave a halfhearted smile. "And here I thought you'd be happy. You said you wanted to be the one to kill me."

Camden glanced between him and Annie, putting the pieces together. He sucked in a heavy breath. "This . . . this wasn't what I had in mind."

Angry shouting echoed from the other side of the fallen tower, growing closer.

Annie grabbed Camden's arm. "Cultists."

"Go." Alexander managed to dig the pocket watch from his coat. He shoved it in Cam's hand, sticky with blood. "Take this. Get out of here."

Camden trembled as he stared at the watch, brows knit together. He shoved it into his pants pocket and swayed as he climbed to his feet. Annie's knee gave out as she tried to stand, and Camden caught her by the elbow. The voices were growing louder. His face fell.

"That's alright," he growled as he hoisted Annie in one arm. He bent over and heaved Alexander over the opposite shoulder, staggering. "I can carry you both."

"Don't." Alexander couldn't fight, but Camden didn't make it more than ten feet before he stumbled. He roared as he tried to lift them again, but his body gave out.

"You've lost too much blood." Annie took on her ice-cold tone again. She knew the truth. "You can't."

"I can." Cam set his jaw, fighting for breath. "I will."

"I don't want you to." Alexander managed to break away and lean against a large chunk of rubble. "Let me do this. Damn it, I'm dying, Camden. Let me go in the way I want to."

Camden held his stare, a thousand emotions passing through his son's tear-stained eyes, before he finally nodded.

"Get her out of here." Alexander's throat grew tight. A deceased cultist's rifle was within reach. He grabbed it, chambered a round, then grinned. "I'll keep them busy. Please, don't stop me."

"I'll take care of Kai and Maya," Camden whispered.

Alexander's armor cracked. "A-and Maya?"

"And the West." Camden kissed his brow. "I'll take care of that, too."

"Good." Alexander inhaled, decades of weight lifting off his broken shoulders. "I'm grateful."

"When you see Mother." Camden smiled at him—truly smiled at him—for the first time. "Tell her I forgive you."

"Yes." Alexander beamed, eyes shining. *Forgiven.* He could die with that. "And remember, your mother loved you . . . so do I."

"I know." Camden wobbled as he scooped Annie off the ground. She clung to him, shoulders shaking, as she buried her face into his neck. "I won't forget it."

Alexander watched as his son turned and picked his way out of the ruins, that magnificent girl in his arms.

The world was theirs, if only they would take it. He prayed that someday they would.

They were just out of sight when six more cultists dropped down below the tower.

"Just a little longer, Cassie," Alexander whispered to himself, aiming at the men searching amongst the rubble. He couldn't remember a time when he'd felt happier. "Then my time is done."

He'd finally get to sleep.

God, he couldn't wait.

Alexander fired, and another barrage of gunfire covered the valley, followed by a never-ending silence.

CHAPTER 66

ANNIE

Annie woke in a dimly lit room, tinged with the smell of vinegar and antiseptic. Grey light poured through the slats in the blinds. Warm. She was too warm. She kicked off the stack of blankets layered over her and sat up.

Waverly. She was at the hospital.

How did I get here? She remembered Camden carrying her out of the ruins. The smoke. Hearing the gunshots behind them, then it went quiet. She didn't remember anything after that.

Alexander. She rubbed away the wetness pooling in her eyes. They were already raw. He'd sacrificed himself to save Cam's life, and they'd left him in the dirt. *If you hadn't, neither of you would be alive.*

Cam. She twisted toward the bed beside hers—the empty bed. Panic burned through the haze lingering in her mind. *Where is he—*

"You're safe."

She knew that voice. Her power surged beneath her skin. When she turned, Maya sat in a rocking chair on the opposite side of her, near her head, a quilt over her lap. She'd been so still, Annie hadn't noticed her.

Maya didn't look perfect today. Her inky-black hair was askew, her eyes as red and swollen as Annie's felt. A cup of what smelled like whisky sat on the small table beside her.

She gave her a weak smile, curling the edge of the quilt around her thin fingers. "Camden is safe, too. He's asleep in the other room."

"Why isn't he in here?" *With me.*

Maya watched her nervously. "The surgeons thought they may still need to operate."

"Not without me, they're not." Annie swung her legs out of bed. "Why didn't someone wake me? I—"

"That was yesterday evening. It's morning now." Maya held a hand out to stop her. "He's alright. We found you both collapsed about a mile from the hospital, covered in blood. We didn't even know to whom it belonged. They wrapped your knee up the best they could."

He carried us all the way here. Annie didn't have any tears left. Five bullets to the chest, and he still got them somewhere safe.

I forgot about my knee. And now that she remembered, it *ached.* She hiked up her nightgown—someone had redressed her—and her knee was indeed wrapped. The swelling had spread halfway up her thigh. Probably torn tendons.

She let her hem fall and glared at Maya. There were so many things she wanted to say. She wanted to scream, to rip the woman's hair out, but what difference would it make?

Maya must have sensed her train of thought, because her face skewed up in pain, voice thick as she croaked, "I'm so sorry."

Annie didn't reply. She just continued to stare.

"He threatened Kai. My only son." Maya wiped her nose on the quilt. "I've been under The Order's thumb my entire life. My father … my brother … they both serve them willingly. They shipped me to Enoch, like a prized mare, to be married off. Kai is all I have."

"You don't have the mark," Annie noted.

"It was never necessary." Maya scoffed at herself. "I always did as I was told. I can't imagine how you must hate me. I hate myself. Kai's the only reason I'm still here."

"I don't *hate* you," Annie replied, and she meant it. "I don't particularly *like* you right now, but I don't hate you."

Maya chortled. "Well, that's a start."

"Is Kai alright?"

"He's wonderful," Maya rocked gently. "And safe. He's happy to have that blasted dragon back."

Annie's heart sank. "Alexander?"

Maya covered her face with the blanket and wept. "He's gone. They found his body. They brought him home to the manor."

He's gone.

He was gone, and Camden wasn't. She would have traded her own soul to keep Cam alive. No, she couldn't hate Maya. She understood her completely.

Maya's words caught her attention. "Who found him?"

"Mr. Price and your friend, Nathan." Maya took a long drink of whisky, then grimaced. "They hunted the last of the cultists through the night. They scattered without Henry keeping them in line."

"And Bale?"

"He's fled." Maya frowned. "We're free of him for now, at least."

For now. Annie sighed and rubbed her face. How long would it take for him to regroup and come looking for them again? Cam had humiliated him. He wouldn't let this go.

She let her hands drop to her lap. "Reika? Jenny?"

"Miss Hall is resting." Maya's lips curled up at the edges. "The doctors say it's a miracle the baby is alive, thanks to you. Jenny is with her. They've taken well to each other."

A little of the tension left Annie's shoulders and neck. This odd group of people had become her family, the family she'd *chosen*, and they were safe. Whole. For today.

Today, they were okay.

A small amount of motion in the corner caught her attention.

Elain sat on the desk along the far wall and . . .

It can't be.

Clarisse was beside her, her eyes solid white as she beamed at her. Her face was no longer weathered. She was . . . beautiful.

A ghost now, just like Elain.

A helper.

Annie swallowed, throat tight, and winced as she stood. Her heartbeat throbbed in her knee, but she didn't care. She needed to see him.

"Thank you." She reached out and squeezed Maya's fingers. "Thank you for being here."

Maya nodded, eyes lined with silver.

As Annie hobbled out of the room, Maya's sobs followed her.

The hall was empty. The only light guiding her steps was the pre-dawn gloom peeking through the curtains. The remaining nurses who'd proven not to be cultists would be changing shifts at this time.

She didn't have to ask where Cam was. She could feel him. His power seeped into the hallway, wrapping around her ankles, warming her calves, guiding her where she needed to go. Weary, yet stronger than she'd ever felt it, like it had reached a new chasm, a new level.

So did hers. Annie could feel the endless well of power inside her, begging to be touched.

The chilled floors bit into her bare feet. She opened his door so as not to make a sound. Her soul nearly broke down at the sight of him in bed, curled up on his side, fast asleep, with the blankets half pulled up over his head.

She couldn't wake him, but she couldn't bear being so far from him, either. She needed to touch him, to prove he was real and not a figment of her haunted imagination, to smell the sun and the sea on his skin.

The bed was small, but so was she. Annie silently slid in beside him. She didn't need any blankets. The room was warm enough just because he was in it.

As she lay her head down, Cam's eyes fluttered open, green at first, then encircled with fire as he looked over her face. They stared at each other for several heartbeats before tears spilled over his cheeks and onto the pillow.

"I almost said yes." His voice was hoarse, nearly gone. "He destroyed me."

Annie brushed her thumb over his lips. He was like a bonfire on a winter night. "I don't care."

His brows furrowed. "I almost ruined everything. *Again.*"

Slowly, Annie pulled the blankets back so she could tuck herself against his chest. It was bare, wrapped in linens, but there wasn't any new bleeding. She pressed her face into the hollow of his throat. "I don't care."

He wrapped his arms around her waist, pulling her tight. His voice cracked. "Annie—"

"I wouldn't care if you *had.*" She stroked down his arm. *He's alive. We're alive.* "All that matters is you and me. We would have fixed it, somehow, together. Not apart. *Together.*"

"Together," he repeated. His brands flared, filling the space with an orange glow. Taking her hand, he entwined their fingers. With the other, he lifted her chin and pressed a soft kiss to the edge of her lips as he whispered, "Take this away from me. *Please.*"

She knew what he meant. Her power didn't wait to tunnel into him, devouring. His gates were open wide. His fire a gaping maw—limitless, eternal—and it would never hurt her. *He* would never hurt her.

She could see straight into the innermost parts of him, filled with overwhelming grief and shame—but more than that—an endless, intoxicating love . . . for her.

Her.

Annie's brands shifted to white, her body humming, as he slid their conjoined hands up her nightgown, resting them over her swollen knee. She let her power go, and piece by piece, her leg knit back together. Perfect. Like it had never been damaged at all.

Cam didn't resist as she rolled him onto his back, peeling back the linens to expose his wounds beneath. The life she'd taken from Alexander had closed the bullet holes, but the deep, deep bruising left behind stretched from his hips to his collarbone.

He leaned his head back and sighed as she pressed a kiss to each wound, letting their entwined power flow back into him. If Death Brands could corrupt by giving and taking, then she could heal. Purify. Sew together all their fractured shards into everything she didn't know she needed until she knew *him.*

The discolored bruising faded, leaving his beautiful, tanned skin beneath.

Her lips moved to his, and she murmured, "I suppose you'll want to know how the others are doing?"

"To quote you." He smiled against her mouth, his fingers hot against her bare thighs. "I don't care. Not right now."

Later, they'd remember everything that was taken from them. Everyone would look to him for guidance, waiting in bated breath for his next word. For now, she would be selfish and keep him all to herself.

And she didn't feel guilty about it one bit.

CHAPTER 67

CAMDEN

Cam set the shovel aside, brushing the last of the dirt off his hands.

It had been a long time since he'd dug a grave, and while his father's wasn't a masterpiece, it was genuine. He'd superheated the tombstone, letting Kai and Maya write their last goodbyes into the granite before he set it into place.

Now Alexander Callahan would rest, overlooking the sea, on a hill outside the gardens on his estate.

My estate. His responsibilities and toil. By law, the West belonged to him now. Especially, now that the council was too terrified of him to argue the semantics.

And my great-grandfather was a Revenant. So, he also had *that* to process. He only wished he'd been able to talk to his father about it. *Really* talk to him, without all of The Order's restraints in the way.

Cam tugged the golden pocketwatch from his coat, brushing his thumb over the leviathan on the face.

Later. Later, he'd try to process all of it. Right now, he had more pressing concerns.

641

Beside him, the black skirts of Annie's gown whipped in the breeze. Mourning clothes. She took his hand and squeezed, her expression hiding all the emotions the touch had conveyed.

With her . . . he could do this. Somehow. He would make this right.

Cam glanced down the hill, where Kai and the girl, Mary, played with Brantley in the strawberry patch. He'd take care of her, too, now. Nathan and Jenny were with them, his arm around her shoulders.

Maya. Kai. Nathan. Jenny. Julian. Reika. The crew of *The Elaina.* Hell, even Magnus. So many depended on him. He'd spent his entire life running from this, but now that he was here . . .

He winced as a sharp pain lanced through his temple. He could still *feel* it at the edges of his mind—the things that Bale had done, the nightmares that haunted him, and the darkness he'd poisoned him with.

Annie's eyes flicked to him immediately. She saw everything. He was grateful for it.

"Mr. Price suspects that he fled North," she murmured, knowing exactly whom he'd been thinking of. "To Sleetfield, where Maya's brother rules as governor."

"I reckoned the same." His fire purred—a predator in wait—as he kissed her wedding finger. His mother's jewel shone atop it, burning in the vibrant oranges and golds of the coming sunset. "I wonder how we're going to flush him out?"

Annie's features turned devious. "We're going after him?"

Cam nodded with a crooked grin. "Jensen Davis escaped. David is gone, too. We can't let the roaches run free, can we?" He looked to Kai and Mary again, letting their laughter soak into him. "We'll never be safe while Bale lives."

"We may never be safe." Annie rested her head against his

shoulder. "The West is vulnerable. You're the governor's heir—"

"I *am* the governor." Cam turned to face her. There was no going back now. The West was *his*. "And you are the Lady of the West now, and I'll take this entire damned planet for you if it means that we can sleep without fearing our throats will be cut in the night."

"You were always so afraid of becoming a monster, Camden." She's seen to the depths of him. She knew what he was. "You dreaded becoming someone who could burn cities to the ground."

Cam grimaced. Half of Enoch was destroyed. The estate house was filled with men, women, and children without homes because of what he'd done.

She grabbed his chin, tipping him down to her level. "Maybe you were *born* to burn cities to the ground,"—she pointed toward the children down the hill—"for them. For Nathan and Jenny. For Reika and her baby. For, as you say, this entire damned planet."

Cam cocked his head. "That's a little dramatic, and a heavy weight to bear."

"*We* can handle it." She kissed him and giggled. *Giggled.* "Lady of the West. I could get used to that."

He burst out laughing.

"*Camden.*" Kai sprinted up the hill, Brantley on his tail. "Mary says you're lying about being a pirate because you have all your teeth. Can we *please* go see your ship now?"

"How dare she." Cam scanned over the dragon. *I wonder if I could make another one. A bigger one.* One big enough for two to ride? "Yes, we can go to the ship now."

Kai squealed and tore off back to the strawberry patch. His brother hid his pain well. He'd make a pirate of him yet.

"You and me?" Cam looped his little finger through Annie's. "Forever. Pinkie promise?"

"You and me," she whispered. He would never tire of her smiles. "Until the stars fall or time takes us away. Even then."

He took her face in his hands and kissed her, long and slow. *Forever.* "Yes, even then."

ACKNOWLEDGMENTS

This is my tenth finished novel, and I've never had one make me cry so much.

Not because the writing itself was difficult, but because it seemed that the world didn't want it written. Health issue after health issue, interruptions, delays, imposter syndrome to the depths I've never felt, but I didn't break me. Not this time.

I'd been waiting so long to continue Cam and Annie's story, but I didn't realize how much I needed to heal alongside them.

I will always thank the Lord first. Thank You for giving me another book to write and for caring enough to stay alongside me.

Sam, thank you for reading this story chapter by chapter and dealing with all my blubbering. You're my ultimate Cam girlie, and I honestly don't think I could keep putting books out if it weren't for you.

To my PA and dear friend, Hailey, this story wouldn't have taken flight without all your tireless work. Thank you for being my rock.

To my incredible editor, B.E. Padgett, thank you for helping me make this story SO much better!

To all my betas, Ashley, Ali, Jewell, and Jill. You're all so amazing and endlessly patient.

Corey, thank you for enduring all of my tears. I don't want to live this life without you. I'm so grateful I'll never have to.

To my darling baby, Lily. Thank you for giving me a reason to be better. I wish you knew how much I love you.

And lastly, to Pasta, my brainless orange cat. Thank you for biting me every time I started to doom scroll. Though your disciplinary methods may be questionable, the results speak for themselves.

And lastly—but certainly not least—thank you to all of my readers. Thank you for cheering me on and being excited to see these characters again. I wouldn't be here without you.

THE DILEMMAS OF A DEAD MAN'S DAUGHTER PLAYLIST

Even in Arcadia album by Sleep Token (on repeat)

Dangerous by Sleep Token (Cam's song)

Eat Your Young by Arankai

KARMA! by SLOWYMANE

The Void by Parkway Drive

Fury by Via Sky

Through the Madness by Teramaze

Specter by Bad Omens (Annie's song)

ALSO BY BRITTANY TUCKER

The Revenant Series:

The Calamities of Camden Callahan

The Dilemmas of a Dead Man's Daughter

The Sunshine Series:

Sunshine's Syndicate

Other:

A Dowry of Snails and Mud

Noah's Not So Super Summer

My First Novel: A Story Plotting Workbook for Tweens and Tweens
(co-authored with B.E. Padgett)

ABOUT THE AUTHOR

Brittany Tucker is the author of several whimsical fantasy series that cater to readers of all ages, from middle-grade to adult. She also co-authored a story-plotting workbook designed for tweens and teens. Brittany frequently teaches writing classes and workshops suitable for all skill levels in her community. She resides on an island off the coast of Washington with her family, cats, and ball pythons.